CARDINAL
GALSWORTHY

EDWARD R. F. SHEEHAN

✢

CARDINAL GALSWORTHY

✢

A Novel

VIKING

VIKING
Published by the Penguin Group
Penguin Putnam Inc., 375 Hudson Street,
New York, New York 10014, U.S.A.
Penguin Books Ltd, 27 Wrights Lane,
London W8 5TZ, England
Penguin Books Australia Ltd, Ringwood,
Victoria, Australia
Penguin Books Canada Ltd, 10 Alcorn Avenue,
Toronto, Ontario, Canada M4V 3B2
Penguin Books (N.Z.) Ltd, 182–190 Wairau Road,
Auckland 10, New Zealand

Penguin Books Ltd, Registered Offices:
Harmondsworth, Middlesex, England

First published in 1997 by Viking Penguin,
a member of Penguin Putnam Inc.

10 9 8 7 6 5 4 3 2 1

Copyright © Edward R. F. Sheehan, 1997
All rights reserved

LIBRARY OF CONGRESS CATALOGING IN PUBLICATION DATA
Sheehan, Edward R. F.
  Cardinal Galsworthy : a novel / Edward R. F. Sheehan.
    p. cm.
  ISBN 0-670-87392-6
  I. Title.
PS3569.H3923C37   1997
813'.54—dc21   97-235

This book is printed on acid-free paper.
∞

Printed in the United States of America
Set in Stempel Garamond
Designed by Pei Koay

What therefore have I to do with men that they should hear my confessions—as though it were they who could banish all that is evil in me? Men are a race eager to learn of others' lives but indolent to correct their own. My memory contains the feelings of my mind because memory is like the mind's belly. Happiness is invisible because it has no body.

St Augustine
CONFESSIONS

⁜

Author's Note

⁜

I wrote this novel as a Romance. The *Random House Dictionary* defines "romance" as "a narrative depicting heroic or marvelous achievements, colorful events or scenes, chivalrous devotion, unusual or even supernatural experiences, or other matters of a kind to appeal to the imagination." Thus this novel narrates much of the tale of Latin Christianity in our modern time, as embodied in the life of a single very gifted, heroic, flawed, and complex man—Augustine Cardinal Galsworthy.

In reading modern novels I have often reacted uncomfortably when authors attached real names to characters from history, and then filled their mouths with fictitious dialogue. Several recent Popes appear in this book; but of course all of their conversations with Cardinal Galsworthy are fictitious. For authenticity I have never strayed far from the true and distinct personalities of these pontiffs; yet out of literary respect I have not given them names. They will appear here as "Stern Pope," "Sunny Pope," "Sad Pope," and "Slav Pope." I have omitted the Pope who reigned for only thirty-three days and whose impact on history was thus not significant.

My exchanges in St Peter's basilica during the Second Vatican Council echo selectively what was truly said. I have occasionally taken very minor liberties with history; also with the geography and languages of the Congo. The cognoscenti will know whether Leo XIII had been indeed the Archbishop Titular of Trebizond or of Damietta. Certain arrangements in the papal Conclave have recently been modernized, but for drama I have favored the traditional protocols in force until 1963.

I am indebted to many authors in several languages for their accounts of the Second Vatican Council, but primarily to the basic documents of that assembly. For various bee images in this book, I am grateful to the writings of Count Maurice Maeterlinck (Nobel laureate, 1911). Above all I am grateful to my editor, Al Silverman, whose idea this novel was, and whose editing was rigorous, creative, and inspired.

E.S.

Greycliffe
October 1996

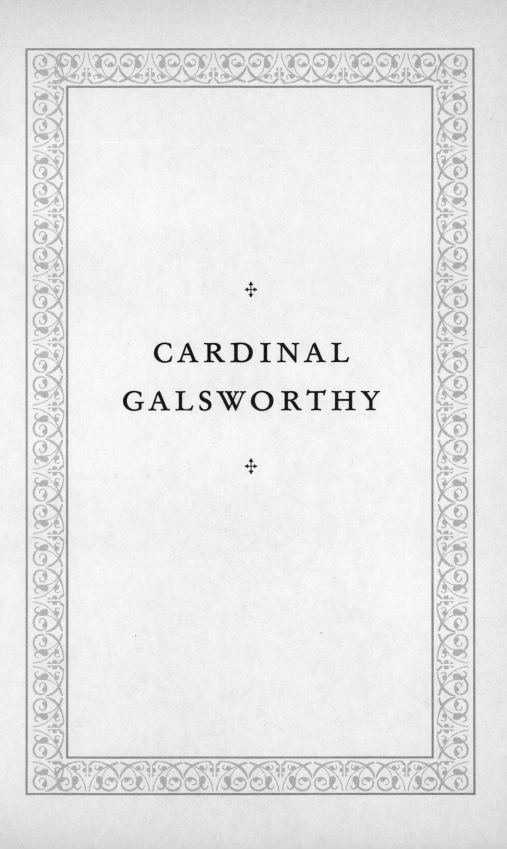

CARDINAL GALSWORTHY

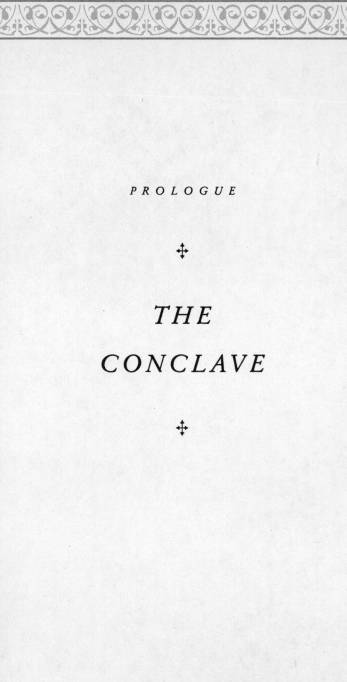

PROLOGUE

✢

THE CONCLAVE

✢

"The cup which my Father hath given me,

shall I not drink it?"

⁜

Often I had reason to brood upon that verse from the eighteenth chapter of St John Evangelist, after I gathered with my brother cardinals in the Sistine Chapel to elect a successor to the Slav Pope. For you see I had more than one mind about the matter. I rejoiced and grieved that I, Augustine Cardinal Galsworthy, was amongst the most favoured candidates to ascend the throne of St Peter. Should I or should I not be Pope?

We were nearly on the eve of the Third Millennium. I had been alone with the Slav Pope when he died, oddly, on the roof of the Apostolic Palace, stung by bees from his apiary. In the moment before he left this vale of tears, he fixed his eyes on Heaven and asked me a riddle: "Will the bees ever taste the honey that they harvest?"

Not so many years before, toward the end of his long pontificate, the Pope had created me Camerlengo, or Chamberlain, of the Holy Roman Church. Thus upon the death of the Pope I became head of the Sacred College of Cardinals and prince regent of the Church during the interregnum— until a new Pontiff should be raised up from amidst his brothers.

As prince regent it was I who summoned my fellow cardinals from around the world to Rome and the Apostolic Palace, where the Conclave assembled to pursue its hallowed task in a Church

Universal ill with discord. I was sixty-nine, an ideal age for the papacy—and too proud not only that my health was so robust but that even into the lengthening shades of life I had kept the elegance of my appearance, the trimness of my tall body, and my face ascetical beneath my silver-white locks of hair, abundant still. The season was July, all wet heat. I opened the Conclave.

Or rather—a fortnight after the Pope's death—I shut the Conclave. In my capacity as Camerlengo I sealed the College of Cardinals inside the labyrinth of rooms around the Sistine Chapel that we might undertake the election with zealous secrecy. Banishing all but cardinals and their chaplains ("conclavists"), with a golden key I locked the apartments from within. Then I strode towards the chapel—the last in a glorious procession of brother princes, we each of us in our full robes of Sacred Purple, progressing through the marble halls under the lunettes and frescoes—preceded by our conclavists with rococo crosses and blazing candles and sweet incense.

In the Sistine Chapel, we heard Mass invoking the guidance of the Holy Ghost, celebrated by the Dean of the Sacred College—an African—the finely wrought Patrice Cardinal Zalula, Prefect of Bishops, in years only slightly older than myself. We were one hundred and twenty electors. To be chosen Pope, a cardinal needed two-thirds of the ballots, plus one—eighty-one votes. We were to cast our ballots in the chapel twice each morning and twice each afternoon until we should elect the successor to the Slav Pope. Our rubrics were scrupulous and elaborate.

The conclavists withdrew to other rooms, leaving the electors alone in the chapel. The cardinals sat along the walls in nooks at shrouded little desks under miniature baldachins. Since I had been a Prince of the Church for nearly three decades, my seniority placed me near the head of the class: by the high altar beneath Michelangelo's Last Judgement.

For each vote (or "scrutiny") the Cardinal Dean sat before the altar at a great table bearing a huge golden chalice. In order of seniority the cardinals filed solemnly to the table, and into the chalice each elector thrust his ballot. Various cardinals, chosen by lot, assisted His Eminence Zalula in counting out the ballots and announcing the results. The first scrutiny chastened me.

I received but five votes. I had not, of course, voted for myself. I had voted for Cardinal Zalula—as rock-like in the Faith as I, more heroic and saintly. Cardinal Zalula received three votes. The other ballots were scattered between various Italians from the sternly traditional to the mildly modern. The learned Archbishop of Turin (who pretended to be both) led the pack with twelve votes.

No cardinal having received the required great majority, the ballots were stuffed into an old stove, mixed with straw and chemicals, then burned: their souls ascending as black puffs of smoke through a twisting pipe to tell the world outside that we had no Pope.

Afterwards, Cardinal Zalula told me, "But my dear Augustine, it was only the first scrutiny. You will be Pope!" I kept silent and thought, Surely I shall never be Pope. *And I thought of the several reasons why I should not be Pope and of the thousand reasons why I must be.*

As the scrutinies proceeded, I craned my neck to gaze from my gilded chair at Michelangelo's vaulted ceiling; at the Sibyls and Prophets and Stories from the Book of Genesis; at God separating light from darkness, making the sun and planets, fashioning fish and birds, creating Adam and Eve, then banishing them both from the Garden of Eden. Then I looked to the Last Judgement—*to the floating, redeemed nude bodies; to the angels astride clouds sounding trumpets; to the writhing damned in Charon's boat sailing off to Hell; and to the thick-waisted, thick-thighed Christ who sent them there.*

I thought: Images from my childhood. *Often during those days and nights, I brooded also about my childhood. May I tell you why?*

PART I

✜

CHILDHOOD

✜

ONE

My presence in the Conclave and my wish for the papacy were the ordained and pitiless result of my infancy and youth. Indeed, as the voting in the Sistine Chapel continued, inexorably I reflected upon the sweet and turbulent romance of my length of life—much as any man might repeat in suspended time or in the instant before his death every footstep of his journey through the bright, dark world.

I was the child of minor nobility. My father was an English baronet who had married my mother for her modest fortune. My mother was American. I happened to be born in the United States on 25th December 1927, but as the years unfolded my birthplace seemed to me of small consequence. I was educated in English and in French; I spent much of my lonely childhood and youth in France. To this day I do not identify myself with any nation, though I hold four passports. When asked, I reply, as did St Paul to his tormentors, even to my auditors who do not understand, *"Civis Romanus sum."* Or: *"Civis Vaticanus sum."*

You will have noticed that I was born on Christmas Day—a happy portent to my parents. Then, like Christ according to the Old Covenant, I was circumcised on the eighth day of my life. (In that Tridentine era, the sacred liturgy began the New Year with the Feast of the Holy Circumcision.) Yet as my childhood progressed I was neglected by my parents, who were embarrassed by my awkwardness and stammer, and who shunted me off to monastic schools in England and in France. I knew few women. I was terrified of women. The small warmth of my life I took from my monkish tutors, who nurtured my learning and (they thought) my natural piety as they nudged me towards a career in the Church. Wordsworth tells us, and I believe him, "The child is father of the man."

Thus my birth—in Washington—was purely the result of chance, because my father, Sir William Galsworthy, had of a sudden been posted there as Second Secretary of the British Embassy. Though they bear but trivial importance, I hear you demanding to know more of his title and lineage. As I write I am leafing through my Burke's *Peerage* (an old edition, One Hundred and Fifth, MCMLXX), never ceasing to find it funny.

"Sir Charles Chetwynd-Pott, K.C.B.E., quondam Her Majesty's Minister to Andorra. . . . Sir Ranulph Twiselton-Wykeham-Fiennes, Third Baronet of Banbury. . . . Sir Mounstuart Elphinstone Grant-Duff, Recording Secretary, Royal Metaphysical Society. . . . Admiral the Honourable Sir R.A.R. Plunket-Ernle-Erle-Drax, R.N."

Ah, here is the entry for GALSWORTHY The heraldry is of rampant lions and unicorns breathing fire; a coronet; a shield with spears, iron bars and prickly chains, a crucifix. Beneath is the family legend: *Lux ex Tenebris*: Light from Darkness: from the fourth verse of the first chapter of the Book of Genesis.

GALSWORTHY. *Lineage*—RALPH WILLIAM, distinguished for his attachment to James II, early joined the Royal Standard, and was present at the battle of the Boyne, 1690. He left issue. . . . ALFRED, served at Waterloo, 1815, 14th Inf. Regt., afterwards went to Calcutta, where he was accidentally shot in the left foot. . . . HENRY FRANCIS (Sir), 1st Bart., G.C.B., late H.B.M. Envoy Extraor. and Min. Plen. in Spain, Portugal, and Bavaria; *b.* 23 Nov. 1808; *m.* 1stly, 11 Dec. 1830, Isabella (*d.* 5 March, 1835), 2nd dau. of 3rd Baron Scone; and had issue. . . .

WILLIAM HUGH JAMES [my father], 6th Bart. [Baronet], of Galsworthy Court, a Baron of the Holy Roman Empire, Kt. of Sov. Order of Malta; *b.* 23 Jan 1901; *educ.* Appleforth and Magdalen Coll. Oxford (B.A. 1923); entered H.M. Foreign Service, 1924. . . . Order of Merit. . . . Order of Pius IX. . . .

My mother, Daphne, I have told you, was American, and though it became common knowledge that Sir William had married Daphne for her money, she remained mysteriously obscure about her origins. As I grew up, I overheard her drop odd and contradictory remarks about her birthplace. She had been born atop a mountain amongst the Berkshires of western Massachusetts. She had been born in a mansion in a valley of the Green Mountains of Vermont. She had been born aboard a yacht in the middle of Lake Champlain.

Etc.

Daphne's fortune, not all that large, she had in truth inherited from her maternal grandfather, who had been famous, for a time, as a manufacturer of chocolate cookies. One winter, when she was twenty-six and still lacked a husband, Daphne took a cruise to South America to escape the cold. At Montevideo, during a dinner party, she met Sir William Galsworthy, then Third Secretary at His Britannic Majesty's Legation. Daphne abandoned her cruise, lingered in Montevideo, and several months later she married my father before the high altar of the cathedral.

The marriage, for my mother, seemed a fair exchange—Sir William got her money; she in turn became "Lady Daphne" and, by strenuous practice, acquired his high British accent. She acquired as well Sir William's fixation on all the shibboleths and icons of England's recusant Catholic nobility. (She had been born, she said, a Unitarian, and converted to Catholicism before the wedding.) In most of his inclinations, Sir William looked to Rome, not Canterbury. To be a Roman Catholic baronet meant grand station in the "old" religion, so much superior to the Church of England. For my father, whatever was "Roman" was good; whatever was merely Anglican, even the Royal Family, was perforce inferior.

My mother adopted the same bias—though not, so far as I could tell, for any truly religious reasons. Once, in Paris, before I was even ten, I overheard her arguing with a distant female cousin about her family tree. "But Daphne, in your maternal line you have many Jewish ancestors," the cousin said. "That's a *frightful* accusation!" my mother shouted, storming out of the salon. So great was her vexation, she did not notice me in the corridor, half concealed behind a pedestal. The revelation about my putative maternal forebears disturbed me less. Already, I knew some of the Old Testament in three languages (English, French, Latin), and it intrigued me that in my veins might run driblets of Jewish blood.

I was an only child. I recall every word of my early and rare conversations with my mother. I was seven, I think, on holiday in England at Galsworthy Court, when one day I asked her, "M-Mother, what does D-Daphne mean?"

"It's a name from classical mythology," she answered. "Daphne was a nymph, pursued by Apollo. The other gods saved her by turning her into a laurel tree."

"A *l-laurel* tree?"

"Imagine that—your mother as a tree."

You might as well be, thought I.

"Frightful," she continued. "Have no fear, your father is no Apollo."

"P-People say that you're beautiful but he's n-n-not."

"Will you stop that stammer, you frightful child? We must work on your stammer, starting tomorrow."

That tomorrow never happened, with my mother or my father. I kept eavesdropping on their conversations, curious to learn how lowly I ranked on any given day. My father said, "But there is little to be done about it, Daphne. The doctors say that he lacks balance."

"That may explain his awkwardness—oh, the things he breaks, the bumping into doors and walls, that Chinese vase, the other day!—William. It does not explain his stammer."

"It may have been your difficult delivery, the doctors say. Or—I hate to mention this, dear Daphne—the time when he was so very small and you . . . dropped him."

"*I* did not drop him, William. It was the nurse."

"Last year, you said it was the governess."

"The nurse, the governess, I can't remember. He hit his head. I mean his forehead. I shan't ever forget the enormous blue bump above his eye. It took weeks to disappear."

"That, Daphne, is your recollection. I was away from Washington, you may recall, at Whitehall when he bumped his head."

"The bump may explain his awkwardness. It does not explain his frightful stammer."

"It could explain both. Or—the doctors say—it could be simple fear."

"Of whom?"

"Of you, Daphne."

"Preposterous. He's far more afraid of you!"

"Stop shouting at me, Daphne. It does not become your station. We're getting nowhere. We must accept Augustine as we would a retarded child— as a cross that God, in His mysterious design, has given us to bear. Now, as for the theatricals . . ."

"Augustine will be heartbroken if we exclude him."

The theatricals. Let me explain.

The year was 1937; I was nine years old. My father was between postings; we were passing the summer at Galsworthy Court, his ancestral seat, in the countryside of Gloucestershire near Dursley. Of Gloucestershire as a great place I know little, but I do vividly remember the late sunsets and long twilights of summer in that patch of England I inhabited so briefly. On the grassy ridge of the Cotswold Hills, where I walked alone at late twilight, I saw the wide valley of a river, and beyond it, Wales. Horses grazed near the road: in relief against a sky of mauve they became dark silhouettes, mythological.

Of Galsworthy Court, I am almost ashamed to speak. Poets and philosophers have written rhapsodies to the special beauty of imperfection and decay, propounding ruins as more beautiful than perfect structures, and asking deeply, "*Why* are they so? *Ought* they to be so?" Our house was Georgian, large and rambling, but beholding it I saw no superior beauty, only an exterior of falling, dirty brick. The inside as well bespoke neglect and ugliness, all shabby, shabby, shabby, a foreshadowing (I recognise today) of the dreariness of England in morose decline.

The house was tree-girt, elms and oaks I think, but the manor had no gardener; the lawns and vegetation grew long and wild, with no flower beds at all, or rather flower beds that used to be, classically, symmetrically arranged, overgrown now with weeds and the rare wild rose. The statuary suggested romantic decadence once fastidiously maintained, naked pagan gods and goddesses in heroic poses, but with their limbs and genitalia fallen off, not from contrivance but indifference. Miniature mock Greek ruins were ruined anew by the rains and fog. Even the grotto of the Most Blessed Virgin Mary was vanishing, chipping away, hiding as though embarrassed behind random vegetation.

Galsworthy Court was maintained, supposedly, by an elderly couple who lived in rooms near the kitchen, the only dwellers of the house during the long absences of Sir William and Lady Daphne. In the rear, those servants kept a kitchen garden, hen coops, and pigpens, to which they seemed to devote most of their labour. They rarely cleaned the interior of the manor; thus my memory of that summer at my ancestral seat is of rooms full of dust and cobwebs, peeling damask, and furniture falling apart. I wondered, If Mother is so rich, why doesn't she make repairs?

One room in the house, at the insistence of Sir William, was decently maintained. That was the library, as large (in memory) as any reading room I later visited at Oxford, the Sorbonne, or Rome. Its walls were lined with the pagan classics in Greek and Latin, the writings of the Church Fathers, the novels of Jane Austen, the Brontës, Dickens, Trollope, the great novelists and historians of France, and the complete works of Cardinal Newman. Often when I opened a volume—during that summer I opened many—its leather binding cracked for lack of oiling. I might have lived in the library throughout the rainy, sunny, fog-filled summer had not my father used the room for another purpose: to stage his theatricals.

For years, even before my birth, Sir William had been acting out his crazed hobby of the theatre. In Montevideo and in Washington he had gathered for such entertainment all sorts of friends and strangers; his taste ran to dramas with a cardinal in the cast, and he played that part himself. Once he staged Shaw's *Saint Joan*, playing Cauchon, the villainous Bishop of Beauvais, in a cardinal's robes. Later he translated a forgotten French drama about Cardinal Richelieu, and played Richelieu. In that summer of 1937 he staged *King Henry the Eighth*, one of Shakespeare's least perfect works, and he took the showy part of Cardinal Wolsey, Lord Chancellor of England.

For his pageant he needed many actors, nor was he too particular in how he chose them.

At Dursley, not far away, was a Roman Catholic orphanage, run by Poor Clare nuns and full of beautiful, abandoned children, many of them fair and blond. (My own hair was a lavish black, my eyes deeply brown, in shadow seeming as raven as my hair; my mother thought my skin in contrast much too pale.) My parents took a keen interest in the welfare of these nuns and orphans. Behind our house, my father even brought in hired men to cut the savage grass, making of it a croquet lawn to entertain the children—all for his true purpose.

On Thursday afternoons, a blue bus appeared at Galsworthy Court, disgorging nuns and orphans for their games of croquet with Sir William and Lady Daphne. My parents invited me to join the fun, but their invitations so lacked warmth I surmised that I was not welcome. From the upper floor, through the murky windows of my room, I watched the festivities on the lawn below.

The boys in their white shirts and short blue pants, the girls in their white blouses and blue skirts, the nuns in their sandals and brown habits, white coifs and starched wimples, their long rosary beads entangled with their rope cinctures—all fairly romped on the grass, laughing childishly together and pretending to play croquet. My parents struggled to keep order, but between the matches they mingled with the children, chuckling; if not hugging and kissing them, then squeezing several fondly on their arms before they served them lemonade and yellow muffins.

I watched from above. When had my parents last joked with me, squeezed my arms fondly? My mother, fluttering about in a green dress and a floppy pink hat, was as radiant as the sky that afternoon with her black curls dangling beneath her hat, her face the hue of a ripening peach, her waist as trim as a birch tree, her legs long and nearly dancing as she moved.

My father wore a blue blazer, trousers suggesting cream, a flat straw hat, and grey spats above his white shoes. His hair was brown, almost red; when he lifted his hat, the sun shone through his meagre locks to a bony skull. His face was pink from drinking too much gin; bony like his skull, remarkable less for his thin and shapeless lips than for his pronounced cheekbones, prefiguring my own. His body was trim but his height was mediocre, making him (to my eyes) shorter than my mother. Beyond Christian charity, his kindness to the orphans as I have intimated had a deeper cause. He needed them for his *King Henry*.

The performance was staged in the library one Sunday evening on a platform before our threadbare tapestry of Wolsey's Hampton Court. My mother played Queen Katharine—Henry VIII's long-suffering spouse whom Henry is trying to divorce canonically with Wolsey's connivance. Only my parents had memorised their parts. The other players read their parts from books, and badly; squires and their wives, a nun ór two, played King Henry, Norfolk, Buckingham, Anne Bullen (Boleyn). But most of the parts, large and small, were read by orphan children.

I hoped at least to be cast as a non-speaking scribe, spear-carrier, torchbearer, but those rôles were awarded to the orphans. I all but begged my father to make me Cardinal Wolsey's train-bearer, but even that part he gave to a blond orphan boy. *I* was assigned to sit in the audience, which consisted of myself and our elderly couple, the keepers of our hens and pigpens.

None of the players wore period costumes except Sir William and Lady

Daphne. My mother, dressed up in a tinsel-cardboard crown and a purplish velvet robe, spoke her part in the fake high English she had borrowed from her husband. Though she spoke with verve, her gestures seemed an imitation of an overzealous diva and therefore silly. And my father? Ah, he was special.

As Wolsey, he was transformed, his ugliness enhancing his sinister performance in his cardinal's robes. His cardinal's robes! By diligence and obsession he had managed to acquire a dazzling costume—all scarlet watered silk and fine French lace; soutane, mozzetta, rochet, and mantelletta; red buckled shoes. Beneath his cappa magna his crimson train stretched twenty feet, borne gracefully to suit his movements by the blond orphan. Upon his head, hiding his baldness and his bony skull, he wore his broad-brimmed *galero,* elaborate tassels dangling from it.

The play begins. Wolsey's voice is deep, arrogant, magisterial, resonant with disdain for the Duke of Buckingham and for all who chafe beneath his power with the King. How rich and mighty, how full of craft and tricks and insolence is this Lord Cardinal!

But with Queen Katharine he pretends sweetness. She tells him, "Sir, I am about to weep. But, thinking that We are a queen, the daughter of a king, my drops of tears I'll turn to sparks of fire."

"Be patient yet," says Wolsey.

"I will, when you are humble. I do believe, induced by potent circumstances, that you are mine enemy."

"Madam, I have no spleen against you: how far I have proceeded, or how further shall, is warranted by a commission from the consistory, yea, the whole consistory of Rome."

"My lord, my lord, I am a simple woman, much too weak t'oppose your cunning."

Yet as the play proceeds, Wolsey's tricks catch up with him and his fortunes wane. The King intercepts the Cardinal's treacherous letters to the Pope, entreating the Pontiff to withhold the divorce. Henry complains of Wolsey's corruption and piles of wealth. Aware of the King's suspicions, my father in full scarlet treads in circles about the stage, biting his lip, striking his breast; springs into a faster gait; casts his gaze upwards, at the moon. I think: *Dear God, how he lives the part.*

"What should this mean?" asks Cardinal Wolsey. "The King parted frowning from me, as if ruin leapt from his eyes. I must read this paper; I fear, the story of his anger. 'Tis so; this paper has undone me—'tis the account of all that world of wealth I have drawn together for mine own ends; indeed to gain the Popedom, and fee my friends in Rome."

Dispossessed by the King of all his estates, palaces, and gold, dismissed as Lord Chancellor of the realm, the Cardinal is plunged in ruin.

"And—when I am forgotten, and sleep in dull cold marble—say, I taught thee. Say, Wolsey, that once sounded all the depths and shoals of honour—found thee a way, out of his wrack, to rise in. Mark but my fall. I charge thee, fling away ambition. By that sin fell the angels; how can man, then, the image of his Maker, hope to win by it? Love thyself last; cherish those hearts that hate thee; corruption wins not more than honesty. Had I but served my God with half the zeal I served my King, He would not in mine age have left me naked to mine enemies."

Those last lines my father spoke with a quavering voice, full of echoes, doom, self-pity; but suggesting, faintly, true repentance—leaving me in doubt. As he uttered the verse, a boy flicked off the lights of the library; into the gloom filed a choir of orphan monks, in black cowls and habits, bearing blazing candles. When my father said, "Had I but served my God with half the zeal I served my King, He would not in mine age have left me naked to mine enemies"—he lay supine upon a slab of wood, clutching at his cardinal's robes and casting them away.

The drama is today rarely done on the legitimate stage; I have seen performances in London and New York, but of those few, with famous actors, none could surpass my father's Cardinal Wolsey. At Galsworthy Court, I thought then, when I was a child, as I think now: He *is* Wolsey, *was* Wolsey, *is* a cardinal, *was* a cardinal, born for the part.

I learned from my father as Cardinal Wolsey one of the deep lessons of my life: the Roman Church as theatre.

I disliked my father, maybe hated him. May I beg you to understand that until his death my father gave me nothing of his love—save his rich images of the Roman Church as theatre?

T W O

In autumn, as Adolf Hitler shook Europe with his threats, my father was posted to Paris as First Secretary at the British Embassy. He never took me inside that sooty palace on the rue Faubourg-St-Honoré; after only weeks of living with my parents in a large flat on the rue de Lille, I was packed off to school in the south of France.

From that moment, I became sealed from the world outside, kept deliberately in the dark about the great events of Europe swirling round me, save when I rarely chanced to see a newspaper by accident left lying about or overheard the monks whispering in corridors or debating in their refectory. I was not allowed to listen to the wireless, but then neither were the other boys: we had no wireless.

My school, in fact, was a monastery of Benedictines, built on a hill beyond the ancient town of Carpentras, not far from Avignon, seat of the papacy six hundred years before. We were but forty or fifty boys, my schoolmates for the most part the progeny of French nobility—the second, third, fourth sons of dukes, counts, barons, who under the rules of primogeniture would inherit neither their fathers' titles nor their fortunes but were destined as if by default for careers in the Church. The Benedictine priests, in their black tunics, belts, and scapulars—their heads shaven but for circlets of hair round their skulls—were harsh and learned teachers. What they taught us, they taught us well: theology, history, mathematics, and—superbly—the classics, in French, Latin, and ancient Greek.

Come, visit the monastery with me, as it was in my boyhood and as I remember it today. (We are told that "memory fades." Memory never fades. Memory *selects*.) Glimpse grey limestone, Gothic in the style of its arches and its windows, pillared cloisters and open courtyards, but older than Gothic as the upper battlements, Romanesque or even Gallic, climbed the side of the hill as though grasping for Heaven. The mass was all parapets and gargoyles; pinnacles and tracery; escarps, merlons, crenels, gables and crockets and ribbed vaults, gloomily ecclesiastic except on blessed days when from soaring lancet arches the reds and blues of stained glass winked brilliantly at the sun.

Surrounding the fortress were fig and olive trees of the *département* of Vaucluse, once the Comtat Venaissin, a fiefdom of the papacy. Our hill—we called it a mountain—was snowy in winter, brown in summer, verdant in spring, scarlet in fall, but even in May and autumn the gales of the mistral might rage at our windows and howl through our corridors and cloisters to chill our bones.

We boys lived largely according to the Rule of St Benedict, rising before dawn to chant Matins and Lauds with the fathers in the abbey chapel, None in the afternoons, Vespers and Compline before we took to bed again. Like that Divine Office, all of our Masses were celebrated in resonant, mysterious Latin, the priest at the altar with his back to us; barely had I been a year in the abbey than I knew the *Ordinarium Missae*, the Ordinary of the Mass, by heart. My life was hard, but—amongst the gargoyles and tracery, parapets and pinnacles and fluttering pennons, Gothic arches and stained glass and the relentless chant of Latin—one might say quaintly beautiful.

Nor did we sleep in dormitories. Like the monks, each boy inhabited his own cell, so spare and tiny that a brutish Spartan might have spurned it. I had a bed with a mattress so lumpy that I cast it away and slept thereafter on the bare slats of wood. I was given but a single black blanket against the cold, a trunk for my clothes, a shelf for my books, and a clay pot for whatever urine I could not contain at night. To move our bowels, we had to climb to privies on the side of the mountain, even in the snows of winter. To bathe, we each of us hauled a tub of cold water to his cell, and kept our bodies clean with crude grey soap made in the abbey by the monks.

Our meals were nearly as frugal. We pupils ate in our own refectory, from custom often silently though speech was not forbidden, beneath our towering lancet windows. We began invariably with a vegetable soup, steaming hot, thick with spinach and potatoes, then ate carrots and more potatoes. Cheese followed, as grey as our soap, likewise made by the fathers. On Sundays and sacred feasts, they added a shank of mutton. For sweets, we ate grapes, figs, or melon, grown by the monks. Their red wine, fermented in the abbey cellars, had the scent and taste of vinegar, but their bread, baked in huge loaves in the abbey ovens, was the most delicious I ever tasted.

As we ate, a chosen boy, high in a vaulted pulpit, read to us from St

Anselm on reason, revelation, and the nature of God; from St Augustine on the bitter fruits of lust; from the Rule of St Benedict: "What are the instruments of Good Works? . . . 44. To fear the Day of Judgement. 45. To be in dread of Hell. 46. To desire eternal life with all the passion of the soul. 47. To keep death daily before one's eyes. 48. To keep constant guard over the deeds of one's life. 49. To know that God sees everyone everywhere. 50. To dash all evil thoughts—should they invade the heart—against Christ forthwith. . . . 53. To show no love of talking, useless chatter, or boisterous laughter. . . . 63. To love chastity. 64. To hate no one. . . . 67. To beware of arrogance. . . ."

In class, we little boys of the lesser nobility, dressed identically in black knickers, white shirts, black ties, hunched over our rude desks and learned the classics by rote. Watch me memorising my Blaise Pascal in sublime French, my Xenophon in classical Greek, and in rolling periods of Latin *The Verrine Orations* of Cicero: "*Quid faciat Hortensius? At hominem flagitiosissimum, libidinosissimum. . . .*" Hear me when called upon to recite: "*. . . h-h-hominem f-f-f-flagitiosi-s-s-s-imum, libid-d-d-d-inosi-s-s-s-im-m-mum. . . .*"

A black father strode through the thicket of wooden desks, towards me. "*Mémoire parfaite,*" he said, "*. . . accent déplorable.*" He fingered a stub of blue chalk, and then—one hand gripping the back of my little head—with the other he traced a big blue **X** across my mouth and chin. My classmates giggled, roared, whistled, pounded their desks with their books and fists.

Not all of the boys—or monks—were so unkind, as you shall see. We rarely left the abbey but on Thursday afternoons, when for recreation we were allowed the liberty of the countryside on long walks.

I loved the mellow Mediterranean sunshine, the dry contours and cloudless skies, the rugged peaks and valleys of the Vaucluse. I loved sniffing the pine and almond in the sparkling air; the slopes and gardens where we strolled through oleander, pomegranate, olive, jujube, fig. I loved the mild-eyed oxen hauling wooden carts of hay and rock. We trod through vineyards; through crops of strawberry, sugar beets, cabbages, and artichoke; orchards of apricot and cherry. Sheep swarmed on the dirt roads, shepherd boys with crooks chastising them; potteries beneath sun-baked orange tile hummed here and there. In woodland, always we sought truffles, digging by the roots of trees and often finding them. I asked myself, Is this Arcadia?

Not for me, alas. I kept falling into ditches, bumping into trees, getting caught in thorn and bramble. I began to judge my schoolmates by how they responded to my distress. Most of them laughed and hooted, and then ignored me, forsaking me in my ditch or ensnared in bramble, dashing ahead as I fell far behind. Or they gathered round me, jeering at my misfortune as I fought thorn about my ankles and cried a little. Sometimes a boy or two would take pity, free me from my trap, with a handkerchief bind my bleeding arm or leg, but none of the boys cared for me so much as the Père Benoît.

Our excursions from the abbey were always guided by a father, though only now and then was the task assigned to Père Benoît.

He seemed old to me, though today I suppose he was not more than forty, a small man with hair dark blond above a face pocked by some disease of childhood, blue of eye, with a chin that came to such a point I could not look at it without the thought, *Arrow.*

Of a spring day, when the other boys, tired of taunting me, had run ahead, Père Benoît ran back in my direction and found me in another ditch. He leant down, grasped my hand, yanked me out, then with his scapular stanched as best he could the bloody wound that a jutting rock had inflicted on my ribs. *"Tu es si innocent, angelique, et hébété."* You are so innocent, angelical, and bewildered, said he.

Thereafter the Père Benoît became my protector. In the afternoons he visited our corner of the abbey and marched me up and down the corridor, guiding my shoulders as he strove to improve my balance, to induce me to walk in straight lines without stumbling or bumping into walls. Now sometimes, on Saturday or Sunday afternoons, with another boy or two we boarded the bus at Carpentras and visited Avignon.

We toured the Gothic Palace of the Popes, then lingered by the portals as Père Benoît recited the marvels of the Avignon papacy centuries ago. Across the great square, another door opened; out filed a pair of nuns in black and white and behind them a queue of schoolgirls two by two (my age? ten? eleven? twelve?) all dressed identically in blue berets, white blouses, blue skirts, blue stockings.

Sprung that suddenly through the portals of their convent, the girls appeared to me so much like creatures from another sphere that I wished against myself, against my habitual and comfortable isolation, to mingle with them—to know them by their names, play tricks on them, be teased by them, laugh and romp with them. They marched closer to us. A girl near the end of the procession, the loveliest I had ever seen, brown hair and brown eyes, stared at me for just an instant and smiled swiftly.

As suddenly I saw myself a tall and ageing man, clad in the red biretta of a cardinal, my dark locks turned to lucent silver, a black cloak trimmed with crimson flung round my shoulders—as though in a cinema, the lens behind me, catching me in half-profile—and in high relief against the line of passing schoolgirls. I asked myself, Is this my destiny? am I condemned to this? am I doomed always to watch and wonder, forbidden for ever to mingle with women or to laugh?

The Père Benoît touched my shoulder, grasped my hand, guided me away, up the steps, through the classical gardens, to contemplate the waters of the River Rhône before the sun set. In the gardens, I emerged from my hallucination of the schoolgirls as I heard the chatter of the tourists, not least three words repeatedly: *"les Juifs"*—the Jews—and "Hitler."

I hardly knew who Hitler was.

When we reached the last balustrade, I gasped at the beauty of the sun as it descended through lingering wisps of cloud and faintest tears of rain upon the umber waters of the Rhône and the ruins of the Pont d'Avignon.

"S-Seeing this, I w-wonder why the p-popes ever returned to R-Rome," I said.

"Ha-ha! *Cher Augustin!*" cried Père Benoît. "Have you been to Rome?"

"Once."

"When?"

"When my m-mother was p-pregnant with me. I didn't get to see m-much of it."

"Ha-ha! *Cherissime Augustin!*"

"What about H-Hitler?"

"*Allons-y, cher enfant, allons-y!*" Let's get going, dear child!

That was a Saturday. Next afternoon, following High Mass sung by the enthroned and mitred Father Abbot, Père Benoît took me and several boys hiking amongst the evergreen and vernal flowers on the mountain's other side. In a sloping meadow, he spread out a black blanket and from his straw basket made us a picnic luncheon—*pâté de campagne* he spread with his long fingers on monastery bread, vinegarish red wine, grey cheese, and green apples that in our trek we had picked from trees. The other boys soon drifted off to search for truffles, leaving me alone with my monk, we two sitting on either side of the picnic blanket. Staring at his countenance, I thought, in English: Arrow face.

For months, neither of my parents had written to me; the other boys mocked me constantly; I had not a friend on earth except this homely monk, yet I longed for human warmth. On an impulse I rolled my body across the blanket and with vigour hugged the Père Benoît about his neck and shoulders. He wrenched loose my grasp, struggled to his feet, and said, "Enough, Augustin."

"I am so alone, *mon père!*"

"And I, too, *cher Augustin,* but as a monk I must not be fond of anyone—save our Lord Redeemer Jesus Christ."

"I have no f-father."

"Must I take his place?"

His question set me on a path from which I have never erred, leading me to heights. For the first time, I used a man. I asked him, "Would you p-please, *mon père*? Would you teach me everything you kn-know?"

My memory was prodigious: I had hardly to glance at a page of Horace, Plato, St Augustine but my brain absorbed it in bountiful detail. By midafternoon, as the other boys still battled with their lessons inside their cells, I had finished mine and hurried to the library and the Père Benoît.

He began my special education by immersing me in the masterpiece of François René, vicomte de Chateaubriand, *Génie du christianisme,* written on the morrow of the French Revolution. We each of us had a copy, so we sat on armless wooden chairs opposite each other and read rapidly, silently, turning the pages until the monk paused to explain to me the importance or the peculiar beauty of a passage, an image, or a lustrous metaphor. Though the book was apparently an apologia, intended to rehabilitate the Faith in the early nineteenth century after the depredations of the Enlightenment and the Reign of Terror, Chateaubriand's deeper purpose was to celebrate the *aesthetic* marvels of Christianity—and to hold them forth as the most ennobling force in the arts and literature. In the *Génie*, Chateaubriand sought not to convince, but to seduce.

"*L'homme est suspendu dans le présent, entre le passé et l'avenir....* Man dangles in the present, between past and future, as though on a rock between two whirlpools. Behind him, before him, all is shadow; barely does he see the few phantoms ascending from the depths, floating for an instant upon the waves, then plunging deep again. Thus does Christianity provide its passions and its treasures to the poet. Like all great loves, it hints of the serious and the sad; it leads us to the gloom of cloisters, thence to the crests of mountains. Yet the beauty that the Christian worships is not fleeting: it is everlasting beauty, the kind of beauty for which the disciples of Plato made haste to abandon this earth."

More [said Chateaubriand], *religion is the true philosophy of the fine arts: it never separates, as does human wisdom, poetry and ethics, tenderness and virtue.* "Oh, how bitterly we remember those days when men of blood presumed to raise up—atop the ruins of Christianity, in the temples of the Virgin, who had consoled so many wretched hearts—the goddess of *Reason*, who has yet to wipe away a human tear!"

Atheism has nothing but plague and leprosy to offer us. "Religion roots itself in the feelings of the soul, in the sweetest bonds of life, in a father's fondness for his son, in the love of wife and husband, or a mother's for her child. Atheism reduces all to the sniffing of beasts; it hardens the heart until nothing can touch it. In our faith as Christians, we are assured that our sufferings will end; we are consoled; we dry our tears; we look upward to another life. In the faith of atheists, human ills are their own incense, Death is the high priest, a coffin is the altar, and Nothingness is God.

"Without Christianity, the shipwreck of society and all its lamps would for ever happen. God is all beauty. I have never been blessed, I must confess, with supernatural light. My conviction emerges merely from my heart: I wept and I believed. . . . *J'ai pleuré et j'ai cru.*"

I *wept* and I believed! From Chateaubriand and the Père Benoît, I learned another deep lesson of my life: the Roman Church as beauty; the Roman Church not only as theatrical but as the source of fierce—may I say almost sensual?—aesthetic pleasure.

Beyond our books, Père Benoît taught me Bach. Earlier in my childhood, my parents had hired tutors to teach me piano, but they despaired of my banging even as I learned, and rather well, to read Baroque, classical, and romantic music. Somehow the monk's presence soothed me, helped me to master my brash fingers, to guide them through the fugues and préludes until the music I produced was, as he remarked, "mature beyond your little years, and—like your nature—sweet."

We sat on a bench before the piano in a dim and vaulted alcove of the abbey's immense library, amongst illuminated mediaeval manuscripts. As we worked our way for the fiftieth time through Bach's "Goldberg Variations," out of the shadows of the alcove stepped the Father Abbot in his cowl and patriarchal white beard. For a moment he pondered us together, and then he said but two words: *"Amitié particulière."* Particular friendship.

The accusation struck the Père Benoît like a lance through his scapular. "Particular friendships" were forbidden by monastic rule. He leapt up from our piano: in doing so his face was illumined by a shaft of blue and amber light thrusting into the alcove through a lancet window of stained glass. I thought, His face is beautiful. He cried, *"Mais, Très Révérend Père!* But Right Reverend Father! This child is a future cardinal!"

"How do you know?" the Abbot asked gently.

"I had a vision!"

"A dream?"

"A vision!"

"As you slept?"

"In chapel! I was deep in prayer. The chapel was empty. Suddenly I heard a sound, the rustling of robes, and looked to the high altar. There, seated on your Abbot's throne, was this child, *notre cher Augustin,* in the red biretta and the full crimson robes of a cardinal."

"But we do not wish Augustin to be a cardinal. Nor, do I think, does God. We wish him to be one of us—a learned monk, dressed for ever in simple black."

"He will be a cardinal!"

"Amitié particulière," repeated Father Abbot quietly, turning his back upon us as he walked out of the alcove.

From that day, Père Benoît and I were separated, never again allowed to be alone together, catching glimpses of each other only from afar such as in chapel. Once or twice, at night when I looked from the arched window of my cell, I saw him below in the cloister, pacing up and down, reading his breviary, glancing but seldom at my window.

Springtime lengthened and grew warm, beckoning to summer to take its place. Sir William Galsworthy, not bothering to write to me, wrote instead to Father Abbot pleading the urgency of his diplomacy in Paris and begging the Benedictines to keep me for the summer.

Classes ended; the other boys went home; I was abandoned in the abbey with the monks. With no one and nothing else to occupy my time, I haunted the library, playing Bach in the alcove among the illuminated manuscripts, otherwise sitting in an armless chair and reading.

French literature was a sea of diamonds, but even as I revelled in the rich ideas, luxurious images, and vehemence of phrase, I brooded on the Père Benoît's figment of me as a boy-cardinal. On and on I read: during the Renaissance, the Church of Rome abounded in boy-cardinals. At age thirteen, a Medici received the Sacred Purple; at fifteen, a d'Este; at seventeen, Cesare Borgia. Forward from Medicis and d'Estes and Borgias I devoured time until I reached the eighteenth century and France of the Enlightenment before the Revolution.

I was dazzled less by saintly cardinals than by wicked ones, as I watched them prance through glittering courts; lavishly patronising poets, painters, and musicians; madly seducing women.

How I marvelled at their countless chaplains, valets, pages, grooms, ushers, runners, footmen, mace-bearers, train-bearers, and mounted equerries; at their princely dinner parties of pâtés and mousses, tourtes and tansies, *blamangos,* oyster loaves, bombarded veal, *pompetones* of larks, triumphal arches of meringue, and Baroque palaces of nougat; at their glorious titles: Grand Almoner of France, Prince of Hildesheim, Prince-Archbishop of Strasbourg, Landgrave of Alsace, Abbot of Noirmoutiers, Abbot of Chaise-Dieu, Illustrious Member of the French Academy, Vicar General of the Sorbonne, Commander of the Order of the Holy Ghost, Commendator of St-Vaast d'Arras, and Superior General of the Royal Hospital of the Quinze-Vingts—the offices of a single cardinal, the Prince de Rohan-Guéménée.

How cheerfully they fornicated! How recklessly they gambled! How cynically they played dice with God, repenting on their deathbeds!

In my childish mind I began to regard the Roman Church not just as theatre and as beauty but as the bourn of majestic riches, luxury, and deceit. On I read . . . and read . . . and read . . . alone.

T H R E E

✛

In the midst of my schooling at the abbey, I
entered my twelfth year of life on Christmas
Day. The year was 1938. By then the Benedictines had despaired of hiding from us the great
events of Europe. In autumn, my schoolmates
returning from their holidays at home had told me
in detail who Hitler was and that he had annexed
Austria and Czechoslovakia. Throughout the
monastery, even the monks spoke openly of
impending war.

My father, in the train of these events so busy
at his embassy in Paris, rarely had leisure to write
to me in the Vaucluse. (My mother did not write to
me at all.) Occasionally he corresponded with
Father Abbot about my grades and conduct. Such
letters as he wrote to me were terse, dictated to his
secretary, typed on embassy paper beneath the
Royal seal, and signed simply, "William." Early in
1939, I did receive from him a longer letter.

My very dear Augustine,

Belatedly, alas!, your mother and I send
you our fondest greetings for your birthday,
Christmastide, and the New Year. We both
of us had frightful colds, were caught up in
the social whirl, and my duties in Chancery
obliged me to leave Christmas Mass at Saint-
Sulpice before the Last Gospel to deal with
urgent cable traffic. However, I have today

under separate cover dispatched to you a quite special gift, which I trust upon arrival will touch and please you.

I do so very much congratulate you, dearest boy, for your studious habits and your high grades. In my recent correspondence with your Father Abbot, I have been discussing your future. I agree with that good Right Reverend gentleman that you shall pursue a career in the Church, but he and I are of different minds as to the direction you should take. The Abbot, naturally enough, wishes you to become a Benedictine monk; I, with equal vigour, rather favour that you should pursue your vocation in the habit of the secular priesthood.

I do not fancy that the vast library of your French abbey contains a copy of Burke's *Peerage,* but if perchance it should, please consult it. You will find that upon the branches of your father's family tree sit several priests and nuns in black, but not a single *Monseigneur* in purple.

I have in mind that when you are somewhat more mature and the proper moment comes, I shall have a word with the Cardinal Archbishop of Westminster and certain ecclesiastical dignitaries at Rome as to your placement in a suitable secular seminary. Do not be hurt, dear boy, if I mention now your physical impediments: I rather doubt, because of them, that I could ever dream of you in the crimson toga of the Sacred College. Yet I see no reason why, if you apply yourself in future as you are doing now, you should not aspire to the episcopal purple of an auxiliary, titular bishopric—perhaps in England, or perhaps more fittingly in some far-flung missionary vineyard such as the Gold Coast or China, all for the glory of God.

Affairs in Europe are becoming so unpropitious that Lady Daphne and I have no more time for our theatricals. She joins me in embracing you.

WILLIAM

For several days, I brooded over that letter. How dare my father decide for me that I had a vocation to Holy Orders? The more I brooded, the more I thought that despite my fantasies of a luxurious cardinalate, God (if He existed) did not intend me for the Church.

Within a fortnight, Sir William's "quite special gift" arrived in a wooden crate: inside wads of straw I found an exquisite plate of porcelain. Embossed upon it were rampant lions and unicorns breathing fire, a coronet, a shield with spears, iron bars and prickly chains, a crucifix: the escutcheon of the Galsworthys. Beneath it was the family legend: *Lux ex Tenebris*: Light from Darkness.

The season now was mid-February; the mistral was howling outside my cell; though lightly clothed in my knickers and white shirt, I dashed alone out of the abbey and up the snowy mountain, through the tombstones of the Benedictine graveyard, clutching my plate of porcelain and embossed escutcheon, sobbing for my father's arrogance and his edict that I must be a priest. Near the summit of the mountain, a jagged rock jutted from the snow: with all my force I smashed his quite special gift into a thousand pieces.

My violence, it seemed to me and soon enough, was a portent of evil happenings. In September, Hitler invaded Poland. In the spring that followed, he invaded France. By then, many of the younger monks had fled my abbey to join the French army. My schoolmates, one by one, vanished also. Again, I was alone in the abbey, now with mostly older monks. At the end of May, Sir William Galsworthy—so I learned from Father Abbot in due course— was killed by the *Luftwaffe* on the road between Paris and Dunkirk.

Valiantly, my father had been amongst the last to evacuate his embassy in the rue Faubourg-St-Honoré, but the details of his death were blurred. In time, he was posthumously awarded the George Cross, but I never learned whether he died defending women and children with a Tommy gun (as one version had it) or (as another version had it) he simply dove blindly from his motorcar into a ditch to escape the bullet that bore his name. His *"Monseigneur"* letter (I shall always call it that) was the last I received from him. I mourned him little.

What I knew of my father's death I learned through the network of the Roman Church; with war, the monks talked constantly of events, sharing them with me. The Germans, at first, did not occupy all of France, only half of her—the north to the Swiss border, then they stabbed southwards along the Bay of Biscay to the frontier with Spain. In the enclave that remained, the dictatorship of Marshal Pétain coped with Nazi pressures as best it could, then succumbed to them. Avignon, Carpentras, the whole *département* of Vaucluse, lay deep inside the "free" zone governed by the senile Marshal of Vichy, but soon I discovered that even in the Vaucluse agents of the Gestapo and the S.S. were everywhere abroad in mufti.

Regular postal service stopped. Eventually, through the Church, I learned the fate of my mother. During the disorder of the invasion, my father had put her on an aeroplane for London before the Germans reached Paris and he took flight on the road to Dunkirk. In the chaos of events they had no leisure to think of me; or they assumed that in the bosom of the Benedictines I would remain safe. In London, the (now dowager) Lady Daphne joined the war effort and became a driver for the Royal Air Force. Suddenly it occurred to me that with my father dead, and as his only child, I had inherited his baronetcy.

I was now entitled, in my fourteenth year, to be addressed in all documents and letters as "Sir Augustine Galsworthy, Bart." Indeed, the monks teasingly began to call me "Sir Augustine." I giggled and responded, *"Non! Je préfère M-M-Monseigneur Augustin"*—My Lord Augustine. The fathers laughed: rare laughter, as the terrors of war drew closer. Rumours swept Vaucluse that the Germans were seizing Jews in the north of France and shipping them eastward to mysterious destinations. First in driblets, then in a flood, Jews from Paris and other regions of the north were migrating to the "free" south in search of sanctuary from the Nazis. One cold winter afternoon, well more than a year after my father's death, a bizarre scene happened at the high iron gate of our monastery.

A crowd of people in summer dress, at least three hundred of them—men, children, women hugging infants—were shouting and banging at our locked bars, begging admittance to the abbey. Peering from the battlements, I asked a monk, "Wh-Who are they, *mon père?*"

"*Des Juifs,*" he answered.

Father Abbot, cowled, white-bearded, patriarchal, whom by now I knew well, stepped from the shadows of the battlements to watch the scene with us. I cried, "*Très R-Révérend Père!* Won't you help these J-Jews?"

"*Non,*" he said.

"*Mais pourquoi?*"

"*Ce n'est pas notre problème.*" It's not our problem.

We repaired to supper, then to chapel for Vespers, chanting from the Book of Genesis of God's creation of the universe, of light, man, and beasts; and Compline, chanting of sleep and waking, life and death, sin and grace. After Divine Office, I eavesdropped outside the Abbot's chambers as he debated with his monks what to do about the Jews outside the gate. Several monks favoured summoning the Vichy police to take them away; rather more pleaded with the Abbot to let them in. "I have made up my mind," said the Abbot finally.

Yet he did not act before I went to bed. Shivering upon my slats of wood, I could not sleep for the weeping and lamentations that rose in the frigid air above the gate and battlements, then echoed through the cloisters to the window of my cell. At dawn, in chapel, we sang Matins and Lauds, shouting praises to God, invoking His mercy, chanting of the rising of the sun and likening it to the Resurrection of the Lord. After breakfast in the refectory, I mounted to the battlements and gazed down at the gate. Of the several hundred Jews I had seen the night before, only fifty or sixty, mostly women with infant children, a few men and boys, a girl or two, had persevered in their vigil, still weeping and lamenting, begging our sanctuary. To what sanctuary had the others fled? I wondered, half knowing there was none.

Suddenly, at my side, stood Father Abbot. Impulsively I grasped his icy, bony hand. He turned away from me, to a monk behind us, and commanded, "*Laissez entrer les Juifs.*" Let the Jews in.

The monk dashed down to the gate, unlocked the chains, and the Jews rushed in. Such a cruel triage, I thought. I demanded of the Abbot, "Why d-did you ignore the hundreds?"

"*Mon cher Augustin,*" said the tall, ancient patriarch, sighing, kissing his rosary, raising his eyes to Heaven. "I had to make a choice. Had I let in the mob, the Gestapo would have found out, and all the Jews you saw—poof! Is it not better, at least, dear child, to save fifty Jews? We'll have trouble hiding *them,* or—poof!"

. . .

From that morning, much of the abbey's energy was devoted to lodging our sudden guests in the cold cellars of the monastery, in fact in caves which the fathers normally reserved for fermenting and bottling wine. The abbey was nearly a town unto itself: the monks also curdled their own cheese, canned vegetables from their own gardens, slaughtered their own sheep, ate the flesh and tanned the hides for manufacture into their own shoes. They brewed their own medicines: when the Jewish infants caught colds, and they often did in those deep caves, the monks treated them with potions and warmed them by the fires of the abbey's ovens.

Above all, the monks—I with them—worked to manufacture credible passports and baptismal certificates to enable the Jews to pretend that they were Christians and to flee Vichy France for Spain, Portugal, and (we prayed) freedom in lands beyond. We forged the certificates of baptism only after Father Abbot had prayed in chapel for at least a week and managed to repress his tormented scruples.

He asked his monks, "Does God allow us to tell so many lies for a higher purpose? These Jews have rejected Christ."

"They never knew Christ," argued Père Benoît. "If you wish to make the certificates true, then baptise them first."

"Conversions for convenience, without faith?" roared Father Abbot. "That's a worse sin!"

"Then the false certificates are the lesser sin." Père Benoît sounded now more like a Jesuit than a Benedictine.

"Oh, oh, oh. . . ."

"Très Révérend Père, la Gestapo. . . ."

"Ah, oui . . . la Gestapo. . . ."

On their printing presses, the monks printed and illuminated dozens of passports, identity cards, and certificates of baptism; then they stamped, signed, and sealed them. They descended to the cellars to dip them into vats of white wine and prune juice to make them in various degrees seem worn and aged before they hung them up to dry on clotheslines near the ovens.

The fathers were as meticulous with names and dates. "Jacob" they changed to "Jean," "Rachel" to "Renée," "Rothstein" to "Rouleau," then added dates of birth or baptism to correspond with the appearance of the documents and the photographs of the bearers: 1905 . . . 1921 . . . 1934. Père Benoît and I worked near each other among the monks dipping documents into the vats; but Father Abbot still forbade us to commune, to resume by spoken or written word our "particular friendship." I chatted shyly now and then with a Jewish girl, my age more or less, brown of eye and ungainly like myself, not pretty.

"What's your n-name?" I asked her one morning in the caves.

"Sarah," said she.

"After Abraham's first w-wife?"

"Did Abraham have a second wife?"

"K-Keturah, I think."

"Aren't you smart?"

"Th-thank you. Where are you f-from?"

"Paris."

"I lived—for a l-l-little while—on the rue de Lille."

"Around the corner from me! Our house is on the rue du Bac."

"Wh-Who lives there now?"

"Nobody."

"I'm sorry that you're J-Jewish, Sarah."

"I'm as French as you are."

"I'm not F-French. I meant, I'm sorry that you're p-p-persecuted."

Eventually, armed with their false papers, the Jews were dispatched from the abbey in stages, in late evening or at dawn, in groups of three or four, to their salvation or their doom.

During such events, again through the network of the Church, Father Abbot was receiving letters from my mother, increasingly hysterical.

In his good time, he showed them to me. At London, Lady Daphne had been reading in the press that the Germans, and very soon, might barge through the wobbly barriers of Vichy and occupy all of France. She conceived a phobia that I would be captured by the Nazis, who would discover that I was circumcised and think me a Jew.

Not such a *wild* fantasy: Christian European males were generally uncircumcised. To the north, in railroad and bus stations, the S.S. were pulling down the pants of grown men and the knickers of little boys whom they suspected might be Jews. I have never ceased to ask myself, If my mother was so ashamed of the Jewish twigs—or branches?—on her family tree, why did she so punctiliously have me circumcised, according to the Old Covenant, on the eighth day of my life?

She stuffed her letters to Father Abbot with sterling notes to finance my flight from France—through Spain and Portugal—to Britain.

"Therefore . . . you must leave," said Father Abbot.

"No," I protested. "This abbey is my only h-h-home."

"But Lady Daphne is your mother."

"I h-hate her."

"Have we monks taught you nothing of Christian love?"

"*You* did—not Lady D-Daphne or my d-dead father."

"But the danger . . ."

"I prefer the N-Nazis to my m-mother."

I was nearly fifteen now, swiftly growing taller. Father Abbot, fearful of the Vichy police, decided to accompany me himself from Vaucluse to the Spanish border, and to disguise me for the journey as a fellow Benedictine. On my final evening in the abbey, I begged him for a few minutes of farewell with Père Benoît.

"*Non,*" said Father Abbot.

At dawn, we set out, I garbed like him in black tunic, leather belt, scapular, shoes, and cowl, the cowl pulled low and forward to hide my childish face. In my small black bag, I carried a fake French identity card and two authentic passports—from the United Kingdom and the United States. Just beyond the gate, I glanced back to the battlements, praying that Père Benoît might stand there, waving me adieu. He was not on the battlements; I mourned for several miles as we walked in autumn sunshine from our mountain to Carpentras.

At Carpentras, we boarded a rusty bus to Avignon; from Avignon we rode a belching train through Nîmes to the Mediterranean, then south towards Perpignan. Father Abbot had brought an extra breviary: as I sat beside him on a wooden bench in third class, I read the Office of the Day, pretending to be a priest and rather liking our little theatrical. At every stop, Vichy militia in uniform passed through the cars with blond men in grey fedoras (Gestapo?), but they did not ask us for our papers, we seemed such humble monks.

South of Perpignan, we got off a bus in the foothills of the Pyrénées. The Abbot said, "We must avoid the border posts. We'll wait till night." At night, we walked amongst the mountains and got lost. Two days later, hungry and exhausted, we entered Spain. Father Abbot embraced me liturgically as though at Solemn Mass, and said, "*Pax tecum. Bon voyage. Adieu, cher Augustin.*" He pointed through the forest and the falling tawny leaves southward to Figueras, then turned away from me to France.

Alone in the wood, I became afraid. I decided not to shed my Benedictine habit, but to prolong my theatrical until I should enter Portugal. Halfway there, I ran out of money. Can you picture me as a mendicant monk on the cobblestones of Valladolid? At Salamanca, I learned that the Allies had invaded Vichy North Africa and that the *Wehrmacht* had occupied all of France. A fortnight later, I reached Lisbon. At His Majesty's Embassy, I found a letter from my mother.

My dearest son,

By the grace of God and His Church, I have heard from your Father Abbot that you entered Spain safely. When you read this letter, speak at once to the First Secretary, and he will cable me that you are safe in Lisbon. He will also pass some money to you and arrange for your transport on military aircraft directly to Scotland, where I have arranged that you shall continue your studies at Appleforth Abbey. That would please your father; I do *miss* him so.

You can not come to London because it is too dangerous—bombs might fall at any moment. Besides, I am so very busy with my secret work for the R.A.F. As soon as I can, I shall come to you in Scotland.

Heaps of love,

DAPHNE

Secret work? I wondered: I thought she was a chauffeur. She never came to me in Scotland.

My several years at Appleforth I refuse to relive: too bleak. Mostly I remember wet moors, rolling fogs, thick stone walls. Inside them, we lived largely on broth and apples; wartime Britain was hungrier than France. The British Benedictines were cold and kindly both at once; I missed the mellow sunshine of the south of France, my Father Abbot, and my Père Benoît. I read more theology, Latin, Greek; Cardinal Newman on the truths of Christianity; Edward Gibbon on the decline and fall of the Roman Empire and the lies of Christianity. I learned also to swim in lochs a little and to drive a truck.

When the war in Europe ended, I was in my eighteenth year. I took the train to London, bought books in the Charing Cross Road, and then went to see my mother.

Nearly a decade had passed since our brief life together in Paris before the war. She dwelt in a large flat in Kensington, decorated in garish Art Nouveau. Yet I preferred the flat to the appearance of Her Dowagership.

Lady Daphne, whose beauty I had admired, had aged so remarkably that even the strains of wartime could not justify her face. Her hair, once black, she had dyed to a curly ginger. Her eyes, once a shimmering brown, had lost their lustre, as much as I could glimpse of them beneath her green lids. Her neck, once long and stately, seemed as wrinkled as a ravaged swan's. We did not conduct a conversation: it was more like an interview, as though I were applying for a job.

"You've grown so tall, Augustine, dear."

"Thank you, Mother."

"And better-looking."

"Thank you, Mother."

"You're a bit less awkward, too."

"Thank you, Mother."

"I adore your tweed suit."

"Thank you, Mother."

"And your stammer's gone!"

"Thank you, M-Mother."

She wore a long gown, the texture of expensive beige, sewn with gems about the neck; it reached to her ankles, touching her gilded shoes. I thought, She thinks it makes her slimmer, but against her ample bosom and broad shoulders, it can not hide her bulk. With no other evidence, I concluded she was in pursuit of some duke or marquis to marry into a title superior to my own. Did she read my mind? Suddenly she rose and said, "I have your Royal patent."

She walked to a writing-desk, pulled at a drawer, took out documents— the proof from whatever Royal office that I had inherited Sir William's baronetcy, and a letter praising my father's valour on the road to Dunkirk, signed by the King. I glanced at them and said, "Sir Augustine Galsworthy, BART! *Lux ex Tenebris!* And my in-h-heritance?"

"It's not large, Augustine. Twenty thousand pounds."

"I'll t-take it."

"Now that you've finished Appleforth, what will you do?"

"I don't know."

"You know of your father's last wish—that you become a *Monseigneur.*"

"I DON'T WANT TO BE A P-PRIEST!"

"Oh, dear. You're being frightful. What did they feed you at Appleforth?"

"Forgive me, Mother. Broth and a-p-ples."

I walked to the door.

"Where are you going?" Lady Daphne demanded.

"Back to France."

"*Where* in France?"

"To the only h-home I have—my abbey in Vaucluse."

Father Abbot, quite ancient, awaited me at the gate of the monastery. I looked about, upward to the battlements, seeking a sharp face. I asked, "And Père Benoît?"

The Abbot sighed. "We let in more Jews. The Gestapo came. Père Benoît talked back to them. He is up there."

Father Abbot pointed beyond the Gallic ramparts to the graveyard of the abbey upon the mountain. He said, "Go, visit his tomb, *cher Augustin.* You may speak to him now."

✥

FOUR

✥

In time my Father Abbot told me, *"Cher Augustin,* you must prepare to leave us."

"Wh-Why?" I cried.

"There is nothing more in this monastery that we can teach you. Shall I grasp in space for some example? What ... what was the heresy of Gnosticism?"

"Gn-Gnosticism flourished in the first three centuries of the Christian era. Amongst its many ef-f-fusions, the common bond was a belief that salvation is achieved by s-secret knowledge—that Heaven is the prize of the p-privileged f-few."

"So all of the Gnostics were early Christians?"

"Mais non, Très Révérend P-Père!" I explained that Gnosticism grew out of pagan philosophy and was much influenced by the ancient pre-Christian cults of India, Egypt, and—above all—the Manichaeanism of the Persians. The Christian Gnostics dabbled in magic, hid behind Christian symbols, and polluted much Christian doctrine. All matter—they said—was a corruption of the Divine; existence itself was an abomination to be fled only by élite knowledge; Christ was an aeon, a bulwark between God and evil matter. "F-Furthermore—"

"Who were the chief Gnostics?"

"B-Basilides, Valentinus, T-Tatian, and—first and f-foremost—M-M-Marcion."

"Who was their chief antagonist?"

"Irenaeus! F-Furthermore . . ." The Gnostics brooded constantly on the nature of evil. To them, the separate worlds of good and evil were for ever waging war, the world of the Divine for ever clashing with the world of matter—the seat of all evil—the kingdom of light for ever locked in struggle with the realm of darkness. Demons abounded in the realm of darkness—but they were for ever embattled by the Great Mother.

"But who was the Great Mother?"

"The goddess of H-Heaven. The Mother of the Moon and S-Stars."

"Did she have a body?"

"Mais non, Très Révérend P-Père!" To the Gnostics, the human body incarnated Evil. Carnal pleasure, even within matrimony, was all wickedness and horror. For salvation, self-denial was all virtue and beauty. Mere physical beauty, in men or women, was most dangerous—the mask of Satan. "Even my namesake, S-Saint Augustine—though valiant in his war against the Manichaeans—was infected by their hatred of the human b-b-body."

"Eh voilà, Augustin! You have read so deeply that you know already as much theology—or nearly as much?—as the rest of us. Thus you must be gone—into a seminary."

"I don't want to be a p-priest."

"Why?"

"I have no v-vocation—no special g-grace. I've seen no sh-shaft of light."

"God more often reveals Himself in silent, hidden, secret ways. Shafts of light? Special grace? We have the vision of Père Benoît."

"Père Benoît!"

"He saw you on the high altar, dressed in the robes of a cardinal. I did not believe him then. I believe him now. He may have been a saint."

"A s-saint?"

"He died, as you remember, a holy martyr, tortured and shot by the Gestapo. Since then, a cult has grown up round his blessed memory. More and more, the peasants, the common people of Vaucluse, are visiting his grave—up there, upon the hillside—reciting the Rosary and the *Salve Regina* and the prayers for the dead, leaving flowers and scraps of paper with their petitions, begging his intercession before the throne of God. A few people—deluded perhaps, perhaps not?—are even claiming miraculous cures. Here at the abbey, we are pondering a petition to Rome that the Holy See consider Père Benoît as a candidate for beatification. There is a troubling question, *cher Augustin,* that I must ask you, since only you can answer it." Father Abbot sighed from his depths. "I was tormented by your particular friendship. Did he ever . . ."

"We never had a p-particular friendship," I protested. "Once, c-crazed by loneliness, I hugged him for an instant, but he broke l-loose from me and said, 'As a monk I must not be fond of anyone—save our Lord Redeemer Jesus Ch-Christ.'"

Father Abbot in his cowl rose from his armchair and dropped to his knees on the stone floor. Kissing the crucifix of his rosary, he raised his eyes and called out thanks to Heaven. *"Mon Dieu, je Vous remercie très humblement de toutes les grâces que Vous m'avez faites! C'est encore par un effet de Votre bonté que je vois ce jour. . . !"* As Father Abbot shouted out his gratitude, I looked through the lancet window of his room to see a trickle of the common people—women, children, old men, a young man, two young men, three young men—climbing the side of the arid mountain, bearing bunches of summer flowers and waving aloft little scraps of paper, towards the tomb of Père Benoît.

Then Father Abbot clutched my arm, led me through the cloisters to the Gothic chapel. In the sanctuary, he pointed to his abbatial throne and whispered, "Père Benoît was deep in prayer. Suddenly he heard a sound, the rustling of robes, and looked to the high altar. There, seated on my throne, was a child—you, *cher Augustin*—in the red biretta and full crimson robes of a Cardinal of the Holy Roman Church. We, the others, wanted you as one of us, a Benedictine monk, in robes of simple black—but Père Benoît, I am now convinced, was sanctified. The visions and prophecies of saints—without exception—are destined to come true."

We walked to my tiny cell above the cloister. Amid my disorderly heaps of books, I sat on the wooden slats that were my bed. I wore a neat black suit, a white shirt and black tie, and patent leather shoes. I said, without my stammer, "Please. Beloved Father. I do not wish to be a priest."

"But all these sacred books! What else could you be, *cher Augustin*?"

"I thought of m-marriage."

"Do you know any women?"

"None except my m-mother—and I hardly know h-her."

"Are you attracted to women?"

"I'm not qu-quite sure. Much of my life has been l-lived in this abbey. I'm t-terrified of w-women."

"You will be more than a mere priest, Augustin. Your father was a distinguished diplomatist—and so must you become. His dying wish was that you embrace the secular priesthood. Recently I spoke with Monseigneur the Archbishop of Avignon. Monseigneur is making the arrangements with Rome. Since you are a baronet, you will be enrolled in the Pontifical Academy of Noble Ecclesiastics, where—in a rare exception—you will be allowed to complete your studies for the priesthood and learn diplomacy both at once. I have, also, corresponded with Lady Daphne, your dear mother, who—"

"D-Dear mother?"

"Who, eager to follow your father's wish, has blessed my disposition of the matter. Within but several years, you will be ordained a priest and enter the diplomatic service of the Holy See."

"But my stammer . . . my awk-k-kwardness . . ."

Father Abbot's eyes, celestial blue, flecked with yellow, blazed from their grottoes, all holy zeal. He said, "God, in His good time—or men, His agents—will cure you of your imperfections." Now he spoke in perfect English—a tongue that hitherto I had been unaware he knew. "Were you anyone else, Sir Augustine, I should abandon you to matrimony—but the prophecy must come true. Next week, you shall go to Rome."

PART II

✣

PRIESTHOOD

✣

F I V E

The Pontifical Academy of Noble Ecclesiastics, founded by Clement XI early in the eighteenth century for youthful clerics of lofty birth, dominated the Piazza della Minerva, Roman goddess of wisdom. In the centre of the Piazza stood Bernini's marble elephant, bearing upon its back an obelisk hewn in Egypt six centuries before Christ and symbolising, with the elephant, the pagan ideal of virile intellect. Behind a façade of cinnamon, Doric pillars, and papal seals, my companions in the Academy were all lords; dukes, barons, and viscounts; Frenchmen, Belgians, Germans, an Austrian or two, much outnumbered by Italians. And they were all of them ordained priests, making me the baby of the house.

Amidst the muffled conversations and shuffling feet in marble corridors, I mused: So ends my childhood—in a funeral parlour! We wore buttoned, tailored black soutanes; sombre footmen in livery of grey served our simple meals and cleaned our spacious private rooms. My bed seemed too luxurious. Missing my abbey in Vaucluse, I flung off the fluffy mattress and slept on the hard slats.

As I pursued my studies, I took the tonsure, symbolising Christ's crown of thorns, and progressed rapidly through the minor orders—porter, lector, exorcist, and acolyte. I pronounced my initial vows of perfect obedience and chastity. I heard lectures in Latin and Italian not only at the

Academy but at pontifical universities throughout Rome, chiefly from Jesuits at the Gregorian and Dominicans at the Angelicum. Most of the texts assigned to me in theology, philosophy, Canon Law, and Church history I had already read. The Academy's courses in protocol, jurisprudence, political economy, and international law were less familiar, but I with ease mastered them.

At the Academy I remained entrapped in my ungainliness, stammering like a stupid child, bumping into Italianate Louis Quinze furniture and marble busts of popes, not least of Leo XIII, himself an alumnus of the Academy, whose likeness reposed on a pedestal outside my rooms. My lordly peers, the greater part of them, indulged my trivial misfortunes, raising me up when I tripped on a Persian rug or collided with a balustrade; but the smirking few laughed less when I took Firsts in every subject and surpassed them all, the kindly and the unkindly lords. I was cheerful to everyone, merry even to half-chums, but I shunned friendships and kept mostly to myself.

Or rather, in that palace I had a single friend, long since dead. On the wall opposite my door, in a gilded frame, hung an oil portrait of Ercole Cardinal Consalvi, another alumnus of the Academy, Prime Minister to Pius VII, and a legend in the diplomacy of the Church. Beneath the painting stood a settee of red damask—the Cardinal's own. Often I sat sideways on it, raising my eyes to feast on his urbanity, on his face so slender and so fine above his crimson mozzetta and long patrician neck. Here in such elegance and grace was all that I was not and wished I might be.

My admiration verged on worship. Beneath my breath I mourned, "Why could I not be born C-Consalvi?"

Like me, he was a nobleman, and more, a marquis. As Secretary of the Conclave which assembled at Venice in 1800 on the morrow of the French Revolution, Monsignore Consalvi induced the cardinal-electors to choose the saintly Benedictine, Barnabà Cardinal Chiaramonti, to the Chair of Peter as Pius VII. At Rome, some few months later, Pius VII raised Consalvi to the Sacred College and appointed him first minister, with orders to restore the Roman Church to France. Consalvi hastened to Paris to negotiate a concordat with General Bonaparte, the First Consul, and his tool, the Prince de Talleyrand, apostate bishop and famous trickster.

In the palace of the Tuileries, the First Consul was enchanted by the Pope's emissary, but Consalvi's suave presence and perfect manners reproached the crude Corsican. Ever the bully, Bonaparte stormed and raged, shouting threats that if he could not control the Christianity of France then he would sever it from the Church of Rome. When Consalvi in full watered silk presented new drafts of the Concordat, Bonaparte hurled them into the fire, retrieved them from the flames, and stomped on them with his soldier's boots. After another of the Consul's tantrums, Talleyrand took Consalvi aside and asked, "Isn't it a pity that such a genius should be so badly brought up? You'd best do as he demands."

Patiently and coolly the Cardinal endured the boorish soldier until he had negotiated a concordat he could present to Pius VII at Rome, whither he gal-loped. On the altars of France, Eldest Daughter of the Church, the religion of Rome was restored. Yet soon Bonaparte decided it was not enough to be dictator and First Consul—he must be Napoleon, Emperor of the French. Pius VII must come to Paris and Notre-Dame to anoint his brow, then sit watching as he crowned himself.

Full of misgiving, the Sovereign Pontiff set out for France, where he remained for months, leaving Cardinal Consalvi behind as regent of Rome and the Papal States. The Tiber overflowed, flooding much of Rome; Con-salvi heaped up sandbags with his own hands, nearly drowning as the flood swept all before it; for weeks it seemed that he was everywhere at once, attending to the hungry, sick, and homeless, a tribune of the people. The flood was but a portent of the upheavals to follow.

Pius VII returned to Rome, humiliated by Napoleon's act of self-coronation but still under the Emperor's spell. The Pontiff, by nature con-templative and trusting, sympathised with the ideals of the Revolution; Consalvi, reared from birth as a legitimist, revered the divine right of kings and of the Bourbons especially. As though to shock the Pontiff into Con-salvi's camp, Napoleon's armies invaded the Papal States and Rome itself. The Pope excommunicated the Emperor: the worst holy curse. Thereupon Pius VII was kidnapped, and—separated from Consalvi—dragged first to Savona and then, extremely ill, over the snowy Alps to Fontainebleau. He remained the Emperor's prisoner for five years, distressed—at times it seemed half-deranged—without Consalvi's counsel and his friendship.

Consalvi was dragged to Paris, where Napoleon told him that the Pope must renounce Rome, the Papal States, all temporal power, and transfer the papacy to Paris or to Avignon. "If not," the Emperor shouted, "I shall destroy the Church!"

"Sire," Consalvi answered glacially, "in nearly two millennia, not even we priests could accomplish that."

Napoleon stripped Consalvi of all his crimson and exiled him to Reims. When the Emperor returned from his defeat in Russia, he went to Fon-tainebleau, where he smashed crockery and bullied sick Pius VII into signing a degrading new concordat; yet as compensation he blundered by allowing Consalvi to rejoin his master. Soon Consalvi set things right—the Pontiff repudiated the new concordat; with Consalvi at his side, his health and spirits rallied. Within two years, Napoleon was on St Helena; Pius VII and Cardinal Consalvi returned triumphantly to Rome. At the Congress of Vienna, Consalvi won back the Papal States and helped not only to restore royalist legitimacy but to redraw the map of Europe, for more than half a century preserving the peace of Christendom.

In times of singular disorder, everything that Consalvi did, whether in diplomacy or as governor of Rome, shone with wisdom and moderation. As Cardinal Prime Minister he patronised the arts, preserved antiqui-ties, founded chairs of science and archaeology at pontifical universities. He endowed musicians prodigiously because music was his commanding passion: on the harpsichord and the pianoforte, he played Bach and Mozart well. (In Vienna as a youth, he had dined with Mozart!) More, unlike so many high prelates of his epoch, Cardinal Consalvi remained chaste. He enjoyed every favour that life might grant him except the Tiara of the papacy and the sweet groans of sex: he kept the rules. His body lies at Pius VII's side in Thorwaldsen's vast Grecian tomb in the transept of St Peter's.

On Sunday mornings, after Mass in St Peter's, I prayed invariably at Consalvi's tomb.

I thought, If I can not be happy, shall I substitute ambition?

I told Consalvi, "I shall b-become you."

Such dreams! Such vainglory! During winter, as I approached my ordination to the subdiaconate, I received a letter—written in a hand so quivering I did well to decipher it—from my mother.

> My dearest son
> I am in Vermont and sick with something. I sold Galsworthy Court or did I tell you. Your dearest father did so love Galsworthy Court and Gloucestershire. Too shabby shabby don't you think. I remember a theatrical. What part did I play. You wished to play some little part but Sir William and I we wouldn't let you? Was it I who dropped you. Was I frightful to you. We were happy in Paris together do you remember. Did we celebrate Purim in Paris I forget. I'm sick with something. I'm in Vermont not sure of my address. The nurse will write it on the envelope? Am I a nymph am I a laurel tree. Come to me in Vermont? Heaps of love
>
> DAPHNE

I did not reply. A fortnight later, I received a cable from Lady Daphne's parish priest. "YOUR MOTHER DYING UTERINE CANCER WISHES SEE YOU STOP FAITHFULLY IN CHRIST REV TERENCE FARRICY." I did not reply. That very year, the most eminent of French feminists had pronounced in Paris, "The foetus is a cancer in the woman's womb." Had *I* caused my mother's cancer? I half hoped so. A week passed, then came this cable: "LADY DAPHNE HAS BUT DAYS TO LIVE BEGS FOR YOU STOP IN CHRIST FATHER FARRICY." I did not reply. Then: "YOUR MOTHER DIED LAST NIGHT STOP FUNERAL FRIDAY FARRICY." I remained in Rome.

On that Friday, at the hour I supposed the funeral might be in progress, I did repair to chapel and I opened my fat missal, flipping the pages vacantly as I sought the Mass for the Dead. I happened upon the Introit: *"Requiem aeternam dona ei Domine: et lux perpetua luceat ei. Te decet hymnus Deus in Sion, et tibi reddetur votum in Jerusalem. . . ."* I could not continue. Like a sleepwalker I groped and zigzagged towards my rooms, numb or quivering—do I remember?—with hatred, sorrow, and remorse.

Throughout the weeks thereafter, I interred *myself*—in researching and composing my dissertation for my doctorate in theology: on Divine grace: Divine grace as it inspires vows: Divine grace as it inspires the priestly vows of permanent, perfect obedience and chastity. Eventually I could not bear the subject any longer, so I shoved aside my Latin and Italian texts, and to soothe my mind and keep my sanity, I interred myself in French.

I regressed to my childhood, to my abbey in Vaucluse, to my mellow afternoons with Père Benoît and aesthetic pleasure. Dreamily I read, yet another time, from start to finish, Chateaubriand's *Génie du christianisme.*

"Man dangles in the present, between past and future. Behind him, before him, all is shadow; barely does he see the few phantoms ascending from the depths, floating for an instant upon the waves, then plunging deep again. . . ." Thus does Christianity provide its passions and its treasures to the poet. Like all great loves, it hints of the serious and the sad; it leads us to the gloom of cloisters, thence to the crests of mountains. Religion is the true philosophy of the fine arts: it never separates, as does human wisdom, poetry and ethics, tenderness and virtue. "Oh, how bitterly we remember those days when men of blood presumed to raise up—upon the ruins of Christianity, in the temples of the Virgin, who had consoled so many wretched hearts—the goddess of *Reason,* who has yet to wipe away a tear!

"Atheism has nothing but plague and leprosy to offer you. Religion roots itself in the feelings of the soul, in the sweetest bonds of life, in a father's fondness for his son, in the love of wife and husband, or a mother's for her child" . . . *or a mother's for her child or a mother's for her child or a mother's for her child.* "In our faith as Christians, we are assured that our sufferings will end; we are consoled; we dry our tears; we look upward to another life. God is all beauty. I wept and I believed. *J'ai pleuré et j'ai cru. . . .*"

Roused by my sobs, another scholar banged on the wall from the next rooms, then ran into the corridor and through my door to console me as he could. He was Arnaud, a comely Belgian viscount, but I rebuffed his pity. *"Que s'est-il passé, cher Augustin?"* he asked gently. I had told no one in the palace of my mother's death, nor could I confide in this half-chum, yet speechlessly I wept on.

"Tell me why, Augustin!" Arnaud pleaded.

"I can not."

"I'm offering you my friendship!"

"I'm not worth your f-friendship."

Arnaud embraced me and withdrew. Soon enough, Lady Daphne's solicitors wrote to me from London, announcing my new inheritance, one hundred thousand dollars, nor did I give the money to the poor. Spring came, earlier than usual and warmer, too. Through my open window I stared for hour upon hour at the obelisk of Egypt, but my inheritance could not console me and my tears would not cease. My Rector, meeting me at meals, became alarmed by my loss of weight, my indifference to food, and my purple eyes. He said, "Galsworthy, deep study is all well and good, but more than ever you sin by your excess of zeal."

"Your G-Grace. . . ."

"I'm to ordain you soon to the subdiaconate, but I can not ordain a ghost. I command you—go on holiday."

"On h-holiday? When?"

"Tomorrow."

The Rector was an archbishop and a prince as well, a huge Bavarian in black and purple with eyes so blue and hair of snowy Alpine white still streaked with strands so blond, so blond: another of the reigning Pontiff's German favourites. He had served the Kaiser as a captain of artillery in the Battle of the Somme, before his right leg was blasted off and he retreated to the service of the Roman Church. I asked, "Where should I go on holiday?"

"Go home to England," said the Prince-Archbishop.

"England is not my home, Your Grace. May I go to France?"

"Where in France?"

"My abbey in V-Vaucluse."

"*No!*" The old soldier stomped his wooden foot. "Those monks made you melancholy. Do you ever smile, Galsworthy? Do you ever laugh? When I was in the army, even in the trenches with the shells exploding, we German soldiers joked."

"Is a G-German j-joke a laughing matter?"

"Oh, *ha*! Go to Florence, Galsworthy. Since you so love art, go to the galleries. Rest your mind. Sit in the sun. *Eat. Sleep.* Walk along the Arno. Stay away from libraries! Except for your daily Office, I *forbid* you to read! You shall not return to Rome for one month."

I glanced across the great refectory of Carrara marble to a distant table where the pleasant viscount Arnaud sat, alone, eating his salad. I asked, "May Arnaud come w-with me?"

"No," said the Prince-Archbishop.

At dawn, I took a taxi from the Piazza della Minerva to the Stazione Termini, where I boarded a train for Florence, alone.

+

S I X

+

In Medici Florence, after but a day or two, I avoided the centre of the city—the galleries, the cathedral, and the Piazza della Signoria. In the piazza, for a few minutes, I lingered to admire Benvenuto Cellini's statue of the naked Perseus holding aloft Medusa's severed head, and Giotto's toothy campanile surging from the Palazzo Vecchio; but in the Uffizi and Pitti galleries, even the most celebrated masterpieces—the Raphaels and Titians; Peruginos and Boticellis; Lippis and da Vincis—I passed with only hurried glances. I spent half an hour at the Accademia, regarding from various perspectives the lithe, colossal nude splendour of Michelangelo's marble David. Obedient to the Prince-Archbishop, I kept away from libraries.

At daylight, I attended Mass beneath the ancient beams and stained glass of the Franciscan church of Santa Croce. For the rest of the mornings, with nothing else I wished to do, I wandered more and more towards the periphery of Florence, through narrow, pink, cobblestoned streets; past rowboats, battlements, and mediaeval houses along the River Arno—until I could see the claret Tuscan hills and far beyond them even the misty mountains of Carrara.

I wandered through thickets and vineyards, delighted by sudden rustic shrines of the Madonna and her infant Child. I sat in the cool shade of poplar and cypress trees, looking to meadows carpeted by flowers, and to the twinkling Arno as it flowed beside sunlit paths in its westward progress towards the sea. Watching the river as it groped between young green vines and grey gnarled olive trees, between the Tuscan hills into a horizon of hazy blue, I wondered about my calling to the priesthood—which I may have heard or perhaps never heard—and whither it would lead, like the river in the distance yonder, vanishing?

Clad as always in my buttoned black soutane, gripping my black breviary, feeling the Mediterranean sun burn the bare skin of the tonsure on my skull, I sat down on a stump of tree in an olive grove and read my sacred Office of the day. In the midst of this, I heard branches cracking, trod upon with the earth underfoot. Startled, I looked up and saw half of someone—a floral skirt, blue shoes, darting behind a tree; I heard hasty footsteps fading until beyond my earshot; or was I imagining? Now only the songs of larks above my head, and the hum of oil presses crushing olives in faraway tiled shacks, intruded on my prayers.

At midday, from Franciscan towers scattered across the plain, bells tolled, ringing out the Angelus: three strokes, a pause; three strokes, a pause; three strokes, a pause; nine strokes. Across the fields, peasants and their children in rough costume knelt upon the soil, bowed their heads, and prayed. The Angel of the Lord announced unto Mary. And she conceived of the Holy Ghost. *Ave Maria.* . . . Behold the handmaid of the Lord. Be it done unto me according to Thy Word. *Ave Maria.* . . . And the Word was made Flesh. And dwelt amongst us. *Ave Maria.* . . .

I knelt together with the peasants and recited the Angelus, still not sure that I believed a word of it. At least my long walks had restored my wish for food; hungrily I got up and—glimpsing Giotto's campanile above bursts of oleander—I returned to Florence, where I took my luncheon in a catacomb.

Solitary ecclesiastics in the Italy of that early postwar era were suspect in public places, ordered by their superiors to avoid cinemas, games, and restaurants—even as they were expected to shun "particular friendships," reserving their emotions and their love for Christ, His Virgin Mother, and the saints also in Heaven who clustered round them before the throne of God the Father, much as in the paintings I had hurried past in the Pitti and Uffizi galleries.

A *trattoria,* near the Arno and my hotel, served my furtive purpose. I approached it down an alley, then descended many steps. Inside, the restaurant was cramped, tomb-like, lit haphazardly by fake electric candles, decorated by dangling Chianti bottles, and rarely full of patrons. I retreated through a curtain of red and yellow beads to an alcove in the rear, dimly lit, which contained but several tables and where I could lunch in solitude.

Today, I ordered prosciutto and melon, a plate of pasta, a green salad, a fresh peach, and a large carafe of chilled white wine. Normally I drank little, but lately I looked forward to my wine and even to an apéritif before my meal or a cognac afterwards (or both) because they made me slightly tipsy and thus drowsy for my siesta, which with luck might last the afternoon:

until I was ready to go out again for apéritifs and dinner, seeking that sort of stupor to last till dawn. As I sipped my wine and nibbled on my prosciutto, the beads of my alcove rattled and a woman entered, alone.

She sat in the other nook, opposite my own, in her floral dress and blue shoes. I watched her, or rather glanced at her, only as she entered my cave and sat, since like any good seminarian I practised "custody of the eyes" and kept them downcast while I consumed my luncheon. When the boy entered with my pasta, she ordered prosciutto, pasta, and white wine; when he came with my salad, and then my peach, she ordered a salad and a peach.

After my peach and espresso coffee, I lingered over my cognac, as she did over hers, and though I kept the custody of my eyes, I knew that she was gazing at me. Finally I rose and walked out of the cool restaurant, glancing once over my shoulder and thanking God that she did not follow me.

When I emerged from the alley into the boulevard along the River Arno, the blazing sun and heat of afternoon hit me with much force and I nearly stumbled. Dazed, full of food and wine, I strode uncertainly up the boulevard until I reached the Albergo Berchielli, where I mounted to my rooms and collapsed on my bed—soft and downy, a luxury I allowed myself on holiday—hoping for oblivion and having it.

This ritual of the cave, the luncheon, the litre of chilled wine, the silent woman in the nook opposite, the siesta dissolving into oblivion, continued for days and days, I should say for at least a week. One afternoon, varying my menu, between my pasta and my salad I ordered a *bistecca fiorentina*: she did the same. When I finished my refreshment and rose to leave, still in faithful custody of my eyes, she rose from her nook also and followed me through the curtain of red and yellow beads.

I mounted the many steps, and hurried through the alley, across the boulevard to the balustrade along the Arno, where the sudden heat of day struck me again with such ferocity that my mind swam for some moments and for support I had to lean against the balustrade. Recovering, I glanced at my right hand which gripped my breviary and my rosary wound around it; I had bruised my knuckles against the balustrade; droplets of my blood mingled with my rosary beads.

I continued to walk along the river towards my hotel, fingering my moist rosary, praying that the woman had ceased to follow me. I paused again by the balustrade, pretending to watch a bird in flight, and glanced behind me. The woman wore sunglasses, and a floral skirt and jacket over her broad hips. Without a word, she grasped my hand with the bloody rosary round it and kissed my fingers: I did not resist. We stood by the Arno staring at each other. Her complexion was dark, her hair very black; she was perhaps a decade older than myself. She asked, "Will you come with me to the seashore?"

"Where?" I stammered.

"Viareggio."

"I c-can't."

I continued to stammer replies to her entreaties as we walked further along the Arno, I several steps behind her to avoid notice. She turned to me: "Where do you live, Padre?"

"I'm not a p-priest," I said.

"Where do you live?"

I pointed to the Albergo Berchielli opposite. I was terrified that we might encounter people in the lobby, but in the hour of siesta there was no one in the lobby or at the desk, and from the bar beyond not even the *swooosh* of the espresso machine oozing coffee, yet I could hear the bludgeon hammering inside my chest as we entered the lift unnoticed. My hands trembled: my bloodied fingers could not press the button.

"*Che piano?*" she asked.

"*Qu-Quinto,*" I replied.

Calmly she pressed the button, and we ascended to the fifth floor. Inside my rooms, I tossed my breviary and the rosary round it towards an armchair, but my aim was poor and they landed in a wire wastebasket. On my way to retrieve them, I bumped my head against the armoire. She laughed and asked, "Why are you so clumsy?"

"My mother d-d-dropped me on my head," I answered.

"I saw you in an olive grove. You were bumping into trees."

"I was looking for a laurel t-tree."

"In an olive grove?"

"My mother is a laurel t-tree."

Slowly, as I stood, she removed my soutane, my shirt, all of my garments, and then as languidly disrobed herself. Sitting on my bed, she embraced me round my waist as I remained standing. She looked up at me and said, "You may be clumsy, but your body is quite fine. Smooth and hairless—like marble."

Yours isn't, thought I. Yet though her hips were peasant-broad and her skin was lumpy, there was a freshness and a softness to her body that I found pleasing. She continued, "Smooth. I saw you, the other day, at the Accademia. You remind me of David."

"I l-lack his grace," I said.

"You're circumcised," she said. "I've seduced many priests, but you're the first who's circumcised." She giggled. "Or are you a rabbi? Are you Italian?"

"*Né rabbino né italiano,*" I replied, laughing, beginning to enjoy myself.

Now my cinema resumed, and I watched myself—not in colour but in a grainy, jerky, black and white—as fondly she addressed my loins. Until that moment, I had observed the rules of Holy Church, keeping the custody of my eyes, drowning my fantasies of Aphrodite with icy showers in the early mornings and in the middle of the nights, sleeping supine on my wooden slats with my arms crisscrossed against my breast, all to prevent emissions against my wish.

I had, of course, abstained from masturbation. Or rather, I had practised it compulsively, much against my wish, only for several weeks—when I was a child and those images of Avignon were still fresh, the portals opened across the square and the schoolgirls two by two in blue berets, white blouses, blue skirts and stockings, advanced towards me, creatures from another sphere, and the girl at the end of the procession, brown hair and brown eyes, stared at me for an instant and smiled swiftly.

Thus today in the Albergo Berchielli, the treasury of my seed seemed to me an embarrassment of riches. She worked slowly, yet so methodically that when my eruption began to stir, it did so with such measured speed that I hoped it might last for ever. Soon we were recumbent side by side. As ever my food and wine had made me drowsy; she caressed and kissed me in many parts, turning me gently as I dozed. When I awoke, I reciprocated upon her softness to satisfy fantasies of my own, but before such amusement became too repetitious, she beckoned me into her catacomb.

Enough of my erotic cinema; but you should know as intimately as I the games I had forsaken throughout my youth. In the midst of all, she asked my age. *"Venti-quattro,"* I murmured, without my stammer. Twenty-four! In her depths, I felt a nibbling at me, as though by a nest of famished eels; when my eruption happened, it seemed to last as long as my chaste youth.

Afterwards she reached down to her floral handbag and took out a green and crumpled pack of Sportazione cigarettes and lit one with a wooden match. Normally I abstained from smoking as from sex, but when she pressed it to my lips, back and forth I shared the black tobacco with her, and now I loved the poignant taste and acrid fumes. Squinting through the fumes she cried, *"Il tramonto!"*: the sunset.

Nakedly we hurried to my window; I stood behind her, my arms around her below her breasts, her raven head not reaching even to my chin, as we watched the sun descend on the River Arno, and—not far from us—the Ponte Vecchio. We could hear the shouts of people in the covered bridge's busy markets and the din of tiny hammers pounding precious ore in the teeming goldsmiths' shops. The bridge had been there for a millennium, all Romanesque arches, ancient plaster and barred windows, tiled roofs over jumbled little shops and dwellings with twisted balconies jutting out above the river, the tiles shaded red during high daylight but apricot and purple as the sun vanished.

In twilight we returned to my chaotic bed, where we resumed our robust exertions. When we shared another Sportazione cigarette and silently she kissed and stroked my cheekbones, I meditated on my Père Benoît and my Father Abbot and my Cardinal Consalvi; in the face of such temptation, they had resisted nonetheless and kept their vows. I meditated on my dissertation for my doctorate in theology: Divine grace: Divine grace as it inspires vows: Divine grace as it inspires the priestly vows of permanent, perfect obedience and chastity.

I wrote the Latin dissertation in my head. Grace is a gift of God, preordained in His eternal mind yet spontaneous also, which He bestows on men to refresh them as if with a celestial beverage in their thirst for everlasting life. Ah, how bountifully in the vats of Heaven had He fermented so many vintages of grace: Natural Grace . . . Actual Grace . . . Sacramental Grace . . . Efficacious Grace . . . Prevenient Grace . . . Elevating Grace . . . Illuminating Grace . . . Sanctifying Grace. Imputed Grace and Irresistible Grace were (of course) heretical Protestant fabrications, since they supposed that no man could resist Christ's favour were he chosen to receive it; but in fact grace would not yield its supernatural reward unless men accepted it with free will and so acted. Grace might be granted directly by God, or mediately through His creation—by reading Scripture, from this joy or that sorrow, from a dream, a sunset, or a song. Her head against my breast, the woman slept. I began to hum the *Dies Irae*.

When she woke up, the room was dark, but in the night we renewed our lovemaking, its result as prolonged and jubilant as before, and though it left me a little tired, I felt the fatigue of a special grace and none of guilt. I asked, "What's your name?"

"Giovanna. And yours?"

"Agostino. Are you from Florence?"

"Lucca. I work in Florence, at a flower shop, but I'm on holiday."

"So am I."

"Then will you come with me to Viareggio? The sea. . . ."

"Let me think about it," said I.

"If you're not Italian, where are you from?"

"I'm not sure. The south of France?"

You will notice that I spoke without my stammer. I wondered, Were my ejaculations therapeutic? She continued, "I've never been to France, but I've thought of going there. I've a grandmother who lives, I think, near Avignone."

"Avignon?"

"What is Avignone like?"

"Heaven?"

"Then one day I must go to Heaven—to see my grandmother."

"I forget your name."

"Giovanna."

"Are you a Catholic?"

"Of course. I'd be a good one, if you priests would make this"—again she kissed my loins—"a sacrament."

"Ha-ha! Pagan religions did! Do it again! HAH!!! Oh, stop! Do *that* again! Ha-ha!" I went on laughing, so merrily that my amusement seemed to me as therapeutic, as much a special grace as my carnal pleasure had been at its highest moments. She said, "It's such fun, seducing priests."

"Ha-ha! Why?"

"*La frutta vietata?*" Forbidden fruit?

"Do you ever fail?"

"Quite often. I enjoy the challenge of their chastity. You'll die from guilt."

"Guilt, also, is a grace."

"*Come?*"

"I'm not a priest."

"But soon you will be."

"Not before I take my final vows."

"Will you ever take them?"

"I've not decided."

"Will you come with me to the seashore?"

"I c-can't."

She turned on the lamp, put on her floral clothes, and left. Still naked, I bent over my bed to make it up, and noticed that the sheets were smeared with traces of her excrement: had she not bathed that day? I tore off the sheets, the mattress, and the springs, and for the remainder of my holiday I resumed my slumber on wooden slats.

When I returned to Rome and the Pontifical Academy of Noble Ecclesiastics, I brooded as much about my jolly laughter in Florence as about my forbidden acts of fornication. I scanned the pages of the four Evangelists, seeking out Christ's sense of humour. I knew that Christ loved irony, but did He ever laugh? Did He ever say anything *funny*? His irony—all I found—was amusing in its way. Still I wondered, could jokes serve as channels of Illuminating Grace? For that matter, could fornication?

I posed the fornication riddle to my confessor, an elderly Sicilian Jesuit who came to us at the Academy on Saturday afternoons to hear and absolve our sins. Through the darkened grille, he asked, "How old are you, Agostino?"

"*Venti-quattro.*"

"I'm astonished that you waited so long to fornicate. Ah, how was it?"

There, in the dim confessional, for an instant, again a nest of famished eels nibbled at my flesh. I answered, without my stammer, "Quite therapeutic, actually."

"*Bene.* Now that you know, you will have to choose. If you wish to fornicate, you can not take your final vows."

"In the history of the Church, many priests ignored that ch-choice."

"If you mean that Holy Church has always winked at fornication—specially here in Italy—I agree with you. Why, half the popes of the Renaissance sired children of their own, and I'd wager three-quarters of the cardinals! But even then, chastity was the ideal—for the fornicators, too—and even then, good and holy priests clung to the ideal. Make up your mind, Agostino. If you can't resolve to remain chaste, you must not take your vows. Now say a good Act of Contrition. *Deinde ego te absolvo. . . .*"

"You forgot my p-penance, Padre."

"Oh, say the Rosary. *Deinde ego te absolvo. . . .*"

When I emerged from chapel, I met the huge Prince-Archbishop. He said, "Galsworthy! You look so well! Wasn't that a fine idea of mine—sending you on holiday? You were so pale. And now—your face—you've such high colour!"

"The Tuscan sun, Your G-Grace. Walks by the Arno, as you c-commanded. Other b-bits of exercise. I even explored a catacomb."

"Odd. Are there catacombs in Tuscany?"

"Of an odd kind, Your Grace."

Jubilantly, the Rector stomped his wooden foot. "Next week, I shall ordain you to the subdiaconate!"

My dreams were calmer now. I dreamed, not so much of dead Lady Daphne or indeed of the woman whose soft body I had enjoyed, but of the child we had conceived. How, even in a dream, could I be certain that I had sired a child of my own?

In May, in the Baroque chapel of the Academy, the Prince-Archbishop raised me to the subdiaconate, vesting me above my alb with amice, maniple, and tunicle, as he intoned, "May the Lord God clothe thee with the garment of Gladness and of Joy." With diffidence, submission to prophecy and to fate, but not with joy, I pronounced my solemn, final, perpetual vows of perfect obedience and chastity. Then we sang the Litany of the Saints. A week later, he vested me in my dalmatic, "the garment of Salvation," and ordained me deacon.

In June, the Prince-Archbishop ordained me to the priesthood. The elaborate ritual took place in the Basilica of Saint Mary Major, Santa Maria Maggiore, on the hill of the Equiline, beneath the Ionic columns and the mosaic friezes and the golden ceiling donated from their depredations in the Americas by the Kings of Spain.

In his full pontificals, the Prince-Archbishop was as richly clad in a golden mitre studded with precious gems; embroidered silken slippers, the right one bursting over his silken buskin and his wooden foot; indeed he was weighted down, wearing tunicle and dalmatic beneath his bejewelled white Roman chasuble.

At the foot of the altar, I lay prostrate in my spotless alb of lace and linen bound by my rope cincture, as I prepared to receive the Sacrament and we all of us chanted the Litany of the Saints.

> *Omnes sancti Angeli et Archangeli,*
> *Omnes sancti beatorum Spirituum ordines,*
> *Sancte Joannes Baptista,*
> *Sancte Joseph,*
> *Omnes sancti Patriarchae et Prophetae,*
> *Sancte Petre,*
> *Sancte Paule,*

Omnes sancti Innocentes,
Sancta Maria Magdalena,
Sancta Agatha,
Sancta Lucia,
Sancta Caecilia,
Sancta Anastasia,
Omnes sanctae Virgines, orate pro nobis.

O Lord, we beseech Thee, hear us.
From all evil, O Lord, deliver us.
From all sin,
From Thy wrath,
From the snares of the Devil,
From anger, and hatred, and all ill-will,
From the spirit of fornication,
From lightning and tempest,
From the scourge of earthquake,
From plague, famine, and war,
From everlasting death.

Make haste, O God, to deliver me.
Let them be ashamed and confounded,
   that seek after my soul.
Let them be turned backwards and put to
   confusion, that desire evils to me.
Let them be turned back with shame,
   that say unto me: *Aha! Aha!*

But even as we sang the Litany and I lay prone and horizontal, I could not keep my glances from the Prince-Archbishop's hands. He wore embroidered silken gloves, and over the glove of his right hand, on his third finger, an amethyst ring so brilliant, large, and heavy, he seemed almost with hardship to raise his arm. I was dazzled by the embroidered gloves and the glinting jewel, and suitably: those hands made me a priest for ever.

Imposition of the hands! The Prince-Archbishop placed both of his gloved hands upon my tonsured head: in his guttural, Germanic Latin, he sang the Preface of Consecration. Amidst fragrant clouds of incense, he vested me in white stole and chasuble. A priest-acolyte removed his ring; others peeled off his liturgical gloves, then restored the ring to his bare right hand. As I knelt, he anointed my hands with the Oil of Catechumens. I kissed his ring. He tendered me a golden chalice, containing wine, and on top of that a paten, a golden plate; upon that a moon-like Eucharistic host, empowering me from that moment to celebrate the Mass and consecrate bread and wine into the Body and the Blood of Christ.

Throughout, a choir of beardless, celestial boys sang *Veni, Creator*

Spiritus. I thought, *Do I act according to my own wish? Do I intend to keep my vows? I choose to be a priest. Do I choose not to be a priest? Must the prophecy of Père Benoît be fulfilled?*

Next morning, in the chapel of my Academy, I celebrated my first Mass.

More than a year passed as I completed my dissertation on Divine Grace. At last, with highest honours, I received my Doctorate of Theology and my Licentiate of Canon Law. After toiling as a clerk at the Vatican, in the Secretariat of State, I was posted as a diplomatist to Egypt—a future I regarded with fear.

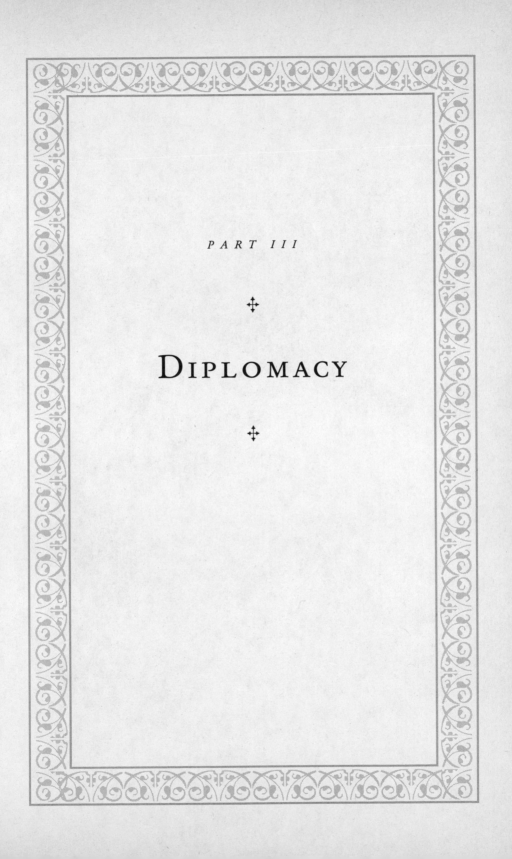

PART III

✛

DIPLOMACY

✛

✥

SEVEN

✥

You can perhaps imagine how callow I felt when I arrived in Egypt to take up my post. The year was 1954; I was twenty-six, as clumsy in my movements as I had been in seminary, but vain secretly about my rich and undulant black hair, my dark gaze, my flared nostrils, and my high patrician cheekbones. More than ever in my mind I had the habit of seeing myself as the innocent and uncertain hero of an endless cinema. In Cairo, constantly I glimpsed and juxtaposed myself against backgrounds that I found bizarre. I walked the teeming streets in a tropical white soutane, and saw my silhouette now not against the ruins and basilicas of Rome but against mythological mosques and minarets, and beyond them the immense shimmering desert.

The season was the spring, already hot. Wretched Egypt was in the grip of hopeful revolutionary passion, governed by young colonels who had recently deposed a lecherous, fat king.

The Apostolic Internunciature, situated in the luxurious quarter of Garden City, not far from the River Nile, was small and insignificant. Our embassy occupied the first and second floors of an old white palace, in the style of Italianate-Ottoman, laden with mouldings of stucco. Our offices, reception rooms, and chapel filled the first floor; we dwelt on the floor above. The palace's uppermost apartments were inhabited by the Salamas, a Jewish

family whom we never met even on the stairways: domestics delivered provisions of food and drink to them in wicker baskets and cardboard boxes.
The Salamas seemed loath to leave their flat, as though sealed inside it, a mystery that as time passed more and more pricked my curiosity.

Only the Internuncio and I staffed the embassy, save for a dark Nubian
manservant who in turban and gown swept our floors and served our frugal
meals. My rank was *addetto,* attaché, in practice a sort of First, Second, and
Third Secretary all embodied in my bumbling person; I even took the Internuncio's dictation, typed his correspondence, and served his daily Mass.

The Internuncio was Monsignore di Benevento, an ageing, diminutive
Neapolitan, so long an archbishop titular and so long exiled to posts of
diminutive importance that he had despaired of any sinecure in Rome and a
cardinal's crimson hat. Though a nobleman and alumnus of the Pontifical
Academy, he had never been a full nuncio; in Roman Catholic countries, the
Holy See's ambassador by right and custom was dean of the diplomatic
corps, but in Muslim Egypt Monsignore Benevento was not dean of anything and thus merely an "internuncio." He was but half my height, a
kindly, learned man, a canon lawyer much practised in the guile and circum-
spection of diplomacy, and—if I may dare to say so—rather too fond of me.

The high pilastered walls of the Internunciature were punctuated with
ersatz Louis Quatorze furniture, the fading oil portraits of nineteenth-
century popes (Gregory XVI, Pius IX, Leo XIII), previous internuncios in
their French lace and watered purple, and huge yellowing mirrors in frames
of swirling, gilded rococo. I had the unpriestly habit of pausing now and
then before the mirrors in the corridors to consider my face. The Internuncio noticed my ritual; in the mirror I glimpsed him as he regarded me
from afar brooding on my own image.

"You are so self-conscious, Agostino," said Monsignore Benevento,
approaching me.

"Another of my v-v-vices, Monsignore."

"A minor vice, dear Agostino, but why do you stammer so?"

"Something in my childhood, Your G-Grace?"

"A trauma, perhaps?"

"My m-mother thought so."

"Why are you so awkward?"

"My father asked me that—a th-thousand times. Oh. Not a thousand
times. I never saw him—or my mother—very much. Not a th-thousand
times."

"The Holy See, as you no doubt know, prefers its diplomats to be polished. How did you survive the Pontifical Academy?"

"My superiors admired my m-mind."

"*Sì!* Now I remember. In Rome, I read your dissertation. Brilliant."

"*Grazie, Monsignore.*"

"I'm afraid that I forget the subject."

"Divine grace, Your Grace. Divine grace as it inspires vows. Priestly
v-vows."

"Ah, so it was. Divine grace! It is reflected in your face, *caro Agostino*."

"*Grazie, Monsignore.*"

"Verging on the classical. Rather like the face of a Roman statue? I mean Christian Rome, of course. And yet ... would you turn your head a little? The profile is of pagan Rome. Still, is not your nose quite admirably straight? Is your mouth almost too sensual? Why, I wonder, is your skin stretched so tightly across your cheekbones?"

"From my struggle, Monsignore?"

"What sort of struggle, Agostino?"

"To maintain my ch-chastity."

"Not easy, I should imagine, in a young man so lustrous and innocent?"

"Not totally in-innocent, Your Grace. Nevertheless ..."

"Nevertheless?"

"N-Nevertheless, here I am, in Egypt, at twenty-six—a priest, your servant, Christ's servant, obedient to my vows, and despite whatever p-past v-vicissitudes, ch-chaste."

"Whatever inspired you in the first instance, dear Agostino, to write of Divine grace and priestly chastity?"

"Curiosity, my l-lord?"

"Curiosity!"

"I wondered whether, throughout my l-life, I should receive sufficient g-grace to keep my v-vows. The drama—the awful struggle of it, as my l-life unfolds—will be, I f-fear, more interesting than I can sometimes b-bear. I wished, if Your G-Grace will forgive the expression, to gird my l-loins for the great b-b-battle."

We were by now in the vestry of our chapel, on the feast of St Augustine of Canterbury, Archbishop and Confessor, Apostle of England. I began to vest the Internuncio above his soutane of black and purple for his morning Mass, according to the Tridentine rite, still the rule of the Roman Church.

He kissed each garment before I put it on him, both of us mumbling the suitable Latin prayers. First came the white amice, signifying the hood against Satan, which I wrapped around his neck and shoulders; then the alb, figure of perfect purity, its folds of lace falling to his toes; then his golden pectoral cross and chain above his alb; then the cincture, girdle of sacerdotal chastity, and the stole, symbol of immortality; finally the silken white chasuble of the day, emblem of enveloping Divine love, and its matching maniple, which I pinned to his left forearm, a sort of liturgical handkerchief to wipe away the tears of this world. Vested, he raised his amethystine ring for my ritual kiss, but suddenly he swayed and faltered as if to faint, brushing his nearly dwarfish body against my torso.

"Are you ill, my l-lord?" asked I.

"No, Agostino."

"Let me help you to your bed."

"I must say Mass!" he cried out, swaying. "Specially on your feast day! Most Blessed Saint Augustine of Canterbury!"

"I was named for Most Blessed Saint Augustine of H-Hippo."

"Does it matter? I'm such—such an ugly, lonely man, Agostino. I must thank our Blessed Lord and Saviour Jesus Christ again for having sent you to me."

"I insist that Your Grace take to b-bed."

"No, Agostino!"

Unsteady and ashen he said his Mass, the experience the more eerie for the supplemental little rubrics which, since he was a bishop, I duly rendered him. I washed his trembling hands with a silver ewer and basin before the Introit, and took care to see that the *bugia,* his special candle, flickered always beside his missal, moving it with the missal to the left side of the altar at the conclusion of the Gradual. At the Lavabo, after he had recited the Creed and offered up the bread and wine for the remission of men's sins, I washed his hands again, fumbling with the crystal cruets, splashing wine and water on the laced sleeves of his alb before they reached his chalice, but— transported by his prayers—he hardly seemed to notice.

"*Lavabo inter innocentes manus meus* ... I will wash my hands amongst the innocent. Take not away my soul, O Lord, with the wicked, nor my life with men of blood." After the Consecration, as he began to drink the blood of Christ (*was* it the blood of Christ? was I so sure?), the blood of Christ mingled with his own. He gurgled just a bit, then vomited blood into his jewelled, golden chalice.

Alarmed, I dragged him moaning and protesting from the altar, up the marble staircase to our residence, unfurled him fully vested on his bed, then telephoned his doctors.

In hospital, his doctors, an Egyptian and a Greek, diagnosed a tumour of the stomach—benign, they thought. There was little in the Internuncio's condition that I found benign in the weeks that followed his return from hospital. He refused the ministrations of our Nubian, and of the male nurse I thereupon proposed to engage. To my duties as stenographer, typist, and acolyte, I now perforce added those of nursemaid.

I disliked entering his bedroom, suffocating hot (we had no air- conditioning) and unpleasant from his smell. Obliged to bathe him as he lay supine or prostrate on his bed, I recoiled from his buttocks, as pink as a baboon's, but dutifully I scrubbed the offal from him as he dozed in a drugged stupor. Even in bed, the Monsignore wore his amethystine ring; whenever he was conscious as I entered his room, he raised his right hand for my obeisance and kiss. For hours I knelt at the foot of his bed, counting the beads and reciting the responses as repeatedly he murmured the fifteen Joyful, Sorrowful, and Glorious Mysteries of the Rosary. When drugged, he raised his arms to embrace me, crying out, "*Agostino! Carissimo Agostino!*"

At last as his vomiting of blood increased, Monsignore di Bene- vento's doctors decided that his tumour was not benign. I advised Rome by cypher. The Internuncio returned forthwith to Italy, on a ship from Alexandria, nursed by a Franciscan friar. As chargé d'affaires, I was left alone to run the Internunciature.

I had not much to do. During the hot days, my Nubian attended me, but at sunset he vanished to dwell with his wife and children in the shantytown of Shubra, leaving me to myself. Habitually I refused invitations to diplomatic cocktails and dinner parties because I felt stupid, stammering, and gauche.

I began to miss Monsignore Benevento: at least *he* loved me. Late, when my lids were heavy from reading sacred theology or pagan Latin verse, I sought refuge at the keyboard of my Steinway, imported from France as part of my luggage and recently retuned by a Greek. From memory I played Bach, pieces he composed for harpsichord alone, or variations on the Brandenburg concerti. I was never gauche with Bach: I played with skill and vigour. One night, as I paused between stanzas, I heard my music answered by someone upstairs, on another piano, repeating the stanza I had just played, prolonging it, completing the piece. I began again, but now the unseen hands played Bach together with me—more precisely and more sweetly.

Of a sudden, that other music ceased. Intrigued, I went to my door, out onto the landing, lay my hand on the cool marble of the balustrade, and looked up the stairway. The door above opened a crack, but I saw nobody.

"Who's there?" I whispered in French: no answer.

I returned to my piano and my Bach, pounded on the keys, yet I heard no contrapuntal music—not on that night or on several that ensued, leaving me utterly bewildered about the Salamas, the family of Jews sealed in the flat upstairs.

Otherwise, except for perfunctory correspondence and the rare ecclesiastical caller, I was at my wit's end to fill my time. I spoke French and Italian as perfectly as I did English, Latin nearly so, good classical Greek, decent Spanish and German. Now I struggled to speak and read Arabic, mostly by myself. I bought gramophone records, books of lessons with English on the left page and Arabic on the right; within a month I could understand the headlines of Egyptian newspapers. I conversed in Arabic occasionally with Ghassem, my Nubian, or rather barked commands at him. *"Gib ash-shai!"* Bring the tea! *"La, en-naharda awz kahawa!"* No, today I want coffee! *"Feyn el bantalon?"* Where's my pants?

The Nubians, though a race of servants, are a regal, handsome people: traits embodied by Ghassem. Tall, with skin of burnished bronze, he had migrated like so many of his kinsmen from the region of Wadi Halfa in Upper (southern) Egypt on the border of the Sudan. His mouth, like the mouths of numerous Nubian men and women, was remarkable—lips not thick or much Negroid but carved as if from stone or copied from the death masks of ancient Pharaohs. His hair was kinky though cut short; in youth his cheeks had been delicately slashed according to tribal rites. Ghassem also practised a ritual of silence, seldom speaking unless spoken to—but one afternoon as I took my luncheon, he broke his ritual.

He told me that his wife was ill, and asked—quietly, not timorously—whether he might bring two of his younger children to the Internunciature as he performed his duties during daytime. I did not much care for children, and I had no mind for miniature and possibly unruly Ghassems romping through my embassy. I refused.

Without a word he accepted my refusal and turned to leave the dining room. So stately were his movements, the swish of his robe as he strode out, the tilt of his head beneath its turban, that instantly I felt remorse. I remembered then that I was, after all, not only a diplomatist but a priest, and that priests are commanded by Christ to love children. I summoned my servant back.

"Gh-Ghassem?"

"*Nam, ya Sidi?*" Yes, sir? he asked.

"You may bring your ch-children."

They were a boy and a girl, Kamal and Fatima, in age respectively eight and seven, the boy clad like his father in a soutane-like *galibiya* though without a turban, the girl swathed in black, both of them undernourished it seemed to me, but otherwise as comely as the rest of their race. Nor did they romp through my embassy breaking china or defacing with dirty fingers the oil portraits of deceased pontiffs and forgotten internuncios. At Ghassem's command, they remained always in the kitchen, perched on wooden stools, talking quietly to each other or—tiny bronze fingers moving laboriously across the pages—straining to decipher verses of the Koran.

The children's presence in the embassy cheered me; over the weeks I brought them sweets from Groppi's or other downtown shops, and notebooks and pencils, that they might transcribe their Koranic verses. The children laughed, accepting my gifts with shy thanks; I found myself entering the kitchen simply to see them smile. In time, they leapt from their stools to hug me, lessening my self-disgust.

More, in the late afternoons, after my siesta, I sought their father's help to thwart my awkwardness. I marched with Ghassem through corridors and salons, seeking to achieve his long stately gait, his regal posture as he sat in a chair, effortlessly, rose from a chair, effortlessly, turned in a doorway to glance in my direction, his chin held high and the tilt of his head so naturally imperious. By force of will and much practice I wobbled less, and walked (I thought) if not quite gracefully then with greater poise. In a way, Ghassem and his children became my family, such as it was. I mourned the sunset, when they left the Internunciature, leaving me to solitude.

Increasingly at night I read aloud to myself as I struggled to repress my stammer, reciting again and again passages from the *Confessions* of my namesake, St Augustine. *Begin*: " 'Too l-late have I loved Th-Th-Thee, O B-Beauty so ancient and so n-new, too l-late have I loved Th-Thee!' " *Later*:

" 'I searched for Thee out th-th-there, and I cast myself, all deformed, upon those well-formed things which Th-Thou has m-m-made. Thou didst call and cry out and b-burst in upon my deafness; Thou d-didst shine forth and banish my blindness; Thou didst send forth Thy f-f-fragrance, and I drew in my breath and now I gasp for Th-Thee.' " *End*: " 'I have tasted, and now I hunger and I thirst; Thou didst touch me, setting me on fire with my passion for Thy peace—when I shall cleave to Thee with all my b-body and my s-s-soul.' " In a rage I threw open the French doors of my balcony and flung the *Confessions* into my scented garden of hibiscus and bougainvillaea.

At dawn, saying my daily Mass, I drew no consolation from consecrating the bread and wine into the body and blood of Christ. I loved Christ (I *hoped* I did) but did I believe that He was the Son of God, that the wafer in my artless hands, the wine in my golden chalice, became in truth His body and His blood? I had begun to doubt the meaning of my own priesthood. For that matter, who was I? Was I English, French, American, *civis Romanus, civis Vaticanus*? Was I even a priest? Had I any identity at all? Did I believe a single word of the Roman creed? If I believed in anything—I was not sure of this—I believed in Divine grace. I clung to my priestly vows: keeping my vows had become the body and blood, bone and marrow, of my life.

More and more, my self-disgust drove me from my embassy. At night, after Ghassem and his children had gone home, I walked the banks of the Nile, often for hours, strolling endlessly along the Corniche in my white soutane, sitting on stone benches to read my breviary, then walking again until at last I was exhausted and I could return to bed and restless sleep.

My walks gave me much to dream about: a sky ablaze with stars, the lamps of Gezira island twinkling from afar, the sails of dhows tacking against the brisk, warm wind. I marvelled at the mongrelised population that seemed to live upon the sidewalks: young men with Negroid lips and blond hair, in flowing *galabiyas* or tight blue jeans; women in black giving suck; hungry, ragged children, shouting, milling.

The city was protean, shifting with alarming suddenness from neighbourhoods of flowering jacaranda and healthy opulence to slums of flattened cardboard and tin cans, meagre electricity, and open sewers, spread out in groping tentacles and strident music: the deep-throated agony of Arabic song, on transistor sets, blaring: *"Ma barrif leesh bahibbak"*: I don't know why I love you.

I walked up the Pyramid Road, past a gallery of garish nightclubs all blue and pink neon to the quarter called Bebsi Cola (Pepsi-Cola), a name that only Egyptians could have thought up. The paths were of dust, moistened by children's urine and heaps of garbage. The plaster hovels were squeezed together, groaning with ten and fifteen people to a room, shrivelled men and young men, grandmothers and wives in black, children as numerous as mosquitoes. Inside pushcarts, men lay curled and fast asleep. Other people slept standing against walls, squatting among cases of soda pop, squeezed into trash barrels and cardboard boxes, snoring.

Wherever I trod in Cairo, the twisted, crowded streets produced a sweet cacophony: grating of cartwheels, braying of donkeys, mendicant musicians strumming on crude lutes, and the melancholy chants of peddlers. "O watermelon, sweet as honey!" "Gas! Gas for sale!" "Odours of Paradise! Flowers of the henna! O maidens!"

I lingered in the old city, in my stocking feet striding through bronze doors into the courtyards of huge mosques, where the scent of jasmine perfumed the odour of so many bodies. Inside the mosques, men and boys sprawled on threadbare carpets; students in flowing robes and striped pyjamas walked to and fro and hand in hand, chattering to each other or studying their lessons amidst crooked pillars, under sycamore beams, tubes of fluorescent electricity, and lanterns of enamelled glass. Students clustered cross-legged on rugs around their sheikhs, committing the Holy Koran to memory. Boys rocked backwards and forwards, chanting their lessons aloud, their voices echoing in gilded cupolas.

The mosques swarmed with paupers, settling on me like lice, howling for baksheesh. *"Raboona yihaleek, ya hawaga, ana maskeen!"* God make you prosperous, O gentleman, I am afflicted! *"Al Allah."* I commit you to God, I answered. "I have recited the chapter of Yaseen for thee, O Pasha!" cried another. *"Al Allah,"* I cried back. More beggars, all of them blind, roved about in bands, beating wooden spoons against copper plates and chanting lamentations. In the crooked streets outside, donkey drivers cracked their whips and shouted, "O Sheikh, take care! Praise the Prophet and get out of the way!" These people were "as poor as the needle that clothes the rich but which itself remains unclad."

Beyond flame trees, the desert sighed, drawing a vast breath, then exhaled, blowing at me over barren hills, pagoda-like minarets and bulbous domes, brown tenements, tin shanties, the skeletons of palaces and fortresses. The bright sky of night turned to rusty copper. Now Cairenes braced themselves against the sandy wind they called *khamseen,* and to escape its blasts I hastened home.

Next day, I abandoned my embassy for a fortnight, took a train south towards Aswan and Upper Egypt, and witnessed the life of the Nile Valley: landscapes of sun-drenched palm; thickets of sinister banyan; potteries in oases of petrified tree and plant; burdened camels and starving donkeys; hoopoe birds with rufous feathers colliding in flight above the cerulean Nile; hordes of *fellaheen,* peasants, crouching in the shade of mud-brick hovels.

Along the banks of the river, in that narrow depression of green land between hazy, grey mountain peaks of desolate rock, many millions of the poor subsisted—tilling their crops of cotton and tomato with stone tools; beating their oxen as they trod round and round and round their water wheels; bathing naked in the river or in the canals, mingling with invisible snails that infested them and then ate their intestines, leaving them eventually hollow shells, ghosts of humankind.

At Assiut, I mingled with families who lived in hovels beneath roofs heaped up with cow dung. "It keeps us cool," they told me, proud of their pristine air-conditioning. Children swarmed, eyes moist with the pus of trachoma; flies feasted on the pus, buzzing, buzzing, buzzing.

At Aswan, just below the cataracts (the High Dam was yet to be built), I boarded a river boat and sailed towards the Sudan to see the Pharaonic temples of Abu Simbel. The ship stopped along the way, invaded at every port by filthy boys hawking green tomatoes and dead pigeons. A boy stood on the shore selling pigeon eggs. I leaned down and took a dozen of his eggs as the ship pulled out; fumbling with my purse, I tried to toss his coins to him, but the coins fell short into the Nile. The boy crouched on the shore and wept. As we glided south, Nubian women in black perched like vultures on the sombre rocks, ululating.

Never before had I been exposed to such vast squalor. I reached out toward the shrieking women, as if I wished to touch them, as if in compensation for my failure to pay the boy. It was as though all the tropics of the poor, the whole of the Third World, crouched there by the River Nile, throbbing, nearly touching my fingers but much too far beyond my grasp.

EIGHT

At Cairo, I received another kind of shock. The revolutionary colonels fanatically distrusted the Western powers—specially Britain, France, and the United States. They considered Roman Catholicism, indeed all of Christianity, as an alien cult, and the Vatican as a sinister ally of imperialist Europe. Now the colonels publicly attacked the Christian schools of Egypt—run by French Jesuits, Italian Franciscans, Irish, Lebanese, and French nuns—as Enemies of the People.

Generations of élite and rich Egyptian Muslims had been educated in Catholic schools, learning perfect French and English, the history and civilisation of Europe, of classical Greece and Rome, the alexandrines of Racine and Corneille, the comedies and tragedies of Shakespeare: but to the colonels the Christian schools were nurseries of a hostile culture and of conspiracies against the Revolution. The Cairene newspapers, mouthpieces of the Revolution, demanded that all foreign priests and nuns should be expelled from Egypt and their seditious schools shut down.

Cables in cypher arrived from Rome, fearful of the worst and instructing me forthwith to undertake vigourous representations to the Foreign Ministry in the name of the Holy See. I felt confused and impotent: I knew hardly a soul at the Foreign Ministry, but I hastened anyway to that heap of Egyptian Gothic overlooking the Nile.

There, of a late morning, after passing from shabby clerk to shabby clerk, I rose eventually to the second floor, where glossy, white-suited young diplomats, scions of the *ancien régime,* shunted me the more from one office to the next. "I'm not a sh-shuttlecock," I protested to their jolly smiles. (The Foreign Ministry was only beginning to be revolutionised; majors and colonels had barely begun to elbow out professional diplomatists from their posh directorates and embassies.) A Second Secretary told me, "I'd like to help you, Father Galsworthy, but our ministry has no power." Another said, "You've come to the wrong place. May I suggest that you see the Minister of Education?"

"Wh-Who is he?"

"An army officer."

Finally I found Ali, an attaché, handsomer than any young man ought to be—running his fingers constantly through his straight black hair, calling attention to its splendour; his skin not truly dark, tanned only by the Egyptian sun and naturally I thought the tint of blondish copper; his purplish mouth carved not like the faintly Negroid mouths of Nubians but more finely; smiling often through his flashing teeth, speaking as did I in a high British accent.

And Ali said, "I was educated by the Jesuits. *L'École Supérieure Jésuite.*" Now he spoke back and forth in French, English, a bit of Latin. "*Ratio Studiorum,* and all that? Xenophon, Homer, Plato, Cicero, the *Aeneid,* and all that? How about the *Exercises* of Saint Ignatius? I don't much care for Catholicism, but mind you, Father, I'm not much of a Muslim, either."

I asked, "May I p-present you with this formal written protest against the government's plan to close the Ch-Christian schools?"

"You may," said Ali. "I'll pass it to the Foreign Minister. It won't do a bloody bit of good."

"Do you know the M-Minister of Education?"

"Unfortunately."

"Would you introduce me to h-him?"

"And waste your precious time, dear Father?"

"Sir, in Egypt, I've t-time to b-burn. Do you know any of the other c-c-colonels?"

"Some few? My late father was an army general."

"Then would you k-kindly make appointments for me?"

"You clearly don't know Egypt or our glorious Revolution, dear Father Galsworthy. They'd laugh at you."

"Then what c-can you do for me?"

"How about luncheon—at my club?"

In his open red Alfa Romeo, Ali drove me over the great Kasr-el-Nil bridge, across the Nile, to the island of Gezira and the Sporting Club.

Those were the days yet early in the Revolution when the Sporting Club was still the preserve of diplomatists and rich Egyptians, before—under revolutionary pressure—it was invaded and taken over by the rabble. (Forgive me!) Already, it was infested with spies of the *muhabarat,* police intelligence, military intelligence, Ministry of Interior intelligence, dressed in mufti or bathing costume, mingling among the foreigners and the rich, eavesdropping on conversations at luncheon tables, in the dressing rooms, in the playing fields, the swimming pool, eager to overhear the hatching of imperialist plots and report them to their masters. One could easily spot police spies; they wore cheap cotton clothes, pointed black shoes, and—so very often—dirty pink socks.

But I race too swiftly before my story. The clubhouse was of brown stucco, reached by a long drive between flamboyant trees and bushes, brilliant yellow and crimson flowers; on either side were green lawns as smooth as glass where balls of wood clicked one against the other and laughing men and women played leisurely at croquet, a game I bitterly remembered from my childhood in Gloucestershire and therefore fled. Up a flight of stairs, I glimpsed a bar and dining room; we emerged onto the terrace, all luncheon tables beneath piebald umbrellas before a swimming pool. Beyond the splashing cosmopolitans rolled vast velvet lawns in the British style, where golden Arab and European youths and older men played cricket, volleyball, tennis, and galloped upon Arabian steeds, swinging long white mallets. And beyond the polo fields, shots rang out from a shooting range: hear the distant, constant bang, bang, bang.

From that first day, when he took me to the Sporting Club, Ali drew me into his society of golden friends, became my guide and teacher in the great dazzling world outside my hollow embassy. You may wonder why. He said, "I like you, sir! If the Jesuits taught me anything, it was to recognise quality. Behind your stammer, Father Galsworthy, you're clearly a man of quality. May I call you Gus?"

"I refuse to be called G-Gus."

"I sense, also, a certain solitude, Augustine?"

"To m-madness, Ali! Now, may we discuss the sch-schools?"

Even before that day, I was not totally the dolt: I could swim a little, almost well, from my boyish plunges in the lochs of Scotland. But in the pool of the Sporting Club, as I splashed and refreshed myself in my proper black bathing costume, Ali from the highest springboard dove like an aureate falcon in swift descent, or pirouetted his tall and exemplary body in the midst of space, then rod-like struck the deep water. Presently I strolled by the side of the pool, sipping a bottle of *gazooza*, soda pop, through a bent straw: Ali sprang from the pool lamenting my uncertain posture and ridiculing the look of me slurping my *gazooza*. "You're pitiful," he said. On the morrow he introduced me to polo, but I was as indecorous at polo as in slurping my *gazooza*. I dropped my mallet swinging, causing my horse to stumble as I flew from his back through dreamlike space.

Slowly I learned at least to ride a horse. By the pyramids of Giza, beneath the paws of the Sphinx in late afternoons or at evening in open desert beneath the moon and stars, in boots and jodhpurs I rode with Ali and his friends, young men and young women, and enjoyed myself finally. As often, at shooting ranges in the desert or at the Sporting Club, Ali taught me

marksmanship. I tried rifles, too bumbling beneath their weight, but gradually I learned to shoot straight with Colt police revolvers, Mauser and Luger
military automatics. When Ali's soft chatter relaxed me and my hand no
longer trembled, I nearly hit the bull's-eye at a hundred feet. From a tiny
cannon, a turbaned Nubian released plastic birds toward the cloudless sky; I
did not miss invariably. It was midsummer now: as the gritty wind blew
across the lawns from the desert not much distant, the whole world seemed
to breathe fire.

Ali was very rich, the son of a pasha; his father had been a general in the
Royal army who had helped to lose Egypt's first war with Israel, had been
tried for incompetence and corruption, then shot himself. Ali's friends likewise were mostly of the *ancien régime,* hating the Revolution as much as he
did: fathers, mothers, sons, and daughters, intermingled with young diplomatists from Europe and cosmopolitan young men and women of Egypt
and beyond whom he found fashionable and amusing.

In the evenings, often till after midnight, we all of us sought the sweetness
of life on starlit Nile cruises, rode horses far past the Sphinx deep in the
desert to Saqqara, or dined in gaudy, coloured tents near the pyramid of
Khefren. Those nocturnal picnics unsettled my peace of soul and my new
sweetness of life. As the company feasted on grilled chicken, *shish kebab,*
white rice in grape leaves, paste-like *homus* with unleavened bread, I sat on a
cushion apart, in my tropical soutane above my jodhpurs and riding boots,
picking at my food and seldom uttering a sound. By now I wondered
whether Ali was displaying me as a sort of mascot to amuse his friends.

The trilingual chatter, in Arabic, English, and French, so common among
rich Egyptians, flowed like the chilled Bordeaux: *"Mush araf izza Mustafa is
coming min Iskanderia bukra, baa-da bukra, ou la semaine prochaine."* I
don't know if Mustafa is coming from Alexandria tomorrow, the day after
tomorrow, or next week.

Following the feast, Ali would often abandon me, taking up a blanket,
slinging it across his shoulder, and vanishing into the dark cool desert with a
toothsome woman. I wondered, How many are his conquests? Do I envy
him above all men?

During Ali's disappearances, other young women now and then
approached me, perhaps out of pity for my isolation and striving to penetrate it by asking me vapid questions about the Pope. They raised their hands
to touch my face, remarking as had Monsignore Benevento how tautly it was
stretched across my cheekbones. I wondered, Does my chastity attract
them? I knew from literature (indeed, from my encounter in Florence) that
chastity in priests was a challenge that adventurous women wished to van-
quish. Lidia seemed to step from that tradition.

Lidia! She was a latecomer to our society. Or rather, I fancied that I had
glimpsed her from afar some weeks before, on a torrid afternoon at the
Sporting Club. As Ali and I walked across the lawns from the shooting range

toward the dressing rooms, I noticed a young woman by the swimming pool in a brief bathing costume, with slim hips and brunette hair, laughing as if only to herself: how heavenly, I thought, yet the image like her laughter was evanescent.

She was there in the gaudy tent that evening, sitting cross-legged on a Persian carpet, gossiping and laughing amongst men and women friends, wearing white ballet slippers without stockings, pantaloon-like blue slacks, and a loose blouse the colour of peach. Dangling down the sides of her forehead were dark brown tresses that I imagined she had imitated from gazing, as I had so often done, at the statues of Roman goddesses. She is speaking in Arabic and French but she looks Italian, I thought. Why must I sit so far apart? Why can not I approach her? How I yearn to know the colour of her eyes.

Suddenly she rose and walked towards me, still laughing to herself. "So you're Father Galsworthy?" she asked in English. "Ali's famous Father Galsworthy?"

"I am not Ali's," said I softly, yet suggesting vehemence. "Ali is my friend, but I am not his p-p-puppy dog. I belong to the R-Roman Church."

I glanced at her eyes: a deep green. "May I know your n-name?"

"Lidia," said she, opening a tin box, taking out a black cigarillo, and lighting it. "Would you like one, Padre?"

"I'd l-love one. Are you Italian?"

"Only half of me. My mother is Syrian."

"But surely you're a C-Catholic?"

"Half-Italian. Half-Catholic—if even that. I hate the Pope."

"Why?"

"He's a mean old man, commanding people—the whole wide world— what to think and how to live."

"Can't we leave s-s-sex out of it?"

"Ha! Can't your mean old Pope?"

"I think I saw you once—at the S-Sporting Club."

"I can see why Ali is so fond of you, Father. You're interesting and f-f-funny."

With her short, unpolished nails, she lightly touched my cheekbones, ran her fingers for an instant through my black and rippling hair. As swiftly: "Will you come swimming with me?"

"Wh-Where?"

"At the club? Or—on Saturday—we could drive to Alexandria."

"Go swimming with you? Alone?"

"Alone—without Ali."

"I'd l-love to."

"Then on Saturday we'll drive to Alexandria."

"Let me th-think about it. Alone? I am a young priest. You are a beautiful young woman. Have you never heard of C-Canon Law? I live by r-rules."

"R-R-Rules! I won't tell a soul, Gus."

"Let me th-think about it. Would you c-call me Agostino?"

Ali, back from his amorous stroll in the desert, approached us to kiss Lidia on the nape of her neck. Laughing, he said, in Arabic, "*Aieeb enti!* Shame on you, Lidia! Lusting for a priest!"

And what of the crisis with the Christian schools? From Rome I received inquiries in cypher about the result of my protests to the Foreign Ministry, but the colonels kept swearing public oaths to close the imperialist acade-mies. I began to badger Ali to lead me to men of power in the Revolution.

"I'm *ancien régime,*" he reminded me. "All that the colonels despise."

"But you know them," I persisted. "You know everybody. You see them at luncheons and conferences, conduct b-business with them day by d-day."

Ali shrugged, as ever sympathetic, but loath to act. We were on the shooting range at the Sporting Club; with a Mauser pistol he massacred a row of clay ducks, but I saw no deeper evidence of his valour. Like so many of the Egyptian rich, he raged against the new order, but his rage lacked steel. He flaunted his Western education, but fear of the Revolution para-lysed him. He belonged to a lost generation who might have carried on from the pashas had the monarchy survived, but he was numbed by the rapacity of the colonels, impotently looking on as the Revolution and its new élite propelled Egypt into a maelstrom of despoiling the upper class and playing dangerous games with the Western powers. Cairo swarmed with police spies; Ali and his peers, if too shrill in their hatred of the Revolution, risked arrest and stinking dungeons.

Slyly I worked on Lidia, hoping that she might influence Ali. From frag-ments of her conversation, I suspected that once he had been her lover; indeed I wondered whether now and again they still were lovers. At our pic-nics in the desert in the gaudy tents, I allowed her to continue her advances to me, knowing that if my will should falter she could become an occasion of sin.

"Are you coming to Alexandria with me—or not?" she demanded.

"I f-forget why."

"To go swimming."

"Alone?"

"Alone!"

"I can't go on Saturday, but next w-week?"

"Promise, Agostino?"

"Will you p-press Ali about the sch-schools?"

"Will you promise?"

"I didn't p-promise. Will you p-promise?"

"But you may?"

"We'll s-s-see."

At my embassy, in chapel, I begged Christ's forgiveness for pursuing His purpose by devious means, assuring Him I was not certain that Lidia had been Ali's lover—and that never, never would I encourage her to grant him her erotic favours in order to promote my mission for the Christian schools.

"Nor need You fear, my dearest Lord, that I will break my vows. Do I not live by Your admonition, 'And there be eunuchs which have made themselves eunuchs for the Kingdom of Heaven's sake. He that is able to receive it, let him receive it.' But how hard it is! Am I becoming of a sudden too fond of holy mischief? Is it wrong for me to manipulate Lidia for Your sacred cause? Dear God! O Lord! I want so to succeed! To impress my superiors at Rome!"

On I prayed—now to the Virgin—for my success. " *'Salve Regina, mater misericordiae! Vita, dulcedo, et spes nostra, salve!* ... Hail, holy Queen, Mother of Mercy, our life, our sweetness, and our hope! To thee do we cry, poor banished children of Eve, to thee do we send up our sighs, mourning and weeping in this vale of tears...!' Ambition, Most Blessed Virgin Mother, is the *ecclesiastical* lust!"

Nights later, at another dinner party in a desert tent—beneath oil lamps, those ancient-seeming lanterns studded with false gems that Egyptians so loved to fashion—Lidia cooked for us. Her cuisine was not Arabic, but chicken tetrazzini. As she tended to her cooking, scuffling on sand and carpets now this way and now that, her feet were bare. Her green slacks were rolled up beyond her knees, so her legs were bare. She had knotted the flaps of her denim blouse together at the front, so that much of her tanned stomach, with its delicate dimpled navel, was exposed likewise. Her skin, I fancied, was as soft and warm as moss in sunshine and as smooth as the marble of all those pagan Roman goddesses I had so much admired since my lonely childhood.

Again, her most casual movements—flavouring the pot of chicken, walking to and from her little stove to set the places on the carpets, clinking a spoon against a wine glass, the raised posture of her head as she laughed and hummed and sang to herself, left me confounded; in my white soutane foolishly I crouched near her, aroused and helpless. "*Come prima,*" she sang, "hmmm hmmm, *come prima*, hmmm hmmm.... *Volare, O O. Cantare, O O O O....*" I asked myself, How much longer can I endure the erotic languor, the maddening sensuality of Egypt?

Before she served us, she whispered to me, "For the last time, Agostino, are you coming with me to Alexandria?"

"I've been thinking about l-later in the m-month."

"I'll drag you there!"

"What of *your* p-promise?"

"I'll work on Ali tonight—at his place."

"His place? I beg you, Lidia, do nothing wr-wrong."

✥

NINE

✥

Late next evening, Ali came to my embassy, and we worked on a strategy to save the Christian schools. (For his change of heart, I asked not why!) He drew charts crisscrossed with vertical lines, horizontal lines, and loops, indicating key officers in the army, in which ministries they sat, and how they might help me. "Forget the Minister of Education," he admonished. "Just another boob in uniform. You need to see Major Mahmoud, Colonel Rifaat, and General Ramadan."

"Do you know them?"

"Slightly—I've friends who know them better. Colonel Rifaat is your best bet, and—I'm told— not a bad chap. He's Vice Minister of Culture, studied for a while in France, and has two daughters in nuns' schools."

Within the week, Ali arranged a dinner party in his ancestral gingerbread palace, not far from my Internunciature, in Garden City overlooking the Nile. He had invited half a dozen army officers; four of them accepted, including Colonel Rifaat. The season was autumn, still so warm that we took drinks and dinner on the roof, an expanse so large it seemed half the size of a soccer field, with a fountain of tessellated faïence in the centre surrounded by a garden of palm and jasmine. All of teeming, nocturnal Cairo sprawled before us: we could see the twinkling bridges, the *feluccas*, dhows, in full sail, the Tombs of the Caliphs, the endless slums, and—at the horizon—the illumined Pyramids of Giza. Besides the colonels, Ali had invited forty guests, including his typical décor of glamourous women.

The Revolution was not yet three years old; Arab Socialism was not yet born; but even as I revelled in Ali's world I heard its death rattle. I wondered, How long amidst such mediaeval poverty can this kind of luxury last? How long can this kind of ducal, Khedival grace remain, with platoons of copper-skinned, fine-featured Nubians in red tarbooshes and silken *galibiyas* serving the two score guests, from burnished silver plate, crêpes with cream and beluga caviar, salmon with sauce *au vin blanc,* mountains of spiced mutton and grilled pigeon, stuffed grape leaves, a rainbow of sherbets, washed down by white Bordeaux, red Châteauneuf-du-Pape, and buckets of *brut* champagne?

After dinner, as most of the other guests drifted off, I sat by the tessellated fountain with Ali and the four colonels, each in an army tunic open at the neck, as we sipped our liqueurs in the humid breeze under a canopy of brilliant stars. I tried to speak of the Christian schools, but conversation was difficult. The colonels, all of them I supposed children of the slums, the village, or the lower middle class, seemed too dazzled by Ali's palace to follow my stammered logic. One of them kept rising from his garden chair to walk about the roof, to finger the faïence appointments, sniff the jasmine petals, admire the glorious view. When he returned to us, the moisture in his eyes seemed to gleam of greed and envy, as though to say, "Ah, if this palace could be mine."

This officer was, in fact, Colonel Rifaat, Vice Minister of Culture, a youngish man, not yet forty, half Negroid, mongrelised of the Hamitic and Arab race—as many Egyptians were—with a neat mustache and a body that was turning fat. At evening's end he asked me, in excellent French, and just as I was beginning to despair, "Will you take luncheon with me tomorrow at my club, *mon père?*"

"*Avec p-plaisir, mon c-colonel.*"

Next afternoon, his orderly came to the Internunciature to pick me up in a military van, and drove me across the Nile to the Officers' Club in Zamalek. Behind high walls, once the gate opened from the throbbing street, I saw at a glance the future of the Arab world, and indeed of much of Africa: rule by army officers. In Egypt, already victorious, they gamboled with their wives and children on the trim green lawns, playing miniature golf and volleyball; in the swimming pool; upon the tennis courts; or they took luncheon from a buffet on a large verandah beneath khaki-coloured tents. Colonel Rifaat, wearing his bathing costume, led me along the smorgasbord and heaped my plate with *homus* paste, grilled beef, and unleavened bread. When we sat ourselves at table, he came straight to the point.

"Some of our officers suffer from an excess of zeal," he said. "The Revolution can embrace all cultures."

"Which school do your d-daughters attend?" I asked.

"*Les Soeurs du Sacré-Coeur.*"

"I'm told that it's to be sh-shut down."

"Wouldn't that be sad? Best education in Egypt! The state schools stink! Still . . . *Sacré-Coeur* is so expensive . . . on a soldier's salary."

"Perhaps I could have a w-word with the Mother S-Superior, *mon colonel.*"

"How kind of you, *mon père.*"

Next day, I arranged matters with Mother Superior, seeing to it that Colonel Rifaat's daughters would pay thereafter but one Egyptian pound, respectively, for every term they studied with the Sisters of the Sacred Heart. The colonel was grateful. In the weeks that followed, I negotiated with him as the Revolution's chosen representative on the status of the Christian schools in Egypt, using Ali as my secret counsellor.

The colonels' key demand was that the schools, should they survive at all, must be "Egyptianised"—becoming, like the press and universities, servants of the Revolution. Most of the schools taught in French and English, scrimping on their Arabic lessons if not ignoring that tongue completely. Now Arabic must become the predominant tongue, just as Arab and Egyptian history must repress the schools' fixation on Christian Europe—its culture, history, and cast of mind—as the summit of civilisation. The colonels wished not merely to diminish imperialist Europe, but to demonise it.

I recognised at once that to satisfy my superiors at Rome, I should have to win my battle on the prickly issues of curriculum, retaining as best I could the languages, literature, and flavour of Christian Europe. The Jesuits, especially, insisted on preserving the *Ratio Studiorum*—their rock-like structure of Greek and Latin classics, Aristotelian logic, Thomistic philosophy. Like a sweating hound I dashed from the Jesuits to the Franciscans to the Mothers Superior, back and forth to the Ministry of Culture and Colonel Rifaat, suggesting, stammering, imploring.

I knew from history that the Roman Church had often failed of her purposes by refusing to compromise. Pius VI in the beginning had tried to placate the French Revolution, despaired, and then condemned it as the Antichrist; Pius IX had repeated such errors in reacting to the *Risorgimento*. I asked Colonel Rifaat, "What if the schools give courses ex-p-pounding the R-Revolution?"

"That won't do, *mon père*. They must *glorify* the Revolution."

"Could they do it in F-French, *mon colonel*?"

In time, the contending sides grew closer. I suggested that in the schoolroom Arabic become coequal with French and English, and that the history of Egypt and Araby at large should overshadow the history of France, England, and classical antiquity. On one principle I would not yield: the final word on what the schools would teach must be reserved, not to the Revolution, but to Rome.

I sweetened my arguments by arranging the placement of various other colonels' sons and daughters in the most coveted of our academies, not least with the illustrious Jesuits, for nominal tuition. In cypher, I kept Rome informed of every twist, receiving meticulous instructions in reply. Ali told me how to convey Rome's wishes in such ways and language to make them palatable to the colonels, but over the crucial problems of curriculum the negotiation veered towards rupture. My telephone rang constantly: calls from priests and nuns fearing imminent expulsion. From my chapel, throughout one crisis and the next, I stormed Christ and Heaven with my agitated prayers.

Finally—after several months—a bargain was struck. In the curricula, Arabic would command pride of place, the Revolution would be exalted as Egypt's deliverance from imperialism and feudal bondage, but the essentials of classical and Christian education would survive. No priests or nuns would be deported; except for a few symbolic closings in Alexandria and Assiut, most of the Christian schools were saved. "We've won, *mon père!*" exclaimed Colonel Rifaat. Ali, proud of his secret rôle, acknowledged that the marvel could not have happened without my fanatical tenacity. In the press, the assaults on imperialist Christianity ceased . . . for a time.

I sent the news of my success, not in cypher but in rolling Ciceronian Latin—ecclesiastical victory bulletins—to Rome.

✣

TEN

✣

My victory accomplished, I wearied of Ali as too worldly, and all but cast him aside. I told him, "I'll call you now and then, see you at the S-Sporting Club...." Towards Lidia, I was even more ungrateful. On the telephone, I told her, "I played too many games with you—and with my vow of celibacy by exposing it to r-risk. Dear Lidia, you're an occasion of sin. For the love of Ch-Christ, leave me alone."

Thus again I thrust myself into the glacial arms of my old companion: Solitude. It was winter now; at night, with little else to do, I regressed to the keyboard of my Steinway and my variations on themes of Bach. One evening, improvising cadenzas on his early cantata, *Gott ist mein König* (God is my King), I was answered anew by those unseen hands on the floor above, prolonging my melodies and elaborating cadenzas upon my cadenzas. Ill, half mad, with loneliness, I ran out of my rooms, onto the landing; gliding my hand along the cold marble of the balustrade, I climbed the oval staircase.

I knocked on the grilled door: no answer. I pressed my thumb on the brass button: a bell rang near the entrance: no answer. I knocked again, rang again, insistently, for several minutes: no answer—until at last a small woman in greying hair opened a window of the door behind the black iron bars of the grille. I said, *"Bon soir, Madame Salama. Je suis le Père Galsworthy, chargé d'affaires de la nonciature apostolique, votre voisin, en b-b-bas."*

She glanced at me, then lowered her gaze, as though afraid of any human creature beyond her iron bars. Behind her appeared a man in a purple cardigan and dark, sparse, hair; near to her in age, I thought, perhaps the middle thirties, and clutching, in blankets, an infant child. The woman hesitated, gazing downward still, uttering no sound. The man brushed past her, towards me, grasped the bars with his hairy fist. *"Entrez,"* he said.

Inside, at once I marvelled at the furniture—enormous, throne-like armchairs, settees, chaise longues, ottomans, some in the style of Louis Quatorze, all so gilded they seemed like monstrous golden pineapples intended to decorate a palace but squeezed now into rooms of proportion far too small. In an alcove, an ancient, bearded man—his head beneath a black yarmulke and his shoulders covered with a white shawl—rocked back and forth, praying, reciting verses from the Old Testament or the Torah before a flickering menorah. Yet he chanted his verses not in Hebrew but in Arabic. Still clutching his infant, the younger man said, "He is my father—a religious Jew. We"—he pointed to himself, his wife, and child—"are not."

"Why is he p-praying in Arabic?" I asked.

"He never learned Hebrew. We speak only French and Arabic in this house."

"Such a lovely ch-child," I said. "Your son?"

"Our daughter. Lisa."

Silently Madame Salama led me to another room, again too small for the proportions of her grand piano. She sat on the bench and resumed her variations and cadenzas of *Gott ist mein König*. Impulsively I sat beside her, struggling with my left hand on the lower scales to match her skill, but I knew I could not. When we finished the piece, I bowed to her—to her husband, daughter, and the ancient Jew—and took my leave. During ensuing weeks, I visited the Salamas nearly every evening after dinner; they never descended to my Internunciature to reciprocate the courtesy, so fearful were they of venturing beyond their iron bars.

For generations, the Salamas had been among the richest Jews of the Levant. As Sephardim, they had emigrated from Morocco to Egypt in the wake of General Bonaparte's invasion, the Battle of the Pyramids, and French linguistic imperialism among the bourgeoisie until in turn that imperialism was eclipsed by the intrusion of the British raj. Over time, they had enjoyed the favour of the khedives and kings of Egypt, acquiring considerable estates along the Nile from the delta in the north to the south near Aswan, boutiques in Alexandria, a department store in Cairo—until the Revolution confiscated them. Now the colonels coveted as well their hidden gold, dollars, pounds sterling, and precious gems. "Until we hand them over," said Monsieur Salama, "we are forbidden to leave Egypt."

Thus the Salamas were sealed in their dwelling above my Internunciature, knowing that the secret police would shadow them should they venture out, depending on servants to deliver them their food—isolated, abandoned, terrified.

How fond I grew of their infant daughter, still in her first year, all tufts of dark hair, eyes so large and luminous I caught my own reflection in them, and skin of such a tawny hue that in its texture I glimpsed her forebears of Morocco and Iberia. I took to playing games with Lisa, tossing to her little rubber balls and zeppelins made of tinsel as she crawled across the regal carpets or sat enthroned in one of those gilded chairs that reminded me of pineapples.

I took to sitting on such chairs as I jounced her on my knee, draped in its black soutane. She cooed! She *loved* me! I tossed her up and down, towards the high ceiling—until my awkwardness gripped me for an instant and I nearly dropped her, catching her at my shoelaces. Is this a dance, some kind of predestined *dance*? I wondered. In his alcove, the ancient Jew ceased his rocking back and forth, his incantations of the Torah; as Lisa nearly crashed, he cried, "*Ya khouri!* O priest! Take care!"

At that moment, my cinema resumed: I glimpsed myself, clad in crimson and in buckled shoes, seated at a piano in a Roman palace, playing passionate sonatas, not by Bach but Chopin, to Lisa as a beautiful grown woman, tresses of Moorish hair about her shoulders, gazing at me with adoration. She lifts her head, and laughs.

Winter yielded to spring: my superior, Monsignore di Benevento, returned to Cairo from his surgery for the cancer in his stomach and his long convalescence at Rome. Leaving Egypt, vomiting blood, he had resembled a gnomish corpse; now he seemed robust, fatter, and more cheerful.

"It wasn't the surgery that saved my life, *caro Agostino*," said the Internuncio. "After the operation, my doctors told me that my cancer was so far advanced they could not be sure they had removed all of it. I seemed doomed, but I was resigned to death, to departing without regret this vale of tears. Then, deep in prayer, I received an inspiration.

"I went to Lourdes. Not only did I splash my face and stomach with the sacred waters of Our Lady's grotto—I drank Lourdes water by the bucket, reciting the Joyful, Sorrowful, and Glorious Mysteries of the Rosary on my beads repeatedly, begging Our Blessed Lady for a remission of my disease and a prolongation of my life, all for the glory of God.

"She did not hear my prayers immediately, or at least she did not answer them. I returned to Rome moribund, but I continued to drink the holy water while I recited the mysteries of the Rosary. Slowly, over months of time, my health improved and I regained my vigour, all for the glory of God. When my doctors examined me only weeks ago, they said that my cancer had completely disappeared, and they pronounced me cured. *Èra un miracolo, Agostino, un miracolo!*"

Said I (dazzled by the event and delighted that he seemed so healthy), "*È molto possibile, M-M-Monsignore!*"

From beneath his purple sash, Monsignore Benevento produced a vial of Lourdes water, uncorking it and sprinkling my face. I made the Sign of the Cross, then in gratitude to Heaven, I genuflected and kissed the amethyst that adorned his right hand. He chattered on, "Here, taste the water, Agostino, gulp it down—I have gallons more. Maybe it will cure your stammer!"

I drank the whole vial. "*G-Grazie, M-Monsignore.*"

"Nor is that all, Agostino. I have a secret I will share only with you. Will your lips be sealed?"

"*Per sempre, M-Monsignore.*"

"Oh, it needn't be for ever! Soon enough the world will know! I am to be created a cardinal!"

"*Eminenza!*" I kissed his ring again.

"For the moment, it is all *in pectore,* in the Pope's breast, but His Holiness himself informed me. He will announce my elevation at the next Consistory. You will ask me how this came about, since I had lost all hope of joining the Sacred College?" Monsignore Benevento giggled. "The Pope loved my story about the Lourdes water. In fact, as you may know, the Holy Father, in his old age, suffers recurrently from hiccups. Now he, too, drinks Lourdes water, praying for a cure."

"And to which Congregation will Your Eminence be n-named?" I asked.

"I will be Prefect of the Sacred Apostolic Penitentiary. A sinecure, Agostino, a mere sinecure—granting Indulgences ... the celestial remission of punishment for sins from the treasury of Holy Church ... sweet, pious little things like that. But I shall wear the Red Hat! If I live, and I expect to, I shall sit in the next Conclave and help to elect the next Pope. Nor is that all, *caro Agostino*! Will you come with me?"

He led me to his study. Laid out elaborately across his rococo desk and chairs were the purple robes of a *Monseigneur*. He giggled again. "Will you take these to your rooms, Agostino? They belong to you."

"To m-me?"

"Your triumph with the Christian schools did not go unnoticed by the Cardinal Secretary. Nor by the Holy Father. They were both—how shall I put it Biblically?—*well pleased*. I myself mentioned the matter to the Supreme Pontiff, but my news came as no surprise. He is, as you know"—he laughed now not with mirth but sarcasm—"omniscient."

The Internuncio helped me to carry my new regalia to my own rooms. He seemed so happy for me that he could not contain his deluge of words. "You will notice, Agostino, that among your new robes there is no black cape—only purple. There was talk at first of making you a Very Reverend Papal Chamberlain—but papal chamberlains wear only the purple sash and the black cape. *I* insisted that you be created a Right Reverend Domestic Prelate to His Holiness—and I prevailed. *Bene, bene,* here are all of your robes in good order—with the *purple* cape! The robes of a bishop, Agostino, though without the *pontificalia*! There are more *monsignori* in Rome, my dear Augustine, than there are choirboys—but your *pontificalia* will come next. You will be a bishop, an archbishop—I shall see to it! How old are you now?"

"T-Twenty-eight, Your Eminence."

"*Benissimo!* Among the mob of Roman *monsignori,* you will be the youngest."

"R-Roman?"

"Did I fail to mention it? Here at the Internunciature, we are *both* to be replaced. Within some months, you will be recalled to Rome. *Carissimo Agostino!*" He hugged me as a father might, then withdrew to chapel to recite the Rosary.

Alone, I tried on all of my new robes. For ordinary dress, I would wear my black soutane with purple buttons, attached to it a shoulder cape trimmed with purple, and—around my waist—a purple sash with tassels. For secular occasions, diplomatic dinner parties, and suchlike, I would add my *ferraiolone,* the violet cape flowing from my shoulders to my shoes. For high religious pomp, I would don my violet soutane, my white linen rochet with sleeves of lace and red, and my mantelletta, a sleeveless purple tunic worn over my rochet and reaching to my knees. *Monseigneur.*

Before the gilded mirrors of my rooms, in my sudden robes I paraded back and forth, agog with my unexpected burst of fortune. What a fine figure I cut! *Monseigneur.* My father's final wish had become a prophecy: soon enough, I should be a bishop. In French, Spanish, and Italian, bishops, archbishops, and cardinals were also addressed as "Monseigneur"—no less than French and Belgian princes of the blood.

Monseigneur Galsworthy. As the days passed, my new robes endowed me with such confidence that no longer did I stumble over my own feet; my awkwardness began to vanish altogether, and I walked with growing dignity and grace. Then a little miracle of my own took place—almost overnight. I had been slipping into Monsignore Benevento's private rooms and tippling his Lourdes water. My stammer ceased. Or rather, it would recur only when my emotions were aroused.

In all documents and letters, I was now entitled to be addressed as "The Right Reverend Monsignor Sir Augustine Galsworthy, Bart."

Monsignore Benevento returned to Rome. During my final months in Cairo, I devoted much of my energy and zeal to getting my afflicted Jewish neighbours out of Egypt. Not a simple task: the Salamas were desperate to escape, but they insisted that they do so with at least a fraction of their riches, lest they face an impoverished future in Europe or America. In my black and purple, I called on Colonel Rifaat.

The colonel, of late, had prospered in the councils of the Revolution, rising from the Ministry of Culture to that of the Interior, sitting there as vice minister in charge of the police. When he saw me, he exclaimed, *"Ah! Monseigneur! Félicitations!"*

"Merci, mon colonel," said I. *"Félicitations à vous, également! Vous serez bientôt ministre!"*

"Ha-ha! Mais non, cher Monseigneur. Vous serez bientôt cardinal!"

"Ha-ha! Très peu probable, mon cher colonel!"

Flummery accomplished, I came to the point. "The Salamas wish to leave Egypt with me, but with some of their wealth."

"How will you leave?" the colonel asked.

"By ship—from Alexandria."

"Too bad. I don't control naval customs. Still . . . perhaps . . . arrangements could be made. How much do these Jews want to take?"

"One million pounds sterling—and some jewels."

"Far too much. Once out of Egypt, they'd give half of it to Israel."

"They're not going to Israel."

"They can take one thousand pounds Egyptian."

"That's nothing, *mon colonel.*"

"The Revolution has its rules. I might specially arrange to bend the rules a bit. Shall we say . . . perhaps . . . they will be permitted ten thousand pounds Egyptian?"

"Still nothing, *mon colonel.*"

"Well, then, *cher Monseigneur,* the arrangements must indeed be special."

I paused. Colonel Rifaat's moist eyes smiled. He wanted a very large bribe. Rigging free tuition for colonels' sons and daughters was one thing, passing money to a vice minister quite something more. During our long silence, I heard the chanted summons of muezzins on minarets beyond the window, and my priestly conscience throbbed. *"Hayi illa as sala, hayi illa as sala."* Come to prayer, come to prayer: the Angelus of Islam.

Yes, but such a bribe would save more Jews, I thought, just as I had helped to do at my abbey in Vaucluse. No. I was not a Jesuit. No casuistry, no argument of the lesser against the greater evil, the good effect juxtaposed against the bad effect, could prevail in my tormented conscience—even to save Jews. I replied, "I'm sorry, *mon colonel,* but I didn't hear your last statement."

"Quoi?" What?

"I was educated in a Benedictine abbey in the south of France. Since we had no showers, we washed in wooden tubs."

"Quoi?"

"Often, I forgot to wash my ears. Alas, my habit lingers, as do the globs of wax inside my ears. I did not hear your last statement."

"Given your sudden deafness, *cher Monseigneur,* I can do nothing for your Jews."

"You . . . ah . . . might discuss the matter with Monsieur Salama directly."

"Where? In your embassy?"

"The Internunciature is a holy place. May I suggest the garden?"

Next evening, well after dark, Colonel Rifaat met Monsieur Salama in the garden below the windows of my embassy. I did not participate in their discussion, but as I prayed in chapel, I assumed that the colonel's gratuity would be extremely high. I never learned the exact amount, for afterwards when Monsieur Salama broached the subject, I told him sharply, "Please shut up."

My conscience eased as the Salamas and I respectively packed our things. I was taking my Steinway, my furniture, and all my books, but the Salamas packed only a few clothes, abandoning the rest of their possessions in Egypt. Well, not *all* of their possessions! In his arrangements with Colonel Rifaat, Monsieur Salama had failed to mention that his apartments contained caches of money and precious gems inside the legs and cushions of his majestic armchairs, ottomans, chaise longues.

Again, I proved to be of service. Madame Salama, as dexterous with her sewing needle as she was in playing Bach, snipped open the seams of my new robes and concealed inside them large sterling and dollar notes, precious emeralds, amethysts, and diamonds. As a diplomatist, I expected my luggage would be immune from the police at the port of Alexandria, yet how greatly I enjoyed such little games, intrigues, dissimulations!

And, once gone from Egypt, how badly I would miss Ghassem, my laconic, faithful Nubian. In our kitchen, I paid him his final salary and asked, "How is your wife?"

"She died, *ya Sidi.*"

"When?"

"A year ago, in childbirth."

"Why didn't you tell me?"

He resumed his ritual silence. I continued, "How many children have you?"

"Five, *ya Sidi.*"

"Where are they now?"

"With my mother."

"How are little Kamal and Fatima?"

"They miss you, *ya Sidi.* You were so good to them."

"Ghassem, if your mother could keep your other children—and we send her money—would you and Kamal and Fatima come with me to Rome?"

"*Nam, ya Sidi.*" Yes, sir. He added, "We have no passports."

"Those will be arranged."

I telephoned Colonel Rifaat.

Thus a little mob surrounded me in Alexandria at the gangplank of my ship—my rescued Jews; my robed Nubian and his two children; Ali and Lidia with him, bearing flowers and farewells.

Colonel Rifaat, so well bribed, had kept his word. The naval customs fussed perfunctorily over the Salamas' luggage, fingering the linings of their garments for gems and cash, but otherwise the family passed into the ship unmolested: Madame Salama holding her infant Lisa, her husband pushing a wheelchair that carried the ancient father in his black yarmulke. My luggage, with its robes containing the Salamas' hidden riches, was borne aboard the vessel untouched. It was autumn now, pleasantly cool, following a summer ghastly hot and hectic. Egyptian warships filled the harbour. Oh, did I neglect to tell you? In July, the Supreme Colonel of the Revolution had nationalised the Suez Canal, much angering the British and the French.

I remained on the dock for my adieux with Ali and Lidia. Ali, dressed resplendently in a white suit, nevertheless had changed since I saw him swimming at the Sporting Club: his raven hair was beginning to recede, and his waist seemed broader, just a bit. He promised to visit me in Rome, but— so ephemeral are the friendships of diplomatists—I knew that he never would. I wished to ask, "Ali, what will happen to your godly looks?" For an instant, before he wandered off, I hallucinated, perceiving him clearly as one day he should become: bald and fat. Lidia lingered.

She wore an azure blouse and a long white skirt, her head covered by a blue hat with a brim so wide it left her face in shadow and dulled the greenness of her eyes, yet her presence was so alluring that I trembled. Just then, a sea breeze blew at the cape of my soutane, revealing its underside of violet. She said, "You look so handsome, Agostino, in your black and purple robes."

"Dearest Lidia . . ." My voice cracked as I grasped her hand. "If only I'd been someone, s-something else . . ."

"Ali and I are getting married."

"Ah? Do you love him?"

"I'm not sure. There's his money and estates, of course—until the Revolution steals them. In our different ways, we both of us loved you, Agostino. At least we have that in common."

As the sands and minarets of Egypt vanished from my sight, I stood on the afterdeck with little dark Lisa asleep in my arms. At Naples, I would return the gems and money to her parents, but then the Salamas would proceed to France, perhaps even to America: would I see them again, ever? Already, I longed for Egypt, regretting the uprootedness of my life, knowing it would continue inexorably until my death, and that to confound my dreams of glory always I would return to the throbbing tropics of the poor.

On the high seas, we learned by wireless that the aircraft, ships, and armies of Great Britain, France, and Israel were of a sudden waging war on revolutionary Egypt. Even as I mourned the war, I rejoiced that throughout my sojourn I had resisted Egypt's ravening sensuality and kept my sacred vows.

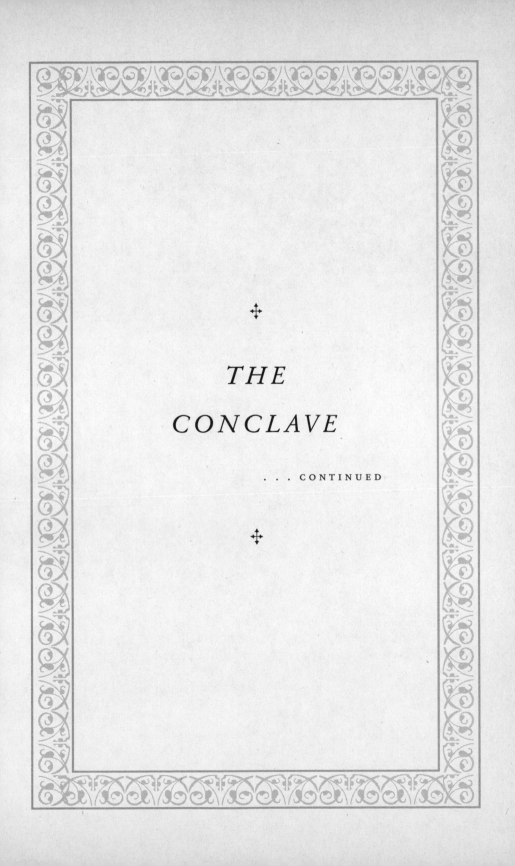

✛

THE
CONCLAVE

. . . CONTINUED

✛

"The cup which my Father hath given me,

shall I not drink it?"

✛

As we cardinals prolonged our deliberations in the sodden Sistine Chapel, holy composure began to wobble. In recent time new popes had been chosen within days, but now we were reverting to the tradition of centuries past, dragging the election out on the eve of the Third Millennium.

Papal decrees laid down that for the sake of holy secrecy the cardinals should keep no diaries of the proceedings. I honoured the spirit if not the letter of that command. In my little cell—compulsively—I scribbled a running account of the Conclave on sheets of foolscap, but at evening before retiring to bed I tore them into tiny pieces and flushed them down my loo. Still I remember much too well every word of my foolscap:

First day. No result. Second day. No result. Third day. Niente. The Sacred College is riven with rivalries and factions. The subtle and indeed sinuous intrigues can not seem to coalesce around any candidate for the papal throne who might please the great majority of his peers. Again the abortive ballots are being stuffed into the potbellied stove, mixed with wet straw, and burned: their souls ascending as black puffs of smoke to the Sistine Chapel's roof to tell the world outside that we have no Pope.

Are we cardinals deadlocked? Rather badly! Surely we must know that in our vivacious debates we are somehow supposed to be guided by the breath and finger of the Holy Spirit. Are we engaging God in a lovers' quarrel?

The balance of power in the Sacred College has passed from the Italians (still the most numerous minority) to the cardinals of the Third World. However, among the cardinals of those poorer realms, emotions and loyalties wage war with one another; not to speak of the divisions amongst the Americans and the North Europeans—throwing up from each cultural and national persuasion "conservatives" and "liberals" of various ferocity.

During the ballotings in the chapel each morning and afternoon, two distinct and contending camps have reared their heads. The first camp is rather soft, born of the reputed loving-kindness inspired by the Vatican Council. The second camp is rather hard, wishing to entrench throughout the Roman Church the harsh and iron discipline of the late Slav Pope.

On and on the scrutinies are read out. The learned Cardinal of Turin—pretending to be traditional and progressive both at once, and in the first balloting the beneficiary of a dozen votes—has been reduced to nine. Cardinal Zalula, Prefect of Bishops, has risen to fifteen, but I have surpassed him with my twenty-three—far short of the eighty-one I need. By turns the archbishops of Naples, Munich, Paris, São Paulo, Palermo, Bombay, Buenos Aires, and Westminster fly aloft like zeppelins and then crash. To undo such misadventures, the written canons of the Conclave urge holy dialogue and more ardent prayer; but as we undertake new scrutinies, still we founder.

Certain incidents cause alarm. Guillaume Cardinal Jaloux, not renowned for his love of Africans, faints suddenly in his gilded chair.

"What on earth has happened to Cardinal Jaloux?" His Eminence of Westminster asks me wearily.

"I assume," say I as wearily, "that the African cardinals spiked his porridge."

We adjourn from the Sistine Chapel. Westminster retires to his cell. I wonder: In the scrutinies tomorrow, will I gain another five or six ballots . . . ?

✛

PART IV

STERN

POPE

✛

✤

✤

Arriving in Rome from Egypt, I did not prosper quickly. At the Vatican, I joined a multitude of ecclesiastical bureaucrats likewise decked out in black and purple, nor did I stir much fuss at the Secretariat of State, to whose service I was now assigned.

I worked in the Apostolic Palace, across the Courtyard of San Damaso from the apartments of the Pope, but my own office lacked papal splendour. It was, in fact, a cubicle in the attic of the palace, rattling cold in winter, ungodly hot in summer, where I deciphered dispatches from nunciatures abroad and translated the Pontiff's orations and encyclicals from ornate Italian into ornate English and flowery French.

One winter's day, I was assigned to accompany a crowd of tourists from Valladolid and Liverpool to a papal audience in the Hall of the Consistory. During the noise of expectation before the appearance of the Pope, and surrounded by pious Liverpudlians, I glanced about the great chamber, a paragon of Renaissance and Counter Reformation grandeur, the Throne Room of the Supreme Pontiff.

High above my head, the ceiling was so richly coffered, so crisscrossed and swirling with carved beams and panels of gilt and gold, the lustre dazzled my eyes and I nearly blinked. Beneath the ceiling, lunettes by the Fleming, Brill, enshrined the most venerated Italian hermits of the Counter Reformation, though I rather doubted that amidst such opulence any real hermit would seek seclusion from the world. The lower walls were intermingled with more paintings of the saints, elaborate red damask, and soaring windows that overlooked the Courtyard of Sixtus V.

Lining the walls were carved armless wooden chairs where the archbishops of Valladolid and Liverpool sat anxiously waiting with other prelates in full fig. The floor of Siena marble was polished to such a sheen that I could admire the reflection of my face above my flowing purple cape. At the end of the long chamber, up a little flight of steps, beneath a caparisoned baldachin, stood the gilded throne of the Pope.

"*¡El papa llega!*" cried the Spaniards. "*¡Viva el papa!*" "The Pope is coming!" cried the English pilgrims. "Long live the Pope!"

Swiss and Pontifical guards entered, in a torrent of such plumage, helmets, boots, yellows, blues, reds, swords, and halberds that the pilgrims gasped. They were followed by papal gendarmes in gala Napoleonic costume and a caravan of prelates in black, purple, scarlet, and then by lackeys in livery of lace and damask, eighteenth-century shoes and stockings, bearing an enclosed, Baroque sedan chair. Oh, in that setting, the *theatre* of it all! A lackey genuflected, opened a door of the sedan chair, and out stepped the Pope, his gold-rimmed spectacles glinting beams of light, his face of mediaeval parchment smiling, his bony palms and prolonged fingers rising heavenward in saintly salutation. *Thunderous applause.*

Over his white soutane he wore a short cape of white ermine, his buffer against the wintry draughts of the Apostolic Palace. Now he removed the ermine, handing it to a genuflecting lackey, without—such is the custom of born aristocrats—thanking him even with a glance. Beneath his golden chain and pectoral cross, the Pontiff circulated amongst the visiting prelates and kneeling pilgrims, offering his ring to be kissed, blessing rosaries and prayer books, handing to the privileged few medals with the likeness of Our Lady of Lourdes, and medallions with the likeness of himself.

I felt an odd sympathy for this ancient, stern Pope. I thought that history had maligned him.

He was infallible in faith and morals, but he had invoked that doctrine only once—by declaring as Revealed Truth the bodily Assumption of the Virgin Mother into Heaven. So humbled by the sacred dignity of his Office that he would invite no other human creature to share his table, invariably this Pope took his frugal meals alone, his imperial solitude assuaged only by the songs of his canaries. Omniscient he was not, but he was deeply learned in theology, history, science, languages, and modern exegesis of the Scriptures. He had been maligned, alas, for his policy toward the Jews.

That this Italian Pope was pro-German was all too palpable. He had been nuncio to Munich and Berlin, where he nourished his ardour for German culture and its unmelodious tongue. After the Nazis rose to power, he had negotiated a Concordat with them to protect the interests of the German Church, which the Nazis soon dishonoured. As Pope, in the Apostolic

Palace, he kept his old secretary, a German. His Jesuit confessor was German. His canaries (so everyone said) were German. His parrot spoke German, the language of his household. His housekeeper was a German nun, who henpecked him.

He was pro-German, but not pro-Nazi. When Hitler invaded Poland, the Pope condemned aggression and racism forthrightly, but even as hundreds of his priests were being shot in Poland, he never identified the Nazis by name, and the style of his pronouncements by degrees became so opaque and circumspect that the Nazis ignored him and the world missed his point. His predecessor had been more blunt, explicitly condemning National Socialism not in Latin but in German, darkening the Vatican and fleeing in horror to his villa in the Alban hills when Hitler visited Rome as the guest of Mussolini. "Spiritually," the previous Pope had thundered, "we are *all* Semites."

The Pope who stood before us in the Hall of the Consistory—so tall and gaunt that he seemed skeletal, in private as nervous as a frightened cat, in pain perhaps from the hernia in his esophagus which gave him hiccups, but moving now among the pilgrims as though in a slow and distant trance—had depended upon diplomacy to thwart Hitler, and his diplomacy failed. He did allow his Dutch bishops to protest with vehemence the deportations of Holland's Jews, whereupon the S.S. rounded up Holland's baptised Jews and shipped them off to ovens in the East. Thus candour gave the Pontiff pause.

Yet he, like my own beloved Father Abbot in the Vaucluse, had not failed to save the lives of Jews. Aghast at Nazi pogroms, he sheltered Jews in monasteries and convents, even in the cellars of the Vatican, overcame his scruples and authorised fake certificates of baptism. Surely his actions were more benevolent than those of the Allies in London and in Washington, who simply shut their doors to Jews, but still he stood condemned for his opacity and silence before the crimes of Hitler.

I was sad that this Pope did not defy Hitler as Pius VII had defied and excommunicated Napoleon. But in the end would words—blunt words, sharp words, the curse of excommunication—have deterred the tyranny of Adolf Hitler, born like Napoleon into the Church of Rome? Pondering, I thought not, so I absolved this gaunt Pope.

Soon he ascended the steps to his golden throne, sat down, exhorted the Spaniards and Liverpudlians in their respective tongues to be stalwart and angelic Christians, stood up, and—with white arms extended, trance-like still, transforming his body into the image of the Cross—imparted his Apostolic Benediction.

Descending to leave the Hall of the Consistory and about to enter his sedan chair, he was diverted by a ruddy, dwarfish, scarlet figure in his entourage—Cardinal di Benevento—who pointed inward amidst the mob . . . to me. With Cardinal Benevento at his elbow, the Pope walked towards me among the Liverpudlians.

Of a sudden I felt dizzy, as if thrust into my own trance.

. . .

In my cubicle that morning, to fight the cold, I had shirked my work and burrowed in the memoirs of Chateaubriand—who with his aesthetic defense of Christianity became at the beginning of the nineteenth century the most celebrated man in France except for the First Consul, Bonaparte himself. Chateaubriand recounted a delicious scene in the palace of Lucien, Napoleon's younger brother:

From afar the First Consul sights Chateaubriand in the crowd. Napoleon walks toward him, though no one knows whom he is seeking out. The ranks of courtiers open like waves of the Red Sea, each courtier hoping that the Consul seeks him. As if playing a game, the mischievous Chateaubriand ducks and hides behind other courtiers until the exasperated Consul finds him. The crowd draws back, then regroups round Bonaparte and Chateaubriand. Leaping without pause from idea to idea, the Consul speaks of Islam and Christianity, geometry, astronomy, of a shifting and a shaking of the planets and the stars.

How I savour that scene, hoping that one day somehow the same sort of fame might be heaped on me.

Now in the Hall of the Consistory, it is as though Napoleon, First Consul and Emperor-to-be, sights me amidst the crowd. He heads toward me, the ranks of courtiers and pilgrims opening like waves of the Red Sea.

As he does so I, too, crave mischief, longing to play a game with him, ducking and scrambling behind the backs of courtiers, obliging the Presence to search for me amidst the crowd. Indeed for a moment I do so, ducking and hiding amongst the pilgrims.

But in the nick of time I emerged from my hallucination of Paris and Napoleon and I ceased my perverse game of mischief. Eerily still when the Pope found me in the crowd, the Liverpudlians drew back, then regrouped round the Pontiff, Cardinal Benevento, and myself, hanging on our every word. I knelt at the Pontiff's feet.

The Pope gazed at me myopically through his glinting spectacles, turned to Cardinal Benevento, and said in Italian, "Eminence, your young monsignor is quite elegant and handsome."

Assuming I was English, the Pope addressed me in that tongue; as Cardinal Benevento, my patron, stood by splashing in his pond of crimson and beamed at me paternally.

"So," the Pontiff said. "Indeed. Monsignor Galsworthy. We were happy to hear of your success with Our Christian schools in Egypt. We thank and congratulate you, Our dear Monsignor, and We bestow upon you Our special Apostolic Benediction." Still kneeling, I crossed myself, and—in the old style, passing out of fashion—I bent my body down and kissed the papal foot.

As he addressed me, the Pontiff's notorious affliction had recurred and occasionally he hiccupped. He turned and frowned at Cardinal Benevento: the Cardinal's Lourdes water had yet to work its miracle on his master.

Moreover, though his grammar was perfect, the Pope's English was so thick with Italianate pronunciation that I could barely grasp it. Knowing that his French was easier, not totally withdrawn from my Napoleonic trance, and groping still for my own identity, I replied to the Pontiff thus:

"Je vous remercie, Saintissime Père. Je ne suis qu'un pauvre prêtre, mais le serviteur éternel de Votre Sainteté. Par vos éloges, Saintissime Père, je suis humblement comblé." I thank you, Most Holy Father. I am but a poor priest, yet the everlasting servant of Your Holiness. By your praise, Most Holy Father, I am humbly overwhelmed.

Then I bent again and kissed his right red shoe.

The Pope stepped back, palpably offended that I had ignored his English benediction and had chosen cavalierly to address him in another tongue. His hiccups ceased. He asked, *"Ah? Vous êtes anglais ou êtes-vous français?"*

"Je ne suis p-pas certain, Saintissime Père." I am n-not sure, Most Holy Father.

"Eh bien, il vous faut bientôt trancher, cher Monseigneur, surtout dans Notre présence." Then you must soon decide, dear Monsignor, especially in Our presence.

I blushed. The Pope turned away from me, complaining of the winter chill. His lackeys came running with his ermine cape and then with his sedan chair. As florid as his robes with embarrassment, Cardinal Benevento abandoned me in my pool of isolation and chased the Supreme Pontiff, enclosed in the sedan chair, through the mob of Spaniards and Liverpudlians, out of the Hall of the Consistory. *Thunderous applause.*

T W E L V E

✠

So abruptly out of favour for daring to address His Holiness in French, my ecclesiastical star stopped rising, and I remained trapped in my cubicle in the papal attic. Not even Cardinal di Benevento could set me free—nor did he care to—until it should serve the Pope's sacred pleasure.

In the afternoons and evenings, time once more lay mournfully on my hands; having so few intimates in Rome, I fancied again that I might die young, of boredom. Throughout that grey and dreary Italian winter, I pined for the radiance of Egypt. Worse, I was running out of money.

As a secular priest, I had taken solemn vows of perfect obedience and chastity, but not—as monks and nuns of religious congregations are bound to do—of poverty. Like any secular ecclesiastic, I could be as rich or poor as I should choose, and—given my high ambition—I had no mind to wallow in holy poverty.

Upon reaching Rome from Egypt, I had taken a large high-windowed flat in the Borgo Angelico, gloomy and nearly decrepit, minutes by foot from the Vatican. I needed space for my piano, my plate, my pictures, my French furniture, and my five thousand books. I aspired, as soon as I might afford, to install a private chapel. My salary from the Secretariat of State was a pittance, but in Rome prices were rising rapidly and I was exhausting my inheritance.

Of the twenty thousand pounds sterling bequeathed to me by my father, I had invested a portion in the City of London stock exchange and in the Paris *bourse,* but I was a neophyte in finance, my choices were injudicious, and I lost money. True, I had also inherited a considerable purse of dollars from my mother, but as my youth slipped slowly away, so did her dollars.

Compounding my financial embarrassment was the presence in my household of my Nubian, Ghassem, and his two children. He was as deferential and serviceable as ever in his immaculate turbans and flowing *galabiyas,* delighting me as he chattered in Arabic in the kitchen with little Kamal and Fatima, softening my loneliness; but he was increasingly restless in Catholic Rome. He missed his mosque, his mother, his other children he had left behind with her in Egypt, and his dead wife. Ghassem longed for a new wife, and to sire more children. In his quiet way, he pressed me to enlarge the remittances I sent to his mother, and to arrange the transport of a new wife, Nubian as he was, to be chosen by his mother, from Cairo to Rome. I loved Ghassem: such petitions I could not refuse. But when he sired new children, where would I put them, and how would I pay?

As I grew more desperate, I realised that I needed a patron—who should be quite rich.

Still in quest as well of my national soul, in the afternoons I began to frequent the Venerable English College, not far from the Vatican across the River Tiber, in the narrow, crooked, Via di Monserrato.

The college housed young British priests pursuing sacred doctorates, and the oldest, largest English library in Rome. In the library, I read copiously the history of the English Church from the Dark Ages to present time, with particular attention to the rupture between Canterbury and Rome during the reign of Henry VIII and the ensuing martyrdom of the Roman Church in England under Elizabeth I.

The priesthood was not merely my vocation (*was* it?); religion was my craft. Something deep inside my psyche compelled me to absorb every esoteric fact, the better somehow to blend my learning with my hunger for high office in the Church. I did not, however, confine my reading to religion. The Rector of the college being more broad-minded than the Roman Curia, I dabbled with delight in the library's collection of Christopher Marlowe, George Eliot, Charles Dickens, Anthony Trollope, T. S. Eliot, the mystical Aldous Huxley, the agnostic Sir Julian Huxley, and the atheist H. G. Wells.

When I emerged from the library in the late afternoons, I paced up and down, up and down, in the long gallery of oil paintings, clad in my robes of black and purple, reading from my breviary the sacred Office of the day. As I mumbled my Latin, the corner of my eye meditated on the oil portraits. They were all of English cardinals, in crimson watered silk, beginning with the era of the Tudors and before: this was, indeed, called the "Gallery of Cardinals." Wolsey, Pole, and Stuart of York. Acton, Wiseman, and Manning. Newman, Vaughan, and Bourne.

Over time, my daily stroll in the gallery became an event for the students: more and more of them queued up behind me, pacing, reading their breviaries. In conversation, I affected the high English accent of my father, until it came naturally, as if part of me. Invariably these young priests, and the Rector with them, addressed me as "Sir Augustine." One afternoon, as I departed the college by the marble staircase, I heard students in the gallery above whispering to each other: "Mark my word . . . wait and see . . . Sir Augustine's portrait will hang here, too . . . as an English cardinal."

Turning left into the squeezed Via Monserrato, I tossed a long black cape, lined with purple satin, about my shoulders, fastened it with a silver chain and buckle about my neck, and, hatless, walked some few steps toward the Piazza Farnese. Winter was turning to spring; it was the Holy Season of Lent, but still the air was chilly, and as I entered the piazza a gust of wind ruffled my cape and my luxuriant black hair.

The piazza was vast, but not so vast as the Palazzo Farnese that loomed above it, a monument of sooty grey and brown, aspiring with Greek and Romanesque windows round an immense, pillared balcony in the centre surmounted by the papal coat of arms. The palace had been built in the sixteenth century by Alessandro Cardinal Farnese, who led a sensual life and sired several children until elected to the papacy as Paul III. Then he grew saintly, convening the Council of Trent, launching the Counter Reformation, fortifying the Roman Church against the onslaughts of Martin Luther throughout much of Christendom.

The Farnese fortress had long since become the Embassy of France. As I gazed at the great façade, the *tricolore* fluttered atop its mast; watching the *carabinièri* and the changing of the guard, I wondered, To whom do I belong—to the Palais Farnese or the Venerable English College? Again I heard the Pope's angry question: *"Vous êtes anglais ou êtes-vous français?"* My dead mother was American. I held a British passport; a Vatican passport; a U.S. passport. Was I American? Was I a Jew?

At the corner of the Via Monserrato, facing the Piazza Farnese, behind Corinthian pillars and a Grecian arch, stood the little church of Santa Brigida, one of Rome's most charming. I stepped inside—into a haze of blue and gold. I felt warmed by the flickering votive candles, by the blue ceiling splashed with golden stars, frescoes of the saints and the Holy Virgin and the high altar in the centre of the sanctuary, above the tabernacle a blinding gilded sunburst. To the left, on the Gospel side of the apse, behind a wooden grille, knelt a dozen young nuns in habits and veils of blue, their celestial faces framed in wimples and bibs of white, chanting in Latin the Sorrowful Mysteries of the Rosary in keeping with the penitential season of Lent.

I walked into the sanctuary, knelt on a *prie-dieu,* took out my rosary, and recited the Sorrowful Mysteries with the nuns. The Agony of Jesus in the Garden. *"Pater noster, qui es in coelis. . . ."* The Scourging of Jesus at the Pillar. *"Ave, Maria, gratia plena. . . ."* The Crowning of Jesus with Thorns. *". . . Dominus tecum. . . ."* Jesus carries His Cross. *". . . benedicta tu in mulieribus. . . ."* Jesus is Crucified. *". . . et benedictus fructus ventris tui. . . ."*

In deference to my rank, the Mother Superior at the head of the nuns ceased calling out the mysteries and let me lead the prayers: she joined her nuns in the responses. As I prayed aloud, I reached into the side pocket of my soutane, extracted a flask of Lourdes water, and tippled from it. While I chanted the mysteries, I pleaded silently for my own intention:

O Lord and Thy Virgin Mother, help me. I'm almost destitute—down to my last hundred guineas and some few thousand dollars, if that. Yes, I am ambitious, but I seek also, Most Blessed Lord, to serve Thy glory. (Do You believe me? Do I believe myself?) Send me a rich patron, and soon.

Now aloud: "... *Panem nostrum quotidianum da nobis hodie....*" Give us this day our daily bread.

The mysteries completed, I crossed myself, kissed my rosary and Lourdes bottle, and rose to leave. By the door of the empty church stood a small, dark man, expensively dressed in a double-breasted coat of herringbone with a collar of black fur, holding a grey Homburg, gazing at me. As I passed through the door, he asked, in American English, "Who are you?"

"Ah, that I knew," I said.

Putting on his Homburg, the man followed me into the Piazza Farnese. "Are you the parish priest?" he pressed. "No, no, you couldn't be, with your British accent. You're British, then, on holiday in Rome?"

"I'd hardly call it a holiday," I answered, laughing. "I'm at the Vatican, actually, in the Secretariat of State."

"May I ask your name?"

"Monsignor Galsworthy."

"May I have the honour of calling on you?"

"If you want to attend a papal audience, you had best apply through the North American College."

"I've attended a papal audience."

"Then why do you wish to call on me?" asked I, increasingly puzzled.

"Forgive me, Monsignor, for being brash. I had finished some business at the French embassy, and as I crossed the piazza I noticed you, staring at the embassy with a troubled look. The wind blew at your cape and your marvellous hair." He lifted his Homburg, exposing his own, sparse hair. "I thought: Why, this is the finest figure of a prelate I have ever seen! I went into the church, and prayed with you as you recited the Rosary with the nuns. It was all so beautiful! I was so moved! Monsignor Galsworthy, I must know you!"

"Really, I—"

"May I call on you at the Secretariat?"

"You'd best write first, for an appointment," said I, quickening my pace toward the Via Monserrato, fairly running from him.

"The name is Northwood!" he called after me.

Next morning, as I struggled in my cubicle to translate another of the Pontiff's rococo allocutions into readable English, my telephone rang. It was a Vatican policeman at the Gate of Santa Anna: "Monsignore, there's an American gentleman here to see you—Signor Norta-vooda."

"Signor *Who?*" I replied in Italian.

"Norta-vooda."

Ah. Mr Northwood. "I told him to write me a letter."

"He has a letter in his hand."

I was about to hang up, but my instinct seized me. My instinct—some voice inside my head—told me, *Choose. Make a crucial choice.* I said, "Ask a Swiss Guard to conduct Signor Norta-vooda to Raphael's Loggia—the far end, beneath the bust."

I could hardly receive Mr Northwood in my cubicle: besides, the inner sancta of the Secretariat were closed to strangers. Nor did my instinct dictate that I should see him in the usual reception rooms: I needed grandeur, *theatre.* My eye wandered to the hat rack in the corner of my cubicle, where my purple cloak hung at the ready for papal audiences. My voice commanded, *Wear it.* It added, *And keep him waiting.*

Slowly I finished my translation, then flung on my cape; knotting the violet ribbons about my neck, leisurely I descended the several marble stairways to the Loggia of Raphael. Ah, that loggia!—the blues of the marble floor and the iridescence of the mural frescoes were bathed in the morning light of spring splashing through windows of high Romanasque above the Courtyard of San Damaso. Far from me, at the end of the long gallery—beyond the bays and pavilion vaults, the arabesques and mouldings, the ineffable taste and inexhaustible fantasy of the paintings, beneath the bust of Raphael on a pedestal of pink marble—stood Mr Northwood, alone.

As I approached him, the whoosh of my self-locomotion billowed my cloak a bit and blended with the splendour of the gallery. My cinema resumed: I saw my face, half of it bathed in refracted daylight, the other half radiant with reflected hues of the loggia. I commanded myself: Don't trudge. Glide. Longer steps, *per favore*! Be like Ghassem and Ali: effortless, athletic. Watch your movements in slow motion, where your feet are, what your hands are about, how your body is postured. Above all, don't *wobble.* Nor did I: never, I knew, had my gait been quite so stately.

When I reached him, Mr Northwood genuflected and kissed my right hand. I drew back and said, "Sir, I am not a bishop."

"Ah, but you will be," answered Mr Northwood. Still kneeling, he gazed up at me with small, black eyes, not quite focussed, as though glazed from medication. He wore a topcoat of soft vicuña cloth; in his left hand, he clutched his Homburg, this one the colour of black, together with an envelope the colour of rich cream. He murmured something, though I am not so sure of this: "I'll see to that."

He had trouble rising. I helped him to his feet—odd, I thought: the man can not yet be fifty. "My bad legs," he explained. Standing, in face and posture Mr Northwood reminded me a bit of Cardinal Benevento, although he was inches taller; still, I towered over him. He continued, "Again, my dear

Monsignor, I beg your pardon for being so presumptuous and brash. You told me to write you a letter. Since no one trusts the Italian mails, I thought it best to deliver it myself." He handed me the envelope.

"If it's about an appointment—"

"But we're having our appointment, aren't we, Monsignor Galsworthy, here in Raphael's Loggia? No, this is an invitation to tea—with me and my fiancée—tomorrow afternoon. I have enclosed, well, a little ... something else."

"Tea? At your hotel?"

"We were staying at the Hassler, but last week we took apartments— separate apartments, you understand—at the Doria-Pamphili palace."

"Are the princely Dorias running a bed and breakfast?"

"Ha-ha! They're short of cash."

"I'm sorry, sir, but I couldn't possibly take tea with you tomorrow. My schedule is full." My schedule was empty.

"Thursday, then?"

"I'm engaged on Thursday afternoons—with the Pope's business."

"Friday?"

"I'll try."

"Friday, then. Four o'clock? Diana will be delighted."

I pray she's prettier than you, I thought. No, that is disingenuous; there was something about him I liked; I wanted to have tea with him that morning.

Walking out, we gazed at the art together in Raphael's Loggia. Mr Northwood said, "Marvellous ... marvellous ... marvellous. I love these frescoes of the Old Testament. God creates Man. Adam and Eve fall from Grace. Moses receives the Ten Commandments. Joseph interprets the Pharaoh's dream. ... Of course, Raphael did not paint them."

"There's an eminent school of art historians who agree with you," said I, mildly impressed. "Raphael may not have wielded the brush, but at the least he conceived and directed the decoration."

"Oh, my dear Monsignor, I don't dispute *that,*" riposted Mr Northwood, bubbling. "However, the true painters were Giulio Romano, Giovanni da Udine, Polidoro da Caravaggio. ..."

"Do you collect art?"

"Rather a lot, in fact. Originals, whenever possible."

"Where do you keep it?"

"At my house in Paris on the avenue Foch—but mostly at my estate, Northwood Hall, across the sea. Ah, that I could own but one of these. Caravaggio. I'd pay the Devil for a Caravaggio."

"Don't you mean Michelangelo da Caravaggio, far more talented and renowned for his daring use of light and darkness?"

"No, I mean *Polidoro* da Caravaggio, my dear Monsignor! Like his namesake, Michelangelo Caravaggio was a bit—shall we say?—too daringly homosexual in his portraits for my unfashionable taste. Ha-ha!"

We reached the marble stairway. I held out my right hand; Mr Northwood grasped it again, raised it almost to his mouth, as if wishing upon it a bishop's ring I did not bear. I said, "Till Friday, then."

"The address is in the envelope."

"I know the Palazzo Doria-Pamphili, Mr Northwood."

"By the way, Monsignor, what's your Christian name?"

"Augustine—after the Saint. And yours?"

"Urban—after the Pope."

"Which Urban?"

"All eight of them—ha-ha!"

Climbing the stairway to my cubicle, I opened the creamy envelope. It contained not only my invitation to tea but a cheque on the Crédit Suisse for one hundred thousand dollars—made out to "His Holiness the Pope." Across the top, in his large, neat hand, Urban Northwood had written, "For the charities of the Holy See."

I hastened to Cardinal Benevento in another corner of the Apostolic Palace. Half out of breath, I asked, "Eminence, what shall I do with this?"

"*Caro Agostino.*" He squinted at the sum, then raised his bald head, his brown eyes twinkling at me. "Oh my, how little scraps of paper can absolve blunders large and small."

"What shall I do with it?"

"Give it to me."

"What will Your Eminence do with it?"

"*Carissimo Agostino.* I shall give it to the Pope—with your humble compliments."

✥

T H I R T E E N

✥

O n Friday afternoon, I took a taxi from
my flat in the Borgo Angelico, rather
far across the River Tiber to the Doria-
Pamphili palace on the Piazza del Collegio
Romano. I wore my tailored soutane of black and
purple, with shoulder cape and sash, and upon my
head I placed a priestly broad-brimmed Roman hat
swathed in claret ribbon with tassels dangling.
Urban Northwood seemed amused and pleased by
my appearance. Diana, his betrothed, straightaway
disturbed me.

She was the most attractive woman I had ever
met—more radiant, even, than Lidia, though she
lacked Lidia's Mediterranean sensuality and enshrined her beauty in a face and head that seemed
almost too diligently sculpted from ice.

I removed my Roman hat. Small Urban wore a
blue lounge suit with pinstripes, and a grey pearl
that pierced his tie of lustrous silver. Tall Diana
wore a woollen skirt that matched her double
cashmere sweaters, turquoise in colour, the outer
sweater draped about her regal shoulders, and a
modest necklace of white pearls. On her left
forearm, she carried a small purse of simple black
leather. Her mouth was carved, her nose was brief
and straight, her bouffant hair so blonde it suggested Nordic golden. And her beauty was mature:
had she turned thirty? She wore no makeup, no

bracelets or brilliant rings: she needed none. Was she fifteen or twenty years the junior of dark, ungainly Urban Northwood?

We began our little gathering by taking tea, sitting on Dante chairs in a little alcove off the Third Gallery, round a marble table daintily laid out, and beneath the most famous painting by Velázquez in all of Italy—his portrait of Innocent X. A butler in livery, blue satin and white ruffled lace, served us black tea and Italian pastries from silver plate. I found the tea bracing, the pastries so rich and sickly-sweet I barely nibbled on them. More, I was so unsettled by Diana's beauty that as of old my right hand trembled slightly and rattled my teacup against its dish. Mr Northwood asked, "I assume, Monsignor, that you opened my envelope?"

"I did, sir, thank you."

"Oh, call me Urban, please."

"Thank you, Urban."

"And the . . . enclosure?"

"I entrusted it to His Eminence Cardinal di Benevento, Prefect of the Sacred Apostolic Penitentiary, who has presented it to the Holy Father."

"There will be more. . . ."

"His Holiness, I am sure, will be well pleased. There are so many claims on his benevolence."

As I spoke, I could not keep my glances from Diana's mythic face and shoulders. Constantly, her ice-blue eyes met my own dark ones. In desperation, I looked away, about the alcove, then fixed my gaze upon the huge portrait of Innocent X on the wall opposite my chair. Diana said, in an American accent so upper-class it seemed half-British, "You seem hypnotised by that painting, Monsignor Galsworthy."

"I know its h-history," I answered.

"*Do* you?" she exclaimed. "I'd love to hear it."

"Or rather, I know the history of Innocent the T-Tenth."

"What sort of pope was he?"

"Quite odd and eccentric," I said. "He reigned for eleven years, from 1644 till 1655, if I remember properly, and was the only issue of the princely Pamphili ever elevated to the Chair of Peter. He hardly seemed qualified to sit there, having served with no distinction as nuncio to Naples and Madrid, but the cardinals were fed up with the nepotism and rapacity of Urban the Eighth, so they elected Giambattista Pamphili to succeed him, praying for economy and calm. Alas, Heaven seemed deaf to their prayers."

On and on I rattled, not so much to display my erudition as to deter my thought from Diana's blue, ironic gaze.

"Innocent," I continued, "was d-dominated and henpecked by his sister-in-law, the notorious widow Olimpia Maidalchini, who cast a spell upon him so eerie he could refuse her n-nothing." Not enough that, overnight it seemed, she acquired an ungodly fortune; she even nominated new cardinals and all but ran the Roman Church. Howls of protest reached Rome from every nook of Christendom. The walls of churches were plastered with pasquinades, reviling Olimpia as *la Papresa*. Certain unkindly cardinals

called Olimpia a seeress, a sorceress, a witch; others whispered of an inces-
tuous *liaison,* a malicious slander upon the poor old man for which no evidence has ever been produced.

"Innocent was partially redeemed, I th-think, by his delicious sense of
humour. One day, as Velázquez painted that very portrait, he stubbed his
toe and dropped his palette. Pope Innocent rose from his armchair,
descended to his knees, and picked up the artist's paints and brushes. 'So
there we are,' His Holiness said. 'Even the Vicar of Christ stoops for
Velázquez.' "

"Marvellous," said Urban Northwood. Diana merely smiled—in disbelief?

"Look at him there," I urged them, not knowing how to stop. Urban and
Diana, whose backs were to the painting, craned their heads and stared as I
did at Innocent X.

"It is not a f-f-flattering portrait. The properties are subdued—the dark,
red velvet in the background and on the papal chair, the chair's gilded frame
and the pontifical regalia that sprout from either side. The folded piece
of parchment that the Pontiff holds between the thumb and forefinger of
his left hand is a touch of genius—the genius of Velázquez, who no doubt
placed it there. But n-notice, nothing in the portrait gleams—neither
the Pope's red bonnet nor his red mozzetta nor the gem on his right hand.
The ends of his lace rochet seem torn and tattered, and the rochet itself
is streaked with an odious yellow—almost the colour of urine. As for
Innocent's persona, remark the long, sharp fingernails, suggesting the talons
of a beast. And the face!—the hard and suspicious ruby lips framed by
that grey goatee; the long, princely nose hinting at centuries of aristocratic decadence; and above all, the eyes. Oh, those b-brown eyes beneath
their arched, sparse brows, glancing at Velázquez as though in a given
instant, from their sockets sideways! The slyness, the cunning, of those
papal eyes! And yet the corruption, the dross, of the surrounding colours!
Were they Velázquez's own sly judgement of the odour of Innocent Tenth's
p-pontificate?"

"My God, they must have been," exclaimed Urban Northwood.

"Nevertheless, when Velázquez finally showed the portrait to the Pontiff,
Innocent smiled and said, 'All too t-true.' "

"Ha-ha!" laughed Urban and Diana quietly.

"Oh, dear, have I t-talked too much?"

"*I* could listen to you for hours," said Diana—did I hear a hint of
mockery?—turning from the portrait to gaze at me and then at her
betrothed. "Forgive me, darling," she told Urban. She glanced at me again
from those misty orbits of ice-blue. "I refused to believe you at first, but
indeed you have found a diamond—this *dazzling* young Monsignor—in the
Piazza Farnese."

After tea, we three meandered through the galleries of the *palazzo* toward
Diana's private apartments and Urban's beyond them; but the paintings and

appointments were so opulent, I might say even gaudy, they reminded me of the Italian pastries I could but nibble on.

Busts of gods, goddesses, and saints reposed on pedestals amid gilded mirrors, candlesticks, and furniture, beneath ceilings that swirled with landscapes, forests, doves, cherubs with wings, and pagan, prancing naked deities. Many of the portraits were all too famous—*Portrait of a Franciscan* by Rubens; *Spain Succouring Religion* by Titian; *Battle in the Bay of Naples* by Breughel the Elder; several masterpieces of light, darkness, and iconography by the homoerotic Michelangelo da Caravaggio.

We descended marble stairs and entered room after room after room of Diana's and Urban's private apartments, passing (as if through ordinary streets, and not even pausing to admire) the illustrious Madonnas, chandeliers and frescoes, tapestries and statuary, draperies and the gold that decorated the Louis Quatorze furniture—until we reached Diana's sitting room, the Venetian Salon.

We lingered there, upon rococo chairs, chatting, bathed in a green haze. The room was done in green damask, not just the vaulted walls but the draperies and cloth on the gilded chairs. The largest painting was of Venice, without a hint of green—Il Giovane's *Piazza of St Mark.* "Don't you adore the pavement?" Diana asked me. "How *red* Il Giovane has imagined it, all the way from the Doge's palace to the cathedral so far beyond."

Red. We withdrew from Diana's green Venetian Salon until we entered a crimson haze and Urban's Dutch Salon. The walls and furnishings were of red damask, the paintings all by Breughel the Elder evoking his homeland; but the main piece was an enormous tapestry by the Gobelins, done early in the eighteenth century—depicting Dutch nobility and peasants mingling on a frozen lake—for Louis XIV in his dotage. From a distant room, a telephone began to ring. Urban Northwood rose from his crimson armchair and, on his wobbly legs, hurried there to answer it. For the next hour, the telephone rang repeatedly, summoning Urban so often from the Dutch Salon that during much of the time Diana and I were left alone together.

"Shall I ring for more tea?" she asked.

"Not for me, thank you," said I.

"An apéritif? Whisky and soda?"

"No, thank you."

"I rarely drink, either, Monsignor Galsworthy. Alcohol makes me drowsy—disrupts my work."

From her black purse, Diana took out a notebook and, with a stub of pencil, wrote for several minutes as I walked about the Dutch Salon, pretending to inspect the busts and pictures but stealing glances at her beauty from different angles, as she sat writing in a Baroque armchair, and I admired her silently. I thanked Christ for the amplitude of my soutane: my loins were on fire. When she closed her notebook, I asked, "Is that a diary?"

"Not really," she replied. "I'm a writer, you see, and compulsively I take notes. I knew about the witch Olimpia Maidalchini, but I'd never heard your story of Innocent Tenth stooping before Velázquez. It's too *priceless* to forget."

I sat again on a damask couch across the vast room from her, ever obedient to my rules: Avoid the Occasions of Sin. Fairly shouting to be heard, I said, "Ah. Have you been published?"

"Two historical novels. An earlier period, actually, than your Innocent Tenth Pamphili. I'm more attracted to the Borgias, the Medicis, the Renaissance."

"I'd like to read them."

She laughed. "You'd never find my books, Monsignor. My publisher did not advertise, the reviewers largely looked the other way, and nobody read them. Still, I write and write and write. Even here in Rome, I write every morning and often half the night. I crave seclusion."

A pause; extended silence; in a swirling, Baroque clock, the pendulum ticked and ticked; I knew not what to say. From the distant room, Urban Northwood shouted at his telephone in a strange tongue: Magyar? Presently I said, "Since you are betrothed, it might be improper on my part to address you as 'Diana.' May I know your family name?"

"Duchesse."

"Echoes of nobility."

"Being American, I have no title and want none. My ancestors in France were of the nobility, or so my father claimed. You, I understand, are a baronet?"

"How did you know, Miss—Mademoiselle—Duchesse?"

"Urban makes it his business to know such things. He went to the British Council and looked for you in *Who's Who*. Pages were torn out, so he followed his intuition and found you in Burke's *Peerage*. This 'Monsignor' stuff is so formal. May I call you 'Sir Augustine'?"

"If you wish. It means nothing to me."

"*Ah, but it should!*" exclaimed Urban Northwood, bursting into the Dutch Salon from his telephone call. "As a baronet, dear Sir Augustine, you have precedence over all knights of the Queen's realm, save Knights of the Garter. Ha-ha!" Hardly had he sat down but the telephone rang again and he was gone. Diana Duchesse laughed. "Poor Urban," she said. "*He* wants to be a duke."

I asked, "At the hands of which sovereign?"

"His Holiness the Pope. Oh, dear. He told me never to mention it. I've been *frightfully* indiscreet."

"HAH!!!"

"What an odd, loud laugh you have."

"Forgive me, Miss Duchesse—"

"Oh, Diana, *please.*"

"Forgive me . . . Diana. 'Frightful' was my mother's favourite word."

"Why do you use the past tense?"

"She's dead."

"I'm sorry. You must miss her so."

"I don't, actually."

"And your father?"

"He's dead."

"Do you miss *him*?"

"No."

Another pause; the gilded clock ticked on; Diana opened her purse again and scribbled notes. (Did I guess, even then, that in the future I would turn up as a character in one of her enigmatic modern novels?) She raised her golden head and asked, "How do you amuse yourself, Sir Augustine—"

"Oh, Augustine, *please.*"

"Thank you! How do you amuse yourself, Augustine, when you are not attending the Pope?"

"In Egypt, where I served for several years, I mounted, swam, and shot. In Rome, I take long walks, read, and play Bach upon my Steinway. A bit of Chopin, too, but Chopin is so romantic . . . and it pains me to remind myself that romance can not play any part in my chosen life."

"No Mozart?"

"I've tried Mozart, but beneath my clumsy fingers, his sonatas come out with the beat of Bach."

"I'm disappointed, Augustine. I prefer Mozart."

"The angels agree with you . . . Diana. Before God, the angels play Bach. Amongst themselves, they play Mozart."

"Ha-ha!" Her laugh seemed forced.

"When I die, and go to Heaven—if I ever get there—plenty of time for Jesus and John the Baptist. First, I must meet Bach and Mozart."

"Ha-ha! *Comme vous êtes méchant, cher Monseigneur.*"

"*Donc, vous êtes francophone?*"

"Probably as much as you are, Augustine. My Italian is not quite as good, but I manage."

"And Latin?"

"Of course."

"Classical Greek?"

"Of course."

"Who educated you, Diana?"

"Sisters of the Sacred Heart."

"Ah. The Jesuits of the other gender."

My loins were calmer now, so I moved to an armchair much closer to her own, facing her. I thought: What a pity, what a *frightful* pity. I wished to tell her, "We are the two of us about the same age. Your hair is blonde; mine is dark. You are beautiful; I am handsome. We were born for each other. If only I were someone, something else."

I think she read my thoughts. She asked, "Why do you keep glancing at my right shoulder?"

"I'm looking for your bow and quiver."

"I have no arrows to shoot at *you,* Monsignor. Diana, you may remember, was not only goddess of the Hunt. She was also goddess of the Moon, goddess of Virginity, and—"

"The Protectress of Women."

"So. Need I protect myself from you?"

My loins were aflame again, but rarely had I been so amused, miserable, or happy. I answered, "Hardly. Diana was Apollo's sister. I am not Apollo, but you, Diana, are goddess of the distant Moon, of, of—inviolable—V-Virginity. Should we ever meet again, we shall do so as brother and sister."

"I'm afraid we must, Monsignor."

"Forgive my flirtation—I am so alone."

"I sensed that, Augustine."

"I'm doomed to it! I think—in the deepest part of me—I prefer solitude."

In the far room, Urban Northwood by now was screaming—Magyar?—into his telephone. We heard him slam it down, then we listened as he hobbled on marble floors to the Dutch Salon angrily and out of breath. He said, "Forgive me, darling, but my plans have changed. I'll return to Budapest, tomorrow."

"Oh, Urban," Diana protested. "Not another trip behind the Iron Curtain? It's so dangerous."

"I'm sorry, darling, but I must."

"How long will you be gone?"

"A fortnight, I'm afraid." Urban brightened as he turned to me. "We have so few real friends in Rome, Sir Augustine. Could you call on Diana, show her more of Rome?"

"I'm terribly busy in the mornings," said I, barely able to believe his invitation.

"So is Diana."

"I might manage a bit of time—in the afternoons."

"Marvellous."

Silence: Diana, no doubt against her better judgement, did not demur. I added, "We'll need a chaperone. Canon Law . . ."

Said Urban, "I'll arrange something with Prince Doria."

"You needn't b-bother Prince Doria," I responded. "I've a manservant with small children."

Thus next afternoon, a Saturday, I called on solitary Diana Duchesse at Doria-Pamphili palace with Ghassem's children in my train.

Kamal and Fatima had grown, though neither was yet in puberty, and Ghassem and I still loomed like pillars above their heads. Both still wore white flowing gowns and brown sandals over bare feet, Kamal in a red turban like his father's, Fatima's face nun-like beneath a black veil. Neither child attended school in Rome or spoke a word of Italian; Ghassem would not allow it. Arabic remained the language of my household; Ghassem tutored them for hours daily, mostly in the Koran.

Like him, they rarely ventured outside my flat in the Borgo Angelico,

except to help their father to carry bundles when he shopped for meat, vegetables, and fish. Ham, pork, and bottles of wine he refused to buy: such
shopping he left to me. The children shared his fear of Catholic Rome, and
now they seemed more terrified than awed by the immensity and opulence
of the Palazzo Doria-Pamphili.

"Such adorable children," exclaimed Diana when she saw them. "Such
sculpted features—so Pharaonic! Are they Hamites?"

"Nubian Hamites" said I.

Not understanding, Kamal and Fatima seemed as afraid of blonde Diana
as they were of her palace. As she and I conversed, they clung to me, hugging
me about my waist and legs, and fairly hiding between the folds of my
soutane. Diana said, "Good heavens, Augustine, how they love you."

"They're my family—all I h-have," I answered, my voice cracking, as I
stooped to kiss their faces.

As the afternoons passed, the children grew less fearful of Diana, I might
say fond of her. When we visited a ruin or a church, she walked ahead,
holding the hands of Kamal and Fatima on either side, whilst I in my black
and purple deliberately rambled a little ways behind for reasons of pro-
priety. The lengthening days of Lent and spring grew ever warmer, the
Roman sunshine ever mellower, more Mediterranean.

Whilst we explored the Roman Forum and other imperial ruins, Diana
wrote copious notes. She seemed to be doing research, but she would not
deign to reveal whether the book she planned would dwell upon Rome past
or Rome present. Each afternoon we returned to the summit of the Capito-
line Hill, where she could not cease to revere Michelangelo's Piazza del
Campidoglio, with its twin staircases ascending classically on either side to
the centre of the Palazzo Senatorio; the pagan deities atop the balustrade of
the Palazzo Nuovo; or the equestrian statue of Marcus Aurelius in the heart
of the piazza flanked by elegant palaces. Then, it being the season of Lent,
we visited churches to pursue our devotions and penances.

The children watched bewildered as Diana, on her knees, climbed the
Scala Santa, the Holy Stairs, by devout legend the steps of Pilate's praeto-
rium, made of marble but for suffering pilgrims planked by common wood.
These venerated stairs (did Christ ascend them?) were in St John Lateran, the
Pope's own cathedral as Bishop of Rome: I mounted them as well, upon my
knees, several steps below Diana, to the domed chapel and the altar beneath
its soaring mural of Christ Crucified.

In all of the churches how warmly the red and amber votive candles flickered, vast blazing forests of them, before tormented images of Christ and the
Virgin; how massively and ardently the processions of acolytes and hooded
monks pulsated through the aisles and sanctuaries; how fervently men,
women, children, Diana, I, mourned or even wept as priests, bishops, cardinals trod the Stations of the Cross and relived our Redeemer's passion, crucifixion, and entombment. How demure and pious Diana seemed in her
sleeved black gowns, illumined only at the neck by twinkling pearls, her

golden head enshrouded for all occasions that were sacred in a mantilla of black Spanish lace.

By the grace of Cardinal Benevento, we gained entry to the private Gardens of the Vatican and even to the ways where the Pontiff trod. That afternoon the air was brisk but the sun shone brightly and already the Roman spring was lush: red camellias in full bloom, lilies afloat on mossy ponds, flamboyant cannas juxtaposed with laurel hedges. With the children we wandered down crooked footpaths, by boxwood nooks with statues of marble and terra-cotta, until—through a fountain's mist, among the ilex trees—we saw the tawny stone and glazed faïence of the Summer Villa of Pius IV.

Diana and I sat there for a while on the balustrade of the tiny piazza, amid the urns and Doric columns, as the children dashed in and out of the villa, romping and laughing between the columns, beneath the Grecian arch, playing tag and hide-and-seek, in their incongruous costumes of Nubia. From her dark purse Diana removed her pencil and little notebook and asked me slyly, "What intrigues are going on in the Roman Curia?"

Said I, "If you quote me, Diana, you'll get me sacked."

"I'm a novelist—not a journalist," she riposted.

"As you see, I live in fear," I answered. "The Roman Curia—and the Roman Church—are ossified. I'm stuck in a job I hate: translating papal allocutions so morose and dense I do well to understand them. I'm a clerk! I was more important in Muslim Cairo than I am in Catholic Rome! I have no power—nor shall I, ever, under this moribund pontificate."

"But I assumed that you revere the Pope."

"His Holiness is immensely erudite—and, ah, such magisterium! However, in his age he is growing so feeble from his hiccups and his many ills that no longer can he really govern the Church. Save for ceremonies, I—most prelates—can not get near him. He is being pulled to and fro by a cabal of reactionary cardinals, his German housekeeper who stands like a storm trooper at his door, and a quack gerontologist from Switzerland who injects him daily with the minced entrails of freshly slaughtered lambs."

"*Agnus Dei,*" replied Diana, crossing herself and laughing in that little piazza of Pius IV. More than ever, I was enchanted by the resonance of her laughter—but quickly her visage darkened as she said, "I'm serious, actually. He is, like Christ, the Lamb of God. He's infallible in faith and morals, and you, Augustine—his Right Reverend Domestic Prelate—should show him more respect."

"He's a mean old man, commanding people—the whole wide world—how to think and how to live."

"Good heavens, how cynical—and *liberal*—you're becoming."

"The Roman Church must change!"

"No—for her glory—she must remain for ever as she is!"

Diana and I were nearly shouting at each other. The children stood by at the portal of the lovely villa, uncomprehending and confused. For a moment as we argued, through laurel hedges and holly-like ilex trees, I caught sight in the distance of the tall Stern Pope, walking stooped upon a favourite path, on either side of him his Italian physician, in formal coat and striped pants, and the veiled papal housekeeper, the German nun. Though the day was mild, the Supreme Pontiff beneath his broad-brimmed crimson hat wore a white coat as long as his soutane, the collar turned up around his neck to protect him against his private chill.

Then Diana saw him, too: she fell to her knees in veneration, tracing against her head and torso the Sign of the Cross. I knelt beside her, likewise tracing the Sign of the Cross, and I said, "Forgive me, Diana. I revere him as you do. I repent my anger—and my ungodly ambition. He is, after all, the Vicar of Christ."

The Pope passed from view.

I laughed. "Ha-ha! Ha-ha! Dearest Diana, with each passing day, we're becoming like a married couple—don't you th-think?"

Said Diana, "Oh, Augustine . . . I do adore your stormy passion."

"I mean, now we're even *f-fighting*!"

Weeks passed, but still, as we approached Palm Sunday, Urban Northwood did not return to Rome. "He calls me every evening," Diana said mysteriously.

She began to attend my daily Mass at daybreak upon a side altar of St Peter's. Assisted by an acolyte, I wore the violet chasuble of Lenten sadness; as a Domestic Prelate, I enjoyed the privilege of the *bugia*, a candle in a short candlestick of silver set beside my missal as I celebrated the Introit and Kyrie, Creed and Offertory, Consecration and Oblation, of the Tridentine Mass in Latin. Diana in her mantilla took Communion from my hands each morning. Afterwards she said, "I've never seen the Mass celebrated as beautifully as you do, Augustine." Holy Week, Spy Wednesday, Maundy Thursday, Good Friday, Holy Saturday, Easter Sunday—sorrow ceding at last to joy and glory in the Resurrection of Jesus Christ—came and went, but still Urban Northwood did not return to Rome.

After Easter, Diana visited my flat in the Borgo Angelico to take tea in the late afternoons. Kamal and Fatima were always present in a nearby room as Diana and I chatted and laughed and she listened when I sat at my piano and played Bach or a bit of Chopin. Later, she wandered about my rooms, peering at shelves, picking out esoteric books and glancing at them, testing my divans and Louis Quinze chairs by sitting on them or running her short, unpolished fingernails across the fabrics. She said, "Your apartment is so *shabby*, Augustine."

"I've some interesting Egyptian curios," I protested.

"You've nothing of value except your books and your piano," she answered. "You badly need new furniture and rugs and some decent paintings. When Urban returns, I shall speak to him."

"I . . . couldn't p-possibly accept. . . ."

"Nonsense. Urban is in awe of you. He's convinced that—one day—you'll be created a cardinal."

"He's so indecently rich, Diana. What is his business?"

"I don't know and I don't care. Well . . . I care but I don't care to *know.* Once, rather vaguely, he suggested he was a financier, another time an entrepreneur or an *homme d'affaires.* Yet another time, under the influence of his medication—his wobbly legs, you know—he mumbled something about manufacturing pencils before the war in Budapest, where it seems he inherited money or made his first fortune."

"Was he born in Hungary?"

"He's as vague about his birthplace. You noticed his high culture, his perfect American English? He travels on a U.S. passport. Wherever he goes, he collects art. He'll collect *you,* if you let him, as another work of art. Which, I must confess, you may be." Her voice rose to a higher, more patrician register of soprano, teasing, nearly mocking. "Oh, those piercing dark eyes of yours, Augustine. That straight nose, with its flaring nostrils. Your high cheekbones, the skin stretched across them like young parchment from your battle—I see *all* such things—to keep your chastity."

"Is it my chastity that attracts you?"

"But I'm not attracted to you, *cher Monseigneur.* Oh, those god-like Grecian locks of blackest hair . . . which, I have no doubt, will turn to streaks of perfect silver by the time you enter the Sacred College. I can read your mind, Augustine. You think I'm marrying Urban Northwood for his money."

"My mind is not quite so mischievous as yours, *chère Mademoiselle.*"

"I have my own fortune, thank God, tiny compared to his. I've told him, 'I want none of your fortune.' "

"He's rather much older than you, Diana, and—"

"Almost . . . ugly."

"*Hélas!* But you love him?"

"That, Augustine, is a secret I shall never share with you."

"Forgive me, but I sense a bargain somewhere."

"Indeed there is a bargain. I've promised him an heir."

We were seated beside each other on the bench before my Steinway. Diana wore a dark blue dress and her single string of whitest pearls; the children chattered Arabic in the kitchen with their father. As we conversed, I played an étude of Chopin's, softly. Diana went on, "You must one day see Urban's estate in America—Northwood Hall. He modelled it on Cardinal Wolsey's Hampton Court—hardly as huge, but sometimes it seems to be. He's still building it! I shall have my own apartments at Northwood Hall. I want to write, Augustine. I crave splendour in seclusion."

Against myself, I began to write letters to Diana, arranging that a messenger from the Secretariat of State should deliver them to the Palazzo Doria-Pamphili early in the mornings. Under the circumstances, I could scarcely send her wine and flowers also, but I struggled to disguise my

ardour by composing verse that was mystical and erotic both at once. For that, I could not achieve the lofty, dazzling imagery of St John of the Cross, so in my sweet agony I cited him as well.

> *Descubre tu presencia,*
> *Y máteme tu vista y hermosura;*
> *Mira que la dolencia*
> *De amor, que no se cura*
> *Sino con la presencia y la figura.*

> Reveal your image clearly,
> And kill me with the beauty you discover;
> For pains that come so dearly
> From love, can not recover
> But through the presence of the lover.

This was, in fact, my favourite model of erotic mysticism: many years thereafter, I cited such verses of St John in my unread book, *The Joy of Celibacy.* However, Diana stopped coming to my flat, nor for several days did she attend my Mass at dawn in St Peter's. At last one morning she appeared at my Mass. Afterwards, as we walked out of the basilica—through the stuccoes and mosaics of Maderno's vestibule onto Bernini's great flight of marble steps—Diana said, "Your letters are sublime, Augustine. A trifle too sublime, I'm very much afraid. I shan't be coming to your flat again to take tea alone with you."

"But the children," I protested, "are always present!"

In the piazza, a light rain fell. Diana flung on her white raincoat, across her stately shoulders like a cape, and in low, black shoes strode swiftly in the direction of the Tiber whilst I chased a stride or two behind her. She said, "It's my fault, really. It's as though, Augustine, I were writing a novel about you in my head—and provoking your childish emotions for each new scene."

"My emotions are no more ch-childish than yours."

"Indeed they are. As for mine, I've at least reached puberty."

"HAH!!!"

"Oh, dear, that strange, loud laugh again. It's not my virtue that's in danger but your own. Now leave me, please. I'm to be the wife of Urban Northwood."

⁜

A fortnight later, Urban Northwood re-turned to Rome. Serenely, Diana accompa-nied him to tea in the Borgo Angelico. Like Diana, Urban (in a grey lounge suit) took the liberty of wandering about my rooms, per-haps forewarned by her that he would find them shabby. He asked, "Where is your chapel, Sir Augustine?"

"I have no chapel, Urban," I replied.

"Ah, but you must, Augustine. Hello, who's this?"

"Ghassem, my manservant. And these are his children, Kamal and Fatima."

We were in the kitchen. Urban said, "Why, he is the handsomest manservant I ever saw! So tall! Such marvellous robes and turban! The children are so fine! And Ghassem's wife?"

"She died in Cairo," said I. "Ghassem wants another wife from Nubia—and more children."

"What are your wishes in the matter?"

"I should help him if I could."

Urban banged on a wall: "What's in there?"

"An empty flat."

"Then we must knock down the wall and enlarge your flat. You need a chapel. Ghassem needs a wife."

"I couldn't possibly . . ."

"Absurd, my dear Augustine. Tell your land-lord to ring me up."

Within the week, workmen appeared, to knock down walls, doubling the number of my rooms; and in their train an architect, a decorator, apprentices. I thought, All well and good and paid for, but have *I* a hundred quid?

Throughout the ensuing month, as labourers painted and refurbished, my doorbell rang often in the afternoons and men arrived with carpets, candlesticks, furniture, and *objets d'art*. The rugs were Damascene or Persian, hardly priceless but of high quality. Among the pictures and the statuary, only some were originals, but all were costly and of exemplary taste.

Here were oil copies of Bacchiacca, of *The Flagellation of Christ;* of Fra Angelico, detail of the nails and crown of thorns taken from His body in *The Entombment*; of Mantegna's *Descent into Limbo*. Here were copies and original, preliminary sketches from the eighteenth and nineteenth centuries, in pencil and in watercolour, by John Sell Cotman, William Pars, Francis Oliver Finch, Thomas Heaphy, Thomas Shorter Boys, William Turner of Oxford, depicting Dionysus and Ariadne; a churchyard in Surrey; landscapes with ruined castles; a rocky coast by moonlight; a tumbling bridge in Shropshire; a ruined abbey in Gloucestershire; a teeming market and towering spires in Wolverhampton; the rue St-Denis in 1802; French valleys, rivers, and cathedrals; the Pavillon de Flore in the Palace of the Tuileries (where Napoleon had lodged Pius VII); the waterfalls and trees and frolicking gods and goddesses of Arcadia; Plato—amidst ponds and cattle grazing and columned temples in the distance—teaching his pupils in the Grove of Academe; and—in Hastings—a fish market.

Most of those were imitations by gifted if lesser painters; but the mounted silver, brass, and copper coins seemed each of them authentic, minted in antiquity—coins of Syracuse, Clazomenae, and Heraclea; engraved gemstones of a Ptolemaic king in amethyst, of a Ptolemaic queen in cornelian, of the head of Alexander in tourmaline; bronze coins from the Roman Republic and Early Empire of heads of bulls, horses, goddesses, emperors in laurel wreaths; more gemstones engraved with the snake-haired Medusa in chalcedony and a naked Diomedes in red jasper; Bactrian coins of Demetrios and Antimachus. All of the coins and gemstones were mounted on crimson watered silk in frames of pure silver.

My new furniture was Italianate Louis Quinze—chairs, divans, desks, and tables much as I had (one sweet afternoon) recounted to Diana of the Academy of Noble Ecclesiastics—capricious, graceful, rococo; curved lines with decorative shells and flowers; cloth of velvet and of damask, red, blue, and purple; yet suggesting lightness, comfort, and fantasy.

For sculpture, on a marble pedestal, stood an admirable bust of Aristotle; upon other pedestals, miniature classical and Renaissance nudes, all of them perfect copies: a Venus cast in bronze, her right hand hiding her vulva; a bronze torso of the Doryphoros, after Polyclitus; an armless Apollo of the Tiber, in the style of Phidias. I mused, Has Diana chosen my new art or did Urban Northwood make most of the selections? To create space for his munificence, I threw out all of my junk.

Now my rooms shone with warmth and elegance. More, my landlord informed me that Signor Norta-wooda, for a period to last two years, had paid the rent for my lodgings.

I fancied that some other sort of compensation would be expected from my side, and I did not wait long to learn it.

The churchly banns of marriage having been announced in the United States, Urban and Diana were now ready to be wed. They came to me one Sunday afternoon in the late spring, ostensibly to tour my restored apartments, but in truth to discuss the ceremony. As Diana poured tea, I thanked them both for their generosity, but Urban was impatient with my compliments and came swiftly to the point.

He wanted the ceremony in the Sistine Chapel, and a cardinal to confer the sacrament. When the ceremony was done, he and Diana should be received privately in the papal apartments, where the Pontiff would bestow upon them his Apostolic Benediction.

Urban handed me an envelope the colour of cream, suggesting as he did so that I should open it forthwith. Inside, I found a cheque for two hundred fifty thousand dollars, drawn on the Crédit Suisse, made out to "His Holiness the Pope." As before, across the top, in his large, neat hand, Urban had written, "For the charities of the Holy See"—but now he had added, "via Msgr Galsworthy."

I slipped the envelope and cheque inside the purple cincture of my soutane. I said, "Thank you, Urban. However, I must tell you that in the Apostolic Palace such matters are not so directly done."

Diana, never more alluring in a suit the hue of pale tangerine and her usual pearls, grew suddenly so radiant that I recognised a blush. She said, "I tried to tell him that, Augustine." She turned to her fiancé and asked with petulance, "Darling, why can't Augustine marry us quietly in the Doria-Pamphili chapel? Why must you insist on a cardinal and the Pope?"

"I'm doing this for you, Diana."

As they argued, I thought, No, Urban—for yourself. What do you want? Respectability? Had Diana been serious—that you covet a papal dukedom? When their voices rose towards vehemence, I pointed to the English watercolours. I asked, "Do you not both admire the subtlety of Lord Oxford, of Thomas Shorter Boys? Let me make some—ah—soft inquiries at the papal court."

Next day, in the chambers of the Apostolic Penitentiary, I sought out Cardinal di Benevento. Pondering the cheque on the Crédit Suisse, His Eminence said, "I shall pass this to the Holy Father when he is lucid."

I inquired, "When is the Holy Father lucid?"

"In the mornings, mostly, after he has received his lamb injections. His hiccups, at least, have diminished of late. He has gained more faith in his lamb injections than in my Lourdes water. My influence, alas, is drying up."

I explained, as delicately as I could, Urban Northwood's wish for a wedding in the Sistine Chapel and a private audience with the Sovereign Pontiff.

The Cardinal exclaimed, "*La Sistina?* But that is the Pope's own chapel! His Holiness would never agree." He waved the cheque: "I must warn you, Agostino, against the perils of promoting ecclesiastical preferments—carried to excess, they can lead to simony."

"I shall never be a s-simoniac."

"We've confidence in your integrity, *carissimo Agostino.* We have rather less in your Mr Northwood's."

"*We?*"

"I mean the Pope. Half the day he may be ga-ga, but when lucid he is as ever shrewd. After your first cheque, he made inquiries about Mr Northwood."

"What did he learn?"

"*Niente.*" Nothing. "That, I fear, is itself a problem. We both of us know that candidates for beatification must exude 'the odour of sanctity.' Your Mr Northwood exudes the odour of doubt."

Nonetheless I persevered, and after some days Cardinal Benevento agreed to receive me with Urban and Diana. As the sole member of the Sacred College with whom I was intimate, only he might fulfill Urban's wish that a cardinal should join him to his betrothed. The Cardinal, decked out at my request in full scarlet, told them gently, "The Sistine Chapel is not suitable. The Pauline Chapel, on the other hand, though rarely used—"

"The *Pauline* Chapel?" Urban interrupted. "True, it's another treasure of Michelangelo's. . . ."

"And marriages in the Pauline Chapel," the Cardinal continued, "are so privileged—almost without precedent."

"Will Your Eminence officiate?"

"That depends upon the humour of the Holy Father."

"Will the Holy Father—"

I stopped Urban in midsentence, before he could demand a papal audience. Afterwards, as we strode across St Peter's Square, Diana told us, "I shan't be married by a gnome."

"Darling," reasoned Urban, "he's not that short, and he's a cardinal."

"He's *awful.*"

There, by Bernini's colonnade, I turned to Diana and raged at her, "How dare you? Cardinal di Benevento is the kindest man in Rome. In Egypt, I nursed him at the door of death. I wear this purple toga as his gift."

"*Je m'excuse, Monseigneur!*"

Yet in the event, Cardinal Benevento was no more willing than Diana. Soon, he told me, "The Pope forbade me to perform the wedding. He was not quite lucid. He quoted Balzac."

"*Balzac?*" I marvelled. "Not Goethe? Von Clausewitz?"

"He said, 'Behind every fortune lurks a crime.' "

"Should I return the cheque?"

"Oh, we've cashed it."

.   .   .

So, for want of a cardinal, it was I (one Saturday morning) who joined Urban Northwood and Diana Duchesse in Holy Matrimony in the Pauline Chapel, at the summit of the Scala Regia in the papal palace. The ceremony, for all the beauty of the chapel and the Mass, was done in circumstances of deep embarrassment to the nuptial couple.

But for the bride and groom, nobody showed up. Urban had invited several of his associates in business with their wives, yet it was clear from Diana's unsettled countenance that she and Urban had been quarrelling: Diana would have no guest she deemed disreputable. At the last moment, the commercial attaché of the French embassy sent his regrets. Not even Urban's Roman landlords, the Prince and Princess Doria, deigned to attend. Finally, barely quarter of an hour before the Mass, I dragooned an altar boy and two Swiss Guards as witnesses. On the ancient organ, a Capuchin monk played melodies from Mozart's *Mass in C Minor,* but we had no choir.

Michelangelo's characters nearly compensated for the nonexistent guests; indeed, the very emptiness of the chapel infused the ceremony with an eerie enchantment. Amidst a mysterious commingling of light and shadow between the columns and the mouldings, Michelangelo's murals dominated us. They were his last paintings, done in his extreme old age, and perhaps his greatest—*The Crucifixion of St Peter,* and *The Conversion of St Paul.* Such violent *movement* in those frescoes!

Lightning bursts from Heaven: a horse rears, hurling the blinded Saul to earth as he hears the voice of the Son of God. In the mural opposite, out of deference to the upright crucifixion of his Lord, Peter by his own request is crucified upside down. The paintings ooze pessimism, and properly: the Renaissance is dying, the Reformation is tearing Christendom apart, and the Wars of Religion loom. The paintings are morose, romantic, and tragic all at once. St Paul and the men surrounding him are seized with terror; the mob of soldiers and the common people round St Peter are hushed with sorrow, doubt, or horror; only Peter glares out at us, as if hinting of the harshness of the Christian era to follow for millennia. In both murals, the very world, its harmony, its yearning for beauty and perfection, seems about to explode.

The couple dressed simply, Diana in long white satin, a double string of pearls, and a white mantilla concealing the fairness of her hair; Urban in a dark, double-breasted suit, a silver tie, and a white flower on his lapel; he was inches shorter than his bride. I wore a golden Roman chasuble, studded with precious gems, borrowed from Cardinal Benevento's fabulous collection. I began the nuptials with a brief exhortation, inspired by Bossuet, reminding the bride that she was about to sacrifice her beauty, perhaps even her health, and the power of loving that women possess but once in life; in his turn the groom would surrender the freedom of his youth, those incomparable years which he could never relive, to drink of the sacred chalice of self-denial and undying consecration to one weaker than himself. Together, the two of them must await not only joy but sorrow, pain, and suffering, in a lifetime to be passed in union as Christ was for ever wedded to His Church.

That said, Urban and Diana exchanged vows, and I blessed them with these words: *"Ego conjungo vos in matrimonium, in nomine Patris, et Filii, et Spiritus sancti."* They were man and wife.

Then I sprinkled them with holy water and blessed their silver rings upon silver plate and sprinkled the rings with holy water in the pattern of the Cross. During the Nuptial Mass, I recited Paul's Epistle to the Ephesians: Let women be subject to their husbands as to the Lord; for the husband is head of the wife, as Christ is head of the Church. Therefore, as the Church is subject to Christ, so also let wives be to their husbands in all things. Husbands, love your wives, as Christ also loved the Church. So also ought men to love their wives as their own bodies. He that loveth his wife loveth himself: for no man ever hated his own flesh. For this cause shall a man leave his father and mother, and shall cleave to his wife; and they shall be two in one flesh. Let every one of you love his wife as himself, and let the wife fear her husband.

When the Nuptial Mass was done, and as the Capuchin played his last melodies from Mozart, there, on the high altar of the Pauline Chapel—and though it had no place in the sacred liturgy—both Urban and Diana seized my hands and kissed them.

The Pope did not receive us.

In Urban's Mercedes limousine (I in my ceremonial mantelletta and soutane of purple, rochet of French lace), we were chauffeured back to Doria-Pamphili palace. In the Dutch Salon, beneath Breughel's paintings and the great tapestry of the Gobelins in the crimson haze, a butler in ruff and satin served us beluga caviar and *brut* champagne. I was the only guest. Throughout the celebration we rarely spoke, but we all three of us must have recognised that thenceforth I was as wedded to Urban and Diana as they were to each other.

I wondered, Was it the will of Christ that I should pray for help as I tippled Lourdes water, and then, as though by purest chance, encounter Urban Northwood in the Piazza Farnese? During Urban's long absence, Diana had told me, "I crave splendour in seclusion." I supposed that, married to such a man, she would have much splendor in seclusion. As I rose to leave, Urban handed me a creamy envelope; I assumed that it contained my stipend, but I did not open it until I returned to my own apartments.

The cheque, made out to "Rt Rev Msgr Sir Aug Galsworthy, Bart" on the Crédit Suisse, was for fifty thousand dollars. I surmised that in future other cheques might follow. I went into the kitchen, where I found Ghassem and his children preparing my solitary luncheon. In Arabic I said, "*Ya Ghassem,* you may write to your mother to send you a wife."

Next day, Urban and Diana Northwood returned to the United States.

FIFTEEN

Soon enough, the austere and magisterial
Pope—seized again by hiccups—sank into his
final illness. He had repaired with his court
to Castel Gandolfo, his villa in the Alban hills,
attended as ever and fussed over by his German
housekeeper, his German secretary, his German
confessor, his Swiss gerontologist, and his Italian
quack doctor, not even a physician really but an
oculist. I recoiled in distaste as the oculist sold
photographs to the world press of the Supreme
Pontiff in his death agony, wearing white pyjamas
but without his gold-rimmed spectacles, his head
propped up by soiled pillows, a rubber tube dangling from his mouth.

Then he died, and (no doubt! without pausing
to rest in Purgatory!) his soul went straight to
Heaven. In keeping with the ritual of the Roman
Church, the Dean of the Sacred College, an
ancient, bearded Frenchman, tapped the Pontiff's
forehead thrice with a silver hammer, thence from
the bedside proceeded to the expired Pontiff's
rings and seals and smashed them.

Thereupon the quack doctor called in a quack
mortician, and the two of them embalmed the
papal corpse. Of a warm October afternoon, the
corpse—vested in a red mozzetta trimmed with
ermine and wrapped in cellophane, reposing inside
a casket of cypress wood—was transported upon a

hearse towards Rome, escorted by an army of priests and prelates in black robes of mourning.

As the procession reached the Cathedral of St John Lateran, the Pope's seat as Bishop of Rome, the corpse exploded, popping open the cypress casket—the corpse a victim of incompetent embalming and bubbling fermentation in the autumn sunshine. At St Peter's, as the Pontiff in a red chasuble and golden mitre lay in state, and scores of candles flickered and mourners in the scores of thousands trudged weeping past his corpse, his face turned green and his remains released a rotting stench.

During his last years, the Sovereign Pontiff had confided to a cardinal that as he walked in the solitude of the Gardens of the Vatican, the miracle of Fátima had been repeated, the Blessed Virgin had appeared to him, and the sun had danced in the sky.

I thought, *Maybe she did: and maybe the sun danced.*

To some Jesuits he confided that, one morning when he awoke, Christ was sitting by his bed.

I thought, *Maybe He was.*

At St Peter's, as I filed past the Pope's body, remarked the greenness of his face, and smelled the rot exuding, I mourned as did so many millions the passing of an august pontificate. Still I sensed somehow that with the botched embalming of the Pontiff's corpse, the Roman Church I so deeply loved and hated—the Church of Michelangelo and Chateaubriand and Mozart and Consalvi; of miracles and visions and votive candles; of Lourdes water and rosaries incessantly recited; of the rococo; of the Baroque; of the Renaissance and the Counter Reformation; of Napoleon's Concordat with Pius VII; of zealous sexual repression; of Tuscan peasants kneeling to the Angelus bell tolling across the fields; of my Gothic abbey in Vaucluse; of the Imperial Papacy—had been embalmed with him.

I had been present at St John Lateran when the corpse exploded. Now I wondered—but why? but why?—whether the Roman Church itself would not suffer, and rather soon, a like combustion.

✚

PART V

SUNNY
POPE

✚

✥

✥

I was intrigued to discover that Cardinal di Benevento and the new Pope were old friends.

For decades the two of them had been shunted off to lonely backwaters of the Holy See's diplomatic service, Monsignore Benevento to Cairo and before Cairo to legations eastward and southward in Djakarta and Ouagadougou; the future Pontiff to Sofia and Istanbul. Over the years, their paths intersected far from Rome, allowing them liberty to commiserate about the whims of imperious popes and the cruelties of being forgotten.

Then a fluke of history happened: God played a little joke.

God the Holy Spirit intervened in the comedy of men, and cast His dice in the Divine game of chance.

In France, His unwitting agent, General de Gaulle, angry at the Papal Nuncio for having collaborated with Vichy and Marshal Pétain, demanded a replacement. More, he insisted that the new Nuncio should appear at noon in the Elysée palace on New Year's Day 1945 to present official greetings in his capacity as dean of the diplomatic corps.

In Rome, amidst much eleventh-hour vexation and thrashing about, the Stern Pope commanded his Nuncio in Buenos Aires to fly to Paris, but that

Archbishop was ill and forbidden by his doctors to travel. At the last minute, someone in the Roman Curia remembered the genial papal delegate languishing in Istanbul. The Archbishop was posted forthwith from Istanbul to Paris, whither he rushed, playing nick and tuck with time and entering the Elysée as noon struck.

For the next eight years, the rotund Nuncio charmed France. Talkative and easygoing, full of north Italian mirth, he served a good table and fine wines and regaled his eminent guests with funny stories in his fluent though imperfect French. And yet tension reigned (as it always had) between Rome and the French bishops and cardinals. Rome was unhappy with radical French worker-priests who toiled with the *Lumpenproletariat* in factories, and most unhappy with the new French theologians who tampered with ancient doctrines to the verge of unorthodoxy.

More and more, whenever bad news arrived from Rome, the Nuncio arranged to be out of Paris, allowing various ecclesiastical guillotines to drop and heads to roll without his chubby, helping hand. His notorious absences from Paris gave rise to three disparate theories throughout the French Church:

1. The Nuncio is a jolly fool.
2. The Nuncio is a jolly coward.
3. The Nuncio is a sly fox.

Finally, in his seventy-second year, as a prize for his obedience and longevity, and not least for staying out of trouble with the French, the Nuncio was created a cardinal by the Stern Pope and "translated" (the ecclesiastical term) to ravishing Venice as Archbishop and Patriarch. There, ever the chatterbox, he reorganised his diocese, cruised the canals blessing festivals and gondolas, revelled in the robes and ceremonies of his rank, gave lavish benefactions to the poor, and became as beloved of the Venetians as he had been of the French.

But when he entered the Conclave of autumn 1958, almost in his seventy-eighth year, the Patriarch of Venice was still considered a nonentity by many of his brother cardinals, with meagre chance of achieving the papal crown. His friend Cardinal Benevento, whose gnome-like appearance and dubious health gave him no chance at all, nevertheless displayed an unexpected zeal for pope-making.

Cardinal di Benevento brought me into the Sistine Chapel and the Conclave of 1958 as his chaplain ("conclavist"), enabling me to observe the papal election with an eye to detail that served me well in papal elections yet to come.

Watch with me as Cardinal Benevento, in his Purple, plays his cunning game throughout the Conclave.

First he shuffles to the reactionary cardinals of the Roman Curia, suggesting by indirection that they have no hope of electing one of their own, because the cardinals of France and northern Europe are too weary of their harshness. The Patriarch of Venice, on the other hand, though famous for his bonhomie, is as *orthodox* as they.

Next he repairs to cardinals of Italian sees, Genoa, Naples, Palermo, all nearly as hidebound as the Roman Curia, arguing that although their party has no chance, the Patriarch of Venice is as *orthodox* as they: besides, he is old. He will create conservative new cardinals, and soon he will die: the conservatives can then elect one of the younger amongst themselves, and Holy Church will continue as before, anchored to the glorious past.

Next he hastens to the cardinals of Bologna and Turin, apostles of change, whispering that the progressive party has no chance, yet the Patriarch of Venice shares their agenda for reform and that into the Sacred College he will pump fresh, reformist blood. On to the cardinals of Germany, the Netherlands, and Belgium, reformists of various intensity, who listen with mounting interest. Finally, to the cardinals of France, who know the Patriarch so well, with such affection, and who in fact hold the balance of power in the Sacred College.

Ten ballotings ensue in the Sistine Chapel. No cardinal can swiftly grasp the essential two-thirds majority. The multitude in St Peter's Square moans with disappointment each time the puffs of black smoke belch from the stovepipe on the chapel's roof.

However, a consensus has formed among the hidebound and reformist electors of the College, accepting Cardinal Benevento's sly argument that the new Pope must be orthodox, innocuous, and old: a bridge, a transitional Pontiff, a *papa di passaggio* who will do nothing new or nothing much, create some younger cardinals, and then expire. Following the tenth ballot, all of the French cardinals move to the Patriarch of Venice. On the eleventh ballot, he is elected Pope.

Appearing on the central balcony of St Peter's in his white soutane, blessing the mob in the piazza, the new Supreme Pontiff seems to me short, ugly, and fat.

Tactfully, next morning, the Anglo-Saxon press calls him merely "a man of girth." At Sissinghurst, Sir Harold Nicolson, prince of snobs, confides to his diary that on television the new Pope "looks like a head-waiter at a Soho Italian restaurant." At Rome, I tend initially to the same distaste, but I am pleased at least by the Pope's smile.

"*È tanto soleggiato.*" It's so sunny, I tell Cardinal Benevento.

Nobody but the new Pope gives credit to Cardinal Benevento as popemaker. Sipping his Lourdes water, grasping his stomach again in mild pain, His Eminence replies, "*Carissimo Agostino!* Sunny? Oh, I should say so! This will be such a *sunny* pontificate."

Unlike his predecessor, the sunny Pope did not care to take his meals in august solitude, but invited all sorts of people to share his table. Soon,

Cardinal Benevento managed such an invitation for me—and he did so publicly, the better to show the Roman Curia that I, Monsignor Galsworthy, his protégé, would enjoy the Sovereign Pontiff's favour.

Again, the theatre was acted out in the Hall of the Consistory, beneath the elaborate ceiling, the glowing lunettes of Italian hermits, the gilded papal throne. As before with the deceased Pope, the new Pontiff's appearance was preceded by Swiss and Pontifical guards; plumage, helmets, boots, swords, halberds; papal gendarmes in gala Napoleonic uniforms; prelates in black, purple, scarlet; lackeys in livery of lace and damask. This Pope, however, was not carried in a sedan chair, but entered the chamber on his feet.

In his costume he seemed like a well-fed fugitive from the Renaissance, or better, the Counter Reformation. Over his white soutane and rochet, he wore a mozzetta of red velvet trimmed with ermine, surmounted by a gorgeous stole, but it was his head that fascinated everybody. He wore a red bonnet, much as had Innocent X Pamphili in the portrait for Velázquez: no pope had appeared thus for centuries.

The audience took place in chilly autumn, not long after his coronation. The whole of the Roman Curia, and all of the cardinals of Italy and France, were assembled for his allocution and blessing from the throne. When he was finished, Cardinal Benevento at his elbow guided him inward through the crowd, toward me.

As Pope and Cardinal headed in my direction, again I lived a sort of Napoleonic trance. The ranks of courtiers, curialists, Italian and French cardinals opened like waves of the Red Sea, each curialist and cardinal hoping that the Presence sought him. Today, however, I played no game of mischief, of hide-and-seek with the Sovereign Pontiff. The courtiers drew back, then regrouped around the Pope, Cardinal Benevento, and me. Kneeling at the Pontiff's feet, I asked myself, Will it always be so for me—literature colliding with life?

The Pope turned to Cardinal Benevento and said, *"Com'è bello ed elegante, il vostro giovane monsignore!"*—precisely the same compliment his predecessor had paid to my youth, elegance, and good looks. The remainder of the new Pope's remarks were rather different, but before he could utter them I replied in Latin, *"Ad pedes provultus Sanctitatis Vestrae, ego sum servus in Christo."* Prostrate at the feet of Your Holiness, I am your servant in Christ. Then, continuing the ancient tradition, I bent my body and kissed the Pontiff's right red slipper. In doing so I remembered Lytton Strachey's sneer at the doctrine of papal infallibility—delightful for "its very exorbitance. Not because he satisfies the reason, but astounds it, men abase themselves before the Vicar of Christ."

The Pope leaned down, grasped my hand, and tried to draw me up. He said, with some annoyance, *"Basta! basta!* No need of that, *figlio mio.* Get up, dear boy, get up."

Despite myself, my love of mischief seized me now. Still kneeling, in Italian I protested, "But even cardinals kissed the foot of your holy predecessor. They knelt when he called them on the telephone."

"*I* never did! Well, at least I never knelt when he called me on the telephone! *Va bene! Basta!* We are not Our predecessor."

"Cardinal Newman kissed Leo XIII's toe."

"And you are not Cardinal Newman!"

"So did his patron, the Duke of Norfolk!"

"Stand up!"

We were both of us nearly shouting. In a trice I stood in my purple cloak, towering over the Vicar of Christ; and the Vicar of Christ in his red bonnet bent back his neck to gaze at my face. Of a sudden the Pope laughed. He said, "You're charming, Monsignore. First you're servile, next you're not afraid to pick a fight, even with the Supreme Pontiff. But why all this chatter of English dukes and cardinals? Our brother here, His Eminence di Benevento, tells Us that you are not truly English, or so you claim."

"*Civis Romanus sum.*"

Now the Pope spoke in English: "It is a good day today."

I replied in English, "I agree, Your Holiness. It is a good day today."

In Italian, the Pope answered, "I'm afraid that's the extent of my English. And yet, now that I'm Pope, I must learn your language. Yesterday, I needed an interpreter when I talked by telephone with the President of the United States." The Pope turned to his cardinals: "Do you suppose, dear Eminences, that the President of the United States knelt while he talked to Us?" The cardinals exploded in noisy laughter. "Would you teach me English, Monsignore?"

"I should be d-delighted, M-Most Holy F-F-Father."

"Charming. Your stammer, too. How very aristocratic! Aren't you a baron or something? Poor me, I'm just a fat, little peasant, born in a farmhouse! Will you teach me to s-stammer in English? Would you kindly come with Cardinal di Benevento to dine with Us—on S-Sunday?"

✥

SEVENTEEN

✥

So, of a Sunday evening in November, I
appeared punctually in the Apostolic Palace
for dinner with the Pope and Cardinal di
Benevento. Just outside the papal apartments, a
chamberlain told me that Cardinal Benevento had
taken to his bed, seized with gastric pains, and that
in his absence I should go home. Suddenly the
Pope stood at the doorway. *"Al contrario,"* he said.
"The Monsignore must teach Us English. And We
are not pleased to dine alone."

Such was the first time I set foot inside the private papal rooms. The Roman Pontiff, in his fur
bonnet and white soutane, a red cloak tossed
round his shoulders against the draughts of those
lofty, marble chambers, led me alone deeper and
deeper towards his inner sancta, unhurried and
amused as I paused to gape and marvel at the paintings, tapestries, and frescoes that adorned his walls
and ceilings.

Everywhere I cast my eye I saw the leavings of
Fra Angelico, Perugino, Pinturicchio.

Scenes of the Creation! The Flood! The
Madonna of the Snows! St Francis of Assisi gives
his cloak to a beggar. St Laurence Martyr is roasted
on a grille. (St Laurence joked to his tormentors,
"You may turn me over now—I am cooked on
that side.") St Benedict takes leave of his parents. St
Thomas Aquinas is enthroned in Heaven. The
Dream of St Dominic's Mother! St Dominic res-

cues the drowning pilgrims. St Dominic confounds the Albigensians. As Judas kisses Him, Christ is arrested by Roman soldiers. With a lance, a Roman soldier, girt in armour of the Renaissance, pierces the torso of Christ. St Dominic in robes of blue and cream hugs the Cross, blood dripping from Christ's hands and feet, *squirting* from His side.

The Crucifixion of the Good Thief! (The Pope touched my elbow, whispering, "Ah, and that thief died a thief—he *stole* Paradise.") In a triptych, Christ crowns His Mother the Queen of Heaven. Christ Gives His Keys to Peter. Christ, crowned with thorns and blindfolded, is mocked by his captors: disembodied hands and rods, the head of a young man, spitting, float in the turquoise air, prefiguring by centuries the surrealism of Dali and Picasso.

Finally, on the wall of the library above the Pontiff's desk, hung Pinturicchio's *Transfiguration of Christ,* His apostles blinded by His light.

Otherwise, though spacious, the papal living quarters were almost Spartan. The Pope led me to his dining room, adorned with a single mediocre painting of the Madonna above a heavy mahogany sideboard with a tarnished silver samovar, urns and pots of wilting flowers, candelabra with candles tilting, a threadbare Turkish rug. "The rug is mine," the Pope said. "The rest is as he left it." I sat opposite the Pontiff at a small table, covered with white linen, on a chair like his, upholstered with red velvet turning to mould and a back of woven cane tattered and dangling loose. The Pope tinkled a tiny silver bell, summoning his supper.

He said, "You should have been with me, Monsignore, the first night I spent here as Sovereign Pontiff. The cardinals locked me in, I couldn't find the light switches, and when I struck a match the larder was empty. No German nun! On half an hour's notice, the cardinals had kicked her out! I passed the night alone, in darkness, dozing in a chair, fingering my rosary, with the ghosts of all my predecessors. It was spooky [*spettrale*]!"

Through the kitchen door, a pair of young and pretty Italian nuns, swathed in grey veils and starched white, entered with bottles of wine and a tureen of steaming soup. As they laid the table, the Pontiff rose and placed a record on his gramophone. He let it play for a few moments, then asked, "Who is the composer?"

"Ernest Amédée Chausson," I answered. "Pupil of César Franck."

"But greater than Franck in talent, *n'est-ce pas*? And the composition?"

"Symphony in B Flat Major. Chausson's only symphony, *Saintissime Père*," I replied in French. "He wrote it when he was thirty-five—not so very long before he died."

"I acquired a taste for Chausson when I was Nuncio to Paris. Ah, such clarity and sunshine! Such strength and tenderness together! Such waves of melody like a rolling sea—majestic, yet with hints of menace and sometimes so very sad! *Ah, comme c'est beau, sa musique!*" ("Oh, Most Holy Father," I wished to cry, "your *French* is not infallible!") The Pope continued, "You're quite right, Monseigneur. Like Mozart, he died too young—out riding his bicycle, hit by a horse."

The Pope said grace, mumbling the prayer in Latin and crossing himself as mechanically as did I. When Chausson's symphony was finished, he got up and played it over, repeating now grammatically, *"Comme c'est belle, sa musique!"* Otherwise, throughout the meal, the Pontiff uttered hardly a word: he was too busy devouring his food and drink.

We began with a broth floating with raw eggs. We followed with pasta seasoned with garlic; *rombo,* a flounder-like fish fried in lemon and olive oil; roasted partridge garnished with basil; *puntarelle,* a chicory salad dressed with a sauce of garlic and anchovy; goat cheese on peasant bread; and a cream pudding thick with prunes. Our wines were a delicate white Frascati, and a bold red Franciacorta from the Pontiff's homeland of Lombardy. I got up from the table as groggy as I had ever been when I emerged into sunshine from my catacomb in Florence, but the Pope despite bountiful lashings of Frascati and Franciacorta was brisk and lucid.

We returned to his library, done in crimson damask, where we sat in satin armchairs beneath Pinturicchio's *Transfiguration,* and the Pontiff said, "Time for my English lesson. I'm too busy to learn the grammar, so we'll have to do with phrases I can use at audiences and with chiefs of state. Also, pronunciation, so I can read a speech in English without sounding silly. No notes, Monsignore, all rote and memory—the way I learned my catechism as a child. Where shall we begin?"

In my torpor I pondered for a long moment. Finally I asked, "The Nicene Creed?"

"Meraviglioso."

" 'I believe in one God, the Father Almighty, Maker of Heaven and earth, and of all things visible and invisible . . .' "

"I belief in won-a God-a," the Pope repeated.

In Italian: "Try to drop the vowels at the ends of words, Most Holy Father." In English: "I believe in one God . . ."

"I belief in won-a God-did-did . . ."

"Much better. The Father Almighty, Maker of Heaven and earth . . ."

"Tee Fatter Almakker-r-r . . ."

That is as far as we got, that evening, with the pontifical English lesson. As though gorged already with my native tongue as he was with his Franciacorta and roasted partridge, the Holy Father relapsed to Italian, chattering (it seemed so vaguely to me) of every subject under the moon and stars. Mistily I wondered, Is he serious about English or upon the heights of his Office is he so lonely he simply wants to talk? More distantly and distantly I heard his voice, as my eyelids turned to lead and I sank deeper and deeper swathed by my purple shroud into the catacomb of my huge armchair, dreaming first of my mother upon a croquet lawn of Gloucestershire, and then of the dark lady of Florence giving birth to my male child. From another cosmos a sound intruded.

"Monsignore . . . Monsignore? . . . MONSIGNORE!"

I stirred. *"Santo . . . Padre?"*

"Are you tired, Monsignore?"

"No . . . Holiness, merely . . . enchanted."

"Then would you sit up straight in Our presence?"

I jerked myself upright, to the edge of my chair. Laughing, the Pope said, "Maybe you need fresh air."

He rose, leading me past shelves and shelves of musty books of theology and Canon Law to a high, recessed window, unbolting it and, with a force marvellously robust for a man of his age, hurling open the shutters.

We looked down upon St Peter's Square: a cold breeze assaulted us, refreshing me instantly, disturbing my black hair and billowing my cape as it billowed his. It was nearly nine in the evening: the basilica, obelisk, and colonnades were still illuminated in honour of his coronation, and solitary or huddling shapes of pedestrians, clerics, tourists, pilgrims crisscrossed the vast piazza; beyond them loomed the hill of the Janiculum, the snakelike River Tiber, and all of Rome in shimmering and mysterious scope. I knew that in their day Consalvi and Chateaubriand had gazed on Rome from the same perspective, but neither of them could have been as blithe as I.

Beneath us Bernini's fountains splashed; according to their custom, the faithful scanned the walls of the palace to the upper storeys, where they knew the Pontiff lived, to see if his lamps burned. Discovering him at his window, they began to clap and cheer, crying, "*Viva il papa!*" He waved to them and blessed them repeatedly, extending his ringed hand in all directions, raising both arms, the palms of his hands, upwards and upwards, as if to exalt their souls, then lowering them in a caressing motion as if to hug them and the whole world. "*Viva il papa! viva il papa! viva il papa!*" Finally he closed the shutters, the chant fading, and turned to me.

He said, "Your noble nostrils flared, releasing steam, when the cold wind struck your face. They flare now, Monsignore, in the stillness of my rooms." He raised his right hand and touched my cheekbones, not with his flesh but with his icy, enormous ring, a bevelled emerald encircled by pimples of gold upon a golden band. Our eyes met; his were very brown. The moment was almost sensual. He continued, "How odd in a man so young—your skin so tightly stretched across your cheekbones."

"Wounds of my struggle, *Beatissime Pater.*"

"Your struggle? For—against—what?"

I wondered, Should I tell him the truth? I was still not certain of the Divinity of Christ, nor indeed that when I said the Mass I truly changed the bread and wine into His body and His blood, but I shared with superstitious fishwives the notion that a pope could gaze directly into men's hearts. Even wicked popes such as Alexander VI, luxurious popes such as Leo X, raging popes such as Gregory XVI, possessed the celestial power to stare inside the souls of men. So: the truth. I answered, "To keep my chastity, *Santo Padre.*"

"*E come va questa lotta?*" And how goes that fight?

"I'm winning it."

"*Meraviglioso!*"

"With great pain."

"Celibacy was never intended to be easy. Have you always kept your vows?"

"My final vows. In Florence, once—just before my subdiaconate—I fornicated."

"And . . . since then . . . in all your pain, do you not find beauty?"

"A certain barren beauty . . . I suppose?"

Sighing, the Pope sat down in his throne-like chair, still staring at me as I stood. I stared back, not into his eyes of brown but at his golden pectoral cross, studded with blue diamonds. He said, "Celibacy in priests is sacred discipline, not dogma. Yet though not Revealed Truth, of all the gems in the priestly crown, none other shines with such lustre. Shunning women, a priest cleaves instead to the Bride of Christ—the Holy Roman Church. Relax—abolish—celibacy in the priesthood? Not so long as We are Pope. Never! Never! Never! [*Giammai! Giammai! Giammai!*] At the Conclave, Cardinal Benevento told his brothers in the Sacred College the simple truth when he assured them of my orthodoxy. However, however, however, [*Nondimanco, nondimanco, nondimanco*] . . ."

He rose again, attaching a pair of spectacles to the tip of his nose, walked far across the library to the last bookshelf, took out a black tome, blew away the dust, and with his fleshy hands flipped through pages as he said, "Did you know that for many years, as priest and professor in seminary, We taught the history of the Church?" Finally, his eyes fixed upon a page, he asked me, "In what encyclical did Gregory XVI condemn the *Paroles d'un Croyant* by the Père Lamennais?"

"*Singulari nos,*" I answered.

"In what year?"

"In 1834. June."

"Why?"

"Lamennais rejected royal legitimist absolutism and exalted democracy."

"With what language did Gregory XVI condemn Lamennais?"

In Latin I recited, " 'False, calumnious, rash, tending towards anarchy, contrary to the word of God, impious, scandalous, and erroneous.' "

"Perfect," the Pope said. "You didn't miss a word. Cardinal Benevento did not exaggerate when he sang hymns to me of your learning. Such language—'false, calumnious, rash, contrary to the word of God, impious, scandalous, erroneous'—shall henceforth be banished from the vocabulary of Rome. *Fuori! Fuori! Fuori!*" Out! Out! Out!

Angrily the Pope repaired to his mahogany desk and sat behind it. "From now on, Monsignore, the Apostolic See—and above all, the Roman Pontiff—will address the world, not with anger but with love. Out with anathemas! *MISERICORDIA!*" Mercy!

He seemed beside himself, in revolt against the very bone and marrow of his predecessors, of papal history from the reign of Peter to his own pontificate. He continued, "It is quite true, Monsignore, that our dear Cardinal Benevento promoted and achieved my election to the Chair of Peter, but he was, if I may say so, merely a little tool in the hands of the Holy Ghost. Years ago, long before I was created cardinal, I knew I would be Pope. My papacy was revealed to me, in . . . in . . . ah . . . ah . . ."

"In a dream?" I asked, thinking of my own and rather different sort of dreams. As the Pontiff hesitated still to reveal his secret, I repeated, "In a dream!"

"No . . . I was quite awake . . . in Istanbul," he replied distantly. "I was celebrating Mass. At the moment of the Consecration, as I transubstantiated the bread and wine into His body and His blood, Christ spoke to me. How clearly I heard His voice! He said, 'Thou shalt be Pope.' That is all He said! 'Thou shalt be Pope.' Ha-ha! God helps those who help themselves. From that hour, I schemed and schemed to win the papacy.

"Can you imagine the humiliations I endured to fulfill His edict? Ignored by popes, fobbed off by the Roman Curia for most of my career to the Siberias of papal diplomacy, because they thought me dull? A monsignore, the *Sostituto* [deputy], my superior in the Secretariat of State, wrote regularly in the margins of my dispatches, 'Stupid. Half-wit. Idiot.' Once, for a minor indiscretion—or was it some silly breach of protocol?—a certain Pontiff made me kneel in his presence for half an hour reciting the Sorrowful Mysteries of the Rosary. Always, I bowed my head, obeyed, played the dunce, the fool, grovelled, and kept my mouth shut. I was such a *convincing* bureaucrat! In France, as Nuncio, I fled Paris so very often whenever an anathema descended from the Pope, not because I was a coward but because the French cardinals hated the messengers as they hated the anathemas, and I needed the French in the Conclave that elected me. Speaking of cardinals . . ."

The Pontiff reached deeply into his robes, took out a golden ring of keys, pulled out a drawer at the bottom of his desk. "Where is it?" he protested. "Where *is* it? . . . Where did I *put* it?" He yanked at another drawer. "Ah!" He held up several sheets of foolscap, waved them at me as I stood.

"The new cardinals," he exulted. "I shall create them on Christmas Eve. Dozens of new cardinals. Every name a secret. Guess who's here, Monsignore."

"The Archbishop of Milan," I answered.

"He heads the list. Well, *shouldn't* he? Also, an African—the first to be elevated to the Sacred College! Guess who else."

"Surely not the *Sostituto*," conjectured I, laughing. "Not he who called Your Holiness 'Stupid. Half-wit. Idiot.' You'll exile him—to Istanbul!"

"Ha-ha! I thought of that!" He waved his ringed hand. "But . . . no, Monsignore. When I said 'mercy,' I meant mercy. I shall create the *Sostituto* a cardinal—and my Secretary of State."

"But why, Holiness?"

"Because he wields such power in the Roman Curia. I can not achieve my visions of the Church without the Roman Curia. Ah, such visions! The cardinals elected me to be an old, harmless *papa di passaggio,* but I have lived my priesthood preparing the fulfillment of my secret wishes. How I shall shock them."

That was all, that evening, that the Pontiff revealed to me of his plans for the Roman Church. Now he led me through room after immense room of the Apostolic Palace, rattling his golden ring of keys and flinging open the lids of strongboxes.

"Look at all this money! Whenever I mingle with the faithful, at audiences or in Saint Peter's, people press petitions at me and envelopes, envelopes, envelopes. I hand them to my secretary, Don Giulio, and so we pass on. When we return to my rooms and open the envelopes, they are stuffed with cheques, coins, and paper money in quantities large and small. When I took up residence in this palace, not a day passed but I found another strongbox, a bureau drawer, a precious vase, stuffed with money. Look, Monsignore! Lire, dollars, francs, sterling, Deutschemarks, all left—all forgotten?—by my predecessor. There must be millions here. What shall I do with it?"

"Give it to the poor?"

"Of course, of course. I surely shan't keep it for myself. I was born poor and I'll die poor. 'Naked came I out of my mother's womb, and naked shall I return thither.' These very robes and gems I wear belong not to me but to the Church. All I own or want is my underwear, my books, and my Turkish rug. The Vatican bank wants this money."

I had heard unpleasant rumours of the Vatican bank. I said, "If you give the money to them, much of it may never reach the poor. The bank will put Your Holiness on the dole, and at Christmas they will send you a princely cheque—for not asking questions. May I suggest that you keep the money?"

"Then how shall I distribute it to the poor?"

"Directly, Holy Father? I've a friend in high finance. Will you allow me to consult him secretly?"

"*Va bene.* I can use you, Monsignore—for more than English lessons. And besides Latin, French, Italian, what languages do you speak?"

"Spanish, German, Arabic, classical Greek. A bit of Hebrew, from my Biblical studies at the Pontifical Academy."

"And theology? Have you read the modern theologians—Gilson, Maritain, Rahner, de Lubac . . . ?"

"Of course, Holiness. Theology, not diplomacy, is my real craft. I enjoy Gilson and Maritain, and—despite his density—de Lubac, immensely. Most others are so abstract and murky they often drive me mad."

"My own faith is simple, so they *mystify* me. My predecessor of holy memory condemned the greater part of them. Yet their voices must be heard. No more anathemas! Henceforth, to start, you are my interpreter. You shall write my allocutions in English and in French. And—soon—I shall assign you to other tasks. Where is your office?"

"In the attic of the Secretariat."

"This palace has a thousand rooms—or is it two thousand? Here in my own apartments, there are so many rooms I've yet to enter all of them. I'm afraid to! This place is creepy [*spaventevole*]! We'll make an office for you in my own apartments. Others will be jealous—but pay no heed. My secretary, Don Giulio, loves me dearly, but he is too . . . protective? The Pope can do whatever he may please."

We reached the door of the antechamber. The Pontiff grasped the knob to let me out. Before he turned it, he gazed at me and asked, "Are you a Jew?"

"Did Cardinal B-B-Benevento . . ."

"His Eminence mentioned that, in Cairo, during your long and lonely nights together, you hinted . . ."

"Surely, Holiness, I am not a Jew on my father's side. He was of the minor nobility, Catholic and recusant, reaching back through the fog of history to before the tyranny of Henry VIII. My mother, an American, claimed before she married to be a Unitarian."

"Ah, the Unitarians. They believe in one God—at most."

"Ha-ha!" I laughed politely. (I had heard the jest a hundred times; as for the Good Thief who stole Paradise, that was a chestnut as ancient as the Church.) "My mother denied that she was Jewish, yet in Washington she had me circumcised—a common practice in America, except that she made it happen precisely on the eighth day of my life."

"According to the Old Covenant. . . ."

"Not long before she died, she wrote me a delirious letter claiming that when we lived in Paris we celebrated the feast of Purim. We never celebrated Purim in Paris or anywhere. I hated England, nor have I seen America since my infancy. Am I a Jew? In rabbinic law, a Jew is anyone with a Jewish mother. Should indeed I be a Jew, then I rejoice, Most Holy Father. I revere the Old Covenant as I do the New."

"The New. The Jews. Matthew Twenty-seven, twenty-five?"

" 'Then answered all the people, and said, His blood be on us, and on our children.' "

"The verse has been misinterpreted, Monsignore, throughout Christian history. As Pope, We shall reinterpret Matthew Twenty-seven, twenty-five. Also, the liturgy must be purged of allusions to 'perfidious Jews.' During the war, in Istanbul—secretly, with Herr von Papen, Hitler's ambassador—I saved the lives of several thousand stranded Jews."

"How, Holy Father?"

"We gave them false passports and certificates of Baptism."

"Why, Holiness, so did I—at my Benedictine abbey in the Vaucluse."

"But you were a child then!"

"I helped the monks!"

"Vaucluse? The Benedictine abbey? I fled there once, from Paris—for a week, during another of the anathemas from Rome."

"If I have a country or a home, it is my abbey in Vaucluse."

"So. Are you a Catholic?"

"I hope so, Holy Father."

"Is Jesus Christ the Son of God?"

"I hope so, Holy Father."

"When you celebrate the Mass, do the bread and wine become His body and His blood?"

"I hope so, Holy Father."

"You sound diffident and sceptical—like one of those cardinals of the Enlightenment, in eighteenth-century France."

Fantasies of fornicating cardinals, playing dice with God, frolicked in my head. I was tempted to reply in French, "You flatter me, Most Holy Father"—but I held my tongue. Better not to tell the Pope the truth too well, lest I lose the game of my ambitions and the goal of my ecclesiastical lust. So I changed the subject. I said, "If I revere Judaism, I also revere Islam. My children are Muslims."

"Your *children*?"

"Well, my Nubian manservant's children. I love them as my own. We celibates are so lonely. Would Your Holiness deign to meet my children?"

"I insist on meeting them. I love children! And I insist on seeing you, dear Monsignore, dear Agostino, dear son, often. If the Pope can't fortify your faith, then in God's name what good is he? I am, as Pope, a pastor most of all."

On marble I genuflected to kiss his gem, glancing upwards at his sunny smile. He opened the carved and swirling door. His antechamber was full of flunkeys, chamberlains, his secretary, Don Giulio, even several cardinals—a pair of chamberlains crouching so close to the door I suspected them of eavesdropping. Now while all knelt down in the monarch's presence, they each of them seemed perplexed, perhaps angry, that a monsignore so young and lowly as myself should dine alone and spend such lengthy time with the Sovereign Pontiff.

"This is Monsignore Galsworthy, Our linguist and interpreter," declared the Pope to his courtiers. "Henceforth when he comes to Us, he shall pass."

I descended the Scala Regia to Bernini's colonnade, thence to my rooms in the Borgo Angelico, exalted.

✛

EIGHTEEN

✛

I was happy also for the new arrangements in my rooms in the Borgo Angelico. Ghassem had written to his mother, and from Egypt she had sent to him his new wife.

Nubians are never afraid to travel: as a race of servants, Nubian men on a moment's notice will leave their rainless, dusty, wretched villages in Upper Egypt and the Sudan to venture to Cairo and Alexandria, to Baghdad and Kuwait and far beyond, in search of work to feed their families. Most of the women remain in Nubia, multiplying the race when their husbands visit them from employment in the north; Ghassem's wife was an exception.

She was Maha, barely a woman but a girl of sixteen—only several years older than Ghassem's children by his dead wife—and a generation younger than her husband, now nearly forty.

Maha had been fetched from Wadi Halfa, on the upper Nile, and put on an aeroplane to Rome, where she met her husband for the first time, at the airport. No sooner arrived, she hastened by bus with Ghassem to Rome's tiny mosque, where a sheikh wedded them in a brief ceremony to which I was not invited.

In my kitchen when I met her, Maha seemed not merely shy but frightened. She spoke hardly a word of Arabic, releasing only high-pitched little squeaks and whimpers in her tribal tongue of

Dongola-Kenuzi. She wore a long black gown and a veil tucked atop her head, but she did not shroud her face: rather, she lifted the hem of her veil across her mouth and nostrils, and modestly turned her countenance away from me when I greeted her in my futile Arabic.

Like Ghassem, Maha was not so Negroid as carved of Pharaonic bronze, with fine Hamitic features, large eyes, and hair that fell beneath her veil in short tresses, nearly straight. Her body was slender; her movements graceful; her cheeks delicately slashed. I supposed that, like most maidens of Nubia, she had been infibulated: her clitoris excised, her labia nearly all stitched up, to ensure her virginity till marriage.

On that first day, Maha seemed as frightened of tall and quiet Ghassem as she was of me. But Ghassem was—as I knew he would be—good and gentle to her. A month passed, and Maha was with child.

I thought, Within five years, my flat will be overrun with children. How shall I support them?

NINETEEN

⁜

Pursuing the Pope's wish to distribute his private treasure directly to the poor, I telephoned the United States and Northwood Hall. A butler answered; after much pushing of buttons, maids picking up extension telephones, muffled dialogue, I heard Diana's voice. "Forgive me, Augustine. I'm flat in bed."

"Are you ill, Diana?"

"I'm pregnant."

"Congratulations," I murmured, mourning that her child was not also mine. "How do you f-feel?"

"My legs ache."

"Ah, the Northwood curse?"

"Urban is abroad."

"In Europe?"

"He never says. He'll call me this evening."

"Would you ask him to ring me up?"

"I miss our fights, Augustine."

Much past midnight, the telephone in my library summoned me from my bed of wooden slats. A voice asked distantly, *"Monseigneur?"*

"Urban? Where are you?"

"Your chapel . . . have you installed your private chapel?"

"I'm installing it still—and Ghassem has his wife."

"Marvellous. . . ."

"I've a new post."

"Not out of . . . Rome, Augustine?"

"In the apartments of the Pope. I need your advice."

I explained. Urban's responses were misty and disconnected, as if he were exhausted from a long day's labour or ill and medicated to excess. "My legs . . ." he mumbled, apropos of nothing I had said. From the pudding of his words, I deduced advice.

He seemed to confirm my judgement that the Pope had best hold fast to whatever cash he found, and surely that his privy purse should be deposited outside the Vatican bank. Of that institution he said only, "Octopus . . . real estate . . . shady characters. . . ."

I wondered, How do you know—have you dealt with them?

He asked, as murkily as before, ". . . Charities of your own, Augustine?"

I answered, "The poor of Rome—and Egyptians who live in huts of cow dung."

"How sad. . . ."

He uttered other phrases I could not grasp, then hung up. Evenings later, the Managing Director of the Crédit Suisse called me from Geneva. He said in English, "This is all most confidential, Sir Augustine. Where are you?"

"In my flat," I answered.

"Splendid. Your telephone in the Vatican might be tapped."

"The Vatican is not the Kremlin," said I with some vexation.

"Sorry, I merely meant that in matters of finance, it might as well be."

"Then why are you calling?" I demanded.

"I've instructions from Mr Northwood to open two accounts—one for His Holiness the Pope, the other for yourself. He has deposited one million dollars in the Pope's account, one hundred thousand dollars in your own. Would you kindly inform the Pope of his account, and—confidentially— convey the identity and the compliments of the donor?"

"Of c-course."

"I understand that His Holiness has at his disposal considerable sums of cash?"

"C-Considerable."

"May I recommend that you bring the money to Geneva?"

"Couldn't I just make deposits in your Roman branch?"

"Then they would be subject to Italian banking regulations, and you'd hardly want *that*. I suggest, Sir Augustine, that you plan regular visits to Geneva to make deposits. You may be confident of our most favourable rates of interest. Have you a diplomatic passport?"

"Of course."

"Splendid. No fuss with customs."

"I shall have to consult His Holiness."

"I'll give you my confidential telephone number. . . ."

I could scarcely blame the Swiss banker for his diffidence towards the financial labyrinth of the Vatican.

Papal history abounded in the abuse of money and the open practice of simony. During the Renaissance, the red hats of cardinals were bought and sold; Cardinal Borgia bribed his brothers in the Sacred College and bought the papacy to become Alexander VI. Under the Medici Leo X ("God has given us the papacy—let us enjoy it"), indulgences rescinding for the faithful their punishment in Purgatory were likewise bought and sold. Indeed, such trafficking provoked the revolt of Martin Luther and the Protestant Reformation. Until the latter nineteenth century, when the House of Savoy conquered the States of the Church, the papal government in central Italy was too often incompetent and corrupt. Only time would show that the secular governments to follow would be far worse.

The Roman Church needs much money for its central government and vast works of mercy throughout the world. But its finances were impenetrably veiled by the Holy See's perennial refusal to admit that it consorted with the demon of Mammon. St Matthew vi:24: "No man can serve two masters: for either he will hate the one, and love the other; or else he will hold to the one, and despise the other. Ye cannot serve God and Mammon."

The Vatican reeked with fabulous, unsaleable treasures: Michelangelo's *Pietà*, the Sistine Chapel, the Pauline Chapel, the Borgia Apartments, Raphael's Loggia. It also owned many marketable assets, often managed without audit in majestic confusion, abuse, bungling, and circumlocution.

I knew all this—and of the common belief that the Holy See was blasphemously rich, controlling many billions of dollars and pounds sterling in real estate, securities, and corporations. At intervals I had heard, or I would hear in future, of the Administration of the Properties of the Holy See; the Special Administration of the Holy See; the Prefecture for the Economic Affairs of the Holy See; such bodies belonging to a maze of overlapping, interlocking, autonomous, competitive bureaucracies that managed the assets of the Vatican and never published balance sheets.

Even most cardinals inside and outside of the Roman Curia were kept ignorant of the budget and finances of the Vatican. Successive popes themselves knew few details, nor did they wish to, so long as they had sufficient funds to keep the Church running.

The notorious Vatican bank was in theory not a bank at all, but "The Institute for the Works of Religion." Yet surely it looked like a bank, once anybody found it behind Swiss Guards and pontifical police in the hidden, tiny Courtyard of the Triangle. The Institute for the Works of Religion was sealed inside a bastion built by Nicholas V more than half a millennium ago, but beyond its doors, tellers in business suits and nuns as clerks—behind booths of glass, beneath a crucifix on the wall, gliding in and out upon marble floors—almost seemed to whisper, "Oh, indeed, we are a bank."

Orders of monks and nuns, ecclesiastical academies, bishops, archbishops, cardinals, diplomats accredited to the Holy See, privileged laity of various nationalities, not least rich Italians, composed the clientèle of the Institute for the Works of Religion. The institute rendered gainful service to the monastic orders, circumventing the Baroque bureaucracy of the Italian banking system, transferring with blithe simplicity funds of Roman mother houses to needy missionaries in distant fields, directly by telex wire or by telephone.

But the Institute for the Works of Religion, over the years, became immune to scrutiny even by the cardinals as a body or by the Pope. Nominally a cardinal presided over the institute, but cardinals as a rule were novices in finance and tended to be manipulated by shadowy lesser clergy and canny laymen. Thus diplomats, corporations, rich Italians used the bank to evade the maddening Italian fiscal regulations and to transfer large sums of money out of Italy to secret accounts in Liechtenstein, Switzerland, Luxembourg, the Bahamas, and the Netherlands Antilles.

Cynics said, "Money is what the Roman Church is really all about." Yet to prosper on earth, the Church had to traffic in finance; it had to fund its immense network of schools and hospitals, run directly by the Holy See or separately by bishops, missionaries, monks, and nuns.

Certainly, I was troubled, sometimes even cynical like so many common Romans, annoyed like them by the Church's constant calls for money; because the Holy See possessed such palpable real estate in Rome, manifold shares in Italian banks and corporations, and lucrative stocks and bonds on Wall Street. Yet still I must stress the sanctity, asceticism, and mystery of the Roman Church as juxtaposed against its bonds to Mammon—since the soul of the Church was deeply about sin, redemption, and salvation as promised by Christ. As for simony and my own scruples, let me speak frankly.

My models in matters of preferment, property, and money were the scrupulous (overscrupulous) Benedictine, Pius VII, and his Prime Minister, my beloved Ercole Cardinal Consalvi. Pius VII and Consalvi were tormented when Napoleon invited the Pope to Paris to anoint him Emperor of the French. They badly wished to ask the Emperor to restore to the Papal States its northern provinces—the Legations of Bologna, Ferrara, and Ravenna—seized by Napoleon on the field of battle; but to seek the Legations as a condition for the anointment would be to demand property in exchange for a sacred act and thus commit the mortal sin of simony.

Both the Pope and Consalvi spent hours prostrate before the Blessed Sacrament, beseeching Christ for inspiration to resolve the dilemma. Finally they decided that Pius VII should go to Paris—Napoleon was, after all, master of Europe, and the Church craved his benevolence—but the Pope must not mention the Legations: he would accept them only if the Emperor should so offer, of his spontaneous free will, after the ceremony at Notre-Dame was done. The Emperor never offered the Legations—a cruel disappointment, but Pius VII and Consalvi avoided the sin of simony.

And so, I knew, must I.

I assumed that eventually Urban Northwood would demand a high price for his continuous benefactions to the Pope, the Holy See, and myself. His psyche thirsted for the recognition and honours of the Church, and from the very hands of the Supreme Pontiff. It maddened me that I still knew nothing of where his money came from. In the depths of night into the grey thrusts

of dawn, upon my bed of slats I was tortured by grotesque dreams of Urban's wealth. I saw him on his wobbly legs, masked and waving a machine gun, robbing fashionable banks. I saw him in impeccable pinstripes, seated in vaulted conference rooms, politely plundering renowned corporations. I saw him in the great art galleries of Europe, wielding a knife, slashing masterpieces from their golden frames. I saw him with dark and hooded men, trafficking in drugs and bombs.

In the early mornings, after I celebrated Mass in my unfinished private chapel, like Cardinal Consalvi I prostrated myself before the Sacrament, begging Christ for guidance. I found these intimate sessions with Christ refreshing, therapeutic, and useful. Indeed, He helped me to justify the decisions that soon enough I undertook.

Following my monologues with Christ, I wrote cheques to the charities of the Diocese of Rome; to the foreign missions of the Sacred Congregation for the Propagation of the Faith; and to a Melchite Jesuit who cared for Christian and Muslim children in Upper Egypt infested with flies buzzing about their pus-filled eyes as they inhabited huts of cow dung. I should guess that within a month of receiving Urban's benefaction, I gave away ten or even fifteen per cent of the money to the poor.

As for the rest, I reserved it for benefactions of the future, to buying ever more precious books and pictures, and to maintaining my Nubian family and the beauty of my rooms and ecclesiastical costume. I resolved to consecrate my life to the cult of monkish asceticism, and my riches somehow to the glory of God and the Roman Church. I would imitate Christ, continue to sleep on my wooden slats or even upon the floor; eat little, drink wine sparingly, do hard penance for my sins, and hold fast to perfect chastity.

Though I lived and worked in surroundings of elegance, pomp, and grandeur, I would zealously endeavour to practise the Corporal and Spiritual Works of Mercy—to feed the hungry, refresh the thirsty, clothe the naked, shelter the homeless, tend the sick, visit the imprisoned, bury the dead; convert sinners, instruct the ignorant, comfort the sorrowing, bear ills patiently, forgive wrongs, and pray for the living and the dead.

I did not mention my Swiss bank account to the Pope or to anybody.

Not that the Pontiff would have fussed. At the Apostolic Palace, when I told him of Urban Northwood's million dollars and the secret pontifical account in Geneva, he answered, "Isn't that nice? What's the man's name? Signor Norta-wooda? Please thank him and pass along Our Apostolic blessing." At once he turned to other things, so absorbed was he not with finance but with the business of religion.

As his renown and popularity grew round the globe, the Sunny Pope continued to receive thousands of letters stuffed with money. And so every six weeks I flew to Geneva and the Crédit Suisse, dressed in a smart double-breasted black suit and Homburg hat, my Gucci satchel bursting with cheques and cash in many currencies. I deposited the treasure in the Pope's account; strolled along the shores of sunny, misty Lake

Geneva; took my solitary luncheon in a fashionable restaurant; and returned to Rome.

During private audiences in his library, the Pope loved specially to hand out wads of dollars, Deutschemarks, pounds sterling to missionary bishops from destitute dioceses of Africa, Latin America, or elsewhere in the tropics of the poor. If the gift was to be very large, His Holiness instructed me to write a dollar cheque in the bishop's presence, then the Pope signed it. Knowing the balance in his account, if the sum seemed too generous, by a prearranged signal I would twist the ribbons of my purple cloak, and the Pontiff would reduce the benefaction.

If I quibbled still, he might raise his voice and answer, "Make it the amount I said, Monsignore! I'm the only Pope in this place!"

In my new dignity as his interpreter, I sat with him in the papal library as his sole aide whilst he conversed with those cardinals, prime ministers, kings, queens, and other heads of state who did not speak Italian or French. Always I took notes, and with fastidious attention to secrets. Much of the time, the Pontiff simply expatiated on his love of humanity. Since the President of India spoke perfect English, I assisted at that audience. The Pope told him, "I so revere your saint, Mahatma Gandhi. I met him once, in Istanbul, and asked, 'What do you want?' Gandhi answered, 'To wipe every tear from every eye.' As Pope, I wish the same—to wipe every tear from every eye." The President of India left the Vatican in tears.

I had to remain behind, and with reasons of my own to weep. If the Pope was kind to me, his entourage was beastly.

Cardinals and chamberlains of the curia were suspicious and resentful of my increasing access to the Pontiff. More than once, at day's end, they encountered the Pope wandering the halls of the Apostolic Palace, asking, "Where is Monsignore Galsworthy? He shall dine with Us tonight." Don Giulio, not yet a monsignore but as papal secretary soon to be one—young, talented, and tireless himself; dark, bespectacled, brooding; hound-like in devotion to his master—despised me not only for displacing him at the Pope's table, but because as a Latinist he was mediocre, spoke French indifferently, and other foreign languages not at all. So many were his slights, I yearned to tell him, "You are the prince of beasts."

I never did, but in ways more circular, I fought back. Directly after the Pontiff's meeting with a foreign cardinal or a chief of state, I would type the minutes in Italian, but I was leisurely in handing them over to Don Giulio. No matter that he complained and stormed, I pretended that the work was not yet done, even as I hinted that it might be as soon as he was civil. He turned more beastly.

Since entering the Pope's apartments, I had been given no office; Don Giulio assigned me to a desk in a corner of his antechamber, but the traffic of visitors and flunkeys in and out became so bothersome, truly I could barely work. After several weeks, Don Giulio gave me a private office, still

within the pontifical apartments but on the other side of the palace—in a storeroom.

The storeroom had but a tiny window—overlooking the rusty orange tiles of jutting roofs, potted evergreens, the Courtyard of the Triangle—and no electric light. I worked illuminated by an electric torch, until after much begging I persuaded the technicians of the palace to install some wiring, which (no doubt at Don Giulio's behest) they attached outside my door. I bought a long cord, plugged it in, and lit my office with a bulb dangling above my desk. The walls of the storeroom were heaped up with dusty wicker crates; one day I pried them open.

Inside were works of art, oil paintings on wood: miniature triptychs, mostly—probably dumped there in centuries past and long forgotten—mouldy and dark with time. When I held them up to my little window, even in the grey light of December, with my practised eye I recognised the nature of my discovery.

They were of the school of Perugino; probably not by the master himself, and surely not by Raphael, one of Perugino's first pupils; not priceless and not all fine, but generally of quality and several of them exquisite. I surmised at once that they were of the High Renaissance, painted probably in the late fifteenth century or early in the sixteenth, possibly during the reign of Alexander VI. As if to rebut the revellings of that carnal pope, the subjects were all celestial—madonnas, the apostles, the Nativity, the Crucifixion, the Ascension into Paradise, saints, archangels, some set against Umbrian landscapes and castles, and all done with Perugino's lucid simplicity.

I thought, No one else wants these treasures, so I must have them. I must take half a dozen or a dozen of the best, clean off the grime and mould, and mount them in my private chapel.

Evenings later, I dined alone again with the Pope. He consumed his soup, pasta, duck, Franciacorta, and goat cheese with familiar gusto, but I picked at the courses and ate little. The Pontiff asked, "What's happened to your appetite, Agostino?"

"I'm fasting—in this Holy Season of Advent."

"*Meraviglioso.* Are you suggesting I should?"

"That, Most Holy Father, is a matter between you and God."

Suddenly he seemed eager to change the subject. He asked, "And your new office? Is it true? Don Giulio put you in a broom closet?"

"A storeroom, Holiness."

"I shall find you something better."

"I rather like it there, actually. It reminds me of my cell at my abbey in Vaucluse. I found some forgotten paintings."

"Are they any good?"

"Some few—from the school of Perugino."

"Well, then, hang them on your wall."

"Of the storeroom or my private chapel?"

"You mean, take them home? You'd have to ask the Prefect of the Apostolic Palace."

"I believe that the jurisdiction belongs to the Prefect of the Apostolic Museums."

"Then ask him."

"The Prefect of the Apostolic Palace might dispute the jurisdiction."

"Hmmm."

"More wine, Most Holy Father?"

"Frascati . . . that's *enough*. Then take them—borrow them—on Our authority. Don't tell Don Giulio."

The Pontiff chattered on, concerned by more sacred things. Next afternoon, when Don Giulio was out of the Vatican on business, I packed the finest triptychs into my Gucci satchel and took them to my rooms in the Borgo Angelico, increasingly a rare museum.

Whenever I found time in the afternoons, I continued to visit the Venerable English College in the narrow, crooked Via di Monserrato. There, in the gallery of the English cardinals, beneath the portraits of Wolsey, Acton, Newman, as I paced and read my breviary, I was approached by an elderly gentleman in a black suit, Roman collar, and purple waistcoat. Ah, I thought, a British bishop.

"Sir Augustine . . . ?" he said shyly.

"Do I know Your Lordship?" I asked as shyly.

"I am Dr Thackery, Bishop of Gibraltar and Rome."

"Rome?"

"Ha-ha. *Anglican* bishop of Rome. High Church, though—Anglo-Catholic, one might almost say. My faithful here are rather few."

From the murk of the gallery stepped a grey woman in a tweed suit, handsome in her tall, broad-shouldered way, who grasped the frail bishop's hand and held to it. "My wife . . ." the bishop said.

"Lady Thackery," said I, not eager to disengage her hand by extending mine, but I tilted my head a bit.

"Sir Augustine," she replied. "Reginald and I have heard so much about you."

"I can't imagine how."

"Our cousins here at the college speak of you constantly," said Dr Thackery. "We understand that you work directly with the Pope."

"In a humble way, Your Lordship."

We paused, each to our own thought, as if we were each of us embarrassed by the schism of Canterbury from Rome and by the four centuries of reciprocal anathemas and hatred. I thought of Henry VIII's confiscation of the English abbeys and cathedrals; of Elizabeth I's oppression of clandestine Roman priests and faithful; of all the floggings, beheadings, martyrdoms; I thought of Sir William, my recusant father, and of his raving bitterness. Lady Thackery coughed and said, "We—we're told that the new Pope is very open."

"Open, sunny, and—believe me, my Lady—delightful," I answered.

"I've a rather important message for the Pope," said Dr Thackery.

"A *message*?" I exclaimed, then pondered for a moment. "I see His Holiness every day. I should be happy to deliver it."

"I'm afraid, Sir Augustine, that wouldn't do," said Dr Thackery. "The message is so secret that I must deliver it myself."

"Surely Your Lordship is aware that no pope has received a clergyman of your communion since the rupture of Canterbury and Rome?"

"Do you forget the meetings of Lord Halifax and Cardinal Mercier less than forty years ago?"

"The Viscount Halifax was not a clergyman, Cardinal Mercier was not the Pope—and besides, the talks failed."

Another lengthy pause. Lady Thackery squeezed her husband's hand with such distress that I nearly pitied her and knew that I must relent. I bowed slightly in their direction as I said, "Your Lordship. Your Ladyship. When I see the Pope this evening, I shall mention your request."

After dinner in the pontifical apartments, I told the Pope of my odd encounter in the Venerable English College. He was surprised, intrigued, then silent. We were seated in his library. He glanced upwards at Pinturicchio's *Transfiguration*, took out his rosary, and mumbled prayers upon the beads. At length he looked at me and asked, "You're English, Agostino—though you deny it fondly—so give me your advice."

"I advise Your Holiness not to see him."

"Why?"

"You know from long experience that the Holy See is obsessed with precedent. Should you receive the schismatic Bishop of Gibraltar and Rome, you would not only shatter precedent—you would be seen as reversing the decision of the Roman Curia to terminate the talks between Lord Halifax and Cardinal Mercier."

"But the talks were intended to reunite Canterbury and Rome."

"Precisely, Holy Father. The curia didn't want reunion then, and it doesn't now. May I suggest that Your Holiness has already alarmed the curia enough? Besides, there is *Apostolicae Curae*."

"But Leo XIII was almost senile when he issued that Bull—pushed into it by the curia."

"Nevertheless, Most Holy Father, the Bull bore the weight of the Magisterium. Senile? May I disagree? For compelling reasons, after careful study, Leo XIII found that the Anglican orders were invalid—because the ordinations of their priests and bishops were improperly conducted and thus the chain of the Apostolic succession was broken. If you see this schismatic bishop, the curia will contend that you have recognised Anglican orders. Risky, Holy Father—perhaps dangerous."

"Hmmm. Dear Agostino, let me pray and sleep."

"Most Holy Father."

I genuflected, kissed his ring, and, bowing, I backed out.

Late next morning, as I typed a document in my storeroom, the Supreme Pontiff appeared, alone, at my door.

"Your Holiness!"

"May I come in, Agostino?"

"Oh, do sit down!"

The Pope sat behind my desk on my single wooden chair, nearly breaking it beneath his weight, below my bare electric bulb, as I stood. He said, "I stayed in chapel half the night, before the monstrance and the Blessed Sacrament, begging Him for guidance. In bed, I had a dream, and He spoke to me again. He said only, 'You have not long to live.' I woke up in darkness, terrified and shaking. I have much to do in my pontificate, and swiftly. The divisions of Christianity, dear Agostino, are a scandal before Christ. Do you suppose that *He* cares—so very much—how Anglican priests and bishops are ordained? I have made my decision, and don't try to talk me out of it. I shall receive Doctor—Who?"

"Thackery."

"Thack-er-y."

I bowed my head and said, "Most Holy Father. When?"

"Tonight."

"So soon?"

"Before the cardinals get wind of my intention and try to stop me. Have dinner with Dr Thack-er-y, then bring him to me."

"With Lady Thackery?"

"Impossible. Now, given the problem of his rank, I'm as worried as any cardinal would be about the proper protocol. Well, for Heaven's sake, the man calls himself the Bishop of Rome. How shall I greet him?"

I reflected for a moment; my love of mischief seized me, not letting go. I answered (in Italian), "Tell him, Holy Father, 'Good evening, Dr Thackery. We have the honour of residing in Your Lordship's diocese.' "

"Ha-ha! Ha-ha! Ha-ha!" The Pontiff fairly rocked in my frail chair, grasping his potbelly with both hands, and roaring. "Ha-ha! Ho-ho! Oh, Agostino! No wonder that Our dear, sick Cardinal Benevento is so fond of you! That's perfect! 'We have the honour of residing in Your Lordship's diocese.' Now teach me that in English!"

I bent over my chaotic desk, wrote down the words, and rehearsed the Pontiff in my native tongue until he left for luncheon. Then I telephoned Dr Thackery at the tiny Anglican cathedral.

That evening, during dinner at my flat, as my Nubians served us roast beef and Yorkshire pudding, in a voice that was nearly vehement, Lady Thackery lamented that the Pope would not receive her at her husband's side. She asked, "Is the Church of Rome so utterly misogynous that its Pontiff can not countenance a bishop's wife?"

"The Pope is not misogynous, Your Ladyship," I answered, "merely uncomfortable that a bishop should have a wife."

From the Borgo Angelico, I walked with Dr Thackery through an icy mist to the Vatican. Upon my advice, he did not wear his robes of office, but only a black fedora and his black suit without his purple waistcoat; I as usual was clad for a papal audience in my black soutane and purple cloak. Thus as we passed through the antechambers, the papal flunkeys paid no heed, thinking that my companion was an ordinary priest. At the door of his library, in his ordinary white soutane, the Pontiff paced, anxiously.

"Your Holiness," I announced in Italian, "this is Dr Thackery, Bishop of Gibraltar and Rome."

"Good evening, Dr Thackery," replied the Pope in perfect English. "We have the honour of residing in Your Lordship's diocese."

Amused and touched, Dr Thackery then did something that I am sure he had not intended. He fell to his knees, grasped the Pope's right hand, and kissed his ring. Rising, he uttered a Latin title of the Pope's long in use before the reign of Henry VIII and the rupture of Canterbury and Rome: *"Sanctissimus Dominus."* Most Holy Lord.

Dr Thackery's secret message was a proposal from the Archbishop of Canterbury that he come to Rome to meet the Pope.

The Pope said, "Yes."

"When, Your Holiness?" asked Dr Thackery.

"We've waited four centuries, so why not at once? Well, within some days? It's nearly Christmas, We have cardinals to create, and—as you'll see—after Christmas We shall be quite busy. Next Sunday evening, shall We say, after dinner, at this hour?"

"I'll ring Lambeth Palace tonight," said Dr Thackery.

A visit from the Archbishop of Canterbury was not a matter that the Pontiff could conceal from the Roman Curia. Many of the cardinals protested violently, but the Pope would not budge. In deference to their opposition, he agreed that the visit should be done without pomp. The Archbishop was bundled into the Vatican, then bundled out, wearing a plain black cassock and a black cape. No photographs were taken of Rome and Canterbury together. They discussed no theology, and surely not the validity of Anglican orders or hopes for reunion of Canterbury and Rome. "How are you?" asked Rome. "I'm well," replied Canterbury. "We love England," said Rome. "We English love Italy," said Canterbury. That they should meet at all was itself miraculous. Finally, in my presence, Rome and Canterbury embraced.

On Christmas Eve, in a glorious ceremony at St Peter's, the Pope created dozens of new cardinals from every clime of the world. Of the older princes of the Church, only Cardinal di Benevento—still sick in bed—could not attend. That night, as I did so often, I visited His Eminence, and told him of the ceremony in colourful detail. The Cardinal gripped his stomach in such great pain he could not talk, so he merely gazed at me, nodding his affection.

Next morning, the Nativity of Christ—and my own thirty-first birthday—from the high altar of St Peter's, before his cardinals new and old, the Pope summoned a General Council of the Holy Roman Church.

+ +

TWENTY

+ +

L ate at night, in the Borgo Angelico, alone
and sleepless among my books, I ruminated
about the world, the Church, the Council
soon to come, and how it might affect my faith and
my peculiar kind of lust.

I knew that—for nearly two millennia, during
much of her history—the Church of Rome had
waged war against the world.

I knew that the Church's popes and theologians
had long held fast to a dark, suspicious, Augustinian view of humanity's wicked nature, of men
and women as the banished children of Eve, as the
progeny of Eden and Original Sin, redeemed by
Christ Crucified, but mourning and weeping still
in a vale of tears—the whole world itself.

I knew that, since the French Revolution—
regarded as the Antichrist by several popes and
many cardinals—the Church had flirted with
liberal reforms only to be disillusioned by the
consequences.

Par exemple:

Pius IX—or "Pio Nono," as his name translated
so funnily and prophetically in Italian—had been a
kindly, charming, handsome cardinal, his epilepsy
notwithstanding. Elected to the papacy in 1846—
prematurely, at the age of fifty-four—he reigned
for thirty-two years, the longest pontificate in history. As a cardinal, Pio Nono had been appalled
by the reactionary royalist legitimism of his

predecessor, Gregory XVI. Italy was seething with nationalists who demanded unity of the peninsula and constitutional rule in the Papal States. Papa No-no began his reign by saying, "Yes."

Too conscious of the despotism and corruption of clerical government, Pio Nono introduced railways and gas lighting, allowed liberty of the press, government by laymen, and a constitution establishing a parliament with plenary powers subject only to his personal veto. For a while, the Papal States prospered; French painters and English poets flocked to Rome. Pio Nono's popularity grew immense: wherever he ventured in his realm, he was cheered by the common people.

For a while! Soon, however, the demands of the anticlericals became unbearable, and like his friend and early patron Pius VII, Pio Nono suffered bitter disenchantment. He abandoned his liberalism: the Holy See, for the remainder of his pontificate, regressed to hatred of the world.

The Italian revolutionaries under Garibaldi, and the Piedmontese under the House of Savoy, were hacking away at the Papal States. By 1870, all of the states save Rome itself had succumbed. Rome remained the last of Pio Nono's temporal domains only because it was defended by a French garrison sent by Emperor Napoleon III. Embarking upon his catastrophic war with Prussia, Napoleon III withdrew the garrison; Rome fell to King Victor Emmanuel, all of Italy was at last united, and the temporal power of the papacy disintegrated.

Mourning as his territories vanished, Pio Nono unleashed anathemas against liberal notions (many of them French) within the Church, and fanatically reasserted "Ultramontanism"—above the mountains, over the Alps, across the great divide of Italy from the rest of the world—or Rome's and his own absolute, universal dictatorship in all things spiritual. It was not enough to condemn democracy, the separation of Church and State, or the privilege of Catholic scholars to pursue free inquiry. Not long before the fall of Rome, Pio Nono promulgated his chilling "Syllabus of Errors"— condemning specially the proposition that "the Roman Pontiff can and should reconcile himself to progress, liberalism, and modern civilisation."

Next, Pio Nono convoked Vatican Council I, which ended by proclaiming the doctrine of papal infallibility. The doctrine was nothing new; it had been assumed in the Church for centuries; it lacked only formal definition. The definition as it emerged from the assembled bishops of the Church was quite narrow: the Pope is infallible only when he explicitly speaks *ex cathedra*—from the throne, as supreme pastor of all Christians—upon matters of faith or morals. Pio Nono never invoked the doctrine in his own pronouncements. Neither did any other pontiff—save the Stern Pope nearly a century later, when he declared infallibly that the body of the Virgin Mary had been assumed into the Kingdom of Heaven.

The debate over papal infallibility passionately engaged some of the age's greatest minds, not only in France and Germany, but in England, where Father John Henry Newman (already in disfavour at Rome) and learned laymen such as John Lord Acton judged the looming definition as embarrassing and—not least because it would further estrange the Church from the world—tragically "inopportune." Like Newman, Lord Acton did not question the Pope's spiritual supremacy, but he believed that unbiased history and illuminating science, far from weakening the Church, would fortify and vindicate her eternal truths. As the debate raged, Acton wrote to Prime Minister Gladstone that "we have to meet an organised conspiracy to establish a power which would be the most formidable enemy of liberty and science throughout the world."

Yet when papal infallibility was proclaimed, even Lord Acton submitted, since "communion with Rome is dearer to me than life."

Throughout the Church, liberty of thought, the thrills of free inquiry, were trampled beneath the boots of piety; Ultramontanism triumphed insolently. Oddly, throughout Pio Nono's reign, the Church and her charities grew immensely across the earth. And Pio Nono's condemnation of revolution, nationalism, and the cult of "progress" seems less absurd as I pause to remember the enormities of Communism, Fascism, and Naziism that followed in the twentieth century. Nevertheless, when Pio Nono died in 1878, the prestige of the papacy among the intelligentsia of the world had hit bottom.

Pio Nono's successor, Cardinal Pecci, was a different sort.

The son of poor north Italian nobles, Pecci yearned from childhood for fame and power. If ambition is the ecclesiastical lust, it blazed in young Vincenzo Gioacchino Pecci with an ardour that reminds me of my own. His early letters home betrayed a brazen wish for advancement in the Church. Gregory XVI consecrated him an archbishop titular and sent him as Nuncio to Brussels when he was barely thirty-two.

However, Pecci fell from favour at the Roman Curia, and was soon banished to Perugia, where he served as bishop (later cardinal) for more than three decades. There, hugely bored, he turned to books, became a poet, and immersed himself in theology, philosophy, science, and finance. Pio Nono's Syllabus of Errors horrified him. At little Perugia, he established his own court, waiting, learning to be patient, cultivating those cardinals and miscellaneous divines as weary as was he of Pio Nono, and as eager that Cardinal Pecci should succeed him. In his dotage, Pio Nono recalled His Eminence to Rome and made him Camerlengo—prince regent of the Holy Roman Church during the interregnum once Pio Nono should go to God. When at last he did, the cardinals elected the Camerlengo as Leo XIII.

There followed one of the most illuminating pontificates in history.

Much abler than Pio Nono, Leo XIII embarked at once on an intellectual restoration, reviving that perennial wish to make the Roman Church respectable to thoughtful men and open to the world. He opened the archives of the Vatican to scholars of every faith, declaring that the Church need never fear the truth. He renewed the Scholasticism of Aristotle and Aquinas as the bone and marrow of the Church's mind. He insisted that faith and reason should go together and that faith could be compatible with science. He abandoned the doctrine of royalist legitimism and declared

Rome indifferent to forms of government so long as they respected the Church. He embraced the enslaved working class, consecrating its right to a living wage.

Brilliant and eccentric, Leo XIII was so fond of snuff that he had to be surrounded by his cardinals as he sniffed at High Mass, and (like Sigmund Freud) of medicinal cocaine that at times he seemed to speak from a seventh heaven. To me, his greatest inspiration was to create John Henry Newman a cardinal.

Newman, out of pure conviction, had defected from Anglicanism to Rome when Rome was everywhere reviled, and in doing so he made himself an outcast, banished (as he wrote) "to the wilderness"—since the Roman Church was "hated by the great and philosophical as a low rabble, or a stupid and obstinate association, or a foul and unprincipled conspiracy."

Leo XIII lent his ear to the Duke of Norfolk's plea that Newman's literary service to the Church should at last be recognised, brushed aside the shabby quibblings of the Roman Curia and Cardinal Manning of Westminster, and elevated him to the Sacred College in advanced old age. Newman arrived in Rome with such a cold he had to take to bed, and he barely managed to attend the ceremony at which Leo crowned him with his Red Hat. During his private audience with the Pope, Newman was so moved and grateful that he kept kissing the Pontiff's toe. Leo XIII raised him to his feet. Cardinal Newman wept. "Don't cry, Your Eminence," said Leo. "Don't cry. . . ."

Leo XIII's successor, Cardinal Sarto, was a different sort.

Humble, pious, and handsome, Patriarch of Venice, remarkable in his physical resemblance to Pio Nono, Giuseppe Sarto appeared to take Pio Nono as his model when he chose the name of Pio Decimo, Pius X.

Pio Decimo had a lovely smile, but a smile tinged with sadness. Leo XIII's doctrines of social and scholastic progress left him cold. What mattered was piety, prayer, devotion; veneration of the Virgin, adoration of Christ in the Eucharist; confession, penance, fasting, abstinence, self-denial—renunciation of the world.

Under Pio Decimo, scholars did not prosper. From the curia's and his own pen, there flowed numerous condemnations, especially of Modernism, "the synthesis of all heresies."

In the mind of Pio Decimo, Modernism was so contagious among priests and Catholic scholars it threatened to destroy the Church. Modernism was agnosticism by a sweeter name: God can not be known with certitude; Christ is not His son; sacraments are mere symbols; the consecrated bread and wine are but bread and wine, not the body and blood of Christ; Sacred Scripture is beautiful poetry and myth. Pius X obliged his priests, professors of theology and philosophy, to take an oath against the heresy—casting the same kind of curse on free inquiry as had Pio Nono. Yet Pio Decimo was so holy that only forty years after he went to Heaven, he was canonised as St Pius X.

The saint died heartbroken in 1914, bewildered that his direct appeals to God could not prevent the Christian powers from embarking on the carnage of the Great War. I regarded St Pius X with reverence and contempt: with contempt because—inside the Vatican—I felt, myself, so choked and smothered by his legacy.

I longed that the Roman Church I cherished and despised would at last throw off the meanness, intrigue, suspicion, pettifoggery, obscurantism, and hypocrisy that surrounded me. The Pope was fond of me. I was full of hope and gorgeous fantasies of the future. Muttering into my books, I prayed that somehow, at the Pontiff's side, at the centre of great events, I might help him in shedding radiance onto the murkiest nooks and transepts of the Church, and—in his Council—to open our morose religion to joy and reconciliation with the world.

Later during that cold winter, as I typed and shivered in my storeroom, again the Pope appeared, alone and suddenly.

"Your Holiness!"

"May I come in, Agostino?"

"Oh, do sit down!"

Today he seemed hurried, and remained standing, although as he strode round and round in little circles, my bare electric bulb cast an eerie pallor across the crannies of his face, and shadows which dimmed the brightness of his smile. He said, "The curia continue to resist, but I have commanded them to begin their preparations for the Council. First, the agenda. We shall have commissions on the sacraments, the liturgy, the clergy, faith and morals, et cetera, et cetera, et cetera. You shall assist at each commission as Our personal auditor [*il Nostro uditore personale*], my very ears and eyes. Keep your head down. Never speak unless spoken to. But you shall report directly to me of whatever happens—inside the commissions, in the corridors, if need be in the water closets."

Startled, I asked, "Holiness, am I to be a s-spy?"

"Espionage, dear Agostino, is not Christian. Just tell me everything that you see and hear."

The President of the Conciliar Commissions—and in charge of getting the Council started—was the Secretary of State, after the Pope highest luminary of the Church, that prelate who as the Pontiff's quondam superior had written in the margins of his dispatches, "Stupid. Half-wit. Idiot." Raised on Christmas Eve to the Sacred College, he was old, all thick white hair and steel spectacles, a man unbearably shrewd and pithy. Despite a lifetime in diplomacy, he could not contain his bluntness or suffer fools gladly. Since he never suffered me gladly, I shall (for reasons of reticence and embarrassment) call him "Cardinal Sostituto."

But even Cardinal Sostituto was a neophyte in the Fear of God cabal compared to Cardinal Baluardo, Pro-Prefect (the Pope was Prefect) of the Holy Office, formerly the Holy Roman Inquisition.

Cardinal Baluardo was chief policeman of the Church's doctrine. The Latin legend on his coat of arms was *Semper Idem*—Always the Same—summing up in four syllables the numerous volumes of his philosophy. The Church would for ever be the same; the Church could never change; because she was founded by Christ, protected from pollution by the Roman Curia, and therefore perfect. Bumptious heretics outside the Faith, and mischievous theologians burrowing from within, could defile the Bride of Christ only should the Holy Office relax its vigilance, not likely.

Old, bald, blind in one eye, with a little goitre on his throat, Cardinal Baluardo was as learned as any dissident theologian who despised him, and invariably more funny. Where Cardinal Sostituto was brusque, His Eminence Baluardo was suave; where His Eminence Sostituto was caustic, Cardinal Baluardo was ironical, patient, subtle.

Well . . . not always. In his breast, Cardinal Baluardo carried a corollary of *Semper Idem* which each day at noon he might have shouted from the central balcony of St Peter's had the Pope allowed him: ERROR HAS NO RIGHTS.

Completing the holy trinity of curialists charged with making the Council happen was Monsignore Samosata, a titular archbishop, more youthful and more dashing than cardinals Sostituto and Baluardo. With his classical features and abundant silver hair, Monsignore Samosata was not merely more comely but, if that was possible, more Roman and more cultured. Epigrams in Latin, exotic allusions to Horace, Cicero, Livy tumbled from his sculpted mouth; whenever he debated in Latin with Cardinal Baluardo, and he often did, Monsignore Samosata seemed to best him. At the Lateran University, he had taken highest honours for his doctoral dissertation, "The Use of the Ablative Absolute in Papal Rescript Clauses." His favourite maxim, which he was too refined to utter, was the ancient warhorse, *Roma locuta est: causa finita est.* Rome has spoken: the case is closed.

Monsignore Samosata was Secretary of the "Ante-Preperatory" Commission, of the Preperatory Commission which would follow that, and he would be Secretary of the Council whenever it convened. His chief task was to compile the *schemata,* or the topics and the working papers that the Council would consider when the bishops of the world assembled. This assignment delighted Monsignore Samosata. He knew too well that whosoever controlled the agenda would control the Council. All the *schemata* would be composed in Latin; when the bishops rose to debate them, they must do so only in the universal language of the Church, and few bishops beyond the walls of Rome spoke Latin well.

Their Eminences Sostituto and Baluardo, Monsignore Samosata, and the other cardinals and curialists heading the various commissions met regularly in the Cardinal Secretary's *sala da consiglio,* a Baroque chamber of red damask, the damask not only on the walls and chairs but covering the table beneath ivory pens and inkpots carved in the pontificate of Pio Nono. I huddled on a stool by the marble doorway, not daring to take notes but committing each word to memory.

The cardinals and monsignori suspected my prowess, and as the sessions lengthened, kept darting hostile glances in my direction. I wondered, Do they so dislike me because the chamberlains who eavesdropped at the Pontiff's door told them I am Jewish? No, I thought: cardinals Sostituto and Baluardo are men of charity, spending whatever money they can beg or borrow on orphanages and street children; besides, in the war, they both of them hid Jews. Or was it because they guessed not only that I informed the Pope of their opinions in comical detail but that I sympathised, and ardently, with his ends? Monsignore Samosata, holding forth in Latin, hurled a Horatian verse at me which I knew was barbed, but otherwise so swift I failed to grasp it. Cardinal Sostituto was habitually more blunt. He asked me, "Are we doing well enough, *Monsignore Quidnunc*?" Are we doing well enough, Monsignor Busybody? Monsignor Spy?

I: "You are doing splendidly, my lord."

Cardinal Sostituto: "Come now, Monsignore Quidnunc, tell us what you really think."

I: "You are doing miraculously, my lord."

Cardinal Sostituto: "I command you to be frank."

I: "Then may I ask a simple question?"

Cardinal Sostituto: "I insist upon it."

I: "What is the purpose of this Council?"

Monsignore Samosata: "That it never take place."

Cardinal Baluardo: "Precisely." (*Laughter round the table.*)

Cardinal Sostituto: "Be serious, the two of you."

Monsignore Samosata: "All councils in the past have required elaborate preparation. Preparing this Council will take ten years."

Cardinal Baluardo: "Oh, I should estimate twenty-five."

I: "But by then, in either case, His Holiness will be dead."

Cardinal Baluardo: "So we shall have no Council."

Monsignore Samosata: "The Roman Church, may I remind you, thinks in—"

I: "Centuries."

Monsignore Samosata: "Millennia."

I: "Yet if, by the grace of God, the Council assembles during this Pope's lifetime, what should it accomplish?"

Cardinal Baluardo: "It should reaffirm the eternal truths of the Catholic faith."

I: "As we know them now?"

Cardinal Baluardo: "As we have known them for nearly two thousand years."

I: "But His Holiness has announced that the Council will renew the Faith—make it relevant and responsive to the world in which we live."

Cardinal Baluardo: "Do I detect a hint of Modernism?"

I: "Does the Church condemn modern scholarship? Did not the late Pope endorse it? Did he not commend Biblical scholars to use every tool of science, of archaeology, anthropology, even of psychology, to analyse the content of the Sacred Scriptures? Did not that Pope—does not this Pope—believe as literally and deeply as does Your Eminence in the Church's eternal truths?"

Cardinal Baluardo (*sighing*): "I can not contradict you. The Pope also believes that the enemies of the Church are as good and virtuous as he is. We are all of us, at this table, here to protect the Holy Father from himself."

I: "The Council that you envisage, if it ever happens, will cruelly disappoint the Christians of the world. Of France, of Britain, of the United States, of—"

Cardinal Baluardo: "What else could you expect from countries where the people are allowed to vote?" (*Laughter.*)

The Pope, when I reported to him, seemed as discouraged as I had become by the dilatory tactics of the Roman Curia. Distantly he asked, "What shall I do, dear Agostino?"

"The decision of Your Holiness to include the curia in his great design is palpably not succeeding. Therefore, Holy Father, ignore the curia."

"I can not. They are the central government of the Church."

"I mean, of course, that you should work around them. Have you read Monsignore Samosata's draft *schemata*?"

We were by the window of his library. The Pontiff led me to a table heaped with documents. He said, "Every word. They are like a catechism from the nineteenth century. Pio Nono could have written them."

"Pio Nono's Latin was less elegant. I advise Your Holiness not to change a word."

"Why?"

"Take these documents and send them out to all the bishops of the world. Ask the bishops for their comments, point by point. The documents will provoke such howls of protest that even the Roman Curia may cringe before the storm. Then bring the bishops of the world to Rome—and open your Council."

"But when?"

"Oh, given the complexity and scope, you will need several years."

"I will be dead in several years. Next year!"

"Two years, Holiness?"

"I'll be dead! I'll be dead!"

✥

TWENTY-ONE

✥

As the bishops of the world were consulted, the Pope—hiding his anxiety behind the benevolence of his smile—relaxed the rhythm of his labours. On Sunday afternoons, I brought my Nubian children to the Apostolic Palace. Maha had given birth to a boy: I wrapped him in a blanket and carried him myself into the pontifical apartments. The Pope: "Aha! The child's name?"

"Mahmoud," said I.

The old man cuddled him, brown and darling, then mounted the child upon his shoulders and, as I steadied both of them, on hands and knees crawled across the marble floors. "I'm a horse, Mahmoud, your horse!" the Pontiff cried. "*Andiamo!* We're off! we gallop off!"

The Pope glanced up at me: " 'Unless ye become as little children . . .' "

"I admire the tableau, Holiness: *Pope as Horse.*"

"Ho-ho!"

The infant shrieked with delight, loving the Pontiff, but the older children were more reserved. Fatima (in her Egyptian gown) seemed so awed by the palace she could not speak, and Kamal (in his Italian suit) so bored that he could barely wait to get out of there.

Fatima now was twelve and ever pretty; Kamal was entering puberty—bronze, well made, graceful in his movements, all I had not been during puberty, but his nose was growing thick, and I knew that he would never be as handsome as his father Ghassem. Nor as placid: he had lost interest in the Koran, no longer prayed much, and against his father's wish increasingly he spoke Italian. Younger Fatima remained pious and obedient, but Kamal was attracted irresistibly to pagan Western culture, watching mindless television, in his room playing American and Italian "pop" music, escaping whenever possible to the cinema.

Yet whenever I carried little Mahmoud to visit the Pope, I dragged Kamal along, if only to get him out of my flat. More and more, Kamal quarrelled with his father, in Arabic or (violently) in Dongola-Kenuzi. Twice, his father slapped him.

In the United States, Diana gave birth to a son. She and Urban invited me to Northwood Hall to baptise the child.

I begged His Holiness for leave, and reluctantly he let me go. I took Kamal as my manservant, to reprieve him from his father's wrath and because I sensed that I might need his presence as the sentinel of my vows should Diana and I ever find ourselves alone.

I had not seen the country of my birth since my infancy in Washington. On the aeroplane, I wondered whether Northwood Hall might at all resemble Galsworthy Court, my lost ancestral seat in Gloucestershire. Diana had compared her husband's mansion to Cardinal Wolsey's Hampton Court. My father's house (you may remember) was likewise large and rambling; all falling bricks and masonry, girt with towering oaks and elms and neglected gardens once classically arranged; with crumbling statuary and a mock Greek temple intended to suggest romantic decadence, but amidst the strangling vegetation grown merely shabby.

We did not pause in any city, but hurried towards the north, the wood, and Northwood Hall.

In a black limousine, a chauffeur in dark costume drove us from the airport to a forest of evergreen; then the earth ascended, and for miles we motored on winding roads past rocky hills through woods of pine, wide grassy meadows, and leafy groves of elm and birch. The season was late spring, blending into summer; the sun shone dappled through emerald leaves and rolling mist and sparkled upon streams and ponds; in the distance, the hills were coloured violet.

"Northwood Park," the chauffeur said.

We passed fields where cattle grazed; then black, white, and mottled horses grazing, and red barns and stableboys pitching hay behind fences hewn of logs.

"Northwood Stables," the chauffeur said.

I thought of Rome and *Pope as Horse.*

On gravel paths, we drove beneath a canopy of trees: I glimpsed ahead the toothy turrets of a great house. I saw clipped hedges and formal gardens; statues of Greek and Roman gods; vast, shaven lawns extending to the encircling forest; flights of steps between balustrades and urns of stone, mounting to footmen in livery before oaken doors of Tudor architecture—Hampton Court of a lesser scale, according to Diana's promise.

"Northwood Hall," the chauffeur said.

As we descended from the limousine and I looked about, I strove to absorb in glances my first experience of that rose-red castle of towers, chimneys, and mullioned windows. Urban and Diana emerged through carved doors and came down the steps to greet me, followed by a governess in costume bearing an infant child, his pink face and white bonnet peeping from the folds of a knitted blanket. *Oh,* I thought instantly, *how I pity this child. How spoiled and corrupted shall be this child.*

Urban in a charcoal suit seemed wobblier of knee. Diana, her complexion more ebullient since giving birth and her eyes a warmer blue, had exchanged her coiffure from bouffant to golden braids entangled atop her head; she wore a loose smock redolent of cherry blossoms, like the scent of her, not enough to hide her faintly thickened hips and waist. We exchanged greetings and perfunctory embraces; Diana marvelled at tall Kamal in his Italian suit. Urban fingered my lapel, protesting my double-breasted clericals and asking, "Sir Augustine, where's your purple?"

That evening, we took dinner beneath the mahogany beams of the great hall, near a fire roaring against the rural chill. I wore my black soutane and violet cloak; Urban was in evening dress, Diana in mauve satin and double pearls. Amidst silver candelabra, domestics in white gloves and livery of blue served us simple courses and vintage wines as we debated the name of the infant son.

Diana said, "We thought of naming him after you, Augustine."

"Please don't," I begged. "Everyone would call him 'Gus.' Why not 'Urban' like his father?"

"I regret my name," said Urban.

You should, thought I. *Your real name is Urban as mine is Vladimir.*

"And yet," he added, "I like the notion of naming him for a pope."

"Perhaps a French pope?" I asked. "From the papacy at Avignon? Clement?"

"Wouldn't everyone call him 'Clem?' " Diana wondered.

"Benedict? Innocent? Gregory? John?"

" 'John' might be nice as a middle name," Diana said.

"I've run out of French popes," said I.

"English popes?" asked Urban.

"There was but one English pope," Diana scolded. "Cardinal Breakspear. Adrian IV. Twelfth century."

" 'Adrian Northwood'?" asked Urban and I together.

" 'Adrian *John* Northwood,' " Diana answered, ending the debate.

Next morning, after celebrating Mass in the Northwoods' vaulted chapel—beneath a painting of St Michael Archangel banishing Lucifer from Heaven—I put on my lace rochet and purple mantelletta, surmounted them with a violet stole, and baptised the son. As if repeating the couple's wedding in the Pauline Chapel, no guests showed up; no friends or relatives of Urban; no parents or siblings of Diana; only several of the servants, hovering. André, the wine steward, acted as the boy's godfather; Maude, Diana's secretary, held the child as his godmother.

I began the ceremony by reminding Urban and Diana that the waters of the sacrament were intended to wash away the Original Sin of humanity's parents in the Garden of Eden—for unless the child was born again of water and the Holy Ghost, he could not be saved. Baptism, to the contrary, would grant the child the grace to earn the Kingdom of Heaven, and—one day—to gaze upon the very face of God.

I proceeded to the Questioning: "Adrian John Northwood, *quid petis ab Ecclesia Dei?*" What dost thou ask of the Church of God? I responded for him: *"Fidem."* Faith. Then the Exsufflation: I breathed thrice in the form of the Cross upon the child's face, whispering, "Go out of him, thou unclean spirit, and give place to the Holy Ghost." I blessed him now, and imposed my hands upon his heart: "Drive from Thy servant, O Lord, all blindness of heart, break all the bonds of Satan by which he was bound, that signed with the seal of Thy wisdom he may be preserved from the infection of vices."

Soon I performed the Ephphetha: with my index finger I took a droplet of my own spittle and touched the ears and nostrils of the child, as Christ had done when He healed the blind and the deaf and the dumb. I said, "Ephphetha, that is, Be opened for an odour of sweetness. As for thee, Devil, begone: for the judgement of God shall draw nigh."

I asked, "Adrian John, *abrenuntias Satanae?*" Dost thou renounce Satan? Godfather André was bewildered. I answered for the child, *"Abrenuntio. I do renounce him*—and all his works, and all his pomps."

I anointed the child with the Oil of Catechumens on his breast and between his shoulders, then cast aside my violet stole, put on a white stole, and asked Adrian John for his Profession of Faith in God the Father, God the Son, God the Holy Ghost; in the Holy Catholic Church; in the communion of saints, the remission of sins, the resurrection of the body, and life everlasting. I told André to say, "I do believe." André said, "I do believe." Then I removed the lace bonnet from Adrian's head to baptise him, from a silver vessel, with blessed water.

Wisps of golden hair sprouted from his tiny skull, and as he gazed at me—as though with knowledge!—his eyes were of the fiercest blue, resembling his mother's. I glanced upwards at the crucifix and tabernacle on the altar. For an instant I entered another trance, ceasing to pity this chid. I knew with certainty that upon this child, crown prince of so great a fortune, the sacrament had already worked its miracle: he would never be corrupted. More, it seemed to me that somehow my bond with him might one day be much stronger than with either of his parents.

Godmother Maude held up the child. Pouring the water on his head thrice in the form of a cross, I said, "Adrian John: *Ego te baptizo in nomine Patris, et Filii, et Spiritus Sancti."* When I invested him with a white cloth symbolising his purity of soul cleansed from Original Sin, and handed to

André a burning beeswax candle illuminating the child's covenant with God, the baptism was achieved.

As though not sure, Diana hesitated, then took Adrian to her bosom. All knelt, Urban with hardship on his weak, trembling legs. Above Adrian and his parents—in a papal gesture—I thrust out my arms as widely as I could, making of my body a crucifix, and then with tracings of my fingers crooked, I bestowed by delegated power the Pope's Apostolic Benediction.

I lingered for a fortnight at Northwood Hall—more than I can say for Urban Northwood. After the baptism, over luncheon and champagne, he announced to Diana and myself that in the morning he would leave on business for New York and Europe. He added, "Must see my lawyer."

"Oh, darling," Diana objected mildly. "Where in Europe?"

"I'll call you often," said Urban.

"Not Budapest again? Those horrid Communists."

"Darling, did I mention Budapest?"

"Or is it Prague? What do you *do* there?"

Urban opened another bottle of *brut* champagne: *boop!*: like a toy cannon. That evening, in the great hall, as we three dined and chatted, Kamal sat on the floor near the blazing fireplace, knees apart and ankles crossed, clad at my command (and much against his wish) in a crimson robe and a golden turban. Indeed he was a sentinel—proof to Urban of my pure intentions in my holiday to follow, of my resolve never to pass a moment in Diana's company without the vigilance of my Nubian.

Diana kept glancing at the brooding youth as Urban jerked our conversation toward titles of pontifical nobility. He asked, "Who were the last Americans to be created papal dukes?"

"The Duke and Duchess Brady," I replied. "That, however, was thirty years ago."

"I assume they contributed to the Holy See?"

"Millions."

"Where did their money come from?"

"Electricity and gas."

"So why have my benefactions not been recognised?"

"But I brought the Holy Father's Special Apostolic Blessing."

"Meagre gratitude, *Monseigneur.*"

Urban grimaced, maybe less from the Pope's impertinence than from other pain. Of a sudden he bent his body and gripped his legs. Across the table I watched his eyes, dilated from his medications and orange in the reflected lustre of the fire. I said, "Perhaps, when I return to Rome, I might broach the subject of a papal knighthood."

"Perhaps you might," Urban rasped, still in pain. "And perhaps I might accept a knighthood as a fair beginning."

"There are so many orders of papal knighthood," Diana interjected. "Do you mean, Augustine, a Knight of Saint Gregory the Great?"

"Knights of Saint Gregory are commonplace," Urban protested. "They make aldermen, plumbers, and garage mechanics Knights of Saint Gregory. Augustine, at the Pope's elbow, can do better."

"Wouldn't a Knighthood of the Golden Spur be nice?" Diana speculated. "Clement XIV gave the Golden Spur to Mozart as a boy. When Mozart grew up, he never used the title. The costume is red with black breeches."

"On *my* legs?" exclaimed Urban. "I'd look silly."

"Then, as a compromise," I suggested, "we might consider the Order of Pio Nono. The costume is blue with ample white trousers. My father was a Knight of Pio Nono."

Urban pounced. "Sir William, if I read Burke's *Peerage* properly, was also a Knight of Malta. I might accept the Sovereign Order of Malta. Knight Commander of the Grand Cross. And my wife a Grande Dame."

Diana suppressed a giggle. "Will the cardinals call me 'Lady Diana'?"

"They'd better. Why must you smile? This is all for you and little Adrian. So, Sir Augustine?"

"I shall look into it," I promised.

At morning, I celebrated Mass alone in the Northwood chapel. Urban had already departed on his business; Diana, who habitually wrote all night, would not rise till noon. Kamal's lodgings were with the other servants in the attic, but I had been given my own apartments in the north wing, on the far side of the mansion from Diana's, facing the formal gardens. When I returned to my rooms from Mass and breakfast, on my dressing table I found a creamy envelope.

Monseigneur,

Thanks for the lovely baptism. Diana and I were moved. As little Adrian matures, I hope that he can benefit from your sanctity and craft.

U.

Enclosures.

Craft? In addressing a priest, one conventionally said "wisdom." As I read the enclosures—two cheques on the Crédit Suisse—I understood. The first was for the Pope: five hundred thousand dollars. The second was for me: fifty thousand dollars. Urban had cut our tithes in half. I knew he would increase them only when I used my "craft" to produce the honours that he craved.

Otherwise, my holiday at Northwood Hall was bucolic and, for its greater part, serene. Since Diana was so often writing, I explored the estate with Kamal in tow, or by myself. The main house, all red and purple brick in a style of exemplary Tudor, contained scores of rooms joined by open court-yards and enclosed galleries; the halls had high windows that admitted much sunshine and looked out to the symmetrical gardens and the birch forest. The walls were covered by red damask or by a linen of dazzling blue; the galleries were not yet busy with paintings, but such art as hung there from the schools of the Renaissance and onwards bespoke both riches and frugal taste.

The gallery near Urban's apartments was devoted to Turner on the banks of the Thames—pencil and coloured sketches, some few finished originals in water and in oil, reliving the river of the early nineteenth century: Richmond Bridge, Lambeth Palace with a pub in front, a churchyard with cows. The common rooms were as well appointed: ewers and goblets of silver, Isfahan carpets, Gobelin tapestries embroidered with nobles and peasants and fleurs-de-lis. Outside, I rejoiced for the woods and the stables.

With Urban gone, I shed my soutane and wore casual dress and a riding costume I had bought specially in Rome. Still lean and vigourous, in perfect health, I resumed the sports I had played in Egypt. I mounted after Mass each morning, cantering a black Morgan on trails deep inside the forest. The stable master kept pistols; on his crude gallery beyond the barns I regained my marksmanship, shooting at tin cans and beer bottles. In the woods, riding horse or hiking, I sometimes paused to swim naked in the ponds.

My hours with Diana did not begin till the late afternoons, when we took apéritifs on the enormous terrace or tea in her library when it rained. I made sure that Kamal was always with us, sitting at a distance apart. Diana's library, still growing, had thirty thousand books, many devoted to the Renaissance. Her appointments as well reflected that interest—heroic nudes in sculpture and on canvas, rare gilded crucifixes, landscapes with rivers and castles, and madonnas in triptychs by artists I could not identify. Diana laughed and said, "That's because *I* paid for them. I can't afford master-pieces. Not an artifact in this room was bought by my husband."

Still in my boots and riding twills, I wandered about the library, pausing at shelves and tables, picking up books at random, until I came to Diana's novels, bound specially in leather. I asked, "Are you writing another novel?"

"Nobody reads my novels."

"I do."

"And you don't understand them."

"I admire your reserve."

"Do you mean my subtlety?"

"Your books are jolly good, actually, for any reader as refined as you are. Only a boor would complain that your characters lack passion."

"Do you mean sexual passion? You won't complain about my next book. I've begun a biography of Lucrezia Borgia."

The rain stopped, so we walked outside, across the lawns garnished with flowers and Greek urns, into the wood, Kamal in his robe and turban long steps behind us. The sun came out, still high above the branches at the ides of June. In a grove of birch, we watched birds—a pair of blue jays, a bobolink, even a laughing gull. Diana put her hand on the crook of my arm. I allowed it to remain there, but I directed the motion of our bodies back towards the house. As we sat on the terrace, the costumed governess brought Adrian to his mother. Diana hugged him gently, kissed his nose and his Nordic skull. The child in his gown of linen slept, then woke, crying.

"I'll warm his bottle, ma'am," the governess said in a Yorkshire accent. "Will you feed him?"

"In the third salon," Diana answered, "while Sir Augustine plays for us." She turned to me: "Adrian must know music."

We strode through halls and courtyards, porticoes and galleries, until we came to a grand piano in a room with furniture of Louis Seize. As Diana sat and with the bottle fed her child, and the governess and my Nubian stood respectfully at a distance, I played a bit of Bach, a mazurka and a fantasy of Chopin, a sonata of the child Mozart; yet although Mozart's notes were simple, my hands were out of practice and the melody turned sour. I am sure the infant thought so: he shrieked to Heaven until the governess retrieved him from his mother and took him off to bed.

After dinner, we retired to the terrace for liqueurs. When a domestic appeared with his tray, Diana asked for lemonade. "I'm writing tonight," she said. I drank rather a lot of cognac as a moon not yet full rose hazily from mist, shedding a sinister pallor across the lawns, the gardens, and the classical statues. Diana took away my glass and led me far across the lawns towards the high maze hedge.

"What do you want?" I asked.

"To escape your guardian," she answered.

She grasped my hand, luring me into the maze. Soon in the centre of the labyrinth we heard the footfall of Kamal, but unlike Diana he could not solve the puzzle and got lost. Alone with Diana, I paused on the gravel path and asked, "Are you bored with your husband?"

"A writer craves solitude. He enables me to have it."

"Ah, your infamous 'splendour in s-seclusion.' "

We were both of us trembling; Diana was much too close. I asked, "So you've ch-changed your mind?" Diana, wearing wooden sandals over bare feet, kicked them off. "In R-Rome, you accused me of ch-childish emotions."

"Scenes change," she whispered. "I need more passion for the book about you I'm still writing in my head."

There ensued a kiss, then an instant of faint mutual friction that I am too diffident to reveal. I said, "I've a bond with you I insanely want to c-consummate. I've never felt so t-torn."

"Nor I," Diana said.

"Still . . . I've another bond . . . to grace . . . that I can not b-break."

I turned away from her, before she seized my hand again and led me from the maze to the open lawns.

The episode introduced a strain. Two days later, I flew with my Nubian to Europe.

Kamal and I did not return to Rome directly, but by way of Florence, where I took rooms in the Hotel Berchielli. Perhaps you wonder why Kamal never spoke: his father had brought him up in his ritual of the servant's silence, but in Florence the adolescent Nubian erupted.

"I won't wear a robe and turban any longer," he told me in broken Italian.

"*Ya Kamal,*" I replied in Arabic, "that is for your father to decide."

"I want my freedom from my father."

"You are still too young."

"Will you buy me some blue jeans?"

"You've that nice Italian suit you're wearing."

"It stinks."

During the next days, Kamal hounded me so often for Western clothes that finally I relented and bought him a single pair of blue jeans—before sending him to Rome ahead of me to face his father's indignation.

Alone, I regressed into my own resentments, mingled with nostalgia. I was jealous of Diana because she had a son. More and more of late, I imagined that in Florence before my priesthood I had sired a child.

The revelation did not happen during any sacrament but in my common dreams. I relived my passion with the stranger, then witnessed her in labour giving birth to a male child. My son, should he exist, would now be learning to read and write, but in my stubborn dreams he remained an infant. I saw only his head, weeks or maybe months after he was born, tufts of black hair resembling mine growing from his skull, his eyes dark also, alert and fixed on me.

My rooms, in fact, were the same in the Albergo Berchielli that I had inhabited when the woman and I conceived my son. The hour now was late afternoon, as it had been then. Removing my soutane, my garb again since I returned to Italy, I waited by the open window, smoking Sportazione cigarettes, tasting with remembered pleasure the bitter black tobacco and the pungent fumes, until I heard her cry, *"Il tramonto!"* Again I stood behind her, my arms enfolding her below her breasts, her raven head not reaching to my chin, as we watched the sun go down upon the River Arno and the Ponte Vecchio. Again the covered bridge—its Roman arches, its ancient plaster and tiled roofs and twisted balconies, the very hue and cry of people in its busy markets—turned apricot as the sun descended.

Darkness.

"What's your name?"

"Giovanna."

"Are you from Florence?"

"Lucca. I work in Florence, at a flower shop. You're not from Italy?"

"The south of France, I think."

"I've a grandmother who lives near Avignone. Will you come with me to the seashore?"

"I c-can't."

Next day, distraught with longing, amidst roses and hyacinth and scented fern, I searched in flower shops for the mother of my child. Rebuffed by the wrong faces, I returned to the Berchielli and the concierge, who directed me across the Arno to an ugly office of private detectives.

"Haven't you more information, Monsignore?" the first detective asked. "A woman with the most common name in Italy? Native of Lucca. Profession, flowers . . ."

"But you'll go through birth records?" I pressed.

"We always start with dates and birth records," said the second private detective. "You're not the first priest in Italy who thinks he has a child."

"You won't confine yourself to F-Florence?"

"Lucca, too," said the first detective. "It won't be inexpensive."

"Shall I call you from Rome in a month or so?"

"Your mystery will take time, Monsignore," cautioned both detectives. "Wait until you hear from us."

I paid the detectives far too much, then returned to the Berchielli for my luncheon and siesta. Next morning, after my Mass in a Benedictine abbey, I took the train to Rome.

+

TWENTY-TWO

+

For the next two years, amidst maddening delays, I worked with the Pontiff (less portly, his colour a bit jaundiced, it appeared to me) while he prepared his Council. Replies poured in from the bishops of the world—dozens, hundreds, thousands of them, as the months passed—assailing the *schemata* of the Roman Curia, protesting their rigour, their narrow legalisms, and their bombastic, bureaucratic, monarchical image of the Faith.

Vatican Council I had ended prematurely in 1870—in hasty confusion as the Italian revolutionaries and the House of Savoy knocked with their guns at the gates of Rome. That Council defined the infallibility of the Pope, but failed for want of time to define the powers of the bishops of the world and how they might share with the Roman Pontiff the universal government of the Church. Now—with Vatican Council II impending—numerous bishops sued for episcopal "collegiality" with the Pope.

Throughout the episcopate and throughout the world, from priests, scholars, theologians, and learned laity, there rose a clamour for reform; a zeal to atone for the great sins of the Church in decades and centuries past; to reach out the hands of Holy Church to the poor, the humble, the confused, the disenchanted of the faithful, even to schismatic and heretical Christians of so many sects, even to unbelievers; to make the Mass and the other sacraments vivid and accessible to all by celebrating them not in Latin but in the everyday vernacular of myriad tongues; to shed the "royal cloak" of the Roman Church and to revert to "Apostolic simplicity."

Yet even prelates who in greater or lesser degree were considered "liberal" began to doubt the wisdom of a Council. They seemed loath to open the Church's old wounds or to inflict new ones in a religious adventure that they feared might burst into unseemly revolution. Even the Archbishop of Milan—a favourite of the Pontiff's; the first cardinal he created; a veteran of the curia under the Stern Pope, pushed out of the Vatican for his "liberalism" during that pontificate in a Byzantine curial intrigue; kicked upstairs to the See of St Ambrose to remove him from Rome and the fount of power—was torn by misgivings. From Milan he warned in a pastoral letter that the Council might cause "expectations, dreams, utopias, velleities of every kind, and countless fantasies."

The Sunny Pope fled such doubts and shadows, taking me with him. Repeatedly he flaunted his own expectations, dreams, utopias, fantasies, by acting out his voluble—some said incontinent—love of humanity. In his library at the Apostolic Palace, he received all sorts of people—rabbis, tribal chieftains from the depths of Africa in exotic gowns, the family of the First Secretary of the Soviet Communist Party. At the Holy Office, pedantic monsignori chuckled at his childish naiveté. At the Pontifical Academy, noble ecclesiastics jested that "to get in to see the Pope, one has to be a Jew, a black man, or a Communist." And still his frustration mounted as Cardinal Sostituto, Cardinal Baluardo, Monsignore Samosata, and other luminaries of the Roman Curia continued to obstruct his Council.

One morning, nearly Christmas, more than three years after his election to the papacy, I found him in his private chapel, kneeling in his white soutane and skullcap before the crucifix and the Blessed Sacrament, weeping quietly, then with his arms thrust out beseeching Christ aloud not only for His guidance but indeed demanding His intervention. In my purple shroud I approached the Pontiff on his *prie-dieu*, knelt beside him, and prayed with him silently. I asked myself: Shall I play the voice of God? I turned my face to him and whispered into his right ear.

"Wait no longer, Holiness," I said. "Cast aside the devilish delays and documents. Convene the Council."

He rose from his supplications, allowing me to lead him from the chapel to the library and his desk. There, together, we drafted his decree. On Christmas Day, again from the high altar of St Peter's, in his golden chasuble and triple crown; before the cardinals and the Roman Curia and the milling tens of thousands and the microphones and the television cameras of the great and anxious world; invoking his supreme authority, veiling his anger and steely will in graceful Latin pieties, the Pope announced irrevocably that all the bishops of the Church would come to Rome and that—during the New Year—Vatican Council II would at last assemble.

Cardinal di Benevento, ill for several years with a recurrence of his stomach cancer, had benefited at intervals from remissions caused (he was convinced) by imbibing his Lourdes water. Finally the water ceased to work its miracle, and inexorably he regressed in frightful pain towards death.

I begged leave of the Pope, strode through chamber after chamber, corridor after corridor, of the Apostolic Palace until I reached the Cardinal's rooms beneath their frescoes of Botticelli and Fra Angelico, overlooking the Gardens of the Vatican and the Summer Villa of Pius IV. There I remained, living, eating, and sleeping—attending His Eminence throughout the death watch.

As in Cairo, often he cried out for me, allowing no other nurse near him. As in Cairo, I disliked entering his sickroom, emptying his bedpan, administering his medications, injecting his morphine, and bathing him, the slight hump that deformed his back, his buttocks pink like a baboon's, while skeletally he lay supine or prostrate on his bed. As ever, even in his death agony, he wore his huge amethystine ring of office; when he awoke, feebly he raised his right hand from the encumbrances of his blankets, the black beads of his rosary, the great sleeves of his pyjamas, for my obeisance and kiss. Each morning, I said Mass upon a table in his room. And again I knelt at the foot of his bed, reciting the responses as he mumbled for ever the fifteen Joyful, Sorrowful, and Glorious Mysteries of the Rosary.

Not always lucidly, Cardinal Benevento relived repeatedly the bleakness of his days in Djakarta and Ouagadougou. "Agostino . . . Agostino . . . have you . . . have you . . . idea of life . . . the horrible solitude of life . . . I mean . . . my life? To be so ugly . . . almost a dwarf . . . shunned by so many . . . for nearly eighty years . . . all my life? You . . . Agostino . . . in Cairo . . . one of the few . . . who did not recoil . . . from me. Remember?"

"Perfectly, my lord," I answered.

"What, Agostino? Am I going . . . deaf?"

From the end of the bed I crept on my knees towards him and shouted at his face: *"CAPISCO, EMINENZA."*

We were interrupted by the tinkling of a bell, the sweet stench of burning incense, and a commotion at the bedroom door. It was the Pope, attended by acolytes, monsignori, several cardinals in full scarlet. Above the Pontiff's head, priests in soutanes and surplices carried a silken canopy on silver poles, since he—wrapped in his red mozzetta and a precious humeral veil—bore the ciborium with the Blessed Sacrament clutched to his breast beneath the veil. Other acolytes carried a carved Baroque crucifix, blazing beeswax candles, the golden thurible with its fiery charcoal and fuming incense, and the holy oils of Extreme Unction. Amongst the crowd were Don Giulio, the papal secretary, now like me a monsignore and Domestic Prelate, Monsignore Samosata (an archbishop, you remember), and Their Eminences the

Secretary of State Cardinal Sostituto and the Pro-Prefect of the Holy Office, Cardinal Baluardo.

Calling Cardinal di Benevento by his Christian name, the Pontiff said, "According to your doctors, Carlo . . ." His voice cracked, so he tried again. "It is time, Carlo."

Cardinal Benevento, now nearly blind as well, raised his head and blinked his eyes, as if at first he did not recognise his master. Finally he said, *"Sì . . . Santo Padre."*

The Pope asked, "Do you wish to confess?"

"Sì . . . Santo Padre."

Acolytes removed the Pope's humeral veil, and he handed to a monsignore the ciborium with the Blessed Sacrament. The Pontiff knelt by the bed, placing his ear close to Cardinal Benevento's mouth, for his last confession. The rest of us bowed to the Pope and backed away; but Cardinal Benevento with all of his ebbing strength raised his ringed hand. He groaned, "Agostino. . . ."

The Pope rose to his feet, and with the others receded. Over my soutane I donned a lace surplice and a violet stole, knelt at the Cardinal's side, and placed my ear to his mouth. I can not tell you what he said because as a priest I am bound in eternity by the seal of the confessional, but I can reveal that his sins I absolved were few. The Pontiff approached again with his golden ciborium and tendering a host to his dying friend: *"Corpus Domini nostri Jesu Christi custodiat animam tuam in vitam aeternam."* May the body of our Lord Jesus Christ preserve thy soul for life everlasting.

Cardinal Benevento: "Amen."

The Pontiff placed the host on my patron's tongue. I had carefully prepared His Eminence's room for the last rites. By the head of his bed I had set a table covered with immaculate white linen and a mediaeval wooden crucifix between a pair of beeswax candles. Now an acolyte handed me a burning taper, and I lit the candles. Upon the table I had also arranged a silver bucket of holy water, a glass of drinking water (half full), a silver dish of water for purifying the Pope's fingers, a linen napkin, another silver dish with six balls of cotton for wiping away the sacred oils, and yet a third silver dish with a fragment of crustless bread. The Pope proceeded to the table to begin the rites, but again with his feeble strength Cardinal Benevento raised his hand to repulse the Sovereign Pontiff. He groaned, "Agostino. . . ."

Sighing, the Pope stepped back, gesturing to me to administer the sacrament. I sprinkled the room with holy water as I said in Latin, "Thou shalt sprinkle me with hyssop, O Lord, and I shall be clean. Thou shalt wash me, and I shall be whiter than snow. Our help is in the name of the Lord."

The Pope and his suite: "Who made Heaven and earth."

I progressed through the lengthy prayers, imploring Christ to banish the Evil One, making place for the Angels of Peace, that all malicious disputations, all harmful powers, all disturbances and dread might take leave of that house. I dipped my thumb into the sacred oil to anoint the Cardinal's ears, nostrils, lips, hands, the lids of his eyes, beseeching God to forgive whatever wrongs he had done with his senses. I tore down the sheets to anoint his feet.

The stench of him struck my face; already, despite my constant ablutions and though still alive, his body was in rot. The Pope and the cardinals recoiled. Hastily I anointed his tiny, naked feet: ". . . and may the Lord forgive you whatever wrong you did by your power to walk."

The Pope and his suite: "Amen."

I could not continue. The essentials of the sacrament were completed. I bundled Cardinal Benevento to his chin in his sheets and blankets to conceal his putrescence. With his ringed hand he pointed towards the Pope, beckoning him to approach, then spoke to the Pontiff in a voice of surprising vigour: "I have known you, Holy Father, for half a century. Have I ever asked for a favour?"

"Never a single favour, Carlo," replied the Pope.

"I've a favour to ask of you now."

"After the Holy Spirit, Carlo, I owe my papacy to you. The favour is granted. Anything, anything, anything. Granted, granted, granted."

"Make . . . make Agostino an archbishop."

A tremor of shock rumbled through Cardinal Benevento's apartments, so palpable I fancied that the frescoes of Botticelli and Fra Angelico might fall like petals from the vaulted ceilings. The faces of Don Giulio and Cardinal Sostituto twitched with dismay. The silver head of Monsignore Samosata—I should be his equal?—turned as violet as his vestments. The three whispered, "*È troppo giovane!*" He's too young! Only Cardinal Baluardo—rock of orthodoxy, scourge of heretics, heir of the Holy Roman Inquisition—seemed equable. The goitre on his throat bobbed a bit, but (it almost seemed) with satisfaction. A mysterious smile faintly illumined his sombre mouth. His composure in its turn astonished *me*.

Visibly embarrassed, the Pope protested, "But Agostino is a boy." He turned to me: "How old are you?"

"Thirty-four, Most Holy Father."

"Agostino is not ready for a diocese," declared the Pope.

Cardinal Benevento's voice trembled. "Keep him . . . in Rome . . . for your Council."

Uncertainly the Pope replied, "As a titular archbishop? Ummm. . . ."

Macabre though the setting was, I decided to fight. I asked, "Was not Monsignore Pecci a b-boy when he became arch-b-bishop?"

Outraged, Cardinal Sostituto demanded, "How dare you compare yourself to Leo XIII?"

Cardinal Baluardo interjected melodiously, "The comparison, dear Eminence, is not *that* offensive. Pecci was thirty-two when consecrated Archbishop Titular of Damietta."

Cardinal Sostituto: "*Titular of Tripolitania.*"

Monsignore Samosata: "*Cyrenaica.*"

The Pope: "*Caesariana.*"

I: "*Trebizond.*"

Such esoteric quibbling—so typical of the Roman Curia—might strike you as unseemly in the presence of a Prince of the Church about to expire, but His Eminence di Benevento's eyes began to dance, as though he relished the debate about archbishoprics titular even more than the rest of us. The Pope said, *"Ah, sì. Trebisondo."* The others said, *"Ah, sì. Trebisondo."*

"Your wish is granted, Carlo," the Pontiff concluded. "Granted, granted, granted. It shall be done! We shall, with Our own hands, anoint and consecrate Agostino in his archbishopric."

"Ah, sì. Trebisondo," murmured Cardinal di Benevento—his last words.

I bent over him to kiss his ring, but he clutched the amethyst, then slipped it onto the penultimate finger of my right hand. He grasped my hand as if to kiss it, then for lack of strength let go. The Sovereign Pontiff swung his golden thurible, releasing fragrant cloud: my benevolent patron was in Paradise.

Thus would I become Archbishop Titular of Trebizond—once the classical Greek colony of Trapezus; then a glorious mediaeval Christian empire; today a grubby Turkish seaport on the Black Sea as grubbily named "Trabzon."

I took elaborate pains preparing for my consecration. In designing my archiepiscopal coat of arms, I altered but little my escutcheon from the House of Galsworthy, retaining the rampant lions breathing fire, a coronet, a crucifix, spears, and prickly chains. As flourishes I added (for my love of France) a fleur-de-lis and heraldic gules. Above the shield soared a double cross surmounted by a flat mediaeval bishop's hat, coloured green, with loops of cord and, dangling low on either side, ten green tassels. Beneath, as ever, remained my family's legend: *Lux ex Tenebris:* Light from Darkness.

Cardinal di Benevento, scion of wealthy Neapolitans, had left a considerable estate. Much of it he bequeathed to the Pope, but my bequest included not only rather a lot of money but all of his books, precious rings, mitres, and pectoral crosses studded with dazzling gems. His mitres would not fit my head, so I ripped out their jewels and had them mounted onto mitres of my own, fashioned with my other episcopal regalia by Annibale, the most luxurious ecclesiastical tailor in Rome.

Once consecrated, in all documents and letters, I would become entitled to be addressed:

His Grace the Most Reverend Sir Augustine Galsworthy, Bart.
Archbishop Titular of Trebizond

Or, less technically:

His Grace the Most Reverend Sir Augustine Galsworthy, Bart.
Archbishop of Trebizond

Pedants added, "D.D., S.T.D., J.C.L.," acknowledging my doctorates of Divinity and Sacred Theology and my licentiate in Canon Law, but I should be vainglorious to pretend that in the Vatican the joy at my elevation was universal. In fact, so far as I could figure out, only the Pope and (mysteriously) Cardinal Baluardo of the Holy Office seemed pleased.

The Pontiff consecrated me in the Pauline Chapel amidst Michelangelo's masterpieces of St Paul blinded by light on the road to Damascus, and St Peter crucified upside down. He was assisted as co-consecrators by the cardinals Baluardo and Sostituto, but His Eminence the Secretary of State was still so indignant that he appeared for his function only by command of the Pope. With comparable ill grace, Monsignore Samosata served as Master of Ceremonies.

The Roman Curia as a body snubbed my consecration. The Rector of the Venerable English College joined the meagre procession of acolytes and prelates into the sanctuary; some few of his students sat in the pews; several Benedictine monks sang the Mass in Gregorian chant; but otherwise no clerics consented to be present.

Only two lay friends sat in the nave: Urban and Diana Northwood, blond

TWENTY-THREE

✤

Y ou are yearning to know the difference
between archbishops ordinary and archbishops titular. Sacramentally, there is no
difference. All Roman bishops share direct succession from the Apostles since the time of Christ. All
bishops enjoy the fullest measure of the priesthood, empowering them especially to ordain new
priests. Most bishops and archbishops rule dioceses or archdioceses, and liturgically they do so
from their monarchical thrones on the high altars
of their cathedrals.

Bishops and archbishops who directly serve the
Holy See as nuncios and delegates—or who labour
in lofty posts of the Roman Curia—do not rule
dioceses of their own, but in the theology of the
episcopate every bishop must possess a diocese.
Therefore even a bishop without a real diocese is
assigned the title of some ancient see that has ceased
to exist—since the onslaughts of Islam, generally in
the Near East, Asia Minor, or North Africa. Until
the pontificate of Leo XIII, such ecclesiastics were
called bishops or archbishops *in partibus infi-
delium:* "in the lands of the heathen." Leo XIII
abolished this barbarism, so that thereafter a bishop
without a true see was simply called "Titular."

baby Adrian in Diana's arms. I mused, How very strange: when I wed them here beneath St Peter and St Paul, nobody showed up, and so it nearly is in the moment of my glory.

Nevertheless, again the ceremony was the more glorious for its solitude. How happy I was. When I was ordained a priest I had asked myself, *Do I act according to my own wish? Do I choose not to be a priest?* Today I thought, *How much I want this.* How majestic I must have looked in my jewelled Roman chasuble above my alb and tunicle; my silken slippers over my silken buskins, both embroidered with gold thread; my liturgical gloves. When I knelt and the Pope anointed me, and he and his cardinals imposed their hands and prayed upon my head—"Lord, grant Thy priest the plenitude of Thy ministry and by this celestial anointment sanctify him"—I became an archbishop.

As I sat on a faldstool below the altar, amid incessant puffs of incense, the Pontiff invested me with the insignia of my archbishopric: my precious mitre, my gilded crosier, and my glinting ring—symbolising my royal priesthood, my duties as a shepherd of souls, and my marriage to the Church. The Pope knelt for my triple blessing, then kissed the amethyst upon my glove. Gripping my crosier, I proceeded in my mitre and full pontificals from the sanctuary to the nave, scattering benedictions, until I reached the Northwoods, the first of the laity to genuflect and kiss my ring.

I was the youngest archbishop in the Roman Church.

Urban Northwood had come to Rome not only for my consecration but to be inducted into the Order of Pio Nono. Valiantly though I tried, I could not win his acceptance in the Sovereign Order of Malta, let alone as Knight Commander of the Grand Cross or his wife a Grande Dame and "Lady Diana." My friend exuded still "the odour of doubt."

Let me explain.

Puzzled by Urban's august benefactions and not telling the Pope, Cardinal Sostituto had pressed the attorneys for the Archdiocese of New York to investigate the nature of Mr Northwood's wealth. Eventually they discovered that he was represented by a rich but murky law firm, located on Wall Street, Burner, Burner, Burner & Burner. An archdiocesan attorney invited a Mr Burner III to luncheon.

Mr Burner III was gracious and (so he wished to seem) informative. Mr Northwood was an ingenious financier. He had made his money before the war manufacturing pencils in Budapest, after the war investing his fortune in American and European corporations through brokerage firms on Wall Street and in the City of London. Not often, he visited Eastern Europe to buy farm machinery, which for moderate commissions he exported to needy nations of the Third World.

From civic pride, Mr Northwood contributed handsomely to the Republican and the Democratic parties, and to certain of their luminaries in office, not least the President of the United States. In Britain, he was generous to the Tories. Having uttered these benign assurances, Mr Burner III became a brick wall. The luncheon dissolved in brandy and dangling questions.

Elsewhere, the attorney heard vague but common rumours that Mr Northwood invested in corporations only to suck them dry, abandoning them to penury by dirty tricks once he seized his gold. Other gossip—murkier still and unconfirmed—had Mr Northwood trafficking in guns. Was he perhaps, for such a purpose, a merchant between Marxist tyrannies in Eastern Europe and new military dictatorships in Arab lands and in the deep of Africa?

When Cardinal Sostituto barked this offal at me, I shuddered. That very week, I had written an allocution for the Pope deploring the global arms traffic and its slaughter of innocent blood. But since the whisperings could not be proved, the Cardinal Secretary relied on moral casuistry and let them pass. It was the Roman Curia's rule that in its self-interest the Sunny Pope should be humoured constantly. This meant, and most of all, that His Holiness must have huge monies for the poor. If the ilk of Mr Northwood wrote the cheques, would it serve to spurn them?

Nevertheless, the Cardinal Secretary—suspicious, cautious, protective of the Pope's honour—managed the investiture of the Knights of Pius IX as a sort of ballet.

Let me explain.

There were, that day, a dozen Knights of Pio Nono to be invested—not all of them Catholic, including a worthy Dutch poet and a Norwegian hagiographer of mediaeval mystics, but the rest of them were were burghers, businessmen like Urban Northwood who had contributed great sums of money to the Holy See. The ceremony of induction obliged the Pope to vest the knight in a silver medallion and a brilliant sash round the shoulder to the waist, over a dark blue tunic above white trousers. Then the Pontiff embraced the knight, kissed him, and blessed him as he knelt.

These knights were not entitled to be addressed as "Sir," nor were their wives "my Lady." Since Knights of the Grand Cross of Pius IX were by right hereditary, Urban Northwood was excluded from the highest rank and had to be content as a Knight Commander. It was during the investiture that the ballet took place—just outside the Pauline Chapel in the Sala Regia, soaring marble with Corinthian pillars and Vasari's frescoes of tiaraed popes and galley ships and human skeletons as harbingers of death.

The papal photographer was present, but under strict instructions from Cardinal Sostituto to avoid taking pictures of Mr Northwood alone with the Pope. When it came Urban's turn to receive his sash, the photographer's camera jammed. After all the knights were invested, they posed collectively with the Pontiff for a group picture beneath the galley ships and human skeletons. On his fragile legs, Urban fairly danced as he manoeuvred to wedge himself between the others and the Pope; but such a picture could be cropped, making it appear that the Vicar of Christ had received him in private audience. As though on cue, Don Giulio intervened, all but lifting Urban from the floor as he dragged him from the Pontiff's side to the end of the line. The Holy Father chuckled at the dance. The photographer snapped his group picture, then vanished from the Sala Regia.

A celebration followed. Flunkeys in livery entered, offering silver trays with sweet cakes and crystal glasses of Frascati wine. In a corner, musicians of a string quartet played Amédée Chausson's last composition, as sweet as the cakes yet melancholy. Urban Northwood seemed jubilant, elegant in his wobbly way beneath his blue tunic and brilliant sash, unembarrassed by his contretemps with Don Giulio, and content for now to be merely a Knight Commander of Pio Nono. For a few moments, Urban and Diana were allowed to chat in French with the Holy Father.

I had shed my chasuble and mitre; now I was vested all in purple, from the *zucchetto* atop my dark locks of hair, to the sash about my limber waist with its lavish tassels, to my buckled shoes and the little train of my soutane. Round my neck I wore a gilded cord descending to my pectoral cross, winking with purple gems. Nuns and domestics of the papal household, with whom I was popular for my gifts and favours, bullied by Don Giulio and Monsignore Samosata into boycotting my consecration, queued up to genuflect and to kiss my ring.

Baby Adrian, now more than three in a little blue suit beneath his golden curls, scampered here, there, and everywhere, between the legs of servants and the scarlet togas of the cardinals, delighting the seated Pontiff and landing, finally, laughing upon his lap. Diana in her long-sleeved black lace, double string of pearls, impeccable blue mantilla to match the colour of her eyes, drifted presently in my direction, followed by Knight Urban. "Your Grace," they said together, bowing, the timbre of Diana's voice less ironical and mocking than in times past—perhaps because, inside her maze hedge, Divine grace had intervened to save my vows? Regarding me in my new regalia, she added, "Good heavens, Augustine, you're smashing."

"You're the s-smasher."

Knight Urban said, "We'll leave tomorrow. Will you dine with us tonight, Augustine?"

"Forgive me, both of you," I answered. "I've another engagement."

"Let's make it breakfast, then," said Urban, disappointed. "I've an envelope for Your Grace. Are you dining with the Pope?"

I glanced across the Sala Regia to a man in crimson and a goitre on his throat. I said, "With His Eminence of the Holy Office—Cardinal Baluardo."

The season was autumn now: the first leaves fell on the cobblestones of red and tawny Rome. That evening, a mile from the Vatican, next to his titular church of Santa Maria in Trastevere, I met Cardinal Baluardo at his orphanage for street children.

It was twilight; we strolled first in the courtyard, beneath the church's tiled campanile of so many tiers with its great clock and tolling bell. Children were everywhere: small and adolescent boys kicking balls and climbing trees, their voices clashing with the cries of girls on the other side of a high stone wall. His Eminence said, "Nuns and friars run this place, but venerable brother Sostituto and your humble servant are the Cardinal Protectors. See the truck?"

He pointed to a rusty Fiat van parked by the gate. "We go out in that at night."

I asked, "To pick up orphans?"

"We find many of the boys and girls in the Borghese Gardens or round the railroad station."

"Begging?"

"Or selling their bodies."

"But they're *children.*"

The Cardinal mourned, " 'The Devil, as a roaring lion, walketh about, seeking whom he may devour.' "

"Peter, One, five, verse two," said I.

"Verse *eight,* Your Grace. Caught you, finally."

"*Ah, sì, Eminenza.* I mixed it up with Saint Peter's allusion in the second verse to 'filthy lucre.' "

"I'm told you've quite a lot of *that.*"

"Malicious court gossip, my lord."

"I hope not," said Cardinal Baluardo. "We need money."

"How much?"

"How much will you give us?" asked the Cardinal.

I pondered. "Eight million lire?" That was then—in 1962—about ten thousand dollars.

"Your Grace can do better."

"Should we say twelve million lire?"

"*Grazie, Monsignore.*"

"*Prego, Eminenza.* I shall write the cheque before I go to bed."

We repaired to the refectory amongst the boys and friars for a simple supper. Cardinal Baluardo's demeanour towards the boys was fatherly but not too fond; as he blessed and touched their heads, they seemed to requite his love, but shyly, kissing his hand but never hugging him. "Are you learning your Latin?" he asked a boy in Latin. "*Ah, sì, Eminenza!*" We two took our soup and pasta at a distance from the boys, beneath a crucifix at a table with cruets of oil and vinegar and covered with linoleum.

Chewing his coarse bread, the Cardinal began, "When the Council opens in a fortnight . . ."

"*Finalmente,*" I replied with satisfaction.

"Years too *soon* for me! As an archbishop, Your Grace will sit in the Council. Most of the curia expect that the Holy Father will use you as his voice."

I protested, "I am not the Pope's ventriloquist. If I address the Council, I shall express my own vision."

"Ah? Then what is your vision?"

I hesitated, thinking, So he wants to know where I truly stand? How can

I tell him when I am—in my depths—still so uncertain? Presently I replied, "To open the windows of the Church."

"To the world? But that is the Pope's vision, and he hasn't the foggiest notion of what it means or what results will follow. If I hear that phrase again—'Open the windows of the Church'—I think I'll throw up. I've some advice for Your Grace."

For the next hour, the Pro-Prefect of the Holy Office used every thrust and nuance of his Roman cunning to warn, cajole, seduce, convince me. He explained that unlike the other powers of the Roman Curia, he had subdued his jealousy and welcomed my elevation to the episcopate because he sensed, at my core, a kindred spirit. He said, "I've taken pains to read your writings, such as they are. Your doctoral dissertation on Divine grace was not only deeply erudite for so young a theologian but completely, admirably, beautifully orthodox. Who trained you?"

"Originally? The Benedictines of Vaucluse."

"Superb masters, the Benedictines. Thank God it wasn't the Jesuits."

"But Eminence, the Jesuits are just as orthodox."

"They used to be. Some Jesuits remain so. The heretical Jesuits of Germany, France, Holland—if they have their way—will destroy the Church."

At length, Cardinal Baluardo conjured up his nightmares. There festered throughout the Universal Church such a diseased and foolish thirst for change that in the end all discipline would vanish; all devotion would dissolve; all belief would be corrupted; all truth would be reduced to the whims of solitary conscience, and the faithful so confused and void they would flee the Church in multitudes. Purity of dogma was the Cardinal's province. More and more—relentlessly!—theologians in northern Europe were insinuating that the ancient doctrines of Christ's Divinity, His Incarnation, His real presence in the Eucharist, did not truly mean what they seemed to say and were but symbols: lovely myth, poetry, and metaphor. The Cardinal paused before he asked, "Are you a Jew?"

"I'm not s-sure."

"During the war, I hid a hundred Jews in the cellars of this orphanage. In the Council, I will favour purging the prayer for 'faithless Jews' from the liturgy of Good Friday."

" '*Oremus et pro perfidis Judaeis. . . .*' "

"Any other changes in the Roman Church I'll fight with claws."

"But Eminence, there must be other changes."

"*Why?* What's wrong with the Church as she is? The Church is flourishing everywhere on earth, even underground, even where she bleeds from violent persecution. Never have we had so many schools and universities, so many hospitals, so many vocations to religion, so many priests and nuns. We've made mistakes, we've committed sins, but they were sins of discipline, not faith. If history proves anything, it proves that we can reform ourselves by discipline—not by bending to insurgents at the bottom—but by prayer, by acts of will, and by vigour at the top."

"But there have been so many Councils throughout the history of the Church. . . ."

"No Council is superior to the Pope—and his right arm, the Roman Curia."

"The Council of Trent. . . ."

"A glorious assemblage, convened to codify Paul III Farnese's wishes for the Counter Reformation to confound the Lutherans. Eventually, the reforms were defined, decreed by Paul III's successors, and carried out. *Why* must we meddle with them? Let me ask Your Grace some questions. You are, I've noticed, an exemplary Latinist. Do you wish to say your Mass in English?"

"I'm not English."

"Oh? In French, then?"

"I can't imagine celebrating Mass in any tongue but Latin."

"So there we are. When the liturgical reformists arrive here, they will demand in the Council that we tear the Tridentine Mass apart, translate the liturgy into a thousand languages, and deprive the faithful of the mystery of Latin, which awes the common people precisely because they do not understand it. Mystery is the bone and marrow of the Faith, but by the time the Council finishes—should the Dutch, the Belgians, the Germans have their way—we shall be reduced to a pottage of foggy piety, muddled rationalism, fatal compromise with Protestants. And another thing . . ."

With his good eye, His Eminence regarded me more gently even as he raged. "I've noticed also Your Grace's love of show and ceremony. During your consecration, I watched your fine eyes dance as you received your ring, your mitre, and your purple gloves. Out! out! out! with all that royal pomp once the zealots of 'Apostolic simplicity' have done with us! They'll descend on Rome with their 'Apostolic' scissors, and they'll snip! snip! snip! at our gorgeous robes and vestments until we're all but naked. *Snip! snip! snip!* By the time they've finished, we cardinals shall be reduced to scarlet shoelaces and you archbishops to purple underwear. Holy Church will be a SHAM! [*La santa chiesa sarà una CONTRAFFAZIONE!*] UNRECOGNISABLE!"

His Eminence was shouting. The boys and friars gazed up from their spaghetti. More placidly he continued, "On . . . on the other hand, we can fight back. Look at me—bald, my drooping lids, blind in my left eye, the greenish splotches on my face, this bag of breeding tissue on my throat. I look like a toad. I'm old. I'm tired. How long have I to live?"

He thrust a finger at me. "Look at you. Day in, day out, I've watched Your Grace. No doubt you have been told this ten thousand times, it makes a shambles of your humility, but I must say it, too. You are the handsomest Roman prelate I have ever seen. No . . . there was another—Merry del Val, the Cardinal Secretary—from my youth, so . . . very long ago. Like him, you're young, and a dazzling stone in Holy Church's diadem. Look at you! Did ever an archbishop wear his ring, his purple, his pectoral cross, as splendidly as Your Grace? I have no mind to hand you over, without a battle, to the other side—to the enemies of my Church! Your lust for lofty office is common knowledge in the Roman Curia. *Magnifico!* One day, the whole world may know you. If you're clever—like Merry del Val—you'll be a cardinal before you're forty. I'd like to help to make that happen! Now listen to me. You have too many enemies in the curia. They're setting traps for you."

"*Tranelli, Eminenza?*"

"Traps! Now listen to me. Throughout history, the Holy See, the Roman Curia—I hate to say it—have been egregiously ungrateful. You are too close to the Pope. You are too much identified with this Holy Father. He's very old, and soon he'll die. Within an hour of his death, his entire household will be evicted from the Vatican. That always happens when a pope dies—the cardinals clean out the place for the new Pontiff and his own cabal. As an archbishop, you can hardly be made a curate in Calabria, but the curia will see to it that you are banished into exile—to some Marian shrine in the Mezzogiorno or some third-rate missionary diocese in ... Uttar Pradesh? Now listen to me. Do you know the Cardinal Archbishop of Milan?"

"I've met him, Eminence, once or twice, when he came to see the Pope. I was never invited to attend their meetings. He's so ... shy? Does anyone know him well?"

"You should."

"Ah?"

"He may be the next Pope."

"Who forced him out of the Vatican?"

"*I* did, with the connivance of my friends. His ideas of the Faith are too far-fetched and far too ... *French!* In the next Conclave, I'll fight his election to the Chair of Peter tooth and claw, but I'm afraid that I may fail. The Pope loves him, favours him as his successor. For the foreign cardinals, that may be enough to win him the papacy."

"I fly to Geneva every six weeks on business for the Pope—"

"Ah, yes, with all your funny money."

"—so perhaps as I come home, I might detour to Milan. No ... wouldn't that seem rather obvious? Should I cultivate him in the Council? Hmmm. Oh, dear. Lord Cardinal, you leave me dazed. You've most of the Roman Curia in your camp. Why do you want me?"

"If you mean, dear Agostino, that I want you to defect to my party, I am scarcely inclined to make such a mischievous proposal. I admire your loyalty to the Holy Father. I do not propose that you abandon him for me, even for the sake of your ambition. I suggest only that you pause to think. Wait to see what happens in the Council. Watch carefully. Reflect on the kind of Church that the Council seeks to fashion. Then examine your priestly conscience. Ask yourself, 'Is this, in my heart and soul, what I wish the Bride of Christ to become?' "

Running through Cardinal Baluardo's words was not only his blunt flattery, but—like a barely visible thread—his soft hint that unless somehow I helped him in the Council, he would have me kicked out of the Vatican once the Pope was dead.

I answered, with my own soft defiance, "I want what the Pope wants. I wish the Church to love the world."

"The Church must *fight* the world," replied His Eminence of the Holy Office. "You may disagree with me today, but will you disagree with me for ever?"

T W E N T Y - F O U R

✤

In October, with a blast of pomp, the Sunny
Pope opened his Council.

From nearly every nation on earth,
thousands of cardinals, patriarchs, archbishops,
bishops, abbots, and their theological advisors,
converged jubilantly, hopefully, fearfully on
Rome, then flowed into the Basilica of St Peter's in
a torrent of ermine, crimson, purple, black, and
copes and mitres woven of gold.

The trains of the cardinals seemed half the
length of soccer fields; when the cardinals reached
their wooden stalls near the high altar, the swirls of
watered silk proved such an encumbrance there
remained no room for their train-bearers, who
were left to seek as best they could space for themselves in the thronged basilica. A deafening
orchestra, an enormous choir of priests and boys,
sang the papal hymn, *Tu Es Petrus*, Thou Art
Peter.

When at long last the Pope appeared at the end
of the procession, burdened (it seemed) beneath
half a ton of encrustations in his cope and mitre,
he was borne bobbing aloft on his *sedia gestatoria*
by noblemen in capes and knickers, they surrounded by scores of their peers in lace ruffles,

iron breastplates, and bloomers of blue and orange, some few of them hoisting on long poles a priceless canopy above the Pontiff, and a pair of them (as though there to battle cobwebs) wielding immense fans of ostrich feathers atop stupendous broomsticks.

Buoyantly taking part in the pageant as Archbishop of Trebizond, it delighted me for my love of theatre, but I brooded on a deeper level with turbulent emotions. The Pope had called the Council to renew the Church's "fervent youth," yet this ceremony went beyond the Baroque: it marched straight out of the Counter Reformation. And by the Roman Curia's design: they saw simplicity—the Pope appearing humbly among his bishops—as a threat to his Office. To them, pontifical triumphalism was more than ever imperative to prove to the bishops, and above all to the Protestant divines invited to observe the Council, that the papacy would never yield its glory or its primacy to mere bishops or lesser Christians.

I reflected, How sparkling is the Pontiff's triple crown as it reposes there on Bernini's altar. Whatever may happen in this Council, I shall remain true to my bountiful Holy Father.

Thereupon the bearded Frenchman—Cardinal Dean of the Sacred College who had tapped the Stern Pope's forehead with a silver hammer and pronounced him liturgically dead—sang an endless Mass as the Sunny Pope presided from his throne. Afterwards, all the cardinals and patriarchs queued in their trains before the throne to kiss the Pope's ring. A pair of archbishops, a pair of bishops, representing the whole episcopal college, kissed the Pope's right knee; Franciscan and Dominican monks in their brown, black, and white habits bent before the Pontiff to kiss his silken slipper.

The Pope read out his profession of faith, required before any Council of the Church. An ancient, illuminated Bible was held before him, opened to the first chapter of St John: "In the beginning was the Word, and the Word was with God, and the Word was God. . . . All things were made by Him; and without Him was not any thing made that was made. . . . And the light shineth in darkness; and the darkness comprehended it not."

Thus liturgically began the twenty-first General Council of the Holy Roman Church.

Now, from his throne, in rolling, mellifluous Latin, the Pope spoke to the cardinals, bishops, abbots—the Council Fathers—and to the world. I had helped the Pontiff to write his address, fussing for weeks with him as we debated drafts; but as an ecclesial scholar the Pope knew every leaf and tremor of the Church's history, so finally the words that emerged from his mouth were irrepressibly his own.

Above all, his words were cheerful. Since assuming the papacy (he said) he had been surrounded by counsellors who, however zealous for the good of souls, reeked of romance with the past and—regrettably!—of doom. Everywhere they looked, they saw ever more evil in the world, and the rampant ruin of souls. "Yet We as Vicar of Christ find Ourselves at variance with these soothsayers of disaster, who never tire of their prophecy that the end of the world is nigh. We have been inspired—on the contrary—by Our revelations, by Our talks with Christ Redeemer in Our nocturnal dreams, to believe that He leads us all, beyond our highest expectations, to better and more brilliant deeds, towards in fact the fulfillment of His superior, wiser, and still inscrutable designs."

Everything (he continued), even human differences of whatever scale, even philosophies of life that irreconcilably seemed to clash, could be composed with love in the bosom of Holy Church, outside of Holy Church, for the good of Holy Church. The Roman Church could never defect from her sacred patrimony of Truth received from her Founder, His Apostles, and the Fathers; yet with youthful zeal she would need to gaze not backwards but to the present and the future as she learned to greet the astonishing changes in the great world not with fear, suspicion, and anger, but with valour, grace, and a fervor to redeem them. "Nor have we any cause—how often did Our predecessor of holy memory, Leo XIII, remind us?—to cringe before the irrefutable discoveries of modern scholarship and science.

"The substance of our ancient Faith is one thing—we know it can never change—but the mode and manner whereby we hold it up for all the world to witness is (We beg you to believe Us) quite something more! Our sacred obligation is not simply to guard the precious treasure of the Faith as if we had only to worry of the past, but also to clothe it in new garments, to invest our ancient and eternal truths with a relevance which corresponds to the needs and conditions of our time.

"The huge challenge of this hour, to Ourselves as Pope, to you as Fathers of the Council, is to craft a language that proclaims the Truth of Christ joyously, not meanly by anathema. All Christians must proclaim His Truth by working in society such as it may be, sanctifying it, dare We say consecrating it? In the past, the Church has condemned error—We tremble to say this—with an excess of zeal. Henceforth, the Spouse of Christ shall prefer to treat the disease of error, not with the bitter medicine of harshness, but with the fragrant balm of mercy. To the human race, bearing the cross of so many cruel burdens, Holy Church must say, as Our predecessor Peter said to the poor man begging his help, 'Silver and gold I have none, but what I have, I give thee: In the name of Christ Jesus of Nazareth, arise, and walk!' "

I glanced across the transept to the stall of senior cardinals and His Eminence of the Holy Office. From beneath his vapours of scarlet, Cardinal Baluardo's buckled shoe stuck out, trembling violently.

I thought of my first conversation with the Pontiff in the papal library: "Such language—'false, calumnious, rash, contrary to the word of God, impious, scandalous, erroneous'—shall henceforth be banished from the vocabulary of Rome. *Fuori! Fuori! Fuori!* Out! Out! Out! From now on, Monsignore, the Apostolic See—and above all, the Roman Pontiff—will address the world, not with anger but with love. Out with anathemas! *MISERICORDIA!*"

Gazing at the shaking foot, I read Cardinal Baluardo's mind: *Oh, all this lovey-dovey, unity of mankind garbage. Does the Pope have a single clear goal, one hard idea of what he wants?* For the first time, I felt my own twitch of doubt—as still I focussed on Cardinal Baluardo's foot.

And I thought, *Now the battle begins.*

During the two months of that first session of the Council, the Pope kept to his apartments. On private television, His Holiness watched the debates whenever he could, but he was otherwise too busy with his ordinary governance of the Church, and blithely he allowed events in the assembly to take their disorderly course.

It was well that he remained in the warmth of the Apostolic Palace. Theological blood flowed on the cold basilica's marble floor, rippling through the stalls and staining the robes of the Council Fathers. One after the other, day after day, cardinals and bishops from beyond the Alps mounted the rostrum in St Peter's to denounce whatever *schemata* had been prepared or influenced by His Eminence of the Holy Office.

Quarrels erupted straightaway about the sacred liturgy. Latin—the progressive bishops said in Latin—obfuscated the beauty of the Mass, which should be celebrated in the vernacular of the common people. Cardinal Baluardo rose to reply that by holy tradition the Mass (not to mention the breviary of the clergy) must for ever be said in Latin; only the Sovereign Pontiff and the Roman Curia had authority to decide such matters; any further liturgical questions had best be referred to the Theological Commission. (Cardinal Baluardo was president of the Theological Commission.) "As for the veneration of sacred relics . . ."

Progressive Dutch Bishop: "How much longer must Holy Church endure the scandal of sacred relics such as Saint Joseph's sandals, the Virgin Mary's breast milk, and Jesus Christ's foreskin?"

(The latter relic reposed in Rome, in the Chiesa dello Santo Prepuzio, the Church of the Holy Prepuce.)

Cardinal Baluardo (*presiding*): *"Satis, satis."* Enough, enough. "Your Excellency has surpassed his ten minutes and is out of order."

Progressive Dutch Bishop: "Whole forests have been chopped down to provide the credulous faithful with relics of the True Cross. Such sacred relics—"

Cardinal Baluardo: *"Satis, satis."*

Progressive Dutch Bishop: "Such sacred relics, my dear Lord Cardinal, should be reverently interred and forgotten [*reverenter sepeliantur et deinceps nulla mentio fiat*]. Might I as reverently suggest the same for the Holy Roman Inquisition's glorious *Index of Forbidden Books*? Furthermore—"

Cardinal Baluardo: *"Satis, satis."*

Melchite Patriarch of Antioch: "Excuse me, but my Latin is terrible, so I'll speak in French."

Cardinal Baluardo: "According to the rules, Your Beatitude must speak in Latin."

Patriarch of Antioch: "According to the rules of my rite, I say the Mass in Arabic. Latin is not the language of the Eastern Church. *Donc, très éminent Monseigneur, je parle en français.*"

Cardinal Baluardo: *"Satis! satis!"*

Patriarch of Antioch (*continuing in French*): "Christ spoke in Aramaic. He celebrated the Last Supper, offering His body and His blood, in Aramaic. The Apostles and all of Christ's disciples spoke in Aramaic. Saint Paul tells us emphatically in First Corinthians, 'If thou speakest in a strange tongue, how can any man say Amen to thy thanksgiving? He knoweth not what thou art saying. Rather should I utter five words clearly for thy faith, than ten thousand in a strange tongue.' Latin—your liturgical but dead language—must yield before the command of the Apostle. People must pray and the Mass must be celebrated in languages that the faithful understand. Until the third century, the Roman Church spoke Greek."

Cardinal Baluardo: "And since the third century, the Roman Church spoke Latin!"

Monsignore Samosata: "May I remind Your Beatitude that Latin is the bond of unity in Holy Church, and never shall we relinquish it—never! never! never! [*nunquam! nunquam! nunquam!*]"

Cardinal Baluardo: *"Nunquam!"*

Cardinal Sostituto: *"Nunquam!"*

Cardinal Archbishop of Palermo: *"Nunquam!"*

Archbishop of Dublin: *"Nunquam!"*

And so the quarrels raged, day after day, week after week. Many of the Council Fathers were as much displeased with Cardinal Baluardo's tome-like draft, *De Fontibus Revelationis*, On the Sources of Revelation, as they were with his fixation on Latin. It had long been the teaching of the Roman Church that revelation is based both on Scripture and Tradition, but the progressive bishops of France and northern Europe violently attacked His Eminence of the Holy Office for ignoring the advances of modern Biblical scholarship endorsed by the Stern Pope. "We can not," they cried, "any longer separate Scripture from Tradition. There is only one source of Divine Revelation—the Word of God, and that we find exclusively in Scripture."

"That view is so very Protestant," Cardinal Baluardo rejoined, "that it verges on heresy."

"You are contradicting the Holy Father's command to avoid the odium of anathema," riposted a French bishop. "You are insulting our Protestant guests—our brothers in Christ."

"I shall joyfully embrace our Protestant brothers when they embrace the Truth," thundered His Eminence, "as it is revealed in holy Roman tradition—indefectible, irreversible, and unchangeable. The Roman Church has remained ever firm in the midst of storms, imperfect in her ministers without a doubt, but without spot or wrinkle in her possession of the Truth. Oh, how weary have I become of your *mea culpas*—this constant beating of breasts by the bunch of you for our Catholic sins, this ceaseless *mea culpa, mea culpa, mea maxima culpa,* as if the divisions of Christianity were all our fault! You assail me like some common, ultramontanist, cisalpine criminal in your transalpine court—the lot of you . . . you northern Europeans, you Germans, you Dutch, you Belgians, you French . . . the whole lot of you and your 'New Theology.' Ah, *satis, satis, satis,* enough enough enough of your New Theology."

"For the sweet love of Christ," implored the Cardinal Bishop of Lille, "will Your Eminence desist?"

"For the sweet love of Christ, I shall never desist in my condemnation of error. Christ gave us His Church to purify the world of error and evil."

Cardinal Archbishop of Cologne: "Since Your Eminence so harps on tradition, I have the duty to point out that neither the Fathers of the Church, nor the Scholastic theologians, nor indeed Saint Thomas Aquinas, ever distinguished between the truth of Scripture and the truth of Tradition. We are all of us trained theologians, and none of us need lectures from Your Eminence about error, evil, the goodness of God, or the wickedness of man. You accuse us of heterodoxy. I accuse Your Eminence of false historicism and fake Scholasticism."

Other Transalpine Bishops: "*De Fontibus Revelationis* should be thrown out with the rubbish! Rewrite it! Start over!"

As Archbishop of Trebizond, I had not yet exercised my right to address the Council. For weeks I tortured over my Latin speech—composing a draft, discarding it, starting again, refining my foolscap through the tolling bells of midnight until morosely I said my Mass at dawn—torn between my loyalty to the Pope and my rising resentment of the transalpine bishops for their shabby treatment of Cardinal Baluardo.

I wished to say that—although they clung to the essence of our ancient Faith—in forms at least many of the Council Fathers aspired to create nothing less than a new Church.

Since the Council of Trent three hundred years before, under a succession of pontiffs mostly wise and sometimes saintly, the Roman Church had faced the world defensively, calling herself Church Militant; erecting round herself a fortress of thick stone walls to defend her tabernacles of Truth within and to repulse without the onslaughts of an heretical, rationalist, and hostile world. More, until our time the Tridentine system had served us well.

Ah, I could hear the murmur of some Council Fathers, specially those from beyond the Alps, insisting that the Church of Trent was moribund, and that unless we mercifully—or not so mercifully—let her die, that unless indeed we killed her with this Council's sword, the Church of Christ in our modern age could never prosper.

To replace the Tridentine Church and her armoury of glory, militancy, triumph, fear, and condemnation, the paladins of the New Theology proposed to tear down our Counter Reformation fortress, to open the gates and battlements of the Church to all Christian men and women and even to unbelievers; to shed the Church's royal cloak; to revert to the simplicity of early Christianity; and to replace the lexicon of condemnation and triumphalism with a new vocabulary which echoed—they claimed with passion—the voice of Christ.

Thus the New Church resounded with language hitherto unfamiliar: we are all—Pope, bishops, priests, and faithful—equally "the People of God"; we are gathered to hear "the Good News of the Gospel"; we are "the Pilgrim Church"; we are "the Church of the Poor." According to some theologians in our assembly, the Mass is no longer simply what we thought—the sacrifice of Christ's body and His blood—but a social "meal" in which the "People of God" share with the priest his formerly unique act of Consecration.

Might I earnestly ask the Fathers, what does this mean? I had heard a few such theologians state openly that the miracle of Transubstantiation is but a poetic superstition—that the bread and wine do not truly become His body and His blood, but only symbolically, metaphorically, and mythologically.

Might I again earnestly ask many of the Fathers, what kind of Church are you seeking to create? Our Lord Cardinal Baluardo is incessantly attacked in the Council for exalting the Magisterium of the Holy See, even as his transalpine critics continue to exalt its Nemesis, the Christian's private "primacy of conscience." The Cardinal's *schema* on the Nature of the Church, we are told repeatedly, is rigid, trite, tendentious, juridical, Scholastical, ecclesiastical, hierarchical, traditional, militant, triumphalist, uncharitable, unchristian, incomprehensible, hostile to science, unsympathetic to exegisis, theologically immature, not even faintly pastoral, and—the worst enormity of all—*offensive to Protestants*!

"May I suggest," said my final foolscap draft, "that some few of you have sinned—by your immoderate and indeed barbarous attacks upon a Prince of the Church who has nobly consecrated his life to preserving the purity of Christian Doctrine? Venerable brothers in the episcopate, beloved Fathers of the Council, what are you about? Do you demand some other sort of priest in the Holy Office? Do you demand some other means and method of administering sacred justice? Do you demand, indeed, the abolition of the Holy Office?"

"If we as bishops can no longer judge, if the primacy of private conscience is to become the new Pope and Roman Curia, if—in your thirst for 'holy liberty'—the great judicial structure of the Church is to be demolished, then what will take its place? Amongst your heady mists of holy sentiment, not once in this assembly have I heard a clear answer to that question. How many of you bishops from beyond the Alps—in the cold darkness of your northern nights, in your zeal that the Church of Christ must speak with tender warmth to the hearts of men—have lent your deepest thought to my unwelcome, inconvenient, most vexing question?

"Not by blind chance, venerable Fathers of the Council, are we gathered in the heart of Christendom, here in the Basilica of St Peter. Look around.

Look upward to Michelangelo's massive dome, to the grandeur of Vignola's domes of the chapels Gregoriana and Clementina. Glance over there to the statue of our first pope, Peter, his foot worn smooth by the fervent kisses of the faithful.

"Open the windows as you must; let in the friendly gusts of robust, fresh air; but reject the symbols of this basilica, however Baroque, and the beauty of our Church, however antiquated, at your peril. Reject His Eminence of the Holy Office, who has guarded the antiquity and the beauty of our Faith with such a vigilance, at your peril. As the Roman poet told us, 'If you seek his monument, look around. [*Si monumentum requiris, circumspice.*]' Can you, brothers, do so much better?"

As I composed my address, I discovered that—from the depths of me— my true mind was emerging through the mists, that I had stumbled upon a crucial moment of my life, and that in the great battle for the Roman Church I was choosing sides.

And yet in the final instant I felt cold feet—cowardice? my ravening ambition? my conscience asked me—and I removed my name from the list of orators at the rostrum of St Peter's.

Instead, during the days that followed, I became all things to all bishops, eager for the love of my career to discern which way the ecclesiastical winds might blow before I committed my body and my soul to either camp.

To the Sunny Pope (whom I dined with often), I communicated sunshine, assuring him that everything was well, that the rancour of the debates merely echoed "holy liberty"—and that before the Council ended, all contradictions would be composed under the guidance of the Holy Spirit.

"Then why don't you say that in the Council, dear Agostino?"

"When the time is ripe, Most Holy Father."

To Cardinal Baluardo (whom I dined with often), I communicated darkness, repeating the essence of my oration—though never revealing that I had written it.

"Then why don't you say that in the Council, dear Agostino?"

"When the time is ripe, Your Eminence."

In the stupor of my cowardice, I began to observe my life as though I were someone else. I watched as a spectator while my cinema resumed— now not in jerky black and white but in lustrous colour.

I glimpsed myself as I moved with stately gait across the basilica's Nervan marble floor, beneath my purple skullcap, in the splendour of my violet soutane and tassels, my golden cord and pectoral cross, my huge archiepiscopal ring twinkling like the lamps, but not so brightly as the gleam of the cardinalate in my greedy eye.

I watched myself mingling during intermissions with the mob of cardinals; genuflecting, kissing their outstretched simple or ornate rings; whispering encouragement and gossip now to the progressive Dutchman, now to the uncertain South American, now to the reactionary Neapolitan; befriending fairly every foreign member of the Sacred College, offering my advice and little favours, running their errands, too knowing that their gratitude might one day help my rise.

Suddenly I turned to the lens and asked aloud, "But is this how Ercole Consalvi, Your Grace's idol, attained his heights—by grovelling?"

Throughout that first session of the Council, I gave several dinner parties in my ample rooms in the Borgo Angelico. My last was the most brilliant; not only for the presence of so many cardinals in their black soutanes trimmed with red and their flowing crimson cloaks; not only for the foreign ambassadors and pontifical nobility in evening dress with their sleek and coiffured wives; but because I mingled the most progressive and the most conservative of the Vatican Council's prelates.

I served my guests a rich buffet around roast duck, washed down by lashings of white and red Rhône wines. The Bishop of Limerick asked for whiskey, but in the presence of so many of the Roman Curia, I was loath to serve highballs. Everyone was dazzled by my Nubians, not only tall Ghassem in his golden turban and *galibiya,* but by his adolescent son and daughter, Kamal and Fatima likewise in quaint Egyptian costume; and by Mahmoud, the Pontiff's darling, now three years old, in his bare feet and nightgown hiding at first between my purple cloak and black soutane, then emerging to play that sort of game amid gales of laughter between the robes of cardinals. Maha, like any good Muslim wife, remained a secret in the kitchen—but soon enough Fatima brought out in downy blankets Ahmed and Khadidja, boy and girl, the newest infants of Maha's brood, delighting even grumpy Cardinal Sostituto.

After dinner and dessert, the prelates and the other guests, tinkling the china of their *demitasses,* wandered through my rooms, admiring my watercolours by Lord Turner of Oxford and Thomas Shorter Boys; the pictures of Dionysus and Ariadne, landscapes with ruined castles, rocky coasts by moonlight, the fish market in Hastings. The coiffured women professed to be enchanted by the mounted silver coins of Syracuse, Clazomenae, and Heraclea; by the heads of horses, bulls, and Roman emperors in wreaths of laurel; above all by the gemstones engraved with the snake-haired Medusa in chalcedony and the naked Diomedes in red jasper.

The Bishop of Limerick, smoking a black cigar, enthroned in an armchair of Italianate Louis Quinze, stared about a crowded room, at the classical marble busts, the bronze torso of the Doryphoros, the armless Apollo of the Tiber in the style of Phidias, the breathing princes of the Church and the papal dukes and counts in their boiled shirts and pearl cuff links and their wives in Dior gowns and diamond necklaces. Petulant still because he was served no whiskey, he asked me, "Sir Augustine, is this the Church of the Poor?"

Cardinal Baluardo, clad like his brother princes in a scarlet cape and even in his red biretta, mingled with progressive prelates from beyond the Alps, trying to be convivial, avoiding discord, rambling in small talk about the marble busts and his orphanage in Trastevere. Since he spoke no German, I interpreted for him as he chatted with a Jesuit in a shabby black suit, a radical theologian from Ludwigshafen. I struggled to change the subject, but inexorably the two began to disagree about the liturgy. The Jesuit did not help, hurling jargon of the new Biblical theology at the Cardinal: *"Formgeschichte . . . Heilgeschichte . . . Redaktionsgeschichte."*

I begged the Jesuit: *"Ich bitte. . . ."*

Cardinal Baluardo told me in Italian: "Your Grace needn't translate. I understand those terms. I condemned them in the Holy Office."

The Jesuit replied in broken Italian: "The liturgy must be rescued from the Holy Office and returned to the people—in their own language."

Cardinal Baluardo: *"Heil—Heil-ge-schichte. Redaktion-s-ge-schichte!* It's muddled Lutheranism, a stew of German idealism, a pottage of Teutonic rationalism, the kind of crackpot garbage that led to Hitler!"

The Jesuit: "How dare you, Cardinal? My brother was shot by the Gestapo!"

Cardinal Baluardo: "A pity you didn't take his place! Error has no rights!"

I insinuated myself between the angry Jesuit and the indignant Cardinal, then announced to all that we should retire to the grand salon for music.

As the guests flowed through the rooms, the cardinals and other clergy of Germany, Belgium, the Netherlands, and France flocked to one another as if to form a phalanx, shunning His Eminence of the Holy Office. Their memories were too keen of Cardinal Baluardo's admonitions, condemnations, accusations of heterodoxy and heresy aimed at northern Europe and themselves. When the company reached the grand salon, Cardinal Baluardo retreated in embarrassment to a corner, standing incongruously beside sculpted Venus cast in bronze, her right hand hiding her vulva. At the corner, Cardinal Sostituto and Monsignore Samosata joined him in solidarity.

I sat on the black bench before my Steinway. For weeks, I had consumed as many hours practising at the piano as I did in writing my abortive speech. My hands were poised above the polished ivory keyboard as I prayed silently for inspiration to make my music beautiful—but even now my guilty conscience, my loathing of my cowardice, intruded. I thought, Time for your deeper instincts to take charge—to make a crucial *choice.* Of a sudden I stood up, and in a strong voice I addressed all of my guests.

"I dedicate this music to our Lord Cardinal Baluardo."

The transalpine cardinals murmured. The pontifical nobility cheered.

Pursuing my impulse, I strode to the corner and grasped Cardinal Baluardo by his ringed hand: "Come, Eminence, sit beside me as I play."

"No, Agostino, no."

"Ma sì, Eminenza, sì."

I led the Cardinal by the hand, and sat him at the end of my bench.

My music—themes from Handel's *concerti grossi,* Bach's Goldberg Variations with new cadenzas, improvisations upon melodies of that master's Mass in B Minor—was precise and fluent, aspiring in quality if not to Heaven, then perhaps nearly as high as the minor cupolas of Rome. When I was done, the applause though not outlandish was palpably more than polite. Standing to bow in my claret toga, I glanced to the corner, where Cardinal Sostituto and Monsignore Samosata were visibly moved, probably less by my music than by my gesture toward their friend.

Cardinal Baluardo's live eye glowed with gratitude.

In December 1962, when the first ballots of Vatican Council II were cast at St Peter's, the Fathers voted overwhelmingly to reject Cardinal Baluardo's *schemata* on the Sources of Divine Revelation and on the Nature of the Church.

The Pope then appointed a mixed commission of progressive and conservative cardinals to draft more "pastoral" *schemata* on Revelation and the Church—to be considered by all the Council Fathers when they should gather at Rome again in the autumn to follow.

Before adjourning, the Fathers also voted enormously for liturgical reform—opening the windows and the altars of the Church to the vernacular and the eventual suppression of the Latin Mass.

The Roman Curia was shaken.

Cardinal Baluardo was shaken.

In my love of Latin, I was shaken. I had obediently fulfilled all of the Sunny Pope's commands in preparing for the Council and throughout the first session. I had been loyal to His Holiness, and resolved to remain so. But more than ever I wondered how I might reconcile my filial devotion to the Pontiff with my new nostalgic sympathy for the vanishing Church of Cardinal Baluardo.

✛

TWENTY-FIVE

✛

And I was much worried by the Supreme
Pontiff's failing health. His jolly face
turned a more sickly yellow, suggesting to
the naked eye that he suffered from anaemia.
Despite the obsessive secrecy of Don Giulio and
the sealed entourage about the papal secretary, I
learned eventually that in fact, even before the
Council, the Holy Father—like his dead friend
Cardinal di Benevento—had contracted cancer of
the stomach.

Inside of him, gastric hemorrhages erupted.
Surgery had been delayed too long in deference to
the Council, so in the corridors of the Apostolic
Palace it was whispered that His Holiness had but
months to live.

The Vicar of Christ did not complain of his
afflictions, yet they prompted me perforce to
meditate on the succession. I had dissembled,
mildly feigned surprise, when His Eminence Baluardo urged me to become friendly with the Cardinal Archbishop of Milan because he might be the
next pope: his elevation to the papacy was increasingly expected not only in Rome but throughout
Christendom. Given his stature as an intellectual,
his decades of experience in the Roman Curia, and

now as head of Italy's largest See, His Eminence of Lombardy was (indeed!) considered "overqualified" to be Pontiff.

At St Peter's, during meetings of the Council, I had deliberately kept my distance from the heir apparent. During intermissions, by the coffee bar at the side of the basilica, he was invariably surrounded by other aspirants to his favour, but I stayed away from him. I did not invite him to my dinners in the Borgo Angelico, hoping he might hear of them and suppose that I did not seek his favour. I thought, I must get him alone: I must make a deep impression to win his favour.

In the Council, much like myself, he sat on the fence. I had read volumes about the humility of heirs apparent, of their saintly hesitation to mount the papal throne, but I laughed at such legends. To me, the Cardinal of Milan was playing safe, keeping his mouth shut, loath to displease any elector of the Sacred College until the Tiara should be his. In the last hours at the Council, he did say a word for reform, echoing cries of others that the *schemata* of the Holy Office should be rejected—but that was the Pope's wish also, so his risk was slight.

Not that His Eminence of Lombardy lacked convictions. On the contrary, as a young priest, and then for years as a *monsignore*, the right arm of the Stern Pope in the Secretariat of State, he had quietly fought Fascism through his chaplaincy of the Catholic Youth, nurturing a generation of Christian intellectuals who assumed power in Italy after the gruesome death of Mussolini. He fell from that Pope's grace not only because he lacked his master's zeal against the Communists, but because—as Cardinal Baluardo fumed to me—he was too sympathetic to new fashions in theology trickling down from France.

From France. I mused that when I had the Cardinal Archbishop to myself, I might be very French.

Yet, as so often when I faced a crux, I acted on presentiment and impulse.

In February 1963, I flew to Geneva on another of my missions to deposit the Pope's money in the Crédit Suisse, remaining overnight to join the Swiss bishops in a symposium about the Council. At morning, as I walked with my Gucci luggage through warrens of the airport towards my jet to Rome, I happened on a flight with a different destination. Hastily, I changed my ticket, and flew for half an hour above the Alps to the airport at Milan.

In a lavatory cubicle, I shed my clerical twills for my soutane of black and purple and my pectoral cross; placed a violet biretta atop my head; threw a winter cape about my shoulders, black but lined with red satin and fastened by a silver buckle. Then I took a taxi to the Archbishop's Palace beside the great cathedral—wedding-cake Gothic, ghostly in the fog; ah, so many misty pinnacles and turrets, gargoyles and caryatids—called the Duomo.

Deep inside the palace, above an immense court of double colonnades, I found the Cardinal's secretariat. His antechamber was thronged with people sitting on every chair, as if waiting for a dentist. I stood at the door with my Gucci luggage, feeling gauche and out of place, until Don Gianni, the Cardinal's secretary (tonsured, bespectacled, almost fat; I knew him slightly from the Council) emerged from the inner sanctum in a buttoned black soutane.

"Your Grace!" he cried, hastening to me to genuflect and kiss my ring.

"Forgive me, Padre," I apologised, mechanically extending my right hand for his obeisance. "My rudeness is inexcusable. I'm in Milan on, ah, personal business, so brashly I brought myself to pay my compliments to His Eminence."

"I'll squeeze you in before his next appointment," said Don Gianni.

"I won't hear of it, Don Gianni. I'll wait with the others and read my Office."

A tinkling bell recalled the secretary to the Cardinal's presence. I crouched in a corner on the threadbare rug, opening my breviary and mumbling the psalm of the day: "*Dominus regnavit, decorem induit.* The Lord is King; He hath clothed Himself in majesty. The Lord hath clothed and girded Himself with power. . . ." Others in the room—old women in shabby hats, young merchants in smart lounge suits—kept offering me their chairs, but in my fashionable humility I remained floor-bound. I thought, They all want something from the Cardinal. Most of them, by means direct or indirect, probably want money.

I waited two hours, past the tolling of the Duomo's bells at noon till at last the antechamber emptied. Don Gianni opened the door: "Your Grace?"

I advanced toward the Cardinal. His Eminence was clad in a simple black soutane, with only a wooden crucifix on his breast dangling from a noose of grey rope. When I genuflected to kiss his ring, his hand was bare. I thought, Dear God, is this the future? Appraising me in my regalia, he said, "*Ah, caro, elegante Monsignore, il nostro molto giovane Arcivescovo di Trebisondo.*"

I replied in French, "*Toujours votre serviteur très obéissant, cher Éminence.*"

My choice of language, if not my costume, seemed to please him. He responded, "*Mais, Monseigneur, je vous en prie! Asseyez-vous!*"

We sat, I upon a tattered leather couch, he facing me upon a modern chair of blond wood. In French he continued, "Had I known Your Grace was coming, I'd have dressed up."

A reproach? His telephone rang. Sighing, he walked to his desk of blond wood, sat down beneath an oil painting of St Charles Borromeo, his ancestor in the See of Milan. No sooner he sat, picked up the telephone, he stood again. He said, "*Ah, Santo Padre!*" It was the Pope. I thought, Don't tell him *I* am here. He remained standing as they discussed the new drafts in progress on Revelation and the Church. The Cardinal's advice was much "*Ma, sì*" and "*Sì, ma*"—salvoes of "But, yes" and "Yes, but"—mingled with erudite circumlocutions ("On the one hand . . . On the other hand . . .") and sporadic pleas for boldness which then he seemed to water down with "maybe" and even contradict with Latin pleas for caution: "*. . . maxima cum prudentia.*"

As he grew engrossed in their discussion, I enjoyed the leisure of studying his person. He was, I knew, in his sixty-seventh year. His pate was bald, his body slight, the lips were thin, the nose was large, the complexion nearly sallow. His voice was high, almost effete, the hands too nervous, and his eyes—arresting. His eyes were black. Not merely Italian dark, but his irises and pupils seemed the deepest, saddest black. I looked about his office, piled with bookshelves of theology in Latin but more in French, modern novels, all in French, tomes on culture and industrial society, all in French, documents heaped anyhow, disorderly. Paintings of opaque gouache—Milanese modern?—hung tilting from his walls. On tables, atop books and documents, teetered great glass eggs. It seemed wherever I cast my eye, I saw glass eggs. He told the Pope, "Monsignore Galsworthy is here with me."

At last he hung up, approached, and sat again on his blond chair. Silence, for several moments: Oh, those black eyes, as they fixed on mine, as though I were the only man on earth who mattered, as though he could gaze so far inside the deepest riddles of my soul. No further proof was needed, really, for I knew in that instant that he possessed the celestial power and indeed he would be Pope. He said, *"Donc. . . ."*

The door opened: Don Gianni again. *Damn!* I thought. Don Gianni brought in a delegation of young men in steel hats—coal miners. His master, after all, was "Archbishop of the Workers." The young men bore signs, ON STRIKE. They queued to kiss the Cardinal's ring, and seemed as confused and disappointed as I had been that his hand was bare. Instead, and shyly, he embraced each of the miners one by one, expressing sympathy with their demands for a living wage and seeming through his mist of convolution to condemn the wrongs of capital. A photographer raced in; the miners tendered the Cardinal a steel hat. He put it on, and in the centre of the delegation had his picture taken. I thought, He looks intellectual and silly.

As the miners trudged out, the Cardinal quietly told Don Gianni to refuse all further calls and visitors: he wished to be alone with me. From the door, again he fixed his eyes on mine: *"Vous voyez, cher Monseigneur, je n'ai jamais le luxe de la solitude."* He wandered about his office, picking up books and papers, waving them, lamenting, "I've not even the leisure to read or write. I'm invited to lecture everywhere, but since the Council, I have no time. Why, next month, I can not even go to Paris for my cherished Jacques!"

"Jacques?"

"My friend and master—Jacques Maritain!"

"Is there some sort of celebration, Eminence?"

"The silver anniversary of his *True Humanism*. I was to deliver the commemorative address."

"I know the work."

"How well?"

"I love specially Chapter Four," said I, "where Maritain redeems Pio Nono. 'The Church faced a paradox, compelled at once to defend herself against attacks on the dissolving Papal States and fundamental errors which claimed to represent the modern mind. Yet those fundamental errors were the fruit of liberal naturalism, and the Church was in depth defending—not her own perishing temporal order—but a constant Christian conception of the world.' "

"*Précisément.* However, in the next paragraph, Maritain quotes Péguy: 'Christendom will come back in the hour of distress.' Then Maritain asks how, in which mode, to which music? That, Monseigneur, is what our Council is all about—and exactly what I wished to say. How I wish I had time to write the speech."

"If you had the speech in hand, my lord, would you deliver it?"

"For an hour in Paris? Of course."

"Then let me write it."

"But Your Grace is so busy with the Holy Father."

"I shall make time at midnight."

"You'd be enthusiastic but full of nuance?"

"Writing of Maritain, could one be otherwise?"

"When could you send me your draft?"

"Next week, Eminence?"

"No later? I must tell Jacques."

I rose to take my leave. At his desk, the Cardinal rummaged amongst his papers and glass eggs for some pious souvenir to give me, and in doing so found a miner's helmet on his chair. Holding it up, placing it like a crown again on his bald head, looking more than ever intellectual and silly, he said, "Ah, such misery in this rich metropolis, *cher Monseigneur!* Hordes of the workless poor from Sicily and the Mezzogiorno, even from North Africa, pouring—gushing—in, and no place for them to live except in slums and shantytowns and open sewers! I have so little—my resources are so meagre—what can I do to save them and their sick children?"

I asked, "Is this helmet my souvenir?"

"That hat is suddenly dear to me," the Cardinal answered. "A medallion of Saint Charles? Saint Ambrose?"

"I'd prefer the hat, Your Eminence." I removed my violet biretta, tried the helmet on. Did I look as intellectual and silly? I said, "I'll pay you for it."

"*Mais, vraiment. . . .*"

"I meant that I wish to make a contribution to your poor."

"*Ah, oui . . . ?*"

Again, those black eyes, scalding mine. I hesitated, undecided. To mark his papal knighthood and my young archbishopric, Urban Northwood in a creamy envelope had given me two hundred thousand dollars on the morrow. Cardinal Benevento had bequeathed to me nearly half that sum. I thought, *Go ahead. Gamble. Toss the dice? Well worth it? Anybody can ghost a speech. Do something he shan't forget when he ascends the Throne. No? Preposterous? Plunge!*

I groped for my cheque-book in the pocket of my soutane, bent over the blond desk, and wrote a cheque on the Crédit Suisse to the Archdiocese of Milan for one hundred thousand dollars—nearly a third of my fortune.

Impassively the Cardinal glanced at it, then lifted a lid and placed the cheque inside a glass egg.

"*Je vous remercie, Monseigneur.* The hat is yours. In the Vatican, I've been told that you are too clever by half."

"A slander, my lord. Too clever merely by a quarter."

A thin smile. He asked, "*Est-ce que vous êtes juif?*" Are you Jewish?

"*P-Peut-être ma m-mère. . . .*" My m-mother m-maybe. . . .

On the aeroplane back to Rome, clutching my steel hat, I wondered whether I had made the right impression. Already, in my head, as though with keyboard variations on a Bach cantata, I was composing in sublime French the heir apparent's speech for Paris.

✛

TWENTY-SIX

✛

In my library at the Borgo Angelico, not so late at night, I wrote the speech in two sittings. In March, the Cardinal of Milan delivered it at Paris. My moonlight labour did not please the Pope.

In the discomfort of his cancer, His Holiness was becoming irascible and suspicious. He continued to work full days, but the intrigues of his court did not improve his humour.

Like any royal court, the Vatican establishment fed on gossip. At Milan, the Cardinal Archbishop mentioned to a friend that I had written his speech. At Rome, days later, the friend passed on the titbit to a supernumerary of the Roman Curia. The supernumerary hurried to the Pope's secretary. Don Giulio was himself tormented by swirling rumours that no sooner should the pontificate expire, he would be removed from the Apostolic Palace and dispatched to a bucolic bishopric. Ever vexed by my young success, he brought the titbit to the Pope, managing to insinuate not only that I was treacherous, but that the Holy Father should raise inconvenient questions about my fortune.

One morning in late March, the Sovereign Pontiff summoned me to his library.

"So you're sending speeches to Milan?"

"Holiness," I protested, "the Cardinal is your favourite."

"Who told you that?"

"You did."

"I'm beginning to have my doubts about him. Will he ever make up his mind? I can never nail him down. Look out the window. See that cloud? Could you nail it to the wall? That's His Eminence for you. In the Council, he disappointed me—as you did, Agostino. I know, I know, you expect him to succeed me, so you offered him your service. You might have had the courtesy—the common courage—to ask my permission."

I stood like a truant schoolboy before the Pope in his white soutane upon his damask armchair. I knelt at his feet, grasped his yellow, thinning hand, and kissed it. "Forgive me, Holiness. You're the only father I've ever had."

The Pontiff yanked his hand away. "Enough of your humble pie. You're too clever by half."

"A slander, my lord. Merely by a qu-quarter."

"Now isn't that funny? Your wit is beginning to bore me. And look at you. Always trying to impress people. Always so perfectly groomed. Do you visit your barber every day? I watched you on my television during the Council. Your stately gait across the transept of Saint Peter's became an arrogant strut. That archiepiscopal ring you're wearing must weigh twice as much as mine. How many silk and satin robes—how many bejewelled slippers, buskins, chasubles, copes, and mitres—have you? You're straight out of Louis XV's Versailles. Why, you even wear your purple gloves and buckled shoes to work! You are so *vain.*"

I had remained kneeling. Now I stood up. "Most Holy Father—"

"I treated you as my son. I gave you far too much and far too soon. I owed no favour to Cardinal di Benevento. Yes, he helped me in the Conclave, but whether or not you may believe it—does Your Grace believe in *anything?*—I was chosen Pope by the Holy Spirit! You've such ambition—scheming, climbing, cunning! How deeply I regret that I anointed you Archbishop of Trebizond."

I don't. The insolence was halfway off my tongue, but by some magic I retrieved it. Instead I stammered, "Most Holy F-Father," and began to bow out.

"Come back here, Agostino."

"*Sanctissimus Dominus?*"

"I meant every word I said, but still I love you as my son and I'm aching and awfully sick."

"Again you gazed inside my soul, Your Holiness—dear God, as Pope you've such a gift! at least I believe in *that!*—and now you don't much care for what you see. Nor do I—at night, when I'm so lonely! Shall I call your doctors?"

"No. They make me worse. You're lonely? Look at *me.* At least you have that imp, Mahmoud. Bring him to me—soon! How is the darling little devil [*caro diavolo piccolo*]?"

"Happy, Holy Father. He still thinks that you're his horse."

"Ha! So . . . now . . . who is Signor Norta-wooda?"

"Why, Most Holy Father, don't you remember? You created him a Knight Commander of Pio Nono."

"When?"

"A fortnight before the Council."

"Why did I make him a knight?"

"He's given you several million dollars."

"Are you accusing me of simony?"

"To the contrary, Holiness. Signor Northwood seems devout, all the money goes to charity, and you never promised him a *quid pro quo.*"

"Ah . . . yes. An account in Zurich?"

"Geneva."

"Have you the statements?"

"In my office, Holiness."

"Go and get them."

I withdrew to the far side of the palace and my storeroom office. Searching for the documents, I found that my desk and files had been disturbed. As I brought the bank statements to the Pope, in the antechamber I passed Don Giulio—sulking, lean, in soiled purple—but when I glared at him he looked away. In the library, the Pope glanced at my documents, turning the pages with distaste. He asked, "Is this dirty money [*denaro sporco*]?"

"Much of it Your Holiness has received directly from the faithful. As for Signor Northwood, I assume it was Don Giulio who impugned his probity?"

"And Cardinal Sostituto, once I raised the question."

"The suspicions of His Eminence have no proof—or I should never have accepted benefactions from Signor Northwood for Your Holiness or for myself. Yes, he's been quite generous to me, as well, Most Holy Father. Shall I refuse his further gifts?"

"Then where shall We find sufficient means to feed the poor?"

The Pontiff grimaced, gripped his stomach in a sudden fit of pain. He gasped, "A . . . moral question . . . so let Us . . . think about it."

However, the Pontiff's leisure for such reflection was running out. His cancer worsened. He no longer invited me to dinner; he stopped eating dinner. He lived on liquids he sucked through tubes. In April, he suspended audiences, took to bed, and ruled the Roman Church in his pyjamas. In early May, when he entered and came out of comas—so delirious from morphine that often he knew not what he said or did, and even fancied he was in Heaven—his entourage seized control of his affairs and governed the Church in his mighty name. "It is the Pope's wish . . . The Holy Father forbids . . . The Supreme Pontiff commands . . ."

At the centre of this cabal, of course, was Don Giulio, still as papal secre-

tary only a *monsignore,* but for the moment more powerful than any cardinal. To the world press, Don Giulio pretended that the Pope was in perfect
health.

In middle May, Don Giulio's phalanx round the Pope closed ranks, shutting all but the few from access to the Holy Father. In my heart I knew that
the Pope was crying out for the comfort of my presence, but his entourage
turned deaf. In a brusque letter, invoking the Pope's authority, Don Giulio
told me not to approach the pontifical apartments, and in fact forbade me to
use my office or even to enter the Apostolic Palace.

So I remained at home in the Borgo Angelico; sulking; reading; writing;
ruminating; reciting in my private chapel the prayers for the sick and dying;
impatient for the next pontificate when I might resume my chase of the main
chance.

Late one night in early June, the telephone in my library rang. It was Don
Giulio, almost sobbing. He said, "The end is near. The Holy Father has
refused more morphine and is offering his agony to Christ. He has become
quite lucid. He begs for you and for the child."

"The child?" I asked.

"Don't Muslims live with you?"

"Mahmoud?"

"The Pope keeps calling for him."

"I'll come at once."

Hastily I dressed in my soutane of black and purple and my pectoral
cross, but without my violet gloves and in shoes that had no showy buckles.
I raced through halls to the servants' rooms, roused Ghassem and his wife,
then fled my flat with little Mahmoud in his socks and nightgown and
bundled in a blanket. Gripping him, I dashed through empty streets, into the
Vatican, past Swiss Guards, up the Scala Regia, across the Sala Regia, and
into the pontifical apartments.

When I entered the Pope's crowded bedroom, the Cardinal of Milan—
clad now in crimson—had almost finished conferring the last rites.

I wondered: Is he back in favour as the heir apparent?

The Cardinal purified his fingers of the sacred oils in a silver dish of
water. He said, *"Kyrie, eleison."*

The Others (*kneeling*): *"Christe, eleison. Kyrie, eleison."*

The Cardinal: "And lead us not into temptation."

The Others: "But deliver us from evil."

The Cardinal: "Grant salvation to Thy servant."

The Others: "For his hope, Lord God, is in Thee."

The Cardinal: "Be a tower of strength for him, O Lord."

The Others: "Against the attack of the Enemy."

The Cardinal: "Let the Enemy have no power on him."

The Others: "Let not the son of Evil come nigh to harm him."

The Cardinal: "O Lord, hear my prayer."

The Others: "And let our prayer be heard."

The heir apparent's high-pitched prayers droned on. The room was rather small—suffocating with the breath of so many cardinals—and severely made: only a Baroque crucifix, an icon of the Madonna above the bed, fading damask walls, a few gilded sticks of furniture. The Pope's bed seemed hardly bigger than a monk's pallet. A white sheet was drawn to his armpits. His head was propped up by a pair of moist pillows. Round his bony fingers were entwined the black beads of his mother's rosary. Inexorably, I thought again of my first encounter with the Pontiff in his library:

"Such language—'false, calumnious, rash, contrary to the word of God, impious, scandalous, erroneous'—shall henceforth be banished from the vocabulary of Rome. *Fuori! Fuori! Fuori!* Out! Out! Out! From now on, Monsignore, the Roman Pontiff will address the world not with anger but with love. Out with anathemas! *MISERICORDIA!*"

I wondered, Was his a foolish dream? In his allocutions, he had constantly quoted Christ: " 'My children, love one another . . . love one another . . . love one another.' " The Pope's wish was kingly: goodness, happiness, love, by decree. If I was guilty of a sin against the Pope, it was not so much treachery as doubt. Not only had I ambition, but a deep intellectual diffidence.

I was beginning to be grieved by the Pope's conviction that love was the key to every human riddle; that all men could be animated by benevolence; that they had only to be treated kindly by the Church so as to act nobly towards one another. This Pope told us to love the world, to gird ourselves for an insurgency of bliss, that we all of us might know a new millennium and a "New Pentecost." I was troubled by the flammable forces in the Church the Pontiff had released, and I wondered whether upon his deathbed he had any thought that in calling his Council he had been inspired—not so much by the Holy Spirit—as (perhaps) by his subconscious lust for mischief.

He had accused me of vanity, though vanity was my lesser vice. Yet he (I thought) was in bondage to a greater vice: he hungered to be loved by the whole human race.

I held to my thoughts in silence, but no sooner the prayers were finished, His Eminence of the Holy Office stepped from the crowd of cardinals to the end of the Pontiff's bed, unable to contain his wrath.

Cardinal Baluardo: "Before God, and before Your Holiness is dead, I have the sacred duty to speak. You have brought the Holy, Roman, Catholic, and Apostolic Church to the brink of ruin. You have—"

The Heir Apparent: *"Satis, satis."*

Cardinal Baluardo: "You have set fires in the sanctuaries of the Church that we may never quench. You have—"

The Heir Apparent: *"Satis, satis!"*

Cardinal Baluardo: "In moments, you must answer to the throne of God. In moments—"

The Heir Apparent: *"SATIS! SATIS!"*

The Pope cried out, "Mahmoud? Where is my little Mahmoud?"

I squeezed through cardinals to the Pope's side. Baby Mahmoud, not yet four, slept on my shoulder. Now I woke him. Blinking, he may have recog-

nised the person of the Pope but not his Office: to the child, the Pontiff was a horse. I thought again, *Pope as Horse.* Suddenly I glimpsed him prancing with the child upon his back through the mists of Heaven.

On earth, I raised Mahmoud above the bed for the Vicar of Christ to see. The Pontiff lifted his arms to hug him, because (he knew) this brown child was the breeding human race. Too late: the Pope's arms fell feebly to his sides. I lowered the child to touch the Pope, but a physician with his stethoscope and then the ancient bearded Frenchman, Cardinal Dean of the Sacred College, intruded on us.

The Cardinal bumped Mahmoud's elbow. The child—like a newborn—cried at the instant that the doctor uttered a moan of sorrow. Thrice with his tiny silver hammer, the Cardinal Dean tapped the forehead of the Sunny Pope, then liturgically declared him dead.

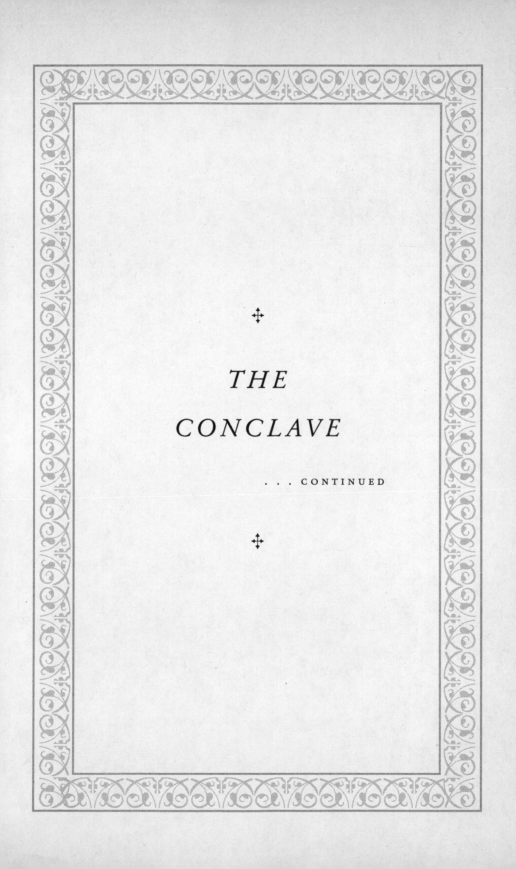

THE

CONCLAVE

. . . CONTINUED

"The cup which my Father hath given me,

shall I not drink it?"

✜

*T*he Conclave on the eve of the Third Millennium continued to deliberate. On I scribbled my abortive diary upon sheets of foolscap:

We have just completed our fifth day of scrutinies in the Sistine Chapel, entrenching deadlock. But my ballots have slightly increased from twenty-three to thirty-two— or forty-nine short of the votes I need to achieve the papacy.

One might wonder why a cardinal as vain and imperious as I, so unbeloved by many of his peers, should show such steadfast and mounting strength. I never cease to ask myself, Is it because more and more of my brother princes in the Sacred College fear as I do the collapse of discipline in the Church and the growing fecklessness of so many of the faithful? Do they recognise at last that only a Pope with a will of steel, in the shimmering tradition of the Slavic Pontiff, can hold the Church together?

But in truth do I possess a will of steel? Am I worthy to lead the Roman Church into the next millennium? More than any other cardinal might imagine, my soul is haunted by the spectre of my self-doubt. Yet I so much crave the papacy!

✣

PART VI

SAD

POPE

✣

✥

TWENTY-SEVEN

✥

Since I was not a cardinal, I was excluded from the Sistine Chapel during the Conclave that elected the successor to the Sunny Pope. All of the cardinals swore oaths of silence never to reveal whatever might take place during each balloting for the new Pontiff. Several princes of the Church, as voluble as they were devout, somehow managed to surmount their scruples.

Within hours of the election, I learned all. The Cardinal Archbishop of Milan entered the Conclave telling his brothers in the Sacred College, "I am in darkness and can see nothing clearly." There is a maxim about inevitable pontificates, "He who enters the Conclave as Pope comes out as cardinal." Oddly, during the first few scrutinies, other candidates for the Triple Crown proved to His Eminence of Milan that the maxim might again be so.

The battle against his papacy was led, of course, by Cardinal Baluardo. His Eminence of the Holy Office had made so many enemies in the Church that he enjoyed no chance of seizing the Tiara for himself, but with ardour he promoted the candidacies of other princes—the cardinals of Genoa and

Palermo, conservatives inside the Roman Curia—cut to his own scarlet cloth.

In the opposite camp, the Archbishop of Milan was considered too much of an enigma; progressives favoured the Cardinal of Bologna, a zealot of liturgical reform and anathema to Cardinal Baluardo. Wet straw was burned with the abortive ballots in the chapel's potbellied stove, and from the pipe above the chapel black smoke belched.

On the fourth scrutiny, with no small assistance from the French electors, the tide turned towards the Cardinal of Milan.

As it did, the Cardinal practised all the pieties of imminent pontiffs enshrined down through the centuries and thoroughly expected of him. He was observed in his Sacred Purple praying alone before the high altar of the chapel, beneath Michelangelo's *Last Judgement*, his frail body bent low in supplication, his face buried in his hands as though like Christ's they sweated blood. His murmurings were likewise faintly heard exuding from his cell, *"Domine, non sum dignus."* Lord, I am not worthy. And—equally imperative—moans from the thirty-ninth and forty-second verses of Matthew, Twenty-six: "O my Father, if it be possible, let this chalice pass from me: nevertheless not as I will, but as Thou wilt.... O my Father, if this chalice may not pass away, except I drink it, Thy will be done." And John, Eighteen, eleven: "The cup which my Father hath given me, shall I not drink it?"

This was, if not quite a dance or ballet, a sort of sacred choreography, a show of ceremonial humility that had to be fulfilled before the aspirant was finally anointed by the finger of the Holy Spirit. On the fifth scrutiny, genuflecting to the Divine wish, Cardinal Baluardo gave up his fight. Like any other rod of the Roman Curia, he recognised that he would do well to be seen on the side of the victor, an old acquaintance if not a friend. Besides, at least his machinations had prevented the papacy of His (more dangerous) Eminence of Bologna.

On the sixth scrutiny, the Cardinal of Milan surpassed with ease a majority of two-thirds of the ballots plus one. The bearded Cardinal Dean proceeded down the line of princes until he reached the Archbishop of Milan trembling at his place in a gilded chair. In Latin he asked the Archbishop, "Dost thou accept thy canonical election to the Supreme Pontificate?"

"Placet."

He did. The scarlet canopies above the other cardinals were forthwith lowered, leaving intact only the baldachin above the new Pope. In the stove, the ballots were burned with dry straw, and white smoke puffed from the roof of the chapel. From the central balcony of St Peter's, Cardinal Baluardo announced to the world, *"Habemus papam."*

A fortnight later—early summer, late afternoon, then while the sun set— as a symbol of the Roman Church's new openness to the world, the pontifical coronation was staged not inside the basilica but on the front steps of

St Peter's. As an archbishop, I was seated just behind the cardinals, and from such proximity I watched the pageant with a devouring eye. I found it sad.

During the Mass, the unsmiling countenance, indeed the anguish of the new Pontiff as he participated in the celebration, was in such contrast to his predecessor that he tempted me to shock. The Pope's face was tied into a Cartesian knot of doubt, unworthiness, melancholy. I could hear him asking God, "Am I doing right? Am I doing wrong? Is this Thy will?" It was clear to me that although in his knotted way he had craved the papacy, he considered it not so much a reward for his tireless service to the Church; not (like Leo X and the Sunny Pope) as an office he should enjoy; but as the ultimate cross that Christ had given him to bear.

Moreover, the pageant was riven with evidence of the new Pope's contradictory and exotic nature. He chose Cardinal Baluardo to crown him, perhaps as a prize for abandoning his opposition in the Conclave. (Already, he had reappointed His Eminence to the Holy Office, and Cardinal Sostituto as Secretary of State.) The Pope's taste in headgear was another curiosity. He had decreed that the fat, bejewelled Tiara of his predecessors should be auctioned off, the money given to the poor—instead, he would be crowned with a diadem at once ancient in its shape (in the style of popes of the Middle Ages) and modern in its allure. Oh, it was a triple crown, all right, but it resembled an artillery shell; a sharpened pencil; it was a cone without jewels, fashioned from metal that might have been brass or platinum but it looked to me like burnished tin.

I thought of our encounter at his palace in Milan, when he crowned himself with the miner's helmet and said he found it dear. I had fought with him, you will remember, for the possession of that prize: "I'd prefer the hat, Your Eminence." (I meant, of course, another kind of hat, of a brighter colour. The man was much too subtle to misconstrue me.) At length Cardinal Baluardo crowned him with the sharp cone and the ageless prayer, "Know that thou art the Bishop of Rome, Vicar of Jesus Christ on Earth, Successor of the Prince of the Apostles, Supreme Pontiff of the Universal Church, Primate of Italy, Patriarch of the West, Servant of the Servants of God, Father of All Princes and of Kings."

The Cardinal Dean liturgically cried out—to remind the Supreme Pontiff of his mortality, that soon enough like the rest of us he would become but dust and ashes—"*Sancte Pater, sic transit gloria mundi.*"

Even that Roman irony did not seem to charm His Holiness, much less make him smile. I thought, The Sunny Pope is dead. Long live the Sad Pope.

I thought, *Pope as Horse:* but no equine image will do for this Pontifex Maximus—thus I must craft another. I recalled the Sunny Pope's question, "Will he ever make up his mind? See that cloud? Could you nail it to the wall?" So: *Pope as Cloud?* No, the nebulous imagery was too unjust and would not quite serve. The Sunny Pope, though plump and homely, once he assumed the robes and charism of his Office, looked every inch the monarch, indeed the Father of All Princes and of Kings. He seemed to me a

Bourbon, some distant cousin of fat Louis XVIII seated upon the throne of France after Napoleon and the Restoration. But this Pope, this Pope—what was he? Not a lion, not a horse, not a king, not a prince of any sort. Yet he had laboured so long at the Stern Pope's elbow that against his wish he mimicked his master's nervous, jerky, catlike ways. So: *Pope as Cat?* No, he was not that feline. *Pope as Mouse?* Insulting! *Pope as Rabbit?* Better, but still too unkind. My hunt for the proper beast was doomed that day. I began to listen to the papal allocution.

Now before a bank of microphones and television cameras the Holy Father addressed mankind: timidly he spoke of the Church's new dialogue with the world and of establishing a "civilisation of love." I cringed. I revelled in the favours of the world, but still I recoiled from it. Men would not be civilised, least of all by love. My boyhood had been spent with the reclusive Benedictines of Vaucluse, and those black monks had taught me to reject the world. If I grasped at Faith, it was to disdain the world. But Christ had come to redeem the world! *"My Kingdom is not of this world."* Renunciation of the world was my deepest image of the Church.

I wondered, When will my conviction inflict its wounds?

The Sad Pope announced that—in the autumn—the Council would reconvene at Rome.

TWENTY-EIGHT

✤

Once the Sad Pope was elected, I braced myself for permanent eviction from the Apostolic Palace. Before the Conclave, I had mischievously spread rumours in the Roman Curia that in the final months of the Sunny Pope's pontificate, I had fallen from his favour. This was, of course, a contemptible ruse—the better to ingratiate myself with the new Pope's men as a serviceable ecclesiastic unburdened by old baggage and ready to do their bidding. My duplicity seemed to fail.

In fact, I had reason to fear that my fate would be more hapless than Don Giulio's. For several days, the quondam papal secretary hung helplessly about the pontifical apartments, gathering as best he might his late master's papers, waiting irritably for the new Pope to be crowned until his exile from the seat of power should be enforced. Don Giulio knew already that he would be consecrated a titular archbishop and dispatched with humbling swiftness to the rocky hills of Sicily. There, safely out of sight, he would serve the remainder of his priesthood as episcopal protector of a Marian shrine stuffed with dubious relics of the Virgin Mother's veil, her locks of hair, and murky vials containing her breast milk and menstrual blood. I had no mind to follow such a path, but I became bitterly resigned to it.

Despite my efforts at Milan to win the confidence of the heir apparent, within but hours of his coronation I looked up and saw the guillotine descending. I was still, technically, a member of the papal diplomatic service; from a clerk in the Secretariat of State, I learned that I would be banished to Siberia. Well, not Siberia, literally—a bit further south, and worse. I was to be appointed Apostolic Nuncio to Ouagadougou, Cardinal di Benevento's torrid, horrid old post in West Africa. Cardinal Secretary Sostituto—still suspicious of the provenance of my finances—had approved the nomination, and it awaited only the new Pope's *placet*.

Thus one Wednesday afternoon soon after the coronation, I went to my office in the Apostolic Palace to pack my prodigious accumulation of books and papers.

Since becoming an archbishop, I had resisted all offers to move me to a finer office befitting my rank. I had grown fond of my storeroom overlooking the Courtyard of the Triangle because it was still a storeroom. Due perhaps to proprietary disputes between the Prefect of the Apostolic Palace and the Prefect of the Apostolic Museums, workmen mysteriously had continued to dump superfluous artworks in my office, and I continued to liberate them from their wicker crates.

My new discoveries—miniature paintings on canvas, triptychs on wood, minor statuary, all inspired by the New Testament or by classical pagan mythology—were not only from the school of Perugino, but even now and then from the schools of Fra Angelico, Pinturicchio, and the other (less talented, heterosexual) Caravaggio. Again, many of the works were mediocre, but you may fancy my delight when I found a canvas, a triptych, or a statuette of quality. Relying on the Sunny Pope's casual blessing, I had gone on walking out of the Vatican with the treasures in my Gucci bag.

Now, with my books and papers, I packed the lingering art I coveted. I had help.

I brought several of my children with me—Kamal, as usual, to get him out of the house. Save to decorate my dinner parties, Kamal had shed for ever his Nubian raiment; today in the Vatican he wore blue jeans. Almost a man, his fights with his father had become so savage that it was sadly clear he must soon leave home to live by his wits in common work. Yet I was content as well, for I found it costly to feed so many mouths and to educate the children in Arabic and Italian at Rome's Islamic school. Demure Fatima by choice wore her prudish gown of black as she held slumbering Mahmoud, in a piebald nightshirt and sucking his thumb.

After little Mahmoud, darling of the Sunny Pope, Maha at home had given birth twice again—now five children lived beneath my roof—and she was moreover pregnant with another child. Even as I envied Ghassem for his unrelenting issue, in my dreams my fantasy of fathering sinfully my own son in Florence vexed me more and more. For several years my Florentine detectives had searched for him with no result, but I kept insisting that they carry on, so certain was I that I had sired issue, and so vivid was his infant face in so many of my nightmares: not nightmares, really, but dreams that were bittersweet, full of loss and yearning.

Now thick-nosed Kamal sang silly Italian pop lyrics as he bound my papers, rising at random to dance alone in little circles or to beat the rhythms upon the lids of wicker crates with the pink undersides of his long brown hands. I was packing a canvas by Polidoro da Caravaggio when knuckle-bones knocked timidly at my door ajar. Quickly, I concealed the treasure beneath straw and burlap, since my visitor was the Pope, in embroidered slippers and his white soutane.

"*Santo Padre!*" I cried out.

"*Je m'excuse, Monseigneur. Puis-je entrer?*"

"*Mais bien sûr, Saintissime Père! Quel honneur! Je vous prie de vous asseoir!*"

I genuflected in the Presence. The Pope did not accept my invitation to sit down, but walked directly to Mahmoud to kiss and fondle his cuddly little head: "*Mais voilà, je connais déjà cet enfant mignon, n'est-ce pas?*" Mahmoud awoke, confused by the stranger's hand. When the Pontiff pried him gently from his sister's grasp and descended to the floor to tickle him and play with him, the child bellowed and took refuge in the pleats of my soutane. The Holy Father said in French, "Alas! I lack my predecessor's grace with little ones." On his knees he gazed up at me and asked, "Do you suppose, Monseigneur, that if I had not been celibate, that if I had married, and fathered children, my theology might be different?"

Ever dissembling, I responded, "I doubt it, *Saintissime Père.* Your theology is based on indefectible Scripture and Tradition."

Again that thin smile, and those black eyes, scalding mine. He said, "You sound like Cardinal Baluardo." He rose to his feet: "In fact, I came to see you because His Eminence is raising such a fuss."

From his side pocket, the Pope took out a document. He said, "On the one hand ... We have this decree appointing Your Grace the Apostolic Nuncio to Ouagadougou. It needs only Our signature to take effect. On the other hand ..." From his pocket opposite, he extracted a torn newspaper clipping. He continued, "This is the notice from *Le Monde* last March about Our allocution in Paris commemorating Maritain's *True Humanism.*"

The Pope handed me the clipping; I glanced at it, an encomium lauding the speech's lucidity and eloquence. "I have never received such praise for anything I wrote myself," the Pontiff said. "I had no time to revise your draft, so I delivered the speech as Your Grace wrote it." He retrieved the clipping, bent over my desk, took a pen, scrawled in French a few words of thanks, and added the papal signature to the torn scrap of paper. "This is for Your Grace." He added shyly (ah, that shyness! such meekness from the Father of All Princes and of Kings!), "If you would *like* to have it."

"I am deeply moved, Most Holy Father." (I very much meant that.)

"His Eminence Baluardo has been waging war with his venerable brother Sostituto, insisting that Your Grace has too luminous a mind to waste in

Ouagadougou. Therefore ... We leave the choice to you ... whether to go to Ouagadougou or to remain here, in Rome, with Us."

"May I inquire in what capacity, Most Holy Father?"

"To assist Us with Our allocutions and encyclicals—and to work intimately with Us to conclude the Council in such a way that will please the Lord."

I thought, Write more speeches for you? Dear God, write rhapsodies about your impossible "Civilisation of Love"?

I answered, "I shall be honoured, Most Holy Father, to remain, at your side, in R-Rome."

Those eyes.

They were too wise, and they stared directly to my mocking thought. He asked, "Monseigneur has reservations?"

I thought, *Tell him the truth.*

"About ... your philosophy, Holiness? It is wonderful to tell the world that we shall create a Civilisation of Love. To such a lofty end, we might do better if we created one right here in the Vatican."

The Pope sighed. "Must I remind you, Monseigneur, that I worked for two decades in the Roman Curia?"

"Then Your Holiness knows more keenly than I ever could that we might as well be living in Byzantium, or in some sealed palace of the Sublime Porte where inconvenient little princes were strangled in the darkness. I never dreamed, before I came to Rome, that the See of Saint Peter could be so virulent with gossip, envy, intrigue, treachery, and vengeance. I must confess to Your Holiness that I have dabbled in those black arts myself—simply to survive. Moreover—"

The Pontiff raised his ringed hand to silence me. "I know, I know. *Assez, assez.* ..."

"The exile of Don Giulio to that fraudulent shrine in the hills of Sicily is but the latest scandal of the Holy See's ingratitude. I disliked the man—he had his faults—but he was fanatically devoted to your saintly predecessor, and he deserved better."

The Pope apologised: "My own secretary suffers sometimes from an excess of zeal. I learned of the arrangement too late."

"It is, may I suggest, a matter of reversing entrenched practice? Your predecessor wished to—all popes wish to—but the system never changes. Has it occurred to Don Gianni that Don Giulio's fate awaits him—when Your Holiness is dead?"

"But all such abuse, *cher Monseigneur,* will vanish—evangelical charity will reign—once we complete our holy Council!"

I bit my tongue. The Pontiff read my disbelief, so he changed the subject. He asked, "Who is Monsieur Nort-vood?"

Ah, thought I, in his famous efficiency the Pope has read my dossier. I replied, as blandly as I could, "A rich American industrialist, Holy Father, a devout Christian, a Knight Commander of Pius Ninth at the hands of your holy predecessor."

"Cardinal Sostituto thinks he's shady [*louche*]."

"The misgivings of His Eminence lack the s-slightest evidence. If I knew them to be true, I should never have accepted Monsieur Northwood's money in the first place. The, ah, one hundred th-thousand dollars I contributed to the charities of Your Holiness at Milan came from Monsieur Northwood."

"And . . . his account in Geneva?"

"The account at the Crédit Suisse is numbered. In the Crédit's secret files, no name is mentioned, only 'His Holiness the Pope.' Since you now hold the Office, we can—if it is your wish—go on using the account at high rates of interest."

"What is Your Grace's advice?"

"Keep the account."

"*Bien,*" decided the Sovereign Pontiff. "Continue your visits to Geneva. Apart from Monsieur Nort-vood's deposits to the account, in what sort of quantity did my predecessor receive contributions from Christians throughout the world?"

"Your Holiness," I said enthusiastically, "the money gushed in."

The Pope seemed troubled. "Will it gush in for me? We desperately need money for the poor—and to finance the Council. The costs of the Council are . . . embarrassing? Do I have the charism of my predecessor? The world press said that at my coronation I seemed sad. Did I look sad to you, Monseigneur?"

"You might have smiled more often, Most Holy Father," I answered with half a laugh, to disguise my reproach.

The Pontiff smiled meekly in response, then moved again with raised hands toward baby Mahmoud in Fatima's embrace. The child whimpered and recoiled.

"Do I need practice?" the Pope mused. "On the other hand . . ."

✥

✥

TWENTY-NINE

In late September of 1963, the Second Vatican Council reconvened. How dimly did I, the Pope, the cardinals, or any Christian of the world foresee that in its complexity—its turbulence, the breadth of its ambition—the Council would adjourn and reconvene again, and then again, not ending finally until two years thereafter? I observed the battles with growing alarm as more and more—from conviction as well as from my hunger for a cardinal's hat—I warmed to the camp of Roman tradition.

The progressives of the Council yearned to shatter the traditions of latter centuries and to restore the Church to the supposed practices of early Christianity. The conservatives were fanatically zealous to preserve the Church defined by the Baroque pontiffs. In such tension the Council Fathers debated a Constitution of the Church on the floor and rostrum in the grandeur of St Peter's. They did so, not in the exuberant mood of the Sunny Pope, but in the sombre shadow—hesitant, cautious, indecisive—of the Sad Pope. *Sì, ma . . . oui, mais . . .* yes, but. The progressive bishops wanted a collegial Church sharing power with the Roman Pontiff. The Roman Pontiff wanted a collegial Church even as he clung to his kingly papacy.

The conservative cardinals and bishops were most unhappy with the draft Constitution, specially that it so poorly pictured the last ends of our human journey—death, judgement, Heaven, or Hell. Why, they complained, Purgatory was scarcely mentioned! And where was the rightful condemnation of souls who die in mortal sin? It was the clear duty of the Council to remind modern man that sin, Hell, and Satan do indeed exist—and eternal damnation for unrepentant sinners.

A Dutch bishop rose to ask, "Must you in the minority forever harp on mortal sin, Satan, Hell, and eternal damnation? None of us has the slightest proof that a single human soul burns in Hell. The new Constitution of the Church liberates us from your hoary Scholasticism, inspires us to joy as the People of God, conveys to us the mystery of the Church in the language of the Scriptures which suffering men—and women—can understand."

Cardinal Baluardo sprang up to give the Dutchman a piece of his mind, but the Pro-Prefect of the Holy Office was barely clearing his throat, heaping even more fervent scorn upon the draft Declaration on Religious Liberty. "The Declaration is badly named," protested His Eminence. "It should refer only to 'Religious Tolerance,' because those who revel in error have no rights. The Declaration, moreover, smells of subjectivism and—worse—theological indifferentism."

How broadly he smiled and chuckled; how palpably he enjoyed the consternation rippling through the basilica. "Since ours is the one true Church, it should be supported by all governments. No, venerable brothers, I do not propose that our true religion should be forced on anyone, but can a single bishop in this basilica deny Christ's promise that only the Catholic Church shall prevail till the very consummation of the world? Can any of you deny that for centuries and centuries—until this present Council—such has been the doctrine of the Roman Church?"

Cardinal Archbishop of Chicago: "We insist on more than tolerance, dear Eminence, we insist on liberty."

Cardinal Baluardo: "Ah! See? You avoid my question."

Cardinal of Chicago: "Eminence, if the act of faith is freely made—and you seem to agree it should be—then in the world as it has become, only freedom can advance the apostolate of Christ. No longer can the Faith be spread by crusaders' swords! Unless we clearly proclaim religious liberty as absolute, how can we claim the Church's rights under totalitarian tyrannies?"

Cardinal Baluardo: "Your Eminence sadly fails to draw the suitable distinctions between freedom of conscience in the singular and freedom of conscience in the plural. In the singular, may I insist, such freedom breeds subjectivism, solipsism, and indifferentism—the plague of modern souls. In the plural, applied to modern society in general and to tyranny in particular, freedom of consciences can serve Holy Church as a palatable expedient."

Cardinal of Chicago: "Eminence, you split unearthly theological hairs—ever your genius."

Cardinal Baluardo: "The highest compliment ever paid to me—for which I most humbly thank Your Eminence."

Cardinal of Chicago: "Man has a natural right to follow his conscience."

Cardinal Baluardo: "A Catholic has a natural *duty* to follow his conscience—provided his conscience is informed by the Magisterium of the Church."

Further disputations followed about the draft Declaration on the Jews. Numerous bishops and cardinals heatedly abhorred any lingering notion in the Roman Church that the Jewish people were guilty of deicide.

"I heartily agree," responded Cardinal Baluardo. "The charge of 'deicide' is absurd because nobody can kill God. As for Holy Church's goodwill toward the Jewish people, many Catholics—this meek Christian among them—saved Jews from the scourge of Hitler. However . . . even as we purge 'deicide' from the vocabulary of Christians, we have the right to demand reciprocal concessions from Jews—not least that Jews should purge their anti-Christian paranoia and certain anti-Christian passages from the Talmud. As Christians love Jews, so Jews must love Christians. . . ."

While the quarrels waxed, often I conferred with the Sad Pope—tendering advice, drafting allocutions, mediating in the papal library between bumptious cardinals, conservative and progressive. I became ever more conspicuous in the Council. The Pope used me to run errands on the floor of the basilica, to hasten back and forth between intractable parties with secret pontifical messages that strained to reconcile the irreconcilable.

Whenever I appeared in St Peter's, I was approached by clusters of cardinals and other prelates thirsty for word of the Pope's thinking, since nobody knew what the Pope thought. I asked myself, Do I know what the Pope thinks? Does the Pope know?

One sunny autumn afternoon, as I sat in my storeroom office doing the Pope's work, the Vatican police rang; a Rabbi Ashkenazi was at St Anne's Gate, seeking an audience. I pondered and replied, "Tell a Swiss Guard to escort the rabbi to Raphael's Loggia—the far end, beneath the bust."

My eye darted to an open closet, where my claret toga hung ever. As I flung it on over my soutane of black and purple, I thought, Not so fast: *keep the rabbi waiting.*

Eventually when I descended the marble stairway to the Raphael gallery and approached the bust theatrically in my toga, I was surprised by the visitor I found. There, cooling his heels—amid the radiance of the bays and pavilion vaults, the arabesques and mouldings, the frescoes of the Old Testament—was a tall Jew of Aryan good looks: his hair so blond, his nose so straight, his eyes so very blue. He wore a turtleneck sweater coloured beige beneath smart grey tweeds.

In deference to the rabbi's creed, I did not extend my ring to be kissed, but merely shook my visitor's hand. The rabbi bowed to the Archbishop.

The Archbishop bowed to the rabbi. We spoke in English throughout. "Rabbi?" I began. "Forgive me—I forget your name."

"Ashkenazi, Your Grace."

"Remarkable. You bear the noble name of an entire tribe."

"The Ashkenazim were more a whole people—a nation, if you will, before the creation of Israel."

"Are your family from Poland?"

"Byelorussia. However, that was long ago. I am a sabra, born in the earth of Israel."

"Or Palestine—before the creation of your state? What can I do for you, Rabbi Ashkenazi?" Against my better wish, I began to finger the contours of my pectoral cross, provoking quizzical glances from my guest.

"I represent the Jewish Agency in Rome," the rabbi said. "We are worried about the Council's decisions on the Jews."

"The Declaration is being revised."

"We hear that it is being watered down."

"Hardly, Rabbi. It may be included in a Declaration on other non-Christian cults."

"You mean Islam?"

"Islam, Hinduism, Buddhism. . . ."

"We Jews will be disappointed—may I say offended?—unless we are treated in a separate document disavowing the charge of 'deicide' and condemning Catholic anti-Semitism, past and present."

"His Holiness the Pope—the entire Church—deplore anti-Semitism. I shall mention your visit to the Holy Father. Beyond that, I can do nothing."

"But you have influence on His Holiness—so I've been informed."

"The Council Fathers will decide the disposition of the Declaration. I have no power."

"We have heard otherwise. Besides . . ."

"Besides . . . ?"

We paced beneath the tableaux of the Old Testament, my purple toga flowing as I strode. The rabbi glanced up to the tableaux. God creates Man. Adam and Eve are expelled from the Garden of Eden. Moses receives the Ten Commandments. Joseph interprets the Pharaoh's dream. The rabbi answered, "We had hoped for a greater sympathy from Your Grace. May I ask a personal question?"

"I'd rather you should n-not."

"Are you a Jew?"

"Is that some titbit from M-Mossad?"

"I do not work for Israeli intelligence. Your Grace's Jewishness is common knowledge."

"Where?"

"In Rome."

"Do you mean in Vatican gossip? My father was of the recusant Catholic English nobility. My mother may have had J-Jewish ancestors, but she

denied it. Were indeed she Jewish, then privately I rejoice that in my
unworthy flesh the Old and New Covenants c-converge. As for influencing
the Roman Pontiff, dear Rabbi, my genealogy is none of your b-business."

"I'm sorry."

"You should be. As a youth, in Vichy France, I helped to save the lives of
Jews. Privately also, I favour a separate Declaration on the Jews, and a
vigourous condemnation of anti-Semitism. However, we are troubled by
political complications."

"You mean that the Arabs hate it."

"The Holy Father is deeply perplexed about the effect of the Declaration
upon Christian Arabs in the Middle East. The creation of Israel caused grave
injustice to the Palestinians. Well, after all, you did expel the Palestinians
from their own ancestral soil. There is, moreover, the problem of
Jerusalem."

"Jerusalem, Your Grace, is the eternal capital of Israel."

"Jerusalem, Rabbi Ashkenazi, must be internationalised."

"The straight Vatican line!"

"I serve the Vatican!"

Our raised voices echoed through the loggia—though may I say without
rancour? I wondered, Is this a brothers' quarrel? On the way out, I deigned
to call the rabbi's attention to glorious details of the Old Testament by
Romano, da Udine, and Polidoro da Caravaggio. God creates Man. Adam
and Eve are expelled from Eden. Moses receives the Ten Commandments.
Joseph interprets the Pharaoh's dream.

Next day, the Israeli press reported that Rabbi Ashkenazi had been
rebuffed in Rome by "an arrogant Vatican bureaucrat."

The Council continued to deliberate, grappling with definitions of
the Church's posture toward the modern world. The Cardinal Archbishop
of Westminster complained bitterly that since the beginning of the Council,
Catholics throughout the United Kingdom were desperately confused,
asking again and yet again, *"What is now the teaching of the Church? What
are we in the Faith now bound to believe?"*

"And may I say," Westminster continued, "that I am quite fed up with
some of the brilliant theologians in this Council? They care nothing for the
teaching authority of the bishops—or even for the Magisterium of the popes.
It is useless to point to a papal encyclical in which Christian doctrine is
stated clearly. They sneer that a pope's encyclical is not infallible."

"But it's not!" rose random cries from the basilica.

"May I hasten to examples?" asked Westminster. "We all of us know that
scientists are busy producing a contraceptive pill. The draft declaration
before us states that Christian married couples should decide for themselves
what is right or wrong, adding murkily that they must act 'according to the
teaching of the Church.' What does *that* mean? The document is as clear as
mud! This Council is sowing devilish confusion amongst the faithful!"

The Holy Office rose to cheer Westminster. "In the section as it is written," said Cardinal Baluardo, "I see Satan's hand. The papal encyclical on sacred marriage, *Casti Conubii*, written but thirty years ago, declared for eternity that contraception by artificial means is a mortal sin."

Assorted cries from the basilica: "But no encyclical is infallible! The discoveries of science and psychology . . . !"

Cardinal Baluardo: "If the primacy of private conscience becomes the norm, if a contraceptive pill is ever accepted by the Holy Roman Church, then all too soon in 'holy liberty' we shall have Catholics who demand that we bless abortion."

Cries from the basilica: "Absurd . . . ! Unthinkable . . . ! Preposterous . . . !"

"I beg you, brothers," implored Cardinal Baluardo, "to desist in questioning the established teaching of the Church—rooted infallibly in Natural Law and Sacred Scripture—on Holy Matrimony. Can the Church have erred for so many centuries? Is this Council to contradict the Magisterium of the popes?"

At that moment, I sat in the apartments of the Pontiff, watching his private television circuit with him, as engrossed by the debate as he was. In French His Holiness said, "This is becoming unseemly [*peu convenable*]. What on earth should I do?"

"You should intervene, *Saintissime Père,*" said I.

"How, Augustin?"

I meditated, deciding presently on the oldest stratagem of diplomacy—that we should play for time. I answered, "Why not remove the question of birth control from the Council's agenda altogether? Your Holiness could appoint a commission of experts to study every moral and medical nuance of the problem. . . ."

"Should We do that . . . ?"

"If I may cite your saintly predecessor, 'The Pope can do whatever he may please.' "

The Sad Pope paused, reflecting, clearly torn between the intellectual pleasure he derived from the conciliar debates and his sublime rôle as Supreme Pontiff. At length he fixed his black eyes on mine and said, "Go down to the basilica, *cher Augustin,* and inform the Fathers of Our resolve to appoint a commission of experts—and to reserve all matters of conjugal morality to Our own final judgement."

I hurried from the Pope's presence. When the Council Fathers saw me emerge in full purple from the side of the sanctuary and then mount the rostrum of St Peter's, requesting of the presiding cardinal immediate leave to speak, they reacted with an uproar—sensing that something of moment was about to happen; some cheering, others releasing groans of dismay. I thought, Now—at last—I shall address the Council. Thank God I waited! What better might I do than make a *coup de théâtre*?

"Venerable brothers, Fathers of the Council," I declared in robust Latin, "I arrive with a command from His Holiness the Pope. The Holy Father is reserving to himself the vexatious question of birth control. He shall appoint a commission of experts to study the matter, and then, in his and in God's good hour, he shall inform you of his deliberations and of his own— irrevocable—c-conclusion."

The papal edict pleased some Fathers, angered many of the others. As the debates on the Church in the Modern World resumed, there followed further demands from progressive bishops that the Church must remove all compulsion from her laws of observance hitherto imposed under pain of sin. "How," asked a bishop of the Indies, "can Christian men and women of the modern world believe that God is good—if we continue to teach them that for eating meat on Friday they shall go to Hell? And will any Catholic truly incur damnation if he takes a drop of water before he takes Communion? Where, venerable brothers, is the proportion between such niggling precepts and the Ten Commandments? Henceforth no mere precept should be imposed under pain of mortal sin. Religion is not fear but love."

Cardinal Baluardo rose to rebut him: "Religion, dear Excellency, is both. Once we remove coercion, Catholics will leave the Church—and abandon her morality—in multitudes."

I mounted the rostrum to rebut Cardinal Baluardo: "May I beg to differ with Your Eminence of the Holy Office? Mother Church should never coerce her children. However . . . I should agree with Your Eminence that if we remove all rules of *obligation,* then defections from the practices of Mother Church will be colossal."

Cardinal Baluardo replied from the floor: "I thank Your Grace for his lovely distinction. 'Coercion' in the temper of our time is too strong a term, and humbly I retract it. 'Obligation' serves, and without obligation the authority of the Church will fall apart."

A Brazilian archbishop then shouted out, "I demand that we define 'the Church of the Poor.' Is it not high time that Holy Church descend from her mighty thrones and showy pomp? We bishops and cardinals are weighted down with silk and jewels, violet and crimson, and for the love of the poor we should throw them in the garbage, evacuate our palaces, live in shacks if need be, and minister to our people in simple black."

From my place on the floor of Nervan marble I replied with vehemence: "What on earth is Your Grace proposing? The splendid dress of prelates adds to the awe and lustre of the Church. More, to the *theatre* of the Church! The poor—above all of the faithful—take delight in the golden altars, the glorious music, the crimson of our cardinals, the ceremony and gracious beauty, as a balm for their dreadful sorrows. Why, if we had your way, we prelates should all of us dress as threadbare Quakers or bleak Calvinist divines in the Shetland Islands. Should the Roman Church turn Protestant—is that what you want?"

A Dutch bishop: "Enough of this nonsense about showy pomp and the Shetland Islands. The Council ought to consider relaxing the rules of ecclesiastical celibacy."

I mounted the rostrum with another mandate in my pocket from the Pope—entrusted to me without my prompting, so militant was he on that matter. "Venerable brothers," I asked the Council, "did I fail to inform you? I bear another announcement from the Sovereign Pontiff. He is reserving to himself all decisions on the law of ecclesiastical celibacy."

But although the Pontiff at his leisure would pronounce upon celibacy and birth control, the Second Vatican Council changed the Church much.

When at last it concluded in 1965—in a Mass on the steps of St Peter's, under a sad December sky—the Council had reformed the liturgy; proclaimed the Constitution of the Church; defined the collegial powers of the bishops; set up episcopal synods to consult with the Pope; and endorsed religious liberty. The Declaration on the Jews was implanted in a broader document proclaiming love as well for Muslims, Hindus, and Buddhists, but vigourously it denounced anti-Semitism and dismissed as repugnant the ancient libel that the Jewish people—at the hour of the Crucifixion and for all time thereafter—shared collective guilt for the death of Christ.

Throughout the Council, I had found my work for the Pope ever more maddening. My pen, as ever facile, enabled me to write a lengthy allocution for the Pontiff in a single sitting—in Latin, Italian, or French, interpolating faithfully from remembrance whatever verse I might need from Scripture. But when I submitted the text to my master, often it was returned to me smeared in the cramped papal hand with so many deletions, insertions, and marginal quibblings that I did well to unsnarl them. Then mischievously I delayed delivery of his texts until the last moment, when the Pope would have no time to change them. Can you hear my telephone ringing? It is Don Gianni, the (now) imperious secretary. "The Lutheran delegation is in the antechamber. *Where* is the Pope's speech?"

"*Io vèngo, Don Gianni!*"

I tried also—with variable success—to manipulate the Pope on other matters. On the one hand . . . the Holy Father believed deeply in the collegial power of bishops and that he should share with them the government of the Church. On the other hand . . . now that he was Pope, he became obsessed with the dignity and primacy of his Office. In the late afternoons, when the Council had adjourned for the day and we chatted in the papal library—refurbished with modern gouache paintings and those many glass eggs—I played chords upon the Pontiff's mixed emotions.

"Your Holiness," I suggested casually, "are you quite sure you're satisfied with the text on the bishops as it stands?"

"Why should I not be, Augustin?" the Pope asked in French.

"It seems to me ambiguous," said I. "Collegiality is all well and good, but the declaration lacks insistence that any consensus of the bishops must be subordinate to the assent and supremacy of the Pope."

"I have been rereading the ancient Church Fathers," the Pope replied, "and they tend to agree with you. So, of course, does Cardinal Baluardo."

"Might we add a paragraph or two—at your command—emphasising papal supremacy?"

"Will you draft them?"

"Tonight, Holiness."

The interpolations displeased the progressive bishops, who accepted them with ill grace. Yet the disquiet of the progressives was serene compared to the dread of the conservatives.

On a November morning in the Hall of the Consistory, I attended an audience between the Pope and the bishops of Poland. As a youthful papal diplomat, the Pontiff had served in Warsaw, but the winter was too chill for his frail body, his mission was aborted, and he learned no Polish. Thus the dialogue in the Hall of the Consistory was conducted in an amusing mixture of Latin and Italian. The Cardinal Archbishop of Warsaw, Primate of Poland—tall statue of a prince, with a face chiselled (it looked) of rock, the more sharply for his years in a Communist penitentiary—spoke for his brother bishops.

"We can not understand the need for this Council," the Cardinal Primate told the Pope.

"We are prayerful that in Poland the decrees of the Council will be applied with zeal," the Sovereign Pontiff replied coolly.

"With something less than zeal," the Primate riposted.

"But the decrees of the Council are universal."

"We beseech Your Holiness to understand the terrible conditions of our nation in its chains and thorns. In Poland, the Communists have reduced us to the Church of Silence. In Rome, we have encountered the Church of the Deaf."

"The *Pope* hears you."

"Yet few cardinals and bishops seem to care that the ancient Faith we have always known nourishes the Polish people in their enslavement. Popular devotions, mass processions, pilgrimages to shrines, the liturgy in Latin, veneration of the Holy Virgin, the mysteries of the Rosary—they are our daily bread. Here in Rome, cosmopolitan bishops and fashionable theologians laugh at us, insisting that all of this must change, that the 'People of God' must converse with the pagan world in an ecumenical salon. There is no such salon in Poland, Holiness, and we don't want one. In Warsaw, we hear too much of 'Scientific Socialism.' In Rome, we hear too much of 'Scientific Christianity.' We Polish bishops warn Your Holiness, the Church Universal is embarked upon a dangerous adventure."

The final embrace of the Primate and the Pope was as chilly as Warsaw's winter he had fled.

Walking back with me to his apartments, the Pontiff asked, "Do you see,

Augustin? I can satisfy no one. I am assailed on all sides. Equally I am like a hermit on a barren mountain, suffering the vertigo of solitude. Like Christ, I am alone on my cross, crying *'Eloi, Eloi, lama sabachthani?'* My solitude will grow. I fear not. My destiny as Pope is to suffer alone—save with the Lord as my companion! [*Mon destin comme pape c'est de souffrir seul—sauf avec le Seigneur comme mon compagnon!*] How are your children?"

"Kamal had another savage argument with his father—they came to blows!—and he has left home, Holiness. I've still six children in the house—and Maha expects another."

"Mais, c'est merveilleux."

"Is it, Holiness? The Council expressed concern for the population explosion. In my own rooms, I have a population explosion."

"Do no Muslims practice the rhythm method?"

"Ha! Blasphemous!"

"And how is little Mahmoud?"

"Happy, Holy Father. Starting his Islamic school. He'll love you yet."

"I pray so, *cher Augustin.* Your Joseph Conrad wrote that 'Fear always prevails'—but he was wrong. Love always prevails."

I rather had my doubts. Beneath the eternal frescoes as we strode, the Pontiff continued his rumination: ". . . Popes die, councils pass, the Roman Curia remains. Here comes His Eminence Baluardo. He's been hounding me to death."

"Hounding you, Most Holy Father?"

"To create you a cardinal."

✜

THIRTY

✜

Yet the toga of the "Sacred Purple"—the princely crimson of the cardinalate—did not fall upon my shoulders promptly. For two years, I had to fight for it.

I wished to become a prince before I turned forty. Still the youngest archbishop in the Church, I craved to be the youngest cardinal. Early in our century, St Pius X created Monsignore Rafael Merry del Val his Cardinal Secretary of State when Merry del Val had just turned thirty-eight; otherwise one had to thrash in the vapours of the eighteenth century, before the French Revolution, to find a Prince of the Church in his boyish thirties.

I brooded often on the career and life of Rafael Merry del Val, another of my lordly models who had suffered the same sort of confused identity that afflicted me.

A marquis of Spain, he had been born in London, where his father was First Secretary of the Spanish legation; he was educated in élite public schools, making English his first language and turning him into more of a Briton than a Spaniard. Destined by his family for the Church, not yet twenty, Rafael was then packed off to Rome, where he pursued his sacred studies—as I would do—at the Pontifical Academy of Noble Ecclesiastics.

Leo XIII took to him instantly, recognising his gifted mind, advancing him rapidly in the papal household and diplomacy of the Church, creating him Archbishop Titular of Nicaea when he was but thirty-four—the very age that I should be when the Sunny Pope raised me to the See of Trebizond. The resemblance between the two of us did not cease in the youthful haste of our careers—or in that terrifying question, "Who am I?"

Merry del Val was a champion swimmer, a dauntless horseman, and so skilled at marksmanship he could hit a penny at thirty paces. He was also, it must be said, the aristocrat *par excellence,* reserved unto coldness, or even (thought his enemies) unto arrogance. Tall and exceptionally handsome, with lush eyebrows, a classical profile, dark hair turning to silver, he attracted women madly; yet I have every reason to suppose that throughout his life he obeyed the rules, kept his vows, and remained chaste. Honeyed of speech, witty when he wished to be, he was as well rich and generous; like the later cardinals Baluardo and Sostituto (whom he inspired) he devoted much of his leisure to the care of street orphans.

As Secretary of the Conclave of 1903, Monsignore Merry del Val became a crucial actor in the election of Leo XIII's successor. Cardinal Rampolla, Leo XIII's Secretary of State, was nearly elected Pope, but at the last moment—invoking an ancient privilege (the royal "Exclusive") still enjoyed by the Catholic sovereigns—his papacy was vetoed by an Austrian cardinal at the (prearranged) command of the Hapsburg Emperor, Franz Josef. Appalled but obedient, the Sacred College turned from the diplomatist to the peasant, the seraphic Cardinal Sarto, Patriarch of Venice, he of the lovely smile tinged with sadness.

Cardinal Sarto recoiled from the papacy, or so it much appeared. With his election certain, he fled to the Pauline Chapel—beneath Michelangelo's frescoes of St Peter crucified upside down and St Paul on the road to Damascus blinded by the light of Christ—where he knelt before the tabernacle, his face buried in his hands, weeping and praying, "O my Father, if it be possible, let this chalice pass from me. . . ." The marvel of this performance—little different from the ceremonial choreography expected of all imminent pontiffs—was (I am convinced) sincerity. Cardinal Sarto *was* humble. Indeed he held himself *unworthy.* He did not *want* the job. Monsignore Merry del Val approached the sobbing figure, placed a hand upon his shoulder, and said, *"Coraggio, Eminenza."* Then he completed the choreographic metaphors, "The cup which thy Father hath given thee, shalt thou not drink it? Come, take up thy cross."

As Pope, Pius X was so bewitched by Monsignore Merry del Val's urbanity that within weeks of the election he created him Cardinal Secretary. Religion, the Pope reserved to himself. Politics, he thrust on His Eminence. The Cardinal's diplomacy—pro-Hapsburg today, pro-French upon the morrow—aspired to prevent war between the powers, and we know that he failed. Moreover, His Eminence encouraged the Pope in his crusade against the Modernists, not seeming to care that the great world considered him an obscurantist as well. Or did he care? Did he care for his identity? Did he suffer my kind of torment for his diffuse identity? Was he Spanish? English?

Italian? More Roman than the Romans? He said, simply, proudly, arrogantly—as St Paul had done and as I should do—"*Civis Romanus sum.*"

No doubt His Eminence longed to succeed Pius X on St Peter's throne as the Great War began, but still he was too young, with too many enemies in the Sacred College. After the Great War, in the next Conclave, his turn came again, and again he lost. Since the death of Pius X, he was shunted to honorific posts, admired but disused. As he aged, he yearned to share the Passion of Christ. When he died in 1930, it was found that beneath his watered silk he wore a hair shirt; among his meagre things was discovered a monastic scourge, caked with fragments of his bloody flesh.

Who was he? What was he? His reserve, his coldness unto arrogance notwithstanding, at the zenith of his power—like Cardinal Consalvi a century before—His Eminence Merry del Val would see anybody. Each afternoon, he opened his palace to all comers—cardinals and ambassadors; scullery maids and chimney sweeps—striding through the crowd in his brilliant scarlet, offering his ring to be kissed, receiving written petitions, passing those scraps of paper to his train of secretaries, handing out money, listening, laughing mechanically ha-ha-ha, ever genial, ever distant.

He remained a legend in the Roman Curia. Everyone remarked on the resemblances: throughout the Vatican it was said that I was the new Merry del Val, the new Ercole Consalvi, or—according to my enemies—a reincarnation of all those young and cunning prelates of the Enlightenment.

The Church of Rome, as I have told you, has ever been obsessed with precedent. For my young cardinalate, I had a precedent in our own century: Merry del Val. In my private chapel, I prayed to him aloud: "At the Vatican, envy and complication encircle me—but I shall b-become you."

Cardinal Baluardo was not simply fond of me: he saw me as—one day—his natural successor and the scourge of heretics at the Holy Office. Monsignore Samosata (he of "The Use of the Ablative Absolute in Papal Rescript Clauses"), now aged nearly sixty, coveted that labour of Grand Inquisitor and the crimson toga for himself. Don Gianni, nearly fifty and though papal secretary still wearing a black soutane without purple buttons, was bitterly aghast at any hint that I might be elevated to the Sacred College. His Eminence Sostituto opposed my cardinalate on principle. "Galsworthy's gold," he nagged the Pope. "The ethics of his money, Most Holy Father? Must we stumble on in darkness?"

Even the Pontiff, in his Christian way, seemed mildly jealous of me. *He* had toiled as only a Domestic Prelate until nearly the age of sixty and his archbishopric at Milan; thereafter he waited four years more to wear the Red Hat. He asked me, "*Cher Augustin,* why do you want this so?" I did not answer. Face-to-face, I never pressed him for my cardinalate.

I schemed.

. . .

But will you believe me when I protest that I was as troubled as Cardinal Sostituto by Urban Northwood's money?

My dreams at night grew worse. Sorrowing that the Cardinal Secretary's suspicion of Urban's trafficking in arms might indeed be true, I was visited on my bed of wooden slats by fantasies of towns and hamlets in East Asia, in Araby, in the depths of Africa, ravaged by napalm bombs, phosphorus bombs, and fragmentation missiles. I saw hordes of helpless women and tiny naked children fleeing from their huts as aircraft strafed them, setting them ablaze.

I saw soldiers and old men turned by phosphorus into charcoal statues. I saw the flesh of infants embedded with shards of bombs which festered there for days and weeks, then at last exploded. I saw the crimson radiance of chemical and bacterial rockets, like the Biblical plague of locusts descending with their malice upon migrating populations.

Awake, I remembered that the Vatican Council had denounced the world arms race, "threatening peace, harmony, and confidence between peoples; diminishing human betterment; dissipating the wealth of nations; endangering the lives of multitudes."

I had drafted that paragraph.

Even as I intrigued to manipulate the Roman Curia—and thus the Pope, by indirection—to win my cardinalate, I became a student of the arms race, not least to assuage my conscience lest indeed had Urban Northwood made his fortune in guns and bombs. I read much about warplanes—French Mirages, British Hawker-Hunters, American Phantoms, Soviet MiGs. I learned about ballistics; tanks, mortars, and machine guns; air-to-air missiles that released profuse steel rods, lethal within their wide scope to human bodies and even to tomato plants; ground-to-ground missiles that liberated cluster bomblets gorged with myriad nails and fléchettes, described by bland bureaucracies as "anti-personnel," yet murdering not only troops but babes and mothers.

To comfort my imagined guilt, I became the Holy See's expert on the global arms traffic. I urged the Pope to share my interest. He authorised me to write burning allocutions condemning all such commerce, which then with only minor quibblings he delivered in St Peter's or from the window of his library to crowds assembled in the piazza for his Sunday blessing. For his signature, and Cardinal Sostituto's, I drafted indignant protests to the governments of the United States, the Soviet Union, France, and Britain, the most egregious of the traffickers among mighty nations.

We were answered with pious reassurances as the governments increased their traffic.

As for the private enterpreneurs—those faceless, free-lance "merchants of death" growing ever more grotesquely rich from guns and bombs in dollars, Deutschemarks, pounds sterling—what little could I do but pray that they should read in the newspapers of the Pope's displeasure, pause, desist, and repent their sins?

Of a June morning, Urban and Diana Northwood without forewarning showed up in Rome—staying on this occasion not at Doria-Pamphili palace but in the Royal Suite of the Albergo Hassler above the summit of the Spanish steps. On a pretext I declined their invitation to dinner, but later in the evening I went to the Hassler to take coffee with them amongst their rooms of red damask, gilded armchairs and blazing chandeliers, busts of Roman emperors and Barberini cardinals, a Gobelin tapestry of Versailles in snow.

Diana (silently embarrassed still, it seemed to me, by our abortive adventure in her maze hedge years before) did not linger over her *demitasse,* but soon retired to her study to continue writing her biography of Lucrezia Borgia—leaving me alone with her husband. Presently I spoke my mind.

I said, "Urban, questions have been raised in the Apostolic Palace about the provenance of your generosity. Would you kindly enlighten me?"

"What do you mean?" he asked genially, as he dropped a pair of white tablets into his black coffee.

"His Eminence the Cardinal Secretary is distressed by certain rumours that you may be an arms merchant."

"*Ha!* I've heard such rumours—inspired, I have no doubt, by my mischievous competitors in business."

"Then you deny that you sell or barter guns or bombs—all that sort of horror?"

"Absolutely. Give me your cross."

I removed my pectoral cross: Urban grasped and kissed it, swearing, "On Christ—without mental reservation."

"Forgive me still," I persisted. "Then how have you made your vast fortune?"

"Pencils in Budapest. Creative finance. Farm machinery."

"In Prague and Budapest?"

"I do not go to Eastern Europe all that often—as my attorney told Cardinal Sostituto's agent in New York."

"Ah, you heard of that luncheon?"

"My Mr Burner III called me five minutes later. Well . . . for God's sake, I pay him . . . ONE THOUSAND DOLLARS AN HOUR!"

Even before Urban's outburst, our voices had been raised. Diana appeared from her private room, still gripping a fountain pen, her reading spectacles dangling from a blue cord over her necklace of grey pearls. Visibly upset, as though indeed she had never heard before her husband's name connected to trafficking in guns and bombs, she said, "I will not allow Your Grace to interrogate my husband."

"I wasn't *interrogating* him, D-Diana."

"You impugned his honour. Since I'm married to Urban and bear his children, I know him better than you or Cardinal Sostituto ever could. His character is beyond reproach. As for his charity, not only the Holy See but people poor and destitute the world over have been touched by his benevolence. Your Grace should go back to the Vatican and tell the Cardinal Secretary that if Urban's benefactions are not welcome—"

"Enough, darling," Urban interrupted pleasantly, but by the vibrato of his voice making it all too clear that I would learn nothing more from him of the sources of his wealth. As he had at Northwood Hall, suddenly he gripped his legs in pain, yet he seemed to recover quickly no sooner had he plopped more tablets into his *demitasse* and sipped the coffee. Again he kissed my pectoral cross, swore "On Christ" upon it, and handed it back to me entangled in its golden chain.

His gesture calmed the three of us. Diana, more serene, retired again to her study. Though still my conscience was uncertain, I deeply wanted to believe in Urban's oath. I changed the subject, reverting to my native vanity and intimating subtly that I could expect the cardinalate.

Brazenly, Urban responded that when I wore the Sacred Purple, he would endow me with a million dollars for my good works, but—alas!—he did not stop talking. No longer was he satisfied to be a Knight Commander of Pius IX. He wished to be a papal duke, and Diana should be a papal duchess, and his child Adrian a papal marquis. As hitherto his voice grew cloudy, suggesting that his tablets contained a potent drug, but by foggy hints he made it clear enough that unless his dukedom was conferred as I gained my cardinalate, I should despair of my endowment.

Urban dangled something even sweeter for the Church, though in such a misty, convoluted tone as to muddle the curse of simony. Before he came to Rome to accept his dukedom—and *of course* these marvels were unconnected—he would contribute three million dollars to the charities of the Pope in his account at the Crédit Suisse.

I left the Hassler upon the horns of a dilemma.

I badly needed money. I had nearly exhausted Urban's previous benefactions on art, rare books, the care and education of my Nubians, dinner parties (with string quartets) for cardinals of the Roman Curia, and immoderate gifts to charities.

The Pope's finances were embarrassed also. The Council had been costly, but to enforce the decrees of that assembly he had enlarged the bureaucracy of the Church—to such profusion that now ecclesiastics were bursting from their office buildings in the Via della Conciliazione before St Peter's and from the Palazzo San Calisto yonder in Trastevere as Roman prices soared. I had continued my visits to Geneva, to deposit at the Crédit Suisse the cheques and currency His Holiness received by air post or directly from the faithful. However, this Pope lacked the allure of his jolly predecessor. He seemed to the world so dour, so intellectual, so uninspiring, that the generosity of the faithful diminished quickly. He needed money more than I did.

Thus—and much against my better wish—I decided to sue for Urban Northwood's dukedom even as I grasped by means more hidden for my Red Hat. Indeed—the dukedom! The Sovereign Pontiff was appalled.

"Augustin," he protested in his library amongst glass eggs, "what on earth is in your head? I am about to abolish the papal nobility."

I all but swooned as the Pope shuffled through the heap of papers on his

blond desk, seeking a certain document. "Here it is," he said after some moments. "My *motu proprio* [personal decree]. I shall sign it today."

"Most Holy Father," I suggested earnestly, "could you reconsider your signature of that decree?"

"*Mais pourquoi donc?* The nobility is an embarrassment in the Church of the Poor. We might possibly retain an order or two of papal knights—but princes, dukes, and duchesses? All those white ruffles, embroidered cloaks, and tight pants? They're meaningless and silly."

"Won't you at least postpone your signature?"

"*Pourquoi?*"

"I'll explain tomorrow. I don't f-feel well."

"And you're suddenly so pale, *cher Augustin!* Do I work you too hard? *Bien.* We'll speak of this tomorrow. Go home to bed."

I genuflected, kissed the Pontiff's ring (a plain gold band!), and backed out of his presence. That night, in bed at the Borgo Angelico, I picked at my conscience. The Sad Pope was as overscrupulous as Pius VII. To avoid the odour of simony, I must: (1) rescue the papal nobility in the abstract; (2) convey to the Pontiff at another time Urban Northwood's offer of several million dollars; and (3) leave it to the Holy Father to meditate, pray, and ignore the coincidence.

All this I did, then waited in impatient suffering. After some months, the Pope sullenly consented to preserve the papal nobility—but only for a year or two. (Inwardly I laughed, loving that, touching my pectoral cross, giving thanks to Christ and deciding to hide from Urban that his dukedom would be brief.) I consulted a list of vacant titles, then debated them with the Pontiff.

"Something simple," said the Pope, glancing at the list. "Duke of Porta Santa Anna?"

"A bit too saintly, Holy Father? Here's one. Duke of Canino?"

"But Lucien Bonaparte held that title—as Prince of Canino."

"I do recall, Holiness, that Pius VII gave the title to Lucien for defying Napoleon. Lucien was a black sheep. So, in a way, is Monsieur Northwood."

"I shan't create your Monsieur Nort-vood a prince."

"Duke of Canino will do."

The dukedom settled, there remained my Red Hat. Cardinal Baluardo, whose health was failing with his eyesight, delivered a macabre ultimatum to the Pope: unless he acted soon, His Eminence of the Holy Office would be blind or dead before I joined him in the Sacred College. The Pope, sympathetic to his old acquaintance and grateful that in the Conclave he had allowed his papacy, dawdled still.

At his orphanage one evening, Cardinal Baluardo confessed that he had exhausted his devices. He said, "It's time for your devices, dear Agostino. Be frank with me." Throwing my fake humility to the winds, I told His Emi-

nence that the problem could be solved only by exploiting the Pontiff's bureaucratic passion.

I explained, "The Pope spent decades as a diplomatist. In his bones he feels that any human puzzle can be solved by compromise, by seeking satisfaction for every party, or—as we so crudely say in English—by splitting the difference. Absurd—but in this case . . ."

"How?" asked His Eminence Baluardo.

"Cardinal Sostituto is your closest friend. . . ."

"I've fought him savagely. He adamantly opposes you."

"So let him. However, you might prevail on the Cardinal Secretary to ask the Pope to raise Monsignore Samosata to the Sacred College—and to create Don Gianni an archbishop titular."

"But Don Gianni is a common priest!"

"Precisely. By hurtling him forthwith to an archbishopric, we might mollify his envy. Monsignore Samosata would not wish me as a brother cardinal, but if he had the Sacred Purple for himself we might deflate his pique. Then Your Eminence would take another step."

"With the Pope?"

"Dear God, no. When it comes to me, His Holiness considers you a broken record."

"*Grazie, Agostino!*"

"You told me to be frank. You would have a word again with Cardinal Sostituto. Tell him, 'All right. Continue to oppose Monsignore Galsworthy on principle, but henceforth make your opposition *pro forma.*' He might do that for you."

"And he might not."

"*Eminenza,* might not you try?"

Months passed as I despaired.

The mills of God grind slowly, but they are swift as they compete with the mills of the Holy See.

Suddenly, whispers swept the Apostolic Palace in windy tempests—as throughout the Roman Curia my proposed arrangements were rumoured to please the Pope.

In early autumn 1967, the Supreme Pontiff called me to his presence, embraced me warmly, and confided that he would create me a Cardinal of the Holy Roman Church.

I knelt to kiss his hand, but he drew me to my feet. He asked, "*Cher Augustin,* why on earth did I wait so long? Day and night, you've worked so hard for me. What would I do without you?"

I thought, The man is unbearably kind. I asked, "And the consistory, Holiness . . . ?"

"Just after Christmas—on the feast of the Holy Innocents."

"Might we not schedule the consistory a little earlier . . . perhaps on fourteenth December—feast of Saint John of the Cross?"

"Does it matter, Your . . . Eminence?"

Trembling with my new title, I thought, *Tell him the truth.* I answered, "I shall turn forty on Christmas Day, Most Holy Father. It would be so sweet—for eleven days—to be a cardinal in my th-th-thirties."

"Ah? . . . ah? . . . granted, granted. Feast of Saint John of the Cross." He kissed me, shyly. He said, "Youngest cardinal in the Roman Church. Oh, my!" He lifted his right hand with its simple ring, brushing my locks of black hair. He asked, "When will Your Eminence turn to silver?"

Soon, in all documents and letters, I would be entitled to be addressed:

His Eminence Sir Augustine Cardinal Galsworthy, Bart.
Archbishop Titular of Trebizond

This left out my titular church. All cardinals are required by tradition to possess a church in the Diocese of Rome. The Pope offered me a choice among the largest and most fashionable, but upon reflection I picked the charming little church of Santa Brigida—with its golden frescoes, blue haze, blue nuns—on the Piazza Farnese, facing the Embassy of France flying the *tricolore,* and just round the corner from the Venerable English College. Indeed, my choice was dictated by these symbols of my diffuse identity. Would I be an English cardinal? French? American? Jewish? I nearly mourned that the neighbourhood did not include the Embassy of the United States with a synagogue next door.

Thus:

His Eminence Sir Augustine Cardinal Galsworthy, Bart.
Of the Title of Saint Bridget
Cardinal Priest of the Holy Roman Church
Archbishop of Trebizond

The Pope had decreed, in the spirit of the Council, that the correspondents of cardinals need no longer conclude their letters with the lovely "Kissing the Sacred Purple." I resented this omission, though I found it less offensive than the havoc he had wrought on the regalia of the Sacred College.

Again in the mood of the Council, the Pontiff had blasphemously (I thought) chopped as though with hedge clippers at the sublime robes of cardinals. The mantelletta—that long, sleeveless outer robe I had worn so proudly over my lace rochet as a domestic prelate and archbishop—was suppressed. The cappa magna—the hooded, crimson cloak of state covering an Eminence entirely, surmounted by ermine in chilly winter, by watered silk in balmy summer, with a train so long and wide it needed train-bearers—was not officially suppressed, but its use was now much frowned upon. Watered silk was frowned upon. Precious rings and buckled shoes were frowned upon. Scarlet gloves were *out.* As a cardinal I would have to make do with a soutane of trainless red, a rochet preferably of plain linen, and a crimson mozzetta above my rochet made of simple wool or even (can you imagine?) of *nylon.*

In my head I heard Cardinal Baluardo raging against the zealots of Apostolic Simplicity and their Apostolic Scissors as I raged with him. SNIP! SNIP! SNIP! I had no mind to be shortchanged. I ignored the Pope's edicts. Or rather, willfully I ordered Annibale, Rome's most élite ecclesiastical tailor, to cut separate wardrobes for me in the old and the new styles. In either style, still I would be a prince, ranking in protocol and precedence with princes of the blood.

My coat of arms as cardinal—to be engraved on all my seals and correspondence and mounted upon my throne in Santa Brigida—would be delectably more royal than my escutcheon as archbishop. How lovingly I designed my coat of arms. I retained my family's coronet, prickly chains, and rampant lions breathing fire, but (for my love of France) I heightened the fleur-de-lis and (for my love of Baroque Catholicism) I added a Roman dome by Fuga. Above the shield ascended a golden mitre, a golden crosier, a double cross surmounted by a great mediaeval cardinal's hat, coloured scarlet, with scarlet loops of cord and, dangling low on either side, fifteen scarlet tassels. Enscrolled beneath, as ever, was my family's legend: *Lux ex Tenebris:* Light from Darkness.

It remained the custom that each new cardinal must publicly receive a *biglietto,* formal notice from the Holy See of his elevation to the Sacred College, and then he must make a speech. My laurels attracted much attention. The Italian press called me glamourous, *il cardinale ragazzo,* the boy cardinal, I suppose not only for my years but for my lithe and youthful bearing. The Rector of the Venerable English College—eager to claim me as a countryman and promising that my oil portrait would hang in his famous gallery along with Their Eminences Wolsey, York, Acton, Manning, Newman—begged me to receive my *biglietto* and deliver my speech at the Venerable College; but it displeased me to be called an "English cardinal."

I decided to stage the ceremony round the corner, beneath the Corinthian pillars and the Grecian arch, on the steps of my titular church, facing the Embassy of France.

I was honoured by the presence of some few friends and several cardinals, but it was grey December, and as I addressed a battery of microphones we all of us rattled in the wind. A mob of *paparazzi* and other strangers—the strangers for the most part young and pretty women, oddly, there not to listen but to gawk, crying *"Che bella figura! Che bel giovane! Bellissimo!"* as though I were a rock star—rippled from the precincts of the church deep into the Piazza Farnese.

The themes of my address I borrowed from Cardinal Newman's *biglietto* speech of nearly ninety years before, when at last his service to the Church was recognised and he was awarded the crimson toga by Leo XIII at the age of seventy-seven. Many of his modern admirers have hailed Newman as a liberal. They dote on his famous retort to Gladstone: "Certainly, if I am obliged to bring religion into after-dinner toasts, I shall drink—to the Pope, if you please—still, to conscience first, and to the Pope afterwards." Yet Newman was no liberal: he was as orthodox and tradition-bound as I had myself become.

Clad for the final day in my archbishop's violet, cribbing shamelessly from Newman's celestial sentences in English, I crafted them into rolling Latin and from memory cried them at the uncomprehending wind and women and *paparazzi* howling and pushing in the Piazza Farnese. With glee and vigour, I denounced liberalism in religion as the fashion and the doctrine of the day—not least its claim that one creed is as good as any other, and thus merely a matter not of truth but of sentiment and fancy.

"Hitherto the great world agreed that religion alone, with its supernatural sanctions, was strong enough to win submission of the masses to law and order; now the philosophers and politicians are bent on satisfying this need without the help of Christianity. Spurning the authority of the Church, they replace it with a secular and Godless education, striving to convince the student that to be orderly, just, sober, benevolent, and industrious is but his own and society's selfish interest. As for religion, it is a private luxury, which a man may have if he will; but which of course he must not obtrude upon others, or indulge to their annoyance.

"Never was there a trap of the Enemy so cleverly contrived and with such a promise of success. Yet I beg you never to suppose that I—as a Roman cardinal—shall stand in trembling fright of that devilish snare. To the contrary. . . ."

Next morning, in St Peter's basilica, the feast of St John of the Cross, the Sad Pope created me a cardinal.

The consistory was small. Only ten of us received the Sacred Purple—including Monsignore Samosata and an archbishop from the Slavic east of whom I shall eventually tell you much. An African, Monseigneur Zalula, Archbishop of Kinshasa in the Congo—in his early forties and very handsome—preceded me in line as the penultimate Prince of the Church. As the youngest, I was the tenth cardinal and the last to be invested by the Pontiff.

The investiture was conducted in the long apse of the basilica, behind Bernini's baldachin, the Pope seated in golden cope and mitre on a formal throne beneath St Peter's Chair. Bernini had also crafted, in flamboyant bronze and gold, this Altar of the Chair, with its colossal figures of the Doctors of the Church: St Ambrose, St Athanasius, St John Chrysostom, and my namesake St Augustine. The monument was crowned by the stunning Glory of the Angels, done in gilded stucco, at its centre the Pentecostal dove of the Holy Ghost, Who (as no doubt you have supposed) inspired the Pope to create me a cardinal.

For many centuries past, even to the pontificate of the Sunny Pope, the ritual of investing a cardinal was the most glorious in the Roman Church. As each new cardinal ascended steps and knelt before the Sovereign Pontiff, his six-yard train of crimson was unfurled, tumbling down the steps. The cardinal kissed the slippered foot of the Pontiff, and after numerous genuflections, abasements, and embraces, he knelt finally. The Pope touched the symbolical Red Hat—the broad-brimmed *galero,* with its fantastic tassels groping back until the Renaissance and even the Middle Ages—to the cardinal's head, intoning in Latin: "To the praise of Almighty God and the decoration of the Holy See, receive ye the Red Hat. . . ."

My own investiture was grossly simplified. Much of the bowing and abasement before the Pope was cut out. I wore no train, only my red soutane, my lace rochet, my red mozzetta, and my red skullcap—and instead of the mediaeval *galero,* I received from the Pontiff only my crimson biretta. In the old style, the Pope did remind me in Latin of my sacred duty as a cardinal to show myself "fearless even unto death" and the shedding of my blood, "for the exaltation of the Holy Faith, for the peace and quiet of the Christian people, and for the increase of the Holy Roman Church, in the name of the Father, and of the Son, and of the Holy Ghost."

Then, as of ages past, I prostrated myself with my brother princes before the Altar of the Chair to prove my humility to God, while a choir sang the Gloria from *The Mass of Pope Marcellus,* and I throbbed with such a bliss that it all but redeemed my bleak childhood.

Afterwards, as the choir continued to jubilate, I proceeded in my scarlet to the assembled elder cardinals and His Eminence Baluardo, now all but completely blind.

"Could you see the ceremony?" I asked him.

"I saw red fog. Your participation was narrated to me, dear prince, dear son, dear brother Eminence, *carissimo Agostino.*" Tears dripped from his dead eyes. I hugged and kissed him: *"Grazie, Eminenza."* He fell to his knees, eager for my first blessing as a cardinal and groping in his fog of red joy for my ring to return my kiss.

Urban and Diana Northwood—both in formal dress, Diana more decorous than ever in a black mantilla—broke through the throng of ecclesiastics, eager to be next to render their homage and receive my benediction.

"Your Eminence," said Urban, genuflecting.

"Duke," I replied.

"Your Eminence," said Diana, genuflecting.

"D-Duchess," I replied.

Diana rose, glancing at my face, then cast her blue eyes demurely to the Nervan floor. Urban, gripping my sapphire and genuflecting still as if unable to stand, gazed up at me with cunning eyes. "And . . . *our* investiture?" he asked.

"Tomorrow," said I, "in the Hall of the Consistory."

He touched his breast pocket: "I've your envelope for you."

"Not *here*."

I hurried away from him, to Benedictine monks in black, all French, from my abbey in Vaucluse. At their head, in belt, scapular, and cowl, stood my venerated Father Abbot, his beard as white as Heaven's cloud and now in his hundredth year.

"*Cher Augustin*," he murmured.

"*Très Révérend Père*," I answered, refusing him my ring and in deference to his sanctity falling to my knees as I begged his blessing and kissed his hand.

In the ensuing silence, I revisited the abbey chapel, where the Père Benoît had glimpsed me on the altar, arrayed in crimson, a boy cardinal.

The Abbot said, "*Grâce à Dieu, j'ai vécu pour voir ce jour.* I thank Thee, Lord, for letting me live to see this day. The holy prophecy—of our dear Augustin as a Roman cardinal—is at last fulfilled."

He fainted, tumbling into the arms of his monks.

A fortnight later, I learned—by a letter from Vaucluse—that my Father Abbot was dead.

On the morrow of my elevation, in the exquisite Hall of the Consistory, the Pope received the new cardinals, all other members of the Sacred College residing then in Rome, and various luminaries of the laity, among them the Duke and Duchess of Canino.

Since Cardinal Secretary Sostituto was now nearly as old and feeble as his venerable brother Baluardo, it fell to me to choreograph the dance when Urban and Diana should approach the Sovereign Pontiff to receive their patents of nobility. Loyal to his simplicity, the Pope did not mount the dais or sit on his golden throne, but merely stood near the stately door before the queue of his guests. His photographer was present, taking pictures of the Holy Father as he embraced his cardinals and the other dignitaries with the Kiss of Peace or offered them his ring. I manoeuvred the Northwoods and their little son to the end of the line, making sure we should be last.

And since the Pope had banished white ruffles, embroidered capes, tight pants—not that Urban coveted the tight pants—again the Duke wore modern morning dress, cutaway and striped trousers; and the Duchess her black mantilla surmounted by a small tiara. I marvelled at baby Adrian, more picturesque, now eight or nine years old—at his skin so pure and apple-cheeked, his curls so blond, the eyes his mother's arresting blue. He wore blue satin, a starched lace collar, and breeches that ended at his knees above his buckled shoes. I told his parents, "He is Gainsborough's *Blue Boy*."

"Gainsborough's blue boy had brown hair," Urban bubbled.

"And Adrian is a marquis," Diana reminded me.

I kissed his classical head and asked, "Why didn't you bring him to my elevation?"

Diana laughed. "In any church, Your Eminence, he fidgets."

The queue ran out and we reached the Pope. The photographer had vanished. A monsignore produced a roll of parchment, handed it to the Pontiff, who handed it to me, and I presented the patent of the Dukedom of Canino to the Duke and Duchess. The Pope traced a blessing in the air, then fled across the floor of Siena marble to the dais and his throne. When the Duke tried to follow him, he was blocked by two Swiss Guards with crossed halberds.

"Insulting," Diana whispered.

I circumvented the Swiss Guards, leading baby Adrian up the steps to the seated Pope. Adrian warmed at once to the Supreme Pontiff, squeezing his waist. The photographer reappeared, snapped a single picture of Adrian, the Pope, and of myself in scarlet, then withdrew for good.

From a distance, Urban Northwood said, "May I inquire of Your Eminence, where is Adrian's patent?"

"Not yet inscribed," I answered. "I shall bring it to Northwood Hall when I come to confirm the child." I thought, You'll pay a pretty penny for that one, too.

"What will Adrian be called?" Diana asked.

"Marquis of the Bells," the Pope replied in halting English.

"Where are my bells?" asked Adrian.

"Ah," said I, "the Pope keeps them hidden in his secret box."

The Pope returned to his apartments.

As we descended the Scala Regia, Urban managed to be cheerful, but he murmured, "Is that what I paid three million dollars for?"

"You paid for nothing," I replied as cheerfully. "In your sweet benevolence, you contributed to charity." In St Peter's Square I asked, "You mentioned an envelope?"

Urban hesitated, then gave the creamy thing to me.

"Darling, at least you're a duke," Diana said.

But not for long, I chuckled to myself.

"I want my bells," said little Adrian.

In the months that followed, I went half off my head.

On Sundays, when I said Mass in the chapel Clementina of St Peter's—containing the tomb of my favourite Pope, Pius VII, and his Cardinal Consalvi—I practised the modish austerity of modern cardinals and recited the new liturgy, which I detested. I appeared in the sanctuary already clad in puritan new vestments over my cardinal's red, my chasuble not the smaller and more comely Roman chasuble I had always worn, but a Gothic white sheet that covered me nearly from neck to ankles in the name of Apostolic simplicity. No longer could I use the mosaic altar of the chapel, but I had to face the faithful as I celebrated the sacrifice upon a wooden table and in Italian: *"Padre nostro, che sei nei cieli, sia santificato il tuo nome. . . ."*

At least that echoed Latin, but the French and English liturgies were atrocious. From all over the world, the Pope was beset by protests from Nobel laureates and lesser minds—even from illustrious atheists—deploring the ugliness of the vernacular liturgies and mourning the loss of the Latin Mass. He replied painstakingly that the beauty of Latin might be well for the élite, but that for the good of souls the Holy Sacrifice must be understandable and close to the common people, above all to the hungry poor.

I abandoned the chapel Clementina for my titular church, where in defiance of the Council I resumed my celebration of the Tridentine Mass.

Upon Sundays and great feast days, I strode up the aisle through the blue haze of Santa Brigida wearing my crimson mozzetta of watered silk above my now forbidden mantelletta. In the sanctuary, assisted by my acolytes, I shed my mozzetta, mantelletta, and lace rochet; vested in my buskins and embroidered slippers, my alb, tunicle, dalmatic, and my Roman chasuble with its rounded beauty; then paused as my Master of Ceremonies crowned me with my precious mitre. I gripped my golden crosier, blessed the congregation, and said the initial portions of my Mass seated on my escutcheoned throne. Behind me, in the transept, a choir of blue nuns and surpliced boys, accompanied by organ, violins, and trumpets, sang Masses by Haydn and Cherubini.

When I proceeded to the altar, there ensued not only the millennial Latin prayers but an abundance of ablutions, incensings, miscellaneous obeisances: priests washing my hands from silver ewers, removing my scarlet skullcap as I began the Preface, placing it upon a silver plate, grabbing constantly for my right hand to kiss the great sapphire of my cardinal's ring.

Santa Brigida was small, but word spread rapidly through Rome of my High Pontifical Mass. Soon crowds of people, young and old—disenchanted of the new liturgy, nostalgic for Tridentine Latin, and aching for the theatre—packed the church, spilled out beyond the iron gates, into the Piazza Farnese, where they knelt or stood in rain or sunshine and listened to me through loudspeakers as I chanted the liturgy and preached.

After the Mass, I vested in my cappa magna, ermine mantle, buckled shoes, scarlet gloves, my red biretta, my grandest ring—the whole shooting match—then ventured to the piazza, scattering benedictions, whilst acolytes bore my train far behind me; and my choir, violins, and trumpets sang on and on of angels, the Holy Trinity, and Heaven. Ah, the heady cheers, the adulation, the rippling human wave as hundreds of my admirers genuflected to cross themselves and kiss my ring.

Not that all of my observers admired me. Young Dutch and German Jesuits in baggy suits of black—even some Franciscans and Benedictines in their proper habits—loitered in the piazza, and instead of genuflecting, they hissed me as I passed.

. . .

As a cardinal, I continued to advise the Pope and to write many of his allocutions. I headed no Sacred Congregation, because he preferred to use me as a sort of minister without portfolio. On a hot evening early in July, he summoned me to the roof of the Apostolic Palace.

We contemplated Rome at sunset. As we did so silently and I glanced at his countenance, his features twitched a little. I wondered whether he was angry at me; for in fact I had heard reports that he resented my shameless showing off and because I had celebrated the Tridentine liturgy without seeking his consent. He said abruptly, "You need humility."

I replied as meekly as I could, "I was so humble as a child, Your Holiness, that I rubbed my nose in that virtue."

"Still, not quite enough? The religious orders—the Jesuits especially— and even your brother cardinals, are calling you a fop."

"Must cardinals dress like truck drivers?"

"No, but if they did, it might delight the Lord."

"I doubt that it would d-delight the truck drivers."

Again he was silent as he watched the downing sun. I have suggested that to the depths of him he was indecisive; but as I observed him now the slight movements of his mouth and jaw betrayed a struggle between his anger and his fondness for me. His features suddenly became more placid, as though for once he had composed his mind. Surely his decision would not be harsh? He said, "We are sending Your Eminence to Africa."

"*Africa?*"

"The Congo."

"In what capacity?"

"As Apostolic Visitor."

"Exile? I do not wish to be an Ap-p-postolic V-Visitor."

"Not your wish, Eminence, but Ours."

I knelt, and—as the sun vanished behind the cupolas—I kissed his feet.

"Most Holy Father."

"Your venerable brother, Cardinal Zalula, has been imprisoned by the dictatorship. Go to the Congo and bring him back to Us."

THIRTY-ONE

So impatient was the Pope to get me out of Rome, I found no time to buy a proper wardrobe for my mission south. So now you see me on a torrid morning, at the summit of a windy hill, not as a prelate of the tropics, but as ever in my heavy black soutane—with its little cape, its crimson buttons, sash and trimmings, beneath my pectoral cross and red biretta—gazing down upon the River Congo.

How wide the river seems, and menacing. How the rapids froth. How hungrily they devour the flotillas of hyacinth plant hastening westwards to the sea.

I had not ascended to that summit for the view, but to meet the President of the Congo. In the moist wind, I turned my back to the river to survey the presidential compound. Long-horned antelopes and soldiers with automatic guns mingled on the lawns. The President had seized the property of the former Belgian governor, building atop the ruins of a burnt-out villa a vast and garish topaz palace that was beginning to fall apart. No matter, he owned more durable palaces in Ionia and France that he had bought with his depredations of the public treasury and (as a reward for his anti-Communism) his dollars from the Central Intelligence Agency. I was not invited inside the palace, but conducted by an officer from the crest of the hill down a grassy slope to a thatch-roofed gazebo.

There, for at least another hour, I was kept waiting as antelopes wandered in and out, and an obese lieutenant sat on a bamboo chair facing mine, fingering a submachine gun. Finally the President emerged from the palace and, alone, walked across the lawn to greet me.

A very young chief of state, he had but several years before held the rank of sergeant in the army, then rose swiftly to the rank of general once Belgium cut the Congo loose and rebellions too bestial to evoke thrust the nation into anarchy. Now here he was, not twenty feet from me, devil of the Belgians, darling of the Americans, crushing the Congo beneath his boot in the name of love, liberty, and anti-Communism.

He wore a fuzzy cap of leopard skin, and horn-rimmed spectacles sitting on his broad nose; he was without a tunic, his starched and beribboned khaki shirt not ample enough to hide his paunch. He exclaimed, *"Mais, Monseigneur, vous êtes si jeune!"*

"But not so young as you, *mon général.*"

Since he was a Roman Catholic, I held out my ring. He did not genuflect, or even raise my hand to his great lips, but grasped my finger, twisting it, and—for at least a minute—he studied my blue sapphire with fussy curiosity. He said, "Oooh, how it sparkles, even without the sun. Where did you get this?"

"In Rome, *mon général.*"

"Is it old?"

"Nineteenth century."

"Mined no doubt in our own Katanga—by shackled slaves!"

"I shall say Masses for their souls, *mon général.*"

"I want one—and just as big."

"I'll give you mine—in exchange for Cardinal Zalula."

"Ah, *cher Monseigneur,* that is quite another matter."

With cautious circumlocution, I explained that I had come—in the name of His Holiness the Pope—to protest the imprisonment of Cardinal Zalula and the expulsion from the Congo of the Apostolic Nuncio. The President responded, "But I expelled the Nuncio because he meddled in our sovereign politics."

"How did he meddle, *mon général?*"

"He protested the arrest of Cardinal Zalula."

"The Holy See has yet to be informed of Cardinal Zalula's crime."

"High treason, Monseigneur. The Church in the Congo is a tool of Belgium. The Church must be *congolisée!* Cardinal Zalula, in thrall to his imperial masters, lacked the wisdom to agree with me."

"The Vatican Council condemned imperialism—"

"In the Congo?"

"—and recognised the right of native cultures to assert themselves, even in the sacred liturgy. But we cannot proclaim you, *mon général,* the Fourth Person of the Blessed Trinity."

"That is a vile invention of the Belgian press."

"Yet do you not demand that in the Creed your name be mentioned with God the Father, God the Son, and God the Holy Ghost?"

"Are my people to be denied the right to venerate their Saviour?"

I suppressed a howl. The President giggled like a schoolboy. He said, in the French familiar, "I love you, Monseigneur"—as he took my ringed hand, squeezing it, and led me about his park to admire his antelope, his jacaranda trees, and his little zoo. The zoo kept caged, exotic birds, pink-buttocked baboons, half-starved it seemed to me, living amid heaps of excrement. Everywhere we wandered, we were followed by thugs with submachine guns. As I stared at the baboons, mourning their condition, suddenly the President seized my red biretta and placed it like a crown atop his cap of leopard skin. He asked, "May I keep this, Monseigneur?"

"No."

"But I need a souvenir of your gracious visit."

"I'll send you a Miraculous Medal, *mon général.*"

Laughing, he gave my biretta back to me, then took my right hand again, squeezing it. He said, "I had a lovely dream last night. I am Emperor of the Congo—by the will of my people."

"You sound, *mon général,* rather like Napoleon."

"Didn't a pope crown Napoleon?"

"Pius VII anointed him, to his deep regret. Napoleon crowned himself— as you just did, with my biretta."

"I will release Cardinal Zalula if the Pope comes here to crown me emperor."

"Popes no longer crown emperors."

"Then Cardinal Zalula will stay in his dungeon."

"Where is his dungeon, *mon général?*"

"Ha-ha! A state secret, Monseigneur."

"I beseech you in the name of the Pope, of Jesus Christ, and your own humanity—to release His Eminence to my custody."

"*Très impossible!*"

We had climbed to the summit of the park and the vista of the great river, its rapids devouring hyacinth. A limousine had followed us upward through the grass; the President laughed gently as his guards shoved me inside that blue Mercedes-Benz. At the window, he said, "Go home to Rome, Your Eminence. In only a little while, I'll send all Belgian priests home to Brussels."

"Your country will collapse."

I was chauffeured off. Not until I reached the outskirts of the capital did I glance at my right hand. My sapphire ring was gone.

I was living in the empty Nunciature, attended only by a Congolese boy. Whenever I ventured from the embassy, I was shadowed by the President's secret police. Early one morning, I eluded them, running down alleys in my black soutane and hailing a rusty taxi.

The capital had but several years before worn a Mediterranean face, shimmering in the heat with milk-white office buildings, bustling with Belgian merchants in short pants on boulevards shaded by palm and fragrant with the shrubbery of jasmine. Now the capital was in quick decay, largely bereft of Belgians and invaded by youths from bush and forest seeking work and finding none; containing a populace of several millions; crawling with beggars; people pushing wheelbarrows, waiting for buses that never came, peering from hovels, lying in the dirt, defecating in open sewers, where children, children, more hungry children splashed and drank the water; men and women walking, shouting, beating beasts and one another with gnarled sticks, as army colonels sped by them and through the midst of them in unblemished limousines, air-conditioned.

I got out of my taxi and entered the cloister-like *Procure,* the headquarters in the Congo of the Fathers of the Sacred Heart. The fathers, forewarned of my Apostolic Visitation and forbidden by the police to talk to me, knelt reverently for my blessing but otherwise seemed so embarrassed by my presence that thereupon they drifted off—murmuring in French or Flemish—to distant rooms. I found a Congolese lay brother hiding in a closet of the vestry.

"Where is Cardinal Zalula?" I asked him.

"On sait rien, Monseigneur." Nobody knows!

"Surely you've all heard rumours?"

"On sait rien, Monseigneur."

"In the name of the Pope, I command you to speak."

"Upriver . . . Monseigneur?"

"Where upriver?"

"A world from here?"

"Where is a world from here?"

"A leper colony?"

"Which leper colony?"

"Iyonda . . . maybe? Lisala . . . maybe? Bumba . . . maybe? *On sait rien, Monseigneur."*

The brother fled. In his closet I found a long tropical white soutane, so I folded it round my arm and filched it. From the *Procure,* I walked to a crowded street market, where I bought cotton shirts and trousers.

A battered truck pulled up; I watched the black driver. He wore a visored cap and a blue boiler suit—or what Americans call "overalls." (Have you noticed that throughout this confession I prefer British locutions and spellings—though I deny that I am English?) I heard my argument with the Pope: *"Must cardinals dress like truck drivers?" "No, but if they did, it might delight the Lord." "I doubt that it would d-delight the truck drivers."* I bought blue overalls and a brown, visored cap.

At dawn, I left for the interior, for the heart of Africa a thousand miles, two thousand miles, away—uncertain, fearful, groping for my destination. Not by aeroplane: I supposed that at the airport I might encounter the President's police. Dressed like a truck driver, I took a riverboat.

"Going up that river was like travelling back to the earliest beginnings of the world, when vegetation rioted on the earth and the big trees were kings. An empty stream, a great silence, an impenetrable forest. The air was warm, thick, heavy, sluggish. . . ."

I read and lived Joseph Conrad's evocation of the River Congo even as my ship plied the mighty stream through Equatorial Province. Save for a pair of Portuguese traders, I was the only white man aboard the vessel, but even from those Europeans I concealed my cardinalate and priesthood. I mingled now and then with the Congolese passengers, several hundred of them, and some were soldiers, in answer to their curiosity confiding that I was a truck driver seeking work in the interior.

The ship was a weird contraption; the prow had been chopped off just forward of the bridge, and now the body of the boat pushed a long brown barge; for cargo we carried a station wagon, military jeeps, and a profusion of fruits and vegetables. The bazaars laid out on the barge deck offered fingernail polish, flashlight batteries, bright blue combs, buttons, sunglasses, cigarettes, soap, wristwatches, cotton underwear, bags of rice, and buckets of huge black fish. No sooner did evening fall than dances began on the cargo deck, little clusters of Congolese throbbing to their own makeshift music. With the rising of the moon the movements grew fervid. A young girl, lacking the customary ashes, smeared her face with toothpaste and, in a sort of reverse vaudeville, turned herself into a white woman.

We were a happy ship, running against the current. My cabin was stifling and in the wet air the broken toilet stank, so I began to avoid my quarters—roaming everywhere over that patchwork vessel, from the captain's cabin to the third-class quarters belowdecks aforeships where the passengers were packed together as though in those buckets of black fish. All the winning qualities of the Congolese—their warmth, charm, and generosity—suddenly confronted me: laughter was my companion on that voyage. Even in the heat, I felt strangely liberated from smothering, pontifical Rome. On Saturday night everybody but me got roaring drunk in the ship's bar, and even I grew tipsy. Yet I could not live without my Mass, so in the middle of each night in my stinking cabin I took my Mass kit from my luggage, and—dressed in my blue overalls—kneeling I mumbled the Holy Sacrifice upon the altar of my bed.

I debarked at Mbandaka—once Conquilhatville, several hundred miles upriver from the capital—hastening by foot to the Mission of Iyonda, a large leprosarium overlooking the river, run by Fathers of the Sacred Heart.

No sooner arrived, I revealed who I was, startled that the priests and nuns should cluster round me to kiss my bare right hand and beg my blessing, despite my costume of a truck driver. The *Procure* had walls inside mounted with tilting crucifixes and broken clocks and yellowing photographs of the King of Belgium. The Flemish faces of the priests reminded me of peasants in Breughel's snowy paintings, incongruous in such tropical surroundings; at dusk, in their white robes, the fathers strolled like ghosts in the gloom of the gardens. But they were less afraid of the police and thus more willing to talk. "Cardinal Zalula is not here, Your Eminence," they told me at dinner, "and he never has been. We've heard that the army is moving him from place to place."

"Lisala?" I asked.

"Perhaps. Communications throughout the Congo have broken down, but the river people whisper that rumour. We'll send one of the fathers with you to Lisala."

"No," I replied. "Better for now that I remain anonymous."

Next day, I boarded another boat for the voyage of several hundred miles from Mbandaka to Lisala.

Just after my solitary Mass, in the middle of the night, the ship made a stop at Makanza: during the stampede to disembark, an old woman was pushed overboard. Young men dove, shouted, and splashed about, but they could not find her. Within minutes, the drowning was forgotten, and the throngs aboard the ship and on the shore resumed their tumultuous commerce amidst an amberish dance of lanterns. Otherwise the night was utterly black, and on we sailed without a moon. The mosquitoes were a plague, the air so sodden that safety matches, even several bunched together, would not ignite. Now and then as we glided upriver a fire along the shore illumined microscopically the tangled corridor of vegetation and gave a brief, ghostly rebirth to a dead tree. But that was all that one could glimpse, despite the spasmodic chants of the forest-dwellers and the thumping of their drums.

With dawn we wove through myriad identical islands, wooded with palm, sycamore, the towering limbo; the baobab trees, and they resembled mangrove, were bulbous, gnarled, groping, twisted, tormented, festooned with vines and each other's branches. Everywhere, along the banks and all over the islands beyond, stood the skeletons of dead trees. Soon, for every living tree, there stood the ghosts of a dozen dead ones, mammoth warped arrows embedded in carpets of moss. In hyacinthine twilight, we passed fishing villages built on stilts. At morning, the currents seemed to cease; the river turned oddly placid; the relentless flotillas of hyacinth plant lay lazily becalmed. At late afternoon, only the blazing little ball of sun, distorted and whirling in its reflection, seemed to suggest the violence latent within the waters themselves. Elephants roared; fantastic birds flew by; baboons gamboled on the shores.

In Lisala, at the *Procure,* the fathers believed that Cardinal Zalula was imprisoned in a remote diocese deep in the great forest of the Congo. By monoplane, a father flew me from the river due south for hundreds of miles over an immense blue jungle. Only once did I see a fragment of human life— a man on a pond paddling a canoe. We landed on a cabbage patch so bumpy we were lucky to survive.

In that sylvan diocese, wayside shrines of the Virgin and St Joseph stood along the roads; the people knelt when they saw a priest, evoking for me pre-Revolutionary France. The missions themselves were in horrid disrepair: Simba rebels had visited of late, pillaging, burning, and killing. The fathers said, "Cardinal Zalula was captive not far from here"—they pointed towards the forest—"but when the rebels approached the army took him away."

Desperately I asked, "Have you no idea where?"

"Upriver maybe?"

"Bumba?"

"Bumba, or much deeper in that forest? Very dangerous—Simba country—so may we beg Your Eminence, *don't go?*"

At Lisala, no boats dared now, for fear of the rebels, to venture further upriver. Already the mission had been strewn with bodies from battles in months past between Simbas and the President's white mercenaries. No sooner I regained the mission than I heard report of a new invasion pending; much of Lisala's populace had fled in fear deep into the forest. I avoided army headquarters, but the priests warned me that presently the army would forbid all travel even by road to Bumba. I found a pair of black truck drivers who agreed—for an exorbitant price—to take me to Bumba.

We left early of an August morning in their junky green truck, the four of us crowded up front in the cabin, the extra passenger being a colossal rooster. The rooster sat regally in the lap of the driver's chum, who was taking the bird to Bumba as a birthday gift for his grandfather. The road ran roughly parallel to the river through a forest of banana trees.

Lisala and Bumba were busy riparian towns a hundred miles apart, but we were the only traffic on the road that morning. It had rained the night before; the road was badly rutted and barely passable. Everywhere along that way the vegetation grew wild, vines and weeds as high as men strangling the rusty road signs erected by the Belgians but tilting now in various angles of collapse. Twenty miles from Bumba, we started up a gully and got stuck in the mud.

The chum handed me his rooster and got out to push, sinking ankle-deep into the morass. A dozen half-naked men emerged from the forest, but even their labour was doomed as we slid deeper and deeper into a ditch.

Suddenly, at the top of the hill, there appeared two open trucks packed with men. A furious blast of horns; a helmeted soldier jumped out and came dashing down the hill, waving a submachine gun and screaming at us to get out of the way. In my lap, the rooster stirred, as the soldier stood there threatening the villagers at the top of his lungs. A smartly dressed young African descended to the mud beneath my window and bashfully introduced himself as a civil magistrate. A bottle of something protruded from his pocket; he seemed slightly drunk.

"Why don't you ask the gentlemen in your trucks to come down and push?" I suggested.

"It's dangerous, Monsieur," the magistrate said. "They're all Simbas and assassins. We're on our way to the prison camp outside Lisala. They're a hundred men, and I have only four guards."

I began to suspect that the magistrate was not only tipsy but terrified. I became terrified, too! The Simbas, I knew, were cannibals.

The Belgians had failed to prepare the Congolese for independence not yet a decade earlier; more, it was the rapacity of Congolese politicians and a ravening thirst for anarchy that caused the bestial Simba Rebellion to erupt in the south—and now still raging in the dank forest and devastated towns throughout much of the Congo. Simba youths, emboldened by drugs and armed with guns from the Russians and the Red Chinese, marched into battle convinced they were invulnerable to bullets.

Witch doctors had immunised the youths by sprinkling *dawa,* or supernatural medicine, upon their bodies. The Simba had only to wave a palm branch, cry out *"Mai, mai"*—water, water—and the bullets of the enemy would turn to raindrops. The religion of the Simbas was a stew of primeval mythology, ancestral fetishism, tribal memories, Messianic fixations, and Marxist slogans. The fable of Simba invulnerability was believed by much of the Congo army: whole regiments ripped off their uniforms and stampeded naked through the jungle backwards at the approach of a dozen Simbas.

The rebellion was not at first anti-European—or anti-Christian—but a burst of rage against all politicians, civil servants, tax collectors identified with the national government. Yet wherever they ventured, the Simbas slaughtered thousands, black and white, finding exotic pleasure in the murder of white priests and the raping and murder of white nuns. Priests and nuns were paraded nude, then the nuns were ritually raped—enormities of deep symbolism for the Simba youths.

It was not simply that some few of these Belgian missionaries had shown contempt for the Congolese—but that this European religion was wrapped in a terrifying mystery of its own. The womb of violence is fear: what unutterable secrets lurked behind the locked doors and veiled tabernacles of the Roman Catholic missions? For the Simbas, secrecy (like the consumption of human flesh) had a special mystical meaning. The flowing long garments of the priests and nuns were themselves a magical force; by tearing them off, the Simbas deprived these white witch doctors of much of their occult omnipotence.

The Simba *Jeunesse*—youth gangs—were the worst of the rebels, howling killers seventeen, fifteen, twelve years old. Tribal memory set them ablaze. Such boys were too young to be bitter from direct experience; their violence was an unreasoning vengeance of inherited nightmares, of all the blood and horror their ancestors had endured from the goons of Belgium's King in the nineteenth century.

Wearing an odd mixture of civil and military costume, or no clothes at all, they stole jeeps and trucks along the way; they ravished women and little girls, cut off the feet and hands of boys and men, saved them as trophies in the compartments of their trucks, severed the genitalia of their victims, hacked open their intestines, and feasted on their livers while they were still warm. Other victims were crucified! Many of the dead were postmen, schoolteachers, small merchants—the sort of people the Congo most needed—but perfect offerings of propitiation and sacrifice to the Simbas' tribal memory and their hungry deities.

The government hired white mercenaries, professional killers, really—Belgians, British, Irish, Americans, South Africans, ex-Foreign Legionnaires, ex-Waffen S.S.—who crushed much of the rebellion by atrocities of their own. They took snapshots of one another atop pyramids of Simba corpses. Their practice upon penetrating a village was to cut the throats of all the wounded, shoot others at random, and put the village to the torch. But the mercenaries were gentlemen compared to the troops of the Congo government when, bringing up their chronic rear, they reoccupied the rebel areas, often surpassing the atrocities of the mercenaries and the Simbas.

In the forest all around me, the rebellion, bestiality, and cannibalism lingered.

On the road to Bumba, as our truck became more enmired in the mud, and the murmur of the Simba youths upon the hill above more restive, I reached into my pocket, touched the beads of my rosary, and thanked Heaven I was not dressed as a cardinal but in my visored cap and dirty overalls. Finally, my tipsy magistrate decided to take a chance. He whistled to the guards: at gunpoint, the barefoot mob of Simba boys and men rumbled down the hill. I sat silently in the cabin, playing my happenstance part of the lonely white man lost in a multitude of Africans, straining to look carefree and perfectly ready, if they wanted a warm liver, to give them the rooster's.

The Simbas put their shoulders to the truck's undersides, and—with a long, low, groaning chant—liberated it from the quagmire. Then they remonstrated with the guards, refused to return to their trucks, and gazed at me with mounting interest. "They want to be paid for pushing you out of the mud," the magistrate said. With *Belga* cigarettes (currency in the Congo), I bribed the cannibals to be good, and they got back into their trucks.

Late that afternoon, at last I reached Bumba. Bumba town, like Lisala, had been partly depopulated for fear of another invasion by Simbas, but it swarmed with churlish government soldiers and swaggering European mercenaries. On the outskirts by the river, the Mission of St André was crowded with refugees from a Simba attack on Buta two hundred miles to the east. The white priests and nuns, the black priests, nuns, seminarians, and catechists of Buta, fearing massacre, rape, being eaten alive, had piled into trucks and fled to Bumba. Not that Bumba was so much safer.

Even from the mission—like all Belgian missions self-contained, immaculate, broad-verandaed, cement-floored, with its own pure water and electric-power plant—I could hear the distant burps of automatic guns as mercenaries and the Congo army continued their hunt of Simba beasts in the jungle yonder.

My arrival at the mission had caused a spot of comedy, bedraggled as I was in my muddy boots and overalls and exhausted as I bore my heavy bags. "Who in God's name are you?" demanded the fathers.

"Cardinal Galsworthy, personal legate of His Holiness the Pope," said I with weary satisfaction.

"We don't believe you!"

I produced the Pontiff's letter beneath his coat of arms, adding, *"Benedictus qui venit in nomine Domini."* Blessed is he who cometh in the name of the Lord.

"Your Eminence!" cried the Fathers of the Sacred Heart as collectively they genuflected.

"I'm in the Congo to find Cardinal Zalula—and I shan't leave Bumba province until I do."

"The army has him, Monseigneur," Father Rector told me timidly.

"I know that—but near here?" I pressed.

"In the forest?" someone ventured.

I withdrew behind a boy bearing my luggage to the Bishop's Room. In my mosquito net that night, I could hear the fluting of Lukulakoko birds and the tom-toms of lepers on the other side of a swamp. Sometime after midnight, a torrential rain began to fall. Earsplitting: from my window I could see the tin roofs flash like huge mirrors when, in the instant before apocalyptic thunder, the stabs of lightning made the mission as luminous as noon and set the river fleetingly ablaze. But at dawn there was sun, heralded by blue warblers and goliath herons exalting in weird formations from the forest.

I emerged from my quarters wearing the white tropical soutane I had filched from the fathers in the capital, but with my crimson sash, my golden chain, my pectoral cross, my red biretta, and upon my right hand my extra ring of sapphire. Hitherto most of these Congolese had never seen a cardinal, so my appearance provoked something of a wow. After I blessed genuflecting waves of whites and Africans, and said Mass in Latin for a throng in the mission chapel, a father paddled me in a canoe across the swamp and I visited the leper colony.

Hundreds of leprous families lived in their separate village of little brick houses built by the missionaries, but most of the families seemed to inhabit thatch-roofed mud huts they had erected themselves in the backyards of the brick houses: evidently the result of some primeval compulsion and not for me to deplore. Lepers from the depths of the dangerous forest kept showing up all day for treatment at the dispensary. I sensed that these lepers knew everything that happened in the forest—and I supposed that were I ever to learn of Cardinal Zalula's fate, might I not learn it from the lepers? By canoe I transported my luggage from the mission, across the marsh, and moved into the leper colony, commandeering an empty brick house, where I cast aside the straw mattress and slept—as I had always done, in Vaucluse and at Rome—upon a bed of wooden slats.

I knew that leprosy could be contagious, but I refused to recoil from it. In those tropics, the disease began with an invisible bacillus festering in the flesh, nourished by malnutrition and dirty sanitation, and it afflicted in milder or more monstrous forms fully a tenth of the people. As in the European Middle Ages, there in the Congo it was still considered a curse of Heaven—or of the tribal gods. Lepers concealed their disfigurement beneath masks and monk-like cowls; not a few announced their approach to the uninfected by clanging bells.

These lepers, also, suffered lesions and deformities of the limbs and feet, "claw hands," tubercular lumps, loss of feeling, atrophy, piebald skin, and repulsive ulcerations. With enough exposure, such leprosy indeed could be infectious, disfiguring not only the extremities of limbs but causing noses and other facial tissue to erode until the profile of a leper became leonine and his eyes went blind.

Early every morning for several weeks, I celebrated Latin Mass in the thatched lepers' chapel; the lepers seemed to prefer Latin to their own Balomingo because Latin was mysterious and they could not grasp it. After Mass I appeared at the brick infirmary in my cardinal's robes, and—deaf to the protestations of my hosts—I worked there helping out, doing menial tasks.

A missionary doctor and Sisters of the Sacred Heart attended the lepers in their beds or those others who hobbled to us from the village and the forest on their stunted feet. The leprous children and their parents knelt in the mud and crossed themselves as I passed them by; small boys with heads shaven to confound their ringworm darted out from behind palm trees to retrieve the cigarette butts that the fathers and the catechists so casually tossed away. Through the nuns I asked a little girl—her kinky pigtails peaked primly in an almost Gothic arch, her nose and mouth already mutilated by her infection—"Who made the world? Who made the day? Who made the night?"

She looked up at me and in Balomingo laughed her answer: "O Baba, we lived in darkness before you came, but last night we sent a man to steal the sun!" So amused and moved was I that I scooped the little bundle up and covered her stunted face with kisses.

Scores of other lepers, young and old, were watching from the edges of the forest or from the doorways of their huts; new mobs of these mutilated came rushing to me, hobbling on crutches and muddy bandages, others pedalling bicycles or bumping along in wheelchairs, everybody begging to be kissed. All priests were witch doctors, but I, towering in my white and crimson robes, was a *sorcier*, a *guérisseur*, a witch doctor with more force. I kissed as many of the lepers as I could, then withdrew as usual to my labours in the infirmary—a small brick hospital, actually. In the ward where the undernourished children were cared for, I volunteered, "These little ones are full of grace." "No, Monseigneur," the missionary doctor answered, "they're full of worms."

It was the operating rooms that moved me most. There, with modern equipment, sat several nursing nuns hunched over recumbent lepers—the ugliest human forms I had ever seen. Under brilliant lamps, the nuns worked with elaborate electrical machines, drilling away in dentist fashion at the dead flesh of their most mutilated lepers. These lepers had no toes, or where their toes should have been they now had only bloated deformations, parodies of toes, like pimples puffed up. Some of the lepers had lost their noses or their ears as well, and several had only stumps for hands and feet. The wound in one man's heel was as wide and deep as a flowerpot, and as red inside; when the electric drill ground away at that, disinfecting the wound by making it even bigger, the odour of the burning rotten flesh was too much for me to bear.

I wept, but since the lepers could not feel pain, they only smiled and giggled back. Their wounds were too horrible to kiss, so I offered each of the lepers all I could—my ringed hand, hoping they might find my sapphire ambrosial and cool to their mutilated lips, if in fact their flesh could feel anything.

In that ward worked a certain nun—Soeur Pauline, in age but fifty though she was nearly deaf, and a bit arthritic also, yet by force of will somehow still robust.

Day after day, I marvelled at Soeur Pauline, at her celestial, ruddy, unwrinkled face beneath her white veil and coif, and her apron splotched with lepers' pus and blood, over her waist bound tight with its white cincture and black dangling rosary beads. Her superiors in the leprosarium, and the fathers of the mission, had for some time been trying to get Soeur Pauline to go home to less brutal work in Belgium, but she refused. For nearly thirty years she had worked there in the leper colony as a nurse and common labourer, on her knees scrubbing floors and water closets, emptying foul bedpans, dressing hideous wounds, from dawn till late at night. I asked her, "*Ma soeur,* why won't you go home to Belgium?"

"Eh, Monseigneur?"

"WHY WON'T YOU GO HOME TO BELGIUM?"

"I've lived in this leper colony most of my life, Your Eminence."

"*Oui, mais*—"

"Eh, Monseigneur?"

"ISN'T THIRTY YEARS ENOUGH?"

"I know nothing else, nor do I wish to. I love my work—helping the lepers. What would I do in Belgium? In Belgium, I'd die. Here, I'm alive, in Christ Our Lord. I am, Your Eminence, the happiest woman in the world."

"But the fathers insist—"

"Eh, Monseigneur?"

"THE FATHERS INSIST."

"Your Eminence can overrule them."

"I've no authority over religious orders."

"Eh, Monseigneur?"

"I CAN'T COMMAND YOUR SUPERIORS TO KEEP YOU HERE."

"You could speak to somebody in Rome."

"I SUPPOSE I COULD."

"Do you know the Pope?"

"MAIS OUI, MA SOEUR."

"Then speak to him."

"REALLY . . ."

"Promise me, Monseigneur.'

"I'LL DISCUSS THE MATTER WITH YOUR SUPERIORS."

"Mille fois merci, Monseigneur."

"ARE YOU EVER PAID, *MA SOEUR?*"

"We nuns are never paid, Your Eminence."

"YOU HAVE THE ODOUR OF SANCTITY, *MA SOEUR PAULINE.*"

"Shhhh, Your Eminence. The other nuns will hear you. You're talking nonsense. I just want to live with my lepers."

I watched her drift off to her daily tasks, descending to her knees to scrub floors and water closets; then emptying foul bedpans, dressing hideous wounds. As the days passed, I struggled to mimic her, in my scarlet robes and upon my knees scrubbing floors and water closets, then emptying foul bedpans, dressing hideous wounds.

If I was a cardinal in Rome, so was I—just as much—a cardinal in a leper colony. I thought: The nuns and lepers are all watching me. Will my legend spread? Am I—as ever—playacting? Still . . . the floors got scrubbed.

As I pursued my menial tasks with my Soeur Pauline beside me, I asked her, "Have you heard any rumours of Cardinal Zalula?"

"Eh, Monseigneur?"

"DO YOU KNOW WHERE CARDINAL ZALULA IS?"

She smiled, illuminating her gentle face with its little nose, nearly heart-shaped mouth, and her large eyes rather like the hue of reddish hazelnut. Up she rose to her tiny feet, for she was a small woman, but sprightly almost no matter her arthritis, wont to hop here and about on her tasks of mercy. She said, "I'll ask the lepers."

Several afternoons thereafter, exhausted from my labour in the torrid heat, I returned to my little brick house and collapsed on my hard bed; but noises from afar intruded on my siesta and my sleep was fitful.

From the forest beyond, I heard the burp of automatic guns—Uzis, M-16s, Kalashnikovs? German Luger pistols? Were the Simba beasts at war again with the Waffen S.S.? In my half-sleep, I dreamt that Urban North-wood (vendor of that death?) stepped from the jungle in his cutaway and silken hat, his wobbly legs in striped pants, and—as he laughed at me—he undertook a frenzied dance.

And I saw my son's infant face—before I was awakened by a gentle knock. At my open door stood my Soeur Pauline together with a leper, barefoot, in short pants, a youth with half a face.

"This is Jean-Marie," said Soeur Pauline.

"Mon p'tit," said I, rising from my wooden slats, walking to him, rubbing my ambrosial gem across his rotting flesh. Jean-Marie to me was a total stranger: I told him, *"Je t'aime."*

"Moi aussi, Monseigneur," said Jean-Marie. "I've seen you scrubbing floors. *Je t'aime."*

Soeur Pauline drew closer to me, and from her breath I sniffed the ambrosia of her sanctity.

"He knows where Cardinal Zalula is," she said.

At morning, Jean-Marie, Soeur Pauline, and I set out through swamp in the leprous youth's old motorboat. We emerged from marsh and chugged eastward against the current into the midst of the great river. The season was late August, feast of the Beheading of St John the Baptist.

The trees grew so densely along the banks they seemed like dank walls. Vines and brightly flowered creepers wound as though stitched by the hand of God into the murals of vegetation; the roots of kingly, wrinkled trees groped like nests of snakes from the banks and deeply into the waters, entangling alligators and hippopotami who basked beneath the fuzzy sun. From within the forest arose the chattering of lemurs and the roar of lions.

Jean-Marie turned his outboard motor into a tributary of the river and then into another vast swamp, a graveyard of dead baobab trees, crowned ever by root-like branches—as though millennia ago Satan had seized all the baobabs in his fist and planted them upside down, thenceforth forcing the thirsty roots to seek their nourishment not from earth but only from the sky.

In the swamp, enormous weeds reached out for us: suddenly we got stuck. So ensnared was his propeller that Jean-Marie removed his shirt to dive beneath the boat, but I restrained him, volunteering for that task myself. Hardly had I touched my robes to tear them off, the leper and Soeur Pauline in full habit were in the swamp together, struggling to disentangle us. As he dove and laboured, the leper's half a face and stunted fingers perforce ascended above the waters; he and the nun gasped for air.

Otherwise the silence among those million trees was so immense that never had I felt so humbled or so at peace and so grateful to the Sad Pope for having kicked me out of Rome. Here, I sensed, in the depths of Africa, I had somehow prematurely found my final destination—but such a thought was swift and fugitive. Finally leper and nun pushed us free.

Soeur Pauline, filthy wet, sat dripping on a plank and opened a straw basket. As we headed into clearer water she served us goat cheese, unleavened bread, and mango juice.

In that tributary we began again to weave between identical wooded islands, the odd fishing village built on stilts, but then for hours we saw not a soul. I meditated on my prey, Cardinal Zalula.

Before leaving Rome, I had read his dossier. Forty-one years before, he had been born of a clan here in Bumba province, and thus his native tongue was Balomingo. His parents were poor lepers: in childhood he contracted the disease himself, but Belgian priests and nuns arrested it. In a mission school, the fathers soon noticed his quick mind, nurtured it with care, and chose him for the Church.

I am ever awed by the Roman Church's genius for detecting talent early and rewarding it eventually with the episcopal mantle and more. Whether the young man be prince or pauper, it matters not. Leo XIII, we remember, was a nobleman; he was succeeded by the peasant Pius X. The Stern Pope, a lord like Leo XIII, was followed by the rustic Sunny Pope. Young Patrice Zalula, former leper, after seminary in Belgium and a parish in the Congo forest, rose in his thirties to a rural bishopric and thence to the capital at Kinshasa and his young cardinalate. His Eminence Zalula's ascent in the Church evoked for me mirror images of my own.

Twilight descended, long before the sun itself, a tiny pink ball whirling like a firecracker in the murky sky, had even begun to set. Jean-Marie shut off his motor, lifting half a finger to his half a mouth, commanding silence, gliding the boat into a marshy cove, towering reeds, to an island like all the others. He pointed upwards to a hill, then crouched wordlessly beside his boat amid the reeds, discharging Soeur Pauline and me to pursue our mission by ourselves. I took my breviary; Soeur Pauline bore her straw basket.

Treading to higher ground, among the dead bokungu and limbo trees, we saw thatched huts and heard rowdy voices in Balomingo. We peered through liana and thorny shrub, sighting finally a dozen soldiers in olive drab, or rather various stages of drab undress, swigging corn liquor (I supposed) from crude brown bottles and very drunk. They fingered automatic rifles, which of a sudden one or two of them for sport shot aimlessly at the setting sun.

"What shall we do, *ma soeur?*"

"Eh, Monseigneur?"

"*Allons-y?*"

"Eh, Monseigneur?"

I grasped her hand. We marched to the soldiers. Even in their dreamlike state they seemed startled by the sight of us. "*Mais, il est cardinal . . . cardinal . . . cardinal,*" said one, touching my red biretta with the muzzle of his M-16, nearly knocking it from my head.

"Where is your commanding officer?" I demanded.

"Asleep," a soldier said.

"Drunk," another laughing soldier said.

"Where is my brother, Cardinal Zalula?"

They pointed their guns toward the hill, crowned by a thatched mud hut. With my arm round Soeur Pauline's shoulder, I walked up the hill, the soldiers protesting, "*Mais non . . . mais non . . . c'est défendu!*" I feared that they might shoot me, but would they shoot a frail, deaf nun? I held aloft my black breviary and my golden pectoral cross: that seemed to daunt them.

Inside the hut, the light was dim and the stench odious. There, sleeping foetus-like upon the earth, barefoot, clad only in a bathing costume, an ankle chained to a stake in the ground, was the man I had come to redeem. From her basket, Soeur Pauline took out an electric torch, illuminating his condition.

Cardinal Zalula's sanitary arrangements were limited by the length of his chain. In a corner lay a heap of excrement, flies and larger insects feasting on it. Beneath a head that was noble and finely featured, his long-limbed body was not ebony but more like moist bronze, undernourished; his left foot lacked a pair of toes, the result I supposed of his arrested leprosy. Sores and wounds covered his torso. I fell weeping to my knees and kissed a wound on his side, as I would (if I could) have kissed the wounds of Christ.

Cardinal Zalula woke, frightened by the nun's electric torch flashing in his face. He blinked, and blinked again, unsure of the veiled nun before him and then of me, his brother cardinal. Painfully he tried to rise, and as he tried I helped him to his feet. At length he cried, "*Mon frère!* Oh, thanks be to God!"

I dug into my pocket, took out my beads: he snatched them, kissed the crucifix, and crossed himself a dozen times.

From her basket, Soeur Pauline removed a wad of cotton and a flask of alcohol, which she used to clean the wounds upon his torso as the Cardinal intoned the Glorious Mysteries of the Resurrection and Ascension, the Paternosters, Aves, Glorias, telling us at last, "*Mon frère! Ma soeur!* They took my rosary from me. On my fingers, for months and months, I've been counting out the prayers. *Mon frère! Ma soeur!*"

The soldiers crowded the doorway, watching us, swaying between silence and fits of laughter. An officer burst in, still donning his captain's tunic, and roaring, "Who are you?"

"The wrath of God, *mon capitaine,*" I answered.

"Why are you here?"

"To save Cardinal Zalula, *mon capitaine.*"

"*Très impossible!*"

In his heavy spectacles, he resembled the President; he seemed drunker than his men. His demeanour lurched, one moment to the next, from tongue-lashings of his men for allowing us to see his prisoner and explosions of frantic bonhomie. "Two cardinals! *Mais, quel honneur!*" He held out a rough brown bottle. "A drink, Monseigneur?"

I drank a mouthful of the foul potion, and passed the bottle to my brother cardinal, but my generosity vexed the captain. He made the Cardinal kneel, then put a Luger pistol to his head. The soldiers likewise drew their pistols, forcing Soeur Pauline and me to kneel as they pressed the muzzles to our temples. In an instant I revisited my elevation to the Sacred Purple: I heard the Pope reminding me in Latin of my sacred duty as a cardinal to be fearless even unto death and the shedding of my blood, for the exaltation of the Holy Faith and the peace and quiet of the Christian people.

Soeur Pauline calmly crossed herself: "At last—I'll see the face of Christ."

Cardinal Zalula serenely kissed my rosary: "Come, Jesus."

Terrified, I said: "Don't sh-shoot."

In a frenzy I leapt up, before the soldiers could resolve to pull their triggers, and—holding high my golden cross—in French I shouted anathemas at them:

"I EXORCISE THEE, UNCLEAN SPIRIT, IN THE NAME OF THE FATHER, AND OF THE SON, AND OF THE HOLY GHOST, THAT THOU GO FORTH AND DEPART FROM THESE MEN OF VIOLENCE—FOR HE WHO COMMANDS THEE, ACCURSED SPIRIT, IS HE WHO WALKED UPON THE SEA AND STRETCHED FORTH HIS RIGHT HAND TO PETER AS HE S-SANK."

Emboldened, Cardinal Zalula and Soeur Pauline rose also, shouting in French and Balomingo apposite verses from John, Luke, and Mark:

" 'BEHOLD THE LAMB OF GOD, WHICH TAKETH AWAY THE SINS OF THE WORLD. IN MY NAME SHALL THEY CAST OUT DEVILS; THEY SHALL TAKE UP SERPENTS; NO DEADLY THING SHALL HURT THEM; THEY SHALL LAY HANDS ON THE SICK, AND THEY SHALL BE HEALED. LORD, EVEN THE DEVILS ARE SUBJECT UNTO US THROUGH THY NAME. AND HE SAID UNTO THEM, I BEHELD SATAN AS LIGHTNING FALL FROM HEAVEN. BEHOLD, I GIVE UNTO YOU POWER TO TREAD ON SERPENTS AND SCORPIONS, AND OVER ALL THE POWER OF THE ENEMY: AND NOTHING SHALL HURT YOU.' "

I (*in Latin*): "Lord, have mercy. Christ, have mercy. Lord, have mercy."

Cardinal Zalula (*repeating me in Balomingo*): "*Mokonz oloyokela. Kristo olondimela. Mokonz oloyokela.*"

I: "Holy Mary, holy Mother of God, holy VIRGIN OF VIRGINS."

Soeur Pauline: "Pray for us."

I: "Saint Michael, Saint Gabriel, SAINT RAPHAEL."

Soeur Pauline: "Pray for us."

Cardinal Zalula: "All ye holy Angels and Archangels, All ye holy orders of BLESSED SPIRITS."

Soeur Pauline: "Pray for us."

I: "All ye holy Apostles and Evangelists, All ye holy Disciples of our Lord, all ye holy Bishops and Confessors, all ye holy Doctors, all ye HOLY INNOCENTS."

Soeur Pauline: "Pray for us."

Cardinal Zalula: "Saint Mary Magdalen, Saint Agatha, Saint Lucy, Saint Agnes, Saint Cecilia, SAINT ANASTASIA."

Soeur Pauline: "Pray for us."

I: "From all evil, O Lord, deliver us. From all sin, from Thy wrath, from sudden and unseemly death, from the snares of the Devil, from the spirit of fornication, from lightning and tempest, from the scourge of earthquake, from plague, famine, and war, from EVERLASTING DEATH."

Cardinal Zalula and Soeur Pauline: "O LORD, DELIVER US."

Slowly, as we shouted out the exorcism, the soldiers began to recoil, lowering their guns. Several of them wept, then sobbed, writhing on the earth, clutching their necks. The captain, either paralysed from fright or too drunk to carry on, collapsed against the wall, and in his stupor fell asleep. I seized his Luger pistol and aimed it at the fetter on Cardinal Zalula's ankle, zealous to free him from his chain. Yet before I could free the Cardinal, a soldier gripped me, hurling me to the ground. On my knees, still clenching the Luger, I screamed at him:

" 'BUT SOME OF THEM SAID, HE CASTETH OUT DEVILS THROUGH BE-EL-ZE-BUB, THE CHIEF OF DEVILS. BUT HE SAID UNTO THEM, AND IF I BY BE-EL-ZE-BUB CAST OUT DEVILS, BY WHOM DO YOUR SONS CAST THEM OUT? BUT IF I WITH THE FINGER OF GOD CAST OUT DEVILS, THE KINGDOM OF GOD IS COME UPON YOU. WHEN A STRONG MAN ARMED KEEPETH HIS PALACE, HIS GOODS ARE IN PEACE: BUT WHEN A STRONGER THAN HE SHALL COME UPON HIM, AND OVERCOME HIM, HE TAKETH FROM HIM ALL HIS ARMOUR.' "

The soldier hesitated. With the captain's pistol, I shot at the Cardinal's rusty shackle, freeing him.

A pair of soldiers raised their rifles to block our flight. At the door appeared Jean-Marie, in his bare feet and short pants, wearing a necklace of hand grenades, the good fingers of his right hand poised as though to pull the pins—as the captain, waking up, asked groggily, "Where did you get those, leper boy [*garçon lépreux*]?"

"In your office, *mon capitaine.* Will I blow you up?"

Jean-Marie posed his question with some excitement. As fervently Cardinal Zalula completed the exorcism, crying out, " 'WHEN THE UN-

CLEAN SPIRIT IS GONE OUT OF A MAN, HE WALKETH THROUGH DRY PLACES, SEEKING REST. AND FINDING NONE, HE SAITH, I WILL RETURN TO MY HOUSE WHENCE I CAME OUT.' "

The captain groaned agreement. The soldiers let us pass.

We four hurried down the hill, I supporting my brother cardinal, the leper walking backwards as he fingered his necklace of grenades to take care we were not pursued. In the marshy cove, Jean-Marie had already scuttled the soldiers' boats, chaotic and half-sunken amongst the reeds.

In the leper's motorboat, swiftly we embarked, beneath a hazy moon, for Bumba.

At the mission—dreading the army—I urged Cardinal Zalula to flee with me at once eastward through the forest to Uganda. Loath to abandon his people, he resisted until solemnly I invoked the Pope's command. My Soeur Pauline was harder to persuade, yet still I hurried.

"But Your Eminence promised to have me kept here!"

"Ma soeur," I pleaded, "soon the Simbas may overrun all of Bumba. I fear for the lives of everybody in this mission, but—you've become so dear to me—especially for yours."

"Eh, Monseigneur?"

"I'M TAKING YOU TO ROME."

"What ever would I do in Rome?"

"I'LL THINK OF SOMETHING."

"I'm staying with my lepers."

Promptly I prevailed on her Mother Superior to order Soeur Pauline to take flight with me and Cardinal Zalula under holy obedience. Thereupon I commandeered a jeep, baskets of food, maps, jerry cans of gasoline; we took no guards or guns. I wore my tropical soutane and accoutrements of crimson which had protected me from death, but my brother Zalula, lacking his regalia, dressed only in a borrowed soutane of simple white. We three took turns at the wheel: we had perhaps a thousand miles to travel.

The roads were terrible; the rains did not improve them; yet for a day or two, we hastened. Abandoning the great river to the south, we drove on jungle paths through labyrinths of palm, eucalyptus, flat-topped bokungo, over frail logs that bridged the streams, through thickets of arched, cathedral-like bamboo. All the villages were identical: mud huts, bamboo fences, primeval graveyards heaped with skulls.

In every village we were greeted by people waving little notebooks—tattered relics of imperialism, the medical histories of the patients, disused today, but the villagers still hoped. Had not we come to them with medicines as the Belgian nuns and fathers once so often did? Had we not at least some aspirin tablets to treat their arthritis, toothaches, glaucoma, diarrhea, gonorrhea, syphilis, malaria, malnutrition, pinkish skin fungus, elephantiasis, tuberculosis of the bone—and the worms, worms, worms—that afflicted so many? Keening disappointment, they knelt to be blessed, but what cures could we bestow with our fickle benedictions?

Whenever we descended the jeep to mingle with these little people of the forest, Cardinal Zalula yielded to me: he hovered on the edges of the crowds, content to chat with scattered children in Balomingo as the mobs gathered round me begging for my hugs and kisses, making much of me in my red. En route, when we stopped to picnic, he acted like my manservant, eager to heap up my sausages on tin plate, spread jelly on my biscuits, or fetch mangoes from the trees.

"But Patrice," I protested, "you're a cardinal, too. I'm embarrassed by your deference."

"Augustin, you saved my life."

"By our exorcism, we saved each other's lives. Tomorrow, *I* will fetch the mangoes."

My Soeur Pauline was less submissive, not ceasing to reproach me for snatching her from the leprosarium, asking once and then again, "Pray as I might—can I forgive you, Monseigneur?"

"But the Gospels say you must, *ma soeur*," admonished my humble brother cardinal.

"Oh, oh, oh," cried my Soeur Pauline, not hearing him, "I'll die without my lepers!"

En route again, inch by inch we climbed a steep and rutted hill, and when we gained the crest, our resolution was rewarded by a vista, a valley of euphorbic frond and misty streams, inhabited by the calls of unseen beasts and haunted by brilliant birds. There, on the summit of the hill, stood a towering cross above an open wayside bamboo shrine, invaded by grass, falling apart, with a crumbling plaster statue of the Virgin. Upon that site Cardinal Zalula and I, both of us starved for the body and blood of Christ, decided to concelebrate a Mass, with my Soeur Pauline as acolyte.

From my Mass kit I extracted my golden chalice, unconsecrated hosts, cruets of water and wine, placing them on a stone table which served us as an altar beneath the crisscrossed tusks of elephants. In Latin and Balomingo, we mumbled our belief in one God, the Father Almighty, Maker of Heaven and earth, and of all things visible and invisible. We proceeded to the Eucharistic feast, and by our hands and mouths, in that ever new and unique event, realised beyond the world and outside of time, the body of Christ was once again mystically slain, ritually consumed, miraculously resurrected.

Did I *believe* that? The dwellers of the forest must have, no matter they were pagans and worshipped other gods, too. As we said the Mass, the dwellers of the forest emerged from the grass and trees and crowded round us on the summit of the hill.

These people were pygmoids, kin to pygmies, not quite as dwarfish—black leprechauns, all of them naked save for elaborate necklaces of lions' teeth and snakeskins, of leopards' claws and live chameleons, of the shrunken bodies of frogs and bats and the pickled heads of monkeys, such

fetishes about their necks and shoulders, dancing. As the pygmoids knelt during the Consecration, from the forest far beyond we could hear the *rat-tat-tat* of automatic guns and Simba cannibals at battle with those mercenaries whom I called the Waffen S.S.

We drove on, zigzagging between stagnant pools created by the feet of elephants, through forests so primeval that only seldom could the sun penetrate the gloom, through fantasies of liana and of vine looping from trees with massive trunks to bushes that flashed with gorgeous flowers to murky grottoes of rock and branch where orange birds were gliding sideways. At night, moths as big as butterflies immolated themselves in the flames of our campfire; in our blankets as we tried to sleep, we heard the jungle speak again with thumping drums and chattering baboons. At daylight, when we resumed our journey, the jungle vanished.

We rode through the skeletons of jungles, all devastation, stumps, and ash. Here the battles between the Simbas and the army and the mercenaries had been waged with such ferocity, so many fires had been set, that animal and vegetative life had ceased, fish no longer swam in poisoned streams, yet people lived in that desolation still, starving.

The swarms of naked children who wandered without their parents had swollen limbs and faces; their bellies had expanded and then popped into pear-sized hernias at their navels. Ulcers covered their mouths, oozing; they crouched and defecated constantly, squirting brown water. Their skin was discoloured, like rotting tobacco; piebald with pustular and peeling sores; their hair was turning orange at the roots, then white, then falling out. Were these children—so deformed they resembled lizards, beetles, puffed-up toads—human any longer?

The Dantesque scene endured for days as we three drove on. We had given away the rest of our food, and our own thirst and hunger made us faint and giddy. In the forest, we had picked wild fruit, but now we found no fruit and we could not feed the children.

Sorrowing, at Mahagi we crossed the border into Uganda.

In Uganda's capital, comfortable at the Apostolic legation, we learned that the mission and leprosarium at Bumba had been overrun by Simbas. Many of the fathers had been butchered, many of the lepers, many of the nuns—raped, then butchered. Hearing of the horror, gasping, uttering no other sound, my Soeur Pauline withdrew to chapel.

Soon, for his own mad reasons, the President of the Congo expelled the surviving Belgian missionaries from his realm.

At Rome, in the weird glory of the Apostolic Palace, I delivered Cardinal Zalula to the Pope's embrace.

And I told the Sovereign Pontiff, "What I have seen—what my brother Eminence has endured—will spread eventually to most of Africa."

"I can not believe you, *cher Augustin.*"

"It's beginning now, Your Holiness, just to the west, in the Nigerian civil war. Millions of the innocent are dying of starvation. Greed, tribalism, and bloodlust play their part, but whatever those plagues can not accomplish, the mischief of the powers—the Russians, the Americans, the Europeans—surely shall. For them, the whole of Africa is a bloody arms bazaar."

"Love will prevail!"

"Amongst the corpses, Most Holy Father?"

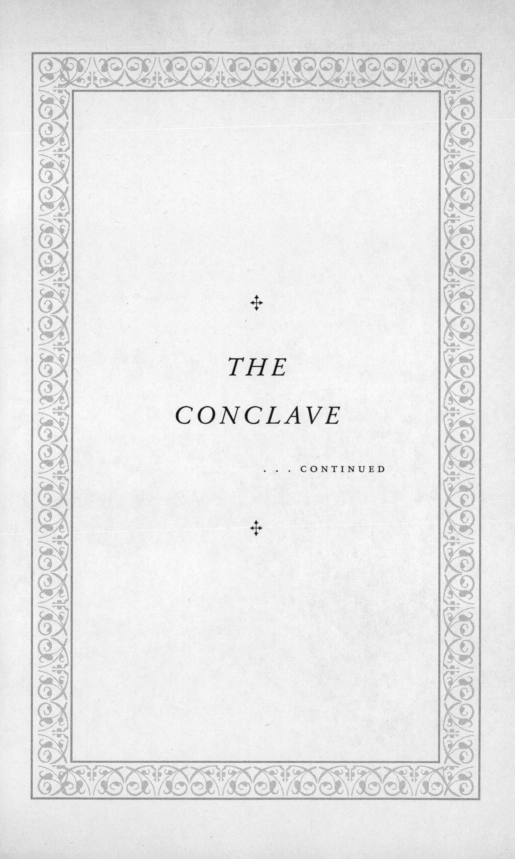

⁜

THE
CONCLAVE

. . . CONTINUED

⁜

"The cup which my Father hath given me,

shall I not drink it?"

⁘

The Conclave on the eve of the Third Millennium continued to deliberate. On I scribbled my abortive diary upon sheets of foolscap:

Sixth day. No result. Seventh day. No result. Eighth day. Niente. *Increasingly I overcome my scruples to the contrary and desire to be Pope. Slyly I embark on various manoeuvres contrived to demonstrate that none of the other candidates has any real hope of election—and intended, of course, to narrow the field to a single cardinal: Augustine Galsworthy.*

Never overtly promoting my own papacy, I urge my conservative party to support a palatable candidate from the progressive camp. Some few cardinals do—nominating the Archbishop of Madrid. He fails—as I surmised he would. Reciprocally some few progressives nominate a palatable conservative—the Archbishop of Genoa. He flops—as I knew he should.

In fatigue tinged with desperation, more of the cardinals turn to me. The electors commonly assume that I crave the papacy; they laugh at my imperious vanity and my putative ambition; but my ability, learning, and devotion to the Church could even my enemies dare to deny?

In the scrutinies, the ballots with my name on them grow to forty—I need another forty-one. As we princes take our breakfast of black coffee and buttered bread beneath Vasari's apocalyptic murals in the Sala Regia, the plump Cardinal Primate of Nicaragua, whose new cathedral I have recently adorned with French stained glass, approaches me and whispers, "Tengo quince cardenales latinos seguros."

I thank the Cardinal Primate, but quietly I protest my unworthiness. As I munch on my buttered bread, again I watch myself in the third person, asking of my conscience: Does Cardinal Galsworthy want the papacy—or in the deep of him does he not want it? Does he know too well the imperfections of his character? Is he not as worthy to be Pope as the other imperfect cardinals?

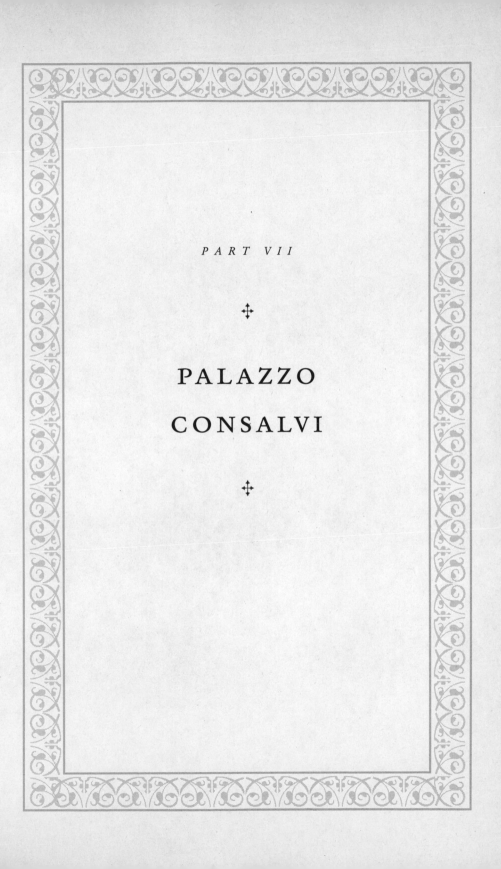

PART VII

✜

PALAZZO
CONSALVI

✜

⁜

THIRTY - THREE

⁜

Upon my return to Rome from the Congo, my life assumed large new shapes. In Africa, Soeur Pauline had told Cardinal Zalula of my menial labour in the leprosarium, dumping bedpans and scrubbing floors. At Rome, His Eminence Zalula revealed to the Pope and many prelates not only such colourful tableaux but also my feats of rescue and exorcism among the drunken soldiers. The Italian press, and then the world press, picked up the stories, embroidering them, and nourishing my legend. The Sad Pope told me, "I missed you, Augustin—not least for your funny vanity."

During my absence in deep Africa, the cardinals Baluardo and Sostituto had died within days of each other, each in his turn being hugged and kissed by the distraught orphans of Trastevere as he took his leave of this vale of tears to gaze upon the tearless face of God. I grieved for them both— for His Eminence Baluardo as the beloved patron of my young cardinalate; and for his brother Sostituto, no less, as a prince of constancy and honour, incorruptible.

In his growing zeal to internationalise the Roman Curia, the Pope had thus appointed a bland Croat to head the Holy Office (renamed "the Sacred Congregation for the Doctrine of the Faith") and a bookish Frenchman as Cardinal Secretary of State. More, the Pontiff now offered to make me Prefect of the Sacred Congregation of the Clergy, and then of Education, and then of the Evangelisation of Peoples, but respectfully I declined the posts (and the drudgery of administration), preferring to remain *ministre sans portefeuille.*

In doing so I retained my daily access to the source of power in the person of the Sovereign Pontiff, enabling him to seek my views on every matter of importance, and enabling me to keep my gemmed finger (so people said) in every papal pie. I did consent to become a Consultor to several important Congregations, above all to the Holy Office, where I could continue the legacy of Cardinal Baluardo by standing guard on the purity of Christian Doctrine—and thither I established my secretariat.

My storeroom office in the Apostolic Palace could no longer contain my scope; besides, I had exhausted its treasures. At the Holy Office, a shabby palace that began its life in the sixteenth century as the Holy Roman and Universal Inquisition, I took over a suite of musty rooms which I staffed with priestly secretaries and young typists of the fairer gender and stocked with tomes of modern theology in many languages. I read the esoteric, turgid chapters vigilantly, not so much to learn anything new in the nature of the Godhead as to detect dangerous heterodoxy.

The Holy Office was situated on the Piazza del Santo Uffizio, to the south side of the Vatican just beyond Bernini's colonnade. Each afternoon, promptly at three o'clock, I emerged from the Holy Office, strode beneath the great pillared and escutcheoned portal of Alexander VII Pontifex Maximus at the centre of the colonnade, and into St Peter's Square. Clad in my black and crimson robes, I was often preceded by two of my Nubians bearing my briefcases. These were little Mahmoud and his brother Ahmed, cherubic and copper, in age now nine and eight, dressed vividly in red turbans above embroidered capes and pantaloons. As we passed the fountains of oriental granite and the Egyptian obelisk from the Circus of Caligula, the appearance of such a cardinal-minister became an event. More and more, tourists gathered to applaud me and take snapshots—those clusters of the faithful and the merely curious genuflecting to impede me and kiss my ring.

I proceeded to the twin portal of Alexander VII Pontifex Maximus at the centre of the north colonnade, up the Scala Regia, through the Sala Regia and the saluting Swiss Guards, and into the papal apartments. In the antechambers, Don Gianni as archbishop and doorkeeper could keep other cardinals out, but not imperious Cardinal Galsworthy and his little Nubians. The boys, fidgeting and noisy, crawled beneath enormous armchairs, wrestled on the marble floors, squabbled and shouted in Arabic, until the Pope himself poked his head from his sanctuary to quell the disturbance. Then he ignored the other (resentful) waiting prelates, beckoning the boys and me forthwith into his presence.

Mahmoud, missing the Sunny Pope as Horse, could not warm to the Sad Pope; Ahmed, of a different mood, sensed childishly this Pontiff's isolation and pierced his shell of shyness. He reached up, tickling the Pope's ribs. The Pontiff reciprocated in his fashion, giggling for an instant, gently, and patting Ahmed's chubby cheek, gently. Then the boys were banished to an antechamber as the Pope and I considered heaps of paper, agreeing rarely— yet the Pope exclaimed, "*Cher Augustin,* I can not rule the Roman Church without you."

My dark hair began in those days to turn to silver, enhancing beneath my scarlet skullcap the landscape of my face, its pale skin stretched ever more tightly across my cheekbones, wounds (as we know) of my hard combat to keep my chastity.

And I changed my residence. My abundant rooms in the Borgo Angelico could no longer contain my books and works of art and brood of Nubians: during my absence to the south, Maha had given birth to twin boys. So I bought a disused building on the Lungotevere in Sassia—around the corner from the Via della Conciliazione, a brisk walk from the Vatican, and facing the River Tiber. The building was a decrepit hospital, hitherto the *Pronto Soccorso,* a depot for medical emergencies, and a palace originally. I resolved to make it a splendid palace again.

The edifice was of the eighteenth century, with soaring windows, framed by wooden shutters, beneath Grecian arches, coloured a sooty, greying brown. The main portal on the street was a heap of grimy Romanesque, all blocks of stone encompassing great iron gates and doors of thick wood. The passageway was wide and gloomy, but the inner courtyard was cloister-like and brilliant when the sun shone, graced with pillars ascending to Tuscan capitals and palm trees shading cobblestones underfoot. At a side of the courtyard stood a building set apart, a sandstone chapel in the Romanesque style, with a charming little porch beneath crumbling orange tiles. The rooms of the palace were numerous and dingy, but I brightened them in the style of the eighteenth century.

I made them over mostly in gilded Louis Quinze, with damasks of red and blue, chandeliers of crystal with candles in them, golden clocks, coffers of red morocco, elephants of bronze ebony, imitation Sèvres vases, imitation Savonnerie tapestries; my English pictures by Lord Turner of Oxford and Thomas Shorter Boys, landscapes with ruined castles, rocky coasts by moonlight; classical statuary mildly erotic, my Baroque crucifixes and Renaissance triptychs of the saints borrowed permanently from the Apostolic Palace; but I added originals, and expensive copies of masterpieces by the likes of David, Ingres, and Hyacinthe Rigaud.

A marble bust of Cardinal Newman and an oil likeness of Pius VII (after David's famous study in the Louvre) dominated my grand salon. Oil portraits of Chateaubriand, Lucien Bonaparte, and Cardinal Merry del Val I conspicuously displayed as well. The place of honour, on the landing of the grand marble stairway, was reserved for an august painting of Ercole Cardinal Consalvi in cappa magna. Indeed, I never called my residence the "Palazzo Galsworthy" but on a caprice I named it for my idol: the "Palazzo Consalvi."

I slept, as I always had, in a small, bare room, below a simple black crucifix, on a bed of wooden slats. I owned no limousine, walked much, ate frugally, and bathed as I had done at my boyhood abbey in a crude wooden tub. Yet my residence became so handsome that unkindly tongues, exaggerating grossly, compared it to Pannini's *Gallery of Cardinal Valenti-Gonzaga,* that fabulous tableau of a periwigged Eminence of the eighteenth century dwarfed beneath his marble arches and walls that swarmed with priceless paintings.

And how, you ask, did I pay for my palace? For the Palazzo Consalvi and my many charities, I eventually used up the million dollars that Urban Northwood had given to me upon my elevation to the Sacred Purple, but as a Prince of the Church I could rely on other benefactors. My fame as a glamourous cardinal grew apace in the world with my reputation as a traditionalist who clung to the old ways, the old liturgy, and the old theology. Moreover as time passed, I did but little to conceal my regret that the Roman Church had been modernised and that the Second Vatican Council had ever happened. As I aged, and gracefully, as my hair grew silver and my opinions were broadcast in the world press, Roman Catholics and even unbelievers from near and yon—who yearned as I did for the aesthetic grandeur of the old Church—sent me increasing gifts of money.

I became a favourite of the nobility of Europe, even of royal houses, not to speak of rich Roman Catholic industrialists in America. My elegant crimson presence was coveted especially at baptisms, weddings, and funerals in the private chapels of nostalgic and (often enough) dissolute nobility in Italy, Spain, Belgium, Luxembourg, Germany, Austria, Portugal, and at the estates of recusant Catholic England. On the royal grapevine news travelled swiftly; it was known that to have this ornament, the cost ("offering") was high—a minimum of one hundred thousand dollars or its equivalent in pounds sterling, Swiss francs, or Deutschemarks, the cheques to be written not to the Holy See but to His Eminence personally for disbursement to his charities as he chose. I gave them their money's worth.

Watch me of a June morning in Bavaria, after the Confirmation of a fair young princeling, descending with the youth and his parents the prince and princess down the steps of an ancient Gothic castle, my little crimson train trailing after me, the castle's ramparts in relief against misty snow-peaked mountains and the onion domes of distant churches, onto a vast green sunny lawn with coloured tents where the Bavarian nobility have gathered for a feast. Leisurely in my lace and watered crimson I glide amidst the crowd, offering my ring to this dowager and that burgher, to this pretty child and that desiccated count, drinking little, picking at my food, chatting a bit in High German, saying nothing much, laughing at leaden humour, performing my part with suave diffidence, until the prince hands me my envelope and I can return to Rome.

How grateful I am to God for casting me so well in such a rôle as I relish my emoluments for my real purpose—since it is in Rome, in my own Palazzo Consalvi, that I shimmer most. More than ever imitating my princely models, the cardinals Consalvi and Merry del Val, I will see anybody.

I open my palace to all comers, between four and six in the afternoon, when in my ordinary black and scarlet I return from my work at the Vatican; we are in autumn now, nearly winter. Often the crowd is so dense that my secretaries must clear my path through the iron gates and the dim passageway, up the marble stairway past the portrait of Ercole Consalvi, to my grand salon. There I am greeted by missionaries in soutanes or black suits, nuns from Micronesia, bishops from the Philippines and Africa, American and British tourists, diplomatists, beggars, vagabonds, even a cardinal or two exasperated by the bureaucracy of the Vatican, impatient to see the Pope, and eager that I should whisper into the pontifical ear. Oh, *everybody* wants something.

But I never seem hurried, greeting my callers in various tongues, at peace for the moment and much relaxed. I have largely suppressed my stammer and replaced it with a soft, mechanical laugh, my reply to most remarks amusing or not. I rarely glance at whoever genuflects to kiss my ring, for by that time I am talking to someone else: "*Ah, Monsignore! E come va il vostro seminario a Livorno? C'è bisogno di soldi—come sempre?* Ha-ha-ha. . . . *Madame la comtesse! Mais, je ne vous ai jamais vu si ravissante! Et voilà, la petite! C'est votre fille? Mignonne comme sa mère!* Ha-ha-ha. . . . *Padre Quien? Ah, sí! Padre Molina y Martínez. Conozco usted desde que Sevilla, verdad?* Ha-ha-ha. And whom have we here?"

First priest: "We're from Philadelphia, Your Eminence."

I: "A good city. In Rome on pilgrimage?"

Second priest: "Rome's, like, *awesome,* Your Eminence! And we spent a week in Portugal, golfing!"

I: "Golfers, eh? Are you any good?"

First priest: "I play in the nineties, Eminence."

I: "My dear Father, you are neglecting your golf."

Second priest: "I play in the seventies, Eminence."

I: "My dear Father, you are neglecting your parish."

Philadelphia priests: "Ha-ha! Ha-ha!"

I (*offering my ring to others*): "Ha-ha-ha. *Mein lieb Doktor! Spat kommt ihr–doch ihr kommt!* Ha-ha-ha. . . ."

Like Bonaparte in Paris, I cast my eye over my many courtiers, debating as to whom in the crowd I shall single out for my attention and favour. Normally I do not look for princes, cardinals, luminaries of literature or cinema—but instead for some humble missionary, priest or nun, who needs my help. This afternoon I sight a tall young priest at the far end of the salon, half-hidden behind a potted flower. I head for him: the ranks of visitors recede like waves of the Biblical sea. I find my quarry as the crowd draws back, then regroups about the two of us, hanging on our words.

"Who are you?" I ask.

"Father Bubu," says the priest, of the colour ebony.

"Where are you from?"

"Rhodesia, Your Eminence. I'm a Father of the Holy Ghost."

"What do you do in Rhodesia, Father Bubu?"

"I run a little school and clinic, sir."

"Do you teach your children their catechism?"

"Every morning."

"What do you teach them about the Eucharist?"

"That it is the body and blood of Christ."

"Symbolically . . . ?"

"Oh, no, sir. That the consecrated bread and wine are truly the body and blood of Christ."

"Do you believe that yourself?"

"With my whole heart and mind, sir."

"Do you need money for your children?"

"My children need milk and books. I could use a thousand quid, Your Eminence."

"Then come to me tomorrow morning at the Holy Office with your credentials, Father Bubu. We might do better than a thousand quid. Ha-ha-ha."

Father Bubu genuflects, but I draw him up, then kneel myself to kiss his hand and request his blessing for all to see, before I beckon others to approach. This afternoon I promise nearly fifty thousand dollars to nuns and other missionaries and to needy bishops from the tropics of the poor. Half of my finance from rich and decadent nobility I reserve for the Pope, chronically in need of cash, but there is always much left. I practise Biblical charity with abandon, knowing I will have more.

I sit down on one of my throne-like French chairs. Ghassem in his robe and turban enters with a trolley of sweet cakes and steaming teapots; his children wander throughout the salon, offering refreshment. Attractive young men and women—painters, sculptors, musicians; prodigies of my patronage of the arts—drift in. A pair of the musicians saunter to the next salon, where they take turns at the Steinway playing Bach and Chopin. As the melodies flood the palace, as the guests mingle and chatter amid the tinkle of their teacups, I overhear a British archbishop: "Cardinal Galsworthy is a blooming *industry*."

Lonely amidst my random courtiers, I sip my tea, mull on the remark, and mutter a bittersweet "Ha-ha-ha." I ask myself, Am I becoming a blooming industry? Am I too deliberately like Leo XIII awaiting his predestined papacy as Cardinal Pecci at Perugia? Why, like Cardinal Pecci, do I insist on having my own and separate court?

And I muse, Could ever a priest so love his cardinalate? Could ever a cardinal so fulfill his boyish fantasy? And for all such pleasure in the years to come, must I only be myself, say my prayers, and abstain from sex? Why must I stage this European pageant? Why was I so at home and so at peace in the heart of Africa? Mother? Father? Who am I? What do I believe? Am I an enigma to myself?

. . .

I posed such stabbing questions to my Soeur Pauline, who had by now become my confidante—indeed, sort of my Mother Confessor. As I grew to know her better, it had astonished me that—beyond her simple love of lepers, her self-abasement for them, having for so long attended to their wounds and mutilations—she should be as well a woman of rich perception.

Barely a day after we arrived in Rome, weary of shouting at her, I bought her a hearing aid. She hated the contraption, and wore it only at my insistence, complaining, "Hearing draws me back into the world—and away from internal prayer."

Soeur Pauline lived at the mother house of her Sisters of the Sacred Heart, on the Borgo Pio, not far from my palace. She refused to attend my crowded tea parties, but she came to me at the Palazzo Consalvi in the evenings after dinner; so impatient was I for her saintly presence that often I descended to the street to wait for her before my iron gate. Ah, at last, there she walked, the chilly wind blustering at her winter habit of grey and white as she approached on the Lungotevere under the mellow lamps.

Often we began our visits by sitting silently together in my private chapel, meditating each of us before the Blessed Sacrament exposed in my golden monstrance. Afterwards, in my library, as a disciple of St Theresa of Ávila, she guided me through thickets of sanctity and mysticism, evoking again and again Theresa's *Way of Perfection* and *Castle of the Soul*, both books written in the sixteenth century.

I invite you to conceive of how much peace this diminutive and vivacious woman provided me—as we sat opposite each other on grand French armchairs, and from her faintly heart-shaped mouth below her eyes of hazelnut she addressed me softly in her low voice; not a voice I should call musical but melodious at least for sounding so serene amidst the sprightly movement of her child-like hands.

Throughout, my Soeur Pauline stressed St Theresa's habits of contemplation and mental prayer. But how could I, a proud and hectic cardinal, attain success in contemplative mental prayer?

"You should start by fasting, penance, and silence," answered my Soeur Pauline.

But I fasted and did penance constantly, I protested. At my work, silence was impossible, save when I fled to chapel.

"Prayer and self-indulgence do not go together," said she.

Did she find me self-indulgent?

"Well, look at this palace, Monseigneur! You should try to *love* more—and love simplicity especially—as you seek detachment from your earthly pleasures. Love and detachment are rooted in absolute humility and obedience."

Ah, humility! I exclaimed. Clearly I needed to be more humble, but as for obedience I was subject only to the Pope—and humbly I did all that he commanded me!

"No doubt, but may I say that Your Eminence is much too self-absorbed? You can solve your stabbing questions—'Who am I? What do I believe? Am I an enigma to myself?'—only when you achieve complete detachment. And I mean detachment from all the vanity of your worldly things, including your own flesh and body. You are too fascinated with yourself. The gifts of contemplation and self-detachment are never granted without valour and suffering. As Saint Theresa said, 'Make up your mind: you came here to die for Christ—not to have a jolly time for Christ.' Begin by being humble—like your brother, Cardinal Zalula."

"Ah, my dearest Sister," I cried out with fondness, "how hard you are on me!"

THIRTY-FOUR

Later in the evening, after my Soeur Pauline had left me, alone I brooded in my library. Hour by hour, I felt more guilty for the fervent part I had played years earlier in encouraging the Sunny Pope to reform the Roman Church. No doubt she needed some measure of reform; but now too late I agreed with dead Cardinal Baluardo that the Church would better have been changed by quiet edicts from the top—not by a General Council where combustible notions were given voice and people were allowed to vote.

In my Palazzo Consalvi, in my titular church of Santa Brigida, and at the Holy Office, I was fighting a lonely war of the royalist rear guard, and how well I knew it. Officially the marrow of the Faith remained the same, but otherwise the Church I despised and cherished in my youth was vanishing.

Gone or vanishing—at the least much mocked wherever they survived—were many of the quaint practices and rich symbols that had given such bright identity to Catholicism in divided Christianity and in the profane world beyond. *Out* were painted statues of the saints, before them flickering beeswax votive candles, incessant recitation of the mysteries of the Rosary, the endless hymns and processions to the Blessed Virgin, the fervid novenas to the Sacred Heart, the zealous cults of self-denial and renunciation of the world.

Throughout Catholicism, churches and chapels were denuded of their icons and turned into meeting houses so bleak they might better serve Quakers. Pictures of martyrs enduring horrors for the Faith, meant to inspire fear and set souls on fire, were derided by the trendy liturgists as too morbid and silly. Human nature was not dark, but sunny; religion must not be terrifying, but chummy.

Out were the delicious Latin prayers and in translation the stately periods of the Gospel in the idioms of centuries past. Christ no longer warned the Jews, "For many are called, but few are chosen." Now He said, "Many are asked; however, not many are picked." *Out* was beauty; the Moloch of ugliness every day devoured us.

Many of my brother cardinals in the Vatican no longer wore their robes to work; they became common, dismal men in grubby black suits. At Masses, my brother bishops no longer wore elaborate chasubles, but mostly plain white sheets, rather like the Ku Klux Klan's. The Roman Church as theatre was being shut down, shrinking the poetry of Faith. Was it Mallarmé who told us, *"Whatever is sacred, whatever is to remain sacred, must be clothed in mystery"*? Day by day I grew more sad, lamenting that the Church of the Council had killed the sense of awe and symmetry and mystery amongst the faithful.

Everybody asked, "What does the new Church stand for?" Everybody knew what the old Church stood for. To replace devotional Catholicism, so many of the little rituals and rubrics—the fragrant puffs of incense at Solemn High Mass; the Communion fasts from midnight; abstinence from meat; fish on Fridays; black chasubles and the macabre and beautiful *Dies Irae* during Masses for the Dead; most of the penances and myriad privations, hoarded like squirrels' nuts and stored up inside the soul as treasure to be spent in Heaven—had best be junked because religion must be easier, more relevant, and *chummy*.

The new pottage of liturgy and theology left everyone confused. Were so many of the lessons from my Père Benoît, my Father Abbot, and the other monks of my abbey of Vaucluse a heap of lies? Must today I feel ashamed because I had believed them? Had the monks repressed and wounded my psyche beyond repair by severing me from the sinful world, forbidding me the comfort of particular friendships, and hurling me alone into the arms of Christ? Must now I love Protestants so much I should pretend their errors and heresies did not matter?

For ecumenism also, I had lost my rapture. Against the tide, I did not wish Catholics to be more Protestant, but Protestants to become more Catholic; yet increasingly I was forced to wonder, What is Catholic? The primacy of private conscience had always been implicit in the Faith, but a conscience informed by the Church's teaching. Now the primacy of conscience, not the Magisterium of the Church, was enshrined by a mob of Catholic moralists and philosophers as the highest guide of human conduct.

I thought: What a tasty recipe for the Church's suicide.

In my murky warren at the Holy Office during daytime or here in my great library at the Palazzo Consalvi late at night, I released little gasps of dismay or horror whenever I read the wordy tomes of the New Theology. "Ooooh, that hurts!" I cried aloud, as I underlined some fresh blasphemy with my bleeding red pencil. A French Dominican had just written: *"Je ne crois plus dans un Dieu créateur."* [I believe no longer in God the Creator.] Liberal Catholic theologians were radically reinterpreting the Bible, demolishing the Faith as we all had known it for nearly two millennia.

The Sunny Pope's Council, ending the seminarian's isolation from the world, had gleefully packed him off to study in secular universities, where he fraternised with heterodox Protestants and was soon enough infected with their theology. Thus in more and more Catholic seminaries themselves it was becoming common wisdom—despite the clear statements of the Gospels to the contrary—that Jesus of Nazareth never considered Himself the Messiah, or the Son of God, or the Second Person of the Holy Trinity, or the Founder of a new faith.

Christ's claims of Divinity (the illumined Scriptural scholars told us) never came from His own mouth, but were poetic fables that His disciples invented in the decades after His death. Nor was Christ born of a virgin: He was unmiraculously and sexually conceived by two terrestrial Jewish parents who regarded Him as purely human flesh and blood. His miracles were fables also: surely He never walked on water. We may hope for Heaven and Eternal Life, but upon this earth we can never prove them, not least because Christ Himself never rose from the dead.

You consider me a sly and venal cardinal, an ecclesiastical dissembler craving money and high art to satisfy my gluttony for beauty. You do not believe that I deeply cared what theologians thought of Christ so long as I could keep my own power and glory. You are sinfully superficial! As I hacked through thickets of the New Theology, with my other hand I clung more wretchedly than ever to the lessons of my youth, and against the exegesis of the modern scholars much of me felt RAGE.

I was at home in the Palazzo Consalvi, in my library and reading still, when my telephone rang after midnight.

"I am suffering, *cher Augustin.*"

"I shall come at once, *Saintissime Père.*"

Over my soutane I flung my black cape, then on foot as always I hastened beneath a moonless heaven, half a mile up the Via della Conciliazione, across the great piazza of St Peter's, through the Courtyard of St Damasus, up the private lift, into the Presence.

He sat at a long table, amongst his glass eggs and gouache paintings and twisted metal statuary and other marvels of his modern art, above a little hill of documents, his face in his hands. He was not wearing his soutane, but a loose white shirt without a collar, his sleeves rolled up, revealing his hairy arms; black trousers dressed his meagre legs, and threadbare blue slippers his thin bare feet.

Without his robes, his mystique of papacy evaporated, reminding me of an underpaid cashier in a two-star restaurant. When he heard my footfall, he lowered his hands, raised his eyes, and gazed at me, full face, weeping silently. He wore plastic spectacles; beneath his bald head, those immense black eyes, thin lips, moist countenance suggested to me another image: the image I had been seeking.

You will recall my conceit of the fat and sunny Pontiff: *Pope as Horse.* At the Sad Pope's coronation, I had fancied my new master in different guises— Pope as Cloud; Pope as Cat; Pope as Mouse; Pope as Rabbit—but the forms were too demeaning and they did not quite fit. Now as he stared at me from his pond of misery with bulging eyes, wide mouth, wet cheeks, his person swam against my wish into a morose and funny hallucination. I thought, *Pope as Fish.*

"HAH!" I cried out.

"Do my tears amuse you, Augustin?"

"Hardly, Holy Father. I supposed—a—a sudden laugh—might cheer you up."

Again he read his papers, and resumed his weeping. Still ignorant of the reason for the Pontiff's suffering, I asked, "Those documents, Holiness . . . ?"

He answered, "The Council, *cher Augustin.* What did it achieve? I expected sunshine to flood the Church, but instead came clouds and storm, searching and uncertainty, darkness. . . ."

I reflected: *Blame yourself for darkness:* but I contained my tongue. Had I dissembled always so well that he had no hint of what I truly thought of him—that I considered him a bureaucratic Prince of Denmark, veering this way, and then the next (indeed like a fish), at first naively confident that the Church could be serene inside the world, now yearning but unable to arrest our chaos?

"Sit down," he said. I sat cross-ankled on the cold floor; painfully with his arthritic hands, the Pope held up a batch of documents. He grieved, "Every Tuesday, I am presented with such papers. . . ."

"*Ah, oui, Sainteté, je sais. . . .*"

"Will they ever stop? From the wide world? Especially from . . . Christian? . . . Europe and America? Petitions from priests . . . and nuns . . . to dispense their vows? Most of them wish to marry."

"Since the Council," I asked, though I knew the answer, "how many priests and nuns have left us?"

"Thousands?"

"Not tens of thousands, Holiness?"

"*Hélas!* And vocations of priests and nuns are drying up."

"What will you do with those documents?"

"I shall sign them."

"May I urge Your Holiness to refuse?"

"But I must sign them. They have been submitted in proper form, according to Canon Law."

I was tempted to leap at him, to prevent his signature, to seize his hands and break the bones. Instead, I responded, nearly shouting, "Let them *keep* their vows—as you do and I do! Does Your Holiness imagine that I enjoy my chastity?"

The Pontiff groaned, pushing the papers, as though unclean, far from him across his great table. Yet I knew that in the morning, removed from my influence, hearkening to other voices, he would relent and scratch his name across those pages. I rose from the floor, rasping, "I'm home to bed."

"Stay a moment and pray with me, *cher Augustin*," said the Pope more calmly.

I knelt at his feet, took out my beads, and recited with him the Sorrowful Mysteries of the Rosary; reliving the agony in the garden, the scourging, the crowning with thorns, the bearing of the cross, the crucifixion of the saint who may, or who may not have been, the Son of God? Refreshed, more cheerful, the Pontiff got up from his chair and rummaged inside his glass eggs, as ever seeking a gift for me. "Would you like a bar of Perugian chocolate—or a fig?"

"Oh, I'd love a fig, Most Holy Father."

Descending to kiss the Pope's bare hand, I noticed a stiff, dark something peeping above the crest of his collarless blouse. *Dear God,* I thought, *he's wearing a hair shirt.*

The Sad Pope continued to favour me not only for my companionship but for my gifts of work. When he needed a quick speech, I drafted it. I advised him on foreign policy, the appointment of bishops, the defense of doctrine—not that he listened to me well. I could digest in an hour a thick dossier that might have baffled more backward cardinals for a week. Constantly in different languages I dictated letters, memoranda, briefs, and bitter critiques of mischievous theologians.

My secretariat at the Holy Office kept growing, a separate centre of power inside the Roman Church's government, allowed to flourish at the Sovereign's pleasure, an international sort of place industrious with aides who wore the cloth, veiled nuns, young laymen in sombre suits, and young unmarried women who dressed more brightly.

I kept obsessively busy; at home I practised loyally at my Steinway for an hour after dinner, and I remained as lithe as any schoolboy by fasting often and taking five-mile walks. Still I slept little, tormented by my own self-doubt—and for that more than ever I sought consolation from my Soeur Pauline.

In my library she told me, "Saint Theresa did not undergo her true conversion until she was nearly forty, only a little younger than Your Eminence. One day, not knowing why, she fell in tears at the foot of the Cross, and felt at last every worldly emotion die inside herself. The shock threw her into a trance. In her trances she saw not only Christ, but the Devil, too—and Hell with all its horrors. Yet always Heaven and its voices returned to speak to her—as I pray that one day they will speak to you."

"But they're speaking to me now—through you—*ma soeur,*" said I.

Truly I needed her—as the voice of my better self, of my conscience, and of my humility not yet born—to do battle with my narcissism. I loved her company because she never nagged me, even when she said, "You show off too much."

Soeur Pauline spent much of the day at a soup kitchen for poor Africans near the Colosseum and the Arch of Constantine, one of my charities. There as in the Congo, in a makeshift building of wood and tin, she scrubbed floors and water closets, disbursed oranges and loaves of bread, and ladled out steaming lentil soup to hundreds of hungry Senegalese, Ethiopians, and Somalis. When not at the soup kitchen, she helped at my secretariat in the Holy Office, where I made sure that she read all of my correspondence and kept abreast of my affairs, but increasingly my wealth distressed her.

"When will Your Eminence embrace holy poverty?" she wondered.

"If I embrace holy poverty," I answered, "I can no longer help the poor."

"Convenient logic," said she, smiling slyly through her tiny teeth and her brownish-ruby eyes. "You could sell your Palazzo Consalvi and all its treasures—and give the money to the poor."

"*Ah, ma soeur, ma soeur. . . .*"

If I was plaintive, her voice was always gentle, with no tremor of mockery or irony. In those gloomy chambers of the Holy Office, she paused to watch a pair of my young typists deposit documents on my desk, wiggling just a bit their little Italian bottoms as they did so.

I must confess that I chose my lay typists and stenographers less for their piety and intellect than for their allure—ignoring too often the reproaches of Canon Law against the propinquity of priests to young women. Against all my rhymes of prudence, I tended to engage grisettes, innocent wenches, fresh-skinned tootsies who could punch keys and take dictation but otherwise not nymphs of wisdom. Though I did not deign to flirt with them, my tone of voice towards them was perhaps too fond as I caressed them with my eyes.

Reading her thoughts, I asked of Soeur Pauline, "Are they too young and pretty, my Sister?"

She said, "Too true, Monseigneur! You have an eye for lovely women—an eye you should shut."

"Ha-ha-ha. But you are the loveliest of them all, *ma Soeur Pauline.* How old are you now?"

"Fifty-two, Your Eminence."

"Yet your colour is so lambent, at moments even luminescent, and—despite your arthritis—you haven't a wrinkle still. Can you imagine how much I love you?"

Though she never mentioned it, I surmised that in her sanctity my Soeur Pauline practised—as had St Theresa—the ascetical discipline of wearing a hair undergarment or perhaps even of inflicting on her flesh the monastic scourge as she repeated the Passion of her Lord. I thought it better not to ask her; but I remonstrated with the Pope for his own monasticism.

The Pontiff's torments were more deep than mine. He blamed himself for the disorder of the Church. Of an evening he told me, "Again and again, I have begged God to give me guidance, but He does not answer. I am supposed to be His Vicar. Why won't He listen? Could God be deaf? I must somehow seize His attention."

To win God's attention, the Sovereign Pontiff undertook the exalted disciplines of so many saints and mystics in previous epochs of the Church. He went on wearing his hair shirt, unyielding to my pleas that already he endured too much discomfort from his arthritis—harsher than my Soeur Pauline's. "Christ suffered—so must His Vicar," he rebutted me. "We must offer up to Him Our suffering for Our sins—and for the sins of the whole Church."

As his arthritis worsened, he increased his disciplines. Now and again, he took to wearing thorns—a spiked garter round his thigh. Nuns and monks in the Apostolic Palace whispered to me that occasionally very late at night, when the Pope was sure that his household slept, through the frescoed rooms and the marble halls they heard echoes of his moans: from his scourge—as he flailed at his back until the blood ran.

I admired the mystics of the past who for the sake of Heaven punished their flesh—St Anthony of Egypt, St Francis of Assisi, St Theresa of Ávila, St John of the Cross, the Curé d'Ars. Pius VII, a Benedictine and my most beloved pope, continued in his overscrupulosity to practise monastic flagellation after rising to to the papacy, even when he became the captive of Napoleon, as if that outrage were his fault. Cardinal Merry del Val, another of my heroes, for all his elegance and pomp, in private expiated for mankind's sins by resorting to the scourge.

In the third century, the troglodyte St Anthony of Egypt was besieged by hosts of devils in the desert, tempting him with fantasies of women and the delights of carnal love. For twenty years, St Anthony repulsed the devils by terrible mortifications of his flesh—hair shirts and scourges and by rolling naked in thorns and brambles and by self-starvation, deigning to eat but bread and water twice a week. In the nineteenth century, the Curé d'Ars wrestled with Satan beneath his bed, and banished him by living on boiled potatoes; and for fifteen, sixteen, eighteen hours a day by locking himself in utter darkness and hearing the confessions of ceaseless penitents. When parched with thirst, the Curé d'Ars abstained from water; he never killed a flea; he never sniffed a flower.

That was the point of self-inflicted torments—not only the expiation of mankind's sins but gifts from Heaven. It was the Infinite for which these mystics thirsted, and they rode gladly on every wave that beckoned to bear them towards it. All great mystics possessed the "gift of tears"—the turning of their sorrows to service of the Lord in hope of miraculous revelations. I suspected that with that kind of yearning, the Sad Pope inflicted suffering on his own person: in doing penance for the sinful Church, he longed that God might cease His silence, reveal Himself, and speak clearly of His wishes.

In such a quest, this most modern of the popes was—eerily—old-fashioned. In some monastic orders flagellation was still practised, hair shirts and thorns were worn, but those traditions were dying out. It may surprise you that I did not mourn their disappearance. Much as I disdained the modern world, I had read enough of William James and Sigmund Freud to become suspicious of self-torture no matter that the motives were exalted.

I believed in asceticism—up to a point. I have told you that I fasted often and lived austerely in my halls of splendour, but I believed also in a healthy body; and you know that when I went on holiday I hiked and mounted horse and swam nude in rushing streams. Christianity was not all lamentation; it was also a creed of Joy; in times past it spawned merry cultures. "Wherever a Catholic sun doth shine/ There's always laughter and good red wine/ At least I've always found it so/ *Benedicamus Domino!*"

The Sunny Pope had possessed that kind of mirth; not this Pontiff. With the insights of psychology, I found hair shirts, thorns, and flagellation in modern time eccentric, unnecessary, and dark: I pressed this view on the Pope.

"But what of holy prudence, *Saintissime Père?*" I asked. "Your chosen path of sanctity is not truly valiant. In a way, it is even selfish."

"I have no choice, *cher Augustin,*" he reasoned. "To get God to listen, I must shriek supernaturally. Is my pontificate a failure?"

"Your intellect is admired throughout the world," I entreated. "Your encyclicals glow with lustrous perceptions of the Faith. Your social doctrines are so progressive they seem years or decades before their time. But your first duty to the Church is to keep your health—the better to pursue a long, I pray a very great, pontificate. Look at you. With your arthritis, at times you can barely move. I beseech you, Holy Father, cast aside your hair shirt, your thorns, your scourge! In all things look to the end! *In omnibus respice finem!*"

The Pope scratched his torso beneath his hair shirt. "Darkness, darkness!" he cried at me. "'*Tam infirmi sumus, per lucernam quaerimus diem!*' We are so weak, We seek daylight in a lamp!"

✛

✛

I played rather a high part in the Roman Pontiff's deliberations about sexual congress and birth control. Moved not least by the pain of mothers bearing too many children, the Pope as we remember had established a commission to study natural and mechanical contraception. As he reigned on and on, the commission continued to debate. Impatiently throughout Christendom, everybody wondered: Will the anathemas of the Church against condoms, diaphragms, and suchlike be softened or revoked?

The Sad Pope was aghast at being forced to resolve the riddle. But he had no choice, since (on my advice) he had removed the question from the quarrels of the Council and reserved the riddle to himself. He knew that whatever his decision, it would define his papacy until the end of time—much as Clement XIV's suppression of the Jesuits in the eighteenth century (for their "perfidious intrigues" against the Bourbon princes) eclipsed all other deeds of his dark pontificate.

Typically, the Sad Pope kept deciding not to decide, seeking solace in his ritual of interring a problem in ecclesiastical bureaucracy. He demanded more opinions, enlarged his commission, then enlarged it again; read volumes of memoranda, studies, petitions, warnings; wrote myriad comments in the margins; listened, discussed, debated, pondered, and uttered no pronouncement.

Still, I have been perhaps unkind to portray my master as a vacillating Prince of Denmark. In truth the Pontiff was not so much irresolute as he was an architect of time—obsessed with weights and measures, the balances of light and shadow, looking for ever beyond the vexations of the day-to-day as subtly he tried to twist distasteful facts to his distant, sacred ends. He did not ignore reality, but reality could never make him rush.

Over several years, I loyally attended irregular meetings of the Commission on Conjugal Morality—held near the papal apartments in the Hall of the Consistory. The Pope presided, sitting not on his gilded throne but at the head of a lacquered Venetian table beneath the Counter Reformation grandeur, the walls so radiant with Brill's lunettes enshrining the most venerated of celibate Italian troglodytes.

Yet the members of the Commission on Conjugal Morality were not all of them celibate. At the Pontiff's behest, chaste prelates and theologians were joined at the Venetian table variously by medical doctors, biologists, sociologists, psychiatrists, women of liberal professions, and professors of philosophy; the Pope occasionally made terse remarks but otherwise was mute. I must be honest. Seated beside the Sovereign Pontiff, I became by turns voluble and cross.

An American physician, a British philosopher, and an Australian sociologist of the fairer gender did not shrink from contesting my defense of traditional Roman teaching. "Look, Father," the American said, "most married couples will do what they please no matter what the Church teaches. Face it! They want sex, not a bunch of screaming kids."

"Do you mean," I asked, "orgasms purely for pleasure?"

"Your Eminence," interjected the British philosopher, "is it not morally possible to sacrifice the good of the part for the good of the whole? Must every sexual act be ordained to produce children? Is it not permissible to exempt some isolated acts of sex in marriage—for the pleasure factor?"

"Not according to classical Christian doctrine," said I, more annoyed by the suave Briton than by the impudent American. "The Church can never sanctify even random acts of mechanical contraception."

"There's nothing mechanical about the Pill, Father," said the American.

"Then let me add, good Doctor, oral contraception also."

Said the Australian sociologist, "I'm a married woman—and millions of married women regard the Pill as a deliverance from bondage."

"No," I responded, "it will inflict worse bondage."

"Come now, Monseigneur," urged a French psychiatrist. "We seek only more compassion for young Christian couples caught in the maddening pressures of our modern world. Where do you see bondage?"

"To evil," said I.

"*Unsinn!*" exclaimed a German biologist. Nonsense!

"May I prophesy," I added coolly, "that the Pill will cause a sexual holocaust? It will encourage fornication, adultery, and recreational promiscuity among Catholics, Protestants, Jews, and pagans—a mere beginning. Easy sex between adolescents will become the rage. When the Pill fails, as we know it can, tender girls will take refuge in the carnage of abortion—which soon enough throughout Christian Europe and America will become as commonplace as dentistry. There's the bondage—to sin and evil, but also to a vast and coarse unhappiness."

Let me confess that in the midst of this argument, half of my mind was elsewhere.

I pictured overpopulated Egypt and the Valley of the Nile, the tens of millions of the breeding poor, tilling their crops of cotton and tomato with tools of stone; bathing naked in the river and its canals, mingling with invisible snails that infested them and then ate their bowels, leaving them hollow shells, brown ghosts of humankind. Huge families lived in hovels heaped with cow dung. Children swarmed about, their eyes milky with the pus of trachoma and flies buzzing and feasting on the pus. Filthy boys sold eggs . . . as my images dissolved.

It was the doctrine of the Church I loved that we should not lessen the numerous guests at the banquet of human life: with more universal social justice, we should enrich the banquet—a symmetry that I prayed for ardently even as I doubted its achievement soon.

Now two Jesuits, a traditional American and a liberal Frenchman, were quarrelling across the Venetian table about sex and Natural Law. The American propounded that—quite apart from Sacred Scripture—pure and natural reason forced us to reject all forms of artificial contraception. "Whatever contradicts innate nature—including contraceptive sex—is unnatural. As Aristotle proved—"

"My dear American brother," interrupted the little Frenchman, "no French couple, when they go to bed together, worry about Aristotle."

"Your American brother," I interposed, "is loyally citing classical Jesuit theory."

"Outmoded and worthless, Monseigneur," the Frenchman shot back. "Today we must help modern Christians to live full and happy lives."

Angry that a fellow Jesuit should scorn the teaching of their Order hallowed over time, the erudite American thrashed in space for some modern scientist who might agree with Aristotle. "Then you should tell your French couples that even Sigmund Freud, in his wise old age, regarded the separation of sex from procreation as a dreadful perversion."

"Freud said no such thing!" exclaimed the French Jesuit.

I pounced. "*Mon très cher père,* Freud said exactly that in his *General Introduction to Psychoanalysis*—when he condemned self-gratification for its own sake. Otherwise, there is no reason why, inside marriage—without condoms or the Pill—sex should not be fun."

"Even," demanded the Australian sociologist, "when the woman is infertile?"

"Fertile or infertile," I replied cheerfully, "so long as she does not close her womb to the possibility of conceiving life."

"The Church will never push modern women to play Vatican Roulette, Your Eminence!"

"Madam, we have replaced the Rhythm Method or your 'Vatican Roulette' with Natural Family Planning—and it works."

"Because it avoids conception?" the German biologist interpolated. "How this Roman Cardinal quibbles! If the Pill and Natural Family Planning have the same effect, why not endorse the Pill?"

"Because the Pill is artificial and demands no sacrifice," I replied with passion. "If a couple can not afford more children, when the wife is fecund they should abstain from sex."

"But they *won't*!"

"They *will*—with self-mastery!"

The American Jesuit: "Whatever the Holy Father may decide, his pronouncement will be binding on all Catholic consciences."

The French Jesuit: "No, Father! Should His Holiness pronounce against the Pill, it will be for couples—counselled by their private consciences—to decide if they must obey."

I: "The Church has for ever taught that the clear voice of conscience, whether true or false, must always be obeyed. Twisting that doctrine—as you do, Father—can lead to chaos. Every Christian has the duty to inform his conscience, lest he fall into error and see evil as good or good as evil. The Church exists to enlighten false consciences—as I pray she may enlighten yours."

The French Jesuit: "A woman who bears or does not bear children may have insights that surpass the Pope's!"

I: "Garbage! The Pope is guided by the Holy Ghost! What are you doing in the Church of Rome?"

The Pope: "Enough, Augustin! You are insulting Our guest. We command you to apologise."

I: "Forgive me, Holy Father."

The Pope: "Directly to Our guest."

I: *"Je m'excuse, Monsieur."*

The French Jesuit: "I'm as much a priest as you are, Cardinal."

I: "You and your gang are destroying my Church."

The French Jesuit: "*Your* Church?"

I: "Ah, that I were Clement XIV—so I could *suppress* you."

The Pope: "AUGUSTIN!"

. . .

I fell silent whilst the others continued to debate, seizing my pen and foolscap, and—in my fine, neat hand—I began to draft a papal encyclical forbidding the Pill and all other forms of artificial contraception. But even as I wrote, a majority in the commission formed in favour of the Pill.

On and on I wrote, as if on fire: "*Neque vero, ad eos coniugales actus comprobandos ex industria fecundidate privatos . . .* and to justify conjugal acts made intentionally infertile, one can not invoke as a valid reason the lesser evil. At times it is permissible to tolerate a lesser moral evil in order to avoid a greater moral evil or to promote a greater moral good, but it is never permissible—not even for the gravest reasons—to do evil so that out of evil may emerge the good . . . *numquam tamen licet, ne ob gravissimas quidem causas, facere mala ut eveniant bona.*"

I somehow heard the Australian woman saying, ". . . and if the doctrine isn't changed, most Catholics will revolt. They *insist* on change."

"That is obviously the *sensum fidelium* [sense of the faithful]," agreed the French Jesuit.

I glanced up from my foolscap: "The Church is not a democracy."

"On the merits," declared the American Jesuit, "we can not change the doctrine."

I echoed the American: "Nor must we ever state—upon a matter so fundamental—that the Church has been in error."

Australian sociologist: "Nonsense!"

French psychiatrist: "*Absurdité!*"

German biologist: "*Unsinn!*"

The Pope: "You have—all of you—much confused Us."

The Commision on Conjugal Morality disbanded. Months passed, but still as he prayed for the guidance of the Holy Spirit, the Pope made no decision.

"Was I wrong that God is merely deaf?" he asked me one midnight. "Is He mute as well?"

"God speaks through men," said I. "Under God, it is my duty to tell Your Holiness—decide."

In the end, the Pontiff took my draft encyclical—with the reports and memoranda he had received from his commission and the great world over—withdrew to his library, locked the door for several days, and wrote his own encyclical on conjugal morality.

Then, late one summer evening, he summoned me to the Apostolic Palace and showed me his encyclical, *Sacrae Vitae*—Of Sacred Life.

I scanned the pages, my hands trembling as I held them. In the midst of much anguished reasoning about Natural Law, I found the crux of his decision: "Each and every conjugal act must remain open to the transmission of life."

I released a grateful sigh.

"We supposed you might be pleased," replied the Sovereign Pontiff.

"Why did I ever doubt you, Most Holy Father? In doctrine, you are a rock. You are so—so sly! Was this decision your purpose all along?"

"Why, Augustin, what do you mean?"

"Why on earth did you take my bad advice—and convene that preposterous commission?"

"We had to show respect for the world's opinions."

"You must have had some other reason."

"We've so few amusements, *cher Augustin.*"

"Ah. So you sought the intellectual pleasure?"

"But the issue was human life!" That thin smile. "As for Our commission, We enjoyed the brawls."

"May I urge Your Holiness to make this document an infallible pronouncement?"

"But only once has a pope invoked Infallibility."

"I beg Your Holiness, summon all the cardinals, mount your throne in Saint Peter's, and speak *ex cathedra.*"

"Do you recall, *cher Augustin,* the declaration of the Council—that when the bishops and the Pope speak as one on matters of faith and morals, their judgement is infallible?"

"I helped Cardinal Baluardo to draft that paragraph."

"Then that paragraph will suffice to bind the consciences of the faithful."

"I beseech you, Holy Father, mount the papal throne."

"Enough. How will the world receive *Sacrae Vitae?*"

"Holiness, it will revile you. The most violent attacks will come from Catholics."

The Pontiff's lips moved, praying silently for a moment. Then he gazed at me and said, citing St John Evangelist, " 'If ye were of the world, the world would love his own: but because ye are not of the world, but I have chosen you out of the world, therefore the world hateth you.' "

You have noticed perhaps that I did not much care for liberal Jesuits. The great curia of the Society of Jesus stood on the Borgo Santo Spirito facing Bernini's colonnade; as Jesuits streamed from its Doric portal, more and more they did so not in their black soutanes but in dun shirts, khaki pants, blue denim, and lumpy tweeds. On errands they crossed St Peter's Square, where as my Furies dictated they sometimes encountered me.

On a radiant autumn morning, passing the Egyptian obelisk, striding toward the Apostolic Palace to assist at a papal audience for the Queen of England, I was delayed by the eternal milling pious, keen to snap my picture and kiss my ring. In deference to the Queen, I wore my cloak of crimson watered silk; my right hand was heavy with a huge topaz; I was escorted by six of my Nubian children turned out in swirling turbans and their brightest livery of embroidered satin.

As the crowd dispersed, I found myself confronted by a Jesuit in a shirt of pea green—the Père St Charles, small, bespectacled, and very bald, my bugaboo from the Commission on Conjugal Morality. The Father did not, of course, deign to genuflect: instead he stood erect and said, "*Voilà!*—the Imperial Cardinalate."

In my haste to meet Her Majesty, I had no mind to quarrel with the Jesuit. Pleasantly I said, "Ha-ha-ha," but the little Father blocked my path.

"I saw your comments in *Le Monde*," said Père St Charles. "Why are you attacking the French Jesuits?"

"I reproached only the French Jesuits who flirt with Marxism," said I, still endeavouring to be civil.

"There is much Christianity in Marxism."

"I never noticed any."

"Many Marxists are anonymous Christians."

"Was Stalin an anonymous Christian? Are you, *mon père,* an anonymous Marxist?"

"Christ never created a cardinal."

"And He never blessed guerrilla warfare."

"He'd be a guerrilla—if He knew you."

"What is your position in the Jesuit curia?"

"Assistant to the Father General."

"I rather wonder for how much longer."

"Is that a threat, Cardinal?"

"Would you kindly," I entreated, "get out of my way? I'm late for the Pope and the Queen of England."

I hurried to the Hall of the Consistory. The Queen, once having exchanged gifts and little speeches with the Pope, proceeded in her glittering tiara and velvet gown down the line of cardinals until she came to me and my turbaned entourage. "How charming," said she, lingering over us longer than she did over the other princes of the Church. "Where are these darling children from?"

"From Nubia, Your Majesty," I answered.

"And you are . . . ?"

"Cardinal Galsworthy, ma'am."

"But We've *heard* of Your Eminence. Wasn't your father a British war hero?"

"I h-hope so, ma'am."

"And good heavens, how elegant Your Eminence—and his Nubians— are! *Most* extraordinary. We must see more of you, dear Cardinal Galsworthy, in England."

For the rest of the day, I felt much flattered, but on the morrow I reverted to fuming about the Jesuits. Of late the Pope did not much care for them, either.

He sorrowed that since the Second Vatican Council, too many Jesuits had abandoned their old vocation as rocks of orthodoxy and gladiators of the papacy. Restored by Pius VII after Clement XIV's suppression, the Society of Jesus lobbied for papal infallibility with relentless zeal until that doctrine was pronounced by the First Vatican Council. But now the Jesuits were obsessed with the sufferings of the poor, with works of social justice, and in the midst of that they seemed less sacred and ever more enmeshed in the foibles of the secular.

They shook off their bonds to Aristotle and St Thomas Aquinas, shut down various of their academies devoted to educating rich men's sons, and scattered from their ample priestly households to live in squeezed apartments or elsewhere in the squalor of the world.

Jesuits took the traditional religious vows of poverty, chastity, and obedience, to which they added a special fourth vow of unconditional loyalty to the Pope, giving the Society of Jesus a unique status in the Church because it was directly responsible to the Sovereign Pontiff. "I would dissolve the Society in fifteen minutes—if the Pope commanded it," said St Ignatius of Loyola, heroic founder of the Society. Yet of late in the name of the new liberty inspired by Vatican Council II, many Jesuits sneered at their archaic rules of blind obedience to the Pope and to their own superiors, and boldly explored uncharted realms. They embarked on startling journeys of theology and discipline, not least a "third way" between celibacy and lust allowing deep sexless friendships with women that did not remain asexual invariably.

For the Pope—himself of the liberal temper—such experiments in religion became a crown of thorns. Since the Council, he had complained bitterly to Jesuits that by so transforming their Society they were defacing the ideals of St Ignatius. He was joined in his lament by a robust minority of Jesuits who clung to the old rules, the old obedience, the old Scholasticism, as repelled as he was by the Jacobins. The Jesuits had long been the largest religious order in the Church, but now in their thirst for change growing numbers of the revolutionaries jumped to the next step—leaving religion altogether to get married. Their ranks in the Society were replenished thinly: life without sexual pleasure attracted few modern young men. As defections from the priesthood swelled, so did the Pontiff's tears.

The Père St Charles lost no time in telling his fellow Jesuits that I had threatened to get him fired from his lofty post as Assistant to the Father General. Already my remarks to Père St Charles during meetings of the Commission on Conjugal Morality had become notorious common knowledge among Jesuits throughout the world: *"You and your gang are destroying my Church ... Ah, that I were Clement XIV—so I could* suppress *you."* How the letters flew, how the fathers buzzed, how telephone lines across the oceans burned with embellished gossip!

Following my encounter with the Père St Charles in St Peter's Square, I became identified throughout Jesuit ranks as head of the reactionary party in the Roman Curia and the Society's public enemy *Numero Uno*—the more dangerous because I had the ear of the Pope.

A tribal loyalty bound the Jesuits as it did any society of men whose inner councils were so secret they verged on the occult. A modern Jesuit might mock the infallibility of the Pope, question the virginity of Mary, doubt the Divinity of Christ; he might be savagely assailed inside the Society itself for the intemperance of his opinions; but should he be attacked by an outsider— even by a cardinal, especially by a cardinal—most of his fellow Jesuits would rally round him. Traditional Jesuits as well felt threatened by my outbursts. Within a month of my row with the Père St Charles, the Society in its holy liberty mounted a major assault on me in Jesuit journals from Paris to Bombay, from London to New York to Montevideo.

My reckless allusion to Clement XIV—particularly—seemed so sinister that it chilled Jesuit bones. The fathers recalled in macabre detail the sufferings of the Society in the late eighteenth century after Clement XIV's Brief of Suppression—not least its dispossession throughout Europe and the Americas—and now they feverishly imagined my future feats of mischief even as they unleashed polemics against my arrogance, the opulence of my palace, and the reputed luxury of my life.

Of course I could not *suppress* the Jesuits—but I could play on the phobias of the Pope to dissolve the Society's pontifical status and to diminish its singular power in the Church. Besides, as a cardinal, I was eligible to succeed to the papacy—and *then*? As the weeks passed, as Jesuit protestations from round the world grew more shrill, the Father General of the Society went directly to the Pope and demanded that I be removed from Rome.

Angrily, the Pope refused.

However . . . in the midst of that storm, another stirred.

My relations with Don Gianni, the Pontiff's private secretary and long an archbishop, had not prospered. Increasingly the Monsignore resented my intimate friendship with the Pope; his bitterness the harsher for my blithe neglect of him as I sailed into the pontifical rooms without knocking, without uttering a gracious word except a fleet *"Buon giorno"* or a mechanical "Ha-ha-ha."

In the high efficiency of that pontificate, the proprietary quarrels between the Prefect of the Apostolic Palace and the Prefect of the Apostolic Museums were reconciled; the art treasures of the palace were counted up and catalogued; but when the assessors reached the storeroom that had once served as my office, a number of antiquities were discovered to be missing. Seizing on the disappearances, and having sound reasons to suspect me, Don Gianni hastened to the Pope and snitched gleefully.

That evening, the Pontiff summoned me for a private chat. "But I had your holy predecessor's permission to remove those paintings!" I protested.

"Did Our holy predecessor put his permission in writing, Your Eminence?" the Pope asked.

"No. He said, 'Take them.' "

"Permanently?"

"He said, 'Borrow them on Our authority.' "

"We are told that among the treasures are some precious triptychs from the schools of Perugino, Fra Angelico, Pinturicchio. . . ."

"And some canvases by Polidoro da Caravaggio."

"You shall promptly give them back."

"Must I, Most Holy Father?" I grieved. "At my residence, the paintings are on display to edify the faithful. Here in the Vatican, they will rot in crates."

"At the least you must return the most valuable. You may retain, for now, the lesser ones—for which you shall receive, in due course, Our authority in proper form, that is to say, in writing. Now leave Us."

Humiliated, next morning I restored all of my borrowed treasure to the Vatican. The convergence of the papal reprimand with the fury of the Jesuits blemished my reputation and added another prick to the Pontiff's crown of thorns. Don Gianni told everybody in Rome about the missing pictures. The Jesuits called me an art thief. Weeks passed, but it did not please the Sovereign Pontiff to receive me.

Then, one afternoon in early winter, the Pope summoned me to the roof of the Apostolic Palace. The Pontiff was wrapped in a black cloak; a cold wind blew; fog rolled in from the River Tiber, enshrouding St Peter's dome and the Hill of the Janiculum in vapours coloured green. I recalled that from that roof I had been exiled to the Congo.

And the Pope said, "For the peace and quiet of the Christian people, you must get out of Rome. The Jesuits want your head. We have defended you for months, with small comfort from the Roman Curia. Showing up for the Queen of England with six Nubians in livery was a bit much for your brother cardinals. Yet Her Majesty seemed enchanted. Since the See of Westminster is vacant, you shall be Cardinal Archbishop of Westminster."

"But I'm not British," I insisted.

"You are a baronet."

"I barely know England."

"You'll be Primate of England!"

"I refuse the Primacy of England!"

The Pope seized my arm. "Then what shall We do with you, *cher Augustin*?"

"Keep me in Rome—to protect the Church and to serve you."

"Impossible. We've another foreign task—less glorious than Westminster."

"If I took it, would I return to Rome?"

"Eventually."

"I'll take it."

"The Church of Holland is riven with doctrinal curiosities—and insolence towards Us. Could the Dutch Church be on the verge of schism? Our Nuncio has returned from the Hague an ill and broken man, muttering tales of horror. Do the Dutch need the fear of God? Hmmm. Oh, dear. *Bien.* You are—from today—Our Apostolic Visitor to the Dutch."

"The *Dutch*?"

"May We suggest, however, that once in Holland you should keep your temper? Proceed quietly! Listen! Observe! Ask civil questions! Strive for holy wisdom when you write your reports to Us! Don't, ah, hurry home."

"Sly Holy Father! With one hand you feed me to the Jesuits—with the other you set me on the Dutch."

✥

THIRTY-SIX

✥

The Pope did not announce my mission to investigate the Dutch Church. In confidence he informed the Cardinal Primate of the Netherlands, but he shrank from arousing public fear of an inquisition. Nor did he deign to advise the Primate of when I might arrive, how long I might remain, or the scope of my instructions. Loyal to his wish, by train I entered Holland quietly, garbed as a common priest.

Besides, the longer I could remain anonymous, the more I thought I might discover. I wondered, Should I shed my black suit? At Amsterdam, I took rooms in a drab hotel round the corner from the Royal Concertgebouw, then ventured to a department store and bought a visored black cap, a double-breasted woollen jacket of navy blue against the wind and cold, trousers of thick corduroy coloured umber brown, and dark red boots. My face was known from the press and television, so to deepen my disguise I put on tinted spectacles that made my dark eyes seem greenish, and I grew my greyish beard, trimming it with care to keep it elegant and short. For my transport throughout the Netherlands, I leased a small Volkswagen truck.

This was winter, 1971. For many weeks, I kept much to myself. Holland, being small, was multilingual; with ordinary people I spoke English. Of course at first I could not speak Dutch, but Dutch was a dialect of Low German, so I read the newspapers with a dictionary on my knees and I began to learn Dutch. Even as I mingled with the people, I remained alone.

On frozen marshes near the North Sea, I spent days and days, ice-skating. In the galleries of Utrecht and Amsterdam, I wandered for a fortnight, so drawn by the pictures of the Dutch masters that I regressed as though in a drugged hallucination deeply and more deeply into the seventeenth century, better and more beautiful than now. At Utrecht, I admired Rembrandt's *Baptism of the Eunuch;* at Amsterdam, I spent mornings mulling on his tricks of light in *The Holy Family, The Jewish Bride, Joseph Telling His Dreams;* indeed, how dreamily I lingered over the four Vermeers at the Rijksmuseum, Frans Hals's Room, the landscapes by Ruysdael and Hobbema, van Leyden's *Worship of the Golden Calf.* At night, I danced in discothèques.

Does that shock you? It should not, if you understand that as a vigourous, chaste man still at the crest of life, I needed sinless ducts for my sexual energy. And so in the discothèques of Amsterdam, the wilder the dances the more I felt release. Nameless in my spectacles, beard, and visored cap I stood at bars, drinking draught *pils,* with toothpicks stabbing at my supper on little dishes—salted herring, eel, pig's knuckle—as I surveyed the mobs of people for separate women who might become my partners. Finding none, I danced alone.

Watch me below the red and amber flashing lamps, amid the throbbing youths and young women, the hippies in their jeans and dirty hair, as they share their hashish, passing the tiny cigarettes back and forth one between the other, and as I dance alone. I pump my arms, flex my body, kick up my legs, savagely. The rock in Dutch blends to rock in German which blends to rock in English, the beat so unrelenting that I ask myself, Do I hope it stops?

> *I'm gonna drive my tank through your picture window*
> *Drop a bomb on your pretty pad*
> *I'll push my bayonet through your pearly teeth*
> *And it don't tickle, baby.*

Now a young woman, no more than twenty, brown of hair and very pretty, emerges from the flashing lamps and dances with me. Her eyes are green, like Lidia's in Egypt. In rhythm we pump our arms, flex our bodies, kick up our legs, outlandishly. I glimpse a dreamy image of myself, dancing in wooden shoes. My movements seem to please her. She sings.

> *I'm gonna drive my tank through your picture window*
> *Drop a bomb on your pretty pad*
> *I'll push my bayonet through your pearly teeth*
> *And it don't tickle, baby.*

The music stops. We walk to the bar, where I order two steins of *pils* and share with her my salted herring, eel, pig's knuckle. She wears a costume of washed blue denim, beneath the jacket a man's white undershirt. She is Swedish, she says in English, from a place called Lund. "My name is—"

With my right hand, I touch her mouth. "No names!" I cry at her. I take out my black Gauloises, light one, offer her a puff, but she extracts a tin from her denim pocket and offers me hashish.

"I smoked hashish once—in Egypt," I tell her. "It gave me nightmares."

"Aren't you good-*looking?*" she teases.

"No longer *y-young.*"

By the visor she tilts my cap, runs her fingers through my silvering locks of hair, as the rock resumes. Singing new lyrics, she drifts away, like her cloud of hashish, to her solitary dance.

Alone, yet not too sad, I walk home to my rooms near the Royal Concertgebouw.

I did not neglect my duties.

I rose at six, hours before the winter sun, put on my vestments, and on my breakfast table celebrated a secret Mass. *"Hoc est enim Corpus meum . . . Hic est enim Calix Sanguinis mei . . .* For this is My Body . . . For this is the Chalice of My Blood." During the days and weekends, I visited libraries, reading whatever books and documents I might find about the old and the new Dutch Church. I visited the universities of Amsterdam, Utrecht, and Nijmegen, stole into classrooms, sat in the back, took notes of lectures by theologians and philosophers. On Sundays all over Holland, I stood in the rear of churches to hear the homilies of parish priests.

One Sunday morning, moved by rumour and curiosity, I drove my truck through the frosty streets of Amsterdam to a canal called the Prinsengracht and a shabby wooden church, not far from the university, called the Pieterskerk. Inside, amidst a décor of sombre Gothic and a congregation composed of hippies, students, burghers, I watched several Jesuits celebrate a New Mass.

They wore no vestments, only turtleneck sweaters, blue jeans, and jackets of dogtooth. They had no altar, only a pool table. They recited no Creed, no Canon, no Consecration of bread and wine; instead without prayers they poured French vermouth into a brandy snifter and fed brown muffins to the faithful. They read from Scripture, raged against American horrors in Indochina, and assisted by guitars they sang pop tunes and new psalms. Ah, the new psalms: "God gives Man freedom!/ And through freedom renders Man/ The equal of Himself!/ This freedom of God's children/ This freedom of conscience/ Is the Revolutionary principle!/ There and not elsewhere is the root of the Revolution!"

It rhymed in Dutch.

After the Mass, the fathers served coffee. I watched the pastor of the

Pieterskerk, a married Jesuit, middle-aged, leave the premises prematurely with his young wife cradling their howling infant child. A *married* Jesuit? Or had he been defrocked? I itched to ask the question, but I was jealous of my anonymity amongst the students and the burghers and I dared not. I felt a hand on my shoulder. Beside me, a voice asked in English, "Haven't we met?"

In a trice I put on my visored cap, turned up the collar of my woollen coat, then addressed the face: "I beg your pardon?"

He was a lean and youngish man, nearly as tall as I, in jeans and sweater; his dark hair grew savagely and his teeth protruded, but his acne—childish and harsh—made him improbable. He persisted: "I've seen you somewhere."

"Unlikely," I grunted.

"Are you a movie actor?"

"I drive a truck."

"Are you English?"

"I hope not."

"Are you a Catholic?"

"My mother was Jewish."

"I'm Frans. Maybe I dreamed your face. I'd like to paint a picture of your face."

"I saw you in the Mass, Father. Are you a Jesuit?"

"And chaplain at the university. I forget your name."

"I didn't mention it."

"If I'm going to paint your picture, I should know your name."

"Gus?"

How I loathed "Gus"—but I would suffer martyrdom for my purpose. Next morning, I went to Father Frans's room in one of those squeezed and gabled stone houses overlooking the Prinsengracht and the university. The room was large and dirty, half for living, the other half his studio; the walls were mounted with his collages, cobbled of pastels and bits of burlap, newspaper, tangled rosaries, and grainy snapshots of nude young men. Books of avant-garde theology lay piled on his upright piano and upon his coffee table, mingling with glossy magazines and pamphlets from the Dutch League of Homosexuals. I picked a pamphlet up and asked, "Are you a member, Father?"

"I'm the Vice President."

"You must be very busy—here in Amsterdam."

"Shall we?"

"Shall we what?"

"Begin your picture, Gus."

I took off my cap and heavy jacket. You might imagine that as I sat for him, I resumed despite myself my persona of Grand Inquisitor. I remained mostly silent. No need to ask questions: as he sketched my face, the Father's philosophy oozed out of him, like the colours from his tubes of paint.

He said, "I had to paint your face because it's such a contradiction. It seems so chaste and sensual, pagan and monastic, all at once. Would you take off those tinted spectacles?"

"No, sir," said I.

"Why not? Oh, never mind—I can see your green eyes. I'll paint you in your spectacles! Why, you could be a spoiled priest. Ah! that's perfect, Gus—your glance of surprised contempt. I must capture that! You're smashing. I love your lustrous, silver hair. I love your angry, flaring nostrils as I wonder about the hell you suffer. I dreamt last night of your pale skin, stretched so—unusually?—tight across your cheekbones. The skin burst open, and underneath I saw a pit, full of snakes and fire. Isn't that *awful*?"

Father Frans dabbed at his easel and never stopped talking: "Isn't life awful? Long ago, people sought refuge from life's sorrows in the dark confessional—stupid. Oh, *you* wouldn't know, since you're not a Catholic? In Holland now, nobody confesses. When students come to me to chat, they never mention sex. Well, it depends on what sort of sex. In Holland now, we all assume that university students—any young man, any young woman— will have sex. Nobody considers it a sin—so long as love is present in whatever sort of sex. When the Americans bomb Indochina—*they* sin. Do they commit mortal sin? Could I ever say so—since I don't believe in mortal sin? Do I believe in venial sin? The Americans are committing mortal sin! Lift your head a little higher, Gus—more towards the light. *No!*—don't smile! I need your surprised contempt!"

And he said, "I p-ss on Rome! I p-ss on what Authority—Rome or anybody—thinks of us! I p-ss on vestments—symbols of Authority! Rome says that homosexual love is sinful. I tell my students that homosexual love is beautiful. I tell my students that it's sinful to suppress such love when one man yearns for communion with another. I hate society! Society forces homosexuals to conform to a corrupt and cruel bourgeois structure! Is homosexuality neurotic? The inhuman bourgeois structure makes homosexuality neurotic! When the structure is destroyed, the neurosis will disappear! In my ministry at the university, I urge my homosexuals to adapt their preference to their daily lives in non-destructive, loving, joyous ways. If you love the other person, you can—you should—have sex with him. Why don't you talk? I know so little of you. Love redeems all! Don't you think so, Gus?"

His telephone rang; he leapt across the room. "Oh," he said to the other voice, "—it's only you." He spoke in torrential Dutch, but I grasped his anguish for a new lover whom he could not quite trust. "Or can I trust him? I do trust him! Will he make a *commitment*? Will he go to Paris with me for a weekend as he promised? You'll ask him? Bless you! You'd better not ask him. . . ."

He returned to his easel. I wondered distantly, yet aloud, "Does God exist?"

"I don't know," said Father Frans. "It's not important."

"What is important?"

"Tolerance. Acceptance. Commitment. Love."

He put down his brushes and seized a book. "When people ask me whether God exists, I read to them from this German book. I might believe in *this* God!" In High German the words of that book tumbled from him, something about God the Infinite showing up at a priest's house in the form of a mouse-grey donkey and the priest kissing Him and crying, "My Lord and my God! blessed be Thy holy name in all eternity! I love Thee dearly!" and then the priest squealing and kissing God the Donkey and pulling Him up a staircase to a little bedroom where he possessed Him thrice in His Secret Orifice.

"Excuse me, Father Frans," I said. "I'm going to be sick."

I rushed into his water closet, where frantically I raised the lid and threw up my breakfast. When I emerged, he asked, "Have I upset you, Gus?"

I sat down at his piano. He sat on the bench beside me. I played the melody from Bach's *Jesu, Joy of Man's Desiring,* but the piano was out of tune and the notes were sour. "It's still beautiful," he reassured me, with his left hand improvising chords on the lower scale as I played on.

And as we persevered he said, "You're the first truck driver I've ever met who plays Bach. Your hands—so long and fine—are not the hands of a truck driver. Is that the impression of a heavy ring on your right hand? Your accent is British upper class. Who are you—what are you—Gus?"

I did not answer, preferring to refute him with my *Jesu, Joy of Man's Desiring.* He asked, too intimately I thought, "How old are you, Gus?"

"Forty-three."

"Only seven years my senior. Do you find me ugly?"

"Your eyes fascinate me, Father Frans."

"What do you see in them?"

"Sorrow."

Rebuffed, he returned to his painting of my portrait. I sat throughout the morning in that disorderly room above the Prinsengracht as he stared at me, dabbing at his easel; but his bell rang often. Students—blond Dutch boys, dark Mediterranean youths—intruded on us, sprawling about on his unswept rug, invading his refrigerator, gobbling on cakes and apples, drinking his beer, muttering to each other in Dutch and French and Italian, clearly impatient for me to vanish.

Several times, vagrants and pitiful old women drifted in: he gave them money, clothes, and hot soup. As he fed the vagrants and old women, and in Dutch and other tongues joked of his romps in bed with his coarse young votaries, he displayed flashes of a frenzied sweetness and even of compassion I might call Christian: against myself, I rather liked him.

So I lingered still—through his tirades against Authority and his odes to Eros of a single gender—until evening when he invited me to dinner. We walked along the Prinsengracht to a proletarian restaurant, where we ate pea soup, smoked sausage, minced tripe, carrots, potatoes, and *wafels met slagroom,* waffles swimming in whipped cream, washed down by steins of *pils.* As he drank his beer, he gazed at me with such devotion that I protested, "Must you, Frans?"

"An artist must know his subject, Gus."

"You're making me uncomfortable."

"But you're only forty-three."

"No longer young."

"Not all my friends are young. I swear that I've seen you somewhere."

"Can't we get out of here?"

He led me to bars in alleys behind the Oude Turfmarkt. I was dazzled by that experience: less dazzled, may I say, by the ageing men in mesh stockings and shiny leather than by the spectacle that Frans called "girl drag"—lesbians who impersonated male homosexuals who impersonated women. The lesbians stood on platforms beneath their strobe lights, in the midst of their disciples, smoking hashish, wearing strawberry wigs, tight skirts, spike heels, strings of fake pearls, scarves the length of night made of pink ostrich feathers, dancing to their orchestras and a familiar beat. They sang.

> *I'm gonna drive my tank through your picture window*
> *Drop a bomb on your pretty pad*
> *I'll push my bayonet through your pearly teeth*
> *And it don't tickle, baby.*

Walking again along the Prinsengracht, Frans proposed, "Come up for a nightcap."

"Some other time?" said I.

"But you'll come tomorrow—to sit?"

"Without fail, Frans."

I turned away from him and hurried to my truck, thence home to my sombre rooms, deciding that I had seen and heard enough of Father Frans: fearful less of his indecent proposal pending than of his opacity dissolving as he recognised my face.

In late March I wrote again to the Pope.

Saintissime Père!

. . . and thus in sending me to Holland, Your Holiness has condemned me to a chilling walk through the modern world.

You can imagine, Most Holy Father, how my anonymous visits to parishes, monasteries, and universities have afflicted me. Dutch Christians yearn to converge with fashion. Too many of them approve the Pill, abortion, homosexual marriage—and so do growing numbers of their theologians. Our dearest doctrines, not least Christ's Real Presence in the Eucharist, these illustrious pedants explain away as they dismiss the metaphysics of Aristotle and Aquinas and end with hollow symbols.

The Dutch aspire to remove all the mystery and ambiguity of ultramontane Mediterranean Catholicism, and—with their Nordic fixation on legality—to bend theory to behaviour. They wish to kill the classical—may I say beautiful?—tension between doctrine and the world.

The religious orders are divided and bewildered. The radical Jesuits, posturing and shrill, prevail. At Utrecht, a Dominican theologian says that Rome has no right to judge his orthodoxy. At Nijmegen, a Marxist Jesuit tells his class that "Jesus Christ was a saint—like Che Guevara."

I wonder: Does Holland foreshadow the future of the Christian West? In effect, the Church here tells its faithful, "Do whatever you may please." In practice, the Church of Holland is in schism from the Church of Rome. Unless Your Holiness acts soon, and harshly, the Dutch disease will spread throughout the body of the Universal Church, infecting everything and butchering souls. Moreover . . .

Hardly had he received that letter, the Pope publicly announced my Apostolic Visitation to the Netherlands.

I shed my beard and tinted spectacles, moved from my hotel into the papal nunciature, and dressed again in my black and crimson robes. The Dutch press erupted, with pictures of me, cartoons of me, and venomous speculations evoking the torments of the Holy Roman Inquisition. By cypher cable I received new instructions from the Pontiff, telling me to rebuke the Dutch for their heterodoxy and impudence but to avoid a schism. I had been in Holland for nearly four months: how well prepared I was for combat! I telephoned the Cardinal Primate at his palace in Utrecht.

"Good morning, Your Eminence," he said coldly.

"I have read in the press," I replied as coldly, "that the Pastoral Council of the Dutch Church will meet at your residence on Saturday. I shall attend, of course."

"But Your Eminence is not welcome."

"You can not snub a legate of the Pope."

I heard a sigh. The Primate said distantly, "I suppose we can't."

Early on Saturday, I debated what costume I might wear to the Pastoral Council. I decided that to dramatise my presence I should appear in full scarlet. Over my crimson soutane, I placed my rochet of linen and French lace, my red mozzetta with its little hood, my jewelled pectoral cross and gilded cord. On my head I wore my crimson skullcap and biretta, on my right hand my blue sapphire. I carried my black breviary entwined by my rosary. In the nunciature's Mercedes-Benz, I was driven to Utrecht.

The Primate's vast residence, Dutch Baroque, stood at the edge of a pond swept by frigid winds and still frozen in early spring. When I entered the palace, I was pleased by the marble halls and sculpture, by the soaring pictures of the saints and the magisterial popes and dour cardinals who for centuries had governed the souls of the decorous Dutch faithful until the Second Vatican Council inspired them to revolt. I found my way to a great hall, all pilasters and foliate capitals; elegant niches with statues of

St Boniface and St Willibrord; murals of the North Dutch school, amongst them a noble painting of Christ before Pilate.

The Pastoral Council was already in progress. I lingered at the marble entrance, waiting to be recognised and suitably received. The hall was crowded with men in lay dress and perhaps a dozen women clad like house-wives: I assumed they were most of them priests and nuns. At the centre of a long table, the ageing Cardinal Primate—in a loose white collar and a bleak grey suit—after an unconscionable delay rose from his place and strode down the length of the hall to greet me. All discussion stopped.

"Eminence," said the Primate quietly.

He did not extend his hand. He bowed slightly. I fancied that I saw my red reflected by his pinkish skull.

"My Lord Cardinal and venerable brother," said I civilly. *"Pax tecum."*

I followed him to the long table, where he invited me to sit at the lowest place, in an armless wooden chair. Instead I walked to the wall and seized a grand armchair. I set it down at the centre of the table, beside the Primate's place, beneath Christ before Pilate. There I sat. Throughout the chamber, voices rumbled at me.

Pretending to be untroubled, I glanced about the hall, recognising from the press, or from my travels throughout Holland, rather many of the faces. Besides the Primate, the six other bishops of the Netherlands assisted, together with all Fathers Superior and Mothers Superior of Dutch religious orders. Only the Bishop of Rotterdam wore a ring, a Roman collar, and a black suit.

They resumed their deliberations. The Cardinal Primate—much em-barrassed by the splendour of his residence—proposed to sell it off. "Besides," he said sadly, "we need the money."

"But we have sold our rich vestments," the Bishop of Rotterdam objected. "Today, hippies are wearing them."

"We have no money for our seminaries," the Primate answered.

"I've closed my seminary," said the Bishop of Breda.

"Why?" I intervened.

"No seminarians."

"How many seminarians has Your Eminence?" I asked the Primate.

"Three."

"Ten years ago, you had thirty times that."

"Cardinal Galsworthy," said the Bishop of Breda, "if we allow our priests to marry, we'll have plenty of seminarians."

"Should we allow nuns to marry?" I speculated.

"Married *nuns*?" exclaimed Rotterdam.

"If priests should marry," asked I with mischief, "why not nuns?"

"My nuns don't want to marry," the Dominican Mother Superior scolded me. "They want to live in the world, do good, and have meaningful relationships."

"What are 'meaningful relationships,' Reverend Mother?" I probed. "It used to be enough for nuns to be brides of Christ. Today in the Netherlands, why should any woman wish to be a nun? If she is to live in the world, she might as well do social work or drive a tractor."

"Some of my nuns," said the Franciscan Mother Superior, "do both."

Thereupon for half an hour, I debated the Father Provincial of the Jesuits, who laughingly dismissed my doubts about the holy "third way" between celibacy and sex—deep friendships. "At the university," I rejoined, "your Father Frans pursues friendships that are a different sort of deep. And why do you allow him to perform homosexual marriages?"

"Father Frans," replied the Provincial defensively, "has a special apostolate for Christian homosexuals."

"And a special apostolate for sodomy? Is not sodomy a sin?"

"Formally sodomy is a sin, Your Eminence—but a sin can be mitigated by circumstance, depending on proportionality and intention."

"What sort of intention?"

"Is there love involved? Commitment? Dignity?"

His casuistry was too crude for the Cardinal Primate: "That is not the doctrine of the Church, Father Provincial, and you know it. Really, you should dismiss that shocking priest from his chaplaincy at the university."

"I do not dismiss people, Your Eminence. I engage them in dialogue."

"I, too, disapprove of Father Frans," volunteered the Bishop of Haarlem. "But in the Netherlands we no longer dismiss, expel, or condemn. We engage in dialogue."

"That is not, however, a courtesy you Dutch extend to Rome," I countered. "Whenever the Pope sends you an order, you ignore it."

"*Not so! Not so!*" exclaimed the Cardinal Primate and several bishops.

"Then what of the Pope's encyclical on contraception?"

"I accept it heart and soul," swore Rotterdam.

I thanked the Bishop of Rotterdam and asked, "You others . . . ?"

"The Pope has made an interesting contribution to the debate on sexual ethics," declared the Jesuit Provincial.

"*Contribution?*" I marvelled. "The encyclical is infallible."

"It is not an *ex cathedra* pronouncement," the Cardinal Primate corrected me.

"It bears the infallibility of the ordinary Magisterium!"

"Only if all the bishops of the world concur with the Pope," Breda growled at me. "We Dutch bishops have dissented."

"We *interpreted*," the Primate snapped at him. "We told our faithful that they should take the Pope's ban on birth control into account—as they decide themselves in good conscience how many children they might have."

"Thus," I reasoned, "you invited them to ignore the Pope. Dear God, what is all that noise?"

I rose from the table and walked to a high window, followed by the Cardinal Primate and his bishops. Just below us, scores of young men and women skated on the frozen pond—shouting, beating tin drums, blowing plastic trumpets, waving signs and banners that reviled me as Rome's Inquisitor. In the midst of them, dressed in jeans and a flowing scarf, skated Father Frans, holding up a sign: GO HOME TO ROME, GUS!!!

Hippies participated, long of hair, unsteady of their skates, passing little cigarettes back and forth one between the other, I supposed hashish. Some wore sacred Tridentine robes—black Roman chasubles, embroidered copes, jewelled mitres tilting from their heads—that the Dutch Church had sold at auction to pay its bills. Round and round they skated in the rich vestments, on that weird pond, mocking me and my Church. I returned to the table to debate the bishops—voicing the Pope's sorrow that so many Dutch theologians no longer believed the consecrated bread and wine to be the body and blood of Christ.

"We can not accept Aquinas's abuse of Aristotle's categories and theories of causation," a Jesuit theologian instructed me. "It is absurd to say that the bread and wine appear to remain the same—but the substance becomes literally the flesh and blood of Christ."

"Then why," I demanded, "did the Jesuits teach that doctrine for four centuries?"

"Those dead Jesuits were not infallible."

"But you are infallible? I prefer Aquinas and the dead Jesuits. The doctrine of Aquinas has illumined the Church for seven centuries—and means exactly what it says."

"Oh," scoffed a Dominican philosopher, "enough of that superstitious folk Catholicism!"

"It is a Divine riddle," I retorted, "not superstition, nor is it a poetic fable or folk Catholicism. You reject the Eucharistic decrees of the Council of Trent—and the reaffirmation of Trent by the reigning Pope. You are deep in error. The consecrated bread and wine become in truth the flesh and blood of Christ. That is the central mystery of the Mass—and if it is false, then all of Catholicism is a lie."

"I accept the doctrine literally according to the Magisterium of the Pope," swore the Bishop of Rotterdam.

"I thank Your Excellency, but I am dismayed by the silence and impotence of your brother bishops."

"Stop insulting us," cried the Bishop of Breda. "We're compassionate—not impotent!"

"Ah, you grey, weak men!" I railed. "You do not lead, you follow! A church that can not denounce heresy forfeits its own faith. Under you frightened, cowardly bishops, the Dutch Church has stumbled to the brink of schism."

"We've a horror of schism!" the Cardinal Primate shouted at me.

"Then act on it," I replied gently. "Expel the radical priests who reject the Magisterium of Rome and the defined essentials of the Faith."

"We can't expel them," said the Cardinal Primate, meek suddenly. "They refuse to leave."

"Because they know that outside the Church they'd not be taken seriously? They cling to the skirts of the Church they scorn. *Kick them out!*"

When I left the Primate's palace, the protesters of the icy pond surrounded my limousine, hitting it with juicy vegetables, tin drums, plastic trumpets, and GO HOME TO ROME, GUS!!!

For the next week, the Pastoral Council continued to debate me. Each evening, I conferred by telephone with the Pope, who kept commanding me to restrain my temper. In the end, the bishops agreed to discipline or expel their most flagrant ecclesiastics. We glossed over our manifold remaining differences in a joint communiqué: "The Church of the Netherlands remains joyously in full communion with the See of St Peter. All outstanding questions of discipline and interpretation of doctrine shall be resolved between Utrecht and Rome in a spirit of fraternal dialogue and Christian love."

For many weeks that followed, I lived at the nunciature, waiting for the Dutch to keep their word. The bishops chided a few of their revolutionaries, told others to be silent, but little changed. The Jesuit Provincial ignored the Pact of Utrecht. His Jacobins continued to celebrate dubious Masses, bless homosexual marriages, question the Real Presence of Christ in the Eucharist, proclaim that "Jesus Christ was a saint—like Che Guevara." Distraught—nine months after he had banished me—the Pontiff terminated my Apostolic Visitation and called me home to Rome.

On the eve of my departure, I visited the Royal Concertgebouw to hear Géza Anda play Chopin and Mozart. I was by now a famous—notorious—man in Holland. In my black soutane and crimson cloak I sat alone in a velvet box, savouring the melodies, serene with them, and ignoring war-like stares. For the finale, Maestro Anda's rendition of Mozart's Piano Concerto Number Twenty K. 466 was so exuberant that the Dutch demanded more. Graciously the maestro repeated the last movement, but I rose and left the hall, not eager to mingle with the Dutch when the feast was over or to suffer their jibes and insolence.

I descended the twisted marble stairway, neo-Renaissance, my cloak of scarlet billowing after me and the maestro still playing as I sang the delightful melodies to myself. Mozart could be dark and sunny, sad and cheerful, forlorn and merry, all at once. Ah, the drama and emotion rising, the cadenzas and twirly bits and the depthless, jubilant imagination! Near the end of the composition, the counterpoint of piano, horns, and oboes suggested mischief and then exploded in raucous laughter. The French horn: bump-bump-bump-bump-*bah*-bah! Bump-bump-bump-bump-*bah*-hah! As if the horn were mocking the piano, as if Mozart were laughing at his own masterpiece! At the bottom of the stairway, in jeans and yellow flannel, stood Father Frans.

"You tricked me," he said.

"I'm fond of you, Frans," I answered softly. "You've a sweetness and a generosity that touched me deeply—but you should not be a priest."

"I'm still chaplain at the university."

"Whatever I might do about your chaplaincy, I shall do on principle—not forgetting my affection and sadness for you."

"I p-ss on you, Gus."

"I bless you, Frans."

I bowed to him and walked into the night, singing, "Bump-bump-bump-bump-*bah*-bah, bump-bump-bump-bump-BAH-bah," still intoxicated by Mozart's joke.

At Rome, I proposed to the Pope that he dismiss the Cardinal Primate of the Netherlands, most of the Dutch bishops, the Prior of the Dutch Dominicans, and the Father Provincial of the Dutch Jesuits.

"I can not drive the Dutch into schism," protested the Supreme Pontiff.

"Holiness," I answered, "essentially they are in schism now."

"But this is a purge."

"I've conferred with the prefects of the appropriate sacred congregations—and they support the purge. I suggest that you invite the Cardinal of Utrecht to Rome, create him an archbishop titular, and assign him to the Apostolic Penitentiary."

"Who would replace him as Primate of the Dutch?"

"May I recommend the Bishop of Rotterdam? A good priest, an exemplary scholar, a rock of orthodoxy."

"I can't face another battle with the Jesuits."

"Nevertheless, I urge Your Holiness to summon the Jesuit Father General. Command him to dismiss the Dutch Provincial and to replace him with a less perfidious subordinate. At Rome, there is in fact a sober Dutch Jesuit—a good priest, an exemplary scholar, a rock of orthodoxy—who would clean those Augean stables of the north, and who would expel from the Society various egregious priests. I brought a list."

"Let me see it."

"Moreover, Most Holy Father, I have drafted for your signature several of the decrees."

"Let me see them."

From the pocket of his soutane the Pontiff took out his spectacles and studied my documents. It was late at night. We were not in the Vatican but at the papal summer palace in the windy Alban hills, drinking porcelain cups of chocolate at a table near a rattling window. In a corner, my Nubian Maha sat giving suck to her eleventh child: a little girl. The Pope said, "I am so tired, *cher Augustin.* My bones ache. I've missed you—and your children—terribly. Thank God I brought you home to Rome. I shall die soon."

"Rubbish, Holy Father. First you must complete a long—I pray a very great—pontificate."

"Where is my pen?"

"Here is mine."

"Why am I so sleepy?"

"Let me help you, Holy Father. No, you sign on the third page. Now this other batch . . . you sign on the sixth page."

"Is this prudent? Is this good? Aah! Done. I want to sleep, Augustin."

"I'll help you along to bed, Holiness. Why, you can barely walk! Lean on me. I'll lift you up. Are you asleep? No matter, I'll carry you. Up we go! Sleep, Holiness. *Ah oui. Ah, oui.* Sleep . . . sleep . . . sleep. . . ."

E ventually at Rome I received an alarming
cable from the United States.

YR EMINENCE
URBAN MORTALLY ILL SINKING RAPIDLY. PLS
COME POSTHASTE NORTHWOOD HALL COM-
FORT HIM W LAST RITES. KISSING SACRED
PURPLE.
DIANA DUCHESSE NORTHWOOD

I wish to be honest with you about my inconstant character in that season of my life. You will
recall that I had ignored cables of a similar sort
when I allowed my mother, Lady Daphne, to die
alone in Vermont. Troubled—and as curious as
troubled for reasons you shall discover—I flew
straightaway across the sea to comfort Urban
Northwood.

This was my eighth visit to Northwood Hall.
The month was August. The mansion, already rich
with art when I first saw it, had become a glorious
museum. The bare spaces in the galleries and on
the walls of the salons were crowded now with
new and original pictures. Within but moments of
my arrival, I remarked several of Claude Monet's
impressions of the cathedral at Rouen, and provincial art from the north of Italy—Lombardy, Li-

guria, the Piedmont—less famous but just as dear: miniatures and larger paintings on wood and canvas by Tanzio da Varallo, Barbieri Francesco ("Guercino"), Caliari Paolo ("Veronese"), depicting Christ before Herod, donkeys, horses, tumbling bridges, landscapes with misty cliffs and Greek ruins, and a woman in red velvet.

The main rooms had been refurnished in the French mode, neoclassical eighteenth century: as a butler guided me toward the apartments of his dying master, I beheld through doorway after doorway the long (indeed indefinite) perspectives, room after room decorated with cabinets and painted panels in the style of Ferdinand Schwerdfeger and Jean-Démosthène Dugourc, evoking Marie Antoinette's fancy for drapery and flowers at the Petit Trianon; marquetry and gilt-bronze tables; other furniture with garlands of ivy and laurel; chiming mantel clocks, in the style of Boulle, encased in giltwood moulding; vivid panels of painted arabesques and of crimson damask beneath pilasters of creamy Doric.

Urban's apartments were the largest in the mansion, separated from the others by courtyards and galleries, the walls the colour of fierce bright blue covered with bucolic paintings by Turner, Constable, and their disciples; the pictures—cottages, graveyards, sunlit lakes—the more enchanting the nearer I approached his bedchamber.

Urban Northwood lay on a large white bed beneath a blue canopy emblazoned with the silver heraldry of his Dukedom of Canino, defunct since the Sad Pope abolished the pontifical nobility five years before. Physicians, nurses, and Urban's little family—Diana, Adrian, grown to adolescence, and Pius, Adrian's younger brother—hovered near him. A night table of stainless steel was cluttered with his tubes and drugs and his needles and syringes steeped in alcohol. Urban exuded a certain odour, which my nostrils warned me was the stench of death impending. Diana, dressed as ever in double cashmere sweaters against the draughts of that palace, genuflected and kissed my ring. She glanced up at me and said, "Your Eminence is late."

"Who's there?" asked Urban faintly.

"Cardinal Galsworthy, darling," Diana answered.

"Sir . . . Augustine? Come . . . here."

I knelt by his bed. Sheets covered him to his neck, but I surmised from the contours of the linen that his body had withered to an elfish lump. I stared into his small, black eyes, dilated and swimming even more than hitherto from his cornucopia of medications. I remembered terse and mysterious allusions Diana had made to his "little fault" and I wondered whether—for much of his life, afflicted by such pain in his sick legs—Urban Northwood had not been a morphine addict. Indeed, might not morphine have induced his thirst for honours of the Church?

The dying man beat his bed with both fists. "Black," he said. "Black . . . black . . . BLACK."

"Urban?" I asked him.

"I believe that Urban is disappointed by your black suit," Diana said. "He expected to see Your Eminence in crimson."

I rose from my knees. "Ah! For the viaticum? I shall go and vest."

I withdrew to my apartments at the other side of the palace. From my black trunk I vested swiftly in my soutane, mozzetta, and other crimson and draped my shoulders with a violet stole—as if dressing for a performance. Clasping a book of Latin prayers, I returned in haste to my moribund billionaire.

When I reached Urban's antechambers and then his room, I found them mobbed. Several pale men in dark lounge suits (his associates in business?) and all of his domestics—butlers, footmen, and maids; gardeners, grooms, and stableboys; in costume, livery, and muddy boots—had assembled to say, "Farewell, good Master!"

His blue bedchamber was ablaze with beeswax candles and burning incense, the silver candlesticks and thuribles and crucifixes and buckets and sprinklers of holy water gripped fervently by American monsignori and bishops in floating purple and already busy at prayer. I knew that, much like myself, these philanthropic ecclesiastics had taken money from Urban Northwood, and I wondered: Can he *buy* his way into Heaven? From the chapel yonder, a choir sang Mozart's celestial *Ave Verum Corpus,* seeming to answer that indeed he could.

I proceeded to confer the last rites, not the Sacrament of the Sick according to the Second Vatican Council, but—by special dispensation of the Pope—the more macabre and more beautiful Sacrament of Extreme Unction according to the Council of Trent. Urban's family and the others crowded me, making my space so close, amidst the smoke of beeswax and the clouds of incense, that I did well to breathe.

Raining holy water on my benefactor and upon all present, I chanted, "*Asperges me hyssopo, Domine, et mundabor: lavabis me, et super nivem dealabor.* Thou shalt sprinkle me with hyssop, O Lord, and I shall be cleansed: Thou shalt wash me, and I shall be made whiter than snow. . . ." I continued in Latin, beseeching God to hear my prayer, to send forth His holy angels from His seat in Heaven to watch over, cherish, protect, and defend for all eternity my dying brother Urban's deathless soul. "*Per Christum Dominum nostrum.*"

It was time for Urban to confess his sins. Would he—at last—unlock the secrets of his wealth? I turned to the others, commanding them all to withdraw. They backed away to adjoining rooms or beyond earshot to the walls and nooks of that huge bedchamber. I knelt, and placed my ear against Urban's mouth, but his voice was nearly indistinct.

"Bless me . . . Father . . . for I . . . have sinned."

"The Lord God be in thy heart," I whispered to him, "and on thy lips, that thou mayest rightly confess thy sins. In the name of the Father and of the Son and of the Holy Ghost."

". . . last confessed . . . ago . . . when I . . . absolution . . . and . . . performed my . . . penance. I accuse myself of these sins. . . ."

You will remark that although he breathed with labour, Urban's mind of a sudden was turning lucid. For the next quarter of an hour, he unlocked his secrets, unveiled his mysteries, and—in answer to my questions—essentially he told me all.

Catholicism at its core is about two things: belief in Christ, and keeping elaborate rules. Whatever you may think of me, you know by now that zealously I believed in Christ and that achingly I kept the rules. No doubt you know as well that the Code of Canon law is brutally forthright about the seal of the confessional. Canon 889: *"Sacramentale sigillum inviolable est; quare caveat diligenter confessarius ne verbo aut signo aut alio quovis modo et quavis de causa prodat aliquatenus peccatorum."* May I continue? Canon 2369: *"Confessarium, qui sigillum directe violare praesumpserit, manet excommunicatio specialissimo modo Sedi Apostolicae reservata."* I should relinquish my cardinalate, shed my blood, die of leprosy and plague, before I would confide or even hint to you of the sins that Urban Northwood confessed to me on his deathbed.

I can freely tell you that I found the remaining rites rather less compelling than the epiphanies of his last confession. I pronounced Urban's penance; he mumbled his Act of Contrition; in the name of God the Father and God the Son and God the Holy Ghost I absolved him of all his sins. His family and retainers again pressed round me. I gave him Communion—the "viaticum" or food for his journey into everlasting life—prayed against the deceit and power of the Devil, then dipped my thumb in holy oil and anointed his eyes, ears, nose, lips, hands, and feet, invoking Divine pardon for the sins he had committed by his flesh. *"Per Christum Dominum nostrum. . . ."* With a sepulchral voice, he interrupted me.

"Augustine . . . ?"

"I'm praying, Urban," I reproached him.

"Open the door."

They were his last words to me—or the last I understood. He mumbled some other words—in Magyar? Then feebly he lifted his right hand, dismissing everybody from the bedchamber, even his wife and younger son, beckoning only Adrian—his dauphin—to stay behind. In a fog of incense and a whispering of robes, we bowed to Urban Northwood and backed out. Fifteen minutes later, the dauphin opened the door. In a brave voice, blond Adrian announced, "My father is dead."

The fog of prayer and ceremony continued on the morrow, in the vaulted chapel, beneath the painting of St Michael Archangel evicting Lucifer from Heaven, and I wore a black Roman chasuble to celebrate the Tridentine funeral Mass as the choir and a chamber orchestra sang Mozart's *Requiem*. How poignant was the Dies Irae: *"Dies irae, dies illa, Solvet saeclum in favilla: Teste David cum Sibylla. . . .* Day of wrath! O day of mourning, See fulfilled the prophets' warning: Heaven and earth in ashes burning. Lo! the book exactly worded, Wherein all hath been recorded: Then shall judgement be awarded. When the Judge His seat attaineth, And each hidden deed arraigneth, Nothing unavenged remaineth ... *Judex ergo cum sedebit, Quidquid latet apparebit: Nil inultum remanebit!"*

We buried my benefactor in his private graveyard, beyond the forest, in

Northwood Park. When all of the prayers and ceremonies were finished, young Adrian remarked to me, "It was like the death of a French king."

Early on the morning after the burial, I mounted horse and cantered through a birch wood. From Northwood Stables I returned on foot towards the mansion, pausing in my riding costume to admire the gardens and the mock Greek ruins. Those ruins evoking pre-Christian myth sloped upward on rocky, mossy steps, to a path of fescue tufts and laurel shrubs ascending in its turn to an Ionic temple, all nymphs of stone and recondite nooks fashioned of broken urns and pillars and full of flowers resembling candelabra growing wild. In a nook, on a stone bench, as if there by chance, sat mourning Diana.

She was not in black but in a cotton dress of reddish periwinkle, with white buttons at the front and a webbed belt round her lithe waist the tint of fresh butter. She wore a single string of grey pearls. We were both of us forty-six. Her bouffant hair like mine was turning silver, but no flecks of age dulled her blue glance. She had been diffident to me since I thwarted her advances in the hedge labyrinth fifteen years before, yet today her voice was intimate. Tentatively I sat on my own mossy bench, facing her.

"You look drained, Diana," I said.

"Not, as Your Eminence might suppose, from mourning," she answered. "You are the only man on earth, Augustine, with whom I can share my deepest thought. I'm glad that Urban is dead."

"You seemed so devoted to him."

"I tried devotion—for a year or two. Adrian was a godly gift. Since the birth of little Pius, Urban never shared my bed. I have lived since then as celibately as you, but my sorrow is not for lost pleasure. I remain ignorant of the sources of my husband's money. In that deliberate ignorance, have I committed sin?"

"Must I remind you, Diana, that I heard Urban's last confession?"

"Then only Your Eminence knows."

"And I am bound by Heaven not to speak."

"So must I die embarrassed by his money? From today I want no part of it."

"Why did you marry Urban?"

"Because I wished to live in Heaven—Northwood Hall?"

She rose, moved to my bench, and sat beside me, nervously twisting her string of pearls, as though half of her even so early in the morning intended to seduce me and the other half was hesitant, perhaps not so much from virtue as from the exhaustion of her death watch. Softly she embraced me; ruggedly I returned her caress, trembling for her stalwart breasts against my torso. Did she want love or merely consolation? From the gardens below came savage cries.

I broke free of Diana, sorry and grateful both at once for the interruption by Divine grace. Squinting through the ruins and the flowers, I saw two boys fighting—Adrian and Pius.

They were on the shaven lawn, beyond the classical statues, at the edge of the birch forest. Adrian had little Pius trapped beneath him, pounding his head on the grass. Pius screamed, "It's not fair!"

"It's fair! Say it's fair! Say it's fair!"

"It's not fair! It's not fair!"

Adrian pounded him again. I pitied Pius. He had been christened with that uncommon name at my behest, to honour Pius VII, my favourite pontiff, but there his claim to lustre ceased. He had nothing in common with his older brother. Like his late father, Pius was small, ungainly, and dark—an ugly duckling.

Diana, by now standing at my side, seemed indifferent to the battle. I protested, "Why don't you stop them?"

"They're *always* fighting."

I cried out, "Adrian, come here!"

Diana returned to her separate bench, languidly twisting her pearls. "I'm pleased," she said, "that you should give Adrian commands."

"Should I?"

"Now that Adrian has no father, Your Eminence must assume his father's place. I shall look to his love of beauty—but you must supervise his moral education."

"Urban once mentioned that."

"Indeed—it was Urban's wish. No creature on earth is—or ever could be—dearer to me than Adrian."

I watched Adrian release his brother, who fled sobbing into the forest. Adrian turned athletically on the balls of his feet, bounding towards us in our Greek temple, running between the statues, then up the rocky steps of the mythic ruins, until he burst upon us.

He stood between two Ionic pillars, still breathing heavily from his fight, his cheek smudged slightly, boasting with his half a smile that again he had vanquished his little brother. He wore burgundy trunks and a torn blue polo shirt that bore the red and gilded crest of his extinct nobility—Marquis of the Bells. His golden hair was long, locks brushing past his blue eyes, other locks cascading behind his ears and resting almost on his shoulders. His etched countenance was illumined by the morning sunlight, dappled as it shone through great flowers. He was fifteen years old, on holiday from school in Switzerland. How remarkably he resembled his mother, specially the young Diana whom I first knew and loved in Rome.

"Adrian," said Diana, "you should be ashamed."

"I didn't hurt him, Mother—I never do."

"What a dishonourable way to mourn your father."

Adrian's voice cracked: "Could anyone mourn Father more than I?"

Diana rose to kiss his hair: "No, dearest, and I'm sorry. I've been showing His Eminence your temple."

"Adrian's temple?" I exclaimed.

"Adrian built it," said Diana proudly.

"Ah, a precocious youth."

"Mother says that you're a precocious cardinal." (Did I hear in Adrian's voice an echo of Diana's old mockery?)

"Ha-ha-ha. Then we shall go well together."

"Together?"

Diana said, "For the rest of your life—it was your father's wish—you shall benefit from Cardinal Galsworthy's guidance."

Adrian mimicked my laugh: "Ha-ha-ha. That depends on the guidance."

Embarrassed, I broke off some laurel twigs and touched them to the youth's brow. I told him, "Your temple is charming, but all laurels wither. What will you build next?"

"A memorial to my father?" asked the youth.

"Of what sort?" asked I.

"I'm not sure. Will Your Eminence guide me?"

I meditated, and as I did I began to devise my scheme for Adrian's life. When I had first seen him as an infant, I thought instantly, *How I pity this child: how spoiled and corrupted shall be this child!* When I baptised him, my pity stopped—because I knew somehow that the sacrament had truly worked its miracle and that he might never be corrupted. I glimpsed him now as a grown man, dressed in rags, begging food; naked, in a dark hole, but not touching earth. Swiftly I prayed for guidance. I answered, "Why don't you build a grotto to Saint Francis?"

During the next several days, as Diana retreated to her writing desk, I spent much of my time with Adrian. In the mornings, we cantered horses. In the afternoons, we strolled in the gardens, conversing of art and beauty as they endowed the life of the soul; or we lingered over melodies of Bach as we took turns at a grand piano in a salon that reeked of Jean-Démosthène Dugourc.

Adrian's French was as fluent as his English. His Latin and Greek were good. His Italian was serviceable. Since a visit to Andalusia, he was learning Spanish. I told him, "You should not speak the languages of Europe exclusively. Eventually you should visit Egypt to learn Arabic. '*Wakati umeketi funga mikanda.*'"

"Arabic poetry?" asked the youth. "What does it mean?"

"Last night, dear Adrian, I had another dream—that you were lost in the depths of Africa and I went there to look for you. It's Swahili, actually."

"Swahili poetry? What does it mean?"

" 'Please fasten your seat belts.' "

"Ha-ha!"

"The extent, dear child, of my Swahili. For now, learn German—so that you may read Goethe and Schiller. You'll love Schiller's *Der Gang nach dem Eisenhammer.* Ha-ha-ha."

"I'll learn Schiller in Switzerland!"

"Dear child, you'll not return to Switzerland."

"Eminence?"

We were strolling again in the gardens. I answered, "Your public school in Switzerland encourages luxury and is much too soft."

"But I like Switzerland!"

"You are inheriting, dear Adrian, a great fortune—the very reason you must flee luxury. I had wished you to attend my own Benedictine school near Avignon. Alas! in the shambles of the Vatican Council my saintly abbey has shut its doors! However, the French Benedictines survive on the rocky coast of Normandy."

"But my mother . . ."

"Your mother and I have discussed the matter. In September, you shall go to Normandy. Be prepared for a hard school."

I grew impatient to return to Rome and my sick Pontiff. An attorney—a Mr Burner III—came to us in a helicopter to read Urban Northwood's will.

It was morning. I sat with Adrian, Diana, and little Pius at the long table beneath the mahogany beams of the great hall to hear Mr Burner III perform his task. We all of us wore black. Diana, at her own request, received no legacy from her husband. Little Pius was humbled anew by a trust fund of only one million dollars devoted partly to his education. He cried, "It's not fair!" and he ran out of the room, wailing.

I knew that the deceased had nursed a deep resentment of the Sad Pope for having abolished his dukedom. Thus I expected that Urban would bequeath to Rome a sum considerably smaller than he might otherwise have done had he died the Duke of Canino. In the event, Rome did not do badly. Mr Burner III: ". . . and to the Holy See, for whatever good works and charity the August Pontiff in his holy wisdom may deem proper—the sum of fifty million dollars."

Mr Burner III proceeded to my own bequest: ". . . and to His Eminence Sir Augustine Cardinal Galsworthy, Bart., Archbishop Titular of Trebizond . . ." There ensued a list of pictures, not least several from Liguria and the Piedmont, miniatures and larger paintings on wood and canvas by Guercino, Veronese, and Tanzio da Varallo depicting horses, donkeys, bridges falling down, and the woman in red velvet; and some nice sticks of furniture, including a cabinet by Schwerdfeger and a chiming giltwood mantel clock in the style of Boulle. I thought: They will splendidly replace my lost treasures by Polidoro da Carravaggio and the school of Perugino. ". . . and for whatever good works and charity His Eminence in his holy wisdom may deem proper—the sum of ten million dollars."

The rest of the estate, including Northwood Hall—with no constraints whatever—was bequeathed to Adrian.

Adrian asked, "How much am I worth?"

"Hard to say, Master Adrian," Mr Burner III replied. "Your father's holdings were so vast, and we have hardly begun our inventory. It may be months before we know the total. Millions, tens of millions, keep turning up."

Domestics entered in blue livery and white gloves, bearing silver trays with pots of coffee, glasses of milk, and a bowl of fresh strawberries. From rooms beyond a courtyard rose the laughter of other servants and the wails of little Pius.

I mentioned that in the Grecian temple I began to compose my scheme for Adrian Northwood's life. I intended that Adrian, fifteen years old and deliriously rich, should emulate St Francis of Assisi.

I supposed that my fantasy would take years to fulfill, but more and more I meant it literally. Was the Tenth Chapter of the Gospel According to St Mark to be taken literally?

> *... and when He was gone forth into the way, there came one running, and kneeled to Him, and asked Him, Good Master, what shall I do that I may inherit eternal life?*
>
> *And Jesus said unto him ... Thou knowest the commandments: Do not commit adultery, Do not kill, Do not steal, Do not bear false witness, Defraud not, Honour thy father and mother.*
>
> *And he answered and said unto Him, Master, all these things have I observed from my youth.*
>
> *Then Jesus beholding him loved him, and said unto him, One thing thou lackest: go thy way, sell whatsoever thou hast, and give the money to the poor, and thou shalt have treasure in Heaven: and come, take up the cross, and follow Me.*
>
> *And he was sad at that saying, and went away grieved: for he had great possessions.*
>
> *And Jesus looked round about, and saith unto His disciples, How hardly shall they that have riches enter into the Kingdom of God!*
>
> *And the disciples were astonished at His words. But Jesus answereth again, and saith unto them, Children, how hard it is for them that trust in riches to enter into the Kingdom of God!*
>
> *It is easier for a camel to go through the eye of a needle, than for a rich man to enter into the Kingdom of God!*

St Francis took the Tenth Chapter literally—yet not too soon. He began his adolescence as a libertine, a worshipper of beauty, wildly attractive, a minstrel with a lute, much fond of wine and fornication. He was converted to Christ by reading St Mark's Tenth Chapter and by visions of Hell as he crouched in holes. At Rome, he began to mingle with beggars, becoming envious of beggars. At Assisi, he gave his clothes and money to the poor and kissed a leper on the mouth. At Gubbio, he washed the rotting flesh of lepers and preached to flowers, fish, and birds. Then he married Lady Poverty.

And he said, "Fire is my brother."
And he said, "The moon is my sister."
And he said, "The enemy is my body."
And he said, "Money is excrement."
Was he not Divinely mad?
I planned that sort of sweet insanity for Adrian.

Over the years, I schemed for it. With his beauty and money, would Adrian become sensual and dissolute or could I seduce him to defy his flesh and shun the world?

I wondered whether one day he might not give his fortune to the Church.

I did not see Adrian as a priest but as a saint.

At Rome, the Pope was glad for Urban Northwood's gift, which he badly needed for the poor and to pay for the Church's government.

Of my own bequest, straightaway I gave five million dollars to missionary bishops, schools, nurseries, leper colonies—many of those in Africa. I reserved one million for the maintenance of my Palazzo Consalvi, the education of my children, and to patronise the arts. The balance of four million dollars I invested through brokers in the City of London so that I should always have enough of my treasure on earth.

M y flair for raising great sums of money for the Holy See contributed to my success with several pontiffs and nourished my power in the Vatican—in the Roman Church at large—as the years passed. Yet I must insist that money was not the root of my friendship with the Sad Pope.

In spring 1978, alarmed by his deepening melancholy and worsening health, and wishing to cheer him as best I could, I gave the Pope a small present. Perhaps also to fulfill my image of *Pope as Fish,* I had a lush little pond built for him in the Gardens of the Vatican, not far from the Summer Villa of Pius IV, stocking it with goldfish. In early summer, I entertained the Pontiff to a private picnic at the pond's edge.

It was Sunday. At early afternoon, I went to his apartments in the Apostolic Palace, finding him in such pain from his arthritic hip that again he could not walk. And from the movements of his torso I knew that as ever he wore his hair shirt. I told him, "*Saintissime Père,* no one picnics in a hair shirt."

"Then let Us be the first."

"I won't have it, Holiness."

Against his protests and all sacred protocol I lay hands on him, prying loose his fingers gripping the collar of his soutane, undid the buttons, and drew down that garment to remove the hair shirt. You will understand my astonishment when I found—contrary to all hair shirts I had seen in monasteries—that this one had a zipper.

"A zipper?" I marvelled.

"We have been called the first modern Pope."

"Ha! The latest fashion?"

Angrily I unzipped the thing, tore it off him. I told the Sovereign Pontiff, "I shall take this abomination home to the Palazzo Consalvi—and burn it. I forbid Your Holiness ever to mortify his flesh in future." His hirsute torso was covered with calluses and wounds, the unhealed sores oozing blood and pus. You might think I should recoil from the foul stench, but the wounds released instead a celestial spicy fragrance that at once I recognised—no less than from my Soeur Pauline—as the sweet odour of sanctity.

I had been standing over him in his ornate chair, but now much humbled I genuflected for a moment and kissed his wounds, for me the wounds of Christ.

I buttoned his soutane. Liberated from his heinous penance, he heaved a grunt, suggesting relief and pleasure. A wheelchair stood ready, but again I raised him up, in my arms bearing him cradled infant-like through corridor after corridor, then down his private lift to the Courtyard of St Damasus, thence through the Parrots' Court, thence through the Borgia Court, thence through the Piazza del Forno and another labyrinth of archways, into the gardens. I knew that he ate little: his jagged flesh and bones weighed upon me no more than might a sack of nails. It occurred to me then that he was my closest and dearest friend. Yearning somehow to reciprocate his sanctity, as I carried him I recited from the Twenty-first Chapter of St John: " 'When thou wast young, thou walkest whither thou would: but when thou shalt be old, another shall carry thee whither thou wouldst not wish to go.' "

"Into eternity, Augustin?"

"Merely to my picnic, Most Holy Father."

"But I wish your picnic. Eternity terrifies me. I have been a bad Pope."

Again I recalled my youth and that day in early spring when in the midst of my spurious romance I showed Diana these gardens. Today the air was warmer but as then the sunbeams tumbled from the sky like little gleaming pearls and the Roman summer was rich with lilies, red camellias, and cannas the colour of magenta. I carried the Pontiff down crooked paths, past the boxwood nooks and the fountain's mist and the statues of marble and terracotta as we approached the Summer Villa of Pius IV and its balustrades and tawny stone there amongst the ilex trees. By the goldfish pond, my Nubians awaited us—my whole family.

At my behest Ghassem and Maha had brought all of their fourteen children—Mahmoud and Ahmed, both of them fluent in Italian, thrusting now from adolescence into manhood; the others in age descending from the girls Khadidja and Suhair to the boy Mustafa; to the girl Rasha; to the twin boys Hussein and Hosni; downward to Wafa, the newest infant girl. (Ghassem's children by his dead first wife had dissolved into black space: Kamal, you may remember, had long since fled his father; Fatima had regressed to the Nile Valley and marriage to a husband whom she had never met.) The Nubians here, the women quaint in their tucked-up veils and the boys exotic in their pantaloons and twirly turbans, bore straw baskets of unleavened bread and *homus* paste, grape leaves stuffed with spiced rice, *farrug mishwe* or grilled chicken, hard-boiled eggs, immense tomatoes the colour of blood, sticky pastries sickly sweet, and plastic bottles of orange soda pop.

No one else shared our picnic. I had elected the Nubians precisely because they were not Christians, because to me they represented the whole dark human race, breeding relentlessly like nests of eels in the tropics of the poor. The Pope had grown to love their company. He was too arthritic to play games with them, but his manner with the children had grown easy as it had never been when he showed himself to multitudes of the human family. Like me, my Nubians loved the Pope; even Mahmoud had warmed to him. They knew nothing of the nature of his Office, nor did they care. To them he was simply a great man: *el baba*, the father. They revered him all the more because they knew how good he had been to me and they knew about life and death and they knew from the look of him that he was dying.

Thus our picnic was a farewell between the Pope and black humanity. Yet the mood was festive; the younger children romped; I sat the Pontiff in the grass against an ilex tree by the goldfish pond. He said, "Move back, *cher Augustin.* Your shadow is frightening my goldfish."

"The goldfish are all dead, Most Holy Father," I answered sadly. "Look, there are the last of them, floating on the surface. Only the minnows remain alive."

"Move back anyway. You're frightening my minnows."

The children offered food to him. He nibbled on a crust of unleavened bread and a piece of egg, caressing infant heads and mourning his goldfish.

He had human chums to mourn as well—in particular a rare sort of politician. The politician had been his protégé years ago when Italy was ruled by Fascism—and when from his office in the Secretariat of State the future Pope encouraged a renascence of Christian principle in the governance of Italy. With the fall of Fascism his friends in Christian Democracy had assumed power, but as the years slipped by the Christian Democrats, like most other Roman politicians, worshipped the golden calf of greed and became as venal as the Fascists had been—corrupt and ravening like so much of Italy, now Catholic more in name than practice.

One eminent politician shone above the others, unblemished by greed, inflamed by Christian faith, devoted to the social doctrines of the Holy Roman Church. And it was he—only months ago—who had been kidnapped by a Maoist gang and held to ransom.

From the Sad Pope's pen public letters poured out, beseeching the Maoists in the name of humanity and Christ to liberate his saintly chum. *"He is a good and honest man ... upon my knees I beg you ... free him simply, without conditions ... I love you."*

After many weeks of papal anguish, the Maoists answered the Pontiff.

They raked his saintly chum with a hundred bullets, trussed up the body, and abandoned the corpse in the boot of a motorcar.

At the great funeral Mass, in St John Lateran, his cathedral as Bishop of Rome, the Pope railed at God. Before the world, with both fists he beat upon the arms of his throne, crying out, "You didn't listen to me! O God! Am I not Your Vicar on this earth? Why would You not hear my prayer? LORD, YOU DIDN'T LISTEN!"

Thus at my picnic by the pond of dead goldfish, the Sovereign Pontiff resumed his rumination about God the Deaf. Yet he longed to be with God the Deaf Who had let him down. And he added, "Through cracks in the temple of God, the smoke of Satan has entered." And he murmured, not in French, *"Adesso viene la notte"*: Now comes the night. And again: "I have been a bad Pope." It seemed fitting that he should say that here, since he preferred the Sorrowful to the Joyful and the Glorious Mysteries of the Rosary. Presently he took out his white beads to relive the Agony in the Garden.

Done, he asked me, "How can I forgive my own deafness? My blindness? The early deeds of my pontificate? How could I have failed to foresee that my lust for change would contribute to the Church's chaos? Tell me, *cher Augustin*! I forbid you to dissemble."

"You wanted too much."

"No!"

"You were too much the visionary. Too ambitious. Too utopian. Odd in a diplomat. You drove me mad with all your prophecies of a 'Civilisation of Love.' No such culture can be achieved on earth. My own practice as a diplomatist has taught me that—at best—we can only badly balance the clashing savage interests, hatreds, and greed of men as we pray for a short peace. Now and then, the hand of God thrusts down in the midst of our predicaments to dispense a meagre portion of His grace—the most we can ever hope for."

Through the grass he crawled to me, then made a ritual and symbolic gesture such as I had done to him and the Stern Pope and to the Sunny Pope also. He kissed my buckled shoe.

The children ceased their games and gazed at us.

I said, "I am not worthy. Your Holiness has always protected me. Why? I am arrogant and overbearing. Intolerant and theatrical. *Je suis poseur!* But never have you failed to shield me from my enemies, specially from treacherous Jesuits. You created me a cardinal! You offered me Westminster! Why?"

"Because I love you, Augustin. I'll die soon. . . ."

"Yes."

"You've a genius to make men hate you. Other men—and women, I suspect?—love you madly. Do you have prophetic dreams at night?"

"Often, Most Holy Father."

"Have you dreamt of yourself as Pope?"

"Vaguely. I see a white soutane, but not the face of the man who wears it."

"In space, our dreams collide. I see your face, but not the colour of your robe."

"I shall never be Pope, Holiness."

"Surely you'll not succeed me—you are still much too young. But later . . . ? Will you . . . one day . . . be Pope? Oh my, look there, across the pond, beneath the trees. How laughing and how beautiful are your children! Does God not wish us to love the world?" He paused, brooding on a thought. He asked, "What must happen in the next pontificate?"

"We shall need a strong Pope, Holiness—one of iron will and discipline."

"Unlike myself . . . ?"

" 'Thou hast said it.' "

He took my candour meekly. Ah, ever sheepish, ever shy, he said, "May I ask another question—about Your Eminence?"

"Holiness?"

"How can you be so charming, Augustin, yet so angry and so harsh?"

I was not with the Sad Pope that August at his summer palace in the Alban hills—on the Feast of the Transfiguration—when suddenly he died.

I was in Egypt with Adrian, now nineteen, showing him scenes of evil poverty as I pursued my fantasy that he should become another Francis of Assisi. On the Feast of the Transfiguration we reached Assiut, in Upper Egypt, so hot we gasped for air, where we visited families who lived in hovels heaped up with cow dung. At the hotel that evening, still recoiling from the sight, young Adrian wept. On my transistor wireless, I learned of the death of the Pope, but so deep was my affliction that at first I could not weep. Adrian asked me, "Why, Eminence?"

PART VIII

✣

SLAV POPE

✣

And the new Pope?

We had been raised to the Sacred Purple on the same December day, when the Sad Pope invested us in the apse of St Peter's—I at the age of thirty-nine, he at forty-seven—and how fitting that it came to pass on the feast of St John of the Cross.

Earlier I had met him at the Vatican Council, but I had ignored him for the most part because he was merely an auxiliary bishop and I was so very busy cultivating cardinals. Then something odd happened.

The Slav College, where he had been living, burned down. I still resided at that time, while an archbishop titular and before my cardinalate, in the Borgo Angelico. The Communist east being miserly with foreign currency, and having arrived in Rome with a gaunt purse, the young bishop appeared at my doorstep with his luggage. "I can't afford a hotel," he told me in Italian, not at all timidly. "Will Your Grace give me lodgings?"

"Come in," I said.

It was an evening in November, during the second session of the Council, raging outside with wind and rain. The bishop was dressed shabbily in a long black coat above the soutane of an ordinary priest, and he wore no hat. He carried a blue umbrella so askew with broken spokes that it would not shut. His thinning hair, the colour of dark blond, had been slicked down unglamourously by the rain. He reached for his shoddy bags, bulging and bound with rope, but I grabbed them.

"Oooh, they're heavy," said I.

"Full of books, Your Grace," he answered.

"In Your Excellency's tongue?"

"In several tongues."

In the salon, I told Ghassem to bring us hot tea. The bishop's Italian was perfect, his voice a rich baritone, but his spectacles were still foggy from the damp: behind them his broad face seemed owlish, and physically that day he failed to impress me. Preferring to stand as we conversed, he had a funny habit of saying something, stepping forward, then stepping back—a sort of slow, shuffling jig, not (that day) endearing. I responded, and it was the simple truth, "Forgive me, Monsignore, but my flat is full with other prelates of the Council—they're sleeping three to a room."

"Ah. . . ."

"I shall gladly pay to put Your Excellency in a hotel."

"No. I'll manage. Sad. I've heard so much about Your Grace. . . ."

"*Mi dispiace, Monsignore.*"

"I'd *hoped* to stay with you."

I sensed a strong will, but I resisted: "I'll call a taxi."

"You'll never find a taxi in this rain. I'll *manage.*"

"I insist that you drink your tea."

Not gracefully, I might say angrily, he picked up his luggage and umbrella and descended to the street. I stood at my window, watching him raise two fingers to his mouth, whistling like a bumpkin for taxis that passed him in the rain. My instinct dictated, *There's something about him. Go and bring him back.* I hurried down to the street and seized his bags again.

"Of course you shall stay with me," I shouted in the howling rain. "You can sleep in my room."

"Where will you sleep?"

"I'll *manage.*"

In my room, I said, "You'll not find my bed comfortable. There's no mattress."

"I'm used to hard beds," he answered.

"Splendid," I decided. "I'll sleep on the floor."

"I'll sleep on the floor."

"I shall sleep on the floor."

"*I* shall sleep on the floor!"

That night, my bed went empty. In separate corners, we each of us slept on the floor.

Dear God, how he snored!

. . .

Thereafter I got to know him better. Soon the Sad Pope raised him to the Archbishopric of Galicia. Almost forthwith, the Archbishop of Galicia became the most vigourous spokesman of Slavs at the Council, addressing the Fathers at St Peter's in a flawless Latin that put most of his brother bishops (if not your meek servant) to jealous shame. The Slav College was in time rebuilt, but on many of his visits to Rome the Archbishop continued to lodge with me in the Borgo Angelico—and, later, at the Palazzo Consalvi. In my library late at night, we ruminated to each other about our distant lives as youths and children.

I was astonished by the similarities. We had both of us lost our parents during unhappy youth and made of Solitude instead our most abiding friend.

It is true enough that as a youth the Archbishop had been an actor, an athlete, and enjoyed the company of young women. At eighteen, he read philosophy at Galicia's university, but then Hitler invaded his homeland and his life was mutilated. Yet he refused to join the partisans who killed Germans and their collaborators. He had been nurtured to despise violence: now he spurned it even against the Nazis. Thus he embraced the cultural resistance wholly. During the day, he toiled as a common labourer in a stone quarry; at night, in barns and the flats of friends, he acted in clandestine Rhapsodic Theatre.

Such theatre has little in common with dramatic art as we know it in the pagan West, relying largely (without costumes, props, or even stage directions) on poetic declamation and the mystery of the intoned word; often in rhymed verse, often with themes mingling the love of homeland with a yearning for Heaven. At midnight, after his Rhapsodic Theatre had performed, he wrote his own verse and plays. They teemed with allusions to Christ's passion and resurrection, symbols of the enslavement of his homeland, of its longing to be liberated from the Nazis—and such suffering was not only to be endured but welcomed as the path to purification and redemption of his people.

Not yet twenty, he cobbled a play inspired by the sufferings of Job as they resembled the agony of Galicia; but for poetical solace he cast his eye as well upon the bucolic beauty of his homeland—exalting the mountains, rivers, rolling fields and orchards, birds of the air, beasts of the forest, bees sucking nectar from the flowers. Like a bee buzzing amongst the petals of an orchid, he burrowed in Messianic Slavic literature, finding prophecies of honey centuries old.

> *Amidst disorder God's fist so well*
> *Pounds and pounds a distant bell*
> *Summoning a Slav not old*
> *To mount St Peter's throne, behold.*
> *Now at last the throne is ready*
> *Lo, we see his hand is steady*
> *And look, his face anointed*

Answering the call appointed
Of that distant pounding bell.
And honey bittersweet shall tell
The Slavic Pontiff's story well.

His mother, whom he adored, had died in his ninth year; he lived with his father, a stern old soldier of Austro-Hungary, in a little house they shared with Jews. The Jewish daughter, Ginka, acted with him in his rhapsodic plays.

Watch them, he in a torn raincoat and a visored worker's cap, she in her long black hair and a green jacket, strolling together, hand in hand, across the town's wet cobblestones.

Ginka and her family longed to flee to Palestine; not without adventure, he helped them to find false passports and fake Christian identities and to get them out. The Nazis were murdering not only Jews but locking up priests and Christian intellectuals in concentration camps and shooting them by the truckload. When he was not yet twenty-one, his father died naturally. In a black, mourning loneliness, he entered a clandestine seminary in the Archbishop's Palace, and—as though as desperate as the Jews to flee the horrors of the day—he plunged into pools of ecstatic mysticism, loving specially the verse of St John of the Cross.

Let your soul therefore turn always:
Not to what is most easy, but to what is hardest;
Not to what most pleases, but to what disgusts;
Not to matter of consolation, but to matter for desolation rather;
Not to rest, but to labour;
Not to desire the more, but the less;
Not to will anything, but to will nothing;
Not to seek the best in everything, but to seek the worst, so that you
may enter for the love of Christ into a complete destitution, a perfect
poverty of spirit, and an absolute renunciation of everything in this
world.
For . . .
To come to know the All, you must give up the All.
And should you own the All, you must own it, desiring Nothing.
In this despoiling, the soul finds its tranquillity and rest—in a vast and
profound solitude, in an immense and boundless desert, the more
delectable for its isolation. . . .

I mentioned mystical pools—but William James evokes a better image: whirling dizziness and delirium, since the verses of St John "play with that vertigo of self-contradiction which is so dear to mysticism."

And so it was with our future Archbishop of Galicia. The youth resolved to enter for the love of Christ into a complete destitution, a perfect poverty of spirit, and an absolute renunciation of everything in this world. He would join the Discalced or Barefoot Carmelites, founded in Spain during the sixteenth century by St John of the Cross; put on St John's brown tunic, belt, scapular, hood, white mantle; cover his naked feet with but sandals only; sing the Divine Office throughout the day and in the middle of the night; abstain from meat and deprive his flesh incessantly; devote his life to deep prayer and delirious contemplation of the All.

Alarmed, his religious superiors told him brutally that he had too fine a mind to waste on mysticism—that he must emerge from his lonely, brooding, selfish melancholy in order to become the kind of priest who not only reads and meditates but *acts:* his brain was badly needed for heroic service to the Church. In agony, the youth consented, thereby embracing the two large themes of his life, one for ever grating against the other: private mysticism and a frenetic zeal for public work.

After the war, his homeland liberated from Hitler only to be enslaved beneath the boot of Stalin, the callow young priest was sent to Rome to obtain his doctorate in theology. At Rome gradually he became less parochial. Russian and German he already spoke; his sacred lessons he learned in Latin and Italian; he lived at the Belgian College, where he acquired French. Unwilling to shed his mystical and ascetical obsession, he learned Spanish also, the better to read every word ever written by St John of the Cross, to whom he devoted his tortured dissertation. Otherwise he was drenched, as I had been, in the Scholasticism of Aristotle and St Thomas Aquinas.

Home again in Galicia, he pursued his passions of the mind, burrowing amongst modern philosophers, some few of them Jews, struggling to blend his transcendental neo-Thomism with the ugly earthly truths of modern life. Thus he concocted his distinct philosophy of the "Sovereign Person." The Sovereign Person acts according to immutable moral rules—unhindered by determinism, naturalism, the Marxist absorbtion of his identity into the grey and lumpy state or proletariat; illumined now and then by flashes of secular wisdom, anthropology, biology, psychiatry; sheltering himself from abandonment either in cruel, selfish, capitalist society or in the dehumanising hatreds of class warfare.

He taught philosophy in universities; books, articles, and rhapsodic plays gushed from his fecund pen. The more the young priest wrote and read, the more he recoiled in distaste from the secular ideals of the Enlightenment and the French Revolution, and specially from Anglo-Saxon liberalism and the technocratic consumerist culture of the United States. He indulged fantasies instead of a restored spiritual and ascetical unity of all of Europe from the shores of Galway to the Ural Mountains under Christianity, forging a philosophical and metaphysical agenda from which he never wavered for the rest of his life.

Not as rapidly as myself, he rose while young to power in the Church— as an auxiliary bishop in his late thirties; Archbishop of Galicia only several years thence. As Archbishop, he displayed a talent, hitherto occult, which no one dreamed he might possess, and which surely he never learned when whirling in the ecstatic vertigo of St John of the Cross—his gift for political manipulation.

He used it against the Communists who ruled his homeland, often foiling their irreligious tyranny by subtle and cunning manoeuvres, not least by playing off bureaucrats one against the other, by his agitation of the populace in the name of piety—immense processions to the Virgin through cobblestoned streets; public Masses that filled fields and soccer stadiums, overflowing; teeming recitations of the mysteries of the Rosary upon the sides of hills and atop the crests of mountains—and by his shrewd and patient sense of timing, the better to extract hard concessions from the Politburo as he practised *Realpolitik* to advance his transcendental purpose.

Unlike many of his brother bishops from the Slavic East, he welcomed the reforms of the Vatican Council, prayerful that they would regenerate the Church by reconciling her traditions to the needs of modern life, so cursed with loneliness and roots torn up, so poisoned by materialism, hedonism, paganism, and adoration of technology, so bewitched by evil masquerading as adventure. And while attending the Council he did not fail to cultivate important cardinals—specially the Americans, Germans, French—and to reciprocate their friendship by inviting them to visit him in Galicia.

Could he have supposed even then that such high friendships would be crucial to his future? Do we glimpse here subliminal campaigning, a faintly Nietzschean will to power? More, some years after he created both of us cardinals, the Sad Pope summoned me and said, *"Cher Augustin,* We had another prophetic dream last night—full of hovering, fleeting phantoms, their faces never clear. We heard a babbling of Slavic voices, making Us regret that when We served as a diplomatist in the East, We learned no Slavic tongue. Throughout the dream, a distant bell kept tolling. Why do We believe that the Archbishop of Galicia may succeed Us in the papacy?"

"But Holiness," I expostulated, "he is not Italian!"

"Oui, mais . . ."

"And no non-Italian has won the papacy since that dismal Dutchman, Cardinal Dedel of Utrecht, became Adrian VI in the sixteenth century!"

"Oui, mais . . . why do you suppose, *cher Augustin,* that We've made the Sacred College so international? There's a—a vapour?—about him, don't you think? We've a favour to ask of you."

"As if I could refuse, Most Holy Father?"

Ah, that bashful and cerebral smile. "The Cardinal Archbishop of Galicia is still something of a bumpkin—unseemly in a man who might be pope. He could use a bit of Your Eminence's urbanity and polish. Season him, *cher Augustin.* Show him the world."

Therefore, at my expense, I showed him several corners of the world, including France—her churches and cathedrals empty mostly save for tourists—but our excursion to America I recall more fondly. In practice, I became his English tutor. He learned quickly, insisting that I speak to him only in my native tongue, even to our translated Christian names. He called me "Augustine." I called him "Charles."

In America (as in France) Charles was bemused by the empty buildings of the Church—bewildered by that immense real estate of red brick and waxed corridors, once so teeming with noisy children and nuns in white bibs and black habits, now being abandoned or reduced by the ravages of cost and declining faith. We visited seminaries, huge fortresses of puddingstone and Gothic towers, once housing legions of young men preparing for the priesthood, now inhabited merely by their ghosts and few living seminarians of flesh and blood.

Many seminaries had been invaded by mischievous fantasies in the backwash of the Vatican Council. "Holy Liberty" became a tabernacle; only change seemed sacred. The rules of centuries, which hitherto had served the Church so well, were thrown out with the rubbish. Bells and rigid study were abolished. Guitars replaced organs. Cassocks were discarded for blue jeans. The past was bad because the future was bound to be better and more beautiful. Therefore the past was mutilated, and then, like a gangrenous leg, amputated.

Psychiatrists and behaviourists pumped dubious transfusions of trendy blood into seminaries and nunneries. Seminarians and postulant nuns were encouraged to discover "Personal Authenticity": to revere their impulses as inspired, to worship the gods within themselves, to scoff at any tyranny outside their Holy Liberty such as bishops and the Pope. So, with impunity they ridiculed Authority, debated their convictions, wondered if they had any, grew disenchanted, and stared at their lumpy tapioca. Then they stampeded out of the seminaries, back to the world.

As we meditated on the puddingstone and the Gothic towers, Charles heaved a sigh and said, "These seminaries—these empty shells—are like a kingdom lost."

Throughout America, in our crimson we sat together in bare grey sanctuaries as parish priests informed their faithful, "Jesus loves you. Love your neighbour."

"They are not teaching the Faith in its fullness," Charles whispered to me.

"Then get up and tell them that the Faith is hard," I whispered back.

"I said that in Chicago. You tell them, Augustine."

"I said that in Milwaukee. It's your turn, Charles."

At evening, in our hotels, he devoured glossy magazines, fascinated as in France by the sensuous advertisements, fashions, perfumes, jewellery, ravaging eroticism. And he watched much television, engrossed by the rock stars and the game shows. "It's worse than Communist television," he said.

"Is that possible?" I wondered.

"At least the Communists don't glorify greed."

"You don't much care for American culture, do you, Charles?"

"I'm appalled."

"Is it that bad?"

"I prefer the fake ethics of the Communists to the flagrant license I see here."

"But Americans are not completely selfish."

"Of course, of course."

"They give to the poor."

"Of course, of course."

"And their democracy works."

"I believe in dissent, Augustine."

"In the Church?"

"In politics. America is too rich."

"My m-mother was American."

At New York, we stayed in a suite of the Waldorf Towers, done in the style of Louis Quinze. This was summer, 1976. From the window of our salon we could see the palace of the United Nations, a tray of blue ice cubes, not quite perpendicular, teetering; beyond it the East River, steel bridges, a Pepsi-Cola sign, black fuel tanks, green barges, but no great ships. Charles pointed, asking, "What's over there?"

"Brooklyn," said I.

"Are there any slums?"

"I helped a black priest in Brownsville, but he's dead."

"Tomorrow, we go to Brownsville."

"But not as cardinals, Charles?"

I called the desk to arrange our costume. Late next afternoon, we took a taxi from the Waldorf wearing overalls and visored caps. We crossed Brooklyn Bridge, crept through traffic beneath an elevated railway, and abandoned the taxi at the edge of Brownsville, a treeless jungle.

We strolled past trash-filled lots and brick and brownstone tenements boarded up or all burnt out. Derelicts wandered amongst meadows of rusty beer cans and leaned in gutted doorways, making no sound. Little girls in Gothic pigtails taunted drunkards in the doorways; little boys with towering exotic curls romped on hills of rotting car cushions, hurling fragments of brick at one another or through windows of tenements already shattered. The landscape was festooned with rubble and decomposing motorcars. The wooden stairways of the buildings rotted as we watched them—and as Charles, his pale blue eyes darting constantly, fingered his rosary and made no sound. We rambled back towards the screeching elevated railway, under it the day as dark as night.

Men and women stumbled from the murky bars, children running after them. A young woman pushed a baby carriage from bar to bar. Below the maze of rusting stanchions, an old woman shrieked obscenities at the wind; an old man howled blasphemies at Christ. Black young men and women, all tinsel jewellery, huge golden earrings, esoteric hair, entered a discothèque beneath neon plumbing. I drifted towards them; Charles followed me, many steps behind.

From the street I descended a round brick staircase, into a blaring cata-comb of rock music, flashing coloured lamps, and jerking black bodies.

> *I'm gonna drive my tank through your picture window*
> *Drop a bomb on your pretty pad*
> *I'll push my bayonet through your pearly teeth*
> *And it don't tickle, baby.*

How I craved the same release I had enjoyed anonymously in Holland—to pump my arms, kick up my legs, jerk my body, whirl in space, fanatically; but since Charles was with me I did all that dancing in my head, communing with this carnal black girl and then the next only in a fantasy. Now Charles was near me, glancing at my expression, too concupiscent I suppose; but then he drifted off to the periphery, where he stood in his overalls and visored cap, stepping forward, then stepping back, in his sort of slow, shuf-fling jig. Through the tumult of the dancing I could not tell, but when his lips moved, I asked myself, Is he talking to someone? To some exotic young man or woman? Or to God?

Next morning, a Sunday, we two concelebrated Mass in English with the Cardinal Archbishop of New York at the high altar of St Patrick's. The Archbishop sent us back to the Waldorf in his limousine; we ascended to our suite still clad in our crimson robes. Charles's mozzetta was frayed, and his wrinkled soutane had buttons missing. In the salon I said, with some embar-rassment, "Ha-ha-ha. Charles, when we go on Tuesday to Philadelphia, I'd like you to look your best."

"What do you mean, Augustine?"

"His Eminence of Philadelphia is your fellow Slav. You should cut a good figure. Will you wear my robes in Philadelphia?"

"But I'm shorter than you."

"No doubt the Waldorf employs a seamstress."

"All right—to please you, Augustine."

"It's not a matter of pleasing me, but of looking to the future—of ful-filling, if I may say so, what well might be the mysterious design of God. In youth, you must have been a marvellous sportsman because you've such an athletic bearing. You'd have a commanding presence if you'd try."

"Ah, not again, Augustine—your 'Church as Theatre.' "

"The decline of the Church as Theatre is a terrible catastrophe. We must use the lures of the world to confound the world. You grew up in Rhapsodic Theatre. Give us more Rhapsodic Theatre! One day soon, the whole world may be your stage."

"Wooow, will it ever happen?"

"Who can prophesy the whims of the Holy Ghost? Anyway, you should be ready. Here, take my cape. No, don't buckle it—let it hang from your shoulders. Now, walk to the door. Splendid. Turn to glance at me. Splendid. Would you sit down in that armchair? Grasp the knobs firmly. Show your iron knuckles. Hold your head a little higher. Now, arch your fingers beneath your nostrils as you normally do at prayer. No, drag the moment out! Splendid. Now get up. Sit down. Get up. Remember, you can command an audience simply by the way you rise from a chair! Sit down. Get up. Head much higher! Splendid. Your forward, backward shuffle when you talk could become another asset—we must work on that, turn it into a prop."

"Like this, Augustine?"

"Marvellous. Your baritone is marvellous also, but remember your gestures when you preach—use your hands and arms for wide, sweeping arcs of emphasis as you act in your Rhapsodic Theatre. You grew up an actor, so be an actor! On the television, how your silver hair should glisten! *Where* did you get those shoes?"

"In Galicia."

"Such shapeless shoes—like the feet of an elephant. Ha-ha-ha. Tomorrow, we'll buy you new ones."

"Augustine, I won't wear buckled shoes!"

"*Placet.* But can't we do something about those thick spectacles?"

On the morrow, after the new shoes, I bought him contact lenses. In Philadelphia, where he preached publicly in my watered silk, he cut a fine, theatrical, commanding figure.

We parted at the airport. I gave him rather a lot of money for his overcrowded seminaries in Galicia, then genuflected to kiss his simple golden ring. Charles did not reciprocate my gesture. Instead his blue eyes seized me, only for a moment, and thus he said, "Control your sensuality."

"Charles, would you accept the papacy?"

"Of course, of course."

May we leap to autumn, 1978? With the Sad Pope dead, I am eligible to succeed him on the Chair of Peter, not a notion that enchants my brother cardinals as we assemble for the Conclave in the Sistine Chapel.

The cardinals of northern Europe, remembering my purge of the Dutch Church, all but shun me. The two Jesuit cardinals, in doctrine as orthodox as I, carry a secret "Exclusive" from the Society of Jesus to prevent at any cost my election to the papacy. The African cardinals, grateful for my benefactions, might have favoured my election, but finally they agree with their peers in the Sacred College that at the age of fifty I am still too young to be Pope.

In the scrutinies, not a single ballot is cast for me. I am reduced, like my patron Cardinal di Benevento in the Conclave twenty years before, to the rôle of pope-maker.

As pope-maker I regressed in memory to the year 1800, and the Conclave held in a lagoon of Venice. Crucial, and may I tell you why?

That Conclave could not convene at Rome because Europe was in upheaval following the French Revolution. Pope Pius VI had died squalidly in French captivity at Valence; rowdy Neapolitans governed Rome. At Paris, the apostate Talleyrand, prince of cynics, conjectured sweetly that the end of the papacy was nigh. Yet slowly the cardinals assembled in Venice under Austrian protection to elect a successor to Pius VI. The Austrians demanded that a cardinal of their party should ascend to the Supreme Pontificate; many princes of the Church, as aghast at Austrian meddling as at the enormities of the French, protested. The Conclave of Venice deadlocked, dragging on in winter.

The cardinals were sequestered in a Benedictine monastery upon the Isle of San Giorgio; week after week, through January and February into March, they went on gathering in the Chapel of the Scrutiny, shivering in their wooden stalls and electing no pope: a scandal to Christendom. Then the Secretary of the Conclave, my own Monsignore Ercole Consalvi, contrived an ingenious solution.

The cardinals of the Austrian party, he suggested, should nominate a congenial Eminence of the opposite camp. Sick and coughing, the pro-Austrians consented. By the mechanics of elimination, Consalvi intended that the Conclave should eventually settle on the quiet Benedictine, Barnabà Chiaramonti, Archbishop of Imola—himself a nobleman, devout, contemplative, ironical, humourous, charming, deeply cultured, and above all a gentleman; since to be a gentleman was essential in any pontiff. For a fortnight longer, the cardinals squabbled, until at last they turned toward Chiaramonti.

He was strolling in the cold and windy monastery garden when they came to kiss his hands and tell him that he was certain, now, to be Pope. He went white with shock. "Don't kiss my hands! I am not yet Pope!" In such a way began the heroic reign of my dearest pontiff, Pius VII, foe of Napoleon, victorious finally.

Today the Church was in a shambles as she had been in 1800. Like Consalvi, I had chosen my own candidate—the Archbishop of Galicia—much in advance; and like Consalvi by tactics of elimination I intended to make him Pope.

I liked him not only for his liberal attachment to the poor and his implacable orthodoxy of doctrine, but because he had a rock-like will, knew exactly what he wanted, and loved hard discipline. As a rhapsodic actor, he would revel in his skills of theatre and he would command by his presence, conjuring the lures of the world to defeat the world. Was he a gentleman? In a *tough* sort of way! And had not the moment come to elect a pontiff from beyond Italy? Should not the ancient verses of the Messianic Slavic poets and the Sad Pope's dream of a Slav as his successor now be fulfilled? In the Conclave, my craft served prophecy.

We were one hundred and twelve electors, drawn from all of Christendom since the Sunny Pope and after him the Sad Pope had increased the

Sacred College. However, Italian cardinals still composed the largest bloc: no sooner we began the scrutinies, two Italians battled for St Peter's chair.

The first was Cardinal Samosata—he of "The Use of the Ablative Absolute in Papal Rescript Clauses"—now nearly seventy, a rod of the Roman Curia, and a member of the College in the arrangement that resulted in my own elevation to the Purple. As Prefect of the Pontifical Commission to Enforce Conciliar Decrees, he had blithely done his best to subvert and butcher the reforms of the Vatican Council. Darling of the nostalgic cardinals, on the initial scrutiny Cardinal Samosata received twenty votes. Despite our previous altercations, and to make the point that tradition must prosper in the Church, I voted for him twice. Besides, I loathed his rival.

That would be Don Gianni, quondam papal secretary, now nearly sixty and Cardinal Archbishop of Florence. During the Sad Pope's decline, Don Gianni as an archbishop titular (also my doing!) had become his *sostituto*, sort of chief of staff, and from that mountaintop he ruled the Church in the Pope's name. In the vertigo of power, he became ever more the snitch and bully; rushing to the Pope with disaster bulletins as discipline in the Church collapsed; guarding the papal door, blocking entry, or trying to, against all intruders such as myself. Finally a year before his death I prevailed on the Pope to create Don Gianni a cardinal and to pack him off to Florence. Don Gianni headed the "progressive" party of Italian cardinals sworn to the reforms of the Vatican Council. On the initial scrutiny, he received twenty-five votes.

The cardinals assembled in the Sistine Chapel twice a day, at morning and afternoon. As the scrutinies continued, a deadlock developed between Don Gianni and Cardinal Samosata. Afterwards, I sought them out in their separate cells.

"*Non sum dignus*"—I am not worthy, said Cardinal Samosata.

"Your Eminence is surely worthy, but he can not be elected," I replied.

"But I have, ah, twenty votes."

"Fifty-six short of the votes you need."

"According to the other cardinals, my votes may increase—depending, of course, on the Holy Spirit."

"The evidence, dear Eminence, suggests that you are not the choice of the Holy Spirit. We need another candidate."

"I fail to follow Your Eminence. Another candidate?"

"From beyond the Alps."

"A non-Italian? That's sacrilegious!"

Minutes later, I called on Don Gianni.

"*Non sum dignus,*" he informed me.

"Your Eminence is surely worthy, but he can not be elected."

"But I have, ah, twenty-five votes."

"Fifty-one short of the votes you need."

"I trust in the wisdom of the Holy Spirit."

"The evidence suggests that the eye of the Holy Spirit may wander from Your Eminence. Would you support another candidate?"

"Oooooh . . ."

"A non-Italian?"

"Are you insane?"

During the next few scrutinies, Don Gianni and Cardinal Samosata battled on, but votes fell away from them, and the electors looked to other Italians who in their turn did not blossom. Days passed. The marble floor of the Sistine Chapel became (as it were) strewn with corpses of dead and wounded *papabili.*

In my Sacred Purple I glided from one cardinal to the next, beneath the Biblical vignettes of Michelangelo's fantastical vaulted ceiling, confiding that the time was nigh at long last again for a non-Italian pope. Occasionally I glanced up at the Sibyls and the Prophets and scenes from the Book of Genesis—at God separating light from darkness, making the sun and moon and stars; separating the waters, fashioning fish and birds; creating Adam, and Eve from Adam's rib, then banishing them both from Eden. The frescoes were lacquered over with the grime of centuries, the smoke of incense and a million beeswax candles, the body heat and breath of multitudes, but still I felt awe and terror. After another abortive scrutiny I hurried from the chapel to Don Gianni's monastic room, where he sat on an iron bedstead beside Cardinal Samosata, whispering.

"The Conclave has gone on so long we are causing scandal," I entreated them. "The two of you are deadlocked hopelessly—and no Italian can win the papacy. Do you want a pope or not? I see but one solution. Your Eminences must join forces to nominate a foreigner."

"We can't!" cried Cardinal Samosata.

"But who?" asked Don Gianni. "His Eminence of Vienna does not want the papacy."

"And His Eminence of Malines-Brussels does," I said.

"I would fight him tooth and claw," rasped Cardinal Samosata. "He is not orthodox. He tolerates heretical theologians, and he has himself abandoned the doctrine of Transubstantiation for—for Trans-Signification!"

Don Gianni glanced at me suspiciously. "Why have I seen you in the chapel whispering so often to the Cardinal of Galicia?"

"He's an interesting possibility," I answered blandly.

"A *Slav*?" squawked Cardinal Samosata.

"But as orthodox as you are," I said gently.

"I can not deny Your Eminence's assertion."

"And he supports the reforms of the Council," Don Gianni murmured.

"Oooooh," groaned Cardinal Samosata.

"Up to a point," I was swift to add.

"He hasn't a chance," Don Gianni said.

"His Eminence of Philadelphia disagrees with you," I replied with more vigour.

"Oh, *he's* a Slav," said Cardinal Samosata.

"But not the nine other American cardinals," I countered.

My observation seemed to chasten them. "Do you mean," Don Gianni asked, "that they'll vote for the Archbishop of Galicia?"

"This morning, His Eminence of Philadelphia told me so."

"What of the French and German cardinals?" wondered His Eminence Samosata.

"The Archbishop of Galicia has been cultivating the French and Germans for fifteen years."

"Disgraceful!" cried Don Gianni. "Lobbying for Saint Peter's chair!"

I laughed a little and then summed up. "Can't the two of you gracefully accept defeat? We must end the chaos in the Church. We need a strong, corrective papacy of stone and iron."

"If you have the Americans, the Germans, and the French," demanded Cardinal Samosata, "then why do you want us?"

"We need more Italians. If we are to change a tradition of five centuries, for form might it not be better that Italians should propose the—Slav? Besides . . . would it not be well for both of you to be seen on the side of the victor?"

In the Sistine Chapel, the scrutinies resumed. On the morning after my encounter with Their Eminences Samosata and Don Gianni, the Archbishop of Galicia received thirty votes; at afternoon, forty-five. He needed seventy-six.

Following the scrutiny that afternoon, the cardinals of Africa, encouraged by me and warming to my candidate, approached the Slav and asked him bluntly whether he would accept the papacy.

"Yes," he said.

Cardinals from Europe and Asia, America and the Latin tropics, pressed in on the Africans and the Slav. Scanning them with those pale—those fierce—blue eyes, Charles asked them deeply, in English and then in Italian, "Do you know the kind of pope I'll be?"

The cardinals withdrew, murmuring and questioning each other, to the squeezed warrens and their monastic rooms. I lingered from a distance at the side, watching Charles as he knelt beneath the high altar and gazed at the *Last Judgement.* Back and forth I glanced at Michelangelo's vision and its effect upon Charles's face.

Amid the floating naked bodies, the thick-waisted, thick-thighed Christ stood on a cloud in final Judgement, His Mother, demure and clothed, seated at His side. Peering upward at the movement and crescendo of the bodies, I felt not joy but dread, since Christ at the centre appeared so implacable a Judge. Round Him were the saved, and angels astride clouds sounding Judgement's trumpets; below were the damned, writhing with snakes in Charon's boat as they sailed off to Hell.

On Charles's face, I saw pity, piety, love, devotion, stone and iron, but not a trace of doubt or torment. I nearly wanted to call out to him the ritual Biblical verses—*"Domine, non sum dignus . . .* O my Father, if it be possible, let this chalice pass from me: nevertheless not as I will, but as Thou wilt"— yet Charles unlike his predecessor did not fit that kind of meek and humble choreography.

> *Amidst disorder God's fist so well*
> *Pounds and pounds a distant bell*
> *Summoning a Slav not old*
> *To mount St Peter's throne, behold.*
> *Now at last the throne is ready*
> *Lo, we see his hand is steady*
> *And look, his face anointed*
> *Answering the call appointed*
> *Of that distant pounding bell.*
> *And honey bittersweet shall tell*
> *The Slavic's Pontiff's story well.*

At morning, in the Sistine Chapel, the cardinals Samosata and Don Gianni rose jointly to urge all of their brothers in the Sacred College to elect the Archbishop of Galicia to the papacy. That afternoon, Charles easily surpassed the number of votes he needed, and—at the age of fifty-eight—he became the two hundred sixty-third successor of St Peter and the Vicar of Christ on Earth.

In one of his last decrees—sealed, and opened only after the Conclave— the Sad Pope had abolished the Tiara.

Thus on the steps of St Peter's, the Slav Pope was anointed and enthroned, but despite long centuries of tradition he was not crowned.

"I don't care about the crown," he told me afterwards.

"I do," I protested. "For are you not the Father of All Princes and of Kings?"

"You needn't worry, Augustine. Even without my crown, I'll be a very kingly kind of Pope."

✛

FORTY

✛

Almost at once, the Slav Pope offered to
make me master of the world's bishops.
How judiciously I weighed that gem,
among the brightest of the Roman Curia. As Prefect of the Sacred Congregation of Bishops, under
the eye of the Pope I would choose all of the
mitred new lords of Christendom. For a week I
prayed upon the honour, and then refused it. At
my behest, the Pope gave the portfolio to Cardinal
Zalula, banished permanently from the Congo, as
hard and valiant in the Faith as even the Supreme
Pontiff.

Thus I remained as I more deeply wished—
papal minister without portfolio: if not an intimate
of the Pope (in his mystical solitude he needed
none), then his staunch and busy counsellor with
my finger in many pies. I continued as Consultor
to several of the senior Congregations, and kept
my musty secretariat at the Holy Office.

Each day at midafternoon, in my black and
scarlet I ascended the Scala Regia and crossed the
Sala Regia and penetrated the phalanx of Swiss
Guards into the papal antechambers. There, Don
Jerzy—the pontifical secretary and a Galician
also—not suffering the pricks of envy that tormented Italian ecclesiastics, opened the Pope's
door with a cheerful, brute grace.

Awaiting me, in the bleached November light,

amongst his books, and in the blurred lineage I thought of all the dead philosopher-kings down the centuries and centuries, sat my silver, radiant, Philosopher-Pope. We were in his private study, disorderly with heaped documents and books in twenty languages, decorated on his salmon wall with but a single icon, the Black Madonna of Galicia.

His salmon wall? During the reign of the Sad Pope, the imperial red damask of the pontifical apartments had been peeled away and replaced with a soupy damask the colour variously of beige and salmon. The Slav Pope, indifferent to chairs and wallpaper, left the décor as he found it, minus his holy predecessor's myriad glass eggs. In our meetings we spoke a mixture of Italian, Latin, French, and English—but English mostly, since the Pontiff wished always to be limber in that tongue for his great purposes. He had ascended St Peter's chair with a vast design: only slowly did I grasp its scope.

And he said, "Augustine, We wish to send a secret Apostolic Letter to all the cardinals and bishops of the world, stating the goals of Our pontificate. Will you help Us to write it?"

"Granted, Holiness. You intend, foremost, to purge abuses in the Church?"

"Of course, of course, but We intend much more in the world at large— to ignite a Christian Restoration."

For the next several weeks, in English and in French, I drafted the secret Apostolic Letter, debating it with the Pope. And I said, "On the morrow of your election, Most Holy Father, *The New York Times* congratulated you editorially and recommended that you rescind the Church's anathema of divorce, birth control, abortion, and homosexuality."

"Ha! Should I scold *The New York Times*?"

"Oh, they weren't being rude—simply inviting Your Holiness to embrace their enlightened secular ethic."

"Then watch me turn that ethic on its head. No to divorce. No to pills, diaphragms, and condoms. No to the butchery of abortion. No to married priests. No to women priests. No to radical feminism. No to sapphism, pederasty, fellatio, and buggery."

In sundry ways, the Pope wished to reverse the march of history, or at least the Enlightenment and the French Revolution. The Enlightenment and the Revolution had made modern society so feverishly secular that it almost craved—he thought—to murder God. In the East, corrupt Marxism had enslaved man in barren class warfare and grubby atheism. In the West, the consumerist mania of the Americans had infected culture everywhere and left the tropics of the poor to fester in open running sewers where swarms of sickly children bathed and defecated.

The Pontiff much admired whichever of his predecessors resisted and condemned the culture of the day. He revered Pius VI for his martyrdom by the revolutionary French; Pius VII for his excommunication of Napoleon;

Pius IX for his anathemas against the Cult of Progress; the Stern Pope for his condemnations of brutish scientism, pagan nationalism, and for his lamentation that "the greatest sin of our century has been to lose the sense of sin."

Under the Slav Pope, the Church would revert to her Augustinian hatred of the world as it is. She would forcefully resist and fight modern culture, specially Western culture which was so deeply sinful. She would protest and subvert the bleak cruelties of Communism, but as stalwartly she would wage war against the gaudy hedonism of Western Europe and the United States. She would remind men and women everywhere that they could find contentment and salvation not in technology or an aphrodisiac society, but only in the sacred and transcendent. As Pope he would exalt a wisdom enshrining spirit over matter, the person over things, ethics over pleasure, defying the world with the scandal of the Gospel.

The Pontiff clung to the Second Vatican Council, regretting that its goodness had been twisted, as sorrowful as I for the chaos that ensued, and as convinced that only a militant papacy could turn the flood. Throughout the Church, he would silence the most egregious dissenters, discipline and banish from their academies whichever theologians deviated from Truth as the Magisterium defined it, and reaffirm the purity and everlastingness of revealed doctrine.

I asked, "Will Your Holiness restore the old Latin Mass?"

"No," answered the Pope. "The liturgy must remain close to the people."

I groaned and mumbled my discontent.

"Stop growling at me, Augustine."

"A cardinal never growls at the Pope."

"All right, all right. I'll consider a limited restoration . . . eventually."

I asked, "Holiness, since we are to be so pure in doctrine, what of social policy?" He answered, "We must race light-years ahead of the liberal democracies—especially the Americans—in matters of human rights. We must, in our own very different way, inspired by the irenic Gospels, become more radical than the Marxists. We must condemn the sins of capitalism, insist that the rich nations do immensely more to help the wretched ones, and hound the democracies to stop their trafficking in guns and bombs that slaughter children."

His vision was universal, his philosophy a seamless robe: if the violence of abortion was horrid, then so was the starvation of children in slums and jungles and the torture of men and women in the dungeons of hideous dictatorships. At the Vatican, he seemed to itch for fame as a Don Quixote, Christ's unfashionable fool, a brash, raging prophet leaping from a page of the Old Testament.

Thereupon he set about his ceaseless travels, summoning all of his actor's craft, crying out to seas of humanity upon six continents of the frugal joys of communion with Christ Redeemer; of the simple need of personal decency and of solidarity between the well-fed rich and the swarming poor; haranguing against cruelty and greed and self-indulgence; conjuring up in the bargain monstrous and glamourous images of Satan.

He ignored Milton's image of "the infernal Serpent, he it was whose guile, Stirred up with Envy and Revenge, deceived The Mother of Mankind"; and the mediaeval devils, too, incarnating all evil, moving in the air and flecks of dust that floated in any stream of light, through the wide world, everywhere, all-knowing, spying out the secret thoughts and frailties of men; appearing in the form of toads, scorpions, vultures, goats, black hounds, primeval snakes devouring their own tails. Oh, the Devil remains the Evil One, Father of Lies, Lord of Deceit, Angel of Darkness, Prince of This World, though today he dresses fashionably. The Slav Pope seemed to agree with the demonologists of antiquity that Satan has the power to change his shape, and in order to deceive he may appear as a beautiful youth, a lovely woman, or even as an angel of light.

The Satan of Today owns many mansions, not least in Hollywood. In his motion pictures, he wears blue jeans and Gucci boots, sings brutish songs, shares drugs with adolescents, and—stylishly—shoots people in the face. Elsewhere he dwells in the Structures of Sin, enslaving whole populations, laying land mines in cabbage patches, dropping poison gas on children. Satan is not merely the Evil Principle dwelling in us all or the Privation of the Good, the True, and the Beautiful: Satan is a person.

And the Pope kept asking, "Sons and daughters, can any of you doubt the existence of the Devil? In my own diocese of Galicia stood the death camp of Auschwitz. We hear that at the gates of Auschwitz, God and Satan wrestled—and that Satan won the match. God can never lose the war with Satan, but at Auschwitz was He not badly bruised? The struggle rages on today as the Devil, like a roaring lion, roams ever about the world, seeking whom he may devour."

As the years of his pontificate accumulated and a fantastic Turk nearly killed him in St Peter's Square, the Slav Pope clung with growing fervour to his convictions of good and evil. After the botched assassination, his keepers would no longer allow him to stroll in the Gardens of the Vatican for fear of some future zealot lurking with a rifle in a tree, on a wall, or upon a rooftop. Inside the Vatican, his keepers now confined the papal walks to the roof of the Apostolic Palace, rimmed with steel plate, where the Pontiff could take the polluted Roman air and keep his bees.

Did I mention that he was a beekeeper? How often, like the Sad Pope before him, did he summon me to the roof of the palace, where I found him in his heavy sealed mask and gloves and apron, over his white soutane, tending his apiary?

He had imported the apiary from Galicia, and kept a colony of black and golden bees that he said numbered in the scores of thousands. The palace roof was a labyrinth of green wooden boxes that resembled cupboards, huge pots of purple and yellow flowers, clover, alfalfa, and young white-petalled trees. The bees lived inside the cupboards buzzing amidst cavities of waxen combs; the Pontiff's chatter was full of allusions to worker bees, drones, queens, drones mating with queens as they flew high in space, the drones dying invariably as they copulated; queens laying millions of eggs; treasures of pollen, nectar, and honey.

More than once, I stood by awed and frightened as bees escaped the Pontiff's cupboards and swarmed about his hooded head. With his gloves he flailed at them methodically, gathered them in wire nets, and forced them into new hives. Sometimes he subdued the bees with rubber bellows puffing black smoke. Bottles of beeswax and raw honey littered the roof.

"Aah," said he of a sudden, "bees and the Enlightenment."

One of the conceits of the Enlightenment was that God, if He exists at all, takes no interest in the universe He created: He contrived the planets and the stars, tossed them into space, then went on talking to Himself. Every million years or so He stretches out His thumb, to stop the planets from colliding, or to plug leaks in constellations. God is not Providence, nor does He care a hoot for humankind. God is but a plumber—a sort of lazy cosmic plumber plugging leaks in constellations. The Pope resented the Enlightenment especially for that devilish conceit. "God," he confided to me one day, "is not a plumber. God is a bumblebee."

"Holiness," I protested, "your metaphor is shocking."

"The cosmos is a beehive," he continued blithely. "The spaces we perceive around us are the cavities between those balls of beeswax that others call the planets and the constellations."

He stared at me through his great hood with its mask of metal and wire mesh, and his voice echoed inside the mask, sounding dream-like.

"The air is full of yellow flowers. Our rivers run of nectar. God is the Bumblebee who begets Himself. He swarms—in solitude—everywhere at once. We hear Him hum: we dread His sting. For we are bees who brew His nectar, and when we're finished we fly to Him. He tastes our honey, then He chooses."

With his thick brown leather gloves, the virile Pontiff gripped my red-caped shoulders and gazed through me.

"This Bumblebee is above the world but in the world—and very busy. With *us*."

Then he sent me to Central America and its civil wars.

FORTY-ONE

Central America was a garden, full of yellow flowers, abounding in volcanoes and mythical birds. In forests and on the shores of lakes, I picked wild orchid and avocado pear. The isthmus was also a tropical Gesthemane, where human agony seemed to blossom in Biblical counterpoint to the landscape's splendour.

My mandate from the Pontiff was to probe for whatever measures the Church might undertake to diminish the torture and killing throughout the isthmus—and to confront and discipline Marxist priests who were defiling the irenic message of the Gospels by blessing revolutionary violence.

According to the Pope's instructions (which I drafted), I was free for as long as I judged proper to roam anonymously through those little nations as I had in Holland and in the larger Congo: to catch the mood and scent of matters. For such a purpose, as always hitherto my only companion in my journeys was my most steadfast friend—Solitude.

At first I wandered about those tropics in my favourite disguise, starting in El Salvador. At the capital, I bought new overalls and a visored cap, hired an old blue van, and drove over gutted roads and volcanic ash eastward to the province of Morazán, guerrilla country.

Near the Río Torola, I paused to work in a teeming, stinking camp for refugees. Posing as a relief worker, I swept floors, dug latrines, fed sick and hungry children. The refugees kept pointing to the hills and the township whence they came, Perquín, high up there and a guerrilla stronghold. Hundreds of their kinsmen still inhabited the place, but for years without a physician or a priest. Seized by zeal to bring the sacraments to Perquín, I hurried to the hills. The bridge on the River Torola was bombed out; I waded across beneath my hiker's pack, forgetting to drink the water, then once inside the revolutionary enclave I continued my quest on foot.

Stupidly, I had brought no water bottle, but for a while I managed. Though full of potholes the road was paved, and I maintained a steady pace; for mile after mile, I saw nobody. The ascending terrain was brown and parched, with escarpments eventually and purple mountains far off; fires were consuming the sides of hills, and everywhere was ash, bare patches burned out. The road was strewn with bullet shells from automatic rifles, and the houses yonder had been gutted in the fighting.

The month was April. It was noon now. In a cloudless sky the sun blazed; my pack grew heavier, I thought like the burden of the Cross, and I thirsted. I called out at the ruined houses, the parched hills, the eyes I was sure were watching me: *"¡Hola! ¡Hola! ¿Alguno? ¡Agua!"*

No answer. I resumed my upward march, removing my heavy pack, shifting it from hand to hand; for a mile, perhaps two miles, three miles, I persevered, hating my folly. Now beneath every pothole I imagined a land mine, so I zigzagged between the holes, then in the shade of a tree sat down, gasping. My mouth was ashes; again I called out: *"¡Hola! ¡Hola! ¡Agua!"* I resumed my climb, stumbled, sat beneath the sun in the middle of the road, as the landscape whirled. Giddily I watched my hand grope inside my pack until it found a flask of sacramental wine, but as I fumbled with the cork I fainted.

I awoke in the waning afternoon, still in the middle of the road, a plump girl propping up my head, tilting a tin bottle of cool water to my parched mouth. When I sat up, I saw the rifle on her shoulder; other guerrillas emerged from the forest. They were mostly very young, a mixture of dark boys in baseball caps and more chubby girls in khaki slacks, all bearing American M-16 rifles, captured in combat I supposed. Older guerrillas wore mustaches, mufti and military dress, and various nationalities of gun. The *jefe* appeared to be a senior guerrilla—"Luis" the others called him—who wore a cocked safari hat and had no front teeth.

"Search his bag," Luis ordered.

The guerrillas spread all of my possessions across the road, examining them microscopically, even my toothpaste, squeezing it out, even my breviary, tearing the pages, even my Eucharistic hosts, strewing them on the dirt and asphalt.

"Are you a priest?" Luis demanded.

"I'm afraid so."

"Where are you going?"

"To Perquín."

"Why?"

"To say Mass."

"Have you permission of the *comandante*?"

"The *comandante*?"

"I have two choices, Padre. I can shoot you—or I can ask a favour."

"A favour, *jefe*?"

"Will you say Mass for us?"

High above us loomed the red-tiled roofs and adobe walls of Perquín town. The guerrillas did not lead me in that direction, but into the forest, perhaps half a mile, to a tiled and gutted farmhouse, where I was told to wait. Two guerrillas were assigned to guard me, an older man with a mustache and a gun and a young woman with braids and a gun. She wore a denim blouse and American camouflage pants; her olive skin was smooth, her eyes were black, and she called herself Dalila. She smiled, showing full white teeth. I asked her why so many guerrillas had no teeth.

"Because we have no dentists," Dalila said. "We have no doctors. The army bombs our hospitals, and our people bleed to death."

She told me the story of the farmhouse. A family of eleven had lived here, growing a little sisal, tending a little corn, minding their own lives. One day the army came and killed them all because they lived in the wrong place: mother and father, grandparents and children, babies, chickens, pigs, and a cow. It was a large house, with a shattered roof on mud brick, shards and bullet shells where the floor had been, beneath the open sky. I pictured infants playing in the corners, the mother cooking dinner, the father drinking too much *guaro*. I did not care to pass the night with those ghosts, but as the sun went down it occurred to me that I was the prisoner of these guerrillas and that this abbatoir was my jail.

Scores of guerrillas came down the burnt-out sides of hills, emerged from trees still leafy, and clustered round me. "Say Mass," the *jefe* ordered.

From the débris of the farmhouse I retrieved a charred table, my altar. I doffed my visored cap; guerrillas illuminated my abbatoir-cathedral with electric torches. From my Mass kit, I took out my silver chalice, my flask of sacramental wine, my Eucharistic hosts, a simple purple stole which I flung about my neck above my denim overalls and my rough brown shirt. Dalila tendered me her water bottle to complete the banquet.

I opened my Spanish missal, and—facing the guerrillas—I began to celebrate the sacrifice: *"En el nombre del Padre, y del Hijo, y del Espiritu Santo. . . ."* With diffidence I pushed aside the Spanish missal and from memory celebrated the remainder of the Mass in Tridentine Latin, proceeding through the Introit, the Kyrie, the Creed, the Consecration, the Agnus Dei, enchanting the guerrillas by the riddle of my words.

At the Communion, I hesitated. So many of the guerrillas, boys and girls, pressed forward to consume the flesh of Christ that I feared I might run short. I broke the hosts into tiny fragments, dropping them like pills onto famished rosy tongues. *"Corpus Domini nostri Jesu Christi custodiat animam tuam in vitam aeternam,"* I chanted. Fed, the guerrillas released a collective sigh, sprinkled here and there with tears.

I saved my sermon for the last. I shouted, *"En el nombre de nuestro Señor y Salvador Jesucristo . . .* In the name of Our Lord and Saviour Jesus Christ, stop laying land mines. In the name of Christ, stop killing people."

My commands in Spanish broke the spell. "When the army stops killing US!" the guerrillas shouted back at me. "When we LIBERATE EL SALVADOR!"

After the Mass, Dalila brought me supper, a ration can of rice and tomato, and a fresh pineapple. With her rough, gun-ready fingers she touched my face; I twitched. Nourished, I lay down on bullet casings and tile shards, beneath the shattered roof and stars, clutching my rosary, and tried to sleep. In those highlands, the night was cool; as I shivered in my overalls, I rejoiced for my insanity in coming to this place. Now I loved the guerrillas, my game with danger, and Dalila, my pretty one of night. I remembered my father's death on the road to Dunkirk.

I prayed, "Lord, when my hour comes, let it come like this. No lingering, no decay: a guerrilla's bullet through my skull, Beatitude." I could hear Dalila, still watching me, whispering in the bush with Mustache, my other guard. I slept badly, and in my wakefulness I remarked more and more guerrillas lying down to sleep on the shards and bullet casings near me. Even in their slumber, they hugged their rifles, as though knowing that if captured they would forthwith be shot or tortured.

At daybreak, I heard an ugly sound, a distant sort of *chop-chop-chopping:* soon I recognised the roar of approaching helicopters. The guerrillas leapt up from sleep, but then the army in American helicopters spat hate at us, stitching our patch of earth with what seemed ten thousand bullets and dropping sheets of greenish chemical not aimed well, setting trees and hills aloof from us ablaze. Yonder to the north, jet aircraft were more surgically dropping bombs on the huddled adobe houses of Perquín town, producing blasts of orange flame aspiring and evil grey smoke.

Now I hunched beneath my charred altar, fingering my rosary; Mustache and Dalila and their companions crouched between trees and in open space, firing their automatic rifles and submachine guns at a chop-chop-chopping helicopter as it made more passes in the mauve sky. A second helicopter, flying so low that hitherto I had not seen it, of a sudden caught Mustache and Dalila and three other guerrillas leaping across a patch of grass, its flashing bullets flailing them precisely through their torsos and their faces, which spurted just a bit of blood as they fell dead.

My services were straightaway again conscripted: I mumbled *"Requiem aeternam dona eis, Domine: et lux perpetua luceat eis,"* and I blessed the corpses as they were buried in bloody dirt beneath the skeletons of trees.

Dazed, I sat down amidst the rubble and awaited my permission to proceed to Perquín town. Late that afternoon, toothless Luis came to me in his safari hat and said, "I've talked to the *comandante.* Permission refused, Padre. You have till sunset to be on the other side of the Torola."

"You're kicking me *out?*"

"The *comandante* thinks you're a spy."

"I came to say Mass!"

"You've said Mass. Now get going, or—"

"I'm going to Perquín!"

"—we'll shoot you. Sunset. The Torola."

"I'll never m-make it by sunset. How will you know I've reached the river?"

"We'll know."

I picked up my pack and ran—out of the forest and onto the road. My flight now was downhill, but I was sure I would fail the guerrillas' deadline. Over the potholes and bullet shells, past the gutted houses and the eyes I knew were watching me, never had I been so swift. Once or twice I stumbled, scraping my right knee. I reached the riverbank just as the sun, its last rays, vanished. In the twilight, beneath my burden, I waded to the other side, gasping.

At the capital, in my black and crimson robes, I visited the army hospital, jammed with peasant soldiers, fresh from the battlefield, their feet and legs blown off by guerrilla land mines. Naked youths, some of them unsexed, lay sprawled about, nurses and physicians pumping them with blood.

I knew a thing or two about guerrilla land mines. The mines lurked just beneath the surface of the soil: the peasant soldier stepped on a blasting cap set off by a sulphuric acid mixed with potassium hypochlorite and sugar. The mine beneath was common garden hose packed with aluminium powder, gunpowder, stones, glass, and human excrement. *Boom:* no toes, no feet, no testicles.

Such jolly data in my head, I walked methodically from ward to ward, preceded by acolytes and a pair of military chaplains in black soutanes and lace surplices, bearing flickering beeswax candles, a golden ciborium, and tinkling silver bells. From the ciborium I offered each amputee the Holy Eucharist: "*Corpus Domini nostri Jesu Christi . . .*": then I blessed the boy in elaborate Spanish and tendered him my sapphire ring to kiss. This was early morning still. From the hospital I was driven through grey cement and barbed wire to the headquarters of the *Policía Hacienda,* the Treasury Police, where I asked to see the torture chambers.

"We do not torture people, Monseñor," a colonel told me sweetly.

Even as we debated, I pictured the events of that cellar. At the Archbishop's secretariat, I had met one of the cellar's victims—a tender young man whom I shall call "Muchacho." A captain stripped him naked and tied his thumbs behind his back. He knocked him down, kicked him in the head, the stomach, and the genitalia. He said gently, "Muchacho, confess that you spy for the guerrillas." Presently he thrust a plastic bag of lime over Muchacho's head, laughing sweetly when he gasped for air. The captain suspended Muchacho from the ceiling by his thumbs, then attached two-hundred-volt electrodes to his genitalia and his teeth. The captain turned on multicoloured hallucinogenic lamps and, shrieking North American rock music, donned plastic gloves, yellow flowers printed on them, then plunged Muchacho's head into a tub of urine and excrement. . . .

Upstairs, I traced a blessing in the air for all the Muchachos in the psyche-delic cellar, then took my leave of the Treasury Police. I was driven through more grey cement to army headquarters, where the senior generals as-sembled to receive me in deference to my princely rank.

"But we have no death squads in El Salvador, Your Eminence," swore the commanding general.

"I've seen the headless bodies, *mi general.*"

"We are fighting atheistic Communism," said another general.

"I've come with a proposal of papal mediation."

"To stop the war?" asked a third general. "You should talk to the guer-rillas, Monseñor."

"We are approaching the guerrillas through their office in Mexico."

"Your Eminence really needn't bother," declared the commanding gen-eral. "We don't want papal mediation."

"Why?"

"We're winning the war."

"Dear God, when will all this carnage end?"

"When we kill all of the guerrillas."

"In the name of Christ. . . ."

I lingered in the capital for another week. The army, the guerrillas, and the death squads increased their killing. In my overalls and van, I drove towards Nicaragua, admiring the exotic birds and vegetation and volcanic lakes, counting scores of headless bodies along my way.

En route in Honduras, I observe a pack of wild children eating from a garbage dump. I collect as many of the children as I can, buy ointments for their lice and ringworm, and in a noisy restaurant feed them fresh vegetables and lamb chops—even as I wonder, Who will feed them tomorrow?

"When we have no food," they tell me, "we sniff glue."

At León, northwestern Nicaragua, still wearing my disguise, I prayed for the hungry, addicted, dead, decapitated, and tortured in fantastical Baroque churches.

How dwarfed I felt by the life-sized crouching lions, the massive monu-ments and walls of marble, mahogany, and whiteness; gilded choirs and golden altarpieces studded with diamonds and topazes from Philip II; the men, women, and angelic children mournfully chanting the responses of the Rosary to the music of clarinet, accordion, and trumpet: *"Santa María, Madre de Dios, ruega por nosotros pecadores, ahora y en la hora de nuestra muerte."*

The temples abounded in towering statues of Christ: ivory, bronze, and plaster, robed in real velvet, bearing His cross of real wood, His head crowned with real thorns, His brow sweating drops of painted blood. Hordes of praying, hungry people milled in those churches. I left them there—weeping, keening aloud for favours, raising their arms aloft to Him— then drove due southward to the capital at Managua, where I ventured to a revolutionary temple to see Christ as a guerrilla.

The altarpiece was surreal, an immense, twisted mushroom sprouting from the earthen floor; here as in a dream the deepest symbols of the Christian legend merged with the mythology of the Revolution. The crucified Christ became the Nicaraguan people: men, women, and babes, a Sandinista soldier at the forefront, bearing a heavy cross and a Kalashnikov assault rifle. Floating above was the risen Christ, a peasant boy in a crown of barbed-wire thorns, his limbs still bleeding from his crucifixion by the bourgeoisie and bearing a submachine gun.

Below the cross was the Virgin Mother of Martyrs, bearing pictures of her murdered revolutionary sons and packing a blue pistol. Hovering about the Guerrilla Christ and the Mother of the Revolution were Liberated Workers and Peasants (the Apostles), blithely toiling in factories, in fields harvesting crops of sugar cane and coffee, all bearing green rifles; the brilliance of day (the Revolution); the darkness of night (the Counterrevolution); bombs the colour of the Stars and Stripes raining down on helpless peasants; the Holy Spirit hovering in the midst of them as the dove of peace and in his claws the legend: ¡SER CRISTIANO ES SER REVOLUCIONARIO! TO BE A CHRISTIAN IS TO BE A REVOLUTIONARY!

From the capital I drove to the interior, due eastward to the province of Chontales, where counterrevolutionaries, in the pay of the North Americans, were waging war against the Sandinista state. Chontales was all sudden bursts of rain and sun, rolling meadows and steep mountains, herds of sickly goat and red bulls, shepherds with grey sheep and cowboys on black horses ceaselessly crossing the dirt roads; the poor lived in huts with thatched roofs, or in shacks sinking in umber mud, numberless naked infants toddling about, or in more humble habitations of twigs at the mercy of the wind, eating tortillas and cabbages.

I wandered amongst the mud and twigs, handing out to grasping hands shanks of beef and bags of sugar. From there I walked up the slope of a mountain until it seemed that all of Chontales lay at my feet.

Squinting with my binoculars to the north, I saw the Sandinista People's Army join battle with the Counterrevolution. Soviet helicopters aloft and earthbound troops with mortars were attacking columns of men and pack animals descending on a valley; the counterrevolutionaries responded with reports of automatic rifles and rockets they fired from their shoulders, but then incendiary bombs exploded and in pink smoke the battle vanished. I scanned with my glasses to the south. In the fading afternoon, the sky was carmine. A cloud, shaped like a winged horse, galloped in slow motion weirdly above the jagged peaks.

In another distant valley, a village puffed blue smoke. Army troops were entering houses of thatch and twig, emerging with peasants whose arms were raised, herding them onto an open field, then setting their huts ablaze. Even on my mountain, I head groans of peasant sorrow. I drove back to the capital.

At Managua, in the papal nunciature, I resumed my cardinalate of black and crimson.

No sooner was my presence known than the Marxist press attacked me. The Sandinista newspapers splashed huge cartoons of me as Grand Inquisitor, the scourge of heretics and the guerrilla Christ, lurking in the cellars of the Holy Office, fondling the cobwebbed instruments of mediaeval torture and chortling, "Soon, my pretties, I shall have work for you again!"

In the name of the Pope, I summoned the bishops of Nicaragua and the paladins of the Revolutionary Church to a conference at the Jesuit university. Ah, such a university: bastion of Liberation Theology, clusters of ardent young men and women flinging Marxist incantations back and forth like Ping-Pong balls— "... *la lucha de clases ... la explotación del hombre por el hombre ...*"—amidst airy concrete buildings that in the awful dampness were eroding swiftly, walls splashed gaudily with the red and black colours of the Revolution, hammers and sickles and slogans: *¡PATRIA LIBRE, VENCER O MORIR! ¡¡NI SE VENDEN NI SE RINDEN!! ¡¡¡MUERTE AL YANKEE, ENEMIGO DE LA HUMANIDAD!!!*

We assembled in the Rector's conference room, beneath the portraits side by side of St Ignatius of Loyola and Vladimir Ilyich Lenin. First to arrive, at the head of his bishops, was the Cardinal Primate of Nicaragua, garbed in tinted spectacles and a tropical soutane of white and scarlet, looking darkly Mayan and quite fat. "Your Eminence!" I cried at him. "Dear brother, let me kiss you! Now do sit down. I expect the others presently."

The Cardinal Primate glanced up at Lenin, grimaced, then took his place beside me at the centre of the conference table—only to glower again when the Revolutionary Padres burst upon us. Those untidy priests were many of them ministers in the Marxist government, filling zealously amongst other posts the portfolios of Foreign Secretary, People's Education, and Universal Culture. (They were not *all* Jesuits.) They wore brown sandals without socks, baggy slacks or blue jeans, and dingy work shirts open at the neck. The Minister of Culture, secular ecclesiastic and quondam Trappist troglodyte, a renowned poet of the Revolution in the canto style of Ezra Pound, wore a floating muslin scarf with yellow roses printed on it and a black beret that I knew he was loath to take off, even when he went to bed. Teasing him, I asked, "Padre, what is love?"

"The Revolution," said the lyric poet.

"What is the Revolution?"

"The Kingdom of God."

"Who converted you to Marxism?"

"Jesus Christ."

"Have you achieved the Kingdom of God?"

"God's Kingdom is upon us, Cardinal."

"Odd, Father, I've been all over Nicaragua—and all I've seen is hunger."

"The hunger is not the Revolution's fault," the Foreign Minister admonished me. "Imperialism—the North Americans—are waging terrorism and bloody war on us."

"Nonsense!" said the Cardinal Primate. "There's food all over Nicaragua, but you give the poor no bread, no meat, no eggs, no cheese. Cattle all over the country, but meat can't enter Managua. No medicines, no cooking oil, barely any rice, beans, squash. It's a simple matter of distribution, but you simply don't know how. You and your *comandante* masters are all incompetent. You Marxist priests should be doing penance, not running ministries."

"We're teaching the children of Nicaragua to build a society of noble work and human dignity," responded the Jesuit Minister of Education.

Cardinal Primate: "You're teaching them hate and class warfare."

Minister of Education: "We teach Marxist theory only in the universities."

Cardinal Primate: "You're lying, Father. You teach your Marxist-Leninist claptrap even in the grammar schools."

"What are you doodling, Father?" I asked another Jesuit.

"Oh, just a little sketch," the Father told me.

"May I see it? Ah . . . a triangle . . . the Holy Trinity—Jesus Christ, Karl Marx, and Che Guevara."

"I'm merely trying to suggest that Che, Marx, and Christ converge in the Revolution and the New Man," explained the Father—inspiring a fresh outburst from the Cardinal Primate.

"For you Jesuits," the Primate railed, "Nicaragua is a laboratory, and we are all your little guinea pigs. [*Para ustedes, los jesuítas, Nicaragua es un laboratorio, y somos todos sus pequeños conejillos de Indias.*] Religion for the lot of you is no longer supernatural—religion for the lot of you is politics, sociology, class warfare, revolution, blood, and 'holy violence.' "

"How dare you, Cardinal, lecture us on violence?" demanded the Minister of Education. "Why haven't you condemned the Counterrevolution?"

The Primate pointed at Jesuits around the room: "You, Father, gave a young Jesuit *Das Kapital* as an ordination gift. And you, Father, gave him a machine gun."

The Minister of Education shouted back: "We have consecrated our lives to the apostolate of the poor."

"Then why are your revolutionary churches empty?" I asked drily. "Why do the poor prefer the old faith, filling the traditional churches in swarming hordes, weeping, raising their arms aloft to robed and painted statues of the bleeding Christ? Is it not because they crave mystery? Do they not deeply loathe your political Guerrilla Christ?"

"How far too fond you are of superstition, Cardinal! And the Pope—"

"I have come here with a command from the Pope. All of you priests who are ministers in the government will get out of the government—or get out of the priesthood."

"WE WON'T OBEY!" shouted the Revolutionary Padres.

"Then I warn you solemnly, the Pope will defrock you. We can not allow your rebellious and sweaty hands to debase the priceless coin of Latin Christianity."

honey than of lava. Perhaps he noticed his erupting anger reflected in the emotions of my face, for at first he struggled to control it. He said, "True ... true ... true ... but enough, Augustine. Indeed you are the *capo* of the anti-Jesuit party."

"Oh, some loyalist Jesuits still prosper, Holiness."

"True also, but when many Jesuits see you coming, they run the other way. And yet ... Your Eminence's indignation could hardly exceed ... *Ours!* In Galicia, We fought with the Jesuits constantly, but at least those Jesuits confessed the *Faith*! As for so many others, will there be no end to their meddling, intrigues, and—sacrilege? Their public questioning of miracles, existence of the Devil, the Divinity of Christ? Their mockery of the Pope? Humble dissent is one thing, the will to destruction ..."

His words were swallowed by his heavy brown beekeeper's hood as he thrust it on his head. He continued talking, his utterances the angrier as they echoed inside his metallic mask. He put on the rest of his apian regalia, his thick blue apron and his great leather gloves, then shoved a glove inside a cupboard. The bees there protested, buzzing up a storm, and some few of them flew out at him. He demanded, "So what shall We DO about it?"

Next morning, in my rooms at the Holy Office, I vested in my full crimson and lace rochet, tucked a manuscript of parchment beneath my sash, and strode majestically out—into the Via del Santo Uffizio along Bernini's gloomy colonnade. Thence I turned right, into the Borgo Santo Spirito, thence into the Jesuit curia confronting the Vatican.

That brown palace of the Counter Reformation remained but a vast shell. The interior had been modernised, made over from Baroque opulence into a maze of dark pipes, stairways of black steel, little bare rooms. I mounted a stairway to the top and knocked on a metal door. It was opened by a British Jesuit in a grey beard and a dirty shirt.

"I've come to see the Father General," I informed him.

"But Cardinal, he is not well," the Briton said.

"I've a decree from the Pope," I answered.

The Briton led me through a warren of squeezed corridors, past quizzical Jesuits of various colour, into a meek bedroom adorned only by books, a wooden crucifix, and an ancient portrait in oil of St Ignatius of Loyola. On a Spartan cot, a floral yellow blanket drawn to the armpits of his pyjamas, lay the "Black Pope"—Father General of the Jesuits.

He gazed up at me with anaemic eyes as he tried to speak. At once I felt pangs of sympathy for his saintly person. Lately he had been felled by a stroke, crippling his powers of speech, reducing him to mumbles, though at moments lucid thought burst from him in lucid sentences. His roots were Basque: a tormented race. In his bed of old age he was decrepit and sallow; as a younger man, a robust missionary, he had seen the Americans drop an atomic bomb on Hiroshima. That epiphany had changed his life, transformed his Jesuits eventually from men of Scholastic piety into reckless

FORTY - TWO

✥

At Rome, on the roof of the Apostolic Palace, I recounted my adventures on the isthmus to the Sovereign Pontiff. We strolled about the roof in the receding afternoon of a sweet Italian spring, behind the ugly barriers of armour plate. He had long since recovered from his bullet wounds: silently I admired how hale he looked in the tawny sunshine. His cheeks were pink apples; his eyes were twinkling mirrors of Rome's benign blue sky; his movements more than ever incarnated virile celibacy. "Ha-ha-ha," he said ever so merrily of this, that, and the other, before we got to business.

His ringed hand touched my elbow, guiding me towards his labyrinthine apiary. In his immaculate white soutane he paused before his green cupboards, peering into them, humming, uttering "*Bzzzzzz-bzzzzzz-bzzzzzz,*" to greet his manifold black and golden bees. I thought, The Sunny Pope: *Pope as Horse*. The Sad Pope: *Pope as Fish*. The Slav Pope: *Pope as Bee*.

Even as I saw such images in my brain, my tongue began to rattle about the perfidy of Marxist and various other insurgent Jesuits, inciting the Pontiff to a change of mood. His humming and his buzzing ceased; his handsome jaw grew visibly more square; his eyes turned a fiercer blue, suggesting depths of his character composed less of champions of the oppressed. News of my intrusion to his room raged like fire throughout the palace: more and more Jesuits crowded in upon us.

Benignly I began, "Has your health improved, Very Reverend Father General?" He mumbled something I could not grasp. I added, "His Holiness, every morning, remembers you in his Mass."

The ancient Jesuit nodded gratitude. From beneath my sash I removed my parchment. Glancing down at it I said, "However . . . the Supreme Pontiff, invoking the fullness of his Apostolic powers, has in his holy wisdom decided to dismiss you, Very Reverend Father General."

The Very Reverend Father mumbled again. The British Jesuit, interpreting, protested, "But why?"

"His Holiness is displeased with rampant tendencies in the Society of Jesus which do not conform to revealed doctrine and which he fears will lead to self-destruction," I explained. "He holds Father General in considerable esteem, but also—for his famed permissiveness—as the most responsible. In his solicitude for the Society's survival, the Holy Father feels compelled to intervene. His further reasons are elaborated in his decree."

"Which you drafted, Cardinal?" asked a voice.

I tendered the decree to the Father General, but his trembling hand would not accept it. Neither would the hands of his disciples. Not gently—indeed almost as though this were an exorcism—I deposited the parchment at the foot of his bed.

"Who . . . will . . . replace me?" asked the Father General in intelligible Italian.

"For indefinite time, dear Very Reverend Father, the Society will be governed by the Pope's personal delegate."

"Who . . . ?"

"Oh, no doubt he will be a loyal Jesuit, a sound scholar, and—for his orthodoxy—quite above reproach? When the Pope returns from New Guinea, he will mull upon the nomination."

"We . . . Jesuits . . . *elect* our . . . Father General."

"When His Holiness decides that an election should be held, he will inform his delegate."

I withdrew.

As I descended the metal stairway, young Jesuits in blue jeans and khaki shorts lay in wait for me on the landings, hissing and hooting. "You took a special vow—TO OBEY THE POPE!" I shouted back at them. At the great door, I noticed in the midst of the angry crowd a young American Jesuit in proper black clericals, chewing rosy bubble gum, but a friendly face. Indeed, I knew him slightly as an expert on the global arms traffic and specially poison gasses. As he advanced to genuflect and kiss my ring, I jested, "You've no poison gasses, Father?"

"Incense is the most lethal of all, Your Eminence," said the Father as he kissed my sapphire.

I walked back to the Holy Office scraping bubble gum from my precious gem.

✛

FORTY - THREE

✛

As I approach my sixtieth year, the shadows of my psyche deepen. I have, I think, mastered my carnal passions. I remain in robust health, but when my godly emotions are engaged my right hand begins to tremble slightly—and occasionally my stammer returns to afflict me. In matters of faith and discipline, I suffer much whenever other Christians doubt the harsh wisdom of the reigning Pope, whom I revere increasingly. I continue to stroll through the crowds who call on me at the Palazzo Consalvi, my ringed hand quivering against my wish.

I ask of a young man, "Ah, so you're a priest? Why don't you wear your Roman collar? Are you embarrassed to be a priest? Do you read your daily Office? Do you keep your vows of obedience and celibacy?" I ask of a young woman, "Ah, so you're a nun? Why don't you wear your habit? Are you embarrassed to be a nun? I suppose that you pray to 'God the M-Mother'?"

Next day, I receive a letter from Diana Northwood.

. . . and therefore I look forward to Adrian's marriage with huge misgiving. When he arrives in Rome, would Your Eminence suggest to him a few moments of reflection? I can not believe that—on so hasty an acquaintance—this Egyptian woman loves him for anything but his fortune. The prospect that she will live with us here at Northwood Hall fills me with dread.

And you know how reckless Adrian is with his money. Would you also as best you can urge some miserly restraint on my headlong son? If he writes you another check, please do refuse it. . . .

My fantasy of Adrian—that he should become St Francis of Assisi—had not prospered.

A year after his father's death, at the age of sixteen, fair Adrian had revealed to me that he consorted with whores in the Parisian quarter called Strasbourg St-Denis. He disliked his frugal Benedictine school in Normandy, avoided chapel, and abandoned faith in any God who intervened in the affairs of men or was even conscious of His own being. God, should He exist at all, was present merely in the mysterious laws that moved the universe and in the principle of Beauty. Jesus Christ was not the Son of God but an interesting hysteric. At The University in the United States, loyal to his trendy disbelief, Adrian had continued to fornicate regularly. Such lurid disclosures of his callow life dealt me ever sharper stabs of anguish.

Adrian and Antonia, his prospective bride, stayed with me at Consalvi palace. They were en route to America from Cairo, where Adrian had gone to pursue a sudden zeal for archaeology. Sunbathing of a weekend at the Sporting Club, he had met Antonia casually, introduced by someone beside the swimming pool. "What do you do?" he asked her beneath the devilish sun. "I'm an interpreter for the United Nations," said she. "How many languages do you speak?" "Six." "Ha! Only one less than I do?" Antonia indeed was exotic, half-Italian, half-Egyptian, slim-waisted, like Adrian, and sylph-like.

She had brown abundant hair, skin of smooth glass, nearly opaque from the Nilotic sun, and her mouth was carved, of the pigment mauve. Her eyes were fierce green baubles, so unusual that at once upon meeting her in Rome I thought of Lidia. (Do you remember Lidia, she it was who invited me to go swimming alone with her in Alexandria—a temptation I kept putting off?) Soon I wondered, Does she lack Lidia's sweet, insouciant enchantment?

At the Palazzo Consalvi, the lovers oozed the sap of youth, so ebullient and painful to contain, Adrian in fashion blazers and Oxford shoes, Antonia in tight slacks and fashion chiffon dresses that he had bought for her. However, Adrian seemed to me strangely nervous, as if he were never at a given moment sure of his beloved's heart. He seemed too ready to render any service that might please her, hopping here, there, and everywhere about my palace.

Nor could he keep his hands from my lustrous treasures, fingering golden clocks, Sèvres vases, bronze elephants, the marble bust of Cardinal Newman, Baroque crucifixes. Of an evening he rushed to his rooms upstairs and brought down pictures he had painted of the Valley of the Nile, displaying them to me and Antonia in the music room: blue-sailed dhows, a mosque door, a horseman galloping toward distant tombs, a ruined palace of Assiut at sunrise, the colossi of Thebes at moonrise, a woman in black, a clay pot atop her head, walking into grey palms and a green sunset. The pictures were muddy: things indistinct dangling somewhere between Impressionism and Baroque time.

"What do you think of them?" asked the artist hopefully.

"You've a pleasant talent, dear Adrian," said I. "As I look at your creations, I can not but remember Goethe's criteria for a work of art. One, what is the artist trying to say? Two, does he say it? Three—"

"Three, is it worth saying?" interjected the artist. "So . . . ?"

I sighed. Antonia in her gilded chair put her hand to her lovely mouth, repressing her amusement. I sat down on the bench before my Steinway, in order to please my guests inventing lively variations of Mozart's Rondo in A. I bade Adrian to sit beside me, inviting the golden youth to improvise cadenzas on the lower scale, but Adrian's hands could not meet the challenge and he produced sullen notes. Antonia said teasingly, "You've no talent, darling, but for making love."

Making love.

Often I invited the couple to hear my Mass at dawn in my charming chapel off the courtyard, but invariably they overslept. I had taken measures to keep them from each other's bed, lodging Antonia on the first floor, Adrian in rooms on the third floor beneath the attic where I housed my Nubians: but were such precautions futile? At night, as I tossed on my cot of wooden slats, I imagined that I heard whispers in the corridors, bare feet shuffling on the marble stairway, doors creaking open and clicking shut. On Sunday morning, when the two failed to appear in chapel, I mounted in my rich Roman chasuble above my alb of lace to Antonia's room.

Her bed was empty. I climbed the grand staircase to Adrian's apartments, where they lay naked and half entwined upon his bed, sharing a cigarette of acrid black tobacco, no doubt having just achieved coitus. Their exemplary suntanned bodies were pale about their buttocks and genitalia, nor when they saw me did they shamefully grab at sheets to shroud their loins. At once the sensuous contrast of their bronzed and pale flesh provoked a tremor of longing through me for all such pleasure I had denied myself. And yet I managed to quell the rage I felt not for the nude lovers but for my own renunciation.

I turned my back on them, walking out as I said quietly, "Adrian. Antonia. Come to Mass."

They dressed and came down to Mass, at the Communion opening their mouths to receive the Eucharist, but I refused them the flesh of Christ. At breakfast, as my Nubians poured steaming coffee and served honeyed rolls, I told them, "I will not have this any longer. I must remove you both from a state of sin. I'll marry you tomorrow."

"But we hoped you'd marry us at Northwood Hall," protested Adrian.

"Adrian promised me a home wedding," said Antonia languidly.

"I shall wed you *tomorrow!*"

Next morning, in the Pauline Chapel, beneath Michelangelo's frescoes of St Paul blinded on the road to Damascus and St Peter crucified upside down, with only two Swiss Guards as witnesses, I pronounced Adrian and Antonia man and wife. Feeling perhaps postponed contrition for the voluptuous scene in his bedchamber, Adrian upon the eve of flying with Antonia to Northwood Hall made a gesture deeply faithful to his nature. He doubled the amount he had intended and wrote a cheque to me for two million dollars. I accepted the gift with grace, but her husband's grandeur released from Antonia a laugh of ridicule.

I thought of Adrian, *Throughout your marriage she will make you suffer much. But must not each of us here on earth bear his heavy cross?* Suddenly I glimpsed Adrian grieving terribly in future time, but I saw not clearly why. I reflected, *Your suffering to come may serve my St Francis project.*

I gave half of Adrian's benefaction to the Pope. As I had for his two predecessors, I continued to visit Geneva, where I deposited the Pope's personal monies in the secret account at the Crédit Suisse. The Holy Father's exceptional charisma attracted bountiful gifts of cash from admirers around the world, but still they failed to balance the deficits of the Vatican exchequer or to finance the boundless charity of the Roman Pontiff.

On the roof of the Apostolic Palace, as he tended his apiary, the Pope inquired, "Augustine, are you Jewish?"

"Holiness," I responded with some annoyance, "you are the third pope to ask me that question."

"Because I hope it to be true, my dearest brother."

"Ah?" said I, half mollified. "My father was of England's recusant Catholic nobility, but I am not English. My mother I believe was Jewish, though she denied it. On the eighth day of my life, she had me circumcised according to the Old Covenant. I am happy to be half a Jew."

"Next week, We shall visit the Roman synagogue to pray with the Grand Rabbi. Will you come with Us, Eminence?"

"Really, Holiness, I'd rather n-not."

And in my library at evening I continued to explore the light and shadow of my dispersed and imperfect character with my Mother Confessor, the Soeur Pauline—long since a saintly presence at my secretariat and my African soup kitchen near the Arch of Constantine; more creaky of joint and limb; but her countenance lambent ever. And I asked, "Isn't it possible, *ma très chère soeur,* that God did not intend me for the path of lofty mysticism that you keep urging on me?"

"At the least He calls on you to be less worldly, Monseigneur," she answered fondly.

"No doubt—but how? You see, my darling Sister, very long ago—soon after I became a priest—I struck a Faustian bargain."

"Sweet Jesus!" she cried, thrice crossing herself. "Not with Satan?"

"No—with God. I sold my soul to God. The thorns of my celibacy so tortured me that I promised God to go on wearing them provided that He in His turn would raise me high in the Church."

"How selfish," said my Soeur Pauline sadly.

"Deeply selfish, my dearest Sister, but as ever I am deeply honest with you. Nevertheless, isn't it uncanny? We both of us—God and I—have kept the bargain. Can you even faintly imagine how much I love being a cardinal? Yet in matters outside of chastity, I have not always acted with the same thorny rectitude. In things of money, several times I've brushed close to simony, but invariably I behaved with sufficient prudence, and I never crossed the River Rubicon into deadly sin. So often, in so many matters, my struggle has been devilish, but there we are—my Faustian pact with God."

"It sounds to me more like a Faustian pact with yourself," she said wisely.

"Have I failed so badly of your sublime expectations, *ma soeur*? Have I made no supernatural progress at all?"

"Your Eminence is still too self-absorbed."

The little nun rose suddenly from her grand French armchair, beneath her veil and coif her normally unfurrowed face so agitated that at once I sensed a predicament of her soul and not my own. "I beg you, Monseigneur," she burst out, "let me go back to Africa."

"Where in Africa?"

"The Congo."

"But all Belgian missionaries have been kicked out of the Congo."

"Then somewhere else in Africa? There are lepers in many places."

"*Ma soeur,* I could not live without the fragrance of your sanctity."

"I've no such fragrance, Monseigneur! But you, I think, are guilty of spiritual gluttony."

"What do you mean, my beloved Sister?"

"You want me all to yourself. You won't share me with anybody—or give me back to Africa!"

Distraught, my Soeur Pauline went home to her convent in the Borgo Pio. In the weeks that followed, she rather went on strike, doing nothing in my secretariat but scrub floors on her painful hands and knees. Exasperated, I told her, "You're arthritic and deaf and in your sixties. Where would you go in Africa?"

"I talked the other day to Italian nuns of the Consolazione. They need more sisters at their hospital in Somalia."

"*Ma soeur,* I can't even remember where Somalia is."

"On the east coast of Africa. I implore Your Eminence, let me go."

I thought, In her mystical gymnastics she demands so much of me—could I ever imitate as she does St Theresa of Ávila?—that I shall never meet her measure. Forlornly I replied, "This will be amongst the hardest penances of my life—giving you up. With my fondest blessing, my Soeur Pauline, go back to Africa."

✥

FORTY-FOUR

✥

At length I flew to Paris, where in the Pontiff's name I addressed a conference on the global arms trade at the glassy palace of UNESCO. Bitterly I denounced the Americans, the Russians, the British, and the French for their sinful trafficking in machine guns, grenade launchers, tanks, howitzers, assault rifles, armed helicopters, and supersonic penetration bombers. From my journeys in Africa and Latin America I evoked horrid images in French of civil populations throughout the tropics of the poor being cooked and ravaged to enrich the salesmen of death and gratify the greed of governments. ". . . and, for the love of Christ, when will you wealthy nations stop selling land mines that blow up children?" I withdrew from the podium in my swirl of black and scarlet amidst deafening applause, doubting that anything would be done.

The month was grey, rain-swept November, late afternoon. From the Place de Fontenoy I was driven in a UNESCO limousine across the River Seine to the Hôtel George V, where I ascended to my suite on the top floor and read my sacred Office by my high window, glancing now and again at the lamps of Paris as they flickered yellowish and blurred through a rolling fog. At evening, with my Gucci bag, a black cloak flung over my soutane, I went downstairs, thence from the hotel beneath my umbrella I walked bareheaded in the rain to a dinner party.

I strode up the Champs Élysées, turned from the Place de l'Étoile down the avenue d'Iéna, and walked past the rue Jean Giradoux and the rue Galilée through the Parisian damp until the equestrian statue of George Washington in the Place des États Unis: there I pressed a button and penetrated the great door of the Embassy of Egypt.

A Nubian led me to a small room, where I shed my winter cloak and from my bag replaced it with my *ferraiolone,* my long cape of crimson watered silk. Before a Baroque mirror I placed my zucchetto atop the crown of my silver head, then put on my red biretta, tilting it back a bit to show my bountiful locks—when a fat man in evening dress crept in, his dark puffy eyes meeting mine in the looking-glass. He asked, "Did the goddess Chastity sculpt that head?"

"I think she helped," I answered. "Who are you?"

"Well . . . to begin . . . I'm the Ambassador."

I turned to confront the puffy eyes and blurted, "Dear God—Ali?"

As Ali answers, I do not quite hear him: instead in memory I conjure up the Ali of my youth.

He is handsomer than any young man ought to be—at the Foreign Ministry running his fingers constantly through his straight black hair, calling attention to its splendour; his skin not truly dark, tanned only by the Egyptian sun and naturally I think the tint of blondish copper; smiling often through his flashing teeth; at the Sporting Club from the highest springboard diving like an aureate falcon in swift descent, whilst I stroll by that swimming pool in my proper black bathing costume, clumsily slurping my *gazooza.*

Now the Ali of this evening runs his stout fingers across my face: ". . . these flared nostrils, this profuse and glowing hair, these austere high cheekbones . . . betraying . . . such . . . self-denial . . . ?"

Reciprocally I touch Ali's skull, its baldness sprouting but a hair or two and covered with wounds and ruts. I ask, "Were you in a crash?"

"Hair transplants," says the Ambassador. "Not, so far, a huge success."

"Where is Lidia?"

"We divorced long ago. The bitch."

"I never thought so. All these years, I've missed her charming laughter and her fierce green eyes—her invitations to go swimming in Alexandria which coyly I kept putting off."

"I need another Scotch. Ah, *cher Augustin,* your slim waist."

"And you, Ali? Are you wearing a corset?"

"My very special *belt.* Come, my other guests await us. Watch your purse, Augustine—half of them are fake nobility."

"Dear Ali, in Egypt when we were young I envied you above all men."

. . .

At the top of the grand stairway, Ali's major-domo in livery announced, *"Son Éminence Monseigneur Sir Augustine Galsworthy, Baronnet, du titre de Sainte Brigitte, cardinal-prêtre de la Sainte Église Romaine, archêveque titulaire de Trebisond, ministre sans portefeuille à Sa Sainteté le Pape."* As I descended with my crimson billowing, Ali at several steps trailed in my backwash, his smile ironical and wet as if to say, "Look everyone, at last—a real prince."

At the bottom of the stairway, I was engulfed by the Ambassador's guests, bowing to me or genuflecting to kiss my ring, for my televised oration at UNESCO heaping me with vapid praise. I responded in their temper. "Ha-ha-ha. *Mais, Monsieur le comte, vous êtes vraiment trop gentil!* Ha-ha-ha. *Mais, Madame la vicomtesse, comme vos jolis mots sont trop généreux!* Ha-ha-ha." I heard myself mechanically repeating my oldest throwaway jokes. "But Madam Baroness, I rather like atheists. With atheists I don't have to talk shop. Ha-ha-ha."

These were, as Ali had warned, aristocrats with titles of dubious antiquity. Tonight they mixed with diplomatists of minor nations, Ethiopian women of hair so garish they might have been soliciting, and French young men in black leather. They drank Johnnie Walker and Bloody Marys and then sat down to dinner beneath a colossal photograph of Egypt's president and yellow chandeliers with bulbs out.

The cuisine was disappointing: indifferent wines, fillet of sole in a lumpy sauce, lamb minced too much. I sat at the head table between plump Ali and the morose wife of the Lebanese ambassador. Handsome Nubians in satin turbans served the courses, then stood with wrists crossed along the walls, waiting for Ali to summon them to offer second helpings which his guests refused. After dinner, before everybody, the Ambassador implored me to play some Bach and Chopin.

In the salon, I sat at a grand piano with flickering candelabra on it, surrounded by implausible lords and ladies, young women of kaleidoscopic race, and a pair of French youths with earrings of blue glass. My ringed hand might tremble when Latin Christianity was attacked, but it never trembled when I played Bach and Chopin: in recent years I had practised ever more fanatically, mastering the emotions of great music as I had with like discipline vanquished my rebellious flesh.

Tonight I played my adaptations of Bach's cantatas, and Chopin's waltzes, mazurkas, and polonaises with precise and sparkling elegance, followed by a brisk, I should not say brilliant rendering of Chopin's variations upon Mozart's aria *"Là ci darem la mano."* In the midst of my music, with half an eye I noticed a beautiful dark-haired young woman dressed in casual chic (jeans of washed blue, boots of brown suede, a turtleneck sweater the colour of chartreuse) and admired her from the distance. I finished with Liszt's showy *Mephisto* waltz—dark, menacing, soaring only to descend— indeed a dance with Satan. At the end of my concert came lusty applause.

The dinner party broke up. After embracing me, but before all of his guests had left, Ali disappeared with an Ethiopian courtesan of immoderate coiffure. Alone, I mounted the grand staircase to go home, yet I heard a woman's voice behind me: "Cardinal Galsworthy?"

In that gesture I had so much perfected down the years, I turned theatrically on the landing of the stairway in my pond of scarlet, gripping the hems of my cape, fixing my black gaze upon the young woman at my feet, she of the chartreuse turtleneck and now great brown eyes.

"Yes?"

"Are you the Monsignor Galsworthy who lived in Egypt?" she asked in American English.

"I'm afraid so."

"You wouldn't know me—you saw me last as a little girl. I'm Lisa. Lisa Salama?"

"I'm struggling to remember."

"We lived above your embassy."

"Ah? Over thirty years ago? I've quite forgotten."

I remembered the Salamas perfectly. As the woman spoke, I returned to Cairo; the unseen hands upstairs playing Bach; my shy intrusion into that household of frightened Jews; my success in saving them and their riches, too, from the devouring Revolution. And Lisa.

Again amongst the chairs that resemble enormous golden pineapples I toss the infant child—all dark and glossy eyes, black and frothing hair, skin so tawny I imagine Moorish ancestors—toward the ceiling, so high that in my awkwardness I nearly drop her. Is this a dance, some sort of predestined dance? She shrieks! She coos! She *loves* me!

". . . and my mother talked of you so often. Our jewels and money you smuggled out in your robes at Alexandria became a legend in my family and—"

"How do you know Ali?" I interrupted.

"We met at a dinner party. My parents—"

"Do pass my greetings to your parents, Miss Salama."

"They're dead. Would you have tea with me tomorrow?"

"Where?"

"At the Plaza Athénée?"

I thought, *Too lovely. Too risky. Refuse.* I answered, "Tomorrow morning I'll say Mass at Notre-Dame with the Archbishop of Paris, then at noon I shall return to Rome."

"I'm sorry, Cardinal Galsworthy. Thanks for all you did."

"Thanks for thanking me."

I turned away and climbed the stairs. On the top step, I turned again and called after her, "Miss Salama? Lisa? I'll come to tea at four tomorrow."

I remembered the Hôtel Plaza Athénée on the avenue Montaigne with confused emotions of nostalgia and embarrassment: before I was ten, my mother had taken me there for tea, but Lady Daphne did not allow me to enjoy the experience because I broke my teacup. I took tea with Lisa in the long corridor off the lobby, on Louis Quinze armchairs beneath a mural after Jean-François de Troy, *La Déclaration d'Amour:* on a vast sofa, a man in stockings and a velvet coat squeezes the hand of a coquettish lady in a dress embroidered with fern and butterflies, too earnestly confessing his passion. I wore my black suit of double-breasted twill as Lisa persisted in her casual chic—jeans and a yellow turtleneck, bracelets and earrings of dull copper. In the distance, a string quartet played Schubert.

"What do you do?" I asked.

"I'm a radiologist in New York," said Lisa.

"Why are you travelling alone?"

"I'm recovering from a love affair."

"What does your lover do?"

"He sculpted."

"Past tense?"

"He shot himself."

"Why?"

"I wouldn't marry him."

"And you feel guilty?"

"Awfully."

"Guilt, also, is a grace."

"Is that Catholic philosophy, Your Beatitude?"

"Ha! 'Your Eminence' is more correct, actually. 'Your Beatitude' is normally reserved for eastern patriarchs and Greek Orthodox metropolitans. Ha-ha! But no matter. Your American accent enchanted me when you said 'Your Beatitude.' Would you say it again?"

"Your *Beatitude.* Ha-ha!"

"More enchanting, even. And you're laughing, Lisa. Laughter is the best medicine for remorse, don't you think? Is that black tobacco you're smoking? May I have one?"

"Oh, help yourself, Your Eminence."

"Since I've known you for—how old are you, Lisa?"

"Thirty-two. And Your Eminence?"

"Ah! Nearly sixty! I've known you since your infancy, so you may call me 'Augustine.' "

"My mother told me that you're Jewish, Augustine."

"Did I tell her that? It's sort of true, actually."

"I know what you mean. I wish I were a better Jew. Paul, my lover, was a Catholic."

"And a suicide? How very sad."

"He was for ever sculpting madonnas, saints, crucifixes. I'll tell you frankly that I've never been comfortable in the presence of Christian symbols—crucifixes especially. It was one of the reasons we broke up. Oh dear, why am I saying this to a cardinal who's been so kind? I suppose you've all your special reasons for Catholic dogma."

"Which dogmas do you mean, particularly?"

"I'd rather not say, Augustine."

"You can at least tell me one, Lisa."

"On abortion? I'm pro-choice."

"And what of the child? What choice has the child?"

"A woman is the mistress of her own womb."

"And the foetus is inhuman—a cancer?"

"In some instances that's exactly how women feel!"

"Devilish! How devilish!"

"I'm a physician, after all, and—why is your hand trembling?"

I snuffed out my cigarette and stood.

"Your romance, Miss Salama, was with a sculptor. Mine is with the R-Roman Church."

"I wasn't attacking your *faith,* Cardinal Galsworthy. How could I—ever—after all your favours to my family? Oh dear."

"I must catch my plane."

She gazed up at me, her large Moorish eyes so moist with sympathy and even with contrition that I felt quite moved. I yearned for my youth in Egypt.

She asked, "Can you forgive me?"

"Are you coming to Rome?"

"I suppose—in a week or two?"

"Where will you stay?"

"The Grand? The Hassler? I'll come to Rome tonight if you tell me to, Augustine."

"Tonight? Why, that's absurd! Tonight? Then hurry, Lisa. Go upstairs and p-pack."

You suspect that in my new infatuation I am harshly tempted to break my vows, but is such disloyalty any longer possible? Have I not outgrown the games I used to play with danger, testing my celibacy by exposing it to risk? Am I not now much too disciplined—too consecrated to my vocation as priest and cardinal—even to consider allowing Lisa to seduce me?

Nonetheless . . . I dissuaded Lisa from taking rooms at the Grand Hotel or at the Hassler and lodged her in Adrian's apartments on the third floor of the Palazzo Consalvi. Lisa, healing so painfully from her lover's suicide, seemed grateful for my company. In her rooms, she left the rococo crucifixes undisturbed and remained there quietly or absented herself from the palace when I held my crowded audiences in the late afternoons. She became, in a way, my hidden treasure, and more and more against my better judgement the mistress of my thoughts. As the days progressed, I suffered during whichever moment I might pass outside of Lisa's presence.

I loved mounting to her apartments in the early mornings after my Mass to take my breakfast with her. I loved the evenings in the music room when I sat at my Steinway and played for her: Bach's French suites, precise, thrusting, and relentless; Schubert's impromptus, melodic, evocative, and sad; Chopin's sonatas and ballades, now so quiet and so slow, now so suddenly violent; now so exuberant, now so menacing, now so melancholy; now so full of yearning, chagrin, misfortune, and disillusion; yet always so lyrical, graceful, and achingly—insanely—romantic, like a lovers' quarrel that can not end.

"Come, Lisa, sit beside me as I play. Add a chord or two on the lower scale."

In candlelight she sat nearby cross-ankled on the Isfahan carpet, as ever in her casual chic, staring at my busy ascetic hands. On a whim she raised her arms and languidly stretched her body. Even as it happened in the corner of my eye, her slightest natural movement of that sort unsettled me.

"I'd never dare, Augustine."

"But your mother was a superb pianist. Did she not teach you?"

"She tried. Today I can't play a note."

"Then stretch your arms again as you just did. You remind me so m-much of Egypt."

On some days we were mostly silent, happy simply for each other's presence. At the Holy Office, I watched the clock, increasingly more impatient to get through the drudgery of my duties that I might see her. On the roof of the Apostolic Palace, I even managed to cut short my audiences with the Pope.

"But We haven't finished yet, Augustine," the Pontiff objected. "Where are you going?"

"Home, Most Holy Father. I'm s-sick."

Not a lie: lovesick. No more initially than from curiosity, early in the mornings Lisa began to enter my little chapel off the courtyard to watch me celebrate my solitary Mass. At noon on Sundays, she stole into the crowd at my titular church of Santa Brigida, a white handkerchief as her mantilla above her turtleneck and jeans, to watch me pontificate in Latin and preach in Italian from my throne.

"I always loathed Mass," she told me afterwards at our cosy luncheon in Consalvi palace, "but not when you say it, Augustine. Your choir is exquisite. You are almost too regal in your robes. I do love to hear you sing your prayers in Latin. Is it because I don't understand a word?"

If she was ignorant of Latin, she was wise about much else. She recognised the schools of art that adorned my walls, talked shrewdly to the particulars, and told me bluntly when she did not care for them. Her range in literature was not quite so wide, running to the likes of Emily Dickinson, Samuel Beckett, Simone de Beauvoir—not my taste, but she defended that sort of modern sensibility with spirit and intelligence, to my delight.

Christmas and the New Year came and vanished. We took long walks in the Roman winter—Lisa in a dark poncho, I bundled in a great black coat and an Afghani cap to disguise my head—from my palace at the River Tiber up the Lungotevere Gianicolense, across the Ponte Sisto to the narrow streets behind the Palazzo Farnese; or we strolled in the abandoned Borghese Gardens, past the marble Daphne and Apollo and the Grecian temple of Aesculapius on its islet in the frozen lake; or we descended into the deserted park on the Colle Oppio, and sat on a stone bench, shivering in the wind, overlooking under the cold sun the Colosseum and the Arch of Constantine.

There, on the Colle Oppio, Lisa slipped her gloveless hand beneath the crook of my arm—the limit of our physical communion. My dreams were more disorderly. My monastic room on the second floor of Consalvi palace stood beneath her apartments: too often during night I watched my body ascend in space until it found its rest in Lisa's bed.

At breakfast, as she poured my coffee, Lisa said, "We're like a married couple except that we don't have sex."

"In Florence, I had sex—when I was young, before my priesthood. I fathered a child."

"Boy or girl?"

"A son, I think. I've seen him in dreams."

"Something else we have in common."

"Darling Lisa, what do you mean?"

"I dream, too, not all that often, of the child I might have had—a little girl?"

"But you've never had a child."

"Oh dear."

"What do you mean?"

"Augustine, must you play the Grand Inquisitor?"

"You didn't abort her?"

"I was barely twenty."

"Sweet Jesus, why?"

"I was immature, mildly neurotic, and quite short of money."

"But your family was rich! *I'd* seen to that! D-DEVILISH!"

FORTY-FIVE

Next morning, when I climbed to her rooms for breakfast, Lisa was gone. She had left me no note of farewell, only upon her unmade bed an open book of verse, St John of the Cross, that I had removed from my shelves downstairs to edify and please her. Faintly with a pencil, she had marked a single stanza.

> *Reveal your image clearly,*
> *And kill me with the beauty you discover;*
> *For pains that come so dearly*
> *From love, can not recover*
> *But through the presence of the lover.*

I thought: How cruel she is. Does she collect victims? An aborted child, a dead lover, now a distraught cardinal? No, it is entirely my fault.

Lisa had lived for longer than a month in the Palazzo Consalvi. For several weeks, I continued my routine as though she had never abandoned me. After my morning Mass, I went up as before to her apartments, imagined her Moorish eyes across the table, and took my breakfast in the void. In the afternoons, I came home from the Holy Office and the Sovereign Pontiff to a palace which even with my Nubians seemed hollow. In the evenings, I sat on the bench before my Steinway, banging at my Bach, my Schubert, and my Chopin, playing Lisa's favourite compositions without rest even as with half an eye I glanced to the Isfahan carpet and saw her sitting cross-ankled in the candlelight.

Come Lisa sit beside me as I play I'd never dare Augustine I can't play a note. Then stretch your arms again as you just did you remind me so m-much of Egypt.

At noon on Sundays, at Santa Brigida, as I preached in Italian from my throne, contrary to my wish my eyes scrutinised the faithful, seeking her dark and frothing hair beneath her funny white mantilla. In the nights, I lay not on my monastic cot but upon her bed, walking beside her as we crossed the Ponte Sisto to the little streets behind the Palazzo Farnese, passed the temple of Aesculapius in the frozen lake, sat down as we admired the Arch of Constantine and she placed her gloveless hand beneath my arm, shivering.

In my aching solitude, I resolved to see her again. At the Holy Office, I sorted through heaps of my unread mail for invitations to visit the United States, finding at last a letter from New York and the Council on Foreign Relations: "Would Your Eminence lecture on the arms race?" Within the fortnight, I fled Rome.

On the aeroplane, I read a glossy magazine for American women. The cover: 7 SECRETS OF GREAT SEX—*learn the easy way to get in the mood*—*tone the muscle that guarantees orgasm.* . . . THE AFFAIR: *Okay, you're caught. What to do* NOW? . . . YOUNGER GUYS—*why they're* HOT!!! . . . DO YOU REALLY KNOW EVERYTHING YOU THINK YOU KNOW ABOUT SEX? *Wanna Bet? (A Quiz).* BUTT SERIOUSLY . . . *Hard, Firm, Uplifting Tricks for a Tighter Derriere** **(Translation: Behind).*

An article inside: "I first had sex at thirteen and I loved it. I rolled around a lot in a big bed with my first boyfriend, learning to feel good about my body. I knew at once that my body was not my enemy—pleasure was my friend and my birthright. I never felt a loss of innocence, only the wonderful power of self-knowledge. But what about all those dark forces still denying us our self-esteem and our sexual self-empowerment? Taboos about 'right' and 'wrong' cause self-destructive guilt in girls. It's not whether we'll have sex—but what must we do to make sex safe and self-affirming? We're more than the property of parental rules or Shame-on-You religions! Sex can be spiritual! Sex is all about communication and healing! We're dynamic, curious, self-aware young women who need more sexual information and better access to birth control and abortion facilities! We need 'protection' only from poverty and rape. . . ."

In my taxi from the airport, the driver turned up his "boom box."

> *Oh yeah, oh yeah.*
> *Let's do it, let's do it, let's do it.*
> *Oh yeah, oh yeah.*
> *Open up your legs, baby, and let me shove it in.*

Oh yeah, oh yeah.
Let's do it, let's do it, let's do it.
Oh yeah, oh yeah.
Open up your legs, baby, and let me shove it in.

Oh yeah, oh yeah, oh yeah.
Oh yeah, oh yeah, oh yeah.
Oh yeah, oh yeah, oh yeah.
Let's do it, let's do it, let's do it.

I rather liked the beat: Bach was repetitious, too. The month was frosty March, 1987. At midday, wearing my Savile Row black suit and my double-breasted greatcoat, I was driven in a stretch limousine from the Waldorf up Park Avenue to a brownstone mansion on East 68th Street, where in a vast mahogany library I was greeted by a mob of academics, generals, admirals, quondam Secretaries of State, and fed luncheon. In my remarks I protested in English as I had in French the guns and land mines that bled the tropics. Then I took questions.

A general: "But we're under attack. What about our right of self-defense? Aren't Communist guns promoting tyranny and killing people throughout the tropics? You should protest to the Soviets, the Chinese, and the Czechs, Your Eminence."

I: "Through different channels I have often done so, General. They blame the arms race on you Americans."

An admiral: "We sell arms only to defend democracy."

I: "If I believed that, Admiral, I'd believe anything. Of course the Communists are terrible—so are the British and the French—but you Americans are egregious."

Various academics: *"Hear! Hear!"*

I: "In the marketing of death, more and more of these machines—the most primitive and the most sophisticated—are produced by American industry. Cheap Hughes helicopters for soft targets, expensive laser-guided missiles for hard targets, on and on. Within but several years, the American military establishment will control the market. Your sales mount so swiftly, into the billions and many billions of dollars, that they chill the soul."

Various academics: *"Too true! Too true!"*

I: "You encourage destitute nations to buy weapons they do not need and can never pay for. You are burying them in debt and blood."

A general: "Nobody's forcing them to buy."

I: "Nobody's forcing you to sell."

Quondam Secretary of State: "We have our own debt and unemployment problems, so we have to sell. I disagree with Your Eminence. The arms are needed."

I: "Because you're manufacturing them?"

Quondam Secretary of State: "Is the Pope as rabid as Your Eminence?"

I: "The Pope calls all arms traffickers 'tools of Satan.' "

A general: "You should tell the Pope that we're doing him a favour. We're defending Western values."

I: "Greed? Hedonism? Pornography?"

From the Council on Foreign Relations I walked down Park Avenue thirty blocks, thence to First Avenue and New York University Hospital in a forbidding skyscraper. On the fortieth floor, I drew up the lapels of my greatcoat to hide my Roman collar and made nervous inquiries at the desk.

"Dr Salama's not in yet, sir," a nurse told me. "She's on the night shift this week."

"At what time do you expect her?"

"Shortly?"

"I'll w-wait."

The hospital was all blinding fluorescent tubes, prophylactic greenness, detergent stench. From the window by the lift, I stared at the East River, remarking as I had with Charles the hideous smokestacks, steel bridges, the sign blaring PEPSI-COLA. When I heard two women talking, I turned to see Lisa in the distance, at the desk with the nurse, wearing a white smock and gripping a batch of X rays.

". . . and a gentleman asked for you, Doctor."

"Did he leave his name?"

"No, but what a sexy British accent. Tall and all in black, kind of lordly, like? Wow."

"Did he stammer?"

"Just a bit."

"Oh, dear."

I got into the lift and ran away: indeed I fairly dashed from the lobby of the hospital to my suite in the Waldorf Towers, where I fell to my knees and cried out the Sorrowful Mysteries of the Rosary, imploring Christ and His Virgin Mother to release me from Lisa's spell. Early next morning, I looked in the telephone directory, found the address of her flat, and took a taxi to East 10th Street in Greenwich Village. A visored Puerto Rican rang upstairs and told me, "Dr Salama's still in bed."

"Let me speak to her."

I seized the receiver: "Lisa, it's Augustine."

"But I'm not dressed."

"P-Put something on."

"No."

"P-Please."

"Come up."

Her flat was charming, done mostly in red, with a fireplace of white stucco, expensive prints of Utrillo and Matisse, and pieces of gilded furniture slightly too large for the proportion of her rooms, as if somehow she had inherited a taste for the chairs resembling huge golden pineapples in her ancestral palaces of Egypt. Barefoot, she wore white muslin pyjamas beneath a robe of green silk, and as we conversed without sitting down she combed her rippling hair. Embarrassed by her loveliness, I looked out of her window to the street and a picture gallery.

"What sort of pictures do they sell?" I asked.

"Junk," said she.

"But people prefer junk, don't you th-think?"

"Augustine, we must stop this."

"Where's your p-piano?"

"I don't have a p-p-piano."

Disarmed, I sat down on her sofa. She remained by the window, still combing her hair, diaphanous amongst beams of morning sunlight. Mournfully I said, "I've never even kissed you, darling Lisa—but my life lacks all passion without your presence."

"Your passion touched me, Augustine, especially in your music."

"Not enough . . ."

"Would you ever have become so fine a pianist if you weren't a priest? Oh, you're quite manly, but you have a nearly feminine feeling for what a woman wants. You respected my mind—but so much more? Gifts, soft flattery, all your little *mots,* flowers in my rooms each morning at the Palazzo Consalvi? You were so courtly! If you weren't celibate, I've no doubt you'd be a terrific lover."

"No doubt. . . ."

"When you stumble on your vows, I've the deepest sympathy for your dilemma. Silly, mean, repressive vows, I might have said, before I met you. Could I say that now? You're the most dazzling man I've ever known, Augustine, but I'm not in love with you. Given what you are, how could I be? I need a cup of coffee."

In her little white kitchen, she mixed instant coffee for the two of us and we sat at a square plastic table facing each other. And I replied, "I imagine now that I'm in my abbey of Vaucluse. 'Please, beloved Father,' I tell my Benedictine Abbot, 'I do not want to be a priest.' Now watch me, beloved Lisa, in a little chapel as I pronounce my final vows of perfect obedience and chastity. Now I'm in a huge basilica on the day I am ordained a priest. The Archbishop anoints my hands. I think, Do I act according to my own wish? I choose to be a priest. Do I choose not to be a priest?"

"What do you mean?"

"I wasn't sure then—and I'm not sure now. I know only that outside your presence I can no longer savour life. Did I withhold my interior consent when I became a priest? Was that an impediment to my priesthood? Should I abandon my priesthood and my cardinalate?"

"Without them, what would you do, Augustine? Put on tweeds and teach Italian on Long Island? You were born to be a cardinal."

"How mean you were to leave that verse of Saint John of the Cross on your unmade bed. Did I never mention his other masterpiece—about the dark night of the soul? That is a common sickness of mystics—loss of joy in prayer, maddening thirst of spirit, crushing desolation, even doubts that God exists. And that is my sickness, dear Lisa, since you abandoned me."

"Would you ever have given so much money to the poor if you were not a cardinal? I hated Christianity until I knew you and the beauty of your Mass."

"Theatre. . . ."

"Was it more than theatre that made it beautiful? My parents hated religious Judaism and they raised me as an atheist. Since meeting you, Augustine, do I feel differently? Your hand is trembling."

"A cardinal can r-resign."

I removed my sapphire ring, dropped it with a little clink into her drained coffee mug. Lisa gave it back to me. She said, "Only your vows can save you from something so delirious and stupid. Go home to Rome."

At her door, mildly she embraced me, raising her mouth towards the flesh stretched so tautly by self-denial across my cheekbones; but within an inch withdrawing as if to say, "No—I must not tempt you any longer." In silence, and more warmly, we kissed each other's hands.

Go home to Rome: others tendered me that advice. Next morning, I celebrated Mass in English on the high altar of St Patrick's, dismally and mechanically, as though the chalice of the Holy Sacrifice contained not the blood of Christ but common wine. It was the Third Sunday of Lent; my chasuble was of penitential violet. In his Epistle to the Ephesians, St Paul railed against fornication and uncleanness, excluding fornicators from inheriting the Kingdom of God. In the Gospel According to St Luke, Christ cast out devils.

The cathedral was full—not, surely, because my appearance had been announced in the press. Even as I prayed aloud I admired the church's lucent Gothic, the sanctuary all beeswax, marble, and red; the vaulted ceiling and the slim columns; the arched and aspiring baldachin wrought totally of bronze, glinting with a sheen so golden as to make heathens bow their heads.

In my sermon, I ignored the impending feast of St Patrick and preached vehemently instead against the pornography of death, the enormities of arms merchants, and the land mines strewn across hemispheres that blew up children. At the Communion, I descended to the edge of the sanctuary, thrusting my fingers into a jewelled ciborium to distribute the hosts to the faithful, and telling each communicant in English, "The body of Christ."

In the midst of the Communion, a commotion ignited at the rear of the nave. A pack of young men and women rumbled up the aisle, brandishing signs and shouting indecencies. When I saw the green of their banners, I recalled reading in the press of Irish homosexuals angry at the Church for excluding them from celebrations honouring St Patrick. See the sign beneath my face.

EQUAL RIGHTS
FOR IRISH GAYS!

Bizarre young men and women romped about the sanctuary, screaming obscenities and blasphemies and scattering inflated condoms the colour of human flesh. I turned away from the faithful and hurried towards the tabernacle, resolute to lock up the Blessed Sacrament to keep it from desecration. I glimpsed another sign.

GUS
DO U WEAR A CONDOM
WHEN U HAVE SEX???

"GUS"? Did they learn it from the Dutch? Suddenly a well-groomed young man blocked my flight.

I asked him quietly, "Are you a believer, dear son?"

He answered me quietly, "I used to be, Your Eminence. Or am I still?"

For a moment I fixed on his blue eyes, so full of deep sadness, and I felt an immense pity for his pain. He snatched my ciborium from me, dumped it upside down, and with his fashion shoe scattered the Eucharistic hosts across Carrara marble. I glimpsed another sign.

GUS
GOD IS COMING
AND SHE'S P-SSED OFF!!!

Before the high altar, an older man exposed himself. I glimpsed another sign.

GUS
GO HOME TO ROME!!!!

When the police came, I was on my hands and knees, scooping up fragments of bread from the floor of the sanctuary, stuffing them into my mouth and swallowing them as I could to save them from further sacrilege. I asked myself, Is this the flesh of Christ?

At that ghastly instant, I decided: *Yes, it is.* As imperious as I had been with faltering others about the doctrine of His body and His blood, I was never certain that I believed it with my heart and mind wholly—but in the desecrated sanctuary I did so now.

✥

FORTY-SIX

✥

Nevertheless, I returned to Rome in a state
of grief. My barren romance with Lisa,
my fleeting disavowal of my sacred vocation, and—worst—the blasphemous riot at the
Cathedral of St Patrick, provoked me to fits of
weeping. For the rest of the season of Lent,
through Palm Sunday, Holy Thursday, Good
Friday, even Easter Sunday and beyond, my life
became constant penance and atonement.

I stopped going to my secretariat at the Holy
Office and remained at the Palazzo Consalvi,
much of the time in my chapel. I suspended my
audiences in the late afternoons. To all callers on
the telephone, even eventually the Pope, Ghassem
replied in ungrammatical Italian, *"Eminenza
malato."*

I abandoned my music, my Bach, my Mozart,
my Schubert, and my Chopin, for me a harsher
penance than my fast and abstinence from food. I
no longer indulged my love of long walks, so
staunch was I to remain a prisoner in my residence;
only once a day, for half an hour, did I pace back
and forth in the little courtyard before my chapel,
reading my sacred Office. Soon I abandoned my
luxurious rooms and I lived in the chapel, taking
my frugal meals there, sleeping fully clothed, in a
soutane of simple black on the tiled floor, saying
prayers, rosaries, and Masses incessantly.

And so loath was I to leave the chapel that

Ghassem was obliged to provide the vestry with a chamber pot and, but once a week, to haul in a wooden tub of cold water that I might bathe. Rarely did I change my linen, nor did I shave my face or brush my teeth. Then I refused all food in the mornings, confining my nourishment to a jug of water, scraps of unleavened bread, boiled turnips or potatoes, when noon struck; and a cup of weak tea with a few salted biscuits late of evening, before I lay down again on the cold tiles to sleep fitfully before my little altar and my rococo monstrance containing the Blessed Sacrament.

I derived no spiritual pleasure from my privations, since I had indeed entered deeply into St John of the Cross's Dark Night of the Soul.

> *Let your soul therefore turn always:*
> *Not to what is most easy, but to what is hardest;*
> *Not to what most pleases, but to what disgusts;*
> *Not to matter of consolation, but to matter for desolation, rather;*
> *Not to rest, but to labour;*
> *Not to desire the more, but the less;*
> *Not to will anything, but to will nothing;*
> *Not to seek the best in everything, but to seek the worst, so that you*
> *may enter for the love of Christ into a complete destitution. . . .*

A complete destitution: of recent years my gravest sin, I saw in looking back, had been my spiritual gluttony. I had presumed—against all the witness of mystics down the centuries, and of my own dearest vanished Soeur Pauline—that I might enjoy the delights of the spirit even as I revelled in the favours of the world. The Kingdom of Heaven's retribution for my arrogance was my own dark night of the soul.

Now that night followed in detail the frightful portents contained in the writings of St John. My first agony was sensual—a fierce repugnance for my vanity, my narcissism, my vulgar ambition; for the gaudy laurels of the great world and of the Roman Church that had been heaped on me; and not least for my repressed but ravening lust for women. Yet in the very denial of my senses—in my new hatred for carnal pleasure, indeed for all created things, even for food and hot water and soap and shaving cream and toothpaste—I found no sweetness nor the slightest consolation in the things of God: only melancholy and more torment.

Still hearing the portents of St John, I hurled open my Bible, to the Book of Lamentations and the woes of the Prophet Jeremiah: "I am the man that hath seen affliction by the rod of His wrath. He hath brought me into darkness but not into light. Surely against me He is turned; He turneth His hand against me all the day. My flesh and my skin hath He made old; He hath broken my bones. He hath set me in dark places, as they that be dead of old. He hath hedged me about, that I can not get out: He hath made my chain heavy. Also when I cry and shout, He shutteth out my prayer. He was unto me as a bear lying in wait, and as a lion in secret places. He hath turned aside my ways, and pulled me in pieces: He hath made me desolate."

Inexorably I began to fear that my soul was lost, wandering on a misty road strewn with sudden prickly thorns and brambles, leading nowhere vastly, because God (did He exist?) had abandoned me. Thus (according to St John of the Cross) I was "like unto a blacksmith who gives up the hammering he has done in order to do it again, or unto a vagabond who leaves a city only to return, or unto a hunter who frees his prey in order to seek the beast but another and another time."

So . . . obsessively I said Masses—Tridentine Masses in Latin for the Sick and Dying, For the Removal of Schism, Against the Heathen, In Time of War, In Time of Pestilence, In Time of Plague. In the mornings, no sooner had I said a Mass than I said another. In the afternoons, no sooner had I said a Mass than I said another. In the evenings, no sooner had I said a Mass than I said another—for truly I was like unto a blacksmith forever hammering, a vagabond who flees a city only to come back, a huntsman who sets loose his prey the better to hunt the beast but another and another and another time.

My dreams grew unbearable. All the women whose flesh I had ever coveted haunted my nightmares, individually, then together, hounding me, howling at me, devouring my limbs, my genitalia, my head, and then when I expired their own tails, for in the midst of their gymnastics they were transformed into snakes and she-devils. Of a sudden then a rodent sprouted hindward from my chest, its feet kicking so wildly, and its body swelling to such proportion that it grew bigger than myself and its front paws scratched so savagely at my breast that I cried out again and again, "WHERE IS THE RAT'S HEAD? INSIDE ME THE BEAST'S HEAD? THE BEAST! THE BEAST! OUT! OUT! OUT!"

I awoke at dawn, tasting thorn and ashes. Feebly I walked to the chapel's porch, glancing to the corner of the courtyard, where as always Ghassem and his younger sons in turbans and *galibiyas* knelt on little rugs, their bodies facing east to Mecca; bending, touching their foreheads to their carpets; kneeling back, mumbling, chanting, invoking the love and mercy of their simpler and more benevolent One True God. Pausing in their devotions, they gasped when they saw their master, I so gaunt and sickly beneath my unshorn beard and my stormy hair, hitherto of such lucent silver, streaked now I had no doubt with snowy white.

In the days that followed, Ghassem's younger pubescent daughters, Najat, Iman, and Samia, encamped in the courtyard, squatting before copper samovars, steaming pots and pans, crying out in Arabic, *"Akl! Akl! Akl!"*— Food! Food! Food!—weeping, keening, tearing at their veils and hair, raising up silver and teacups and plate, begging me to eat, but I refused.

Do you recall Kamal, the little boy astride a wooden stool in my kitchen at Cairo, learning the suras of the Koran—then the adolescent addicted to Italian fashion and silly pop tunes—then the young man who quarreled violently with his father and who at length left home? Kamal had gone back to Egypt, where he prospered at Alexandria as a chef in an Italian restaurant, yet throughout his absence he longed for Ghassem, yearning to kiss his father's hands, begging his forgiveness and blessing. Now Kamal returned to

Rome, in his manhood (more than forty) not finely made like Ghassem but in bearing huge, thick-nosed, and thuggish. Ghassem welcomed him with joyous sobs.

Soon after he was lodged in the Palazzo Consalvi, Kamal took the measure of my crisis, and to prevent my collapse he decided to act. Well that he did, since in recent days a command from the Pope, written beneath the embossed and golden Keys of Peter in the Pontiff's hand, had arrived at the palace. It said, *"Viene."*

With his father meekly in tow, Kamal invaded the sanctuary. He dragged me, protesting, out of the chapel and up to the palace kitchen, where with Ghassem hovering he forced me to consume fresh bread and thick soup. Then against my imprecations father and son dragged me to my rooms, where they tore my foul soutane and undergarments from my body and pushed me into a hot tub. Then they opened my mouth and scrubbed my teeth; with shears and razors they trimmed my barbarous hair and beard. Thereupon they vested me in clean linen and a fine caped black soutane, with punctilio adding crimson sash and tassels, my golden pectoral cross and chain, my zucchetto and my largest sapphire ring. Thereupon they led me down the marble stairway to the street. Shutting the door on me, they cried in Arabic, *"Ruuh wa shuuf el baba!"* Go and see the Pope!

For some minutes I stood motionless and dazed on the sidewalk of the Lungotevere, the alien sun of springtime beating harshly upon my face. Finally I took my handkerchief, blew my nose, and heaved a sigh, wondering whether the Pope's *"Viene"* might inevitably in the event have restored me to my senses? Slowly I began to walk, turning the corner of the Lungotevere into the Via della Conciliazione, creeping painfully up that boulevard and into the Vatican.

"How dare you ignore my order to come to me at once?" the Pope demanded angrily as soon as I reached his presence.

Standing, I bowed my head and hunched my shoulders, accepting his just reproach in silence.

"You're a ghost, Augustine," he said more kindly.

"I've been doing penance, Most Holy Father."

"As well you should?"

"Your Holiness knows . . . ?"

"Has the Pope no ears?"

"I have been practising the privations of Saint John of the Cross."

"Ah, your *monkish* mood?"

We were, as had so often happened, alone on the roof of the Apostolic Palace, where of a radiant afternoon in May the Supreme Pontiff stood amidst his elaborate apiary of green cupboards, wearing his white soutane, poised to put on his heavy gloves and apron and his great mask. Impulsively I dropped to my knees, tracing the Sign of the Cross upon my face and breast and shoulders, begging the Pope before he donned the hood of bee-keeper to hear the confession of my sins.

"*Veni, Sancte Spiritus . . .*" intoned the Pontiff.

"*Emitte Spiritum tuum. . . .* Bless me, Holy Father, for I confess to Almighty God and to you, Father, that I have sinned."

The Pope blessed me: "The Lord be in thy heart, and on thy lips, that thou mayest rightly confess thy sins. *In nomine Patris, et Filii, et Spiritus Sancti.*"

"Amen," said I.

"How long since your last confession?"

"Six months."

"Of which sins do you accuse yourself?"

"Covetousness and lust."

"Let's dispense with the forms, shall we?" the Pope asked impatiently. "I believe that I may know some few of the details."

"How, Father?"

"Does your confession concern the young woman who visited you in the Palazzo Consalvi?"

"I'm afraid so. She . . . dearest Lisa . . . a Jew . . . like me."

"Scandalous. Not that she was Jewish—but young and beautiful."

"Ah, so young and b-beautiful, Holiness. How did you find out?"

"By stealthy means, certain Jesuits informed me. In their eternal craft, they have long since taken occult measures to know all that they can of Your Eminence. Jesuits have attended your afternoon teas at Consalvi palace, *n'est-ce pas?* And—for a year or so?—they have even from time to time followed you in the street."

"And tapped my telephone? Do their moles in the Holy Office read my mail? Bloody s-spies!"

"Charity! We are hearing *your* confession! They saw you walking furtively on the Ponte Sisto, near the Palazzo Farnese, and on the Colle Oppio with that lovely young woman. They followed you home to the Palazzo Consalvi. They allege that the woman resided with you for some weeks. True or false?"

"True."

"Did you . . . ?"

"No."

"*Deo gratias.* However, these certain Jesuits have understandably surmised the worst, and they are beginning to whisper—more than whisper—not only of your gross hypocrisy but of your 'grave scandal.' They will never forgive Your Eminence for slamming Our decree of dismissal on the foot of their Father General's bed."

"I didn't *slam* it."

"We believe Your Eminence. Though We have, of course, forbidden it, public mischief may soon be made of your indiscretion. Hints of the scandal may appear in the liberal Jesuit press, and in that event the secular press would make much of it. By your own account, my dear Augustine, you chafe against your vows of chastity."

"They drive me mad, Most Holy Father."

"We know that earlier in your cardinalate you were prone to employ nubile stenographers at your secretariat, a dangerous and uncanonical practice. We were aware of the Roman truism, 'If you want to meet a beauty queen, visit Cardinal Galsworthy's rooms at the Holy Office.' No doubt you often cast yourself into the path of temptation and of peril to your vows of perfect chastity. But We so admired your abilities that when We assumed the papacy We decided to overlook your previous imprudence. Have you ever broken your vows of chastity?"

"I fornicated once when I attended seminary, Most Holy Father, before I took my final vows. In Florence, I sired a son."

"A *son*?"

"I have seen his face in many dreams."

"And since Florence . . . ?"

"I swear—on Christ—I have kept my vows."

"Then since Florence you have committed—by your foolishness—but venial sin. You are a most virile man, after all."

"Not so virile as Your Holiness."

The Pope sighed. "*Grazie.* Celibacy was never intended to be easy. We each of us should meekly thank Our Lord and Saviour for whatever cross He wishes us to bear. In New York, you may remember, before We were elected to the Chair of Peter, We noticed Your Eminence's sensuality and We warned you to master it. Alas, your sexuality is the cross that Christ has given you to bear . . . so can you bear it? Do you wish to relinquish your priesthood?"

"I'd die," I murmured.

"Do you wish to resign your cardinalate?"

"I'd die."

"Ah yes, you'd die, dearest Augustine. Nevertheless . . . the Fathers Superior of other religious orders—especially the Franciscans and the Dominicans—have seized upon your recent misadventure and they have joined the Jesuits in demanding your exile. We are assailed from so many sides! We can not easily govern Holy Church without a minimal consensus of Our religious orders, not to speak of certain of your brother bishops and cardinals here in Rome who have resented you so long for your egotism, your arrogance, your glamour, and—in the Church of the Poor—your glorious Palazzo Consalvi. Your enemies insist that out of simple prudence We must separate Ourselves from you—and We must be seen to do so. No priest or cardinal can command the Pope, so of course We have ignored their counsel. What stopped you from seducing that young woman?"

"Divine grace?" I asked uncertainly.

"No *doubt,*" the Pontiff assured me. "Your allocutions for Us on Divine grace used to be sublime. And yet for some months We have noticed your strange distraction and—in your allocutions for Us—a growing mistiness of thought. Do you need rest? A period of reflection and retreat? Is that your problem? Should you resign your papal ministry and go away to write a book?"

"A book, Holiness?"

"A wonderful, beautiful book?"

"About what?"

"Divine grace?"

"Resign my ministry? Leave Rome? To write a book? For how long?"

"For as long as it takes—to write your book."

Now bees inside the Sovereign Pontiff's hives and cupboards began to stir and buzz and storm, rioting to be released from their captivity that they might seek new food, fresh nectar among the pots of purple and yellow flowers, alfalfa, clover, and fragrant white-petalled trees.

The Vicar of Christ peered inside their cells, and as in a trance he said, "The swarm. Quite soon, many thousands of my bees will migrate. They will buzz about my head, then they will abandon to the generation that comes next these fine honeycombed palaces, their homes and the fruits of their labour, eager for hardship and danger in some new and distant place. They may not all of them know ruin, but they will be poor, as their prosperous city is scattered abroad under the law of bees superior to their own bliss."

Out gushed the apian portents: the Pope could not contain them.

"Look, my dear Augustine, that hive there is preparing to swarm—to renounce and immolate itself to the cruel gods of its race! Do you hear their song of ecstasy? Aah, if I could know what they seek! Is the God of bumble-bees the Future? Stand up, Augustine, and look closer! Never is a hive more beautiful than on the eve of its migration. Over trees and houses and churches, over haystacks and lakes, rivers and towns and villages, they will fly to their far destination, which I can never know—only that they return to nature, exile, and death. The swarm! They go!"

Shuddering, deprived of speech, kneeling again at the Pontiff's feet, I thrashed in my mind through Scripture, asking finally with Simon Peter, "Lord, to whom shall I g-go?"

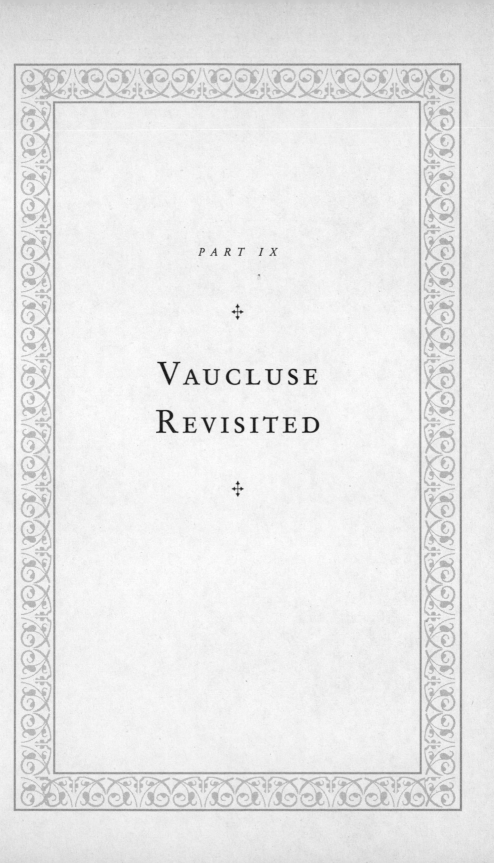

PART IX

✥

VAUCLUSE
REVISITED

✥

FORTY-SEVEN

At the Pope's command, I withdrew wretchedly to France and my true home, my abbey in the Vaucluse. To the vast relief of Monseigneur the Archbishop of Avignon—embarrassed by a fallen cardinal in his diocese—I forthwith shed my crimson and reverted to anonymous common black, oddly cheerful of a sudden to be known in that province simply as the "Père Augustin."

During France's drastic de-Christianisation and the decline of the monastic orders, my abbey had not only been abandoned but in consequence was falling apart. An old caretaker visited occasionally, but otherwise I lived without companions amid the encroaching ruins, in my indecorous soutane beneath my shabby grey-white beard, my mood still penitential, a stranger to passersby.

Despite its disrepair, I loved living in my old home. I foraged about, found a rusty bedstead, and slept on wooden slats in my bare old cell above the cloister, the cloister with its Gothic arches and Corinthian-like gargoyled pillars much overgrown with vine and weed. In a potting shed I found a sickle, and I hacked away at the willful vegetation until unencumbered I could sit on the wall beneath the arches and the singing birds to read my sacred Office.

I swept and cleaned the abbey kitchen, and walked regularly with a wooden basket the several miles to Carpentras to buy my wine and meagre food. The chapel's roof was pocked with holes beneath a sky of shocking blue, but I swept and restored the sanctuary as I could to celebrate my Mass at dawn upon the high altar. I haunted the chapel, since I lived with scruple according to the rule of St Benedict, chanting to my own echo Matins and Lauds, Prime and Terce, Sext and None and Vespers and Compline, increasingly at peace, beseeching grace.

I had no electricity; at night I read squinting by a kerosene lamp. The library had been emptied of its illuminated tomes, but between the bare dust-laden shelves in fulfillment of the Pope's command I lay recumbent with heaps of paper on the cold flagstones and composed my meditations on grace from memory. I exalted the mysticism of the seventeenth century, before the Enlightenment when despite huge evils the culture of Europe was still drenched with Christ, and the riddles of grace and theology danced at the centre of men's thoughts. I wrote with relish of the most illustrious divines of France, Monseigneur Bossuet, Bishop of Meaux, and Monseigneur Fénelon, Archbishop of Cambrai, who waged holy war over the paradoxical and baffling nature of God's grace.

As Rome, the cardinals, and Pope Innocent XII watched with alarmed confusion, Bossuet in pamphlet after pamphlet attacked Fénelon for teaching that the love of God, at its highest, meant deliberately excluding all thought of one's own eternal happiness: indeed, that in the extremes of desolation—the "dark night of the soul"—a man might even consent (for the love of God!) to his own everlasting damnation. In counter-pamphlet after counter-pamphlet, Fénelon defended his orthodoxy, insisting he had not truly said that, or that if he had truly seemed to say it he had truly meant something slightly different, or truly something significantly different, etc., etc., truly etc.

Old Innocent XII (sighing, pacing, wringing his hands, weary to tears of the disputation and of Bossuet's screaming emissaries) responded in a papal Brief, rebuking Fénelon gently, leaving the maddening riddles of grace unresolved high somewhere in celestial cloud, and in bewilderment exclaiming of the quarrel, "*Come cacciano via infiniti libri, questi francesi!* How they carry on in their endless books, these Frenchmen! Do they never sleep?" He added in cutting Latin, "*Erravit Cameracencis excessu amoris Dei! Peccavit Meldensis defectu amoris proximi!*" The Archbishop of Cambrai errs by loving God too much! The Bishop of Meaux sins by loving man too little! Brooding on the riddle's poetic depths—could any man so love God that to prove it he would gladly roast in Hell?—I lay aside my piles of foolscap and looked out the abbey window to the countryside of Vaucluse.

The month was June, late spring becoming summer. I could not resist the fragrance of the apricots and roses, so in my humble soutane, fingering my rosary, mumbling penitential psalms, I began to take long walks, revisiting my boyhood haunts.

Aubignan; Gigondas; Beaumes-de-Venise. Venasque; Bédoin; Crillon-le-Brave. Montmirail; Vacqueyras; Notre-Dame d'Aubune. No village or hamlet along the dry dusty twisting roads was too far for my foot. Strewn across the landscape were orchards of apricot, olive, and cherry; as I trod along, I watched poor peasant boys, truffle hunters with their truffle dogs, darting into wasteland and ascending mountains, seeking live oaks, beneath whose trunks they might most often find their treasure. I walked amidst the foothills of the Alps, beneath Mont Ventoux—Windy Mountain—hovering on the horizon to the north, ever visible when I passed a break in the dense cane hedges or the towering trees of cypress. To the south loomed the Monts de Vaucluse and the Montagne du Lubéron with vegetation so terribly sparse and cliffs so fantastically eroded that in their wild desolation they mirrored too perfectly my monastical and ascetical mood.

Villages teetered on the cusps of mountains, fashioned of rock cottages, roofs of red tile, sheds of yellow ochre, abandoned windmills, the ruins of châteaux. Could you ever picture how ruthlessly blue was the sky of the Midi as the barbarous sun of afternoon shone down upon hamlet, pasture, vineyard, and orchard? Aah, those stark hills, those steep and jagged ochre cliffs, tossing up from a landscape of bleak limestone this sudden hamlet and that forgotten village so gaudy and so red; aah, this hidden corner of *la belle France*, this secret nook of the Vaucluse, this lost kingdom (I pretended) unto itself!

A kingdom? A kingdom of truck farms: asparagus and figs and table grapes and melons and cauliflower and celery and spinach and artichokes and peas and green beans and new potatoes and carrots and cabbages and crates of strawberries and apricots and cherries and tomatoes the colour of blood: the truck farmers hauled the fruits and vegetables across flat fields or down steep foothills and sides of mountains westward through the valley of the River Rhône to the depots of Avignon, whence they were transported by rail to Lyon and Paris and eaten by multitudes on the morrow. Yet the farmers who did not live in lowlands watered by canals relied on the rains, nor were the rains generous in that summer; too many peasants remained at the mercy of nature, despairing when the sun blazed on and no rain fell, fearful despite their constant barriers of cypress tree and cane thicket that the chill north wind would also ruin them.

All of nature still cringed before the mistral, of which in the nineteenth century the likes of Stendhal and Vincent van Gogh had raged so bitterly. It roared and hurtled suddenly out of the glacial Alps yonder, down the corridor of the valley of the Rhône like a ferocious bellows, often at the force of hurricanes, not dying until the Mediterranean swallowed it finally. Against the mistral, every olive tree, the very walls of houses, bent southward. Yet for all the barriers, the cypress trees and cane hedges, the long sloping roofs of barns and dwellings, no soul or beast could escape the mistral. It came howling round the door, through the cracks of my abbey walls, down the chimneys and towers and through the holes of my tumbling roofs: as it blew on, I like the farmers of my province wondered, Will it drive me mad?

Did the people of the Vaucluse never pray for gentler winds and more generous rain? They used to do: perhaps their prayers were answered. My corner of Vaucluse was the old Comtat Venaissin, a thriving papal fiefdom for six centuries until the Revolution. Even for scores of decades afterward, the Faith prospered with the apricots and truffles.

For the feasts of the Ascension and the Assumption and all the festivals of the Virgin, priest and people made processions throughout the countryside, singing hymns, children scattering flowers, everyone praying aloud at shrines and chapels along the roads and on the slopes of hills. For the feasts of All Saints and the repose of departed souls, everybody lit bonfires. At night from the summit of any hill, one could see the whole countryside aglow with bonfires. Even atop mountains such fires blazed, each lonely shepherd tending his flame.

The calendar abounded in Masses, processions, and the jubilations of special feasts. Carpenters celebrated St Joseph's Day; blacksmiths St Elegius Day; cobblers St Thomas Day; seamstresses celebrated St Clare, Patroness of Women with Sore Eyes. In late September, everybody celebrated the Feast of St Michael Archangel, Patron of All Police Officers, who had chased Lucifer from Heaven.

In my boyhood, the Angelus had tolled from my abbey tower thrice a day, at dawn, noon, and evening, ringing across the rich fields, calling humble farmers and their children to kneel on the soil and bow their heads in thankful prayer. Now all such devotions had disappeared. By the roads and on the hillsides, the wayside shrines to the Virgin and St Joseph and St Michael were everywhere neglected, ignored, and falling down.

Country boys no longer aspired (as once so many did) to the sacred priesthood: in the sensual French culture, perfect obedience and perpetual chastity were crosses too repugnant to take up. At Carpentras, a pair of elderly ecclesiastics soldiered on, but their limbs were too brittle to venture outside the town, and my rural kingdom was void of priests. Some few people still visited Carpentras for baptisms, marriages, and funerals, but otherwise throughout the land only a skeleton of the Roman Church remained. It was as if the bare bones had been preserved in order to fulfill a jest of Voltaire's: how awkward were Christianity to vanish altogether, because then the world would have nothing left to laugh at.

Feasting alone on the theological riddles of the seventeenth century at my ruined abbey on the mountainside, while all around me the people of my province were perishing from famine in their souls, I began to reproach myself for my supernatural gluttony. Throughout my priesthood and my majestic cardinalate, never had I lived as a pastor—never as a simple shepherd of souls. In prayer I asked the Holy Ghost, Cannot I obey the Pope's command to write my tome on grace in future time? Would I not serve Thee better now if I brought Thy grace to faithless souls—by becoming a pastor? The Holy Ghost (I thought) responded, *"Mais oui, mon Père Augustin! Deviens pasteur!"* (I was delighted that He spoke in French; according to Bernard Shaw, the Devil's native tongue is English.) Suddenly, with boyish zeal, I made myself a pastor.

With the amused consent of Monseigneur d'Avignon, I established at my abbey a sort of parish, or rather something more resembling a foreign mission in a faraway heathen land. I did not wait for parishioners to come to me, but I went out into my pagan kingdom and whacked the bushes, seeking them. I became like a mendicant friar of the Middle Ages, begging people not for alms but for a tiny portion of their forgotten Christianity.

At the Place du Marché in Vacqueyras, at the Place aux Halles in Bédoin, beneath La Grande Fontaine in Beaumes-de-Venise, shamelessly I stopped strangers on the cobblestones, handing out from my ragged Gucci bag white rosaries and coloured pictures of the saints, entreating them to visit me at my abbey for Mass on Sundays. When nobody showed up, on weekdays I trudged with my Mass kit into fields and truck farms, where alone I tossed a purple stole of mourning about my black soutane and celebrated Latin Masses on the stumps of trees or even kneeling upon the grass, praying that out of simple curiosity farmers would gather round me.

Slowly, in ones and twos, they did, some even kneeling on the soil, some even tracing across their brows and torsos the Sign of the Cross. Slowly, my madness worked; people in my little kingdom began to approach me. Nobody knew I was a cardinal; indeed few would have known or cared what a cardinal was.

On Saturday mornings, unannounced I celebrated Mass between hectic vendors' stalls in open public markets, among cobblers, fishwives, blacksmiths, small farmers selling hares and thrushes, shorn wool and figs, olives and apricots and beeswax and lavender honey; and above us soared those abandoned windmills, the ruins of châteaux, those steep and jagged ochre cliffs beneath my sky so mythically blue; and as I prayed I sorrowed more than ever for the France of the seventeenth and eighteenth centuries, before the Enlightenment and the Revolution when all common men and women still believed so fervently in the world of the life to come.

At my abbey, I revived the practice of tolling the Angelus, pulling at the tattered rope and ringing the cracked bell in my Gothic tower, calling the peasants of my province to prayer at dawn, noon, and evening; but as I squinted out across the fields I saw no kneeling faithful, only crawling tractors and busy dump trucks. Nevertheless on Sundays now, more and more of the curious—not only coarse farmers but bourgeois clerks, postmen, agronomists, schoolmasters, wives, children, grandmothers—crowded into the abbey chapel to hear my Mass in sacred vestments, which I took pains to celebrate today in French, the week following in Latin, rejoicing at their hushed reverence as I chanted my mysterious tongue.

In my sermons, I fed them the Faith in its harsh and joyous fullness. God made you to know Him, and to love Him. God made you to serve Him in this world, and to be happy with Him for ever in the next. You were born into Original Sin, but Christ can redeem you. If you refuse Christ Redeemer, son of a Virgin, Son of God, you can not be saved. If you love Christ, you must obey His rules. If you break His rules, you may lose Heaven. Modern culture is rotten, but His Church can lift you towards beatitude. Fornication, adultery, unnatural contraception, cheating your bosses, oppressing your workers, spurning your poor, are grave wrongs. Sodomy is a mortal sin. Abortion is murder. The mercy of God is boundless, but it is dangerous to play games with His benevolence.

I echoed Chateaubriand with passion. Unbelief will debase you to the sniffing of beasts; atheism has nothing but plague and leprosy to offer you. In our faith as Christians, we know that our sufferings will end; we are consoled; we dry our tears; we look upward to another life. God is all beauty. *Nous pleurons et nous croyons.* We weep and we believe.

After Mass I led my people out of the abbey, singing hymns, children scattering flowers, onto the mountain and the great limestone tomb of my martyred Père Benoît. There I told them of his torture and murder by the Gestapo and of the miracles that on the morrow of the war he may have performed from Heaven: canes and crutches of the once halt and lame still littered the mountainside, decaying. Then I led the people in crying out the Joyous Mysteries of the Rosary, seeking the intercession of Père Benoît and all the saints against their sorrows, before the throng descended the mountain and went home, leaving me alone again.

But even on weekdays as time passed, people returned to the abbey chapel, entered my darkness in a wooden box, and confessed their sins— their fornications and adulteries and abortions and sodomy, their little lies and large thefts. In autumn, from the ramparts of my abbey, at midnight on the eve of All Saints and All Souls, I delighted at the bonfires blazing here and there across the landscape, one or two atop mountains.

The mistral recently had diminished, but as winter descended on my kingdom, the gales returned with anger. In late November, I was trudging with my Mass kit alone along the road below the mountains, between Vacqueyras and Beaumes-de-Venise, wrapped in my great black cape against the cold, when the rainy wind struck me with such force that it knocked me down.

With both arms I clung to the trunk of an olive tree, nearly losing my Mass kit and releasing sobs when the tempest tore open the leather flap and scattered my consecrated hosts across the wild. Trucks approached; I beckoned to them for transport; they passed me by. Finally an old truck stopped. As I struggled against the wind to climb inside the cabin I could not see the driver's face, but when I took my seat beside him I recognised my son.

FORTY-EIGHT

Even should you try, I rather doubt that you could picture the turbulence of my emotions at that moment. I felt suddenly dizzy, as though very drunk, or as though really I were whirling in the vertigo of self-contradiction so dear to mystics!

My *son*? Oh, how the resemblance shocked me: it was as if I looked into a mirror to see myself in my middle thirties. A foot from me were the lofty cheekbones, the flared nostrils, the black and lavish hair of my vanished youth. With my own brown eyes the young man looked back at me, but he did not seem to recognise himself at the age of sixty, and he uttered no surprise.

"*Merci, mon fils,*" I heard myself saying.

"*De rien, mon père,*" he answered.

"*Le vent!*" The wind!

"*Ah oui, mon père, le mauvais vent.*" Oh yes, my father, the evil wind.

Must a cardinal's son become a truck driver? No, but if he did, might it delight the Lord? Does it d-delight the Cardinal? Does it d-delight the Cardinal's son the truck driver? We rode on through the mistral toward Beaumes-de-Venise, beneath the toothy Mountains of Montmirail, the olive trees and walls of houses all bending to the south, my son—but was he, truly?—staring at the twisting road, I stealing glances at his face and body. He wore a rough red cardigan, corduroy

pants the colour of beige, and black muddy boots. His body was much
thicker than my own, nor even seated did he seem as tall; his hands were
large and brutish, oily at the nails, and callused—from labour on the soil?
Furtively I kept looking at his face. Finally I said, *"Je suis le Père Augustin."*

"*Merde, alors.*"

"*Merde?* And you?"

"Agostino."

"Ha! Italian?"

"My mother. . . ."

"Does she live around here?"

"She's dead."

"And your father?"

"Never met the bastard."

"What was your mother's name?"

"What is she to you, *mon père?*"

"*Je m'excuse, mon f-fils.*"

"Giovanna."

In silence I returned to Florence and my rooms above the River Arno.
She: *". . . Giovanna. And you?"* I: *"Agostino. Are you from Florence?"* She:
*"I work in Florence, at a flower shop, but I'm on holiday. If you're not
Italian, where are you from?"* I: *"The south of France?"* She: *"I've a grand-
mother who lives near Avignone. What is Avignone like?"* I: *"Heaven?"* She:
*"Then one day I must go to Heaven—to see my grandmother. Will you come
with me to the seashore?"* I: *"I c-can't. . . ."*

My son lit up a *Gauloise bleue:* aah, those poignant vapours of black
tobacco. He asked, in the familiar, "You want one, *mon père?*"

In the weeks that followed, I learned of Agostino's life in flowering
detail, though not easily. I happened upon his past in fragments, from his
grunts and outbursts as I visited him at home or bought him calvados in
cafés or rode about my kingdom with him in his rusty Citroën truck.

Attended by a midwife, Giovanna had died in labour, giving birth to
Agostino in a little house by the road between Carpentras and Avignon. For
six years he was reared by his great-grandmother, she dying of old age
inconvenienced by his whooping cough and potty training. Thereafter he
was shunted throughout the Vaucluse from cousin to mean cousin—until he
broke all bonds of family in his fifteenth year, abandoned school, and went
to work.

Such a youth could not be happy: he drifted from odd job to odd job,
from truffle hunter to mason's apprentice to blacksmith's apprentice to
ochre mining to scavenging in caves for mushrooms, until he was called
to his National Service at a dreary barracks in the north of France. Returning
to the radiant Vaucluse, he tilled a tiny plot of land he did not own on the
slope of a mountain, and he bought a truck, but the mountain was rocky and

his truck-farming did not flourish. Neither did his marriage to a housemaid: she bore him two sons, yet she left them eventually to his indifferent care and fled his stormy temper to live more sweetly at Marseille.

Agostino drank too much wine and calvados, gambled away too much of his money playing *belote* and blackjack with coarse Algerians in dismal cellars at Carpentras and Avignon that reeked of black tobacco, cheap red wine, and the stench of urine. When he wanted sex, he sought out whores. No, my son was not a clod: his roughness was redeemed largely by his lovely gardening, of which I shall speak. Still, for the hardness and hardship of his life I blamed myself, or more specially my grave and careless sin of begetting him at Florence.

Agostino's little house nestled at the crook of hills far across the road from my abbey, but within my sight when I climbed to the belfry of my Gothic tower. Whenever free of my priestly chores, I walked down the mountain and across the road to the dwelling of my clandestine son.

Outside, the house seemed quaint, with ragged ochre walls, rude brown wooden shutters, and a sloping roof below a leafy trellis; even in the midst of winter, under the sun of the Midi the pots of terra-cotta blossomed incessantly of geranium, marguerite, and zinnia.

More, in the grounds about the house Agostino cultivated a rich garden; planting, watering, hoeing, and pruning it with craft and fondness often. How I delighted in strolling on its paths, so scented with fruit trees; apple, quince, and Duchesse d'Angoulême pear; with tomato and radish; spinach and turnip and cress; with patches of cabbage, gooseberry, candytuft, larkspur, and purple narcissus; buttercup, bog orchid, and evening primrose prospering anyhow randomly.

The interior of the house I found less charming. Sticks of furniture stood wobbly or broken on tile floors dark with scuff and scraps of food; heaps of unwashed laundry lay here and there about, like the discarded copies of old newspaper, *Le Commerce du Midi,* Agostino's only literature, for he read no books. From the kitchen garden the odd chicken and grey rabbit wandered in and out. Mildly the house exuded a barnyard smell. Here from the garden come Agostino's two boys.

My grandsons! The elder was Jean-Luc, just turned fourteen, well-made, athletic, handsome, with hair so auburn it was nearly blond. He went to school in Carpentras, played soccer, all over the Vaucluse, and with such devotion that he seemed to think of nothing else, save that he was puzzled by my steadfast visits. Did Jean-Luc wonder why a learned priest should take such interest in his grunting father? Pascal, his brother, ten only, snatched my heart.

Pascal's head was mine in miniature, with my raven hair, carved nostrils, exaggerated cheekbones, though his eyes unlike my own were green and not quite focussed, blurring but only faintly the beauty of his face. His body beneath his dungarees and jersey was small and nearly undernourished. His movements so lacked grace that I must call them awkward. Not as jerky-awful as mine had been at the age of ten: Pascal might trip on his own feet, but only rarely did he collide with walls and furniture. He had not, thank God, inherited my stammer.

Insofar as anyone kept house, the task fell on little Pascal. I began to show up in the late afternoons, when he had come home from school, to help him. Cheerfully as in the leprosarium at Bumba, I washed the laundry and the windows, swept the place, descended to my hands and knees and scrubbed the floors—Pascal's small clumsy hands assisting my labour eagerly as he sang songs in Provençal, a dialect I had learned at the abbey in my own childhood. *"Entre setanto et quatre-vint, pau de gènt reston sus lou camin. . . ."* I asked myself, Am I beginning to be happy?

The house had electricity and running taps but no water closet; a stinking privy beyond the kitchen garden served that purpose. From Carpentras I brought in carpenters and plumbers to install a water closet; then I had the leaky roof fixed, before the washing machine, refrigerator, and new furniture were delivered. In March, when I emerged from the water closet to wash my hands, Agostino in his rough clothes stood suddenly beside me before the basin and the looking-glass, gazing first at my face and then at his own. In the mirror, our brown eyes met.

Of late I had shorn my beard to mere stubble; thus the contours of my face became so identical to Agostino's that I knew he recognised me in that instant as his father. He drifted off to other things, uttering not a word.

You ask, But surely Agostino knew from the beginning? Perhaps from the beginning he had suspicions, but he never voiced them; nor ever once did I broach the matter of my paternity. I sensed that it would be better and more beautiful to leave all such things unsaid, and that I should never share the secret with my grandsons.

I never hugged or kissed my son. Our unspoken bond seemed to please Agostino, and it suited me as well because all three of that family came to consider me as theirs. When I entered the yard, Jean-Luc cried out, *"Bon jour, mon père!"* and he went on kicking his soccer ball against the house, merry for my presence. Likewise Agostino continued whatever he was about, hoeing his garden or playing a game of solitaire at a rude table in the yard, grunting maybe but otherwise uttering no sound. Pascal rushed to me, laughing and shrieking and squeezing my waist, begging for my kiss.

Oafish with so many others, Agostino was tender with his sons. When he came home drunk after losing again at blackjack, he ignored their taunts, swilled more wine, screamed the bloodiest of curses, and never raised a hand to strike them. When he was sober they cooked his supper, pinching him and hugging him as he ate his soup. Aah, how they loved him, and I saw why.

They knew somehow that his vices were not deeply wicked. Agostino held me up for gambling money, but he had no greed. If I asked a favour, he granted it. Since his kitchen garden fed only his own household, he earned his living, such as it was, by trucking fruits and vegetables from the great farms to Avignon. When he had no trade, he gave me his truck. Or he drove me through my parish as I made my rounds. When I celebrated Mass in a public market or upon some sunny cabbage patch, he loitered at the fringe, smoking Gauloises, bored and irreligious.

Agostino had been baptised, but he had received no other sacrament; nor had his sons. Riding in his truck, I told him, "I must instruct Jean-Luc and Pascal in the Holy Faith."

"*Merde, alors.*"

"But I'm a priest, after all."

"Jean-Luc's religion is soccer."

"As yours, dear son, is blackjack? Will you at least allow me to give Jean-Luc some books?"

"Religious books?"

"With very pretty coloured pictures?"

Agostino grunted, whistled, released a "Ha-ha-ha" uncannily like my own.

"And you'll read them, too, Agostino?"

"Ha-ha-ha."

"Pascal, of course, is special. I wish to educate him properly. Would you let him live with me at the abbey?"

"Oh, *mon père*, not in that spooky abbey."

"Only for several days a week. And it's not spooky."

"But Pascal is mine."

"I am so alone up there."

"*Comme tu veux, mon père.*"

"Thank you, dearest, dearest son."

"Can you lend me five hundred francs, Father?"

In the afternoons, I climbed my Gothic tower, looking out for Pascal as he returned from school and ran up the mountain towards the abbey, too often stumbling. In the desolate library, I helped him with his lessons, drilling him in grammar, mathematics, science. Then I asked him, "Who made you?"

"God made me, *mon père.*"

"Why did God make you?"

"To know Him, to love Him, to serve Him in this world, and to be happy with Him for ever in the next."

"How did Adam and Eve lose their innocence?"

"By Original Sin."

"What is Original Sin?"

"Gluttony? Lust? Disobedience?"

"What is the Holy Eucharist?"

"Our Lord and Saviour Jesus Christ, body and blood, soul and Divinity, appearing as common bread and wine."

"*Pas mal, très cher enfant!* Tonight, before you go to bed, read your catechism again about Original Sin. Now come with me, beloved child."

I took his little hand, leading him through the abbey as aloud I relived my childhood, first in the void refectory, beneath the arched and soaring windows, where again I tasted the vegetable soup, the grey cheese, the huge delicious loaves of bread, and from the crumbling vaulted pulpit a chosen phantom boy read to us from St Augustine of the bitter fruits of lust. In my classroom, amid the missing thicket of wooden desks, I recited Cicero—"... *h-h-hominem f-flagi-tiosi-s-s-imum, libid-d-d-inosi-s-s-im-m-mum* ..."—and with blue chalk a black monk traced an **X** across my mouth, and the other boys roared and whistled at me, pounding their desks with their books and fists.

We walked through cloisters to the chapel, all limestone dust and mildewed stalls and toppled statues of the saints and sunshine flooding down on us through the gutted roof. I lingered in the nave as Pascal mounted the high altar to the Father Abbot's cobwebbed throne and boyishly sat down upon it. Silently I recalled the Père Benoît's vision of me in crimson biretta and full robes, a boy cardinal.

"That is where it started," said I distantly.

"*Mon père?*" asked Pascal.

"My cardinalate," I mumbled.

In that moment, the vision was repeated. I saw the child seated in a shaft of sunlight, incarnating my own self; jet-haired, cheekbones etched, nostrils sculpted, his skull and frail body swathed in crimson, as luminously as fifty years before when my Père Benoît had glimpsed me likewise. I gasped and trembled. Pascal, in his dungarees and jersey, stared down at me.

"*Mon père?*"

"Nothing, child. I never want it back."

"*Mon père?*"

"My cardinalate," I mumbled. "I am too happy as a simple priest."

We returned to the library, where we resumed his lessons with my new and borrowed books, sitting on armless wooden chairs, facing each other. In the months that followed, I became the Père Benoît, force-feeding the voracious child as I might a Christmas goose, filling him up to bursting with theology, history, the rudiments of Latin, and exalted French. I said, "Repeat from memory that passage of Chateaubriand."

" '... and thus does Christianity provide its passions and its treasures to the poet. Like all great loves, it hints of the serious and the sad. It leads us to the gloom of cloisters, thence to the crests of mountains. Yet the beauty that the Christian worships is not fleeting. It is everlasting beauty, the kind of beauty for which the disciples of Plato made haste to abandon this earth.' "

"Perfect, dear boy."

"Who was Plato, *mon père?*"

"With Aristotle, the greatest of the Greek philosophers. We'll start his *Symposium* soon. Now off with you to bed."

He ran out of the library, tripping on the threshold, a ghost of my childhood. I thought, I must also cure him of his awkwardness. I'll march him mercilessly up and down the corridors and teach him to walk straight.

Pascal slept in his own cell, down the corridor from mine above the ruins of the cloister. On the weekends, he accompanied me in his father's truck, all over my parish, my acolyte as I celebrated the sacraments in fields and fish markets. One Sunday morning, when he put on a new blue suit and took his First Communion from me amongst the flowers and the blazing beeswax candles of my abbey chapel, even Agostino showed up—straining at first to look bored but at the end visibly affected by the ceremony and asking, "Father, why does little Pascal make me so proud?"

After a time, pursuing his resolve to reconquer pagan Europe for Christianity, the Pope visited France and Avignon.

The month was April, already warm. My kingdom emptied for the event, much of the populace pouring westward into Avignon to assist at the papal Mass. Moved like so many others by curiosity, Agostino took Pascal and Jean-Luc down to Avignon in his junky truck. Alone, I watched the ceremonies on colour television in an empty bar at Beaumes-de-Venise.

I knew every stone upon which the Pontiff trod—from the Église St-Pierre into the rue Peyrolerie into the Place de l'Horloge, thence into the Place du Palais before the Palace of the Popes.

Preceding him as he marched the streets were schoolboys bearing myriad blazing torches, schoolgirls hoisting a sea of flags with the white and yellow papal colours, bands and orchestras of drums and trumpets, soldiers in blue and khaki bearing rifles, civil functionaries with satin capes and plumed hats, a batch of cassocked, surpliced priests and acolytes bearing crucifixes and candlesticks, the scores of French bishops and archbishops in their brilliant purple, and all twelve French cardinals in their princely red. From the Cathedral of Notre-Dame des Doms and the belfries of a dozen churches, bells pealed and pealed; on the banks of the River Rhône a hundred cannon roared at the vast azurine heaven.

The Sovereign Pontiff, as robust and apple-cheeked as when I saw him last, clearly pleased by the plaudits of the French, strode leisurely at the end of the procession in a rich white chasuble and a golden mitre, his left hand raising his gilded shepherd's crook, his right hand blessing everybody along his path. When he reached the grand Place du Palais and the cheering multitude, and behind him loomed the spires and toothy parapets of that immense and ancient Gothic fortress called the Palace of the Popes, I thought, Why, this is a scene from the fourteenth century.

In a rush I witnessed the mediaeval splendour, the endless outdoor pageants and fantastical interior of the palace during the epoch of the Avignon popes, awash with colour and venal ecclesiastics revelling in licentious banquets; at their centre a succession of pontiffs in thrall to the French crown, munificent patrons of the arts, and not all of them wicked. My brain danced with popes and anti-popes—Clements and Benedicts; Gregorys and Innocents and Urbans—and specially the ineffable John XXII, he thundering (heretically) that the souls of the Just will enjoy no Beatific Vision before the final Day of Judgement.

And yet was the fourteenth century not glorious in its way, when the successors of St Peter were all of them cultured Frenchmen, distant by choice from the squalor of Rome? The pious assailed too many of these pontiffs for wallowing in luxury and vice; Christendom was infected with schism, simony, depravity, and plague; but were not the centuries to follow—I mean our modern time—much worse? As I chewed on my question, the Slav Pope addressed the multitude.

"... *de la France, Notre chère, mignonne, très bien-aimée France, Fille Aînée de l'Église* ... of Our dear, darling, most beloved France, Eldest Daughter of the Church. Here, on the very ground where Frenchmen ruled the Roman Church for nearly a century, We have returned to summon the whole of France to embrace again her illustrious Christian past. France must once more be faithful to her hallowed origins. In Christianity, France finds the source of her grandeur and of her radiance throughout the world. France knows that her most cherished ideas—the rights and dignity of man, liberty, fraternity, justice—can not prosper or survive except in a culture steeped in Christ. For it is by the spirit that we live, and is not all else doomed to death? Dearest France, beloved Daughter, come back to God."

I thought, In my other life I should be standing there, at his right hand, in my majestic red.

I wondered, Who wrote his speech?

At midnight, under a half-moon, I paced the jagged battlements of my abbey, straining to read my sacred Office and missing Pascal, sleeping in his father's house. Of a sudden from the road a cortège of motorcars climbed my mountain's twisting path, drove through the high open gate, and stopped in the courtyard near the limestone stairs. Gendarmes with automatic guns jumped out, followed by agitated priests in black soutanes.

Peering, I recognised Avignon's Chief of Police in a visored cap. From one of the motorcars stepped a tallish man in a wide black Roman hat and muffled from head to foot in a dark cloak: in a trice the gendarmes hopped here and there about, forming a phalanx round him. An ageing priest in rimless spectacles mounted the stairway towards me. I asked myself, Is that the Archbishop of Avignon?

"*Bon soir, Votre Éminence,*" he said.

His greeting shocked me. Aah, it had been so long since anyone had addressed me as a cardinal.

"*Monseigneur?*" I answered.

"Is it too late for Your Eminence to hear confessions?" he asked with an odd solicitude.

"It is never too late, *cher Monseigneur,* to purge sin."

"Then I have a penitent for you."

✧

✧

FORTY-NINE

I retreated through the moonlit cloisters to the nave of the chapel, where I shut myself inside a mouldy oaken box, groped in the darkness for my violet stole, kissed it, placed it round my neck, and sat on hard wood. Within moments I heard whisperings, then a single pair of feet shuffling in the gloom towards my box. As my penitent entered his cubicle and knelt, I drew back the panel and pressed my ear against the grille.

"*Veni, Sancte Spiritus . . .*" I said deeply.

"*Emitte Spiritum tuum . . .*" said my penitent deeply back. "Bless me, Father, for I confess to Almighty God and to you, Father, that I have sinned."

I blessed him: "The Lord be in thy heart, and on thy lips, that thou mayest rightly confess thy sins. *In nomine Patris, et Filii, et Spiritus Sancti.*"

"Amen," he mumbled.

"How long since your last confession?" I asked.

"One week."

"Of which sins do you accuse yourself?"

"Augustine . . ."

There, of course, I must stop. I have reminded you before of the scourge inflicted by Canon Law on any priest for breaking the seal of the confessional—excommunication by the Pope. There is the additional detail that in this instance my penitent was the Pope.

I can freely tell you what His Holiness said in

the presence of others, after he had recited his contrition and I had imposed his penance and absolved his sins. We withdrew from the chapel into the adjoining cloister of gargoyled pillars and Gothic arches, where the court-yard was growing wild again with vine and weed, below the wan half-moon, wrapped in cobwebs of vernal mist. The Pope all swathed in black seemed at a loss for what he might do next, swaying slightly in his forward, backward shuffle as he murmured prayers.

We were joined in the cloister by Monseigneur d'Avignon and his elderly ecclesiastics and by the Chief of Police and his young gendarmes laden with guns and truncheons. Suddenly the Pontiff walked round the cloister, offering his ring to be kissed, his left hand digging into a pocket and pro-ducing brass medallions and tangled rosaries for the genuflecting youths. Presently he turned and pointed to me, telling everybody in French, "I have wronged this man."

"*Tout au contraire, Saintissime Père,*" I protested.

With a rising voice, the Pope continued to heap reproaches upon himself.

"He was my most trusted cardinal minister, but I banished him from Rome. He angered other priests because he believed that the Church must be ruled by hard discipline and zealous attachment to her rich traditions. Some few of his brothers in the Sacred College, long envious of his flair and boun-tiful talent, urged me to humble him in lesser work away from Rome. He became the victim of intrigues by some scheming Jesuits because he carried out my orders to dismiss their holy but errant Father General. For all his human frailties, he has devoted his life to lustrous service of the Church. I dissembled when I told him that I was releasing him from Rome to write a book. In fact, I yielded to the craft and pressure of certain Jesuits and kicked him out. For that, I could not absolve myself—so tonight in the confessional I came to him on my knees, begging his and God's forgiveness for my cow-ardice and pride. At Rome, I am thwarted on all sides by lukewarmness and faint hearts. I want him back—as my rod and my staff."

The Pope shuffled towards me. "Augustine, I can not even remember what your book was to be about."

"Divine grace, my lord," said I softly.

He smiled, nearly sheepishly, for a moment reminding me of his prede-cessor. "You can finish it in Rome."

How stricken I was to hear that penance. I stammered, "I p-prefer, Your Holiness, to remain in the V-Vaucluse."

"*Pourquoi?*"

"I've become a simple pastor here. I have never been so happy."

"Your pastoral experience will increase your wisdom as my minister in Rome."

"I beseech Your Holiness. Leave me in this abbey."

Vexed, the Pope replied, "For a week, Augustine—to pray upon the matter?"

Before the clerics and the police, the Supreme Pontiff knelt for my blessing and kissed my bare hand. But no sooner had he left the abbey than I saw how cunningly he had conjured up my vow of perfect obedience by urging me to prayer. In the chapel I asked of Heaven, Have I a choice?

In the library next afternoon, Pascal seemed bewildered by my agitation, but we got through his lessons. During the next few days, I wrote and threw away three letters to him, then wrote a fourth.

> *Mon très cher Pascal,*
> When you read this, I will be gone from the Vaucluse probably for ever and you will not see me again. I can not explain the reasons. Nor could I ever bear to face your tears. Forgive me.
> I pray that you will continue by yourself to pursue the mysteries of knowledge with the same hunger and thirst that you have shown to me. I have dreamed that you might study for the sacred priesthood. This is a decision that only you can make, without my influence. I can confide in you that against my wish I was pushed into the priesthood by my parents and my Father Abbot during my unhappy childhood. I do not regret it now—it may have been the will of God—but for many of my youthful years it deepened my suffering.
> Learn the world as I never could when young, yet do not let the world seduce you. Never become a priest because you believe that it would please me. But if you clearly hear the call of Christ, then you must serve Him. Go when you are eighteen to Monseigneur the Archbishop of Avignon, and at my expense he will place you in a seminary.
> Always you will be at the centre of my prayers. My parents never loved me. You are blessed, my very dear Pascal, to have a father who loves you deeply in his way.
> Your
>
> PÈRE AUGUSTIN

Next morning, when I knew that Pascal would be at school, I walked down the mountain and across the road to my son's house. Jean-Luc, now entering manhood and no longer at any school, was in the yard with Agostino amidst the marguerite and zinnia, kicking his soccer ball about. With rusty shears, his father pruned a quince tree. When I told them of my imminent departure, Jean-Luc did not seem to react and went back to kicking his ball. "Father . . . ?" said Agostino, as if bewildered by my news.

"For the rest of your life," I told him, "you will receive a modest monthly cheque from the Crédit Suisse at Carpentras. Over time, a jolly sum. Spend it on your boys—not on whores and blackjack. I can not see you or your sons again."

"The washing machine broke down," said Agostino vacantly.

"Then buy a better one," said I. "You need a new truck. Speak to Monsieur Marceau at the Crédit Suisse. Otherwise you must never discuss my benefactions—or me—with anybody. Would you give this letter to Pascal?"

"Won't you wait for him, *mon père?*"

"You must tell him, dearest son."

"Won't you stay for lunch?"

"Can we do it now?"

Agostino and Jean-Luc together prepared our luncheon—lentil soup, a roasted hare with asparagus and new potatoes, and table grapes and apricots. As I chewed my portion, Jean-Luc rose impulsively from his place and wordlessly hugged and hugged me until his father told him to finish his potatoes. Heaps of unwashed linen again lay here and there about, but in a corner of that common room stood Pascal's little desk and books—Latin grammars, Cicero, Vergil, Chateaubriand; Plato's *Symposium* and *The Republic* both in French—arranged neatly. A grey rabbit wandered in and hopped on Pascal's notebooks, dumping. Agostino and Jean-Luc flew at him, hurling the beast into the kitchen garden and moaning as religiously they cleaned up the mess and put Pascal's nook in perfect order. I thought, To them it is a sort of shrine.

Right after luncheon, I took my leave. I told them, "Go to Mass at least occasionally. *Adieu, Jean-Luc.*"

"*Adieu, Père Augustin.*"

I turned to Agostino—myself—not hugging him or kissing him, but I touched his brutish hand.

"*Adieu, mon fils.*"

"*Adieu, mon père.*"

As I descended the hill, I looked back. Father and son stood by the rosaceous quince tree, at the edge of the yard, watching me go. Jean-Luc held his soccer ball against his hip; Agostino with one hand gripped his pruning shears and gently crooked his other arm about Jean-Luc's neck.

At the abbey, I packed my final things, then climbed to the belfry of the Gothic tower to glimpse my parish, indeed my kingdom—Arcadia, so mountainous, green, and ochre—for the last time? Can you imagine how often I had climbed that tower to watch for Pascal when he returned from school? I saw him now—and no, not in memory or in another supernatural hallucination.

In his black jeans and white shirt Pascal ran stumbling up the mountain, calling out my name, much taller than when I knew him first because now he was an adolescent and still awkward. In his hand he waved a scrap of paper which I knew must be my letter. "*Père Augustin! Père Augustin!*"

Agostino and Jean-Luc ran after him, reaching him at last below my tower. Shouting, Pascal protested my disappearance, but against my expectation bravely he shed no tears. His father and his elder brother led him down the slope, and for the final time I heard him cry, "*Père Augustin . . .*"

That evening, I returned to Rome.

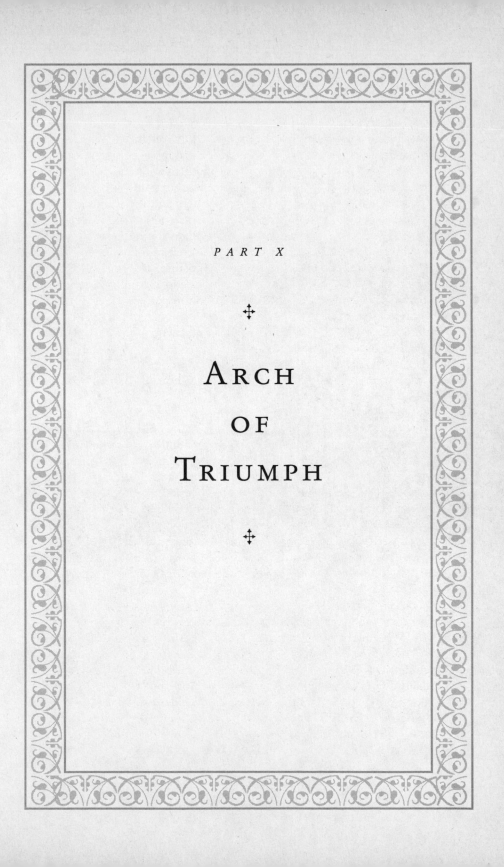

PART X

✤

ARCH

OF

TRIUMPH

✤

✜

✜

The Pope's meek pilgrimage to the abbey of
Vaucluse became a legend in the Roman
Church. The Archbishop of Avignon and
his geriatric votaries, the Chief of Police and his
robust gendarmes, talked heedlessly of all they
had seen and heard. On many tongues, every particular of the pontifical tableau was repeated and
embellished.

The Pope, disguised in swirling black over sack-
cloth and ashes, arrives in mysterious secrecy
amidst the moonlit Gothic ruins, prostrates himself before the fallen Cardinal, weeps and begs forgiveness, then kisses the Cardinal's feet. Images are
conjured up of the eleventh century, of the Holy
Roman Emperor Henry IV grovelling before Gregory VII in the blizzards of Canossa; indeed it is
nearly as if the Slavic Pontiff in his lavish love of
theatre wishes it were exactly so. The tales (did the
Pope foresee this?) are published by the French
and Italian press, then broadcast the world over.

Nor does the legend suffer because for all of my
vaunted arrogance and vanity I had lived for some
years in the Vaucluse as a homely pastor, running
with the rough and tumble of common folk, venturing even to the snowy crests of mountains to
confer the sacraments on the sick and dying. Had
the Pope (in his saintly cunning) foreseen or perhaps intended so? The legend no doubt helps the
Pope as he signals to Christendom that a policy of

the iron fist has been restored at the Holy See—in the person of the rehabili-
tated and implacable papal minister, Sir Augustine Cardinal Galsworthy.

I did not return to my cramped and musty secretariat at the Holy Office.
Instead the Pope bestowed on me a new secretariat in rooms below his own
inside the Apostolic Palace. On their bayed walls and vaulted ceilings, these
vast apartments were opulently decorated with sacred and pagan frescoes by
Baldassare Croce and Guidobaldo Abbatini—floating virgins and haloed
troglodytes vying for the eye with lecherous satyrs and randy unicorns.
These chambers teemed with busy clerics and demure stenographers, the
latter not lovely wenches but ageing nuns, alas!

The Pope heaped further laurels on me, not least by creating me Co-
Titular (with himself) of the immense basilica of St Mary Major—in the
heart of Rome near the railway station, a neighborhood notorious for its
whores and pickpockets—pleasing me not only because I had been ordained
a priest in that temple but because such papal favour had no precedent.
More, the basilica so delighted me for its architecture and decoration that I
contributed handsome monies to its maintenance and sang Solemn Mass at
its high altar on the great feasts.

Whenever I could, I visited my basilica—with princely gait striding down
the nave in my crimson, pausing to chat with nuns, housemaids, urchins, pilgrims, offering my ring to be kissed—rejoicing for its foundation in the fifth
century and for its grandiose mixture of the Romanesque and the Baroque
done during epochs of blurred time.

In the thirteenth century, a great transept had been added; in the eighteenth, to please Benedict XIV, Ferdinando Fuga had stuck on his famous
columned façade and portico with the Loggia of Benediction. And yet since
the fifth century the interior had remained much the same, all mosaic and
marble and the timbered ceiling, coffered and gilded during the Renaissance
by the wicked Alexander VI. In the nave, how stately and humbling was the
lengthy vista of Ionic columns, inviting the eye to behold the distant sanctuary—an Arch of Triumph—prefiguring the journey that the souls of the
Just must undertake through the valley of the shadow of death to the Ely-
sium of eternal life.

The high altar at the centre of the sanctuary seemed to float beneath a
great baldachin upheld by columns of glorious porphyry; overhead, glass
mosaics of mellow colours bathed the crux of the basilica in a mist of awe.
Throughout the edifice stood triumphal monuments to Nicholas IV and
Clement IX and other pontiffs, and polychrome busts of fabled cardinals, all
ennobled by luxurious sculpture. Complex iconography enshrined the lives
of the Virgin, mediaeval saints, and Jewish kings. The campanile, Romanesque, was the tallest in the Eternal City. Everywhere in my basilica, I
rejoiced at the decorative hand of Michelangelo.

. . .

You will assume that I paid a certain price for my new grandeur, but now that I had accepted my fate as a Roman cardinal, I paid it gladly. I became—is the image too blunt?—the Pope's high executioner. I sat often with the Supreme Pontiff urging him to boldness as he took grave decisions that much of the world called imperious if not cruel.

For the world itself had changed dramatically since my exile to the Vaucluse several years before. In Russia and in Eastern Europe, Communism had collapsed, the result in no small measure of the Slav Pope's tireless subversion. His radiant mystique inside his homeland, his relentless rhetoric and intrigues upon the global stage, had deepened the universal thirst for justice and encouraged bloodless insurrections throughout the Marxist empire. In the Third World also, Marxism had been discredited for its shabby fraudulence, and in such a backwash Liberation Theology wobbled on its last legs. But these grand victories produced fresh thorns that pricked and tormented the Slavic Pontiff.

He had expected that once the East had cast off its chains and fetters, it would heed his call to Christ, indeed that in gratitude to Heaven for deliverance from nuclear midnight the whole continent of Europe, West and East, from the English Channel to the Siberian tundra, would renew itself in fervent Christianity root and branch. Instead, no sooner had the East been liberated from the Marxist curse than in its fantasies and wish-fulfillment it flung itself into the arms of the Americans, too eager to embrace their bogus heaven here on earth of greed, consumerism, vulgarity, violence, drugs, and lust.

Even as the world changed, the Pope and I were fanatical in our resolve that the Roman Church should remain the same, a steady flame of permanence in every raging human storm, or (in the ancient image) the impregnable Rock of Ages. To that purpose we reaffirmed the authority of Rome throughout the Church, nor did we bother to be dainty as we went about it.

First, we dealt with bishops. Angry at the gnawing dissidence in the Church and at many of his bishops for failing to arrest it, the Pontiff took into his own hands the choice of all new brothers in the episcopate everywhere—burrowing into stacks of files, swallowing torrents of detail, muttering and thrashing about until he found the sort of men who satisfied his thirst for loyalty and rigour.

The Pope was helped not only by my eager hands but by the Prefect of the Sacred Congregation charged with nominating bishops, Patrice Cardinal Zalula—he of the foetid sores and chains and fetters on the River Congo, as tall and stately and more finely wrought than I, his sibling Eminence, yet deferential to me still because I had saved his life. Initially our triumvirate met in the papal library, but as the Pope yearned more and more to escape his confinement in the Vatican, we took to gathering late at night at Consalvi palace, where the Pontiff arrived in a limousine garnished with opaque windows and stuffed with armed guards.

Making bishops for the vast world exhausted the three of us. Don Jerzy, the papal secretary, piled the evening's dossiers across the Damascene carpet of the grand salon, beneath Bacchiacca's *Flagellation of Christ* and the water-colours by Thomas Shorter Boys and the paintings on wood by Tanzio da Varallo of horses, donkeys, and bridges falling down. Nubians in silken robes glided in and out, offering silver trays of black coffee and unbuttered biscuits.

"I am so tired. . . ." the Pope groaned.

"May I recommend more division of labour?" said I.

"I shall choose every bishop by myself," replied the Pontiff.

"I mean—this may sound crude—why don't we chop up the world?" I persisted. "His Eminence Zalula might winnow more of his wheat from chaff in the Mediterranean and in Africa. I might take on France, Britain, northern Europe, North and South America. Your Holiness might reserve to himself all of the East. For any bishopric, Your Holiness will retain as ever the sanction of consent."

"Can't you at least leave Latin America to me?" asked Cardinal Zalula.

His question, friendly and mildly defiant both at once, made me pause. Hitherto so humble towards me, my brother Zalula had his own opinions about the governance of the Church, not always identical to mine, and as he matured in the Sacred College he felt more bound to voice them. Now—standing beside my albescent marble bust of Cardinal Newman—and his black eyes flaring, he asked again, "Aren't France, Britain, and most of Europe enough for you, Augustine? Couldn't you entrust the Americas to me?"

"But Patrice—the Americas are my province," I protested, secretly admiring him for fighting back.

"Since I am the *Prefect,* after all—"

"Enough," the Slav Pope interrupted. "I don't care to see my favourite cardinals bickering. Augustine, you may have the United States, Mexico, and Central America—subject to my close supervision! Patrice, take Canada and all of South America."

"*Placet,*" said Cardinal Zalula.

"*Placet,*" said I, even as I reflected: Is he becoming my rival? But I shrugged off the thought as I told the Pontiff, "Now as for the new arch-bishops of Munich and Berlin—"

"No goofy theologians," growled the Pope.

So it was. As I swam through dossiers, I sought ability, scholarship, and loyalty to Rome, but even when ability and scholarship were dubious I chose loyalty to Rome. From nooks of the Church I plucked the odd bright star, but more often callow or ageing monks, somber seminary professors, dreary canon lawyers, parish priests with modest knowledge of theology—all safe men—and made them bishops. Urbane ecclesiastics throughout Europe and the Americas groaned with protest.

At Utrecht, scores of illustrious theologians signed a manifesto and sent it to the Pope, complaining bitterly that Rome had ravaged hallowed traditions of the northern churches—filling their vacant sees with sheepish loyalists, ignoring the counsel and indeed the right of many clergy to elect their own bishops. Worse, throughout the seminaries of Europe and the Americas, Rome was crushing free inquiry as it asserted the Pope's doctrinal supremacy in forms that reeked of tyranny. "Human conscience is not a mouthpiece of the papacy. The papal Magisterium depends upon the conscience of the faithful. To ignore the clash between the papacy and private conscience degrades Christianity."

Outraged, the Pontiff appointed me his plenipotentiary, dispatching me on another of my migrations around the world, armed with all powers to enforce the law. Most cardinals and bishops received me cordially. But as the weeks progressed and on I flew between Europe, America, and the far tropics, I confronted so many radical theologians, elusive rectors of seminaries, mushy-mouthed divines of universities, that I began to wonder whether my mission was futile.

I soldiered on and said, "The Roman Church must reclaim her radiant identity. Dissension in the Church has degenerated from self-criticism to self-destruction. Why are so many of you ashamed to call sin and evil by their real names? The Pope will no longer countenance subjective theology. Revealed doctrine is not a ball and chain, iron bars, or shackles on illumined thought. To the contrary, my dear Fathers, doctrine serves the deepest truth, for it is a gift to believers from the Authority decreed by God. Orthodoxy is not a brick wall that shuts us in, but an open window to the Infinite."

I brought them disturbing news—telling professors of Biblical and moral theology to conform their teachings to the papal Magisterium or to resign their posts. At pontifical universities, I fired noisy upstarts.

I warned the survivors that they must accept the Divinity of Christ as the Church had always taught it, or they should seek different work. No longer would it pass to harp on Christ's humanity, adding footnotes to his Divinity until it became mythological and funny. Nor could they any longer smudge the classical conceptions of the Eucharist, Original Sin, the Fatherhood of God, the virginity of Mary, the resurrection of Christ, Heaven as a real place, Hell as a real place, or Satan as a real person.

Wherever I went in Europe and America, I was besieged by people with petitions to the Pope to repeal the law of celibacy, allow a married clergy, and ordain women priests. I answered, "But His Holiness has ruled on celibacy. No repeal of holy celibacy—nor will there be. Women priests? The Sovereign Pontiff has spoken—infallibly—on that subject. *Never.*"

I added, "The Roman Church is not a smorgasbord—you can not pick and choose such delicacies of faith as you may fancy, refusing to eat the rest. Show courage! Swallow the Faith whole!" Of Americans I asked, "Why are you so selfish, indeed narcissistic—immersed in your own petty hurts and feelings? Few of your cravings—for a married clergy, women priests, and such—infect the poor tropics, abode of most Christians."

I told all fractious Jesuits, "Stop bitching and obey."

Americans called me "God's tough guy." Frenchmen called me *"le gendarme du pape."* Germans called me *"der Feldmarschall."*

More and more, I loved my work. Wherever I ventured—and before large crowds—I celebrated the Tridentine Mass in Latin, revived throughout the world at last with the Pontiff's blessing to vie with the unmysterious and ugly rites of the vernacular. In London, I may have shone as I sang the Latin and then addressed the Cardinal Archbishop and all the bishops and priests of England at Westminster Cathedral.

And I said, "The world has invited us to commit suicide, but we have declined the honour. We have only to look to the Church of England and its sister communion in America in order to thank Heaven that we have been spared their unkindly fortune. Liberal Anglican and Episcopalian priests have mocked and defiled their own sweet traditions, and thus droves of their disenchanted faithful are throwing up their arms and walking out. In trying so earnestly to be relevant and fashionable, in yielding to the ravening spirit of this world, the Church of England has ordained women priests and (in too many cases) sanctioned homosexual unions—even as it floods its ever more empty pews with pious sociology and (God help us) multicultural rock music.

"As the world urges indulgence of abortion and homosexual practice on the Church of Rome, it invites the Roman Church to cease being herself. For the common cause of Christianity, may we beseech the Church of England to stay the hand of suicide? As for ourselves, my brother bishops, dear Reverend Fathers, never, never shall we yield to the world that would devour us."

My brutal words sent waves of shock and recognition through Britain. In the wake of such tremors, numerous intellectuals, cabinet secretaries, Anglican priests, and even members of the Royal Family, deserted the Church of England for the Church of Rome. The Queen—whom I had dazzled at the Vatican—was said to be cross. No, said others, my proper wrath had pleased Her Majesty.

At home in Consalvi palace, I received the correspondents of *The Times* of London, *Le Monde* of Paris, and *The New York Times.* I told them, "Latin Christianity has nourished the élite and comforted the poor over an enormous arc of human history. In an inconstant world, the Roman Church is an immovable rock. If she evolves, as she slowly should, such changes must be only as perceptible as a glacier's, creeping with the most majestic gravity beneath the eye of God. The Church marches not to human time or vogue but to the music of her own geology and eternal principle.

"Why, even in permissive France, Britain, and the United States, as families fall to pieces and people yearn for a lost moral universe, abstinence from young sex is coming increasingly into practice, though it is not yet fashionable. Let us rejoice in little victories—before the greater victories sure to come. . . ."

. . .

Early during our century's final decade, in mid-December on the feast of St John of the Cross, I celebrated the silver anniversary of my elevation to the Sacred Purple. At the age of sixty-four, I remained among the youngest members of the Sacred College. To glorify the event, new laurels were heaped on me.

At Paris, the President of France invested me with a symbolical French passport and the Grand Cross of the Legion of Honour, the highest rank of that order founded by Napoleon. At London, as if not to be outdone, the Queen overruled the vigourous protests of her counsellors and created me a viscount, with the right to sit in the House of Lords—the first Roman bishop to enjoy that privilege since the Reformation. It was rumoured that Her Majesty took her unprecedented decision after a chat with His Holiness on the telephone.

However, I did not go to Buckingham Palace to be invested with my peerage by the Queen. Her Majesty's Ambassador to the Holy See delivered the patent to me at the Palazzo Consalvi. The Ambassador inquired, "Will you exercise your right to sit in the House of Lords?"

"No," said I, the ambivalent new viscount.

"May I ask Your Lordship why?"

"I'm not English."

In all documents and letters, I was now entitled to be addressed:

His Eminence
Augustine, Lord Galsworthy
Of the Title of Saint Bridget
Cardinal Priest of the Holy Roman Church
Archbishop of Trebizond
Co-Titular of Saint Mary Major
Grand Cross of the Legion of Honour
Camerlengo of the Holy Roman Church

Are you pleased also by that last title? As though to surpass the President of France and the Queen of England, the Pope created me Camerlengo of the Holy Roman Church. As Camerlengo, I would supervise all revenues and properties of the Vatican. Upon the Pontiff's death, I would become head of the Sacred College and prince regent of the Church. I would rule the Holy See during the interregnum and assemble the Conclave to elect a new Pope.

Throughout Rome, tongues wagged over this fragrant garland. It was interpreted as a brazen signal from the Slav Pope that he wished me to succeed him in the papacy. No pope had the right to name his successor. Many had tried, but in the event most were thwarted because so often the electors of the Sacred College decided differently. Ruminating, painfully remembering the past, I asked myself aloud, "Is so much favour dangerous?"

✛

✛

FIFTY - ONE

I hear you asking, What has become of Adrian Northwood? Could you ever suppose that I had forgotten him? Even from my exile in the Vaucluse, I corresponded with Adrian faithfully. As I had feared, his marriage to Antonia, the radiant Egyptian, had not flourished—especially since the birth of their child, little Urban II.

At Northwood Hall, Antonia's teasing laughter towards her husband and his meagre talent as an artist grew into a habit of mockery that she could not quite control—making her arguments with Adrian ever more bitter. On a snowy winter morning, she shrugged at his request that she drive baby Urban, just turned six, to an appointment with the dentist.

"No," she said.

"Please," said Adrian. "I'm late for class."

"Why go? They laugh at you."

"Less than you do."

Their golden son ran in, romped round their bedroom, and ran out.

"You drive him," she said.

"A child needs his mother at the dentist's."

"A child who prefers his father? You're too fond of him."

At the great doors of Northwood Hall, Urban II hugged his father's boots, begging him not to leave, but by now Adrian was indifferent to the dentist and dashed to class at The University, where he served (ingloriously) as adjunct professor in the Academy of Art. Thus Antonia drove little Urban to the dentist in the snow. On the road, a mile beyond the gates of Northwood Park, she tumbled off a cliff. Her body flew out of the car as it overturned, and she landed so violently on the rocks that she died instantly. The boy—their only child—died inside the car: little Urban was decapitated.

Blaming himself, Adrian undertook a harsh change of life. He fled his mother and Northwood Hall, driving aimlessly thousands of miles to the south, until deep in Texas on the border with Mexico. No doubt as an atonement, on the shore of the Rio Grande he established a shelter for refugees from Central America's civil wars, where he fed and clothed mobs of the hungry poor. His atonement angered the Mexican police, who excelled at seizing such refugees for ransom and resented Adrian's attempts to obstruct their traffic.

One blazing afternoon, in Matablancos across the Rio Grande from his shelter, the Mexican police caught careless Adrian without his papers; they accused him of smuggling drugs and hurled him into a penitentiary, without hope of release until he paid them huge sums of money. When Adrian refused, the police tortured him relentlessly.

They dragged him down dismal corridors into a cement room, where the chief of the Judicial Police stripped him naked, bound his thumbs behind his back, set fire to his eyes and nostrils with Tabasco sauce, and applied a cattle prod to his genitalia. Adrian did not yield. Sentenced to indefinite confinement, and separated from his money, he was forced to beg for his food.

Then he was confined in a blue tower with a cult of Satanists chanting occult rituals—howling of Oshun, the voodoo god of money, sex, and power; chicken heads, magical stones, quarter-moons, fishhooks, female garlic, spider webs, rooster hearts, he-goat testicles, and other demonic charms—that chilled his blood. His torture was resumed, but he did not yield.

Fed up, the police transferred him to another penitentiary upriver at Reynuestro, where goons aloft on cocaine and heroin bashed him with delirious ferocity all about his head and feet and body and then locked him in an earthy hole: leaving him there for days and weeks to reflect in darkness, feeding him only rancid mush, and rejoicing when his dysentery started and he languished in his own excrement. Lying naked with his back on moss, diarrhea, mucus, blood, Adrian entered another sphere. He enjoyed a mystical experience—rising gently (as certain saints have done) a foot or two into the honeyed air as he communed with Mozart, Schubert, Goethe, and his other gods of Beauty.

In time he descended to stinking earth; and at last to save his life he deferred to his tormentors and telephoned his lawyers to pay a great ransom.

Even when he returned from Mexico to Northwood Hall, Adrian never admitted to his mother that he had been tortured, but Diana had only to behold the change in his appearance to know that he had suffered horrors. In his letters, Adrian told me everything.

I invited Adrian to Rome to participate in the celebrations of my silver anniversary. But I was as dismayed as Diana had been by his appearance: he had lost his beauty.

As Adrian mounted the great stairway of Consalvi palace gripping his tattered luggage and wearing indifferent dress, I stood hidden behind a pillar watching him: glimpsing that August morning in the gardens of Northwood Hall when the youth ran up the rocky steps of the mythic ruins and paused between Ionic pillars, breathing heavily, smiling half a smile, wearing burgundy trunks and a torn polo shirt that bore the gilded crest of his defunct nobility—Marquis of the Bells—strands of his golden hair brushing past his blue eyes, other locks cascading behind his ears and resting nearly on his shoulders, his sculpted countenance dappled by the morning sunlight.

Now, though he was only in his middle thirties, his hair while still profuse had changed its hue, hinting of its golden past but mostly tangled locks of grey. His cheeks were hollow. His mouth was thinner, elongated at the corners into downward creases that suggested churlishness—or pain too long endured? Thickish wrinkles encased his eyes, still a shocking blue but blazing as if from caves. As he paused exhausted on a stair, his tall physique seemed stooped; when he resumed his climb he did so cautiously, as though his feet hurt. I stepped from behind my pillar to embrace Adrian fiercely and kiss his cheek.

"Augustine! You look so marvellous!" exclaimed the young man.

"Ah, if I could say the same of you, b-beloved Adrian."

"Don't cry, Eminence."

"May I k-kiss you again?"

"*¿Cómo?*"

"May I kiss you again?"

"I insist upon it."

"You've a superior kind of beauty."

"*¿Cómo?*"

"Still speaking Spanish?"

"What?"

"DID THOSE BASTARDS MAKE YOU DEAF?"

"For a while my world became a silent film. I hear perfectly now. Most of the time? Diana insisted on the best doctors."

"Come into the music room."

"What?"

In the Vaucluse as a penance I had never touched a keyboard, but since returning to Rome I had resumed my rigourous practice; to celebrate Adrian's presence I sat at my Steinway and played variations of Schubert's First Piano Trio in B flat, a favourite of Adrian's since childhood. Adrian sat on the bench beside me, upon the lower scale seizing the part of the haunting, mournful cello. Da-dum-ta-*dee*-dum. Da-dum-ta-ta-ta-*dee*-dum. No composer could sustain a melody as Schubert could: not even Mozart. The themes waxed sweetly, but then Adrian's deafness intruded and he garbled notes, ruining our music. With both fists he banged the keyboard furiously and withdrew to his old apartments on the third floor of the palazzo, I chasing after him, protesting, "DEAR BOY, IT DOESN'T MATTER."

Next day, at noon, feast of St John of the Cross, the Pope put on a chasuble of white and silver and said Mass in the Pauline Chapel to honour Cardinal Zalula and me together for our quarter-century in the Sacred College; but Adrian remembered his marriage to Antonia before that altar and he did not deign to attend. Afterwards, scores of cardinals and archbishops came to Consalvi palace in full red and purple for an elaborate buffet luncheon, but Adrian was late in making his appearance and when he descended the marble stairway he wore torn jeans and a face of stubble.

His mood throughout the rest of the luncheon was no more festive. It had become common knowledge in the Vatican that my considerable wealth and global charities sprang from the Northwood fortune; several prelates, hoping to cash in, approached Adrian picking at a piece of fish to plead their godly causes. The Archbishop of Liverpool was notably tenacious. Adrian told him, "Buzz off, Your Grace."

After luncheon, the prelates in their brilliant swirling robes descended the grand staircase past the oil portrait of Ercole Cardinal Consalvi in cappa magna, crossed the windy courtyard in the December cold, and crowded into my little chapel for Benediction of the Most Blessed Sacrament. Adrian sat alone on a wooden chair at the edge of the sanctuary, now in his bare feet. When I raised the golden monstrance of the Holy Eucharist for the Adoration, Adrian descended to his knees, and as he did his face glowed unnaturally.

Filing out, the Cardinal of Westminster, a Benedictine monk with deep knowledge of such matters, took me aside and said, "Lordship, that young chap of yours has the odour of sanctity."

I grasped Westminster's wrist: "Eminence, he is Saint Francis."

For several weeks, Adrian remained my guest in the Palazzo Consalvi. For much of his youth he had been a sceptic, indifferent to his sacred obligations, but now he attended all of my Latin Masses loyally and sat often in the rear of Consalvi chapel, reading Scripture. He took all of his meals at the palace, joining me in the dining room even for early breakfast because his apartments upstairs reminded me too much of Lisa, and I was loath to enter them. However, late one night, a disturbance happened.

Sleeping tranquilly in my cell on the second floor, I was awakened by screams from above. Hurling on a robe, I rushed to the rooms upstairs to find Adrian writhing on his bed. Clad only in white briefs, the young man was babbling in Spanish and English; from the defensive flailings of his arms and legs he appeared to be reliving his tortures.

He shrieked, "*¿CÓMO? ¿UNA CHICHARRA? ¿CÓMO? NO TENGO DINERO. TU TIENES DINERO. NO TENGO DINERO. ¿CÓMO?* A ROOSTER'S HEART? BUT I DON'T WANT A ROOSTER'S HEART! A FISHHOOK? I DON'T WANT A FISH-HOOK! *¿AJO HEMBRA?* FEMALE GARLIC? WHAT'S FEMALE GARLIC? BUT I DON'T WANT YOUR FEMALE GARLIC! *¿ERES NORTEAMERICANO? NO SOY NADA. ¿CÓMO? NO TENGO DINERO. EL HOYO EL HOYO EL HOYO.* THE HOLE THE HOLE THE HOLE. *CHICHARRA CHICHARRA CHICHARRA.* CATTLE PROD CATTLE PROD CATTLE PROD. *EL HOYO EL HOYO EL HOYO.* THE HOLE THE HOLE THE HOLE. . . ."

His torso and legs were covered with the scars of wounds. His soles had bubbles on them that I supposed had never healed from the beatings of his feet. I remembered that in the Congo I had kissed the wounds of Cardinal Zalula as I would have kissed the wounds of Christ. In the Apostolic Palace I had kissed the wounds of the Sad Pope as I yearned to kiss the wounds of my Redeemer. Now faintly for a moment I kissed the bubbles on Adrian's feet, before I roused him from his nightmare and held him closely until he fell backward into placid slumber.

At breakfast, as my Nubians served chilled orange juice and American corn flakes, I asked him, "What will you do with the rest of your life?"

"I've not the vaguest idea," said Adrian. "I've no future as an artist—I learned that in Mexico. I must get away from my mother."

"Why hasn't Diana written to me lately?"

"*¿Cómo?*"

"WHY DOESN'T DIANA WRITE?"

"Your Lordship needn't shout. She's angry at you."

"*Angry . . . ?*"

"She thinks that you're manipulating me to give all of my fortune to the Church. She blames you for my misadventure in Mexico."

I felt stabs of guilt. As Camerlengo I had to grapple with the crushing deficit of the Holy See, but my fantasy to wipe it out with huge helpings of the Northwood fortune I had expressed to Adrian only in murky hints and glances. I was more culpable in having pushed tormented Adrian towards Divine insanity in the image of St Francis. I recalled my letters to Adrian in Texas: "Where your secret voice will lead you, I know not, but whatever the cost, go there. If at times you are tempted to folly, then do compound the folly and follow the voice, however far. Are your *sublime* follies yet to come?"

"Your mother is talking nonsense," I answered.

"What?"

"NONSENSE."

"Is it?"

"Dear God, what ever shall I do with you?"

"Should I return to Mexico?"

In a distant room, the telephone rang. Ghassem, old now and limping, in red turban and white gown, stood presently at the pillared door. *"Ya sidi?"* I withdrew to take the call, returning after a quarter of an hour. "My private secretary," I said, resuming my breakfast. "Jolly heap of trouble in East Africa. We're trying to do something."

"¿Cómo?"

"East Africa."

"What?"

"Famine."

"Where?"

"TEN MILLION CHILDREN IN EAST AFRICA MAY DIE OF HUNGER."

"Really? Should I read the newspapers?"

Next morning, on my breakfast table, I found a creamy envelope with a scribbled note.

Augustine,
    Read the newspapers. Off to Africa. Will write to you. I do love Your Lordship.
    Yours,

ADRIAN

P.S. Use enclosed for famine?

Included was a cheque to me on the Crédit Suisse for several million dollars: given Diana's anger, not what I had intended, leaving me—without Adrian—lonely and morose. From Africa, he at first wrote often, his letters rife with macabre detail, but then his distant voice ebbed into saddening silence.

✥

FIFTY-TWO

✥

Of a hot and rain-swept afternoon, the Pontiff summoned me to his armoured roof. From behind his wire mask, he ruminated about his apiary. The season was July. He said, "My worker bees are massacring my drones. Look here, Augustine. . . ." Darkly, waving his great leather gloves at Heaven, on and on he talked, fantastically.

When the skies were blue, and nectar oozed from the flowers, the worker bees had indulged the idle drones, so often sleeping, rising from their repose only to feast on the vats of honey, cluttering the combs with their waste. Ending their forbearance, the worker bees have rampaged, becoming suddenly—in their natural republic—judges and executioners. The fat lazy drones are being roused from their dreams by an army of wrathful virgins. Bristling with stings, the virgins are tearing the bewildered parasites to pieces, severing their wings, impaling their bellies, wrenching off their legs, and as for their eyes—mirrors once of the exuberant flowers, of the hyacinth light and the innocent pride of early summer—the virgins gouge them out.

Most of the drones succumb to the onslaught; they are borne away by their executioners to graveyards beyond the hive, victims of nature's unyielding carnage. Others, whose wounds are less, find shelter in nooks, huddling together, but they will each of them die of starvation. The workers sweep the hive, strewn with the corpses of useless drones, and all memory of the slothful race evaporates.

But even for the surviving bees, when summer blends to autumn, the flowers will wither and food will be scarce. Labour will cease, births diminish, deaths multiply, night will lengthen. Inclement rain and winds, the mists of morning, dryness and then drought, will decimate hosts of workers who can not return from their airy flights, for they will perish of toil and hunger.

The Pontiff added, "Africa torments Us more each day. Famine in Ethiopia—again? And Somalia? Will it never stop? All those children— *poof*? Within the fortnight, to prove Our prayerful solidarity, We shall go there."

Within the week, however, the Pope fell ill. Of late, he had suffered fevers, taken tumbles in his bathroom, cracked his tibia and ribs. Now his doctors discovered a tumour in his bowels the shape and colour of a pink grapefruit, which they hastened to take out, announcing that it contained no cancer.

Recuperating, the Pope dispatched me to Africa in his stead. As he bade me farewell, he mused, "Isn't sending you in my place nearly as good, Augustine? Are you not—probably—the next Pope?"

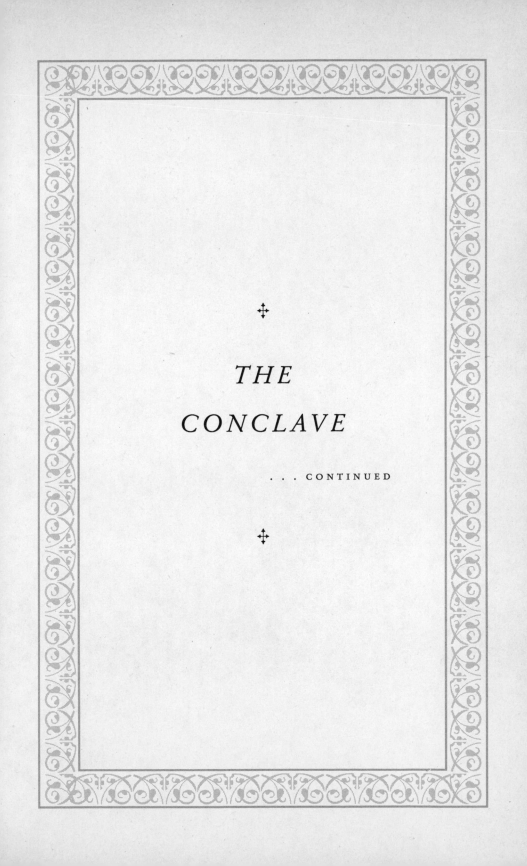

THE

CONCLAVE

... CONTINUED

"The cup which my Father hath given me,

shall I not drink it?"

✚

The Conclave on the eve of the Third Millennium continued to deliberate. On I scribbled my abortive diary upon sheets of foolscap:

Ninth day. No result. Tenth day. No result. Eleventh day. Niente. However ... this morning my ballots rise to fifty-two—meaning that I need another twenty-nine.

At luncheon, I barely nibble at my leg of chicken, refuse a second glass of white Frascati, and avoid all but banal conversation with my brother princes.

In the second scrutiny of the afternoon, my ballots grow to sixty-one—only twenty short of the eighty-one I need for my papacy. My saintly brother, Patrice Cardinal Zalula, is next; but at thirty votes his candidacy is the more and more dwarfed by mine. Most cardinals do not believe that the Roman Church is ready for an African pontificate; and besides, Cardinal Zalula has no wish to be Pope.

Their progressive Eminences of northern Europe, who despise me, and many of the conservative Italians, who yearn to retrieve the papacy for Italy, are thrashing about in an unnatural marriage of convenience to produce a live body who might thwart me.

Despite them . . . is my pontificate inevitable? Already in the Sistine Chapel I begin to hear whispered allusions to Sacred Scripture as cardinals gaze at me, I standing lonely and apart at the foot of the high altar, my head raised to the Last Judgement. *I ask myself, Must I soon begin my sacred choreography, that dance of ceremonial humility hallowed down the centuries—and that I know needs to be fulfilled before I can be anointed by the finger of the Holy Spirit?*

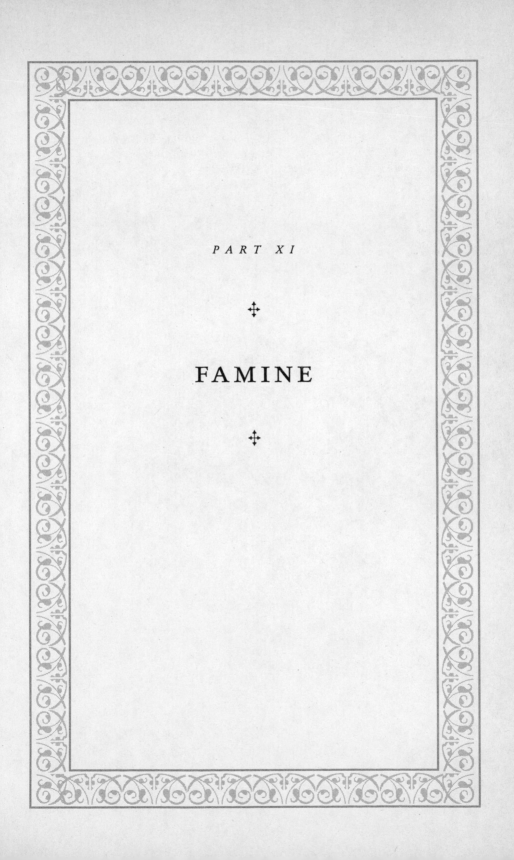

PART XI

✣

FAMINE

✣

✤

✤

The Slavic Pontiff had instructed me to remain in Africa for as long as it might take to dramatise before the world his foreboding about the famine. With growing ferocity it spread like plague: from the hovels of Addis Ababa southward and eastward through vast Ethiopia, across Harerghe province and the deserts of the Ogaden, to the beaches of the sea and much of Somalia.

I landed at Addis Ababa in a hired aeroplane filled with foodstuffs—a symbolic meal for the starving from the Vicar of Christ—accompanied by a pack of impudent young men and women with cameras and microphones representing Italian and British television. Were they not however a necessary evil—for how otherwise might I fulfill the papal mandate to show mankind the dreadful hunger? At their bidding I cascaded from the aircraft in all my red, to be greeted on the runway by the Patriarch of Ethiopia—the Abyssinian Orthodox pope.

He was a youngish bearded man with a chiselled brown face; half afloat he seemed to me in muslin veils and white vestments, or rather half weighted down by silver chains and golden icons, atop his head a rimless hat that gleamed like burnished ivory.

We embraced and exchanged the kiss of peace. For his higher theology this schismatic pontiff had been tutored by divines at Yale, and he spoke as the result a schoolmasterish sort of American English, credentials that did not endear him to the Marxist dictatorship when he returned to Ethiopia. He was thrown with several other bishops into a smelly dungeon not much bigger than a broom closet; there he languished for seven years, emerging only when the Counter Revolution triumphed and the dictatorship tumbled into the wreckage of the nation and the people's hunger. We drove into the capital in his dented Mercedes limousine under a pitiless rain. I asked him, "Should I address you as 'Your Holiness'?"

"You should," he answered, "but 'Your Beatitude' will suffice. We are the most ancient Christian sect. We live by the Old Testament as we do by the New, so we abstain from pork and other unclean meats, honour both Saturday and Sunday as the Sabbath, and circumcise our infant boys. Everywhere you look, our culture is Biblical. Christianity has flourished in Ethiopia for nearly two millennia. Saint Matthew came to Abyssinia soon after the Ascension of Lord Jesus Christ."

"Isn't it sad, Beatitude," I said with my love of mischief, "that we can not agree upon the natures of Lord Jesus Christ?"

"Christ has one nature—the Divine," said the brown pope.

"Christ has two natures—the distinctly Divine and the distinctly human, mingled in the Hypostatic Union."

"There is no 'Hypostatic Union,' Your Eminence! Christ's illusory humanity is subsumed by His Divinity!"

"The Council of Chalcedon—"

"The Council of Constantinople—"

On we quarrelled about the Council of Chalcedon and the Council of Constantinople and the Hypostatic Union and the Monophysite Heresy, conjuring up anew the bloody wars that raged in Africa and Asia Minor over the body and soul of Christ during the fifth and sixth centuries: as we did I looked through my rain-lashed window at the streets of Addis Ababa. In the gutters beggars swarmed; sickly black cows lay mooing on the grass of boulevards; at the crossroads eerie mothers flew at me with starving infants, beating on my window and exposing their shrivelled milkless breasts; wild-eyed madmen wandered between the motorcars, barking like dogs at Heaven.

Through a thicket of beggars we entered the walled compound of the Patriarch's cathedral, and as the rain turned to mist we stepped out of the Mercedes into a Verdi opera. To honour me, a throng of boys, men, acolytes, and monks—in white robes and turbans, beards and black habits, red stoles and blue vestments and round puffy headpieces; wielding crucifixes, staves, rattles, cymbals, tinkling bells, and pounding drums; hoisting umbrellas of kaleidoscopic colour—advanced on us in fervent waves.

On sedan chairs they bore us up the steps to the Shrine of St George, where before a gilded door they seated their pontiff and me on raised thrones. For an hour in the mist they danced and sang and ululated, lamenting the misfortune of the famine, thanking the saints and angels for my presence, and praising God, all in their liturgical tongue of Geez. We repaired to the cathedral and a Mass of three hours, sung by His Beatitude and a mighty choir, in Geez. As the milling faithful prostrated themselves to venerate the icons of St Matthew, St Mark, St Epiphanius, His Beatitude and I ascended to a sanctuary hidden behind brocaded curtains where alone I watched him consecrate the wine and leavened bread, in Geez. After the Mass, we withdrew from the cathedral to his secretariat and another dream-like opera.

The Patriarch's antechamber teemed with monks and bishops—tall, stately, handsome men in silver beards and dark flowing garments and those rimless bloated hats—all waving petitions and metallic crosses at me and contending for my ear. "Bread!" they keened. "Our people need bread! Bread! bread! bread!"

They pursued us into His Beatitude's inner sanctum, a great long room with tattered rugs and shabby chairs along the sky-blue walls, at the end a little desk covered by a clean white tablecloth, where the schismatic pope stood beneath the portraits of his predecessors yellowing and long since dead. There in his pedagogic English he delivered an impassioned aria, entreating the Pope of Rome to save his Christian people.

I sat apart from him on a lumpy armchair brooding in my watered scarlet—and then I rose theatrically to reply that even as I spoke the Roman Pontiff was appealing to rich governments and commanding the charities of the Church Universal to feed Ethiopia. The doors opened, admitting rough labourers who bore aloft my sacks of wheat and corn. I handed the Patriarch a cheque for ten million dollars, signed by my Pope. The monks and bishops queued to embrace me. The clanking gang from that other world of television recorded all, to shame and move mankind. As I left the compound in the Patriarch's Mercedes, under the stone arch and the beating rain, a mob of beggars stopped me, pounding on my roof and windows and rocking the limousine as one might a cradle.

I was besieged by grotesques—lame men leaning on broken branches; one-eyed men with grey flesh bulging from their dead sockets; men with legs as thick as church pillars, hobbling with elephantiasis; ill boys in muddy bathing costumes, their eyes brimming with creamy pus, clinging to the horns of diseased goats; leprous women missing fingers and their noses; and I saw beyond them more abandoned mooing black cows, all sores and hunger. I wondered, *Am I not truly in the Book of Exodus, wandering in the land of lice and locusts and plagues of frogs?*

I kept my windows shut, too saddened by such evil poverty to touch it with my princely hand. Finally as we inched forward my chauffeur drove us free. Glancing back, I imagined that I glimpsed Adrian at the edge of that mob.

I flew from the capital hundreds of miles eastward to Harerghe province, where I was awaited by young Germans of Caritas, the Holy See's global hand endeavouring to soothe tropical mankind's thirst and hunger. At Dire Dawa town we set out in Land Rovers for remote hills and valleys oppressed by war, sucked dry by drought, being devoured again by pestilence and famine.

Abyssinian Christianity I had left far behind; this wilderness was Islamic, inhabited by the Oromo people and infested with guerrillas fighting for autonomy from the feeble central government; marauding, killing, blowing up wells and granaries. Would that sort of suicidal devastation never cease? Burnt-out Russian tanks and artillery pieces littered the sides of roads; till yesterday the Marxist dictatorship had waged war against these peasant tribes, herding them into collective farms that failed, uprooting them in forced migrations, massacring them from MiGs and helicopters when despairingly they rebelled.

Now in the highlands some little rain had fallen, but in the deep valleys and across the plains I saw only withered bush and empty riverbeds and clouds of dust.

For several moments in that bleak world my soul seemed to rise above my body: I became a crimson bird of prey, a fantastic vulture swooping high above those violet hills and valleys, looking down upon legions of old women as they turned that majestic country into desert.

The old women were climbing the naked sides of hills and mountains in search of firewood. They had to eat: in Dire Dawa they could exchange the sticks and branches for pittances of paper money to buy their meagre food. The greater part of the ancient kingdom until our century had been adorned by dripping forest, but of recent years all shade was vanishing—the soil eroding, yielding no crops, only rocks and mud when the rains came—as the women and their menfolk continued to cut down the eucalyptus, cypress, and locust trees whose twigs and splinters they could sell for cash.

From high above I watched the women stumble from the hillsides weighted down like beasts of burden with bundles of sticks upon their backs; then they heaped them onto donkeys or into carts drawn by horses, the donkeys and the horses so sick and skeletal that some few of them dropped dead. Oh, the women wished to feed their animals, and fed them as they could, but could they barely feed themselves or the children running after them?

We ventured deeper to the interior until the gutted roads ran out, but still over the rocky hills and between the numberless stumps of trees we kept driving on, to the villages of Woba, Bilisuma, Fadis, Farso, Fellana, Midega, Melkabello, Jello Bellina, where the cries of the people never varied: "Our crops have failed. Our barns are empty. We have no bread."

At Jello Bellina, all dust and flies and mud-brick hovels, hordes surrounded us, imploring food, the children tugging at the hems of my white tropical soutane, at my crimson sash, standing tiptoe to brush their bony fingers across my golden crucifix. I fled them into the village store, run by miserly Pakistanis, crammed with food, but the villagers had no money so they could buy no food. I bought a tin of sweet biscuits and crouched in a corner of the store munching them for luncheon, but my brash companions of British television came after me commanding, "Come on, Gus, get off your arse! Give us some footage! Ham it up!"

I went back to the merchant and bought every tin of biscuits in his store, then with Pakistani boys in tow laden with the tins I returned to the sunny throbbing road, where I fed the mob. From separate mud-brick roofs the British and Italians aimed their cameras, shouting at me to stand on wooden boxes above the screams and grasping hands, to enlarge my gestures, to hug and kiss more starving children; to weep, to shout out lamentations, to *ham it up*—and I did. I pitied these hungry peasants; but did I not relish my new theatre? In the Land Rover again, as we drove through dust and more fallen eucalyptus toward the next hungry village, my Germans told me, "Terrific television, *Eminenz.*"

One of my Germans, Wolfgang, a fine youth with golden hair, made me remember Adrian before his torture. I said, "You resemble an American friend. He's somewhere here in Africa, but I can not find him. By chance do you know an Adrian Northwood?"

"We all know Adrian, *Eminenz.*"

"Ah? Where is he?"

"In Fechatu."

"Where is Fechatu?"

"Beyond those mountains, *Eminenz*—sixty kilometres?"

"What does Adrian do in Fechatu?"

"Drives a truck. Feeds people. Attends the sick?"

"May we sleep in Fechatu tonight?"

We reached Fechatu as the sun set: a bleak little village—bleaker without Adrian. In Italian, the old headman told us, "He's in Djibouti. Or did he say Addis Ababa? He brings food and medicine to many villages—but we are all so hungry and his truck's too small. He's gone to buy a bigger truck."

"When will he return?"

"Tomorrow, Padre."

"We'll wait."

We slept on straw mats in the headman's mud-brick hut. Beyond in the night, hyenas quarrelled. At morning as we walked about, we learned of Fechatu's affliction from an inscrutable disease that resembled malaria but had no cure. Young and old contracted fever, fell deliriously into coma, and within three days died. Men, mothers, and their infant children languished recumbent in the shade of dwellings, of flat-topped acacia and locust trees, expiring. The village was a heap of dust and horseflies, mud brick, thatched roofs, tin roofs, battered metal drums the pleasant colour blue, grey abandoned tractor tyres, unfed goats and camels chewing thorn. Adrian's dwelling was larger than most others—a rounded hut made of mud and straw below a roof of woven thatch shaped like the head of a mushroom.

I stepped inside. Again I felt stabs of guilt. Adrian lived in squalor. Had I not once urged him to it? For furniture he had only a broken metal chair, some mats of dirty straw scattered on the earthen floor, and a bamboo table

piled up with letters. Flies buzzed. Dangling above the table was an oil lamp
that enabled him to read in darkness, but he had no books. Stuck to the mud
walls were colour snapshots of the rose-red turrets, the mock Greek ruins,
the Elysian gardens of his Northwood Hall. I read the letters.

They were from his mother, elegantly written, but bitter and full of
reproach. In her advancing age, he had thrust her aside, interred and abandoned her in the cheerless grandeur of his huge estate, as he ran slumming
about the world. ". . . and when will you cease hallucinating about the allure
of human suffering and the glamour of the poor? Worse, was it not the sinister advice of His Eminence Augustine Cardinal Viscount Galsworthy, my
ineffable former friend, that provoked you to fly directly from Rome to
dismal Africa, for month after month remaining there? I swear to you on
Christ . . ." I found Diana's diatribes less interesting than her son's
responses.

Or rather, the drafts of his responses: beneath her letters lay much
foolscap, his sentences and long paragraphs scribbled and crossed out,
rewritten and crossed out, written anew, over, and again, protesting his
attachment to her in prolix locutions, pleading the famine for his long
absence, and—rather mildly, I thought—defending me. ". . . but he is (I
think) a good and holy priest. In former times his very presence ravished
you—can you deny that, darling Mother? His Eminence devotes himself not
just to seeking money for the Church but (I hope sincerely!) to the zealous
care of souls. . . ." I wondered, did Adrian half believe his mother's accusation that I coveted his entire fortune for the Church? And what other son on
earth wrote drafts of letters to his mother?

Emerging from his hovel, I decided I must wait for him. He did not
appear that day. By wireless to Dire Dawa my Germans appealed to Caritas
for wheat and corn for Fechatu, but famine prospered throughout the
province and Caritas had no more trucks. Fechatu's only hope for food was
Adrian. During that day and the next, in the devilish heat we did well to
breathe; we lay down in the shade of a locust tree, sharing our sweet biscuits
and warm Pepsi-Cola with the children. On the third day, I decided we
could wait no longer.

Upon his table, I left a note for Adrian: ". . . and so—forgive me—I took
the liberty of reading your correspondence. More than ever, your mother
wrongs me. I can not command you to heed the call that summons you to
heroic sanctity, nor will I try. Somalia—hungrier than Ethiopia? is that possible?—awaits me. Shall I never see you in Somalia?"

From Dire Dawa, a United Nations aircraft flew me eastward, above the
desert of the Ogaden and over the Somali border, to the sea and Mogadishu.

FIFTY - FOUR

My encounters with starving Ethiopians, broadcast by British and Italian television throughout Europe, inspired sorrow. Such gruesome pictures, blending with the alarums of the Pope at Rome and the Red Cross at Geneva, kindled the charity of ordinary people and provoked rich governments to send great shipments of grain and medicine to subdue that famine. But now the anarchy of Somalia was coming to a head, imposing new claims on the world's benevolence.

Intrigued by my performance with the urchins of Ethiopia, American television dispatched crews from New York to join my cheeky Britons and Italians as they pursued me in Somalia. Flattered, I felt rather like a Field Marshal whenever I left the pure white compound of Caritas for the treacherous streets of Mogadishu. I was driven in a Land Rover packed with bodyguards, Somali youths in fashion jeans or those skirts of plaid they called *macawis,* fingering pistols and assault rifles—hardly to my taste, but essential, so everybody said, for the safety of my person in that civil war of clans.

On my roof sat more boys with bazookas and rocket launchers. Before me and behind me rumbled white Toyota trucks stuffed with laughing adolescents, manning mortar cannon and mounted machine guns, wearing T-shirts boasting in English: COOL and A VIEW TO KILL and I AM THE BOSS. They were chewing flowers of paradise—the green, pungent, narcotic leaves and twigs of *qat*. Following in our backwash were my votaries of television and their own loud flotillas. The streets of the capital seemed all sun and rubbish and busy brown rats. Italy had ruled Somalia once; as we sped past shell-pocked Italianate buildings and rows of shanties, from the distance near and far I heard the random exchange of gunfire.

At the vanguard of the armoured parade, astride the roof of the first Toyota, brandishing a submachine gun, was my chief centurion—a Somali of no more than twenty with a thick face, a shaven head, high boots, and quasi-military costume: he called himself "Mussolini." I shrank from Mussolini instinctively, afraid that on a whim at any moment he might turn his knives and guns on me: surely he wielded too much roiling, brute power. Thrust on me by others, Mussolini was too often at my elbow, pushing weaker Somalis—hungry children, for example—away from my sympathy. He did that at Medina Hospital, but I suppose he had to.

Ah, Medina Hospital—barracks of cement, ovens nearly, beneath the cooking sun—and how its thousand patients sighed and groaned as I trod from ward to ward. The beds had no sheets; the floors seemed never to have been swept; feces oozed from water closets bereft of water. Had I expected to see so many gunshot wounds—this boy without a testicle, that woman with half an abdomen, now an infant child, her feet blown off?

An Egyptian surgeon halts my progress: "I can't operate, Father—no electricity." Somali nurses and physicians press in on me, speaking English like the Egyptian, intoning horrors, waving lists of things: "We have no medicines."

"What do you need?" I ask.

"Soap, iodine, syringes, catheters, elastic bandages, plastic gloves ..." a nurse cries out.

"Antimalarial drugs, antitubercular drugs, simple analgesics ..." says a Somali doctor.

"Thoracic drainage devices, colostomy bags, Heimlich valves, major surgical instruments, minor surgical instruments ..." pleads the Egyptian surgeon.

I try to write it down: "Surgical instruments, colostomy bags, plasma substitutes, penicillin, ampicillin, morphine ... ladies ... gentlemen ... I shall ask Caritas."

"Oh, Father, please! Take our lists! Caritas promised us medicine last week!"

"I think it came," I tell them. "The aeroplane was pillaged."

Filled up with their entreaties I walked off: the wards spilled out into the sunshine of a barren yard, where many beds with people in them stood haphazardly in the dust. Ten thousand squatters, having fled the famished countryside, were encamped on the grounds in countless huts of sticks and green plastic—a scene that undulated from the shadows of the hospital across the sandy hills to the edge of the dazzling sea. Nearby, in an enormous tent of more green plastic, the international Red Cross was feeding children: I stepped inside. As the sun shone cruelly on the shiny roof, it made the heat within unbearable and cast an unearthly radiance, turning all of the gaunt children—hundreds? thousands? of them—from brown to a brilliant green.

Swiss nurses walked among the children, serving them a nutritious porridge of grains, beans, and olive oil. A German with me bore a sack of Dehydration Treatment Salts, ideal for curing diarrhea, so for want of something better I distributed the pretty orange packets to the nurses and the grasping mothers. The children, thinking that my gifts were candy, rushed to me, demanding candy. As I refused them and their numbers grew, I forsook the green haze for the freedom of the yard—but by then a mob of men and women and their children came roaring at me from their sordid huts, down the sandy rolling little hills, from as far as the sea I thought, demanding tea and bread.

"Mush andi akl! mush andi shai! mush andi aish!" I have no food! I have no tea! I have no bread! I shouted back at them in Arabic, a language which as Muslims most Somalis understood. My protests did not convince them; the parents snarled at me; the shrieking children clawed at my white soutane, tearing off red buttons and my crimson sash. Mussolini and my bodyguard closed ranks around me. Mussolini raised his submachine gun, swinging it as a club, striking several of the children brutally. Sorrowing, I returned to my compound.

As for my compound—please do not suppose that in that seething capital I shared the squalor of the poor. The Caritas mission inhabited the embassy of Arabia's king, long since abandoned by his diplomatists to the bloody civil war. The embassy was a palace, as luxurious during famine as it had been during peace.

We were, indeed, an enclave, an islet, our own little fortress kingdom, floating spoiled and jolly upon our dirty sea of want. White gleaming walls and steel doors protected us; then walks and drives, embroidered by hibiscus, rose to the broad verandas of the palace—itself all floors of marble, chandeliers of gems and crystal, tiled baths with golden fixtures, expensive teakwood, furniture of *faux* Louis Quatorze, vast and pompous rooms.

Mogadishu had no electricity, but we had generators, refrigerators, and air-conditioning; china, cutlery, and cooks; our meals were hearty and delicious, our French Chablis and Russian vodka fastidiously chilled. I was given the Ambassador's suite, overlooking the courtyard with a mosaic fountain and a monstrous swimming pool. In my salon stood a grand piano, much out of tune, forbidding me to play.

The others did not need my music, for often during night we tendered dinner parties, and our guests—Red Cross and United Nations people, Europeans and Americans from lesser agencies of relief, all young—brought Somali rock orchestras. After dinner we withdrew to the tessellated courtyard, where coloured lanterns illuminated the swimming pool, and the youthful revellers—having changed to bathing costume—swam and danced. Oh, they deserved to do so, for during daytime they all of them risked death by gunshot wounds, and even now at night as they had their fun they could hear the rat-tat-tat of Kalashnikovs and Uzis beyond our sealed walls.

The European women, so exuberant and pretty, imitated Somali women by painting their hands and feet with elaborate floral patterns done in henna dye, no doubt to ward off evil. Perhaps also to calm their fears of death tomorrow, when not swimming or dancing rock they smoked cigarettes incessantly; I surmised that amongst themselves some few of them chewed *qat.* Invariably in a corner of the courtyard I stood apart from all such lovely women in my white and crimson, reserved though gracious when they and gentlemen approached me to render homage. The Germans, as you remember, called me *Eminenz;* the British called me "Lordship"; but— during day or night, not in deference to my priesthood but to my age—all Somali guards and servants called *baba:* Father.

Mussolini called me "baba." He was for ever begging me to take him with me when I returned to Italy—so that he might venerate the monuments and birthplace of his adopted namesake. He had grown up, he too often told me in his bad Italian, watching old newsreels of his idol addressing multitudes from the balcony of the Palazzo Venezia and strutting through the streets of Rome.

"When you go back to Italy, baba?"

"Not soon, Mussolini."

"You take me to the Romagna, baba?"

"Why to the Romagna, Mussolini?"

"Benito Mussolini born there, baba. Buried there, baba. *Uomo bravo.*"

"*Uomo bravo?* His own people shot him dead, then hanged him upside down beside his whore at a gasoline station. *Mussolini èra una bestia. Una bestia brutale.*"

"*Brutale, sì! Brutale, va bene! Brutale, benissimo!* You take me Italy, baba, or . . ."

"Or . . . Mussolini?"

"I shoot you dead."

Mussolini's problem, it occurred to me, was that he thought he was Mussolini. (His real name, I think, was Mustafa.) Early one morning, before we left the compound to resume our visitations to the starving, I stood at the window of my salon and watched him prancing in the courtyard—alone, wearing his dusty boots and khaki jodhpurs, jutting forth his chin, his legs spread out, his hands and elbows akimbo at his hips; then he marched up and down along the swimming pool in a kicking goose step, his right arm extended in the Fascist salute; and throughout, twigs sprouted from his pink mouth as he chewed *qat.*

And yet, more than ever I needed his protection the more deeply I became enmeshed in Somalia's hunger. Distraught that so little food was getting through, increasingly I ventured to the docks of Mogadishu, where surrounded by my guards I watched armed gangs—those ceaseless tides of adolescent gunmen—loot the ships and trucks at will. From their clean white lorries, soldiers of the United Nations—Pakistanis and Sri Lankans—looked on, hugging their rifles, and did nothing. I walked up to their commander in his blue helmet.

"Why don't you stop those thugs?" I raged.

"Sir, we've no mandate to use force," the Brigadier responded in his Pakistani lilt. "Only if we're fired on can we fire back."

"But surely you can threaten them!"

"We have no such mandate, sir."

For the next week, I hounded the minions of the United Nations at their luxurious compound by the sea, urging them to resort to force. As the peer of secular princes in a country that had no government—indeed, as the emissary of the Pope—in protocol I outranked everybody, and the minions dared not ignore me. Finally they bent their quibbling regulations, cobbled together their own armed columns of Somali thugs under the rubric of "technical assistance," and unleashed them on the docks.

Some minor fighting followed: for several days the brigands were chased away. During the peaceful intermezzo, I took over.

As trucks of Caritas, the United Nations, and the Red Cross converged on the seaport, I in my white and scarlet stood by the docks, directing traffic, telling the drivers where to queue their trucks, barking orders at everybody in English, Italian, and Arabic. Again I glimpsed my eternal colour cinema, making me quintuple the size of life.

I ran up gangplanks, hopped on cranes, hastened from ship to ship, organising the debarkation of all those sacks of rice, wheat, beans, maize, and powdered milk; all those crates of soap, plasma, insulin, penicillin, and morphine. Swiftly I decided to ignore the bills of consignment, dividing the food and medicine equally amongst the queuing trucks: not content to watch the Somali labourers hoist their cargo, I thrust in my hands to help them heap up the sacks and crates, for hour upon hour, fanatically. *"Heave-ho,* mates! *heave-ho!"* I sang out, jubilantly. *"Heave-ho heave-ho!"* they chanted back, jubilantly.

I reckoned to my Germans that within five days we had liberated five thousand metric tons of food and medicine—or enough to feed scores of thousands of Somali children for several weeks. In the terrible wet heat, never had I felt so sweat-drenched, tired, or fulfilled.

I returned to the Caritas compound with enough food and medicine to undertake a further mission, very dangerous—to cross No Man's Land in the capital's northern zone and replenish the needy Hospital of the Consolazione, run by Italian nuns, not far from the sea.

Down the hibiscus-scented drive, through the steel gate and the high wall, our convoy set forth—Mussolini at the head with his blue submachine gun on the roof of his Toyota, following him our armada of a dozen vans and trucks, flying white and yellow papal flags; bumping over several miles of trash and rubble until we reached the devastated streets and boulevards, like Berlin on the day that Adolf Hitler shot himself.

In No Man's Land, as we crossed the line of demarcation dividing Mogadishu between its warring clans, my Somali driver ran over a machine gun. When we reached the northern sector, we were at once surrounded by fifty armed and screaming boys, threatening us with death for crushing their gun. Scores of thin and hungry little children converged on us as well, all begging for our food. Receiving none, they joined in shouting, "SHOOT THEM! SHOOT THEM!" Mussolini and my other bodyguards crouched behind their trucks, aiming their rifles at the boys and children.

"DON'T FIRE!" I roared at Mussolini, leaping from my Land Rover, running to a truck and hurling with all my force sack after sack of rice and wheat at the rabid boys and children. An older man frisked me, thrusting with his bronze rapacious fingers beneath my robes to grope not only in my trouser pockets but at my buttocks and genitalia. In my shirt pocket, he touched my purse of several thousand dollars, ripping my soutane as he plucked it out. The boys and children attacked the man, demanding their fair share—forgetting us.

We drove on.

The Hospital of the Consolazione stood on a plateau, before it a wide piazza of pure white sand, the hospital itself all bleached high walls and lofty towers, once a military prison built by the defunct dictatorship, and in the cellar torture chambers. Virginal, blue-veiled Italian nuns—so many of them young, unwrinkled, beautiful—wept and sang hosannas as they rushed across the immense and windy plaza to kneel before me and kiss my ring. "The Holy Father loves you," I told the twenty sisters. I traced his vicarious benediction over their bowed and wimpled heads, then almost with passion I kissed them each.

My trucks backed up to the hospital's doors to unload my medicine and food—great tins of plasma, antibiotics, morphine; our remaining sacks of rice, wheat, black beans. When we visited the wards, thronged with men and boys and rosy gunshot wounds, I could not bear the stench. I followed the sisters out to the dunes of the sea, where they laid out a picnic luncheon in my honour.

Not far from us, a hundred children, boys and girls, trudged along the beach. The nuns conjectured that they were orphans from the north, roaming in search of food. Suddenly beneath their tread the beach began to blow up.

Small plumes of sand erupted in dull reports as the children scattered now this way and now that—toward the grassy dunes above them or downward to the foamy waves of bluest sea, shrieking, but in their haste they hit more land mines. To this day, as I write it down, I can hear their screams, see their little toes and feet being blasted off, brown flesh and bits of rag burping from the puffs of smoke; and their blood, their carmine blood, staining the creamy sand.

From our picnic blankets the nuns and I stood up, crying out together, "*Salve Regina, mater misericordiae! Vita, dulcedo, et spes nostra, salve!* Hail holy Queen, Mother of mercy—our life, our sweetness, and our hope! To thee do we cry, poor banished children of Eve, to thee do we send up our sighs, mourning and weeping in this vale of tears!" And as we did so we hurried to the periphery of the carnage, snatching as we could this body and the next, bloody but still breathing.

On the dunes, as I walked back toward the Hospital of the Consolazione bearing a mutilated child, I said quietly to the television cameras, "This is also your fault. Those mines were planted in that beach by cruel Somali warriors, but they are the sin as well of you in the West—Americans, British, French—who sent them to this poor nation. Now you're sending food and medicine—thank you—but you allowed your governments to traffic in all this blood for alliances and money. You dumped those land mines on this country." I turned and pointed to the beach. "Can you see those dead children?"

At dawn, I left the capital for Baidoa, nearly two hundred miles to the northwest, at the interior of Somalia, and the infamous centre of the famine. My guard was smaller now—an armed truck before my Land Rover, another in my wake, but I could not shake off Mussolini. He sat on my front seat, wedged between my driver and another thug, all three of them aloft on their twigs of *qat,* and talking, talking, talking.

As Mussolini jabbered he turned now and again to smile at me with jagged teeth, beneath his shaven head and black eyes, swollen and dancing in their orbits. I tried to contemplate the flora and fauna—the herds of goat and camel along the unpaved roads, the coarse savannah grass, the euphorbia plants whose flowers had no petals, the stunted scattered trees of camel-thorn dead from drought—and then to read my daily Office; but as the journey proceeded Mussolini was loath to grant me peace. "*Andiamo al Italia, baba? A Roma, baba? Alla Romagna, baba? Insieme, baba, Lei ed io?* Oh, baba, baba, baba!"

He began to quarrel with his companions, whacking each of them in the face; he practised his Fascist salute, punching his fist through the roof; he sang what he said were Fascist hymns in his terrible, contralto Italian. At midday we reached Baidoa.

For my sins of luxury at Mogadishu, the Caritas residence on the main road rebuked me. It was a primitive villa behind an iron door and a cement wall; all squeezed, dark stucco, malodourous from sticks of wood burning in the kitchen, and with such an economy of space that I was obliged to bunk in a sultry room with three snoring Germans. We were deprived of plumbing, attending to our hygiene in the broken lavatory with buckets of soapy water. We could not, thank God, accommodate my bodyguards, forcing Mussolini to seek his lodgings across the road.

Baidoa was even more hungry and more violent than Mogadishu. It seemed that a machine gun was mounted on every roof; men were mowed down as they came out of coffeehouses for reasons I could not fathom; on the roads, spectral women and children teemed in slow motion. At the municipal cemetery, hundreds of corpses—infants, so very many of them— were interred each day. Early in the mornings, in my white and crimson I loitered by a shattered wall at the edge of that graveyard.

Not daring to intrude on the mourners' Muslim sorrow, as the bodies were hurled into common pits I mumbled Latin prayers—from the Tridentine Masses against Cattle Plague and In Time of Famine. "*Da nobis, quaesumus, Domine* . . . we beseech Thee, Lord, to banish this dire famine, that the hearts of men may know that all such scourges proceed from Thy wrath and are stayed by Thy mercy." The farms of Baidoa were plagued as well by drought, so for good measure I added the Mass for Rain. "O Lord, we do humbly beseech Thee, deign to pour down, upon this poor parched earth, Thy showers from Heaven . . . *fluentis caelestibus dignanter infunde.*"

Perhaps for rain I prayed too well. Within but several days the heavens opened, turning Baidoa into a pudding of mud. At the villa in the late afternoons I lay on my iron cot, my bones stiffened by the damp, receding into troubled sleep, waking up, and dozing off again. I dreamt that I sat in the Sistine Chapel, impatient for the other cardinals to elect me Pope. The ballots were collected and read out, but the results were barren, and we had no Pope. At last—unclearly—something happened. I saw a walking white soutane, but not the face above it, yet as a disembodied hand held up a looking-glass . . . and I nearly glimpsed the face . . . another hand shook my shoulder.

"Lordship?"

I woke up.

"Adrian?"

He stood above me, smiling for an instant. Did I say Adrian? Do I mean St Francis? Believe me, he was St Francis. He wore a long brown poncho wet with rain, resembling the habit of the Friars Minor, and a monkish hood about his head. His blondish beard was turning grey, in repose his mouth turned downward, and his eyes were sunken deeper still from enduring pain. Groggily I asked, "Why are you here?"

"I heard that you were, Eminence."

"And Fechatu?"

"Fechatu at last has food. They didn't need me any longer. I gave them my truck."

"What will you do?"

"I'm looking for a job."

"Dear Adrian, you can work for me."

"Doing what?"

"Feeding empty-bellied waifs."

"I'll take it."

"Dear God, your hearing's better."

"*¿Cómo?*"

✛

FIFTY-FIVE

At Rome, the Pope undertook a hunger strike to dramatise his solidarity with the starving children of Somalia—and of the Sudan, Angola, Liberia, and Mozambique, where other bestial civil wars had produced like famines, killing millions. For a week the Supreme Pontiff ate only unbuttered biscuits and sipped cups of black unsweetened tea.

At Baidoa, I emulated him, for ten days living on tea and biscuits. My fast was not difficult, and busily I went on feeding my empty-bellied waifs. My pinched childhood at my abbey in the Vaucluse, my endless walks, my repose at night on hard wood, all my monastic penances to scourge my lust, had prepared me well. Forgive me: I'm boasting. But at the least you should understand that in my sinful vanity I ate little anyway—and in consequence my body, like my beliefs, was as hard as rock. At night, as I lay awake on my empty stomach, hearing my Germans snore and the ceaseless burping of automatic guns beyond my window, I brooded on the reasons for the Somali famine. Yes, there had been drought, but even with the drought, the starvation could not in truth be blamed upon the wrath of God.

The famine was man-made, caused by the Counter Revolution against a ghastly dictatorship in the mould of Mao and the devastation in its wake as myriad clans and sub-clans feuded for supremacy, armed with the very guns and bombs that the Russians and the Americans after them had bestowed on the bloody dictator. Nor could the hunger be blamed on overpopulation: huge Somalia was underpopulated. I blamed the rich West as much as I did the Somali thugs and politicians. You of the rich West dumped arms on manifold poor nations like Somalia, but also in your luxury you largely refused to share your other plenty with pitiful nations throughout the tropics—until famine hit them and you did a wee bit. Such also was the judgement of my Pope.

Often from Baidoa, in the tiny dark office of the Caritas villa, I turned on the wireless telephone and talked to the Pope. The machine, I surmised, was some sort of computer, relaying my voice to Mogadishu or to Nairobi in Kenya before bouncing it off a satellite and sending it to Rome. By punching a few buttons I could dial the Pontiff's private telephone directly; likewise he rang me up in remote Baidoa.

"I watch you nearly every night on television," said the Supreme Pontiff. "Your images are electrifying Europe and America—quite as I intended. Is it possible, dear Augustine, that God will grant my prayer—and finally the world will end all war and famine? Ha! Some of the cardinals, I suspect, are jealous that you're such a star. Must your guards be so nasty to the children?"

"I can not control them, Most Holy Father," said I.

"Then get new guards."

"Do you want me dead?"

"Is Baidoa that dangerous, Augustine?"

"Can't you hear the shooting?"

"Sweet Virgin Mother, shall I call you home?"

"No, Holiness! When I entered the Sacred College, I took a vow 'even to the shedding of my blood.' "

"Can't you wait—as We did—until you're Pope?"

Adrian slept in the villa's smoky kitchen. He seemed still too frail from his Mexican torture, so I forbade him to participate in my hunger strike. Otherwise he vied with me in his exertions against the famine.

We began early each morning by visiting the Bakaraha, Baidoa's great open market, groping from a valley and across a bridge until it blended into a little hill of shacks and doum palm. In the wooden stalls, as the heavens drizzled or the sun blazed down, plagues of horseflies feasted with impunity on golden dates and grey shanks of mutton amongst prodigious quantities of soap, shampoo, mouthwash, plastic chairs, French spark plugs, Egyptian cigarettes, Italian toothpaste—and mountainous sacks of stolen grain that read A GIFT OF THE PEOPLE OF THE UNITED STATES OF AMERICA. Corpses of adults and children lay randomly about, having heaved their final sighs the night before, but we stepped over them, content to leave the labours of inter- ment to Somalis. Men and women resembling zombies wandered up and down the labyrinthine paths, begging food, receiving none, but likewise we ignored them.

Live children were our prey: as their shrunken bodies toddled from the shadows of the misty marketplace or stood in mud beneath the pitiless sun, raising their tiny palms and seeking scraps of nourishment, we scooped them up and loaded them whimpering or silent onto the rear of our red Isuzu truck. When we had a full truck of children, we drove off—to the feeding centres of the Red Cross, the United Nations, Irish nuns, but today all were overwhelmed and they refused our children. I remonstrated with the Irish nuns. "How dare you refuse?" I thundered at the Sister Superior.

"We're running out of food, Your Eminence!" she shouted back at me.

"You've plenty of provisions from the Red Cross!"

"They didn't tell you? The Red Cross warehouse is empty! Last night, it was looted again!"

"Sister, *please.*"

"Oh, come in, Eminence, and see for yourself."

I followed her inside her cement hospital, where again I flinched from the human stench and the spectacle of children throughout the rooms and corridors lying serenely head to head in the last languid hours of their starvation. We drove on to a long stone wall and an iron gate and an Islamic orphanage within the grounds of a colossal mosque. The turbaned sheikh came down a hundred steps to greet me, clenching my hand through the iron bars, but he would not unlock his gate. "What can I do, *Eminenza*?" he asked me in Italian. "Look!" In his robes he turned away from me, pointing to a courtyard of muddy earth and patchy grass, where hosts of naked orphans buzzed, running about or rather most of them merely seated vacantly beneath pavilions of thorn and bramble, clutching bowls of bright red plastic, all waiting for their porridge. "I can feed them today," the sheikh lamented through the bars, "but who will feed them tomorrow?"

As for Caritas, we had no feeding centre; from Nairobi on charter aircraft we flew many tons of food to Baidoa airport, but constantly our trucks were intercepted by gunmen on the airport road or hijacked by our own Somali drivers; and what little food and medicine got through we had given to the nuns and mosques. In despair we drove our children to a field of weeds on the main road, not far from our villa, and encamped them there with nothing. Adrian jumped back into our Isuzu, saying, "Wait here."

"Where are you going?" I shouted at him.

"What?"

He rumbled off. I remained in the field with Mussolini, my other guards, and my forty waifs, wondering what Adrian was about, murmuring to myself, "There they go again"—whenever fresh bursts of gunfire broke out from the street beyond or from the further coffeehouses in the town. At the edge of the field crouched a dozen youths—all plaid skirts, M-16s and Kalashnikovs on their shoulders, before a campfire—boiling their noonday tea in tin cans. As they drank they sang a sort of chant, almost Gregorian in its resonance. "Da-da-DAH-da, da-da-DAH-da. Da-da-DAH-da, da-da-DAH-da." I thought of the *Dies Irae,* and to get away from Mussolini and his dreams of Italy I wandered deeper into the weedy field, not far from the crouching gunmen, chanting with them. *"Dies IRae, dies ILLa, Solvet SAE-Clum in favILLa, Teste DAVid, cum SiBYLLa . . . !"* Day of wrath! O day of mourning, See fulfilled the prophets' warning, Heaven and earth in ashes burning . . . ! Hours later, Adrian returned.

Our truck was full of sacks of grain and powdered milk, cans of olive oil, cups and bowls, forks and spoons, pots and pans, metal poles, yards and yards of green plastic sheet—whatever might be needed to make a feeding centre. I asked Adrian, "Where did you get it?"

"¿Cómo?"

"DID GUNMEN SELL IT TO YOU?"

"I told Your Lordship not to shout. Does it matter how I got it? Let's feed these waifs."

In the weeks that followed, our green tent thrived. From Baidoa and the countryside, orphans and more orphans, children and more children on their mothers' backs, descended on us in relentless waves. How proud I was of Adrian, quondam Marquis of the Bells, as I watched him run the place, so well prepared by his labours with destitute Latinos on the Rio Grande, wearing in rain his monkish poncho or in fine weather his gunman's T-shirt, I AM THE BOSS. How he hopped about on his bare wounded feet, mixing in metal vats his various porridges of rice, wheat, maize, beans, and oil; serving them in those bowls of bright red plastic to our helpless waifs and such quantities of other children as famished as their mothers, adding as their beverage tin cups of milk; attending to the sicker cases by pricking their piebald flesh with needles and feeding them through tubes.

Observe an abandoned naked child, not yet five years old, crouching at the edge of our encampment, whimpering and waiting to be fed. He defecates, or rather he squirts a geyser of brown water mixed with blood and blobs of mucus. He is all skull, save for his wisps of hair the colour orange and falling out. His teeth, a dazzling white, protrude; he no longer has a body, only a shrivelled baked potato beneath his skull, and what used to be his limbs we might compare to withered twigs. Where his navel used to be we see a pear, or what physicians would call a hernia; so many sores and ulcers cover him he seems now not a baked potato but a toad. We know that worms are chewing on his bowels, but does he suffer also from malaria, pneumonia, hepatitis, meningitis, tetanus? If he lives, can he avoid *cancrum oris,* an affliction of the underfed that will eat away his face?

Adrian emerges from our tent, picks the child up, and carries him to a little bed, where he attaches his new patient to dangling plastic tubes, seeking to cure his dehydration with solutions of water, salt, and glucose, though probably the task is doomed. Besides, we are overwhelmed. Repeat this scene of spastic toads, of defecating baked potatoes, a hundred, six hundred, a thousand times: like the Red Cross and the Irish nuns, we begin to turn away more tides of starving children.

I help out, often on my hands and knees, feeding the waifs, cleaning up the mess, but unlike me Adrian avoids cameras. He seems eerily detached, pretending always to be deaf whenever the oafs of television order him about or even on occasion when I chat with him fondly.

"Do you remember, dear Adrian, of my dream so long ago at Northwood Hall—that you were lost in the depths of Africa and I went there TO LOOK FOR YOU? And do YOU REMEMBER . . ."

"What . . . what . . . what?"

I persevere in my macabre theatre, to edify the West holding up this phantom of an infant and now the next, my robes all bruised by sweat and porridge, in the background my feeding centre mobbed with raucous naked children and their mothers in an otherwordly greenish haze. I come upon another waif.

"Hello, darling child," I tell her. "Yes, you've parasites and diarrhea, but God in Heaven loves you still. Let me scoop you up and kiss you."

British television: "Hold the imp a little higher, Gus."

American television: "Couldn't you weep a little, Gus?"

Italian television: "Right, Goose. *E più alta la testa!*"

Mussolini became more hard to manage, hounding me so much for Rome and the Romagna that I shunned him at the villa and the feeding tent. Perhaps grasping finally that he would never go to Italy with me, he hallucinated of a solitary pilgrimage that I would finance. Nor had he a passport. "I'll steal one, baba." For our protection in Baidoa, we had been paying Mussolini and his thugs five hundred American dollars a day; now he demanded twice that. "But Baidoa is so expensive, baba. *E tanto pericoloso!*"

"*Va bene*, you mouthy little Fascist," I snapped at him. "Here, take your bloody dollars and be gone."

The month now was November. From the capital, Caritas sent German nurses to help us at Baidoa, allowing Adrian to itch for Buffa, a crossroads some hundred miles to the south—where the famine was known to be worse! With misgiving I informed Mussolini of our mission soon to Buffa: thus he raised his price for our protection to two thousand dollars a day. The sum seemed so exorbitant that even Adrian grew cross. At the villa that evening, he asked me, "When does Mussolini go to bed?"

"He never goes to bed," I answered. "He spends all night in the coffee-houses, making speeches and chewing *qat*."

"I know half the gunmen in Baidoa," said Adrian. "I'll hire another bunch."

On that errand, he hurried out. I sat sat down at the desk of our little office, opening a bundle of correspondence addressed to me at Rome and forwarded by Caritas: much business from the Vatican, and finally a letter from Adrian's mother. My right hand trembled as I opened it.

My dear Lord Cardinal,

In the sixth chapter of St Matthew, our Divine Saviour tells the multitude, "Take heed that ye do not your alms before men, to be seen of them: otherwise ye have no reward of your Father which is in Heaven. Therefore when thou doest thine alms, do not sound a trumpet before thee, as the hypocrites do in the synagogues and in the streets, that they may have glory of men."

I recalled those verses of the Evangelist as I watched Your Eminence on television amid the starving hordes of Ethiopia and Somalia, feeding the multitude. Once, I think, I glimpsed my son near you as he ran away from the camera, unwilling to be photographed, hiding his head. As for your own theatrical performance, for my Scriptural reasons I could not applaud.

I will never forgive you for separating me from my son, first by encouraging his follies in Texas and Mexico, and then for having inspired his wanderings in dangerous Africa. It has been so long since I have seen Adrian that I wonder, Will he ever return to me at Northwood Hall?

How bitterly I recall the day that I met you at Doria-Pamphili palace. You wore an impeccable soutane of black and purple; I wore turquoise sweaters and white pearls. In one of those enormous gilded mirrors, by chance our eyes met—mine of ice-blue and yours so dark I wondered, Are they sinister? You were quite handsome. We were both so vibrant, and so young. My hair was so very blond, yours so very black. We were so madly attracted to each other.

I had *heard* all your little Mozart jokes. I pretended to be amused because I assumed that you needed Urban's money and you were trying to impress me. Your stammering story about Velázquez and Innocent X was one of the oldest chestnuts in the lore of art—except that it never happened to Velázquez and Innocent X. It was Titian who dropped his paints and brushes, and the Holy Roman Emperor, Charles V, who picked them up. Innocent X never said to Velázquez, "Even the Vicar of Christ stoops for Velázquez." It was Charles V who said to Titian, "Even Caesar stoops for Titian." Anyway, the story is probably apocryphal—much like Your Lordship-Eminence.

The other evening, as I walked through my rooms at Northwood Hall, I glimpsed myself in a Baroque mirror: a stooped arthritic woman, skin wrinkled and turning to parchment, entering deeper and deeper into the darkness of old age, alone in this immense house without my son. I brood morbidly about the reasons. In my research of late, as I reread Shakespeare's *King Henry the Eighth*, I came upon the passage in which Queen Katharine upbraids Lord Cardinal Wolsey. "My drops of tears," she tells him, "I'll turn to sparks of fire." Wolsey tells her, "Be patient yet." The Queen replies, "I will, when you are humble. I do believe, induced by potent circumstances, that you are mine enemy."

Thus do I believe of Your Eminence: you are mine enemy. You have ever pretended devotion to my husband and to me; yet as the years have passed, your real wish has become too clear—that my son should play fantastical rôles you have imagined for him so that in the end you might take his fortune for the Church. As a mother, I shall never cease to reproach myself for having entrusted my son's moral education to Your Eminence. As a writer, though I loathe excessive speech, with utter justice I can accuse you, Lord Cardinal, of treachery.

I have read in the press that Your Eminence may succeed to the papacy. Should that happen—and may God forbid—I shall continue to revere the Office, even as I recoil from the priest who wears its robe.

Kissing the Sacred Purple,

DIANA DUCHESSE NORTHWOOD

I took up my pen and foolscap, intent on writing a serene and reasoned answer, refuting the injustice of Diana's accusations, but my hand faltered as I recognised that it would do no good. Mourning, I asked myself, Is this the woman whom I loved in Rome?

In an hour, Adrian returned. I said nothing of his mother's letter: I had already burned it in the villa's stove.

At midnight, we escaped Mussolini. Under Adrian's new guard, we set out in our Isuzu truck—laden with food and medicine—for the crossroads some hundred miles to the south at starving Buffa.

FIFTY-SIX

✛

At Buffa next morning, along the main road, peasants sat at campfires beneath the trees of camel-thorn, boiling grass for breakfast. Buffa had suffered not only famine but much war and slaughter. Behind the Caritas compound stood a little mortuary of mud brick piled with human skulls and children's bones, and beyond them the shallow graves of bloated corpses with their hands and feet sticking out.

So I slept at night with ghosts, but at least without my snoring Germans. My hosts in Buffa were French—a young man and a young woman, both nurses—and one Belgian: my Soeur Pauline.

Do you remember that some years before, the Soeur Pauline—unsatisfied with Rome and me—had begged to be sent back to Africa? In the capital she worked at length with Sisters of the Consolation; yet as hunger raged more brutally in the provinces, loyal to her valour she volunteered for Buffa.

She was busy in the village when we arrived, but when she returned to find me in the compound she embraced me and cried out, "Ah, Monseigneur! Monseigneur!"

"*Ma soeur, ma soeur ...*" I cried as gladly, clutching her.

The little nun had advanced well into her seventies; age had faintly gnarled her arthritic fingers; her movements seemed more stiff and painful, but was not her will more stalwart? As in the Congo and at Rome, still she spurned the fashion of modern nuns, wearing steadfastly her ample habit all of white, bound tightly with a rope cincture, black prayer beads dangling from it; beneath her veil her face and eyes remained rubicund and lucent, barely ravaged by the years.

"This is Adrian, *ma soeur*," said I.

"Can you nurse the sick?" she asked him.

"What?" said Adrian.

"Sometimes he's deaf, like you, my Sister."

"In Buffa with its guns, it's better to be deaf," she said.

I soon agreed with her. Only miles to the south and west, the army of a local warlord fought barbaric battles against troops still loyal to the deposed dictator. Trucks packed with armed men and boys of either camp passed through Buffa, pausing long enough to rape and plunder, steal goats and cows, set fire to crops of wheat and corn and the thatched roofs of houses. Our wireless telephone at Buffa was likewise broken down, forbidding me to talk to Baidoa, Nairobi, or Rome. Indeed the gunfire was so constant, the paths and nooks of that village so plentiful with danger, that after but a day my rude companions of international television became untypically faint of heart. They took flight back to Baidoa and Mogadishu—not much safer—leaving me cut off from the great world.

At Buffa as in the Congo the Soeur Pauline bore always a large straw basket, often plucking from it high-protein biscuits and various potions to comfort her sick and hungry; but amidst such warfare her ministrations were not easy to bestow. Her French companions were haggard from so much butchery about them; incessantly they smoked black tobacco, and their hands (like mine, again) trembled as they tended dying children in our small mud-brick infirmary.

Our whole compound was as grim—by the road a mud-brick edifice for storing food and medicine, then a yard and huts of mud plaster below roofs of twig. Our dining room of sorts was all wet branches and woven thatch, a shelter from the angry rain where Adrian and I slept on the earthen floor. Even in the early mornings, when at dawn I celebrated Mass in that crude refectory with Adrian as my acolyte, we heard gunfire from outside the compound. Yet for half an hour, my sacramental grace refreshed them all. I told the French nurses, *"Bon jour, Bernadette. Bon jour, Jean-Marc."*

"Bon jour, Monseigneur!" they answered.

"Good morning, Adrian. *Bon jour, ma Soeur Pauline.*"

"Bon jour, Monseigneur!" replied my acolyte and nun.

"Voici ce matin la messe en temps de guerre."

Thus I said the Latin Mass in Time of War, evoking Christ's prophecy that "nation shall rise up against nation, and kingdom against kingdom, and there shall be pestilence, and famine, and earthquake"—begging His deliverance. Next morning, I said the Mass in Time of Pestilence: imploring Him to stay the hand of the Avenging Angel that "he make not the land more desolate nor destroy every living soul." Upon the morrow, I said the Mass Against Evildoers: "Crush, we beseech Thee, O Lord, the pride of our enemies, and humble their impudence by the power of Thy right hand . . . *dexterae tuae virtute prosterne.*"

Believe me, we needed the protection of such prayers. Outside, the warfare waxed more fiercely. Russian guns fought American guns; automatic Russian rifles fought semiautomatic Russian rifles; American bazookas fought Israeli Uzis. The clan of the Rahanwein battled subdivisions of the clan Darod; the sub-clan of the Marehan rampaged against subdivisions of the clan Hawiye—on and on in that vast apiary of nomadic clans and sub-clans and divisions of divisions of divisions: compounded, inscrutably!

In that environment, Adrian and my Soeur Pauline took to each other as bumblebees and sunlight take to honeyed flowers. Soeur Pauline had imported from her long residence in the Congo the notion that she was endowed with *dawa:* immunity to bullets. She communicated her enchantment to Adrian, who with the passing days took for granted his own invulnerability to bullets. Either that, or he did not care whether he lived or died.

From the compound, I followed the two of them one morning as far as the road, but against the bullets flying between the doum palms yonder I dared not venture further; so I blessed them both and then turned back. On they walked towards the swarming village, laden with vaccines and syringes to inoculate thousands of small children against tetanus and typhoid. Out there on the long road, gunmen might shoot at the French and me, but they never seemed to shoot at little veiled and wimpled Soeur Pauline, or at Adrian in his jagged jeans and torn T-shirt—I AM THE BOSS—in the shadow of her protection. Early that afternoon, the pair of them returned, unscratched and joking. "We vaccinated three thousand children," said the Soeur Pauline.

"Miraculous," I rejoiced.

"Eh, Monseigneur?"

"Miraculous," I repeated.

"Eh, Monseigneur?"

"WHERE'S YOUR HEARING AID?"

"I dropped it somewhere here—in the refectory—during Mass."

"LET ME LOOK FOR IT."

On my hands and knees, I searched for her contraption upon the moist earth.

"A cardinal need not crawl on his hands and knees," said she.

"Here it is!"

"Is Your Eminence becoming less self-absorbed—like Adrian?"

I hoped so. Late that night, as the others tried to sleep, I sat alone with Adrian in the refectory under an oil lantern, I muttering as ever against each new round of shooting in the countryside beyond. I sang, *"Dies IRae, dies ILLa, Solvet SAEClum in favILLa."*

Adrian: *"Teste DAVid, cum SiBYLLa!"*

I asked, nodding towards the gunfire, "Is this your 'glamour of the poor'?"

"You sound like my mother, Lordship."

"Do you miss your mother?"

"What?"

"Like Soeur Pauline, YOU NEED A HEARING AID."

"Stop shouting! No, like Soeur Pauline, I love shutting out this world."

"Do you miss Diana?"

"Here—cut off in such a place—I miss her letters."

"And how you must surely miss your Northwood Hall, dear Adrian."

"I miss my gardens. My mock Greek ruins. And my birds. I was never so happy as with my father watching birds in Northwood Park. 'Look, son, a snowy owl. Look son, a laughing gull.' Ah, the woodcocks, whimbrels, yellow warblers. Blue heron? Indigo buntings, golden plovers? Ruby-crowned kinglets, green-winged teals. Buff-breasted sandpipers. Bobolinks. Blue grosbeaks, snow geese, a marble godwit. Screech owls? Bonaparte's gulls! I miss my mythic ruins, my rocky, mossy steps, my laurel shrubs. Nymphs of stone. Ionic pillars. Broken urns—with candelabra flowers?—growing wild. Statues of the gods on the shaven lawn at the edge of my birch forest. Never so happy as with my father in the birch forest. 'Look son, a laughing gull.' Did my father make his money by selling guns?"

"Dear God, I can not say."

"You heard his last confession, Eminence."

"So in Christ I must keep silent."

"What?"

I did not respond. Beneath his greying locks, Adrian's blue eyes flickered in their sombre grottoes; as he continued talking, his voice seemed cheerful, then almost fey. "*¿Cómo?* But he's been dead for twenty years. I went to Mexico—and endured torture—to atone for the death of my wife and son. I came to Africa—and who knows what might happen?—to atone for my father's arms trafficking."

Thousands about us were starving, but soon in Buffa with shells and mortars falling it became too dangerous even for Adrian and Soeur Pauline to leave our compound. Indeed they tried to leave, but I was stronger than the two of them together and I restrained them as I said, "You may be invulnerable to bullets but not to shells and mortars."

Nevertheless, next day, through all the fighting, an old man—his hair and beard dyed henna-orange according to Somali custom—came to us upon his camel bearing an infant child. "I'm from Ufuro," he told us in Italian. "Fifteen kilometres, but it took five days. Here is my granddaughter, little Faduma. Her parents have been killed. Save her?"

In the thatched infirmary, on stainless steel, the nurses Bernadette and Jean-Marc examined little Faduma, removing her saffron wrappings to discover another skull above shrivelled baked potato, withered twigs for arms and legs, and in her rags a wet patch of brown water, mucus, and blood. Bernadette said, "She doesn't weigh three kilos. Her brain is dead."

"Her brain is not dead," protested Adrian, touching the child's eyes. "Look—when I open her lids—Faduma moves her eyes."

"She has hepatitis and pneumonia," insisted Bernadette.

"She won't live till morning," agreed Jean-Marc.

"Adrian and I will save her," decided Soeur Pauline.

From that moment, Faduma belonged to Adrian and my Soeur Pauline: fondly they bathed her, weighed her, attached her flesh to intravenous tubes of water, salt, and glucose; keeping watch on her in the infirmary that night with Mahmoud, the crouching grandfather. At dawn, she breathed still, though barely. Would that we had only Faduma to worry us in the days that followed.

We began to be attacked, and we knew that we might be killed. Our thuggish guards, sprawled with automatic rifles on the roof of the mud-brick store, did their best to defend the compound, armed villagers of Buffa bravely helping them, taking aim at marauders from the tops of trees. The marauders were men and boys in military dress, troops of the clan Darod, eager to capture all of our dwindling provisions for their hungry army.

May I swear that we all of us would have been overrun and butchered had not God thrust down His hand to our predicament to shed a portion of His grace?

God, as we know, acts through men, His agents. In the event, though I hesitate to say it, His agents were the American Marines. Ten days before, on my little transistor box, I learned that the Marines had landed at Mogadishu and seized the airport at Baidoa. Now their armoured columns groped out to the south and Buffa, which they reached in late December, chasing the warring clans back into savannah grass, camel-thorn, doum palm—from which convenient cover they sniped at the Marines.

By our restored wireless telephone, we learned that Caritas would send us trucks with grain and medicine to relieve Buffa's famine. On Christmas Eve, Adrian, the Soeur Pauline, and I mounted our red Isuzu truck to drive out on the main road to greet the convoy.

It was midafternoon. From the brown sky, a warm drizzle fell. I drove, my Soeur Pauline squeezed between Adrian and me on the cabin's black seat. Ah, in the distance, beneath camel-thorn and doum palm, there came the convoy. We drove forward to the outskirts of the village, honking and waving, but the first trucks kept rolling—and the road was so narrow that within moments we became wedged between a pair of trucks trying to proceed in the direction opposite. The convoy halted.

Behind us and ahead of us, gunfire erupted. At first we heard the burping of automatic guns and then the bursts of bazookas and maybe of grenades also. Adrian asked languidly, "Are we under attack, my lord?" Men with assault rifles rushed past us. From the roofs of the trucks, the convoy's guards responded in kind, with their rifles and submachine guns now raking the bush at the side of the road, now aiming at the mob of plunderers climbing the trucks and grasping for the sacks of food.

We were in a grove of sorts, everywhere about us coarse savannah grass and those plants of euphorbia whose flowers bore no petals. From such vegetation, at the roadside near Adrian, Mussolini emerged: in his khaki jodhpurs and muddy boots, beneath his T-shirt—COOL—and his unnatural eyes suggesting a dream of *qat*. He aimed a German Luger pistol at my head—but Adrian, too quick for him, raised his body from the seat to shield my Soeur Pauline and me. Mussolini's bullet struck Adrian in the back of his skull.

Instantly at a sharp angle I zoomed our truck into thorn bush at my side of the road: as the shooting everywhere continued louder, I drove wildly further into a meadow of stunted grass, zigzagging, until at last the sound of gunfire faded. My Soeur Pauline, keening, cradled Adrian in her close embrace, but his bloodied head responded with no sound.

With my right hand I touched the rosary low in the pocket of my soutane, and silently I prayed:

Lord, whenever in the past I sought Thy favour, Thou didst grant it. When I asked for daily bread, grace to keep my vows, honours of the Church, You bestowed them on me a hundredfold. Did You not put Adrian here on earth as a new St Francis to feed the hungry and serve Your sacred name? Let him live and prosper in Your cause! I beseech Thee, Lord, Who hath never yet refused my prayer, do not refuse it now.

When we reached our compound, Adrian was dead.

Most of the food and medicine reached Buffa.

In our thatched refectory, as we gathered Adrian's things, the Soeur Pauline clasped and kissed me as my mother Lady Daphne never had, consoling me as she could.

"Ah, Monseigneur, Monseigneur. . . ."

"*Ma soeur, ma soeur . . . ma mère, ma mère. . . .*"

"Your face . . ." said she.

"Does it show such anger?"

"And sorrow . . . more than sorrow . . . terrible surprise."

"At GOD!"

The Marines brought in a helicopter to fly me with Adrian's body to Nairobi. I begged the Soeur Pauline to come with us, but she echoed Heaven and refused. She could not abandon baby Faduma—still breathing.

At Nairobi—just before I returned to Rome—I prayed over Adrian's body, then put it on an aeroplane for the United States and Northwood Hall. I believe that you will understand my reasons for not flying there with him to face his mother.

PART XII

+

THE
CONCLAVE

. . . CONCLUDED

+

⁜

The Book of Joel tells us that it shall come to pass afterwards that the Lord God will pour out His spirit upon all flesh; and that His sons and daughters shall prophesy; and that His young men "shall see visions"; and that His old men "shall dream dreams."

Adrian, I am certain, had seen visions. More, in his will he had bequeathed much of his fortune to the Church. However, as it came to pass, his surviving younger brother, the ugly duckling Pius, contested the will in the American courts. I wondered, Will the matter ever be settled? After Adrian's saintly and heroic death, no longer did I much care.

But wait: the other part of Joel's prophecy says that old men "shall dream dreams." Surely I qualified now to fulfill the Prophet Joel. When I returned to Rome from Africa, in age I had reached my middle sixties, and how very often did I dream dreams?

Some few of my dreams were of the papacy, but we shall come to that predicament. Against my prayers and deepest wishes, I continued also to dream of Lisa—sitting at my feet in Consalvi palace, as I played for her my transpositions of themes by Bach, and ballades by Chopin, full of yearning.

Indeed, amidst such dreams Lisa returned to Rome, appeared at my basilica in a white mantilla, and when my Mass was done she told me, "I was wrong, Augustine. You have continued to haunt me. Have you kept my rooms for me at Consalvi palace?"

In my robes I laughed and ran away from her, through the streets of Rome, dove into the River Tiber, and swam across the heaving waters into my palace, where I interred myself deeply in the crypt of my chapel, locked my tomb from the dark inside, then I swallowed the key.

Ha! Awake, Lisa's reappearance never happened—and it never would. Her farewell in New York City was more final and more beautiful than dreams.

By now she was nearly forty, to me still young. Probably she had much forgotten me—when she married or took another lover? Despite myself, but obedient to the Prophet Joel, I aged and dreamed.

Some little time passed.

On a late afternoon in June, the Slav Pope summoned me to his presence on the roof of the Apostolic Palace. When I came out of the lift, the roof appeared to be deserted. The Pontiff was not taking his daily stroll— hobbling, leaning on his cane, beneath the white-petalled trees—nor did he hover in his great hood above the green cupboards, tending his apiary. I heard a groan.

I hurried through the labyrinth, and found him in the apiary supine on the floor. Over his soutane he wore his thick apron, but only one of his rough gloves, and his beekeeper's hood lay away from him upside down. His face and right hand were all swollen flesh, the colour of magenta, covered with stings and lumps. I wondered swiftly, Did his heart fail? did he stumble against the boxes, angering his bees? Not a bee buzzed now: had they swarmed and taken flight? I knelt to grasp his body and prop him up, but he seemed blithe to remain supine because his gaze, a puffed-up violent blue, was fixed on Heaven.

He asked, not so much of me but I supposed of God, "Will the bees ever taste the honey that they harvest?"

As I pondered his riddle, his eyes shut and he died.

FIFTY-EIGHT

So ended a long—may I say very great?—pontificate. The world sighed, not all of the sighs wet with tears. In New York, a famous feminist remarked, "Sorry he got stung, but it served him right." I favoured another view: God, wanting him in Heaven, commanded the bees to send him hence. In the Basilica of St Peter's, before the College of Cardinals and watching Christendom, as Camerlengo and prince regent of the Holy Roman Church I sang his requiem in Latin and preached his eulogy, first in Italian, next in English, over his robed and wounded corpse. Then I set about to organise the Conclave that would elect the new Vicar of Christ—a duty I scrupulously pursued in the secrecy of the Apostolic Palace.

More, during the days that followed the papal funeral, in my Basilica of St Mary Major I celebrated Latin Masses for the Election of a Pope, for Humility, and for the Gift of Tears: "that by our sighs and floods of tears we may wash away the stain of sin and quench the flames of Hell." I made a show of those occasions.

From the glass and concrete railway station, I walked in my mourning purple scattering benedictions, behind an army of acolytes and bishops, to the Via Gioberti—all vagrants, money changers, pickpockets, loitering workless sallow youths of Sicily and North Africa, ageing ugly nasty little whores in stiletto heels and short pants—thence into the sunny piazza, thence beneath Fuga's balconied façade into the apse and the august vista of Ionic columns, beckoning me to the far sanctuary: portending the pilgrimage I must one day undertake through the valley of the shadow of death into the Kingdom of the World to Come.

When I mounted the marble pulpit and surveyed the throng, I remarked the faces not only of most of the world's cardinals but of a score of traditional Anglican bishops and indeed of several members of the British Royal Family who had abandoned the Church of England for the Church of Rome—the divines and dukes and princesses by their presence clearly yearning for my papacy. I had no mind to disappoint them. I declared that as we bid adieu to the twentieth century, the Conclave should enshrine the dead Pope's discipline and constancy of doctrine, but it must do more. It must choose as Sovereign Pontiff a priest on horseback.

As great as he was, the dead Pope had left unrealised his dream to gird the Roman Church against the culture of the world that was rising on the ruins of rationalism and the Enlightenment. In the eighteenth century, at the zenith of the Enlightenment, a demented monk had shouted at Pope Benedict XIV that the Antichrist had been born in the mountains of the Abruzzi. *"How old is the Antichrist now?"* Benedict XIV asked quietly. *"He is three years old!"* the monk howled. *"Then let my successor deal with him,"* replied that wry Pontiff. Today however the Antichrist is here, grown up, amongst us, and the new Pope must grapple with him—much as saints and mystics wrestled physically with Satan.

"Who is the Antichrist?" I asked in English. "The Antichrist is largely modern Western culture—where the unborn are spurned, abortion is a secular sacrament, the sick elderly are offered suicide, the Third World is an arms dump, the poor are told not to breed beyond the convenience of the rich, and where no authority is revered save within the Self.

"The world as it exists is repugnant to faith—but still the Church falters when so many of her priests imagine that by softening, sweetening, suffocating the rules of faith they can bend her beliefs to modern culture, itself so eager to crush the claims of faith. The Roman Church can prosper not merely by resisting pagan modern culture passively but by shouting from the housetops without embarrassment or shame—again and still again—her hallowed title to Divine truth. Only a Pope on fire with such conviction can grapple with the Antichrist."

Next morning, I entered the Conclave.

As I strode through the marble corridors towards the Sistine Chapel under the lunettes and frescoes—the last in that majestic procession of brother princes, we each of us in our full robes, preceded by our conclavists with rococo crosses and blazing candles and sweet incense—silently I thanked Christ for every joy and sorrow of my life.

"O Lord," I prayed, "I do graciously thank Thee for imposing upon my body the heavy cross of my sensuality. For too long I resisted my vocation to master my unruly flesh. Yet in my revolt against my sacred vows, I embarked upon my bittersweet enchantment with Thy holy Church, lasting throughout my lifetime and thrusting me at last close to Thee. Aah, what a *romance* my life has been!"

"The cup which my Father hath given me, shall I not drink it?"

The season was hot July. We were nearly on the eve of the Third Millennium. I was sixty-nine: an ideal age for the papacy.

You know also that on the Conclave's eleventh day, in the scrutiny of the afternoon, my ballots grew to sixty-one—only twenty short of the eighty-one I needed to be Pope. It appeared that the Slavic Pontiff's anointment of me as his heir apparent was at last producing an inexorable result. You remember that my saintly brother, Patrice Cardinal Zalula, was next; but at thirty votes his candidacy was the more and more diminished by my own. Besides, most cardinals did not believe that the Roman Church was yet ready for a black Pope. And Cardinal Zalula was too humble to aspire to the Supreme Pontificate.

On the Conclave's twelfth day, the curious marriage of progressive cardinals from north Europe and nostalgic Italian Eminences longing to retrieve the papacy for Italy—unnaturally conjoined to thwart me—began to erode badly. Their candidate—the faintly liberal Archbishop of Pisa—could garner but thirteen ballots.

Still, the cardinals of north Europe, forgetting nothing and forgiving nothing, remained so bitterly opposed to my papacy that they hatched a desperate plot—by sponsoring several candidates at once; by voting for cardinals from Latin America and the East, they gathering each but two or three votes, yet collectively they blocked me. The four Jesuit cardinals carried another secret "Exclusive" from the Society of Jesus to obstruct at whatever price my ascension to the Chair of Peter.

The two Benedictine cardinals favoured me. Like them, the cardinals of Africa—and their venerable brothers throughout the tropics of the poor—owed me much. Indeed, were the Conclave a political convention, I should have called in my notes.

Through my brokers in the City of London, my portfolio of bequests from the House of Northwood—and from benefactors among the nobility of Europe—had thrived handsomely, making me quite rich. I had generously shared my fortune by helping to finance hospitals and schools, cooperative farms and monastic seminaries, in the dioceses of cardinals from Peru to Zimbabwe. Papal decrees prohibited the electors from casting their ballots from motives of friendship or past favour. Indeed no Eminence owed me his ballot for the pontificate: to suggest so would reek of simony. To all such cardinals in the Conclave I was merely nice, never appealing to their powers of memory, always struggling to seem indifferent, never voting for myself or promoting by hint or murmur my own papacy: fatal.

You wonder whether my rise to within twenty ballots of the papacy was due only to the late Pope's benediction. Hardly: I had also to thank my brother, Patrice Zalula. Our past quarrels over the selection of bishops he had long forgotten. Without a word or glance of prompting from me, how quietly zealous he was in urging my cause!

I watched him whispering at frowning faces in the Sistine Chapel, or as we cardinals took coffee together in the Sala Regia, or in the corridors at late evening as he glided in his mozzetta and lace from prince to prince or detained them gently at the doors of their cells. I thought, How tall and bronze he is; of such grace and dignity in his movements; his manners of such natural charm and courtly resolution; this devout Prefect of Bishops; this exiled tribal boy from the great forest of the Congo; this *former leper* lacking toes—is he not a marvel of his race?

The cells of the cardinals throughout the sealed enclosure of the Conclave had been chosen by lot, but happenstance ordained that Cardinal Zalula and I should draw the cells numbered fifteen and sixteen respectively, side by side in the apartments of the Swiss Guard. These were "bed-sitting rooms" of Spartan comfort: cluttered with silver helmets and spiked halberds, furnished with iron cots, lumpy sofas, and frayed linen. In the middle of the night, as I lay awake on my naked bedstead, and I heard Patrice mumbling prayers in his sleep, I rejoiced for the day that I had saved his life— when I had landed on that little island in a tributary of the River Congo, aboard a motorboat with a leprous youth and my deaf nun, the Soeur Pauline.

Atop the hill, in the thatched mud hut, I shudder and shrink anew from the stench of excrement, from the sight of my brother cardinal lying foetus-like upon the earth, clad only in a filthy bathing costume, his ankle chained to a stake, a pair of toes missing from his quondam leprosy. I fall weeping to my knees to kiss his wounds, as I might have kissed the wounds of Christ.

At dawn I rose from my cot, and barefoot in my red pyjamas I peered through the curtains of Patrice's glass door. In his own red pyjamas, he knelt on the tiles, his back to me, his arms spread wide, before his Baroque crucifix, intoning again and again in his native Balomingo, "*Mokonz oloyokela, Kristo olondimela, Mokonz oloyokela.*" Lord have mercy, Christ have mercy, Lord have mercy. An hour later, when he came out of his room fully robed and he walked beside me to Mass in the Pauline Chapel, I caught the scent of his flesh. He had the odour of sanctity.

After Mass, as we all of us took breakfast of coffee and bread beneath

Vasari's apocalyptic murals in the Sala Regia, Cardinal Zalula continued to lobby for my papacy in tones too discreet and far for me to hear. I asked myself, Is he about this at least in part because in the Congo I saved his life?

During the scrutinies that morning, my fortunes rose by nine ballots. Still I failed by eleven ballots to pluck the crown. But my papacy seemed to my brother princes to be imminent.

Again in the Sistine Chapel I heard allusions to Sacred Scripture in louder whispers as cardinals gazed at me, I standing lonely and apart at the foot of the high altar, my head raised to the *Last Judgement*—now my right hand trembling slightly. Again I asked myself, Must I go on with this, my greatest theatre—my sacred choreography, that dance of ceremonial humility hallowed down the centuries—and that now more than ever I know needs to be fulfilled before I can be anointed by the finger of the Holy Spirit?

Before all the cardinals I withdrew across the Sala Regia to the Pauline Chapel, where—below the shrouded tabernacle, beneath St Paul blinded on the road to Damascus and St Peter crucified upside down—I knelt and prayed, my body bent low in supplication, my face buried in my hands as though like Christ's they sweated blood.

In a low whisper, I recited the imperative verses from St Matthew Twenty-six and St John Eighteen. " *'O my Father, if it be possible, let this chalice pass from me: nevertheless not as I will, but as Thou wilt. O my Father, if this chalice may not pass away, except I drink it, Thy will be done. The cup which my Father hath given me, shall I not drink it?'* "

I added, as I knew I must, and striking my breast thrice, as I knew I ought: "*Domine, non sum dignus.* O Lord, I am not worthy. *Domine, non sum dignus.* O Lord, I am not worthy. *Domine, non sum dignus.* O Lord, I am not worthy."

When I rose from the sanctuary and turned to leave, a dozen watching cardinals at the rear of the chapel hurried out. That evening, after supper (I wondered, the Last Supper of the Conclave?) I paced the halls of the labyrinth around the Sistine Chapel, bemused by the buzzing of my brother cardinals as they sat in their cells and gossiped. No, gossip is not quite the word. I heard conversations more akin to music, to the *recitativo* of an opera, not so much by Mozart as by Rossini, the pitch and vibrato of voices resounding—now as tenor, now as baritone—against the marble walls in the sodden heat.

". . . but he has no pastoral experience."

"He was a pastor in the Vaucluse."

"He has grave defects of character."

"He played games with his vow of celibacy."

"Shocking."

"I'm convinced that he kept his vow of celibacy."

"In our age—more shocking?"

"His late Holiness wished him to be Pope."

"Our best reason not to elect him?"

"We'll have to speak to him in Latin."

"A dialogue of the deaf?"

"He'll revive the Imperial Papacy."

"Are we electing an emperor?"

"Is he bound intimately to Christ?"

"Did he discover Christ after receiving his Red Hat?"

"He's an excellent theologian—and deeply devout."

"But is his idea of the Church too aesthetic?"

"And too theatrical?"

"He is still fighting the Enlightenment!"

"And the French Revolution!"

"His orthodoxy is beyond reproach!"

"No, he is something of a Gnostic."

"He believes in Heaven only for the élite."

"Who hate this world?"

"Easy to hate this world—in the Palazzo Consalvi?"

"But he has such *flair*."

"And his finger in every pie."

"By indirection, he is manipulating the Conclave."

"Half the cardinals have taken money from him."

"He is not a Medici!"

"Nor Alexander VI!"

"Do we need another Renaissance pope?"

"He calls himself 'a priest on horseback.' "

"Do we need another Napoleon?"

"He thinks he's Cardinal Consalvi."

"He *is* Consalvi."

"No—he thinks he's Cardinal Merry del Val."

"He *is* Merry del Val."

"Neither was elected Pope!"

"He's the most cultured man in Rome."

"Is he overqualified for the papacy?"

"Do we need an American Pope?"

"He's not American."

"His mother was American."

"He hates American hedonism and cultural imperialism."

"So—the first American Pope."

"No—since Adrian IV—the first English Pope."

"He'll be the first Jewish Pope."

"The second, Your Eminence. You forgot Saint Peter. . . ."

In the second scrutiny next afternoon, my ballots rose to within seven of election.

That night, in my cell, lying on my frugal cot, I examined my sleepless conscience and then at last dozed off into a horrid nightmare . . . of memory . . . of which I shall tell you presently.

Before dawn, I woke up trembling. To escape the horror I leapt from bed into my lavatory and began to shave. Regarding my face in the looking-glass, I saw how aged I had become. My hair, though still abundant, had lost most of its silver as it turned to snowy white; my classical nostrils flared less for the slight wrinkles near them; my dark eyes beamed the tiniest flecks of yellow. My body as I have told you remained robust, but would my skin— like Diana's—soon enough faintly suggest parchment? The razor in my right hand shook more than ever spitefully.

Overnight, several of the elderly cardinals were seized by heat prostration. By its indecision and its length—a fortnight now—the Conclave was scandalising Christendom. We *had* to produce a Pope. I avoided luncheon in the Sala Regia and mounted to my cell on the floor above, where I sat on my armchair reading my Office and chewing an apple. After a quarter of an hour, knuckles rapped on my glass door. I admitted two Jesuit cardinals—an Italian and a Frenchman.

"We wish to vote for you," they said.

"Dear God! You're breaking ranks with your brother Jesuits?" asked I, astonished.

"As Pope would you suppress the Society of Jesus?"

"Must I remind Your Eminences that no cardinal can make promises in exchange for the pontificate? Your question suggests a bargain. A bargain smells of simony. According to Canon Law, simony incurs automatic excommunication. Do you wish an excommunicate as Pope?"

The Jesuits threw up their hands, turning on their heels to leave. I detained them, saying, "However . . . I might, without reproach, speak of the future in the vaguest fashion."

"Eminence?"

"Were I elected Pope—may God forbid—I should not hope to suppress any order of the Church."

"May we—canonically—ask further, would Your Eminence abolish the Society's unique pontifical status?"

"In the pure abstract, improbable—so long as the Society should be loyal to the Sovereign Pontiff."

They seemed relieved. Slyly the Frenchman asked, "Is it canonical to ask what name you will take?"

" 'Clement XV?' "

"But the last Pope Clement suppressed the Jesuits!"

"Ha-ha-ha! Tweaking your ear, Eminence! Maybe 'Innocent XIV'—or 'Urban IX'—*noms plus beaux, n'est-ce pas?*"

That audience improved my humour. Minutes later, Cardinal Zalula (with a triumphant smile that belied his singular humility) led to my cell a delegation of African and Latin cardinals. He said, "All of the Americans— and most of the French—have been suddenly inspired by the Holy Spirit.

Your Eminence is certain, now, to be Pope." Dazed, I sat down on my arm-chair. The cardinals queued to kiss my hands.

"Come now!" I protested as I let them do so—but echoing Pius VII when the cardinals kissed his hands on the eve of his pontificate: "I am not yet Pope!"

We adjourned to the Sistine Chapel for the scrutinies of the afternoon. Cardinal Zalula as Dean of the Sacred College sat before the high altar at his great shrouded table bearing the huge golden chalice. In order of seniority each Prince of the Church strode to the altar—swore an oath to God that he voted solemnly according to his conscience for the worthiest candidate to succeed St Peter—then proceeded to the precious chalice, thrusting into it his ballot.

Again I voted for my brother, Cardinal Zalula—as rock-like in the Faith as I, more heroic and saintly. When we all of us had voted, various cardinals, chosen by lot, thereupon assisted His Eminence Zalula in extracting the bal-lots and announcing the results.

As the ballots were drawn—and the name "Augustinus Cardinalis Galsworthy" was relentlessly called out in Latin—secretly I rejoiced. Yet from diffidence if not humility I craned my neck to gaze from my gilded chair at Michelangelo's vaulted ceiling. Again I wished to gasp at the Sibyls and Prophets and Stories from the Book of Genesis; at God separating light from darkness *("Lux ex Tenebris")*; at God making the sun and planets, fashioning fish and birds, creating Adam, and then Eve, banishing them both from the Garden of Eden—but I could not.

So I glanced above the altar to the *Last Judgement*. Likewise I wanted to be awed by the aloft and redeemed nude bodies; the angels astride clouds sounding trumpets, the writhing damned in Charon's boat sailing off to Hell, and by the thick-thighed Christ who sent them there—but I could not. All of the frescoes of late had been restored, erasing shadow, turning sombre colours gaudy, and replacing mythic grandeur with pictures that nearly seemed cartoonish. As though to compensate for glory lost, my mood turned sombre.

The Cardinal Dean continued counting out. My ballots reached eighty-one.

I had been elected Pope.

All of the cardinals had to be counted. The assistants to the Cardinal Dean continued to echo and cry out the scrutiny. As they did so, I—the Pope-elect—sat staring at my hands, repeating in whispers, *"Non sum dignus.* I am not worthy. *Non sum dignus.* I am not worthy. *Non sum dignus.* I am not worthy."

The counting ended. I had ninety-two ballots. Only twenty-eight cardi-nals had spurned me. A murmur rose from the Sacred College as Cardinal Zalula ascended from his table, strode solemnly to the altar, genuflected, and walked to me beneath my baldachin on the Epistle side of the chapel.

As he approached me, I knew that as soon as I consented to my election, the cardinals would tug on cords to lower the canopies over their chairs, leaving intact only the baldachin above my head. Having voiced my consent, I would glance to the black stove, where the ballots would be burned with dry straw, white smoke would puff from the roof of the Sistine Chapel, and the world would know that the Roman Church had a new Sovereign.

Then I would retire to a little chamber called "the Room of Tears" to be vested in my white soutane. From the central balcony of St Peter's, the Cardinal Dean would announce to mankind, *"Habemus papam."* I would bless the kneeling multitude. Within the fortnight I would be enthroned with the ageless prayer, "Know that thou art the Bishop of Rome, Vicar of Jesus Christ on Earth, Successor of the Prince of the Apostles, Supreme Pontiff of the Universal Church, Primate of Italy, Patriarch of the West, Servant of the Servants of God, and Father of All Princes and of Kings."

I remained seated until Cardinal Zalula stood before me to ask in Latin, "Dost thou accept thy canonical election to the Supreme Pontificate?"

From my golden chair, I rose to reply. In unison the other princes rose and turned towards me, awaiting my consent. Between the act of rising and the opening of my mouth, awake I dreamt my nightmare of the hour before dawn.

In my abbey of the Vaucluse, I implore my Father Abbot, "Please, beloved Father, I do not wish to be a priest." At the basilica of St Mary Major, in the moment I am ordained a priest, I think, Do I act according to my own wish? I choose to be a priest. Do I choose not to be a priest? My mother lies dying in Vermont, but I refuse to fly to her. At Florence, I enter my deep catacomb. On a road of the Vaucluse, I encounter my son. In the heart of Somalia, I read Diana's letter, calling me treacherous and apocryphal. At Buffa, I see Adrian shot dead. At the Palazzo Consalvi, my Soeur Pauline tells me, "Begin by being humble—like your brother, Cardinal Zalula."

Cardinal Zalula repeats his Latin question: "Dost thou accept thy canonical election to the Supreme Pontificate?"

"Nullo modo fieri potest," I answer. In English I add, "I can not."

In many tongues, one hundred and nineteen cardinals cry at me, "WHY?"

"Non sum d-d-dignus."

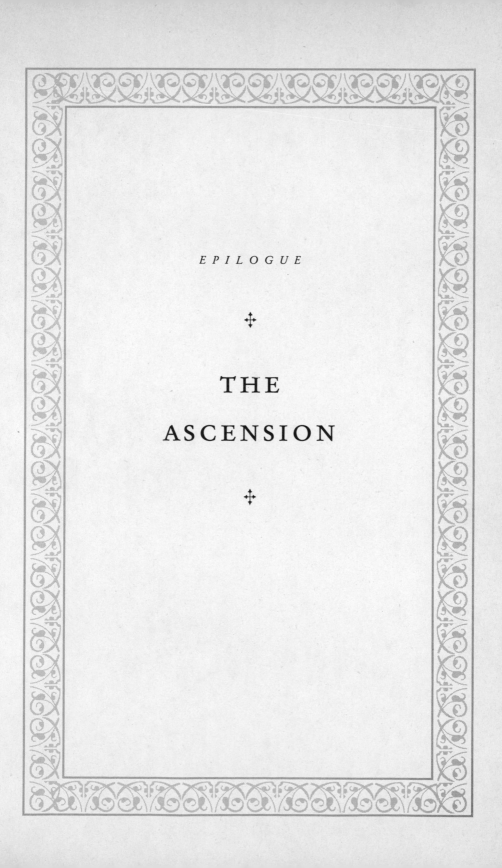

EPILOGUE

✜

THE
ASCENSION

✜

S everal days later, I knelt at the feet of the new Pope—former Prefect of Bishops and Dean of the Sacred College, quondam leper, the once Patrice Cardinal Zalula.

I refused all of his offers of high appointment in the Church, even his plea that I should accept my own archdiocese in France. I sought but a single favour.

I had been promoting the beatification of my Père Benoît, martyred during the war by the Gestapo. Now I begged the Pontiff to liberate the cause of the Père Benoît from the bureaucracy of sainthood and to declare him Blessed.

"Dear brother, it shall be done," promised His Holiness.

Then I bent my body to kiss his feet, and I backed out of his presence.

I did not resign my cardinalate. No earthly force, nor Satan with his works and pomps, could ever tear me from my holy priesthood and my Sacred Purple. However, I prepared to leave Rome. All of my Nubians—parents, children, and grandchildren—gathered in the grand salon of the Palazzo Consalvi to bid me farewell. Old loyal Ghassem—so lame he could barely walk, and now nearly blind—wailed without shame, certain that on this earth he would not see me again. Kamal, his eldest son, long my major-domo, asked me in Italian, "When will Your Eminence return?"

"Some day," I said.

For lest you think too highly of me for having refused the Supreme Pontificate, you should know that I had no mind to sell Consalvi palace and my books and treasures and to give the money to the poor. You also know me well enough to recognise that my character did not contain that kind of valour.

From Rome I flew to the Vaucluse, where for several recent years I had financed the restoration of my abbey. Indeed, the Benedictines had filled it up again with forty youthful monks who shaved their heads and celebrated the old Mass in Latin and practised traditional monastic work and penances: a grand revival of the Faith in the midst of pagan France and another of my sweet victories as a cardinal.

I told no one of my coming. Dressed in my black suit, at noon on Sunday I mounted anonymously to the Gothic chapel's choir loft and watched the monks sing High Mass at the altar below my gallery.

There amongst them, in a black tunic, belt, and scapular, his head shaven but for a circlet of dark hair round his pale skull, knelt a certain young novice—my own Pascal. Amongst the crowded congregation, heads bowed reverently, knelt Jean-Luc, his elder brother, and Agostino, his father—my dearest son. I saw the three of them only from the distance of the loft. Before the Mass was finished, I left my abbey and returned to Avignon.

From Avignon I flew to Paris and thence to Nairobi, where I arranged to travel overland to the interior of Somalia.

The American Marines had long since abandoned maddening Somalia in confusion and disgust. Civil war was being waged anew, and again the people were going hungry.

My Soeur Pauline, now aged nearly eighty, throughout the wars and famines had remained at Buffa—so thither I went.

She was absent from her compound, but I had all sorts of time to wait for her. I shed my black suit, put on my caped soutane of white and crimson—my biretta, sash, and pectoral cross—and walked out onto the muddy road.

It had rained the night before. From the brown sky another warm drizzle fell. Peasants as in those years past sat at campfires beneath the trees of camel-thorn, boiling grass for breakfast. As I walked through such a wilderness I felt a little giddy, bouncy, so light of foot and body that I fancied I might ascend an inch or two into the dank and misty air. From the distance I saw my Soeur Pauline—in her white veil and habit, black rosary beads as ever dangling from her waist—walking towards me on the road, bearing in the crook of either arm a starving child.

Knowing she was deaf, I raised my arms to Heaven and shouted out—not to her but to her Master, hoping that He might enjoy my theatre—"Take me, Lord. I b-b-belong to You."

Rome; Europe; Africa; the Americas
1992–1996

ABOUT THE AUTHOR

Edward R. F. Sheehan has led a varied life as a journalist, diplomat, novelist, academic, and dramatist. He has contributed to leading American and international publications, including *The New York Times* and *The New York Review of Books*, from Europe, Africa, the Middle East, Mexico, and Central America. In 1973, he won the Overseas Press Club Award for distinguished interpretation of foreign affairs. As a Fellow at the Center for International Affairs at Harvard University from 1974 to 1978, he founded and chaired the prestigious Middle East Seminar.

Mr Sheehan's play *Kingdoms,* about the conflict of Napoleon and Pius VII, was produced at the Kennedy Center in Washington and at the Cort Theatre on Broadway. The eminent critic Clive Barnes named it one of the best plays of 1981. *Cardinal Galsworthy* is Edward Sheehan's fifth novel. Of his last novel, *Innocent Darkness*—the story of Adrian Northwood—published by Viking Penguin in 1993, *Publishers Weekly* said in a starred review: "It is a haunting, almost allegorical tale of politics, religion, and high art . . . a remarkable creation." The *Detroit Free Press* called it "one of those exceptionally rare books that we put down because we don't want it to end."